LONG KNIFE

James Alexander Thom

BALLANTINE BOOKS • NEW YORK

A Ballantine Book
Published by The Random House Publishing Group
Copyright © 1979 by James Alexander Thom
Map copyright © 1986 by Anita Karl and James Kemp

www.ballantinebooks.com

Library of Congress Catalog Card Number: 85-91880

ISBN 0-345-38074-6

First Ballantine Books Trade Edition: August 1986
First Ballantine Books Mass Market Edition: July 1994

OPM   18   17   16   15   14   13   12   11   10

George stood for a moment enjoying the incredulous expressions on the faces of the young officers, gentlemen, and ladies, then said to Sanders:

"Tell 'em they may continue their dancing, but to remember that they now dance under the flag of Virginia, not England." While Sanders announced this in his clumsy French, George sent a few of the half-clad, mud-smeared frontiersmen through the room to collect swords and pistols, then turned to go out. But a handsome dark-eyed man, who had been standing in the company of two beautiful women, suddenly left them and came forward.

"Sir," he said in correct but strained English, "several of us here are Spanish citizens from St. Louis, and we are merely guests here of the French. Are we to be detained?"

George looked at the elegant little man, then said: "If you'll be patient, I'll attend to your situation. For the moment I must advise you and all the others not to stir from this house, for your safety."

George watched, over the man's shoulder, the younger of the two women who were with him, and felt a bittersweet pang in his breast. She was dark-eyed, oval-faced, transfixed by terror, but beautiful. . . .

By James Alexander Thom
Published by Ballantine Books:

PANTHER IN THE SKY
LONG KNIFE
FOLLOW THE RIVER
FROM SEA TO SHINING SEA
STAYING OUT OF HELL
THE CHILDREN OF FIRST MAN
THE RED HEART

CONTENTS

Show me a hero and I will write you a tragedy.
—F. Scott Fitzgerald

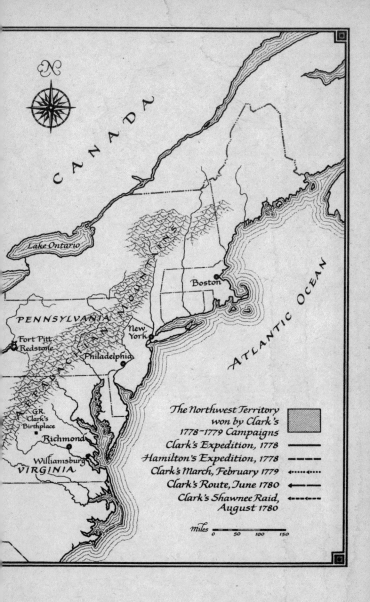

The Northwest Territory
won by Clark's
1778-1779 Campaigns
Clark's Expedition, 1778
Hamilton's Expedition, 1778
Clark's March, February 1779
Clark's Route, June 1780
Clark's Shawnee Raid,
August 1780

Miles
0   50   100   150

CANADA

Lake Ontario

PENNSYLVANIA

Fort Pitt
Redstone

Philadelphia

New York

Boston

APPALACHIAN MOUNTAINS

ATLANTIC OCEAN

G.R.
Clark's
Birthplace

Richmond

Williamsburg

VIRGINIA

PART ONE

1809

1

CLARK'S POINT, INDIANA TERRITORY
1809

THE OLD GENERAL FELT IT COMING AT SUNSET ON THAT FINE COOL evening, while he sat on the porch of his log house on the bluff overlooking the Ohio: a greater melancholy than any he had faced in the thirty years of his decline.

He set his jaw and drew himself up straight in his hickory chair. This awesome, poignant mood had tried to overpower him on many such evenings of late, and he feared it, and wished he knew how to brace his spirit against it. It wasn't death he feared; he had been impatient for that for years. No, it was this eternity of days passing by, each one finding him more helpless to set things right.

The wild beauty of this place seemed to make it worse than it had been when he lived at Mulberry Hill across the river. Now melancholy seemed to come up the hill through the sighing treetops on the breeze from the broad river. It was in the rippling grass in the clearing and in the deep rushing of the Falls of the Ohio far below. It was in the sight of the sun going down at the end of another summer. Still another summer gone by, with all those injustices still unresolved.

The sunlight blazed directly into his eyes and flashed up at him from the surface of the river, but he did not shield his eyes or turn away. Here on this high place, it had become his habit to stare down the evening sun.

On the brassy glare of the river, above the falls, alongside the Kentucky bank, lay the dark oblong silhouette of Corn Island. There, he thought. Right there on that island it all started, in 1778. A conquest like none the world ever saw. Half a million square miles of domain, taken by a hundred and seventy starving woodsmen, who had the audacity to deem ourselves an army. The memory made him sit straighter; his eyes grew moist

3

and a proud smile played on his mouth. But then, as always, followed the bitterness, and with the bitterness that old undeniable craving. Indeed, he thought. I have not touched any this long afternoon. It's time.

With his cane he whacked three times on the wall. A Negro appeared in the doorway, lean, grizzled, clad in dingy white cotton. "You call for me, General?"

"Aye, Cupid. First, fetch me a jug of rum out here. Then, if you'd be so kind, sir, lay up by the hearth enough wood for the night. Make it the walnut. I like the smell o' that. I feel in my bones, Cupid, this is going to be our first real chilling night of the season."

"I do believe it is, sir."

The general shivered. It seemed he had never once been warm enough since that winter campaign in '79. "Then, if you'll kindly poke the fire up good for me, and light a lamp on the table adjacent, then I should say you'd set me up well enough for a tolerable night."

The old black man smiled. "You going to read, then?" Illiterate, he was perennially fascinated by the sight of the general looking at one thing, a book, for hours at a time.

"Maybe. But I have correspondence needs doing. If the rum doesn't take me first . . ." I shouldn't have said that, he thought; it isn't seemly. But, by my eyes, if only they was somebody to whom you could say whatever was in your thoughts . . . some kinds of things you can say to a nephew, some to a niece, and some to an Indian, and some to your old comrades when they come around, but if you have no mate, there's some things as just have to go unsaid . . .

The servant was poised with his weight on one leg, not sure whether he was dismissed; the general seemed primed to say more. His dark blue eyes were squinting through the sun and his mouth was open, as if he had not finished out his remarks.

I wonder if old Cupid could understand my discontent anyhow, the general was thinking. How would a slave take it to be told that his lot is happier than his master's? But no. You don't complain to people. Least of all to a servant. He had always believed it was the obligation of a gentleman never to complain, always to encourage, no matter how bleak the prospects might be. "If you'd bring me that rum?" he said instead.

The brick sun now sat on a purple horizon. Beyond the village of Louisville on the river's far shore, the fields and forests of Kentucky had deepened to lilac, the westerly contours flushed red-gold. That a world which looked so like a paradise could be so full of injustices was a major cause of his melancholy.

Before the stroke it had not been so bad. In those days when he could still move around, still mount a horse, still go hunting and fowling with his nephews, the Croghan boys, still dig for answers in the mysterious Indian mounds; in those days when John Audubon would come and stay and ask particulars about this bird or that bird in the region; in short, until his body had betrayed him and made him a prisoner of his house and porch, it had been possible to put that wretched business out of his mind for days at a time. In the woods, on the trails, on the river, with hearty companions at his side and gun on his arm, the neglect and stupidity of an ungrateful country didn't matter. But when he could only hobble about on a cane and hurt in every bone socket and sit wrapped in a cloak of retrospection, then the past had a way of growing bigger than the present and he could think only of the way things should have been.

On the river below, a convoy of four flatboats was making for the channel of navigable rapids past the falls, seeking apparently to make a run for it in the remaining light. The calls of the sweepmen rose up faintly from the valley, the words unintelligible but their anxiety audible in the turned-up ends of their calls.

Westward they go, day after day, the old general thought. To all that land out there.

All that land out there. That we the Clarks have given them. William and me.

He thought, as he did so often these days, of his famed youngest brother, William. Now there is a man for you! Got the glory he deserves, he did. And has been as good to me as all the fates has been bad. We ought to have been the two richest men west of the Alleghenies, him and me. But any dollar I make already belongs to the creditors, and those bloodsuckers do take it. And then William, he makes it up on my behalf. Selling off land to pay debts and suits . . . Riding about making endorsements and promises . . . Petitioning for me in Richmond and at Congress . . .

The thought of his brother's devotion gave the general a bittersweet pain in his breast, and brought the melancholy a little closer. It was better to think of William in terms of his great triumph than in terms of that eternal dreary business of the debts.

The servant brought a tray with an uncorked jug of rum, two

drinking glasses, and a carafe of spring water on it. He placed it on a bench along the hewn-log wall, and poured the amber rum three fourths of the way to the top of one glass, as the general liked it. As had become their custom, he then poured a shot for his own evening indulgence into the second glass.

"Here's to William," said the general, raising the glass to the level of the setting sun. "I took the frontier to the Mississippi and then he carried it on to the blue Pacific. Here's to William, I say." With a breathy slurp he drained the contents.

"To William, sir," said the Negro, to whom this toast was by now familiar. Swallowing the rum with a shudder, he turned and went wobbly-legged down off the porch toward the woodpile which lay neatly corded between two tree stumps in the clearing. The general watched him and chuckled. Old Cupid couldn't handle more than one shot.

The four flatboats were slipping fast in a single file down through the channel now in a glory of sun-reddened water, and General Clark watched them go and smacked his lips and sighed and felt the beloved comfort of the liquor rise to his head and pursue the rheumatic ache outward through all his limbs. He pulled the old deerskin lap robe closer around his waist and began to feel quite cozy. Perhaps this might be a tolerable evening after all. Wincing from a painful shoulder, he tipped another measure of rum from the heavy jug into the glass and then held the glass on his lap and watched the boats. He remembered his own little convoy of boats setting out down the same main channel under the ominous eclipse of the sun, in '78, full of heroes-to-be, going against the forts at Cahokia and Kaskaskia and Vincennes and, he had hoped, north to the British stronghold at Detroit. Detroit, he thought, The one conquest I wanted more than anything.

He remembered, too, the boat of the Lewis and Clark expedition setting out down that same waterway, just six years ago, in 1803. And he remembered William returning from the Pacific in 1806. He could see him as clear as yesterday: leathery, serene, the look of infinity in his eyes, full of such descriptions of spaces and mountains as would make your heart race.

This is indeed a place of brave beginnings, the general thought, sipping more slowly now.

But of endings, too.

The Negro staggered up the porch steps and went into the house with his arms crooked under a load of logs. Then he emerged and descended into the yard again to go for more.

The general watched his thin form in its faded homespun move like a ghost on a backdrop of dusky trees.

The topmost arc of that brick-colored sun now slid from view into the western forest and the woods nearby opened up with the quizzical peeps of countless tree frogs. Somewhere nearby a screech owl called once and then was still. Wingbeats and twitters rushed past the end of the cabin behind General Clark as a flock of martins sailed through the clearing and down toward the river.

The western sky now retained a tinge of rose. An errant draft of evening air whirled a whiff of wood smoke to the general from his own chimney. The servant, crooning low to himself, clumped heavy-laden across the porch and into the house once more, came out to see if his master needed anything, said his goodbye, and went singing down the hill to his shack. His voice faded into the far drumming of the Falls and now General Clark was alone on Clark's Point, commanding the twilight.

He sat there drinking until stars appeared in the southeast over Kentucky, sat imbibing slowly and steadily in solitary decorum, reviewing his campaigns, calculating his debts, mulling over the slanders and abuse he had suffered by his opposition to the land syndicates and their bogus claims; he sat framing phrases for the petitions and letters that he must continue writing to Thomas Jefferson, to the national Congress, to the legislature of Virginia; he sat daydreaming of the snowy mountains, high plains and evergreen forests his brother had seen in the Far West, envisioning them as clearly as if he had beheld them with his own eyes. He looked at the distant lamplights of Louisville across the river, the Louisville he had founded in 1784 when the Revolution was finally concluded. He pondered on his endless weary efforts to administer for his veterans the tracts of land that had been given them by Virginia as rewards for their gallantry in the campaign. But always his thoughts returned to the indifference and ingratitude shown him by the government he had served so well. *I won their war in the West for them,* he thought, *and ever since I've been paying the bills for it as well.*

Fifteen thousand dollars in receipts and vouchers I sent them in '79, he thought. *And they lost 'em and say they can't reimburse me without 'em.*

What a damnable muddle it all is, he thought. *It is simply impossible to do anything straightforward and swift, once civilization sets in. You can count on men as men. But from their government you can count on nothing but hollow praise and* empty promises. Set your head to do a thing direct and right, and then by God you may expect to flounder with it while your government makes debate and intrigue over it, cavils over its costs, and subverts it motives.

By Heaven, he thought, my misfortune is to have lived too long.

His mind quit its other meanderings then and began to play upon that single notion, while crickets shrilled in the valley and a wolf howled in the darkness somewhere north of the river. The general sighed into his glass and sipped and considered when he should have died.

Of all the musketballs and shot, all the tomahawks and arrows that whistled through the air I breathed before I was thirty, not a one touched me. My life had a charm on it, those days. Not a single missile of war touched me then, when it should have, when I was winning. *That* must be the time to die: When you think you've got everything to live for. A hell on earth it is, he thought, to triumph too early and be thwarted ever after. Spoils a life, it does.

There must have been some ideal time to have taken a lethal blade or bullet. Lord Dunmore's War? No, that was too early. So too was the defense of Harrodsburg. The assault on Fort Sackville? No, it would not have succeeded had he fallen. Against the Shawnees at Piqua? Perhaps that would have been the time, or when he had fought Benedict Arnold in Virginia in '81.

But no. None of those. The ideal occasion would have been in taking Fort Detroit. That had been his main ambition in the war, but the fates never cooperated. And as long as I had been still desiring it, I reckon I should have been most unhappy to get shot down.

"Hah!" He clambered to his feet with a suddenness that hurt his joints and set his head swimming. "By God, sir," he muttered, laughing, swaying on his feet. "Shame on you! Toying with that morbid idea!" He groped down for the slipping deerskin lap robe, and in doing so knocked the tray off the bench. He heard the glass break, and the stoneware jug rolled with a small hollow thunder, its contents glugging out onto the porch floor. Alarmed to hear precious liquor spilling, the General lurched hastily about in the dark trying to locate the jug. Then a bolt of shame went through him and he drew himself up to his full height. He stood there composing himself, trying to erase from his mind the spectacle he knew he must have presented.

Scrambling so desperately after a fallen jug! He turned and hobbled on his cane into the house, stooping to go under the lintel.

The room was warm. Its log walls were mellow with flickering light from the great fireplace. Furniture and glass and memorabilia glinted in lamplight. On a shelf of a glass-front cupboard, couched on a scrap of red velvet, gleamed a tiny silver medallion. No bigger than a dollar, the figure of a running athlete in it. He gazed at it for a long time, remembering.

A stewpot hung over the coals on an iron arm in the fireplace, but its aroma did not tempt him. He was too agitated to eat. He stood by the cupboard for a few more seconds on aching legs, undecided between his hearthside chair and the door to his bedroom, wherein a candle burned unwinking in the close air. There was sweat on his brow. His bowels gripped and burned.

At length he went out the back door into the darkness. The stars were intense overhead. Sweat on his face and flanks chilled him. He went to the outhouse, had a scalding evacuation while holding his face between his hands, then returned indoors.

From the pantry he selected a quart of peach brandy distilled in Louisville, leaving the expensive Jamaican rum and the more stupefying corn whiskey on the shelf. He removed his wide-brimmed hat and hung it on a peg beneath the long rifle, straight sword, and tomahawk he had carried through the Revolution. He uncorked the brandy and set it on a table among letters and inkwell and quill, turned up the lamp wick, drew his chair closer to the table and eased into it, spreading the deerskin robe over his legs again.

For a while he sat there erect, hands on his aching knees, drawing deep and difficult breaths and absorbing the warmth from the fireplace. His eyes, so dark a blue they appeared to be black, gazed into the shadows from under the sad, downward-sloping folds of flesh that hooded the eyelids. His hair, which had receded back to the crown of his head, was silvery, with a few still copper-red strands, and tufts of white were combed back over his ears. Dome and forehead were pale, and beneath was a face which, though weathered to cordovan, flecked with tiny broken capillaries, and mottled with age spots, was yet patrician, strong, and handsome. The nose was long and narrow, delicately winged. His lips were thin but sculptured sensitively, resolute yet not hard; they parted as he inhaled, closed as he exhaled. Despite his age no flesh sagged under his square-cut jaw.

Thus he sat in repose for a long time, pate gleaming like an egg in the lamplight, face grave, aristocratic, and profoundly sad.

He stirred after a while, looked at a point high on the wall, groaned a single word—"Teresa!"—hauled in a deep breath, and then expelled it with a plosive sigh. Then he clenched his jaw, reached for the brandy, and poured it into a glass which shimmered through tears. He snuffled once, drew up as if again bracing himself against sentimentality, fiercely threw the liquor to the back of his throat, and poured another measure.

From a small brass scuttle on the hearth he scooped a handful of poplar stump punk and cast it into the coals, then watched the flames change to emerald and blue. A tall clock ticked in the gloom at the other end of the room; the fire fluttered and shifted in its coals; the frogs outside continued their piping queries. General Clark scanned the letters and documents, old and recent, that were spread in orderly stacks over the tabletop.

He reached for a recent one from Jefferson which needed attending to. A few months earlier the president had written, asking Clark to find for him in the Ohio Valley the bones of certain extinct mammals which he wanted to present to the National Institute of France. Of the mammoth in particular the president wanted ribs, backbones, leg-bones, thigh, horn, hips, shoulder blades, and parts of upper- and under-jaw teeth.

The general gave a wry smile and shook his head. Tom Jefferson knows precisely what he wants, he thought. And I always fill his order. Whether he wants a fossil or a frontier.

Jefferson's letter concluded:

> ... I avail myself on this occasion of recalling myself to your memory, of assuring you that time has not lessened my friendship for you. We are both now grown old, you have been enjoying in retirement the recollection of the services you have rendered to your country and I am about to retire with an equal consciousness that I have occupied places in which others could not have done more good; but in all places and times I shall wish you every happiness and salute you with great friendship and esteem.

He stared at the letter, hands trembling at the edges of the paper, his breathing accelerating.

" 'Enjoying,' you say!" he growled. "By thunder, Mister President, I am thankful you cannot see just how I enjoy my retirement!" He started to crumple the letter, shaking as if with ague, but then smoothed and refolded it. "Well, I shall give you your old bones, my friend," he muttered. "Tusks and backbones I've got already, piled in front of my house. I shall always give you whatever you want, as I have always, now, haven't I? As I know you would do for me, and have, whenever you could. But *try*, Thomas! I daresay you know my needs are desperate. You're the President. Surely you can do something for *me* now."

The time was long past when General Clark had been surprised to hear himself talking aloud in his solitude, addressing those of whom he was thinking. He had been alone almost all his life, alone, relying on himself; even when surrounded by his troops who were prepared to die for him he had been essentially alone, with all responsibility on his own shoulders, with every course of action depending upon his sole judgment. West of the Alleghenies, the Revolutionary War had been *his* war.

And now, now in 1809, though every knowledgeable man who journeyed down or up the Ohio would stop and walk up the hill to pay homage to him, though his brothers devoted themselves to his problems, though his sister Lucy Croghan regularly came from Locust Grove across the river to inquire after his needs, and his little niece Diana Gwathmey came every other week to sit beside him for hours and listen to his tales and his grumblings, he was still alone. Some of his old Illinois campaigners, those still fit to travel, would come up when they could, talk fowl-shooting or bone-hunting with him, sit with him on the porch, drink a little, give him news of their lives, then depart, leaving him again alone. It was strange about them: Virtually every one of them had become a physical ruin, many had died young, and all who still lived looked twice their age. They had been the toughest men imaginable during the campaigns back in '78 and '79; indeed, they would not have survived the campaigns had they not been. But almost immediately after their victory over General Hamilton, the Scalp-Buyer, they had begun to deteriorate. The hardships of that winter march against Vincennes seemed to have taxed their whole life's store of vigor, leaving them unsteady, frail, bone-sore, and prey to any malady that came by. They, like he, had ruined themselves for their country.

There were certain other old warriors who could come to Clark's Point and momentarily alleviate his solitude. These were the Indian chiefs, former allies of the British, whom he had fought or won over by eloquence and tact in the great councils at Cahokia. Every year some of the old chiefs would come from their distant villages, some of them five hundred miles across the wilderness, ride up the road to Clark's Point, sit and talk with him, and smoke the pipe of peace. They called him "the Long Knife, our father who speaks with one heart and one tongue." Of all his visitors, it was these whose company touched him most, these former adversaries with their somber visages and their information from another kind of world, and it was when their bright blankets and feathers had vanished into the forest shadows that his loneliness would return at its most poignant.

Despite the brandy and the deerhide robe, the old soldier felt chilled again, chilled as much by the sense of his own feebleness and solitude as by the actual coolness of the night. Rising unsteadily from his chair, he took a poker in hand, jabbed at the logs in the fireplace until sparks and flames shot up the chimney, then laid two more split walnut chunks against the backlog. He lowered himself back into his chair, spent by the effort; his heart was thudding painfully and light specks were swimming behind his eyes. As the fire began to strengthen, he recovered his breath somewhat. But this new reminder of his infirmity depressed him further. The loss of his legendary physical power was one of the worst of the relentless and undeserved misfortunes which had dogged him through the latter half of his lifetime.

Now he put his hand on a piece of paper that pulled like a magnet at the corner of his eye. It was a draft of a petition he had made to Congress three years before, asking for title to the two and a half square leagues of Ohio Valley lands that had been offered him in 1778 by a great Indian chief. The general deemed this petition the most abject correspondence of his life. He had never felt so pathetic and frustrated as when he had penned this appeal. He could not even bear to read it when he was sober, and would have destroyed it by now, were he not so meticulous about his accounts and papers. But he had read it and reread it countless times while deep in his cups, as now, savoring a rich and righteous feeling of self-pity. He had written it as a last resort, after every other hope for reimbursement had been given up.

The paper rustled in his hands as he read.

> . . . *My reason for not soliciting Congress before this was the great number of Petitions before them, and the prospect*

I yet had of a future support, but those prospects are vanished. I engaged in the Revolution with all the Ardour that Youth could possess. My Zeal and Ambition rose with my success, determined to Save those Countries which had been the Seat of my toil, at the hazard of my life and fortune.

At the most gloomy period of the War, when a Ration could not be purchased on Public Credit I risked my own, gave my Bonds, Mortgaged my Lands for supplies, Paid strict attention to every department, flattered the friendly and confused the hostile tribes of Indians by my emissaries, baffled my internal enemies (the most dangerous of the whole to Public Interest) and carried my Point. Thus at the end of the War I had the pleasure of seeing my Country Secure, but with the loss of my Manual activity and a prospect of future indigence, demands of very great amount were not paid, others with depreciated Paper, Suits commenced against me for those sums in specie, My military and other lands earned by my Service as far as they would extend were appropriated for the payment of those debts, and demands yet remaining to a considerable amount more than remains of a shattered fortune will pay—this is truly my situation—I see no other resource remaining, but to make application to my Country for redress . . .

To have been reduced from the glory of victory to so low a condition as to beg like that! And even then, the Congressional Committee on Public Lands had defeated that petition, and the grant of land—land he already considered his—had been refused him.

The irony, the enormity of it enraged him more every time he thought of it. That tract of land had been offered to him in simple friendship by the Piankeshaw chief, Tobacco's Son, known among the Indian nations as the Grand Kite of the Wabash, who had chosen to make his people friends of the Americans rather than mercenary scalp-takers for the British. Tobacco's Son had given him the deed in a ceremony of dignity and eloquence, with a warning to all other tribes to esteem the gift and never cause that tract of land to taste blood. And he had decreed that the Indians would retain title to a road through that land to the door of the Long Knife's house, so that any Indian could come in safety to get his counsel. He had accepted the deed from Tobacco's Son, taking it in trust for Virginia, whose government he served, and soon afterward, the Assembly of Virginia had agreed by unanimous vote that he had the right to it. But later when the claims of Virginia had been transferred to the new federal government, the national Congress had refused to give him the grant, or even so much relief as a pension.

The thought of it never failed to make him seethe. He sat here now before his blazing hearth thinking of it, heart pounding with indignation, eyes smoldering. Tossing down still another glass of the brandy, he hauled himself to his feet and flung the heavy robe into a corner of the room. He leaned upon the table's edge with his fists clenched and glowered at the petition on the table.

"By God, it is a disgrace," he began in a low and hissing tone. "I gave to a brown savage nothing more than honest words and an invitation to friendship, and he offered me an estate. But . . ."

The general now raised his fists to the ceiling, and brought them down with a crash on the table, shouting: "I gave to the United States half of the territory they possess, and they suffer me to remain in poverty!" His fists struck the table again, then a third time, and suddenly he was blinded by a sunlike flash and felt a pain as if a tomahawk had been driven into his brain. The right side of his body seemed to depart in one instant; there was an intense silent scream inside his head and he felt himself falling.

Alone in his log house on a wild point of land above the Falls of the Ohio, felled by a stroke, General George Rogers Clark lay, his mouth open, drooling on the rough board floor. In a fragmented dream, he saw his soldiers standing with raised tomahawks over kneeling Indian braves. The dream began over and over. In some fragments, the soldiers struck the captives; in others, they spared them and let them go.

The General had fallen close to the hearth. His left foot was inside the fireplace. The room began to fill with the smell of seared leather. The embers ate through his boot and soon the flesh of his foot and leg began to burn.

AT DAWN A PUAN INDIAN CHIEFTAIN CALLED TWO LIVES, WHO WAS in his fiftieth summer, rode eastward along the dirt road on the north bank of the Ohio. His pony's unshod hooves made no sound as he rode toward the Falls. On the far bank of the river lay the big village the American white men called Louisville, its buildings square and blue in the pearly morning light. Many boats were tied to poles in the river next to the town's bank, looking very small at this distance. Smoke drifted from the houses, out over the river. In past years Two Lives had been in Louisville to trade, but he did not like to go there. Louisville had many smells and Two Lives did not like them. There were sour smells from the places where whiskey and brandy were made. There were smells of rotting animal guts and tannin from the buildings where the white men butchered animals for meat and made their hides into boot leather. There were rankling odors of lye and of limestone dust, and other aromas which made Two Lives breathe through his mouth and close his nose. Even now across the wide river, he imagined he could smell the town.

Two Lives rode up a street now between the silent log buildings of Clarksville, where the mills stood still and few men lived anymore. Two Lives knew that his great friend Clark, the Long Knife, was not happy about the stillness of his town, because he had founded it to be a great trade center with a boat canal past the Falls. But although Two Lives was sad for the Long Knife's disappointment, still he preferred the quiet and the emptiness of Clarksville to the noises and smells of Louisville across the river.

The pony began climbing the road up the bluff toward the house of the Long Knife, and as he climbed, the rushing of the river and Falls subsided below, absorbed in the foliage of the giant oaks and sycamores. Up here it was wild and clean and still, and Two Lives was happy that the Long Knife lived up here now instead of in the town. Bluebirds, finches, jays, juncoes, martins, and towhees flew crisscrossing the path, in search of their morning food, and at one place halfway up the bluff the rider startled a grazing doe, which fled in surefooted leaps up a steep bluff covered with ferns. The white flag under its tail vanished into a green thicket far above, and Two Lives smiled with pleasure in the knowledge that if he had been hunting, that foolish deer would have become easy venison. But Two Lives had not come to hunt, nor would he have hunted on this land, which was known among the tribes to be the Long Knife's land, and therefore like a sacred place. Two Lives had been trading a few miles down the river, and had come up the road this morning only for one purpose, to see the Long Knife and bring him greetings from his tribe. Two Lives was anticipating this meeting with great pleasure, as he always did, because the Long Knife once, thirty-one summers ago, had spared him from the tomahawk. It was thus that Two Lives had gotten his name: this

peaceful second life he lived was the life Clark had granted him
to live.

Two Lives was almost to the meadow when a shot rang out.
Reflexively, he dropped low along the pony's back and turned
it in its tracks, listening. He had heard no ball cut through the
foliage near him, and so presumed that the shot had not been
fired at him. It had come from the top of the bluff, somewhere
near the house of the Long Knife. Perhaps he is hunting,
thought Two Lives. As he urged his pony out of the woods and
onto the meadow, he heard a feeble, croaking cry. Alarmed now
for his friend, he kicked the pony into a trot.

Two Lives almost wept when he found the general on the
porch. The old soldier was lying on his side, trying to reload the
flintlock pistol which lay beside him on the porch floor. Wad-
ding, ramrod, and powder horn lay scattered next to it. His face
was dirty and gray and streaked by sweat. Its expression was
grotesque; the right eye drooped almost shut and the right side
of his mouth hung slack, with a string of saliva drooling from
it. His open, wild left eye was inflamed. His right arm was limp
and useless alongside his body. A whiskey jug lay on its side on
the ground among the bones of the ancient animals. Two Lives
jumped from his pony onto the porch and stooped to raise his
friend's head from the floor and look into his face. It was then
that he saw the burned trouser leg and the remains of the boot,
and the bloody, seeping left leg covered with flies and ashes and
flakes of blackened skin.

The general only now seemed to become aware that someone
had arrived to help him. His bloodshot left eye searched the Indian's face and then seemed to show a glimmer of recognition.
The left corner of his mouth drew up in a lopsided smile, then
he sighed and sagged, uttered some incoherent words, and went
into a spasm of shuddering.

Two Lives leaped up. He cupped his hands around his mouth
and broke the stillness of the morning with an ululation that
could be heard far down the valley. He fired his own musket
into the air, then finished reloading the general's pistol and discharged it. Finally hearing halloos coming from the woods below, and seeing the general's old black man bustling up the hill,
Two Lives stripped off his blanket, spread it to cover the shuddering old soldier, and found a pillow to put under his head.
Then, pausing to pick up the liquor jug and throw it out of sight
into a thicket, he plunged down into the woods to get roots and
herbs for a burn dressing.

It was a momentous day for Two Lives. The plight of his great friend had filled his eyes with tears. But in his breast shone a sort of reverent gratitude. Somehow, it seemed to Two Lives, the Great Spirit had sent him here at this moment to help save the life of this great white man who once had spared his own.

THE GENERAL LAY ON HIS BACK ON THE TABLE IN THE BIG ROOM OF his house, drenched with sweat. His long white nightshirt stuck to him. Rivulets of sweat kept running off his temples and down into his ears, where they tickled annoyingly. Occasionally a powerful bolt of pain would stab upward from the jumble of aches, shivers, fires, and numbnesses in the region of his left leg, and he would clench his jaw and his fist to refrain from crying out.

He didn't know how many days had passed since that great pain had pierced his head and he had fallen on the hearth. He had lost track of the days since his friend Two Lives the Puan had found him. He had been in and out of a hell of fevers and deliriums and nightmares.

Now he knew where he was and what was about to happen.

The room was steamy. Water was boiling in a black kettle in the fireplace. The surgeon, Dr. Ferguson from Louisville, stood beside the table rattling his instruments and scowling at the infected leg. His face was flushed and there was a sheen of sweat on it.

Dr. Ferguson looked up and saw the general's one open eye peering at him.

"General Clark, I had better get started. The longer we wait, the more danger for you . . ."

"Just stand where you are, sir. When the music arrives, you may begin. Only then."

The surgeon passed an imploring look around the room, from one of the general's relatives to another. His sister Lucy was there, and her husband, Major Croghan. They looked at each other, then back to the surgeon. "Wait," said Major Croghan. It was quite obvious that, even flat on his back, half paralyzed, full of infection and fever, his speech scarcely intelligible, the general remained in command.

The doctor shrugged, raised both hands, palms upward, and let them fall to his sides. Then he turned and whispered to his assistant, a stout young man with yellow eyelashes. The assistant bent to the surgeon's bag and brought forth some long, black leather straps and belts with loops and buckles. Without a word, he went to the table, passed the longest leather across the general's chest, and was stooping to draw it under the table when the patient suddenly flung it off with his left hand. "Put those away, lad," he warned. "I shall not need to be trussed up like a goat for this."

With a sigh of exasperation, the surgeon came close and bent over his face. "May I suggest, General, that it is for your own safety? I have seen men leap under the knife and throw themselves clean off the table . . ." Hearing this, Lucy Croghan pressed her knuckles against her mouth and made a small strangling sound.

"Lucy, come here," the general said, groping in her direction with his left hand. When her hand touched his, he drew her close to the table and held her by the wrist. She was a tall, sturdy, long-nosed woman, her red hair fading to gray. "Hear me," he said. "Have you ever known me to lose the control of myself? When sober, I mean," he added with a pained chuckle. "Trust me, Lucy, I am as sober now as I have ever been. Have that man stay clear of me with his bloody harnesses, then."

The doctor shrugged again, and motioned to his assistant to put away the leathers.

The door opened, throwing bright daylight across the ceiling. George Rogers Clark Floyd, one of the general's many namesakes, stood silhouetted in the doorway. "Yes?" said Major Croghan.

"Sir, the musicians is here."

"Is Dick Lovell there with his old drum?" asked the general.

"The same, sir," said young Floyd. "Right on the porch."

"Ah," said the general. "Then I reckon I am ready, Bones."

"Have them play," Major Croghan said, "until told to stop."

The door closed. Dr. Ferguson raised the nightshirt to expose the ghastly leg. He cleared his throat, waved away some flies, took up a large knife and tested its edge with his thumb, picked up a bone saw, some steel clamps, and a cauterizing iron, and went to the fireplace. He swished the implements in the boiling water and put the end of the cauterizing tool in the coals.

Outside could be heard the murmur of many voices, and one voice snapping drill commands. Then a slow rattle of drums sounded around the house, and fifes joined in. The general squeezed and released his sister's wrist, and with a grim, one-sided smile began snapping his fingers to the cadence of the music. "Dickie Lovell drummed us through to Vincennes," he said. "We'd not've made it without 'im."

"I know," said Lucy.

"The tourniquet, if you will," the surgeon said, advancing on the table with the steaming tools before him. He paused and looked at the general. "Will you reconsider and have some whiskey, General Clark?"

"For once, no, thank you." He kept snapping his fingers.

"It would be no disgrace, you know."

"Damn, I know that. Who claims it ever is?" Some of the big men in the room laughed nervously. They were a rugged breed but genteel, and, at this moment, very much on the edge of their emotions.

The surgeon smiled. "As you wish, then."

The assistant had turned the stick to tighten the tourniquet. The surgeon drew an invisible line with his fingertip across the thigh. The leg was big-boned, sinewy, and slab-muscled even now; the knee and ankle were gnarled and enlarged by rheumatism and arthritis. The doctor thought of the legendary marches this officer had led on these once-magnificent limbs. He faltered, surprised that he felt a lump in his throat and a stinging of his eyelids. What a pity, he thought. Then he swallowed hard and with a deft pulling stroke of the hot knife laid open the skin and sliced an inch deep into the stringy thigh muscle, then stepped back to give his beefy assistant room for the expected struggle.

But the general did not lunge, or even twitch. His great frame stiffened; his back arched; then he let out a long shaking breath and lay ready again, his eye on the rafters, his thumb and middle finger still snapping in time to the solemn music. Shaken through by a strange surge of love and admiration, the doctor blinked, gulped, returned his knife to the red-welling cut, and continued his work. Lucy Croghan stood trembling at the head of the table with a clean piece of cotton cloth and wiped the sweat off her brother's forehead and out of his eye sockets. She could not bear to watch the cutting, but gazed past the surgeon's bent head and out the window, looking at the crowd that had gathered in the clearing.

The people surrounded the house at a respectful distance, most of them bareheaded in the afternoon sunlight: gaunt-faced old veterans, young blue-coated militiamen, barefooted children, red-nosed pioneer women with their arms folded across their waists, slaves in ragged gray, hawk-faced Indians whose lean brown shoulders and haunches gleamed with bear grease in the sunlight. They had materialized as if by magic from miles around at word of General Clark's trouble. Two drummers and two fifers posted around the house kept up their grave, persistent cadences. The solemn drums and whistling fifes evoked a sense of battlefield apprehension in the sun-drenched clearing. The senior drummer, Dick Lovell, a forty-year-old farmer, small and hollow-cheeked and wiry, had the honored post at the front door. Now and then he would remember that terrible winter march of '79, would feel the unspeakable cold in his bones, and would shudder, and tears would stream from his eyes. He loved this old soldier in a way that one loves not even his own brothers, and he tapped his drum with his heart full of prayer, as if his music were the one thing that could keep the general alive. After all, General Clark had summoned him in particular for this occasion, and for Dick Lovell it was a sacred duty.

After some time it seemed to dawn on the entire crowd that although the amputation must be well in progress by now, they had not heard a single outcry from the house. They began to glance at each other's faces and saw the swimming eyes and the working throats, and suddenly a heartening cheer went up all around the house, then another, and then a third.

The demonstration was over that quickly, and the waiting resumed, but now the entire circle of people felt themselves bound together in a certain kind of pride that they had never experienced before.

The three cheers had sounded through the window at the most critical time for General Clark: just as the surgeon had cleared the muscles away to expose the bone to the saw. As the hideous instrument had begun to whine into the thighbone, laboring through the very armature of him as if he were but a piece of broken furniture, the full comprehension of his loss had swept through him, increasing the pain against which he thought he had so well braced himself. In that moment he had felt at last overpowered by a tide of despair, thinking: Now as everything else has been taken away from me it appears they must divide up my own personal carcass and carry it away piece by piece ... And with that bitter thought he had been ready to scream out like a weakling or simply let go and die.

But then, through the drum taps and the shrilling of the fifes, there had burst into his consciousness those rousing American huzzahs—just like the cheers his men had given when they raised the American and Virginian colors over Fort Sackville thirty years before.

Those cheers from the friends and the strangers in the yard saved him. Though he had for years considered himself ready, even eager, to die, he thought when he heard those cheers: I can't let all these people think a little thing like a leg could do me in. And so he returned as he had so often in his life to draw upon that reserve of fortitude which lay beyond the known mortal limits, and steeled himself once again for the grim business of enduring.

The fifes and drums played on, for still another hour, as the surgeon continued his slicing and sawing, his suturing, his tying-off, and the hideous, hissing cauterizing with its roast-meat smell, and his assistant carried off basins of blood. The general no longer let himself consider this phenomenon of being dismembered; he concentrated on the rhythm of the drums, and on the formidable task of remaining conscious, fearing somehow that if he slipped away he would never be able to come back. It's nought but pain, he thought. You can't let people think you'd die of pain. If this butcher bleeds me to death, then that's out of my control, and so be it. But pain, now, I'm responsible for that ... He would look up at Lucy from time to time, and verify her presence. If he did not look at her for a while, his roiling mind would play a trick on him, and he would begin to imagine that the feminine hand that was soothing his brow was not hers but instead the shapely small hand he had held in his own so long ago, the hand of his betrothed, the shy-eyed Teresa de Leyba. Where is she now? he thought. Is she even alive? In this wilderness lives are just swallowed up by distance, and names remembered like myths. Like de Leyba, like Vigo, like Father Gibault, like Bowman and Kenton and Boone. . . .

Two Lives stood by himself on the fringe of the crowd outside. The brisk, measured music of the fifes and drums went on. Shadows had lengthened in the time the Long Knife had been in the house with the white medicine man.

It is a long time to have pain, Two Lives thought.

He looked around at the people who were watching the house: the settlers, the hunters, the black men, the Indians. People he recognized as relatives of Long Knife came out and sat on the porch, talked to those in the crowd, returned to the house, looking grave but calm.

Standing among these people, Two Lives marveled to remember that there had been a time, up until thirty summers ago, when he and most of the other Northwest Indians had not even known that there was this person, Clark, the Long Knife. In those days before the Long Knife came, the tribes had believed what they had been warned of by the British: that the Virginians and Kentuckians were all bad, that they were mad to own all the hunting grounds above the Ohio, and that they should all be killed and scalped and driven out.

That was what Two Lives had believed in his first life.

And now indeed the Americans *were* moving in over the Wilderness Road from the mountains of the East and coming in boats every day down the big river, and were building deeper and deeper into the great hunting grounds. So in those warnings the British had been right, too.

I do not understand how there can be two truths, the chieftain thought. I know only that the Americans were greater than the British and Long Knife is the greatest of them.

After a while some of the white men came out of the house of the Long Knife. One of them was carrying something wrapped in a sheet. He put it in the back of the medicine man's wagon.

Two Lives swung onto his pony and rode from the meadow into the shade of the trees along the road down toward the river. He stopped halfway down the hill and sat on his pony in the humid green shade where the ferns grew, and he waited. Soon he heard the wagon coming down.

He held up his hand. The two medicine men looked at each other and spoke. The young one with yellow eyelashes pulled the reins and stopped the wagon.

The older medicine man stood up in the wagon and waited for the Indian to speak.

"I am Two Lives, of the Puan Winnebago."

"I know. It was you that brought help to General Clark, eh?"

The Indian nodded, rode close to the wagon, stopped, and pointed at the stained bundle in the back.

"That is the leg of Clark?"

"Yes, it is."

"What will you do with it?"

"Well, we'll . . . we'll just dispose of it."

"Two Lives will take it," he said.

"What, you bloody heathen!" cried the younger medicine man, rising to his feet and raising his whip. Two Lives looked into the young man's eyes until they fell and he lowered the whip and sat down.

"Why the devil would you want that leg?" said the older medicine man.

"Hear me: I am alive because of the Long Knife. For more than thirty years I have been alive because of him. My people have been at peace with the Americans because of him. Now he is alive because of me. I should have these bones for my people. You are only going to throw them away."

The older medicine man looked at the younger one, then at the long bloodstained bundle in the back of the wagon. He turned in the seat and, straining, lifted the bundle. "No," he said, "I was not going to throw it away. I was going to keep it myself." The assistant looked at him in surprise. "But," he went on, "I see that it would be right for your people to have it. Here."

Two Lives took the bundle. It was heavy. The smell of it made the pony step about nervously. Two Lives and the old medicine man looked into each other's eyes.

"Good," said Two Lives. He turned his pony and vanished among the leaves of the forest.

Dr. Ferguson was quiet for a while as the wagon rattled on down the mossy road. Then he exhaled and clapped his palms on his knees. "Well," he said. "I tell you, Jack. There's one to amuse your grandkids with someday."

"Damned savage deserves that rotten limb," grumbled the young man. "Probably his nasty poultice that infected it."

The surgeon gazed at him, thoughtfully. "Well, there's no way of knowing, but I doubt it. Anyhow," he sighed, "that's some souvenir for 'im, it surely is."

AFTER SUNSET THAT EVENING, FOUR FINE FIDDLERS FROM LOUIS-ville came up to Clark's Point to join the drummers and fifers. For an hour into the night, marching around the house by torch-light, they serenaded the general, with music gentler and more elegant than the martial tunes they had played in the afternoon.

He lay between clean sheets on the bed in his bedroom, feeling very weak. Lucy had set a chair beside his bed and she stayed there quietly in the candlelight, talking with him when he wanted to talk, going to fetch things when he asked for them, and seeing that his visitors did not stay long enough to tire him. The Gwathmeys had come up, his eldest sister Ann Clark Gwathmey and her husband Owen Gwathmey, who in the face of the general's suffering was for once not complaining about his boils. They beamed at the general and hardly knew what to say. At last he raised his hand and said, "Is my little sweetheart here?"

"Aye," said Ann. "On the porch. We weren't sure as you'd want a child in."

"Would you fetch 'er here, please?"

The girl, just ten years old, was brought to the bedside, wide-eyed, freckled, and red-haired, coming with a strange, awkward step which betrayed a conscious effort to restrain her customary joyous rush to him.

"Ah, Diana!" His eyes lit up and he held his hand to her.

She worked her mouth for a moment, then said, "I came to see you."

"I'm real glad, Missy. Now, I've a hard day, and I'm not the best company. But tomorrow maybe I'll tell you a good story."

She smiled and tugged at his hand. The strange terror of the moment was suddenly gone. "What about, Uncle George?"

"Why, maybe I'll tell you a story of an Indian chief named Two Lives. And maybe he'll sit with us and help me tell it."

Her blue eyes shone and she turned to her mother for confirmation. "That sounds real fine, doesn't it?" said Ann Gwathmey. "Now you run on out, and ask Georgie to come in."

George Gwathmey, tall and the most studious of the general's nephews, loved to talk by the hour with his uncle about the biography books they shared, biographies of kings and conquerors. But this evening the lad sat saying little, politely trying to keep his eyes from straying to that part of the bedsheet under which the left leg should have been outlined, apparently awed beyond words of the ordeal his uncle had survived in the afternoon. The general tried in vain to talk of Frederick the Second to put the young man at ease, but it was with little success and the effort was taxing on his mind, which seemed now to yearn toward wandering and reverie. The last visitor was another favorite nephew, George Rogers Clark Sullivan, who was anything but tongue-tied, and showed promise of talking the old soldier into his grave. Lucy sent the youth away before long, and the general half-dozed for a while. He dreamed of dancing with young ladies in a room lit by scores of candles, a room which sometimes seemed to be in Williamsburg, sometimes in St. Louis, and sometimes in Kaskaskia, though all the young ladies he danced with in the dream had the same face, with the same dark and downcast eyes. Then he awoke, the music was

still playing outside, and beyond the barrier of pain in his thigh
he imagined he could feel his foot moving to the dance.

Then he remembered that the foot was no longer there.
Awakening to that knowledge brought back an awful poignancy.
As a young man he had keenly enjoyed dancing, and almost all
of his genteel memories, the few he had, involved occasions
when there had been dances. He thought now about the absence
of the leg, and wondered what had been done with it. But he
didn't ask. He was sure that such a question would shock Lucy
too much.

She, who had been watching him closely, leaned near, her
chair creaking, and dabbed away tears that were coursing onto
his temples. She realized that she had never before in her life
seen a tear on his face.

A messenger came, bringing the compliments of Senator
Breckenridge with a promise that he would come to visit in a
few days. Lucy thanked him, and as it was too late for him to
return home, went out to arrange bedding for him on the front
porch.

"George," she said on returning, "this place is so small. And
so remote from everyplace. We shall have couriers and musicians camped all over the premises tonight. There's even a party
of Indians hunkered off the porch, waiting to see you."

"Are there now! What tribe, d'you know?"

"Several. I don't know which."

"Is Two Lives still here?"

"I didn't see him."

"In any case, say I should like to talk with them. Have them
come up. And Dick Lovell, too."

"Not tonight, no indeed. I forbid it. You have to sleep."

"Aye, I reckon. But come morning, then. Say I would like to
talk with them then. And the other musicians, too, them as stays
the night."

"Yes, my dear. I'll tell them."

There was silence for a moment and she stood looking down
at him in the candlelight. He turned his head on the pillow, his
eyes on her face. " 'My dear,' is it? By heaven, Lucy, you've
never called me that . . ." He settled back, and gazed at the ceiling. "Nor has anyone, I recollect, since Mother. Rest her soul.
Well, it has a rare sound to my ears." He blinked rapidly. He
heard the chair creak as she sat down.

"Well, there is a reason. All you Clark boys, I'll swear,
you're scarcely the kind to inspire endearments. A clan of

blamed heroes, the lot of you. Two generals. Two captains. Two lieutenants." She shook her head and smiled. "And only Jonathan and William ever had the good sense to settle down and marry. I'll wager *they* hear sweet words now and then."

"Aye," he whispered. "But you know, Lucy, I'd have married, had things been a little different."

"Mhm. Well, you should've. Ought to have this place full o' your own youngsters."

"Well, Lord knows you Clark girls made up for me in the breeding department. All four of you. As it should be. As fine-looking a covey of quails as ever I saw."

He turned his head and saw her gazing at him with her head tilted and a wistful smile on her lined face. He was buoyed by this rare exchange of banter, and touched by the deep, familial affection it veiled. He reached for her hand and held it. "Y'know, Lucy, this country has done right well for itself, having the Clarks."

She saw the wetness welling up in his eyes again, and bit the inside of her lip to keep from groaning with the richness of her emotions. It was a minute before she could speak.

"Well, listen now, George. You'll be coming to Locust Grove to live with us, as soon as you can be moved . . ."

"Lucy, I cannot . . ."

"Hush now! You should have years ago, instead of coming to this God-forsaken place. That . . . that . . ." She glanced toward his truncated leg, despite herself. ". . . Y'd never 'a' hurt yourself that way had you been with us. You must come, George. You'll always have a carriage to take you in to Louisville. And people around who . . . who care for you . . ."

His hand squeezed feebly on hers. He was too weary to argue the point with her just now. He knew that she was right, that he would be even more helpless to sustain himself now than he had been. But it depressed him to realize it. His selection of this solitary place to live had been his last gesture of independence. In giving it up, he knew, he would become a mere ward in the fullest sense of the term. Locust Grove was a magnificent place, full of young nieces and nephews, a staff of thirty servants and workmen, a cheerful and busy place. William Croghan was an enterprising man. To visit there was always a pleasure. But to go there and move in as a dependent—why, it would be unthinkable.

While he lay thinking of these dreary matters, the musicians concluded their serenade, and soon they were moving about and talking low on the porch. The prevailing music outside now was that of crickets and frogs and a whippoorwill. Lucy was beginning to arch her back against weariness.

"Eh," he said at last. "We will discuss it soon. Now, before you go to bed, Lucy, will you please do me the favor of bringing me a moderate portion of that Jamaica rum from the pantry?" She did not answer, and, looking to see her staring at him with an edge of reproach in her eyes, he added, wincing, "The pain it's coming on fierce now, sister."

"And you, who declined it when they were actually cutting."

"True, Lucy. But there were people watching then. Be a kind lass, now. You might just fetch me the bottle, so I won't have to trouble you for more in the night . . ."

Now there's another thing to be considered, he thought when she was out of the room. Here I can have it whenever I please and no one's to fret. But what fuss and cajolery there'll be to have my daily bottle there in a house full of them who cares.

She did not bring in the bottle, but the glass she bore was, to his pleasant surprise, brimful. She put her arm under his head and raised him to help him sip it. For her sake, he drank it with a seemly delicacy instead of tossing it down. She lowered his head to the pillow and sat on the edge of the bed, looking at him with canny eyes, again with that thoughtful tilt to the head. Lying with hands folded on his chest and the warmth of the rum spreading through him, he studied her aspect, and finally said, "Now, then, sister. Out with it."

"Oh, something you said. Tell me, George, as a hero: How much of bravery is just a matter of knowing you're watched?"

He slowly worked his lips into a wry smile. He was delighted and intrigued by her question. "Why, I would reckon, sister," he said with deliberation, "at least a half." He was quiet for a minute, then he went on: "Don't ever tell another soul. But why I had the musicians out there was because if I'd had to holler, their damn screechin' and bangin' would ha' drowned it out. Heh, heh!"

And when she had kissed his forehead, blown out the candle, and left his bedroom to go and rest on the cot by the fireplace in the cabin's main room, General George Rogers Clark lay pondering that wily question of hers, smiling at it between the onslaughts of pain.

It was true. There were endeavors he could remember which had succeeded simply because, having once launched them so boldly, he could not afford to be seen failing at them.

For the essential business of leading, he thought, is that you have to keep your people believing it can be done, even if your own reason concludes it's impossible. That's how I played it, from the very beginning, from the day I first went back East to persuade Governor Henry to let me do it . . .

PART TWO

1777–1780

2

Caroline County, Virginia
November 1777

Their horses snorted steam into the cold, drizzly air; hooves squished in the sodden ground of the meadow; saddles creaked. The two horses seemed to hang close together as if for comfort in the dankness, and now and then George's left foot in its stirrup was pressed against his father's right. Both then would rein the horses a few feet apart and continue along the fencerow.

"This will be in corn," said John Clark, with a sweep of his arm. "Over there I'll graze army beef for General Washington. Dickie and Edmund had some of the hands out here cutting fence rails last month, as you see. We've not had the weather to erect 'em yet." He fell silent and squinted ahead, absorbed in thoughts of next season.

George glanced at his father's profile, the long straight nose, deep-set eyes, the skin all freckles and furrows, not wrinkled much yet; he was not yet fifty. His torso and thighs were solid and compact. He seemed quieter and more thoughtful than he had been before George's westward sojourns beyond the Alleghenies. George had no doubt that worry over his sons' fates was largely the cause of John Clark's gravity. Jonathan, his eldest at twenty-seven, and a captain in the Continental Army, had been nearly killed by smallpox and other sickness while serving in the Southern theater; John, barely twenty and a lieutenant, had been captured by the British at Germantown a few weeks earlier and his fate was as yet a mystery.

They came to an angle in the fencerow and George glimpsed, through the trees, the clearing where he had grown his own first crop of tobacco at the age of fifteen. Ten years ago it was, but he could remember the weight of the sun on his back, the rank smell of the dark leaves. Ten years seemed as remote in the past

31

as the forest gloom beyond the mountains now seemed remote in the distance. Another world. He had crossed a threshold of his life when, poring over crude maps during lulls in the defense of Kentucky last year, he had conceived the idea that the British could be invaded in their own western outposts. Since then he had been carrying that vision with him, and it had occurred in every detail in his imagination, its possibility coloring everything he saw, directing his every action. The other settlers in the Kentucky land, brave and hardy as they were, saw only as far as the end of the day and the edge of the clearing, as if their minds were stockaded; they saw the Indian raids only as something to be endured, rather than stopped or controlled at their source. In that sense, George thought as he glanced again at his father, this stable and patient John Clark is like them. He is cautious and looks forward only from one season to the next.

Suddenly John Clark turned to face his son, even as he was being observed so thoughtfully; there was an anxiety in his eyes. "Has Dickie spoken to you, about joining your expedition out there?"

"No," replied George. "Nary a word."

"He's talked of little else since you came back from Kaintuck. He's quite fired with your scheme."

"He would be a good lad to have along."

"I must ask you to discourage him, though."

"He is eighteen now, is he not? If he doesn't join me, I'm sure he will go to join Washington almost as soon."

"I can't spare him, George."

"With all respect, Father, I doubt you'll have a choice in the matter. I mean, he may go to the eastern war as Jonathan and Johnny have. Or he might join me and I can keep an eye on him, eh?"

"As you did on your cousin Joseph last Christmas?" The question came loaded with a sarcasm unusual in John Clark's nature. George was stung by it; he spurred his horse a few yards ahead in anger, turning his back on his father. Then he reined in and waited for him, cooling his temper.

"I am sorry I said that, George."

"I'm sorry, too."

"But you must understand it's a worry on your mother. Not knowing whether her own nephew is dead or a prisoner in some Shawnee town."

"It couldn't be helped, Father. You know I always take every precaution. But I'm sure you don't know what an undertaking it was to transport five hundred pounds of gunpowder through those parts. It's remarkable that we made it at all. I'm deeply sad about Joe. But such things happen. You must understand, Father, I'm commandant of the whole Kaintuck militia, and I've lost many a brave man. I've shewed you the Kaintuck, and you saw it's land worth defending. Joe fought, and we mightn't've got the powder there had 'e not."

"Aye. And so now you propose an adventure a hundred times as foolhardy."

"No, sir. Only a hundred times as important. And with a hundred times as many men, I expect. Believe me, sir, I know exactly what I shall do every step of the way."

"So you're a prophet now as well, eh?" Again that sarcasm, but followed by a sigh.

"If to believe one can control events is to be prophetic, maybe so."

John Clark reined in his horse and sat looking directly at his son, obviously no longer thinking just of the next growing season. His cloak flapped against his leg in a gust of raw wind. For this inspection tour of the four-hundred-acre Clark estate, George was wearing his customary buckskins and fringed leggings and a fur hat, and to his father he looked more like a thinly clad savage than a son of the Virginia gentry. The shape of his long, muscular limbs and powerful chest were evident in the light garb. His pigtail of copper-red hair and the ringed tail of his hat hung together down his back.

"Aren't you cold, George?"

"No." The youth laughed. "You sound like Mother."

"Well, I don't know why you're not. I'm frozen clear to my fundament." He grinned, his lips bluish, his big horsy teeth yellow. "What d'you say we go back to a fire and a toddy, son?"

"Good enough. Listen," he said, as they turned the horses homeward. "Here's a story you'll like: A white man shivers in coat and boots on a day like this, but his guide, a Delaware, is naked but comfortable. The white man inquires, 'How can you bear it?' The Delaware asks him, 'Is your face cold?' 'Yes, but I don't mind that,' says the white. 'So,' the savage tells him, 'me all face.'

"Well, Father, I suppose I've come to be like that: all face. I don't mind it."

Laughing, they urged the horses into a canter down across the meadow and into a leafless copse, splashed through a shallow brook, jumped a stone fence, and galloped up the slope of a small knoll where dry yellow grass waved. The sky was the color of gunmetal and the drizzle was changing to a spitting snow as the wind rose. Topping the knoll, they saw the house nestled among its outbuildings, its chimney smoke whipping away like spindrift. Cupid, a tall, skinny buck slave loosely draped in one of John Clark's castoff blue coats, met them at the porch and took the horses to the stable.

Inside the door George and his father were jumped by seven-year-old William, whom they snatched up from the floor in their powerful arms and tossed back and forth between them until he was helpless with laughter, then handed over, reeling, to Lucy, a lithe ten-year-old with the long Clark nose in the middle of a delicate face. The two children went off to the kitchen, clowning self-consciously for their big brother, who, for all his affection and familiarity, seemed an awesome wild stranger from a wild land each time he returned from the west.

Richard and Edmund were sitting before the fireplace in their stocking feet, drying their boots. Their faces were flushed from exposure and smudged with ash and soot. They had been in a field at the corner of the farm all day burning stumps and brush from recent clearing. Edmund, only fifteen, appraised George with a rather timid smile: Richard, eighteen, almost six feet tall and currently trying to break the family of calling him "Dickie," greeted him with a look of manly complicity. George went to them and backed up to the fire. "Hallo, boys! I've seen men come in from Indian skirmishes looking smarter than the two of you."

"It's dirty work, that's what," said Richard.

"It is indeed. Now if you wish to see some really dirty work, you should come out and see folks try to clear a field of those big Kaintuck trees. Big around as a house."

"I do intend to, George. Say, now . . ." He rose and stood close beside George, dropping his voice. "I'd appreciate it if you'd put in a word with Pa to that effect. I fear he's going to be ag'in it . . ."

George put an arm over Richard's shoulder and grinned, gazing across the room to the sideboard where their father was decanting amber whiskey into two glasses. "Oh, 'a word to that effect,' is it? A petition to King John of the Clark kingdom? You feel I have some influence in his court, eh?" He turned and squatted on the hearth and laved his hands in the heat of the fire. Hearing his father's footsteps approaching behind him, he continued, "That you should settle with Father. All I'll say is that any Clark would be a welcome addition to any party of mine."

"So he's broached it t' you, I see," grumbled John Clark, seating himself on a wooden chair beside the hearth and giving George a glass. They touched the rims of their glasses. "To Virginia," said Mr. Clark, glancing shrewdly aside at Richard. "Why anyone should want to leave her is beyond my ken."

"To Virginia," agreed George. "Including her new county of Kentucky, where I predict all good Clarks will go."

"What! Not to heaven?"

"Aye. Just the place I'm speaking of," said George.

"Mm-hm. Well, if it's such a heaven, pray tell me why you must go there with an army."

"Ha, ha! Well said! But I'll wager you'll come there one day, all of you, once Henry Hamilton and his bloody scalp-takers have been smoked out." He sipped the whiskey and winked aside to Richard.

"It's a wild scheme, that's all it is," said John Clark. "You can't go out there a thousand miles and capture forts from the British and the savages. By heaven, give any red-haired stripling from Virginia a gun and a survey chain, and he imagines he's George Washington all over again."

"Washington defended a border of near four hundred miles with seven hundred men in the French and Indian campaigns," George said.

"Aye, and it's as I say, you think you can do something comparable."

"Well, sir, it's a worthy example."

"I'm not a soldier, George, as all my boys seem to want to be. But I have read enough history to know that it takes cannon and a great number of men to storm forts."

"True. But surprise makes one man worth ten. Richard," he said, turning to his brothers, who were listening in awe, "and you, Edmund, I'll remind you not to discuss this outside the family."

"La, la, la," came a woman's voice from the kitchen door. "Intrigues and strategems, in our own home! Or have I entered the Continental headquarters by mistake? Wash up and come to the table, all you generals."

For the occasion of George's visit, Ann Rogers Clark had cooked an entire wild turkey, which Edmund had bagged the day before at the edge of the clearing. He had brought it home headless; the ball from his long rifle had neatly decapitated the great bird at a distance of some twenty yards. Edmund, cheeks flaming with shyness and pride, was coaxed to explain why he had aimed precisely at such a small part of such a large creature.

"He'd caught sight of us," Edmund said. "He was tryin' to sneak off in th' brush, and alls I could see was his dang ol' head. So, I shot it off."

George clapped his hands together and gave a whoop of approval. "Now there's a sharpshooter!" Little William mimicked his glee, clapping and crying, "Edmund is a sharpshooter!"

Ann Rogers Clark, majestic and firm-jawed even though haggard from twenty-seven years of bearing and rearing her ten children, gazed at her son George for a moment, very thoughtfully, then tucked a damp strand of gray hair back under the edge of her dust cap. "You're our guest of honor, George. Would you say the grace, please?"

A hush fell around the table; heads bowed and eyes closed. George did not feel especially solemn and reverent. He was too exuberant with his sense of purpose, and felt playful here in the bosom of his family, and decided that he would extemporize rather than recite the usual invocation. He paused and looked around at the ruddy faces, the heads of red hair, all colors of red: some copper, some sand, and some so dark a red they looked almost black. He looked at the brown basted turkey and the steaming bowls on the table. He caught Frances Eleanor, who was almost five, sneaking a look at him with her luminous eyes, and she shut them quickly.

"Our Father," he began, "accept our humble thanks for the marksmanship Thou hast blessed Thy humble servant Edmund Clark with, and for putting this noble gobbler within its range." He sensed someone at the table trying to suppress laughter. "Our gratitude for our health and for the tranquility and happiness of this house. Now, Lord, if Thou wouldst know how much we appreciate the bounty on this table, just watch us Clarks eat. Amen."

He looked up to see both his father and mother, their lips compressed, shaking their heads and looking at each other. The children were smirking but afraid to laugh aloud.

"Lord forgive my son for his jocularity," John Clark implored heavenward, then stood up, and with a keen-edged knife began laying open the turkey, and the clatter of a spirited feast began.

"Where will you stay, George?" asked John Clark.

"I'll lay up at the Gwathmeys' a day or two, but expect I'll have to take lodgings at an inn."

"Will you have time to pay a visit to Gunton Hall while you're here?" asked Mrs. Clark.

"No, but I shall see Mr. Mason in Williamsburg. He's helping the governor and Tom Jefferson advance my proposal in the Assembly."

"Ah! Tom, too?" exclaimed John Clark. "Well, you've certainly enlisted enough old friends and neighbors to your cause."

"I wish you'd enlist *me*," interjected Richard.

"Time will answer that, and I suggest you be patient," Ann Rogers Clark said severely. "And as for you, George, don't be coveting Edmund's markmanship for your army. Grace of God this war will end before he's of age!"

"Amen," said John Clark.

3

WILLIAMSBURG, VIRGINIA
December 1777

A CARRIAGE DREW UP BEFORE AN INN IN WILLIAMSBURG. SEVERAL soldiers were in its path, arguing, laughing, and exchanging money. They jostled each other out of the way as the driver urged the team alongside the building. A slight young courier in well-cut velvet clothing and polished pumps stepped down from the carriage, and picked his way among the puddles and the heaps of dirty snow to the door of the inn. In the doorway stood the innkeeper and a comely golden-haired chambermaid, both peering up the street.

"I have a message for Major Clark," said the courier. "He's said to be lodging here."

"So he is," the innkeeper said, and pointed a fat hand up the street. "Here he'll be coming now."

The soldiers in the street had burst out in cheering. The girl was hugging herself and jouncing up and down, her bosom and ringlets bobbing. "He'll be the first," she squealed.

The courier looked up the wet, gray street and saw four men in shirt-sleeves running abreast at remarkable speed, sprinting and lunging like racehorses. As they drew near the inn, a tall, wide-shouldered youth suddenly surged ahead of the other three, and passed the door twenty feet ahead of them, laughing, his shoes scarcely seeming to touch the street, the pigtail of his copper-colored hair flying. The others then thundered past, their soles slapping the cobbles as they drew themselves to a heaving, panting halt amid the taunts of the soldiers. The girl was watching the red-haired one, who had stopped a few yards farther on and was now coming back, grinning, carrying his strapping frame with an easy grace, and seeming to be hardly winded. "What did I say?" the lass exulted.

"There is your Major Clark, sir," said the innkeeper. "It's the fourth race he's won this hour. Major!" he called.

The young officer came over, and the courier noticed that the wench inhaled to raise her bosom at his approach, as if in salutation.

"This man has come to see you," said the innkeeper.

The courier and the young officer bowed slightly to each other.

"I come from Governor Henry, sir. May I speak with you?"

"Ah! I've been waiting for you, then. Is he ready to see me?"

"Yes. I've brought a carriage."

"That's good. Have we time for me to wash myself down and dress myself up? Nell here can bring us an ale. Would you, Nell? Now, sir," the young officer said, taking the messenger by the arm and leading him into the inn, "tell me your name, and . . ."

"Heyo, Major," one of the soldiers called. "Don't forget the purse." He crossed the street and spilled a handful of coins into Major Clark's hand. "You're the very devil on your feet, sir."

"Thank you kindly. As I had to be, to outpace such fellows. Goodbye. Well, now," he said, jingling the silver as they climbed the stairs. "Not bad for an hour's exercise, eh? So tell me, how is the great Patrick Henry these days? I'm sorry; what was your name?"

"Jonathan, sir. Jonathan Herring."

"Jonathan! I have a brother named Jonathan. He was with Henry in the Revolutionary Convention. He's serving with General Muhlenberg now . . ."

They entered Major Clark's room, where he dropped a towel in a basin of cold water, stripped off his shirt and began wiping his torso with the damp towel. The messenger was awed by the power and symmetry of the young frontiersman's physique. As he toweled himself, the long muscles knotted and rippled, sharply defined by his leanness. He was deep-chested, small in the waist, with a thick, sinewy neck. Red hair lightly covered his chest and abdomen and forearms. Nell came in with two tankards while he was drying, and blushed mightily at the sight of him. Herring smirked as she went down the stairs.

"I do believe, Major, that the wench has some feelings for you."

"Do you." The major said only that, but a hard look that flashed in his dark eyes made the courier wish he had not made the remark. He found himself a little confused by this; the young officer seemed so affable, so sporting, hardly the sort to take offense at some harmless remark about a bawd. So Herring sipped his ale in silence for a while as Major Clark dressed in a clean linen shirt and red velvet coat which appeared to be fresh from the tailor's. Herring took note that the only other garments that hung in the room were a long hunting coat and leggings of soft buckskin, decorated with colorful designs in quill and trimmed with fringe, and a wide-brimmed sweat-stained hat. These garments were redolent of wood smoke and old perspiration, and appeared to have been worn so long as to be permanently impressed with the shape of their owner. They imparted, somehow, an air of wildness and savagery to the clean, precisely civilized decor of this room in a Williamsburg inn.

Herring wanted to restore the amiable mood they had begun with. "Tell me," he ventured, "what is it like out there in the Kentucky country?"

The major, buckling on his sword, paused and gazed westward out the window. After a while, he answered:

"If you can, imagine trees six feet thick, and leafage so dense overhead that the sunshine never reaches the ground. These from one horizon to the other. Can you envision oceans of cane and grass high enough to obscure a mounted man? Streams like crystal, and game so profuse that you could nearly shoot blindfolded and hit something? Earth so rich you have to jump out of the way after you plant a seed in it?"

Herring, man of the city though he was, thrilled at the thought of such abundance and at the hushed timbre of Major

Clark's voice as he described it. The descriptions sounded like hyperbole, but the enthusiasm was genuine.

"That's what it is like out there," he continued. "But just now there is a bloodiness about it as would make your nape crawl. It's a part of the day's work to keep your scalp on your skull, and I am not exaggerating."

He drained his tankard, took a tricorn hat from a box and put it on, then tucked a roll of papers under his arm and rushed Herring out of the room with him. "Now, then," he said as they tromped down the stairs and out to the waiting carriage. "If the governor is going to help me tame that savagery out there, we mustn't keep him waiting, eh?"

GOVERNOR HENRY, WIRE-FRAME SPECTACLES PUSHED UP TO REST on the top of his head, raised his glass of port to touch the one he had poured for Major Clark. They drank, and sat down on chairs facing each other across the hearth.

"Your health is better," said Clark.

"Much better," said the governor, dipping his long nose into the glass, inhaling, then sipping.

"My father sends his compliments, and thanks you for your many past kindnesses."

"Return my best wishes when you see him next," replied Henry, who had served John Clark as a lawyer on several past occasions. "Now, I understand you have had a harrowing year since last we met, young man."

"Any venture west of the mountains is harrowing in these times. We've done what we could in spite of that."

"I've not heard the particulars of your journey back with the gunpowder. Only that your assemblyman Mister Jones was killed. Most regrettable!"

"Aye. Well, sir, we got the powder through, all five hundred pounds of it, and again I thank you for it. I doubt there'd be a white man alive west of the mountains by now had you not secured it for us. Anyway, with a certain amount of hardship we boated it from Pittsburgh plumb down the Ohio to Limestone. We were ambushed by Indians several times along the way, but no harm done that far. On Christmas Day, though, nigh Harrodsburg, going overland, we were set upon by another band. That was a grievous Christmas Day, indeed. John Gabriel Jones was killed, and within a few miles of home. Three others of the company, among them my cousin Joseph Rogers, were taken captive and we've heard no more of them."

"Ah, that's a sad thing."

"That hurt me deep, sir; I had persuaded him to join our party."

Governor Henry studied Major Clark, who was frowning into the dregs of his port, the left side of his face ruddy in the glow of the fire. The governor felt a rush of sympathy and admiration for him. Then the youth swigged the rest of the port, worked it over his tongue, swallowed, and returned his gaze intent to the governor.

"Anyhow, I organized a government for Kentucky, as I wrote you, and made military discipline for its defense. Made as my captains four of the keenest Indian fighters as ever slipped through the woods. Daniel Boone, Jim Harrod, John Todd, and Ben Logan. What men! By God, sir! But by spring, as you know, the Indians resumed their raids across the Ohio in big bands, led and outfitted by the British. Hamilton at Detroit is supplying 'em with scalping knives and paying a bounty for all the scalps and captives they can get."

The governor nodded and stared grimly into the fire.

"Since then," Clark continued, "it's been pretty much one routine, defending our forts against siege, getting what food we can, chasing Indians about the woods—or being chased by them—dressing our wounded, and burying our dead; that seems to be most of our business. Them able to bear arms are spread so thin among the settlements that even the ladies sometimes have to spell them at the firing ports. Disease takes as many as the fighting, though, cooped up as they are in those stockades with their animals. And not able to get out and plant or harvest, why, you can imagine they're on rations not fit for a rat. But get by they do, and live a life while they're at it. You'd be astounded at some of the tales. Why, a fellow was killed and scalped one day in March, and his widow was married up a month later by a gent whose own wife had been massacred some short time previous . . . Boone's leg was broken by a bullet in a raid outside Boonesboro, but a big free scout named Simon Butler—mark that name well—toted him into the fort with them at his heels . . .

"Now that's the Kaintuck as it is today, and to defend it long with those few men as we have is desperate at best. If John Bowman hadn't arrived with that company of militia you sent, I couldn't have left to come here now. Settlers are returning back over the mountains in numbers, and that hurts us sorely.

Part of my way back this journey, I escorted a party of seventy-six, besides women and children."

Governor Henry was nodding gravely, his lips compressed in a thin white line.

"You know as well as I do, Governor, we have to keep strong settlement out there to keep the British and their Indians off the back door of the colonies," the frontiersman went on.

"I do. I do."

"That country has to be kept secure."

"That I know, too. I marvel at those that stay. But now, George, I know you, and I know you don't come and get a man's ear merely to lament a situation. You're here to suggest some remedy, I presume."

"Correct, Excellency," said Clark with a sly grin.

"Very well. I'm receptive to hearing it. Mind you, I can make no promises. Virginia's picking her own purse and getting naught but lint."

"You've read my letter, about what my spies learned of the enemy post at Kaskaskia on the Mississippi . . ."

"Yes. And your somewhat incredible notion of invading it." The governor shook his head, looking into his wineglass.

"Not so incredible as it might seem, though, precisely because *they* would think it incredible. They expect no offensive from us there, and their defense is lax. Most of its British garrison is habitually up at Detroit. Rocheblave commands the place with a collection of idlers, Creoles, and scoundrels, and they themselves are some disenchanted with the British rule. Our risk in taking it would be small, compared with the amount of mischief we could stop by doing so."

"Go on. I am still listening."

"Rocheblave, as the functionary for General Hamilton, gives presents and bounties to the Indians thereabouts, and incites 'em to raid our settlers in Kaintuck. And Kaskaskia has cannon to control that part of the Mississippi against any communications we might desire, and at the same time hold it open as a supply route for the British at Detroit and the Wabash posts . . ."

Governor Henry raised his hand. "One moment. I respect your appraisal, both of Kaskaskia's importance, and of its vulnerability. But my doubts arise from our own circumstance. Such an expedition would require—what? Seven hundred? A thousand men?"

"Five hundred would suffice, I think. At the very least."

"And how much provision? How much artillery? How many

boats? Horses? Perhaps we have all got unreasonably encouraged about the war, since Saratoga. You know, I presume, that Virginia is hard pressed—nay, unable—to spare men or goods, even *shoes*, for Washington, who's wintering at a place in Pennsylvania called Valley Forge. Why, his own army is starving and naked. As I see it, moving against a fort no one ever heard of, nearly a thousand miles away, would require not only more men and matériel than we could justify, but more than we *have*."

"But to capture that country with a small force now would cost a fraction of its next year's defense if we don't."

"I wonder if you heard me," Governor Henry said. "It's not that I don't like your plan. It is simply not possible for Virginia to provide for it. The Assembly would never authorize the diversion of such a force."

The frontiersman sat back in his chair for a moment, and the governor imagined he could actually see a rapid series of calculations pass behind the glittering dark blue eyes.

"That being so," said Clark, suddenly leaning forward in earnest again, "militia should be raised just for the duration of such a campaign. They should be woodsmen for the most part. Hunters. Swift and quiet. It requires little to equip such a man for a campaign of, say, forty days or thereabouts. That, sir, with a few boats and some ammunition, would be enough, and it would not draw off much from your eastern war here. As for the Assembly, they need only be told that it's for the defense of Kentucky, not for an offensive so far afield. For that matter," he added, "I'd fear for the secrecy of any mission that had to be voted through a legislative body."

The governor nodded at the astuteness of the remark. He sat now leaning forward, an elbow on his thigh, chin in his left hand, index finger laid over his mouth and the end of his nose, tapping one foot on the floor, and stared with his ever-fierce eyes at this audacious youth. Three words Clark had said kept sounding in his head. *Woodsmen. Swift. Quiet.* The governor realized that Clark was talking about warfare in the Indian fashion. And as he looked at the young man's hard, lean form and eagle's visage, he imagined a long file of such tall men in buckskin slipping silently through wilderness shadows, all their provisions on their backs, long rifles at their sides. The governor got up from his chair suddenly and began to pace, head forward, lips pursed, hands clasped behind his back.

For a long time Governor Henry had been encouraging General Hand, the commander at Fort Pitt, to launch an offensive westward. Such an expedition, if done in the orthodox manner, would be ponderous, with cannon, with baggage convoys, with livestock led along to be slaughtered for meat ... A slow affair, costly, almost impossible to do in secrecy ... But this, now ...

Woodsmen. Swift. Quiet.

The governor turned back toward the hearth, and rubbed his hands before the fire. "George," he said. "Have some more port. Then let us spread your maps on the table here. I should like to be made familiar with your whole conception before we broach it to Tom Jefferson and the others."

Clark rose, lithe as a panther, smiling but careful not to seem exuberant. Good, he thought. And Jefferson will see it my way, I am sure.

He knew both of them were thinking of those lands above the Ohio, originally Virginia grant lands left under British control by the French and Indian War.

They'll agree to any campaign which might strengthen our claim to that, he thought. "Thank you, Excellency," he said, tipping the decanter over his glass. "Let me show you what I have in mind ..."

4

WILLIAMSBURG, VIRGINIA
January 1778

GIVING HIS CLOAK TO A SERVANT AT THE DOOR OF THE GOVERNOR'S residence, George was ushered into the drawing room. He was surprised to see there all four of the men who had carried his appeal to the Privy Council. He had met frequently and in secret with one or two of them at a time since his first discussion with Governor Henry almost a month earlier. Now, they were all here gathered around the sideboard and there was an atmosphere of subdued excitement in the room. They all stopped talking and turned cheerfully to him with raised glasses. Jefferson, his boyhood neighbor, immediately proposed the toast.

"Gentlemen! To Virginia's westward blade!"

"Well said!" cried George Mason, eyes twinkling as usual at the sound of a good phrase.

"To Colonel George Rogers Clark," said George Wythe. "May his name become the bane of Henry Hamilton."

George laughed, and feigned surprise. As he had expected, then, it obviously had been approved. "What is that 'Colonel'?" he said, as he accepted a glass and their handshakes.

"Why, George," said Governor Henry, a smug expression on his face, "who else should lead this expedition but its original advocate? The colonelcy comes with your orders."

"*I* am to lead it?" he said, still pretending to be astonished.

"Come now," said Jefferson, throwing an arm up over his shoulders and looking archly at him from under his bushy red brows. "You haven't fooled us a whit, hanging back all modestlike and playing hard-to-get. Why, you'd be mortified if we'd put your scheme in anyone else's hands, now, wouldn't you?"

George grinned and bowed. "I'm delighted to accept, of course . . ." he said in a found-out tone that made the four prominent conspirators erupt in laughter and backslapping.

"Now, George," said the governor, "here are the *public* orders for your enterprise. The Assembly has authorized it on this basis." He gave him a letter and stood sipping brandy, watching him read it:

Lieutenant Colo. George Rogers Clark

You are to proceed without Loss of Time to inlist Seven Companies of Men officered in the usual Manner to act as Militia under your Orders. They are to proceed to Kentucky & there to obey such orders & Directions as you shall give them for three Months after their arrival at that place, but to receive pay &c. in case they remain on Duty a longer Time.

You are empowered to raise these Men in any County in the Commonwealth and the County Lieutenants respectively are requested to give you all possible assistance in that Business.

Given under my Hand at Wmsburg
January 2d 1778

P. Henry

"Well, that should alarm no one," George said. "Yet it gives me all the authority I should need to raise a force. And rather a lot of elbow room for contingencies."

"And here are your *secret* orders," the governor said, handing him a thicker packet. "They're a bit more explicit, and ought not bear any surprises, as you all but wrote them yourself," he added with gruff humor.

George Mason, portly and clear-eyed, rocked back and forth on his heels and looked up at him with thoughtfulness. A long-time friend of the Clark family, Mason had overseen much of George's schooling, both in practical disciplines and in gentle-manly principles. That look of his evoked memories of long, sunny afternoons at Gunston Hall, divided among books and maps and the strenuous athletic competitions among the youth of the local gentry. One of Virginia's eminent men, Mason was the author of the Bill of Rights of Virginia's first Constitution. But to the young frontiersman he was still teacher and mentor, and one whom George would as much wish to please as his own father and grandfather. Mason smacked his lips. "Now, m'lad, you're on your way to an audacious adventure which is sure to try your every resource. God be with you, and however much you trust in yourself, never be too proud to get down on your knees to Him. Do you understand me?"

"I do, sir."

"Even if you succeed in this, there's no excusing pride."

"I shall succeed in it, sir. . . . But I hasten to add that I state that out of confidence, *not* pride."

Mason grinned at him with tight-bitten lips, gripped his broad shoulders with both hands and made as if to shake him. "You're solid as an oak. I'm so pleased with you!"

George opened his coat pocket and drew forth two silver me-dallions, one depicting a wrestler, one a runner. "D'you remem-ber these, sir?"

Mason beamed. "Aye! You still keep them! Well, I am touched!" Eyes filling, he smoothed between thumbs and fore-fingers the trophies he had awarded George more than ten years ago, then handed them back.

Mr. Wythe came over then, crisp and dry as a lawbook, pale-faced under his powdered wig, with the physique of a sparrow and the beak of an eagle. He was one of the men who had signed the Declaration of Independence and, like Mason, had been a member of the Constitutional Convention. Clark respected and appreciated him, but felt no warm attachment to him as he did to all the others.

"I should like to assure you," said Wythe, "that Tom and George and I are drafting our letter guaranteeing those rewards of land we discussed to the volunteers in your expedition. Three hundred acres to each, in addition to their usual pay, if you succeed. And proportionately more to the officers by rank, of course." He paused and gave a small wry smile which reminded Clark of a tenderfoot at Harrodsburg the previous fall who had eaten an unripe persimmon; it was difficult not to laugh. "I don't envy you, my boy," Wythe went on, "when you finally *do* tell your recruits where you're taking them."

Clark looked down at Wythe and nodded. "I've given that occasion a great deal of forethought. I agree. It's going to require a strong hand and a wise head. I think I have the hand," he mused, raising his big, brown, long-fingered right hand, watching it close to a hard fist, then open. "I reckon I shall have to trust in Providence to give me the wisdom."

"As all must," Wythe said. He was blinking, and his lips had gone a bit unsteady. Clark was surprised, seeing this first outward sign of any sentiment in Wythe. And suddenly, after all these weeks of meetings, he felt at last a bridge of warmth across the reserve of this great jurist.

Wythe gripped his hand, and with his left palm squeezed his elbow. "By God, sir," he breathed, "if I were younger, *I* would go with you!" And then he stepped quickly away and gazed into the fire.

GEORGE ORDERED THE CARRIAGE STOPPED WHILE STILL SEVERAL blocks from the inn, and climbed out to walk the rest of the way. He was simply too charged with energy and anxiety to sit any longer in a conveyance.

The carriage rattled away over the cobblestones into the darkness, disappearing and reappearing at intervals as it passed through the small pools of lamplight. It was late. Most house windows were dark. He stood in the blackness for a few minutes, clenching and opening his hands, inhaling the bitter cold air through his clenched teeth, shifting his weight from one foot to the other, and looking above the rooftops and chimneypots at the lucid cold stars. He put his right hand inside his cloak to lay his palm on the letter of secret instructions Governor Henry had given him, and felt as well the rapid thudding of his heart.

It had been this way ever since he left the four great conspirators at the governor's residence: He had been calm while there, somehow as calm and authoritative and confident as those august men, or even more; but once alone he had grown as taut and vibrant as a fiddle string, heart and imagination racing, his whole body silently shrieking its need for release through action.

He began walking toward the inn, walking faster and faster, his bootsoles and heels rasping and clicking on the street. The cold air stung his face and lifted his cape behind him; he seemed to walk in a wide saucer of blackness under a lid of starpoints, ringed by a horizon of barking dogs. The tension built in him faster than he could walk it off, a kind of savage bright eagerness which held off around the dark edges of his consciousness a throng of nameless and unadmitted fears, as a campfire in a wilderness holds off the wild things. He knew what those fears represented, but would not let his consciousness use their names, which were *disappointment*, and *death*, and worst of all, *failure*.

He had to anchor his thoughts to something before they should run away with him; coming into a fringe of strong light from a tavern window, he stopped and drew out the secret version of his orders, unfolded the sheet, and read it again, to attach his mind to words, as he was unable yet to attach his physical self to action.

> *In Council W^{ms}burg Jany 1778*
> *Lieut Colonel George Rogers Clark*

You are to proceed with all convenient Speed to raise Seven Companies of Soldiers to consist of fifty men each officered in the usual manner & armed most properly for the Enterprize & with this Force attack the British post at Kaskaskia.

It is conjectured that there are many pieces of Cannon & military stores to considerable Amount at that place, the taking & preservation of which would be a valuable acquisition to the State. If you are so fortunate therefore as to succeed in your Expectation, you will take every possible Measure to secure the Artillery & Stores & whatever may advantage the State.

For the Transportation of the Troops, provisions &c down the Ohio, you are to apply to the Commanding officer at Fort Pitt for Boats, &, during the whole Transaction you are

to take especial Care to keep the true Destination of your
Force secret. Its Success depends upon this . . .

As he read in the lamplight, he was watched from the
mouth of a pitch-black alleyway by two rancid and swarthy
town thugs, who saw by the cut of his garments that he was
a gentleman of substance, alone and unguarded. They el-
bowed each other in the darkness and then posted themselves
in a niche from which they could ambush him when he resumed his walk. One drew a knife and the other a lead-loaded
leather sap.

. . . It is earnestly desired that you show Humanity to such
British Subjects and other persons as fall into your hands. If
the white Inhabitants at that post & the neighbourhood will
give undoubted Evidence of their attachment to this State
(for it is certain they live within its Limits) by taking the
Test prescribed by Law & every other way & means in their
power, Let them be treated as fellow Citizens & their persons & property duly secured. Assistance & protection
against all Enemies whatever shall be afforded them & the
Commonwealth of Virginia is pledged to accomplish it. But
if these people will not accede to these reasonable Demands,
they must feel the miseries of War, under the direction of
that Humanity that has hitherly distinguished Americans,
& which it is expected you will ever consider as the Rule
of your Conduct & from which you are in no Instance to depart . . .

"I claims them boots," whispered one of the thugs, a short,
scrawny man with a patch over his left eye. "I ain't had warm
feet for a month!"
"Shush!" hissed the other. "Look you, he's a big lad. Better
take 'im quick. Might be he's armed."

. . . It is in Contemplation to establish a post near the
Mouth of Ohio. Cannon will be wanted to fortify it. Part of
those at Kaskaskia will be easily brought thither or otherwise
secured as circumstances will make necessary.
    You are to apply to General Hand for powder & Lead nec-
essary for this Expedition. If he can't Supply it the person
who has that which Capt Lynn bro^t from Orleans can. Lead

was sent to Hampshire by my Orders & that may be deliver'd you. Wishing you Success.

                                    I am Sir your hble Servt
                                              P. Henry

My anxiety, he realized as he folded the letter and returned it to his pocket, *is just that I can't quite comprehend yet that they listened to me and said yes. My God, my God, what I have ahead of me.*

He had taken half a dozen steps when he sensed swift movement behind him, even before he consciously heard it; reacting with that rush of bristling readiness which had become second nature to him in the Indian campaigns, he spun about and dropped into a widestanced posture, poised on the balls of his feet, facing the dark forms that were advancing on him.

One look at his coiled attitude and killing eye and the two thugs went cold with fright and forgot their motive. They backed off toward the shadows.

George saw the glint of lamplight on a knife, and touched the hilt of his sword, but felt no urgency to drawn it. Suddenly in this confrontation he had grown completely calm, with a keen and happy serenity in which no doubts existed. Mirth bubbled up in him like an intoxicant.

"Hey now, you two!" he roared into the night after their retreating shapes. "Hey, now, gents, you want a fight? Then come and let me sign you up . . . Ha! Ha! You can be my first volunteers! Gain yourselves a medal or two, and a plot of ground for your old age, eh? Ha, ha! Ha, ha!"

He turned and strode on toward the inn, leaving behind him the echoes of his own voice, the renewed barking of unseen dogs, and the sounds of window casements flying open. And from the darkness beyond the tavern lights a snarly voice yelled back:

"Ho, you crazy coxcomb! God blast yer eyes!"

And its cackle of laughter trailed off in the darkness.

NELL LAY AWAKE IN HER LITTLE ROOM UNDER THE STAIRS OF THE inn. For hours she had been listening to hear a carriage stop outside, but none had. She was hopelessly wide awake. She had turned over a hundred times under the great thick down comforter, trying to find the magical position which would make her too drowsy to think about the red-haired young officer. She had sensed today that his sojourn here in Williamsburg was about to end, and that he would soon be gone without ever having known of her yearnings. This morning, going to his room to change the linen, she had found him cleaning his long rifle, and all his books were off the shelf and in his trunk. He had looked up at her, smiled pleasantly enough, then returned to his maintenance of the weapon, preoccupied and seemingly not even aware of her presence. And then this evening the carriage had come to take him away again, and there had been something about his manner which had made her feel that his efforts here, whatever they might be, were coming to a conclusion.

Suddenly now she heard the front door of the inn open and close, and she recognized his footsteps, that soft, swift tread, going up the stairs above her alcove. Her heart sank, then raced.

He had not rung for her. If she was to see him she would simply have to go to his room unbidden. The thought of being so bold frightened her even more. What if he should leave before morning? she thought.

Nell slipped out from the bed's warmth, and the icy air chilled her through the thin nightdress. She put her feet into the slippers beside the bed, draped a blanket around her shoulders and clutched it with one hand, picked up a candlestick, and opened her door. She lit the candle at a sconce in the hallway and, trembling with cold and apprehension, quietly mounted the stairs, carrying the small flickering point of light, followed by the huge leaping shadow of herself on the stairwell walls. She turned at the top of the stairs and rapped delicately on his door. Often in her daydreams he had opened the door and taken her into his arms. She breathed deeply, waiting. There was a pause, then the door handle turned, the door opened a few inches, and Nell gasped. She was looking into one dark blue eye and the barrel of a flintlock pistol.

He lowered the pistol. "What is it, Nell?"

She worked her lips for a moment and finally was able to say, "I wondered, do you need anything, sir? I heard you come in . . ."

"No, thank you, Nell, but that's a fine lass. Wait . . ." He disappeared behind the door, then reappeared. "Here, with thanks for your kindness." He extended a silver coin to her with his bare arm.

She shook her head. "No. I don't want that."

"Of course, you do, girl." He pressed it into her hand.

"Are you going away?" she whispered, suddenly feeling as if she would fall apart inside.

"Early tomorrow." He paused and looked at her tremulous expression. He remembered what Herring, the courier, had said about her. George had been too preoccupied with his plans to pay much attention to her during his stay. Now, it was obvious that she wished to be asked in. He reached out and placed his hand against her cheek and neck; his thumb touched her small, warm ear. He had a sudden impulse to draw her into the room; she seemed pliant and soft; she seemed to be wilting against his palm. No, he told himself. He needed to think and be alone with these documents and comprehend everything. He leaned out of the doorway and kissed her forehead, then withdrew and pushed the door shut. It was a minute before he heard her blow her nose softly and then shuffle down the stairs.

He turned away from the door then. He knelt and placed some fresh hardwood on the embers of the fire, shook his head ruefully at the thought of the many long, lonely and comfortless nights that surely must lie ahead, then stood up, went to the table, picked up his letters of instruction from Governor Henry, slapped them lightly several times against his palm while gazing toward the western window, then returned them to the table. There was no sound but the popping and rustling of the fire and the moan of wind around the corners of the house. For a moment he thought of going down to Nell's room under the stairs and simply letting himself succumb to the affection and coziness which she seemed so eager to offer.

Instead he dashed his naked torso with icy water from the pitcher, rubbed down, and began pacing the room, thinking of what lay ahead. He had planned every step of it over the last few months, planned and refined his plans, and knew exactly what must be done, and how. But now that it was authorized and had become more than a daring dream, the details and difficulties of it were staggering to contemplate.

With an advance of twelve hundred pounds in depreciated Continental currency, he was to raise an army, in a commonwealth where manpower was nearly exhausted, and lead it to a place seven hundred miles deep into the hostile wilderness, and there discipline it into a swift and obedient fighting force. From there he was to lead it down still more trackless miles of rivers and wilderness, to attack a fort near the Mississippi, secure that fort and lesser ones nearby, win over or neutralize several tribes of hostile Indians, and then—then, perhaps—move north and east to storm the British base of western operations at Detroit. That last notion he had not even revealed to Wythe and Jefferson and Mason, for fear of being thought mad. And he had only hinted at it to Patrick Henry.

Now running the whole sequence through his mind for the first time as a clear and imminent duty instead of a grandiose reverie, he saw that somehow he had assigned himself a task that would consume every ounce of his energy and every moment of his attention for months to come.

He was accustomed to being the man in charge of impossible tasks; he had been that through all the years of his adulthood, and having been that, he could not imagine himself as anything less. He had never had a home since leaving his father's Virginia roof at nineteen years of age to cross the Blue Ridge Mountains; now he could anticipate more homeless years as a campaigner without any sort of domestic solace.

Thank God for one blessing, he thought. There being no prospect for ease or apparent glory in this task, I shan't be importuned to take along anyone's political favorites, but can choose the sort of officers I know to be right for it.

There were stealthy footsteps on the stairs outside his door again, then a soft knocking. By Jove, he thought, this time I just might take 'er in ... His loneliness had deepened. "Nell?" he said softly at the doorjamb, his hand on the bolt. A pleasant excitement was building in him.

"Nay, sor," said a raspy male voice. Surprised, George stepped back to his table and picked up the pistol.

"Who, then?"

"I'm Davey Pagan, sor," said the voice. "I'd like a word wi' you."

"I don't know the name. Can it wait till morning?"

"I'm 'ere now, yer ludship. I come t' talk about yer offer."

"What offer?"

"T' sign up an' be yer first volunteer, sor, an' get me a plot o' ground."

What the devil? George thought, cocking the pistol and sliding back the doorbolt.

He was astonished at the ugly, battered face that looked in, its one eye staring with equal astonishment at the barrel of the pistol. It was one of the footpads he had confronted on the street a few minutes ago. For a moment George was at a loss for words. "Are you sure you know what y're about?" he said at last. "How did you find me?"

"Just followed you, guv'nor. May I step in, by yer leave?"

Reason told George to keep the scoundrel away, but there was something so engagingly direct about the man, and something so remarkable about his unlikely arrival at this hour, that he signaled him in at gunpoint, glancing into the corridor as he did so. "Where's your partner?"

"Oh, 'e weren't for joinin' nothin', guv'nor. So 'e went 'is way."

"And you're sincere? You'd better be, man, or, by Heaven . . . Davey what? Pagan, you say?"

"Aye, Pagan. And I'm sincere if y'r offer is half decent. I need a berth that goes somewheres. I've 'ad enough o' goin' nowhere a year at a time an' sufferin' all the way. Tell me if you please about this fight we're goin' to." The rascal looked warily at George's imposing physique and the ready pistol, but could talk cockily enough withal.

George was amused and intrigued. He went behind his desk, laying the pistol at his right hand. "I'm going over the mountains to fight Indians," he said. "Have you the guts for that?"

"Hm. Indians? Never done that. Me pet enemy is Englishmen . . ."

"With luck, we'll get at some of them."

"Why, guv'nor, I'd go through a herd o' Indians t' get me an Englishman."

"You feel strongly. Why so?"

"Why, sor, because I was snatched off the street in Boston by a British press gang back in '68 and throwed aboard a British frigate, an' every day since then I been flogged, kicked, maimed, abused, and fed swill, or nothin' at all, under one whoreson tyrant of a British skipper after another."

"What can you do?"

"Why, I'm a good boatwright, sor, and a right fine carpenter, and nobody better with rope and marlinspike."

"Can you shoot?"

"I fed me brothers and sisters on game afore I went t' sea."

"Sounds fair to me. One more thing. You look a bit bandy-legged t' me. Are your legs good enough for something in the nature of, say, forty miles a day?"

For a moment that one gray eye widened. Then Pagan said, "I never been called on to do that. But by my eyes, guv'nor, if it ain't worse'n twelve hours aloft reefin' frozen mainsheets in the teeth of a gale 'round the Horn—that's where I froze these two digits off, y' see here?—if she ain't too much worse'n that, I can do 'er."

George sat back and scrutinized the fetid, nervous little sailor for a moment, and came to the conclusion that he was a better man than he looked. And that he had come out of the night in such a startling manner seemed like some sort of an omen. "So be it, then, Davey Pagan," he said, pouring rum in a cup and sliding it across the table to him. "You're my first volunteer. My name is George Rogers Clark of the Virginia militia. Here's the king's shilling, so to speak, and our first seven hundred miles or so's by riverboat, so might be you're just my man. Drink up and be off, now. Here's travel money to Redstone, where I'll be recruiting, and if I don't see you there you'll carry my curse to your grave."

" 'Ere's to that, Mister Clark," said Pagan, tossing down the rum with a grotesque grimace of appreciation. "Ah . . . About that land for me old age . . ."

"Aye. Three hundred acres for every man if we succeed. Though I don't know what that means to a seafaring man."

"If I don't see another drop o' sea brine till my dyin' day, it'll be soon enough for me, sor. Well, I'm off now. Good night, an' . . ."

"Pagan."

"Aye, sor?"

"Obtain a rifle if you have none. It's what you'll live by."

"I've just th' one, sor, a fine Deckard, at me home place. I'll get it on m' way to Redstone. Addyoo, guv'nor!" He saluted, and slipped out the door, leaving a chuckle and a whiff of body stench where he had stood. George shook his head and grinned. Likely he'd never see the man again. He felt, though, that he would.

With rum before him and the fireplace beginning to take the chill out of his room, George now drew a chair up to his table and in the pool of light from a candle began writing the recruitment orders. He wrote carefully on the new sheets of costly linen paper. He wrote to Major William Bailey Smith, a veteran of the Boonesboro defense, instructing him to raise two hundred recruits on the Holston River and march them over the Wilderness Road and down the Kentucky River Valley, to a spring rendezvous on the Ohio River. George folded a hundred and fifty pounds of the paper money into the letter, sealed it, and set it at one end of the table. Then he drew another sheet of the paper into the candlelight, dipped the quill into ink, and wrote to one

of his favorite comrades, the garrulous and affable but iron-hard
ruffian Leonard Helm. He and George had fought side by side
in Dunmore's War. Helm was fearless; men would follow him
anywhere just to be worthy of his esteem. George instructed
Helm to raise a company in Fauquier County and bring it to
meet him at the Redstone settlement on the Monongahela.
He put that letter and more money aside, then penned a third
letter to Captain Jospeh Bowman. He told Bowman that he
should raise a company of men in Frederick County, and that
he should gather those men as swiftly as possible and march
them overland to the Redstone settlement by the first of February. There they would meet George, and Helm's new detachment, go down the Monongahela to Pittsburgh to obtain their
boats and arms and provisions from General Hand, and then
start down the Ohio by earliest spring.

He sealed the last letter, capped the inkwell, leaned forward
on the table, and raised his glass. He looked at the candle flame
through the liquor, watched its distorted arrow of light, and
thought.

A tall order indeed. The settlers will be reluctant to spare
men for the defense of Kentucky. They've scarcely enough to
defend their own lands and they'll soon be needing to get out
next spring's crops. But Bowman and Helm and Smith have a
way about them. If anyone can help me raise a force, they can.
The brutal truth is, there are always some white men with a
need to get some Indian-killing, some bloody revenge, out of
their systems before they go back to clearing their fields.

He tossed the liquor to his throat, stood up, and paced about
the room. At this hour, there was nothing more he could do, but
he was agitated still by an excess of energy. He lifted his sword
down from its peg on the wall and pulled it out of its scabbard.
It rang slightly as it came out. He flexed his wrist, turning the
blade to reflect the light of the candle and fireplace.

A carriage rattled by under his window and from it came a
snatch of woman's laughter. Someone returning from a ball. He
thought of fiddle music, of reels, of bare arms and milky bos-
oms and adoring eyes, of glittering crystal, of such wisps of
laughter as that he had just heard in the night. There surely will
be none of those delights for a long time to come, he thought.
Again the warm and vulnerable Nell came to his mind, down
there one flight of stairs below, perhaps still awake and waiting
and thinking. The carriage wheels diminished into silence outside.

Then George lowered the sword to rest at his side, and leaned upon it as if on a cane. Suddenly he was lonely, unbearably lonely, frightfully lonely. The weight of his responsibility and the dank gloom of the primeval forest nights awaiting him came into the room and tried to crush his soul.

With a groan, he jabbed the point of the sword into the floor. Then he dropped to his knees, clasped his hands over the hilt, lowered his forehead to rest on his hands. He knelt as he had been taught to do in his family, but for a time his mind resisted trying to assemble the notion of his family's God and he thought instead only of the dark forest, its breath of eternal decay, the scents of its eternal renewal.

Then he thought of what the great solid George Mason had said to him. And, having made himself humble enough to do so, he closed his eyes and prayed for strength, wisdom, and luck.

5

On the Mississippi River
May 1778

At her brother's request, Teresa de Leyba unwrapped her *guitarra* and began picking out one of the simple *passacaglias* of her repertoire, sitting grave and demure under the sun-awning in the stern of the broad river galley. Her spirit was not in the playing. She had grown depressed by nearly two months' travel up this enormous brown Mississippi River. She was intimidated by the dark, inscrutable, and uninhabited shorelines, bored by the eternal slow rhythm of the rowing, and dispirited by the prospect of an indeterminate stay in some tiny village a thousand miles up the river from New Orleans. It seemed that her life, begun so bright and promising twenty-two years earlier in Spain and woven into a delicate tapestry of education and daydreams during her schooling in the convent at Malaga, now was being unraveled to a hopeless nothingness as the career of her brother and guardian, Don Fernando de Leyba, led her farther and farther from civilization and into the crude and insignificant outposts of the Louisiana Territory. As the family fortunes in Spain had dwindled following their father's death, Fernando had come to the New World seeking colonial posts. After a sojourn in the oppressive but exciting New Orleans, he was now to rule as the Spanish Lieutenant Governor of Upper Louisiana and commandant of the garrison at St. Louis. Teresa knew the appointment seemed to him the beginning of life, but to her, it seemed, it must be the end. The notes of the *guitarra*, which would quiver and resonate so beautifully within the walls of a courtyard or sitting room, were merely absorbed by the space out here, plinking and plunking pitifully, accenting the imperfections of her playing and the puniness of the silly instrument with its delicate ivory and mother-of-pearl inlays. Furthermore, the soundboard was beginning to crack and warp from the months of humidity in New Orleans and on this river journey, and that too was ruining the tone of the piece.

But Fernando was not aware of this, she understood as she looked furtively at his elegant profile; he was too preoccupied with their approach to St. Louis. Nor was his wife, the Lady Maria de la Concepcion y Zezar, who throughout this long river passage had languished pale and sunken-eyed among the cushion, dozing fitfully, turning her head in bad dreams and waking to cough into a scented kerchief. So, although it was always Fernando who asked her to play and her sister-in-law who implored her to continue, Teresa's only attentive audience was made up of her little nieces, Rita and Maria Josefa, and the twenty sweating black oarsmen who glanced at her with eyes as timorous as her own, breathed hard and grunted with the strain of rowing, and now and then murmured and chuckled among themselves. Teresa could not imagine what they must be thinking about her and this frail little string-box of hers, but they did watch and listen disconcertingly when she played, with an animallike attention which somehow made the delicate Spanish airs seem even more incongruous and vain. Could they be laughing at her when they chuckled like that? She found that possibility too mortifying even to consider.

In the distance, off each quarter of the galley, a guard boat rowed by Spanish and half-breed soldiers moved at the same ponderous pace, always there. A breeze puffed down the river into her face, bringing smells of rotting shore vegetation and the pungent body smells of the blacks who shone with their sweat in the afternoon sun. Teresa stopped playing and held her own perfumed handkerchief to her nose.

The long, slim shape of a pirogue detached itself from the low western shore of the river now, and came angling downstream toward them across the glittering sunglare of the river surface. As it drew near, Teresa made out the forms of five Indian men who were paddling it, and two bare-breasted Indian women who sat amidships on either side of a dead animal of some kind, dark and huge as a Spanish bull. When the pirogue came parallel with the Spanish galley, some twenty feet away, one of the Indians carefully stood up to take a curious look into the big vessel. He was stark naked, sinewy, gleaming with animal grease, totally hairless except for a bristling crest of black hair on the crown of his head with a white feather tied in it. A rush of shame and confusion shot through Teresa when she realized that her eyes had fallen on his exposed hairless groin with its strange fleshy knot of organs, the first she had ever seen; and as she turned away with a gasp, she heard some throaty and snorting laughter burst from the blacks on the oars. When she opened her eyes again the pirogue had drifted out of sight; Fernando was gazing after it, bemused. Lady Maria, her sickly face strained with disgust, pulled her husband's sleeve to draw his attention away, and Teresa realized that it must be because of the nakedness of the squaws. Teresa fanned herself, feeling flushed and prickly at the thought of what they had just seen. To imagine men and women going naked, out of doors, and in each other's company! It was appalling, barbarous, and carnal in the extreme. And she had heard, before leaving New Orleans, hideous tales of the blood-thirstiness of these savages, of their penchant for settling differences with knives and other sharp weapons. The image of blood flowing over naked flesh flashed through her mind, an intimidating and unbearable image which was immediately replaced by visions of the sanguinary and dolorous crucifixion paintings she had seen everywhere during her upbringing in Spain. A tipsy French courtier in New Orleans once had alluded in her presence to the veiled bloody cruelty of Spaniards. And though her *duenna* sister-in-law had hustled her out of earshot immediately, Teresa had remembered that remark ever since, sometimes becoming quite unsettled by it. Somehow now, during this voyage, those thoughts came to her ever more dreadfully, associated with her fears about the legendary Indian savagery. It seemed as if all the comforting layers of religion and civilization were being peeled off one at a time, like clothing, with every mile that the galley moved up the Mississippi into this wilderness, and that the life ahead of her surely would prove to be more raw and elemental and obscene than anything her sequestered upbringing could have prepared her to imagine.

They had embarked at Kaskaskia the morning before for the remaining sixty miles up to St. Louis. Kaskaskia, though on the east side of the Mississippi, had given Teresa a foresight of what she might expect in this part of the world, and it had been a bewildering impression. A ball had been held in their honor at the home of the merchant Gabriel Cerré by the leading French and Creole citizens of Kaskaskia. Teresa had been surprised by the amounts of imported wealth and finery these people owned—the silver snuffboxes, the silk and velvet and taffeta dresses, the slippers, the chocolates, the crystal and silverware, the clocks, the satin-lined trinket boxes, the mirrors . . . Teresa had heard Kaskaskia referred to as the Versailles of the West; and while it definitely was no such thing, it did boast of more Old World trappings than she would have expected here. Yet, under the glitter, within and around the well-built stone houses, there was a crudeness, a slovenliness, showing through the veneer so plainly that it had wounded her sensibilities. During the evening she had looked into a pantry to find a drunken French gentleman pressing himself upon a half-breed girl servant. She had been set back on her heels by the liquorish breath and overpowering body smells and grotesque awkwardness of the swains, both French and Spanish, at the dance, and by their unbelievable propensity for drunkenness. She had found in a hallway a youth in silks, the son of a great wheat-trader, passed out on a smelly pile of uncured animal skins. And at one point in the evening, the ball had been disturbed by the uproar of a drunken band of Indians who, surprised stealing vegetables from a nearby town garden, had escaped by firing their guns into the air and filling the night with war whoops which were sufficiently ferocious to frighten the equally besotted whites back into the protection of locked doors for a few minutes. It had taken the de Leybas some time to comprehend the farcical nature of this incident, and Teresa had lain awake most of the night thereafter, hearing every sound in the village street outside, fearing that she would not survive till the dawn without being scalped and ravaged, despite the assurances of their hosts, Monsieur and Madame Cerré, that it had been only a sham.

Those had been her impressions so far of the Illinois country, and now they were nearing St. Louis, the capital of Upper Louisiana, a mere village on the western bank of the great Mississippi, on the edge of a vast, unexplored land tenuously claimed by Spain, a mere river's breadth from the troubled country where unfriendly England held sway over a few hundred half-civilized French settlers and thousands of fickle savages. To the east, she had heard, American colonists even more barbarous than the Indians were waging a sporadic war to obtain independence from the British, and there were rumors that this conflict could sweep someday even into this remote Mississippi Valley, which was coveted by every faction as a water road for munitions and supplies. It was a frightening prospect all about, and Teresa de Leyba, timid, introspective, delicate, and vulnerable, could no longer even pretend to share her brother's enthusiasm for his new adventure.

"There lies St. Louis, Excellency," said the vessel's captain, coming astern to point northwestward at a cluster of stone houses standing on the western bluff of the river a few miles ahead, tiny, gleaming white in the late afternoon sunlight.

"St. Louis, at long last," breathed Don Fernando, rising stiffly to his feet, stooping to stand under the awning, stroking his neat goatee. His velvet pantaloons and the white stockings on his slim legs were rumpled and soiled from the long repose in the dirty river-galley. "And that on the far bank, up that stream. That, I presume, would be Cahokia?"

"Cahokia, Excellency. Creole French and Indians under the English flag." He shook his head and then made a scornful gesture toward the town with two fingers. "That the mongrels should stay on their side of the river."

"Enough of that, Captain," said Don Fernando, taking the hand of his wife, who had risen to stand beside him. "Load the six-pounder and signal the fort that we are here. St. Louis, Maria," he said gently to her as the captain went forward, scolding the Negroes to a faster cadence. "You'll be able to rest soon and be strong again." She lowered her kerchief from her face to give him a feeble smile. Teresa rose and stood beside Maria, placing her hand at the small of her back. She jumped and flinched when the little swivel-cannon in the bow of the galley spat orange flame and a cracking roar rolled away over the river and returned in echo. The acrid smell of burnt gunpowder was still in her nostrils when a puff of smoke appeared from the village at the top of the bluff, followed a moment later by its report, then another and another and another: St. Louis saluting her

new governor. Tears of appreciation stung Teresa's eyes and
momentarily swept away her lassitude as she looked at her
brother, the proud young grandee silhouetted against the setting
sun. Suddenly this valley looked rich and mellow and spacious,
and perhaps full of a new and different kind of promise after all.

Can there perhaps, she wondered, be other men in this land
as noble and fine as he? Mother of God, that there should be.
She flushed as she made this frivolous prayer, but prayed it
nonetheless. Maybe, she was thinking as boats came out from
the foot of the bluff to meet them, this is not the end of my
world at all.

"Teresa," Don Fernando said, now turning to her, obviously
feeling expansive, "little sister, I feel that you are going to find
much happiness here, more than anywhere before." He so
wanted her to; she knew that. Perhaps, she thought, it is possible.

6

PITTSBURGH
May 1778

GENERAL EDWARD HAND OF THE CONTINENTAL ARMY, WHO WAS
thirty-four years old but moved with no more spirit than an old
man, walked with George Rogers Clark as far as the great open
log gate of Fort Pitt and stood there with him looking down
over the woodshingled roofs of the town of Pittsburgh to the
wharf on the riverbank where the young colonel's ten boats
hung to their moorings, filled already with men, bristling with
long rifles. The Ohio River here blended the waters of the Allegheny and Monongahela and then, broad and green, curved
away to the northwest and vanished into the fresh springtime
emerald of the forest. The sky was azure from horizon to horizon; the shrilling of locusts stretched like an invisible skin over
the shimmering fields of the valley. Far downstream a hunter's
single gunshot struck like a pulsebeat on the air.

George took a last look back inside the fort, where regular soldiers in buff trousers and blue coats and a ragged assemblage of civilians had gathered in curiosity. They stood about on the beaten, dusty yellow parade ground and lounged against the palisades and blockhouses, somehow looking soiled and stupid in contrast with the vast clean wilderness outside the fort.

My God, but I am happy to be quitting this place, he thought. Nothing here but disappointment and subterfuge.

General Hand stood nibbling his thin lips and gazing with ennui down at the boats. The flesh hung gray on the shapely bones of his face, and a day's stubble on his chin glinted in the morning sun. He had hardly met George's gaze, even while hosting him and filling his requisition for boats and munitions. General Hand's aspect was distinctly that of a failure. His effort four months earlier to lead a force of more than five hundred soldiers against the British trading post at Sandusky had become bogged down in snow and floods and illness and the weight of its own baggage; he had overrun a few Indian villages deserted except for old women, and thus had returned to Pittsburgh to be ridiculed behind his back as the leader of "the squaw campaign," had asked to be relieved of his command, and was awaiting his successor now. It was discouraging even to look at him, and George was as anxious to be gone as the general obviously was to see him leave.

"My thanks, sir," said George, careful as always to keep the pity out of his voice, extending his hand.

"Good fortune to you," said the general, at last looking directly at him. "Let's pray there'll be a bigger contingent awaiting you when you get down to the Kentucky."

"I'm sure there will be. Goodbye, sir."

There had better be, George thought, as he made his way past the massive earthwork redoubts of the fort and down the dirt road among houses and garden plots toward the wharf. He had expected to have more than three hundred men underway to Kentucky by March; now it was late in May and he and his captains had managed to enlist a mere one hundred and fifty. Everywhere they had gone to recruit, they had met the resistance of leading citizens who demanded to know by what authority their own meager manpower was to be taken away for the defense of remote Kentucky. News that Daniel Boone and a party of twenty-seven salt-makers had been captured by an Indian force in February had demoralized many of the settlements, and the borderland disputes between Virginia and Pennsylvania had dimmed George's hopes of signing up any Pennsylvania volunteers. The whole frontier had sent up an uproar of disapproval against his recruiters, and men already recruited were being encouraged to desert. Many had.

There'll be danger of even more slipping away until we put distance between us and these settlements, he thought. That was why he had decided not to prolong the futile enlistment effort any longer; this little band would more likely shrink than expand if it waited longer here.

Despite the disappointments of the recent months, his confidence quickened as he turned his back on civilization and strode down the hill toward his flotilla. Out there, he thought, one can control the course of things, and not be undermined by schemers.

He turned heads as he made his way to the river. Women in doorways and gardens watched him; men with barrows and mules nodded to him; Indians and bushlopers in smoke-blackened deerskins stopped and turned as he passed. He was aware of the impression he created; he carried himself at full height and deliberately expressed all his energy and power in his movements. Without the epaulets and insignia of the regulars' uniform to proclaim his rank, he knew he had to inspire obedience by sheer force of bearing. He wore now a fine high-collared coat of soft doeskin which reached his knees, edged in fringe and emblazoned Indian-fashion on the back with elaborate designs in red and white beads and quills. At its throat showed a clean white linen stock. Into the brass-buckled swordbelt at his waist were thrust a long, slender tomahawk and a flintlock pistol. His chest was crisscrossed by two leather straps, one supporting a large sheath knife and a powder horn, the other a pouch for rifle balls and personal effects. His long legs were sheathed in fringed deerskin leggings and on his feet he wore deerskin moccasins decorated with narrow bands of blue and white beadwork. His red hair was pulled back over his ears and bound into a queue, and his glinting eyes were shaded by the wide brim of a round-crowned soft black felt hat pinned up on the right side. Cradled in the crook of his left arm was his long Kentucky rifle, slim as a walking-stick, with its gleaming blond stock of flame maple. Even so heavily accoutred, he moved with a swift, easy gait which brought him quickly down to the water's edge and onto the sun-warped, fishy-smelling planks of the wharf, where his captains stood waiting for him.

"How went the muster?" he asked, returning their homespun salutes.

"Real good, George," drawled Leonard Helm, a bow-legged, barrel-chested man with a flat red face and tobacco-stained white whiskers. "Nary a one run off last night. Reckon all the chaff's done blowed off this bunch by now."

"I surely do hope so. Loaded to go, are we?" George stroked his jaw and looked over the heavily laden boats, which were nuzzling the wharf with their blunt prows. Captain Joseph Bowman, his young first officer, stood waiting in the command boat holding a furled flag. Davey Pagan was in the stern, leaning on the rudderpost, his good eye squinting against the sun. Each of the boats looked like a floating thicket of upraised rifles and oars, with ten to fifteen ruddy, craggy faces peering up at him, shrewd, patient, glum, or mocking. "Boah, he's some perty, ain't he?" twanged a voice from a nearby boat. Chuckles began, then stopped instantly when his eyes swept the boat. He stepped quickly to the edge of the wharf and stared through narrowed eyelids into the men amidships, so directly that the man who had made the remark must have thought he was recognized.

"That's true, boys," George said loudly, breaking into a grin, "we don't have cannon and we don't have cavalry, so we'll just have to win 'em with our good looks—and that's why I picked all you beauties!"

A wave of surprised laughter swept through the nearby boats. George leaped nimbly onto the bow thwart of the command boat, and shoved it away from the wharf with a mighty heave. He took the green-and-red-striped Virginia flag from Captain Bowman, unfurled it, erected it in the bow, then stood waving toward the west. "Cast 'em off, boys, we're headin' for Kentucky!"

A general cheer went up. The captains scrambled off the dock into their boats; the ten vessels swung off willy-nilly into the current. Then the steersmen strained against their sweeps, oars dipped and found their cadence, and the boats fell into file and headed for mid-channel. A few rifles were fired into the air spontaneously, their puffs of blue smoke dissipating over the river; here and there laughter and war whoops sounded. Davey Pagan started up a chanty, and soon every oar in the convoy was dipping to its rhythm. A fresh morning breeze ruffled the surface of the river and started a cheerful rataplan against the prow of the speeding boat. George stood in the prow bareheaded, looked back at the little oncoming fleet, and watched the bluish bulk of Fort Pitt diminishing astern. Eager fellows, he thought. But what an assortment.

He looked them over carefully. Half the men in each boat were rowing, bareheaded and stripped to the waist. Their sinewy white shoulders and backs were beginning to shine with sweat in the sun. He could feel the forward surge of the boat each time they stroked in unison. If they're not slackers now at this work, he thought, I reckon they'll strive when they learn I'm leading them straight against the scalp-takers. Vengeance is a good wage to work for. How I wish I could tell them now! But I don't need to yet. They're getting to know each other. And they're going to like me a great deal if I can manage that. By Heaven, they'll want for discipline; most every one is used to being a law unto himself. Look at 'em. Not one I'd reckon thinks he's an ordinary man. Let 'em get a triumph or two under their bonnets, and they'll have the worst case of swaggers you ever did see.

He had watched that kind of spirit evolve during the defense of the Kentucky settlements the year before. Even in the most desperate days, when the women were running ammunition in skillets and there was nothing in the forts to eat but tainted meat and musty corn, every repulse made the defenders celebrate themselves as charmed beings, superior to the folks back on the seaboard side of the mountains. He had seen the survival-cockiness of the long hunters; he had seen that giddy sense of invincibility develop in farmers who had conserved their own hair a few times while snatching an Indian scalp or two instead.

Most of the men in this string of boats now were already veterans of such tests. He had interviewed each recruit personally at Redstone Fort or at Fort Pitt, and knew there was scarcely a greenhorn among them. They were trail-hardened and cunning and knew how to shoot the eyes out of a squirrel. Hardly a one had the look of a soldier about him, but they were, he knew, dangerous as a den of bobcats.

All they need to learn, for our cause, is how to follow orders and fight together, not as individuals, he thought. I could lose too many if each one tried to fight his own war, and I can't afford to lose any.

The sound of a child's voice from one of the boats reminded him of the presence of another element he had not initially planned for: the families of several of his recruits. There were about twenty families in the convoy. Some of the militiamen had signed up mainly because they were interested in Kentucky as a destination, or because they had friends or relatives already in Kentucky; some had had to bring their families simply because they were adrift and landless and had nowhere to leave them. Helm and Bowman, finding recruits so scarce, had signed up some such family men, on the condition that they could bring their families at least as far as Redstone Fort. George himself had invited two likely-looking adventurers who had been hanging about at Redstone, and had agreed to bring their families along part of the way in return for three months' service in the militia. The scarcity of recruits had been that desperate. At first the presence of these women, children, and oldsters had seemed to be an unwanted burden, but then the idea had come to him that they might instead prove an asset. They could do planting and other work at the new base camp and thus free all the men for drill. George knew of course that he could not have made these dependents stay behind anyway, as they were as free as himself to venture to the frontier; he had no authority to order them back. Better to have them come along under our protection than follow at a distance, he thought. Besides, every family that settles in Kentucky helps to solidify Virginia's frontier.

So there they were, huddled in the prows of several of the boats, these little homeless families with their precious pots and tools and bags of seed corn—all they would really need to start new lives. They were some added baggage for the military expedition, but not really very much. And their presence for the meantime would help keep the men civilized.

The oars steadily munched the river and the sun rose toward its zenith. The planks of the boats grew hot to the touch. At noon George ordered the rowers relieved, and the boats drifted on the current for a few moments while men changed positions in the cramped spaces. Murmurs, curses, and laughter, bumping and scraping sounds drifted with strange clarity across the water. Those going off the oars blew and sighed happily like pack horses, stretched and flexed their arms, pinched sweat out of their eye sockets, stood at the gunwales breaking wind and pissing over the side. Those going into the rowers' seats now removed their shirts and hats, and some of them had tied rags around their heads to absorb the sweat of their brows.

In minutes the vessels were underway again, awkwardly at first, with some clumsy clacking of oars and good-humored taunts, until all had found the rhythm and the going became mechanical. George lounged now in his shirt-sleeves, quietly observing the men and contemplating their suitability for the expedition.

Here and there among the soiled tan buckskins and homespun hunting shirts he had seen a blue military coat, but these were frayed, patched vestiges of some earlier service, or secondhand articles which somehow had worked their way into the possession of these civilians. George entertained the suspicion that a few of the men might be deserters from the discouraged and unlucky armies of the east, but there was neither means nor reason to prove those suspicions. Anyone who might have left that service only to enlist in this won't find it a bargain, he thought. They shan't avoid serving their state, in any case. He studied faces. Most of the men were older than he was. Many of the faces were gaunt as skulls, with sunken eyes and hollow cheeks. The faces were leathery from years of exposure, with deep seams under high cheekbones and wrinkles radiating about the eyes from seasons and seasons of squinting into sunlight or brilliant snow. There were eyes fierce as a hawk's or merry as a chipmunk's. There were full beards or grizzled chin-stubble; here and there was a lipless thin mouth that grinned perpetually like a fool's. Many a face had its perpetual quid-lump like a carbuncle in the cheek; those heads would turn periodically and spit brown gobs into the river.

Despite the sun's heat hammering down on the boat, George suddenly shivered with a cold chill of pure, savage anticipation and looked down the broad fluid avenue of the river. He scanned the distant banks, where only the white branches of sycamores and the fuzzy-looking, pale flower catkins of cottonwoods broke the dense green foliage of the towering hardwood forest. A shrill cacophony of birdcalls and cicadas pervaded those leafy walls. Distant tanagers and jays flickered like orange or blue sparks against that backdrop of green; now and then a heron with slow, flopping wingbeats would rise from one place along the shadowy banks and skim a few yards to settle again. Far downstream a cloud of black smoke appeared to be swirling above the river, but it soon swept near and turned rainbow-iridescent in the sunlight, proving to be not smoke but a cloud of hundreds of thousands of passenger pigeons. They vanished over the trees with a velvety thunder of wings. On a putty-colored estuary at the mouth of some nameless creek a family of three black bears on a fishing expedition paused and looked up to watch the strange passing convoy with its rising and falling oars.

During the morning's passage, there had been breaks in the forestation of the riverbank: small, stump-dotted clearings running down to the river's edge, with rows of waxy-green young corn standing knee-high, perhaps a human figure standing in a field or in a cabin door, brushfire smoke climbing lazily out of a newly cleared field. Then as the miles were consumed and the river led steadily away from the Fort Pitt outpost, those few riverside farms had appeared empty, the fields overgrown with brush, here and there a scorched chimney standing amid the collapsed timbers of a burned cabin. George had watched the sullen interest of the men in his boats as they rowed past these mute scenes.

And now as the midafternoon sun burned its way down through the hot pearl-blue of the western sky there were no more clearings at all, only the unbroken wilderness. Likely there were Indians along this riverbank, invisible, peering out, watching this handful of armed boats go by.

George had ordered his captains to stay in midchannel. The width of the river itself was the best defense against any ambush; boats in the middle of this wide stream were barely within the range of the smooth-bore muskets of the Indians, who usually had a tendency to undercharge their weapons anyway because of their perennial shortage of gunpowder.

Joseph Bowman, sitting on a powder keg and leaning on the gunwale on one elbow, seemed to keep his gray eyes trained on the riverbank constantly, as if trying to penetrate the foliage. His pupils were so pale he sometimes gave the impression at a distance of being sightless. With those ghostly orbs he could deliver a most eerie and disconcerting stare, and had learned to use the feature as an instrument in leadership; with an unwinking stare he could usually rattle or intimidate any unruly subordinate and thus regain control over him without a word. Bowman wore a three-cornered felt hat which now shaded those eyes and his small sharp triangle of a nose. His lank yellow hair, not pigtailed, hung loose over his collar.

He turned his gaze inboard now, stretched with intense effort, sighed, then leaned close to George. "If you was a savage, in the business of purveying American scalps for a British lord named Henry Hamilton, and you seen this great armada floatin' nice an' sassy down this river, what might you think?"

"Well, I expect I might count how many people were in these boats, then I'd tot how much a hundred and seventy scalps would amount to in British mirrors and knives and trinkets, and then I'd set foot to Chillicothe or Piqua to enlist some help in acquiring those scalps."

Bowman grinned, but shook his head. "I wouldn't," he said. "I'd more likely say t' m'self, 'Now, lookie, Red Eyes, that ain't no simple ordinary passel o' Virginia gentry goin' down to put in a corn crop in th' Ohio bottoms, that there's a war party.' Then I reckon I'd go a-trottin' off to Detroit and tell Big Chief Hamilton what I seen."

George smiled and raised his eyebrows, then gazed off toward the shore. "What is it, Joseph? D'you feel you're being watched?"

"I do that," Bowman said. "Six times this mornin' I've felt my back draw up."

"Six exactly, hm? What a remarkable faculty! Maybe we needn't post sentries, having you."

Bowman's tense look softened; he grinned and fell back to his scrutiny of the far shore. "I don't reckon a party our size has much worry," he muttered.

"No. Not till we draw near the Shawnee country. For now, Joseph, I'd recommend you enjoy the scenery. While you may."

The boats swung into a great bend in the river now; the sun, which had been burning on George's side throughout the afternoon, now beat upon his shoulders. He turned and gazed straight ahead. *This I remember,* he thought. *Some twenty miles now we'll wind to the west and then run south a hundred or so. We've made about thirty-five miles already. That isn't anything to be ashamed of.*

I'd reckon there's enough daylight left to make it to the next big bend before making camp tonight, he thought. He turned and looked at the straining backs of the rowers.

"Hey, gents!" he roared. "I'd say we're warmed up by now; what d'you say we hit a stride now, like we were goin' to someplace nice!"

A few groans came in reply, then curses and a laugh or two, and Pagan began chanting in a quicker time. "*Haaay-up! Haaay-up! Ho!*" The rowers swung the oars at the harder pace; the boat thrust ahead toward the afternoon sun, and the other vessels sped up to maintain the file.

Good, George thought. *Good boys. Good, good, good.* He stood up in the bow again, faced downstream, and pulled his hat brim down to shade his eyes. And he grinned as the wavelets pattered rapidly, more rapidly against the hull.

* * *

THE AFTERNOON SUN HAD DESCENDED TO THE TREETOPS BY THE time the flotilla reached the place where the river curved southward. Inside the curve of the river now, George recognized a gravel beach where he and his father had camped in 1772, the year that John Clark had journeyed out with his son to see for himself the magnificent lands of this Ohio valley.

He stood up now, told the men to rest on their oars, and summoned his captains to bring their boats alongside.

"Damn, George," Helm said as his boat came up, "seemed like you been tryin' t' run away from us all day! Been chasin' you what? Fifty miles?"

"About that. Gents, about a league down on the left bank there's an island where I want us to put in for the night. I think we're due for some hot victuals and a swill o' rum. What d'you say, boys?"

"Yowhoo!"

"You bin a-readin' my daydreams, Cunnel!"

"Rum? Hi, you're a kindly soul, Mister Clark!"

"Where's Private Butler?" he asked.

"Ah'm right cheer, suh," came a voice from Captain Harrod's boat, and a young giant, auburn hair bleached by the sun, naked except for a breechclout, stood up. He was nearly six and a half feet of muscle and sinew, with a great, downsloping, peeling nose that nearly touched his lower lip. Butler was regarded as the best guide and hunter in the West, a peer of Daniel Boone, and was a legend among the Indians, who called him "He-Whose-Gun-Is-Always-Loaded."

"Si, d'you reckon you could rustle up something big and sumptuous for the stewpot, if Mister Harrod was to take you ashore here with a small party?"

"Wouldn't doubt it at all, suh."

"Good. Put 'em on the east bank, Bill. No sense rousing any Indians if we don't have to. Wait for 'em, and then whatever they bag, boat it down to the island. I want to keep a few miles between any shooting noise and our camp, just in case."

"Shouldn't need more'n one shot, suh, I reckon," said Butler with the grin of an oaf.

"Haw! Listen at him!" came a mocking voice from somewhere, and laughter went up in the nearby boats.

Butler looked around and his grin grew still wider. "Ah *promise*," he said, sitting down amid more laughter, and the boat pulled away toward shore. The convoy began sweeping down the middle of the river again in single file, full of good-spirited chatter. The right bank was now darkening almost to black; the crowns of the huge trees on the left blank glowed vivid with the last rays of sunlight.

The boats were scarcely ten minutes down the river when the echo of a rifle shot came rolling down the valley. One shot only. The men listened and grinned, heard no more shots, and grinned more. George smiled and felt the mirth welling up higher and higher and he finally had to bite his lips to keep from whooping with laughter. God damn that Si Butler for a showoff, he thought.

The island was an egg-shaped four acres or so, bordered with tall reeds, with a half-acre thicket near its upstream end and the rest covered with lush grass. A great snarl of driftwood left high and dry by some past flood lay barkless and bleached on the north bank, a ready treasure of seasoned fuel. George led the boats to the shoreward side of the island and had them run aground among the reeds, reasoning that only two or three sentries thus would be required to watch the vessels and the eastern shore as well, which lay some thirty or forty yards away. The distant western shore, now silhouetted against the cloudless crimson-gold sunset sky, was the land of the customarily friendly or neutral Delaware tribes; nonetheless, he saw no reason to let his beached boats intrigue the eyes of any Indian bands that might be roaming that side of the river. The island was a scenic, agreeable, and secure site. As there were no tents to pitch, making camp was a simple matter of carrying wood to the center of the bivouac area, digging a latrine trench on the downward side of the island, and rigging a screen of brush and blankets to give the women and children some privacy.

The big cooking fire was no sooner set ablaze than Captain Harrod's boat bore down on the island. The troops running down to the shore to greet it were at first dumbfounded, then hilarious, to see not one but two deer, a buck and a doe, being hoisted ashore. Simon Butler stood in the prow of the boat looking smug and benign.

"Hey, how's this happen, Si?" someone called. "We only heard one shot."

"Well, heck, boys," he replied with an innocent smile, "y' done heard me promise Mister Clark just one shot."

There was an uproar of hooting and catcalls and incredulous laughter as the carcasses were brought up for butchering. The men from Harrod's boat were importuned by the others for an explanation, but responded only with sly grins and shrugs.

A second cooking fire was built, and soon both carcasses were dressed and turning on spits, filling the cooling evening air with their savory aroma. About fifty naked men at a time were bathing cautiously in the swift, shallow dark water near the boats. George directed that a keg of rum be set up and broached near the fires. The last twilight drained out of the western sky and fireflies began winking over the grassy island and along the nearby riverbank. Whippoorwills and spring peepers filled the night air with their calls, and it seemed to George that the soft voices and laughter of these woodsmen were as harmonious, as much a part of the natural voices of this wild valley, as those of the night creatures. He was immensely calm, tired, and happy. His face felt hot and dry from its daylong exposure to the wind and sunlight, and his haunted stomach growled and his mouth watered for the roasting venison.

Nearby, little Davey Pagan was being gibed about his chanties and his rolling gait. A nasal-voiced woodsman named Jonas Manifee was building his reputation as a comic by miming Pagan's sea-leg saunter and one-eyed squint, and pouring out his conception of Pagan's nautical jargon. "Ahoy, me lubbers," Manifee's voice twanged, "batten down th' mizzlemasts, an' swab up th' poop! Land ho, two points out baft o' th' starborn brow! This 'ere's Davey Pagan yer forepoop swabman talkin'! Blow me down, blow me down!" And Pagan perched on a fallen log by the rum keg, shaking with his cackling laughter, beside himself with delight at all this attention. Before the food was ready he had been dubbed "the Forepoop Swabman," and it appeared that he was destined to become a regimental mascot of a sort.

Stars were brilliant in a velvet black sky when the feast began. Ravenous, warmed by rum, full of Colonel Clark's praise for the orderly swiftness of their first day's progress, they ate, gazing and blinking into the great beds of coals, commenting among themselves on what had become the prevalent theory about Simon Butler's one-shot bag of the two deer.

"Gosh damn, he must of just caught 'em in the *fragrant delecto*," twanged one loud voice in the periphery of the firelight. "That's th' onliest way 'e could of done it. Ain't that why he's ashamed t' 'splain it? Nobody but a pure villain'd 'fess up to a dipperdation like that."

Another voice overrode the laughter. "Always figgered that's how I'll meet *my* end." It was Isaac Bowman, one of Joseph's brothers.

"Ye goan die happy, hey, Isaac?"

"Wouldn't go no other way. 'Ceptin' . . . 'ceptin' maybe fightin' Injuns fer ol' Virginny. Heh . . ."

Several of the men glanced at George when they heard those unexpected, emotional words, and there was a stillness in which the words seemed to linger for consideration.

George arose slowly and stood in the fire's glow gazing into the bank of ruddy faces. In the midst of this rich camaraderie, which made this band of strangers seem somehow tribal, that reminder of duty and the dangers ahead enhanced the sense of being alive, made it stand out against the shadowy sea of oblivion upon which a man's living soul seems to float. George was profoundly moved by the notion, felt a pang from it. It was as if these faces in a ring of firelight made a sun of life in the black, hushed wilderness. He wondered how many of these roughnecks of his were sensing the same thing, or some like sentiment; a glance around at the reflective faces indicated that most were sharing it according to the natures of their individual souls. George raised his cup. They seemed to be expecting him to say something. Isaac Bowman's last word was lingering in the stillness.

"Here's to Virginia, gents," George said.

"Hyeah, hyeah!" Cups were raised. It had been the right thing to say.

"And here's to Simon Butler, our Nimrod!"

"Hyeah, hyeah!"

"And as for the scalp-buyers of King George, who have been like a blackberry seed in our back teeth too long: Boys, here's to us, who's going to spit 'em out!"

"Hey, hey, hey!" The cheers went up several times. The men did not suspect how precisely the remark hinted at their mission, but it was perfectly tuned to their feelings, and they could take it as a compliment as well.

"All right, gentlemen," George said then. "Drink up, and bed down. I see some of you nodding, and we'll be on the river before sunup."

As he strolled off into the darkness toward his bedsite near the boats, he caught Simon Butler's eye, and with a motion of his head summoned him to follow. They stopped near the river. George looked at the huge head, faintly limned by fireglow. He seldom had to look up at anybody.

"Yes, suh?"

"Now, Simon," George said in a low and confidential voice.

"You don't have to tell me if you don't want to but I've searched my head and I can't figure how you did it. I can keep it to myself."

A chuckle deep as a bear's grunt came from the hulking scout. "Well, fact was, Cunnel, me an' a feller named Craze come up on them deer grazin' t'gether. Figgered two'd feed these yayhoos better'n one, so I pointed th' doe t' him, and got a bead on th' buck myself, an' tole him, 'Count o' three,' and we both fired th' self-same instant. That simple, suh. Hit was Cap'n Harrod's idee t' pull some legs when we turned up, so we all kep' shet on it."

George grinned with delight. He clapped Butler on the shoulder. "Go and sleep," he said.

He drained one more cup of rum, spoke with the sentries at the boats, took a long last look over the encampment, which was nearly swallowed in darkness now that the fires were down, then lay on the grass with his head on his pouch and a blanket drawn up to his waist and watched the pulsating stars. A warm, tingling languor stole up through his long legs. Now and then the lush stillness was broken by the sound of some sleeper's cough.

Could make the Wheeling settlement late tomorrow, he thought, and pick up the rest of our provisions from Fort Henry there. Don't reckon anyone'll try to desert there. They're pretty happy so far, seems to me, and right congenial about each other's company.

If Smith has a couple hundred like these waiting downriver, we'll have three hundred and fifty who'd be the match of twice their number of Regulars. That's not many, but with surprise and the Lord's just concern, Kaskaskia should be ours before two months are out.

He had been arriving at a decision during the long quiet hours in the prow of that boat. He was not going to establish his base camp at the mouth of the Kentucky as he had planned; instead he would meet Smith and his Holston Valley recruits there and continue on down to the Falls of the Ohio, where a place called Corn Island showed promise of making an ideal base site and could, even without cannon, control the navigation of the Ohio. It would also be a hundred miles closer to his tactical objective on the Mississippi, and to the mouth of the Ohio where he later must construct a fort.

This stately Ohio, and the veined network of tributaries feeding into it, were engraved like a map on his brain. In this wilderness, these were the roads of war and supply and commerce. In his mind's eye he could trace not only the rivers he had surveyed and seen personally, but also the ones which he had viewed only in the rough sketch-maps of surveyors and scouts, or heard of at fireside parleys. At Pittsburgh he had bent for hours over maps compiled from the sketches of various past travelers in the river country. George had, with the help of those sketches, finally inked in on his mind's map the vague and doubtful headwaters and tributaries which had theretofore been blank gaps in the network. What a kinship he had felt, what a sense of gratitude to the unknown mapmakers, as he pored over those folded drawings with their narrow veins of river and stream.

For a while George looked at the stars and pondered upon the nature of streams and the ways in which they establish themselves in terrain, and then begin to reshape the terrain and the habits of nature, and even history itself. One trail of streams had been very much in his mind for months. It was the route the French *coureurs de bois* had traveled a hundred years before, and the Indians centuries before them: From one point in the plains, where the Miami tribes roamed, the great Wabash flowed southwestward toward the Ohio River Valley and the Maumee meandered off in the opposite direction toward Lake Erie. There it was, a direct water road from the Ohio River to Detroit, a road he hoped to follow within a year, because the conquest of Detroit had not left his mind, despite his recruiting disappointments.

But first there was this business of the Illinois country.

Rivers, he thought, as the Ohio whispered and gurgled a few feet from his ear. For a moment his mind dwelt on the notion of a gunboat fleet that could patrol the Ohio to prevent war parties from crossing into Kentucky. That merits some further thought, he promised himself. Then, with the current of the river, his thoughts flowed beyond the present war and into a future Ohio Valley, where green corn would fill the bottomlands, where breezes would ruffle the plains from horizon to horizon, where tobacco leaves would grow broad in the heat of summer, where cattle would graze on endless meadows and fine running horses would chase alongside fences, where great cities of white stone would stand gleaming peacefully at the junctures of rivers under the perpetual sunshine of peace. And on a high bluff above such a city, on the white porch of a great house, he envisioned himself sitting solid and mature, with a serene,

finely gowned woman in a chair beside him, fanning herself
languidly with a flowered fan. But he could not see her face,
could not tell what she looked like; her face would fade out of
focus when he tried to look at her. The face was a blank and
vague place, like something as yet uncharted on a map of an
unexplored land.

He slept in his deerskins on the ground at the river's edge,
while the stars wheeled silent above.

THE CONVOY REACHED THE WHEELING SETTLEMENT LATE THE NEXT
day, acquired a few more supplies, and encamped on the heights
outside Fort Henry overlooking the river. The small populace of
the town was agitated by the numerous reports of increasing Indian activity to the west, and George forbade his men from cir-
culating in the village where all the talk was so demoralizing.

The next morning he had his boats in the current again before
daybreak, and that afternoon the flotilla reached a region of
magnificent bottomlands which, reluctantly, he passed without
stopping. These were lands he had cleared and planted six years
earlier during an idyllic and profitable year. He had built a small
fortune there at the age of nineteen, with his corn crop, through
a nice cash trade in surveying, and ultimately through a very
profitable sale of the improved land. Now he sat silent and
dreamy in the prow of his war boat as it glided by this familiar
place, and scanned the shore.

Soon, his eyes falling on a sun-drenched slope near the edge
of the forest, he felt a rush of good memory; he put his hand on
Captain Bowman's arm. Bowman turned and was surprised by
the rapturous expression in those usually piercing eyes.

"Joseph, you remember Chief Logan the Mingo."

"Who of us don't?" Bowman exclaimed. Logan had been a
staunch friend of the white men until 1774, when a border ruffian named Greathouse had murdered every one of the chief's
relatives. Logan then had taken up his tomahawk with a vow
not to lay it down until he had taken the lives of ten whites in
revenge for each victim; and the terrorism associated with Logan's revenge had become a part of the reason for the ensuing
campaigns known as Dunmore's War. George had fought in that
campaign as a militia captain, alongside Bowman, William
Harrod, Leonard Helm, Simon Butler, and Matthew Arbuckle,
who was now commander of Fort Randolph at the mouth of the
Kanawha River.

"Well, you see that big beech tree up yonder at the top of that meadow?"

"I see it," Bowman replied.

"That's where I first met Logan. Before he took up the tom-ahawk."

"Aye! I 'member you tellin' me about that! You was surveyin', you said . . ."

"And I felt—well, like you said—I felt my back draw up, and I turned around and there Logan stood, no more than twenty foot away. Rifle restin' over his arm. I reckon we stared at each other five minutes without a sign. Oh, what a man, Jo-seph! I guess you never saw him. But he was tall, and straight. Joseph . . ." he lowered his voice, somehow almost ashamed to be heard talking this way about an old enemy, "you could've put Logan in a room with all those periwigged dandies in our Assembly—yea, even Tom Jefferson and Governor Henry themselves!—and he'd have looked like a god among 'em!"

Bowman listened to this in wonderment. He had heard Logan described as a murderous savage, but never a god. And he had never heard George Rogers Clark wax rhapsodic like this about anything, except the splendor of some fertile new valley or lim-pid waterway.

"So," George continued, "we spent the entire afternoon, Logan and I, sittin' at the foot of that selfsame beech tree up there and smoking tobacco. We spoke of just about everything there is under the sun. Probably wasn't another human soul in fifty miles of us, but there we sat holdin' council like we were in the Roman Senate or some such thing. I tell you, that day passed and it seemed like an hour, if that. I reckon I probably learned more in that day than I ever learned from anybody, even my grandfather or George Mason . . ."

Bowman nodded in amazement and gazed toward the distant beech, as if trying to see two ghosts under it smoking their pipes. "Such as what did you talk on?" he asked.

"Well, it is strange; I can remember we talked about every-thing that matters, but I can't recollect much specific. Now, there was God. I don't think we spoke of God or the Great Spirit, by name at all, but . . ." he lowered his voice further and glanced at the backs of the rowers, "I got satisfied that there's no difference between 'em, except in name . . ." He did not know how, or whether, to explain to Bowman how his own family's Episcopalian God had, in effect, shifted shape during that afternoon, to become less like a single sublime personage and more like a boundless current of spiritual power, flowing everywhere on the face of the earth. No, perhaps it would not be wise to try to express that to Bowman. ". . . No difference except in name," he said again.

"Hm," Bowman grunted and nodded, choosing not to comment.

"I remember one thing," George said. "There was a kind of a . . . a *sadness* about Logan's friendship with the white men. I doubt I have his eloquence to say it. He loved the white people, you see, but to him that love was a tragical thing. He said that his people need wilderness to range in, while we Virginians have an equal passion for tillable land, and he seemed to know . . . I remember how he said it: 'The two cannot be at once, for there is no world big enough.' He said it was a good thing but a sad thing to care for the white man; he said it was a situation as bad as loving someone's squaw. What d'you think of a 'savage' who thinks like that, eh, Joseph?"

Bowman shook his head, lower lip thrust out, frowning. "That was Logan, by your account. Mighty fine. The recollection I have of Logan is his belt of thirty white people's scalps. Whole families found murdered. To me, *that's* Logan."

George nodded. "I know." He gazed back toward the meadow, which was fading out of sight as the boats swung into another long bend. "But he was justly outraged. He sent a message to the peace parley after the campaign; wouldn't come himself. It said something that moved me all the way through. It said: *'There runs no longer a drop of my blood in the veins of any living creature. Who is there to mourn for Logan? Not one!'* You know, I went home to my family last winter while I was at Williamsburg, and . . . if I had entered that house and found—God forbid!—my entire family murdered, and by someone I had trusted . . . And not a drop of Clark blood left! . . . That's what Logan found. My God, Joseph! A man is alone enough in this world as he is; who should bear having no relatives?" He saw in his mind the Clark table, surrounded by redheads. He thought then of Joseph Rogers, his cousin, dead now or living a prisoner in some Shawnee town, probably with no expectation of seeing his family again. He sighed, and suddenly found himself feeling very naked of soul under the quizzical gaze of Bowman. He turned to stare ahead down the river. After a while Bowman cleared his throat.

"Well, it ain't hardly a just world, George."

"No. So I reckon what a man's to do is, see as clear as he

can what *is* just, and do that. Anyhow, I do wish you could have seen Logan as he was that day."

TWO MORNINGS LATER, ROUNDING A BEND IN THE OHIO A FEW miles above the Kanawha River, George saw dirty smoke spreading like a stain across the river, hanging low in the wet air which lingered after a drenching predawn rain. There had been little talk in the boats this morning; the men had been growing sullen and uneasy in the previous twenty-four hours, partly because of the damp discomfort brought on by alternating rain showers and steamy sunshine, partly because of the hard and relentless rowing which had made some begin to feel like galley slaves, and partly because they knew the river was carrying them along the edge of the region controlled by the hostile Shawnees.

An ominous murmur went up in the boats when the woodsmen saw the smoke. "It must be coming from Fort Randolph," Bowman said.

George turned and called, "Faster." The pace quickened and the boats sped down the middle of the stream. He had a foreboding. This place at the Kanawha's mouth, though known as Point Pleasant, had been a place of ugly tragedies. Here in October of 1774 the Shawnee chief Cornstalk had cut off an encampment commanded by General Andrew Lewis, lured five hundred frontiersmen—nearly half of Lewis's force—into a trap, where his braves killed nearly fifty of the whites, including two colonels and four captains, in a hot day-long battle, before withdrawing across the Ohio. Cornstalk had yielded to a peace treaty soon afterward, and had remained friendly for the next three years, even resisting British pressures to make war on the American in 1777. But then in November of that year, while staying at this same Point Pleasant as willing hostages of its commander, Captain Matthew Arbuckle, Cornstalk and his son had been murdered in their cabin by a band of soldiers infuriated by the scalping of one of their hunters across the river. The place had a history ill-befitting its name.

Now here on Point Pleasant sat the precarious Fort Randolph, still commanded by Arbuckle, and George urged the rowers onward, dreading what he might find under the pall of smoke, listening for gunfire, watching for some sign which might indicate whether he was speeding into a trap. He glanced back at the men in his boat and saw that now they looked tense and eager instead of sullen. The hot wet air seemed to crackle with a sense of impending danger, and he sensed their urgent lust for vengeful action against Indians.

The oars swished; the fort came into view, and beyond it the mouth of the Kanawha. The stockades appeared to be intact. The curtain of smoke was rising from the blackened ruins of some riverbank cabins, which were still smoldering. There was a smell of wet ashes mingled with that of the smoke. A great deal of yelling could be heard, and as the boats drew abreast of the outpost, a dozen frontiersmen came spilling out of the gate and down among the smoking cabins to the waterfront to greet them. It was apparent that Fort Randolph had survived a very recent raid. "Joseph, pass the order no one's to leave the boats."

"Oh, by God, but you're a joyous sight to see!" exclaimed the red-eyed, square-faced Captain Arbuckle as George leaped onto the shore and took his hand. "It was more than two hundred of them, mostly Shawnees, George. All day yesterday."

George frowned and shaped his mouth for a silent whistle. "That's a bunch," he said. "Where would they be now?"

Captain Arbuckle pointed southward up the Kanawha, while his bleary-eyed, muddy, bandaged defenders gathered around and surveyed George with hopeful faces or held the mooring lines and talked excitedly with the men in the boats. "Their trail leads up the river," Arbuckle said. "Likely they're headin' up to hit the Greenbrier settlements. I sent a runner up th' other side of the river this morning to try to get ahead of 'em with a warning. Now, look . . ." He pulled a blood-spattered piece of paper from his coat. "They left these on some of the bodies after they scalped 'em."

George unfolded the paper. It was a printed English handbill suggesting that the settlers might save their own lives by deserting the rebel cause, swearing allegiance to the king, and moving up to live under protection of the British headquarters at Detroit. His eyes flashed. "As well as you can, Matt, keep these away from your people. I expect there's some would be tempted; they've seen so much of this."

"Not mine," said Arbuckle with resolution. "Soon's they saw you comin', they hollered, 'Hey, here come the reinforcements! Now we can go after them whoreson savages!' You are a godsend, George. I'd say we can catch up with 'em in . . ."

"One moment, Matt. You presume I'm at leisure to do that . . ."

Arbuckle's expression suddenly went from eagerness to incredulity, and it was a moment before he got his words together.

"W-Well, what in damnation else?" He moved his lips word-lessly and fluttered his right hand vaguely toward the upper Ohio.

"It might be that I have business farther down the river . . ." George said. How he wished he could explain.

"The hell you say! What business . . ." Arbuckle's mouth was gaping like that of a fish. "With due respect, George, but a man come through here from Fort Pitt not a week ago, an' he said you were making an army for protection of the settlements, and if this ain't such a case, I'm damned . . ."

George in turn waved his hand downstream. "The *Kentucky* settlements, Matt, those are my orders . . ."

The defenders had crowded close to hear this and were be-ginning to scowl at him and mutter their disbelief to one an-other. George looked toward his boats. Many of his men were standing up in the vessels, clutching their rifles, talking vehe-mently with those on shore. It was obvious they thought this was indeed just the sort of situation they had come for, and he knew too that they were sick of this endless rowing, spoiling for some action and ready to help avenge the atrocities they were hearing about from the people on the shore.

For an instant, George faltered, listening to the angry protes-tations of Captain Arbuckle. He was tempted to stop and help. It would be feasible to pursue the war party up the river, to de-stroy or scatter it. Defensively, it made good sense, as here was a large Indian raiding party virtually at Virginia's back door, seemingly much more immediate and valid a threat than his ob-jectives seven hundred miles farther west. And the Indians might be expected to strike Fort Randolph again on their return from the Greenbrier outposts. Surely in two or three days here he could stage a successful retaliation and then get his fleet back on its way down the Ohio. Not to do so would be almost inexplicable under these circumstances.

But, no. I'm on an offensive, not a defense, he thought; I can't spare the time or risk any men.

Arbuckle stood before him, his face now hard and challeng-ing. He's bound to presume me a coward, George thought; that's the worst of it. The people around them were beginning to mill about, grumbling and tentative. Glancing over the scene, George noted a few freshly dug graves on a rise of ground be-fore the fort, smelled the stink of burnt rubble, and had to steel himself.

"D'you need food, or powder?" he asked Arbuckle. "I can't spare much, but . . ."

"God damn it, no! I need your regiment, that's what I need!"

George put his hand on the captain's solid, dust-smudged shoulder. "Listen," he hissed. "You'll understand soon enough. What I'm doing will put a sure end to this, but I simply can't stop along the way, d'you hear me? I wish I could, but now, Matt, get your people back away from my boats, and that is an order!" Arbuckle turned, slowly, toward the people as if to assuage them, and George, still haunted by the anguish in his old friend's eyes, stalked off quickly toward his boat. "Cast off!" he roared in a pained fury, elbowing through a knot of inhabitants who stank of smoke and breath and were clutching at him and yelling, seemingly a crowd of claws and fetid mouths. As he broke through them and put one foot in the bow of his boat, two of his own sergeants leaped out of the boat and onto shore, yelling something incoherent. He sprang into their path. "Get back in that boat," he ordered. Both were large men, nearly his height and, he knew already, strong-willed and impulsive. The larger, holding his rifle across his chest like a quarterstaff, advanced as if to go through George; the other side-stepped toward the clamoring inhabitants. "Did you hear me, Crump? Get back in the boat!"

Sergeant Crump stopped. "Beggin' yer pardon, Colonel, but I think this is what we come here fer."

"You're in my pay, Crump, so you'll obey my orders." The crowd was gathering close, watching their faces. In the hush a cardinal's song trilled. Then Crump grimaced.

"Orders be damned!" he snarled; then he snatched off his hat and dropped his head forward, thrusting his skull under George's nose. "Look!" The crown of his head was a ragged, puckered pink scar; in its center the bone of his skull shone through like old ivory. He slammed his hat back on as the crowd murmured and growled, and he started to move forward again.

Suddenly he felt a wrenching pain in his hands, and before he could yell, found himself disarmed, his own rifle pointed straight at his chest, its hammer clicking back.

"You're right lucky to be alive, I see," said George in a quiet voice. "And now if you want to remain that way, you'll get back aboard this boat and lean on an oar. You too, Key," he said, waving the rifle barrel at the other sergeant. Both clambered meekly back over the gunwale, not taking their eyes off his face. He shoved the vessel off and leaped aboard in one move, and soon the boats were again moving downstream. All the people on shore had begun talking the incident over as if they had attended some play at a fair. George tossed a salute back to Captain Arbuckle, who stood at the water's edge; the captain stood there expressionless and did not return the salute.

George turned away, looked once at Joseph Bowman's puzzled, accusing eyes, and passed Crump's rifle back among the rowers, who were saying nothing.

"Hear this now," he said as the fort began to fade into the smoke and mist. "You'll soon enough have all the fighting and vengeance you can dream of. But you'll have it to suit *our* purpose, and any man who chooses to go his own way will have to get past me. For your sakes, don't try it." A full minute went by, the dripping oars rising and falling. Then he said, "Are there any questions, boys?" After a pause, a familiar voice came from among the rowers.

"Sir, just where in th' ring-tailed hell *are* we goin' in such a hurry?"

George grinned and waited for a moment. "Sergeant Crump," he replied, "when I'm ready to answer that, you'll like the news. I assure you, it's going to be more satisfying than chasing a pack o' Shawnees up the Kanawha."

"Wal, I'm a-takin' yer word f'r that, sir," Crump's voice came back.

Good, thought George. Crump and I are all settled up now and it shouldn't be necessary to punish him. The incident may have done us all some good, in a way; they're learning not to take me lightly, and they really must learn that.

He thought of the hideous scar on Crump's head. That'll make him the center of attention for the next few bivouacs, he thought. We've got us a real showpiece.

Now, he thought. Now to see if I can mollify Bowman.

7

ON THE OHIO RIVER
May 1778

SERGEANT CRUMP WAS INDEED THE CELEBRITY FOR THE NEXT three days. He was repeatedly asked to doff his hat and show his scalping scar, as few of the men had ever known anyone who lived to tell of his own scalping. Crump considered it a badge of honor and, gruffly at first, then cheerfully, obliged all the awestruck and curious. But at the breaking of camp on the fourth morning, one of the older woodsmen apparently decided that Crump had enjoyed all the glory that was his due. He sidled up to him as they were loading the boats.

"I say now, Mister Crump," he remarked in a carrying voice, "may be my eyes is deceivin' me, but seems to me they's more o' yer skull a-showin' this mornin'."

"What?" said Crump, reaching up toward his hat.

"Wal, hit reminds me of when I was a tad," the man began, "and my ma would darn my socks. You rec'leck how a sock looks stretched over a darnin' egg, with th' egg showin' through whar th' hole is?" The big sergeant's eyelids narrowed and this nostrils widened, but the woodsman politely, conversationally, continued, as George and a few men nearby paused to listen: "Wal, when Ma'd pull down tight on thatair sock, why it'd stretch an' more o' that egg'd show. So I was just curious to know, maybe yer scalp is gittin' stretched, as if, mought be, uh, yer headbone's a-gittin' bigger?" The listeners broke out in laughter.

Sergeant Crump's whole huge self seemed to swell at that, and one of his dirty hammer fists began to rise to the ready. But George stepped between them.

"Let's get aboard, gents," he said cheerfully. "We aim to reach the mouth of the Kentucky by afternoon, and there Will Smith'll join us with his people."

The prospect of seeing their party enlarged put the men in high spirits. In the last few days they had cautiously passed the mouth of the Scioto River, a major artery for Shawnee water traffic, then the Miami and Little Miami rivers, upon whose banks stood the major Shawnee towns of Chillicothe and Piqua. Though they had seen no Indians around any of the river mouths, they deemed it almost certain that their flotilla had been observed, and in this region, so near the Indian strongholds, they knew the Shawnees could quickly put hundreds of warriors on the river to come against them. The two hundred men Smith had promised to enlist would make the flotilla much less susceptible to attack.

George summoned Captains Helm, Harrod, and Montgomery to his boat before casting off. "Ride with me this morning," he said. "I'd like us all to be up front when we meet Smith."

They talked little as the convoy found midstream and rowed southwestward in the ponderous current. Lounging in the prow of the boat, they watched the darkness leach out of the sky astern, watched the eastern vault brighten and ripen to the color of persimmon, watched the high forested river bluffs turn from black to golden green. Somewhere in the woods a panther coughed and roared. In the first flood of light from the orange sun, wraiths of river mist drifted like silvery ghosts, and the following boats appeared to be afloat on a river of cloud. From both riverbanks, filtered by distance, spilled the rasping of crickets and the exuberant morning calls of thousands of songbirds. The officers, rough and uncouth-looking as they were, contentedly sniffed the river-damp air and enjoyed the dawn as if entranced, until George at last sat up, leaned his elbows on his knees, and cleared his throat.

"Gentlemen, when we put ashore at the mouth of the Kentucky, we'll unload the salt kettles we brought for those people, and that'll make some room. But then we'll have to squeeze up pretty tight, because we shall have to double the number of men in each boat. We'll be riding low in the water then."

"I don't mind some company," Harrod said.

"Me neither," said Montgomery. "My boys'll be glad t' see some fresh labor to spell 'em on them oars."

"I reckon a couple more days will put us at the Falls of the Ohio," George said. "You may know of Corn Island, on the south bank. Here." He spread a rough map. "If this island is all I expect it will be, we're going to put up a base there first thing. Cabins, blockhouses, and stockades. We can't spare but a few days for building, so civilians and troops alike will work. Then we'll put the civilians to planting a late crop while we whip this bunch of poachers and bushrangers into an army. D'you follow me so far, gentlemen?"

"I folly *what*," replied Helm, "but I'm a razorbacked roothog if I folly *why*. Sir, I fear I just fail t' see what buildin' a fort on an island plumb downriver at th' Falls has got t' do with fightin' off Indians who been raidin' on the Kanawha and th' Licking an' th' Kentucky. There ain't anybody *out* there, I know of, is there? Other'n fur traders an' vagabonds . . ."

"Beggin' your pardon, Colonel," Montgomery joined in. "My people been hornswoggled too, ever since we left Matt Arbuckle standin' back there on th' riverbank with his mouth hangin' open."

George nodded from one to another as they quizzed him in turn, but said nothing.

"George, I'll tell you a little observation," William Harrod said. "Ever' time I run across you last year, seemed like you was porin' over some dang map or other. Now, I always figured, this boy is whuppin' up some real bodacious caper. And now, ever since I been on this river with you, I've had a curious idee that I've got myself smack in th' middle of it, whatever it is. Might I be right, George?"

"You might be."

"Well, I would sure like t' know about it."

"I know you would."

"Well, then?"

"Soon as we make camp on Corn Island, you'll know."

Harrod gazed at the distant riverbank. The profusion of grizzled brown whiskers that covered all his face below the level of his livid nose hid any facial expression, but his shoulders were tense and hunched. Finally, he said, as if talking to himself, "Seems t'me like the Kentucky River's where y'd put an army. There y' could get quicker t' any o' th' settlements where you was needed. Y'd be a few days' march from any of 'em. Humph."

George glanced quickly at the other officers. They were saying nothing, but they were looking at old Bill Harrod's craggy profile thoughtfully, and no doubt were agreeing with the common sense of his observation. Harrod soon became aware of their attention; he turned to look each in the eyes. Then he smirked and punched George's knee with his fist.

"Well, you know me, m'boy. Show me th' smarts of it, an'

I'll do anything." The rest grumbled and relaxed then, and the discussion was closed.

By midday a damp breeze was turning the leaves along the riverbank pale side up. A slate-gray overcast crawled up the river to meet them. They rowed another half an hour in a windless stillness and then, as if they had passed through a curtain, found themselves in a deluge which obliterated both banks of the river and turned the water's surface to a hissing, silvery froth. The rowers sat with water to their ankles despite the others' steady bailing. Grain sacks and powder kegs were wrapped in tarpaulins and set up on the thwarts. The boats were moved into tighter file so that each would be in view of the one ahead and the one astern, and the convoy moved on through the rushing oblivion, every man, woman, and child drenched through, every hat brim spilling water like a gutterspout.

George led the convoy closer to the left bank so that they might not miss the mouth of the Kentucky in the blinding downpour, and suddenly, on a grassy bottom, a few yards away, a lone human figure in wide hat and blanket materialized out of the sheets of rain; he was staring toward the convoy which must have looked to him as much like an apparition as he did to it. He turned as if to flee, then came about, and drawing his long rifle out from under his blanket, raised it and aimed it at George, who had risen to stand in the bow of the boat.

"Who be you?" came the man's voice, almost blotted up by the rushing of the rain.

"George Rogers Clark with militia."

The man turned, with a wave of his arm, and began running westward along the bank, feet squishing audibly in the sodden turf. He vanished in the rain, but in a moment shouts were heard not far ahead, and in minutes a lean-to grew out of the curtains of rain, with a small orange cook fire glowing within, then a few more brush shelters and a tent, and a score of white men were running down to the shore to greet them, shouting cheerfully, and George knew he had, at last, reached the Kentucky River. He jumped ashore, sinking almost to midcalf in muck, and in the hubbub of excited voices now issuing both from the boats and the camp, called out, "I'm looking for William Bailey Smith!"

"I am here, George," came a raucous, twanging voice from a tall figure now strolling down from the tent. Wearing a three-cornered hat, a deerskin draped over his shoulders like some unfinished cape, Smith came to Clark, shook his hand solemnly, then looked at him through forlorn and wavering eyes. He was emaciated, gray under his weathered skin; a drop of rainwater hung at the end of his blackpored beak. His underslung jaw moved as if on a cud. "Shore glad you got here, George. You wanta get them folk o' your'n under some shelter?"

George ordered the boats beached and covered and the troops and families into the lean-tos. Something seemed awfully wrong with Smith, who usually rampaged and squawked about like a blue jay. As they walked through the rain among the smoky hovels toward the tent, George peered about the wretched little camp.

"Lot of trouble down along the Holston," Smith mumbled as they went up. "Folks down there's more concerned about Cherokees 'n they are about any redskins from over th' Ohio. Hard t' get any of 'em to come away."

They stopped at the entrance of the tent. George looked hard at Smith's miserable face. Then he looked back through the ragged little camp, where his soldiers and civilians now were crowding in around the cookfires, their voices filtering through the sibiliant rain. He felt a sudden, dreadful comprehension. "Where's the rest of your army, Mister Smith?"

Smith squinted into the rain and sighed.

"George, I done my goddamndest. But what you saw is all I could raise."

George's heart felt as if it had dropped through a trap-door. He clenched his fists at his sides and clamped his teeth shut to keep from yelling in frustration. He glowered from under his dripping hat brim toward the river, suddenly feeling drained and chilled. After a painful silence, he took a deep breath and cleared his throat, and his hands relaxed at his sides. "Will, d'you know we're desperate? D'you have any notion how desperate our situation is?"

"I'm sorry. I done everything I could. I beat doors and wheedled like a . . ."

"How many? Thirty?"

"About twenty able-bodied."

"Any good?"

"They look like a herd o' yayhoos. But I'd ruther have 'em fer me than agin me."

George gazed over the camp, listened to the whooping and laughter, saw old comrades pummeling each other and yelping in the delight of recognition, their buckskins dark with rainwater, mud to their knees, eyes red from the smoke of wet wood, but all seemingly impervious to their discomfort. He followed Smith into his tent and accepted a cup of rum, sat on a cask looking out at this crowd of backwoods ruffians. Less than two hundred, instead of five hundred! He drank his rum down, thought over everything he knew about the enemy outposts along the Mississippi, four hundred miles farther yet into the wilderness, thought of the hundreds of miles he had come since Fort Pitt, and somehow, to his own surprise, began to feel elated, almost mad with an absurd confidence that was swelling up inside him. He took a long look at Smith's woebegone bird-eyes, which now were searching his own.

"Will," he said, "d'you reckon you could fold up this camp by sunup tomorrow?"

"Humph. I could quit this mud hole in twenty minutes. Where to?"

George again emptied the cup, and banged it down on Smith's field table.

"Corn Island!"

8

ON THE FALLS OF THE OHIO RIVER
June 1778

THE RAIN WAS GONE, THE SUN WAS HOT, THE RIVER WAS RUNNING high and swift, when George Rogers Clark, bending over the gunwale to scoop up a hatful of drinking water, tensed suddenly and listened to verify the sound he thought he had heard.

It could have been just the wind in the trees. No one else seemed to have noticed anything yet; perhaps he thought he was hearing it only because he knew he should be hearing it soon. He sat up, drank, then listened and detected it again, he was certain: under the hushing of the wind, a deeper sound, like very distant thunder, now growing louder, sustained, uninflected. And the water did now seem to be running more swiftly. He reached back and put a hand on Captain Bowman's arm, awakening him from a hat-shaded snooze.

"The Falls!" George cried. "Pagan, get toward that left shore!"

"Larboard she goes, sor!" Pagan answered, and Jonas Manifee's nasal laugh rang out, followed by: "Weigh th' mainyard jivits! Blow me down! Blow me down!"

George drew from his packet a homemade map, and laid it out on the bow of the boat, weighted down with his pistol, to consult it one more time before the dangerous approach to the rapids. There was excitement in the boats now as the roar of the waters ahead grew audible and the boats bore in toward the south shore. Few of the men could swim, and perhaps in every man's mind there was a vision of being swept in the laden boats over a great waterfall. George found his own heart beating fast and high.

The river, here running almost due west, curved northwestward ahead, and as the boats swung into the bend the broad stream took on a strange aspect; the left half of it seemed to run straight up against a forest; the right seemed to drop out of sight as if going over a great sill. On the map there showed, in the outer edge of the bend, an island shaped rather like a long mitten, nearly half as wide as the river itself; the northern half of the stream fell away in a long, complex chute of rapids, which a note on the map said was about three miles long. That forest wall, he thought, must be Corn Island. As the boats drew nearer, he could now see mist and white water beyond the lip of the Falls. To get into the water north of the island obviously would mean being carried helpless over the Falls and through a three-mile maelstrom of churning chutes and channels. The safe way obviously had to be a landing on the southeast corner of the island, about a hundred yards off the south bank of the river.

The boats now glided toward that point. The rapids roared between the bluffs on both sides of the river. The island lay low alongside the Kentucky shore, but obviously was high enough never to be inundated. All the officers and the men not engaged in rowing now crouched forward in tense and excited attitudes; it was an intimidating scene of grandeur and natural power.

The men laughed and shouted with relief when the boats swung at last into the lee of the island and the terrible Falls were obscured beyond its green woods. The boats reached shore in calm water and were tied up.

The island was not quite a mile long and about five hundred

yards wide at its greatest breadth, separated from the Kentucky shore by a few yards of swift but smooth water. George led his officers in a hurried exploration around the island on foot, stopping on the north shore to study the great rapids, which seemed to be formed by the river's flow over a limestone escarpment some twenty feet high.

At a place where the forest gave way onto a heavy growth of cane, he stepped off the site of a stockade. Smoothing a patch of the rich black earth with his moccasin, he then bent and drew in the dirt with his knife point a plan similar to the fort at Boonesboro, but smaller. "Each of the long sides will comprise three barracks buildings," he said. "At this end there will be two buildings for the families, with the stockade gate between them. The entire rectangle will be enclosed in palisades of upright logs, sharpened at the tops. We shall begin felling trees immediately and start building the cabins tomorrow. I suggest we draw up our guard details and work parties at once."

He slipped his long knife into its sheath, stood up amid his officers, looked at the distant bluish bluffs which stood high beyond the waving heads of the cane stalks, and listened to the voices of the militiamen and the steady rush of the Falls. An excellent place someday for mills, he thought, with all this falling water. The ground was dappled with dancing sunlight which angled through the quivering foliage. Overhead, puffs of light-limned cloud sailed up the valley. George took a deep breath. "Well, gentlemen, we are here. We are on land after these leagues of floating, and I must ask, have you ever seen a more picturesque and benign place?"

They grinned and looked around. Leonard Helm scratched his sweaty chest through the open collar of his shirt. "Y'd have to take care not t' git too contented here," he said, casting a sly glance aside at George. "Not if we're supposed t' to be gittin' on, as I suspects we are."

He's fishing for those secret orders, George thought. I cannot put off telling them any longer. "We've about five hours of daylight left," he said. "We've less than a third the manpower we expected, so we shall need to work 'em three times as hard. We'll want as many trees dropped and trimmed as we can get today. Tonight we'll gather the men right here for a big feed and powwow, and it's then I'll tell them what you've all been beggin' to know: I mean our mission." The officers all tried to speak at once, but George raised a hand. "When we picked up Smith's recruits, I sent runners up to Harrodsburg and Leesburg and those places, asking their leaders to ride down and meet us here. I should like to have them here when I announce. If they aren't here by tonight, I shall tell the men anyway. But I hope they'll arrive." He looked at Bill Harrod and Joseph Bowman, clasped his hands behind his back, and smiled. "It has been a long time since I saw your big brothers, boys. I tell you, I have the fondest hopes they'll come down. Now, gents, I want to hear this place ring with the sounds of industry for the next few hours. Bill, there's deer on this island, and I wouldn't be surprised if some of those Nimrods o' yours could bag tonight's banquet without even going ashore. If you'd put a few on that, please."

To George's surprise, the men did not complain about having to work out the rest of the day. Relieved to be out of the confining boats and off the monotony of rowing, inspirited by the magnificent place where they now found themselves, they fell to in high spirits. Soon the island was resounding with the solid *chunk . . . chunk* of axes in hardwood, cheers, yells of warning, the great crackling rush and thump of falling trees, the *thud, thud, thud*, of mauls on splitting wedges, the sonorous and rhythmic ripping of two-man ripsaws. At the west end of the island, where the game animals had fled from this noisy invasion and were trying to swim or wade the narrow channel to shore, hunters' rifles cracked periodically. George went among the working parties, watched the skillful broadax handlers straddle huge logs, squaring them into timbers as easily as whittlers; he saw sinewy men with razor-sharp axes lop the limbs off fallen poplars and ashes. He smelled the tang of fresh oak chips and the delicious aroma of sassafras sawdust. Here a ten-year-old boy swung a mallet, driving eight-inch lengths of split hickory through the sharp-edged hole in a small anvil to make the pegs which had to suffice here on the frontier where nails could not be had. "A good tune yo're beating there, Dickie," George smiled. The lad was Dick Lovell, an orphan he had found at Redstone and enlisted as the regimental drummer. The boy beamed, and pounded another peg through the hole.

A few feet away a one-legged old man, an elder in one of the families, sat on a log and deftly sharpened axes and saws and augers with a variety of files and stones, while a butterfly with iridescent blue-black wings stood on his hat folding and unfolding, as oblivious to the man's labors as he was to its presence. Dust-motes swirled in the leaning afternoon sunbeams, and pungent steam billowed near the shore where women had set up kettles to boil long-unwashed garments.

George summoned Private Butler, who had returned from hunting, and went with him to the north shore of the island.

"What is the channel, Si?"

Butler pointed his long arm straight upstream and cleared his throat elaborately. "Wal, suh, you have t' paddle up th' river 'bout a mile fust, an' it's a hard row. Then you 'proach t' 'bout two hunnerd yards o' th' north bank. That gits you inter the proper channel fur enough up from th' Falls. Then y' turn around quick an' come fast, stayin' 'bout a couple hunnerd yards offshore. Y'row a-hellin', t' keep from gittin' sideways, an' y' beeline f'r that gap thar—y' see th' white water 'bout halfway crost? You dassn't miss it—an' go inter that, an' hang onter y'r hat, suh, cause hit's like th' world falls out from under you. Then y' go asplooshin' an' asplashin' mebbe five hunnerd yards, abearin' sorta right toward the shore, t' avoid that big knob-rock y' see down thar, go smooth another half-mile er so, astayin' in that northerest channel thar; then that drops you through another chute o' white water right under yon high bluff-point, see it? At th' bottom o' that, they's a big ol' churnin' eddy that y' have to ride out of, an' y' do that by tryin' t' row right at th' foot o' th' Falls. Th' current will carry you then straight inter th' last funnel; you sort of fall through that for a long spell, an' then th' river jest sort of spits y' out slick as a cherry pit inter the smooth water below, an' ye're home safe. Soaked through, prob'ly, but safe." After that long discourse, Butler had to spit into the river, and his gob headed off toward the Falls. George looked at him, retraced by eye the channel he had described, then looked at him again, took off his hat, and rubbed his forehead with his fingertips. He cleared his throat, then said:

"As simple as that, eh?"

Butler grinned, nodded, and spat again into the river.

"Well," George went on, "would you say that boatloads of troops could make it down that route without spilling?"

Butler gave him a thoughtful sideways look, then gazed back down over the roaring waters. "Wal, suh, some o' them likely might spill in th'r drawers. But a loaded boat would go through thar, yes, suh. If th' helmsman knows how t' git inter that gap thar, an' the water's runnin' high like t'day. Yup. It would be possible."

"I thank you, Si. Now, promise me you won't tell any of the men about our conversation here?"

Butler gazed at him through his canny light blue eyes, and shifted his quid to the other cheek. "Certainly, Cunnel." He grinned and grunted, looked over the rampaging rapids, and shook his head. "They wouldn't b'lieve y're thinkin' 'bout such a thing nohow. Heh!"

COLONEL JOHN BOWMAN, JOE'S BROTHER, APPEARED ON THE south bank on horseback before sunset; with him were James Harrod, the founder of Harrodsburg, and a score of gentlemen and leaders from the Kentucky frontier settlements. They picketed their horses and were ferried across to the island, where they enjoyed a maudlin, back-thumping reunion with their brothers and friends, and gulped cup after cup of rum taffia as the sun descended in the spume of the Falls and the entire island seemed to ripen in an enchanting, cross-lighted glow of warm gold.

George, warm and expansive with rum, led the officers and gentlemen away to the north shore where he had stood with Private Butler a few hours before, seated himself with them on the bank, the thunder of the Falls behind him, the laughter and voices of his little army audible from the center of the island, and read and explained Governor Henry's secret orders, then sat and awaited their reactions.

They were silent at first, looking at him with ruddy faces that could not mask their astonishment. Then they began to stir with excitement and eagerness, and agreed that the plan, if carried out in total surprise, could be successful. John Bowman, like his brother a man of eerie indigo eyes, made it clear at once that he was not enthusiastic. Several of the gentlemen exchanged glances. John Bowman's jealousy of George was well known. "I worry for the small size of your army," he growled, "and it pains me I can't spare a man for you."

"We didn't expect *you* could, John," drawled Jim Harrod. "But, by Jove, if you can do it, George, the salvation of Kentucky is in reach!"

Among those who seemed particularly agitated by the prospects of the raid was a fine-looking young lieutenant named Hutchings, from Smith's contingent. He said nothing, but his whipstock of a body seemed to strain with eagerness and his intelligent face fairly shone with excitement. That one, George thought, might well make a special mark in this campaign. I'll watch him.

At twilight, in the new clearing which would become the parade ground of the fort but was as yet only trampled earth littered with woodchips and leaves and studded with fresh stumps, stacked logs, and half-hewn timbers, a huge bonfire blazed, its flames leaping ten feet high; around it, sitting, standing, lounging against tree trunks, even perched in the branches of trees at the clearing's edge, more than a hundred and fifty men were gathered. They drank their ration of rum, laughed, told tall tales, and sang in small groups, waiting for Colonel Clark to come out and say what it was he had assembled them to hear. Davey Pagan had produced a hornpipe out of his shirt and was playing a jig for a small group of stomping, whooping dancers. But they had rowed and worked hard all day and soon flopped to the ground, laughing, and Pagan returned the pipe into his shirt. From a sentry-post fire on the shoreward side of the island a jew's-harp faintly buzzed and twanged. Near the big fire a fifer then drew his fife out from his knapsack and began playing sweet, nonmilitary airs, home songs full of longing, and the crowd of tired men was subdued and mellow when George came out to speak to them. He mounted a platform made of raw new planks fastened on barrelheads, the officers standing on the ground around him, waited for complete stillness, and then began:

"Now I ask: Is there a man here who's not somehow suffered the wrath of an Indian raid? Who does not know of a woman widowed, or a child orphaned, by savages out of the woods?" Throughout the mass of fire-warmed faces ran an angry, assenting murmur. "We have at least one among us," he went on, "who has personally felt the scalping knife . . ."

"Don't we know that, though!" cried a raucous voice from the shadows, and a roar of laughter went up all around. Sergeant Crump, leaning against a tree near the fire, threw a ferocious gesture in the direction of the voice, but was grinning. George laughed with them, but soon his face darkened and the troops grew still.

"Many of you were free to join this company because you'd been made homeless by torches and fire-arrows, or because you lost your families. Many are here wanting revenge on the savages." The glowering eyes attested. He raised a fist, and shouted:

"You shall have it!"

A cheer went up, but it was followed by a loud, sarcastic voice from the rear.

"Yah! But when?"

The eyes demanded now. The only sounds were the distant rush of the Falls and the crackling of the bonfire. George knew the men were remembering his refusal to help at Fort Randolph; he waited and let them think of it. Then, turning slowly so that they all might see, he drew from his tunic a piece of folded paper. He shook it open and held it high, and the nearer ones could see printing on it, and ruddy streaks and spots.

"You see this," he said. "This is a piece of British paper, with the blood of an American woman on it." He turned again, letting them gaze on it. "This was left on the body of a woman whose womb had been ripped open by ..." he paused, "by British steel!"

A fierce, confused muttering swept around him; the men's hatreds were fixed upon Indians, and here he was talking of British.

"This is British paper, printed with a threat to Americans," he resumed. "That knife was of British steel. *Both* were delivered at Point Pleasant by the hands of a Shawnee warrior." He paused to let that imagery sink in. "Now, gents: It is true, the Indians do not like us. We all know that." He swept his arm full circle. "They call this their country, and they see us coming in to take it. They have always tried to stop us from that. They make a general war against us, now and then resting on a treaty. But they have a natural fear of us. And why should they not? We cut down forest, we kill and drive out game, we build cabins and stay." The men shifted and frowned. What they did not want now was to hear of legitimate Indian grievances. "But I ask you this: Why, with this war for freedom, are there suddenly so many *more* Indian raids than ever before? I ask you, why is there an English paper handbill and an English steel knife in the hands of the red warrior?" He paused again and let them think on that, then he continued.

"The Indians carry British knives with red handles and bloody blades. When they get those knives, only the handles are red; the blades are clean and new. Do you know that the savages are given those red-handled knives by the British lieutenant governor of Detroit, a dandy named Henry Hamilton? *Henry Hamilton.*" He repeated the name so that even some half-listening Indian-hater with a mind gorged on bloody vengeance might grasp it. Then he lowered his voice to a menacing, steely hiss, which the men strained forward for, but could hear, to a man.

"This British Henry Hamilton, this 'civilized' English gentle-man who is in charge of Detroit ... D'you know that *he* gives these red knives to the Indians? D'you know that *he* assigns British officers to lead them south against Kentucky? That he pays the Indians a bounty for every American scalp they bring back to him? D'you think Hamilton does not know the differ-ence between a man's scalp and the long hair of a woman, or the white hair of a grandmother, or the fine hair of a child? Of course he can tell the difference! But he pays his bounty equally for them all!"

The men were seething. Their eyes glowed like coals with the reflected firelight. They were all turned inward now, turned as much to their inner burning fury as to this tall red-haired or-ator beside the bonfire in the center of their circle, who now re-sumed in that menacing, sharp-edged tone:

"Now consider this fine, red-coated British gentlemen, who hires Indians to come and kill women and children in Kentucky. He has agents who help him with this bloody business. His In-dian agent is Major Jehu Hay, a renegade American. Jehu Hay. This is another name to remember.

"But for now let us consider only Henry Hamilton, this learned English gentleman. Lads, I know witnesses who have seen that man curry the favor of Indian chiefs by ..." here his voice fairly curdled with contempt, "by stripping himself to do their war dance and lead their war song!"

He stopped again and raised the bloody paper above his head and listened to the outraged babble around the fire. He had given them a series of unforgettable pictures for their minds' eyes: mutilated women and children, bloody leaflets of propa-ganda, red knives, and now the ridiculous vision of a lordly En-glishman's white nakedness posturing around a war post.

"I demand to know," he boomed, "who are the *real* savages in this game? A warrior with a passion to preserve his lands, or a British official, calculating to buy that passion for his own use, trading for it with guns and knives, pots and cloth, mirrors and liquor? Oh, I make no excuses for a blood-crazy, painted savage who guts a praying woman and throws her unborn baby in the fire. But I'll tell you who the real savages are! Their names are Henry Hamilton, and Jehu Hay, and Philippe de Rocheblave, Hamilton's agent on the Mississippi. Boys, *those* are the people who murder your families and burn your prop-erty! I mean Hamilton the Scalp-Buyer and his Indian agents!" He snarled this through bared teeth and his piercing eyes drilled the message home. The men leaned in toward him, their hearts pounding with rage at this revelation, which they seemed to understand for the first time; but they were not sure what it had to do with their presence here.

"Men," he began now in a confiding sort of tone, "I don't know of anybody lower than a British fop in a white wig hiring Indians to fight a war that he's too weak or cowardly to fight for himself, do you? Why does he have to buy them with gifts, or prance with 'em in a war dance, if he isn't weak? Why, he *wouldn't*, if he had the strength of a man about him!" The men were looking at each other and nodding.

"And so in case you haven't guessed it by now for yourselves," he said loudly, "I'm going to tell you what we've come so far to do." An attentive silence settled in the crowded, firelit circle; he passed an intense dark stare around, to make each man feel he was being addressed personally. "I have the pleasure to tell you now," he said, "that each one of you who serves with me will get a passel of three hundred acres of new land if we're successful. . . ." A great murmur of astonishment went up. Without stopping to dwell upon that happy news, which confirmed the rumor they had heard of it, he waved them to silence and went on:

"You're strong men. You want revenge. Now you shall have it . . . but *not* by ranging over Kentucky, picking off a few hired Indians at a time! No, by heavens! In the name of the Commonwealth of Virginia, I am authorized to take you into the Illinois country and strike once and for all at the center of the British vipers' nest!"

He had chosen his words carefully. He expected, at worst, an immediate hubbub of consternation, at best, a patient attendance for more explanation.

Instead, the men, the whole sweat-stained, haggard, unshaven force of them, mulled on this staggering portion of brave but appalling news for a mere three or four seconds, then rose to their feet whooping and cheering.

He felt almost faint with relief. He stood there on the crude platform sweating and smiling as the men began to come forward, milling about their officers, whooping, swearing, and whistling, asking for facts.

"Hey, boys!" he yelled, "look at this!" He crumpled the bloody handbill into a wad and threw it into the bonfire where it vanished in a small, bright yellow flare. "So much," he shouted, "for your British terror!"

9

Detroit
June 1778

THESE TWO ARE EVEN BEGINNING TO SMELL LIKE INDIANS, thought Lieutenant Governor Henry Hamilton as Major Hay and Captain LaMothe talked with Chief Black Bird and the other Chippewa chieftains and prepared to leave Hamilton's office. Musky and smoky, he thought. Hamilton stood for a moment, hands clasped behind his back, head tilted, a baleful, sideways, heavy-lidded gaze lingering on the two agents and the four Chippewas. The upper lip of his sensual mouth drew up slightly in an unconscious expression of distaste.

He especially disliked Hay. Not just because Hay was a renegade American, but because his courage was questionable, and because he was stocky and uncouth and given to base humor, and was said to consort with squaws.

LaMothe, on the other hand, Hamilton could respect and trust, even though he disliked his arrogant and sinister manner. Captain LaMothe was indeed the only French-Canadian militia officer he could trust. LaMothe looked like an Indian. He was hard, dark-skinned, graceful. He spoke all the tongues of the Lakes tribes, was utterly merciless in warfare, and had an unflinching reptilian eye which never betrayed his feelings. Hamilton suspected that LaMothe was responsible for Major Hay's success with the Indians to a greater degree than Hay would ever acknowledge. And LaMothe for many months had been proving himself a brilliant, foxy leader of the Indians in the small-scale raids against the American settlements south of the Ohio in Kentucky, those bloody, terrorizing skirmishes which kept the immigration of the Americans at a minimum and produced a steady trickle of scalps and prisoners into Detroit.

Henry Hamilton did not like to deal with the fickle and brutal Indians, but he was getting ever deeper into it. He had held several great war councils with the Indians in Detroit in recent months, dispensing tens of thousands of pounds' worth of gifts to the tribes. He and LaMothe and Hay had even stripped to their drawers to join in war dances, which memory never failed to make him shudder or smirk at himself. He was confident that within a year he could enlist enough Indian loyalty through these techniques to conduct a thorough, sweeping offensive through the Kentucky lands and drive all the rebel frontiersmen back eastward over the Alleghenies. Even the major American stronghold at Fort Pitt, he believed, could be taken, and then this obscure war he had been waging in the West, with too few British regulars for the expanse of wilderness, would assume a significance that would redound to his reputation.

He shook hands with the departing Chippewas and accepted the salutes of Hay and LaMothe. The door closed behind them and he stood glowering after them. Then he turned and went to his desk, lifted a small chased-silver snuffbox, pinched out a quantity of the brown powder, dusted it onto the back of his left wrist and, gazing out the glass window at the four blanketed Indians who now stood in a knot just outside on the parade ground gabbing gravely with Hay and LaMothe and passing around a new flask of English rum, he drew up the snuff with two quick sniffs. He always resorted to the snuff after parleying with Indians in a closed room. Though a great part of his success with the chiefs was his habit of treating them as individuals and friends—even delighting them sometimes by drawing fine pencil portraits of them—he still had never managed to accustom himself to their odor.

Would God I had never started such dealings, he thought. An endless business, buying the services of these bloody murderers like piecework one trinket at a time.

Hamilton, who had been in charge of Detroit and responsible for the conduct of all affairs in the Northwest Territory since 1775, had advocated the use of mercenary Indians against the American settlers, and had been authorized to do so in 1776, over the strenuous objections of many in Parliament. "But who is the man," Lord Chatham had pleaded in Parliament, "who has dared to authorize and associate to our arms the tomahawk and scalping knife of the savage? They shock every sentiment of honor. They shock me as a lover of honorable war and a detester of murderous barbarity!"

Ah yes, Henry Hamilton would think whenever he reflected on Chatham's speech. But how else would you have me uphold the interests of His Royal Highness in this barbaric place? Honorable war indeed!

There were others who wanted him to stop hiring Indians to go against the colonists. Lieutenant Governor Abbot, for one, and Abbot never stopped harping on it.

Hamilton went behind his desk and sat down on the dark green velvet upholstery of his chair. He sucked the inside of his cheek. The afternoon sunlight slanting in the window outlined his powdered wig like a halo and cast the reflection of his blood-red coat among the inkwells and books and candlesticks beside him. He caught a glimpse of himself when he turned to lift some manifests and records off the credenza behind him. His eyes had a tired, cynical cast about them, under the dark eyebrows which ran across in a perfectly straight line. He tended to keep his head forward these days and glower out from under those brows. His jaw, long and narrow, always had a dark shadow of whisker-stubble on it by afternoon unless he could find time to sit for a shave at midday, and that gave him a rather swarthy, piratical look most incongruous with his powdered silver wig and fine gentlemanly features. He held the gaze in the mirror for a moment, surprised by the sullenness of his aspect. This Indian business is changing me, he thought.

With a sigh he lifted an inventory ledger onto his desk and opened it to a marked page. Among the goods listed for the Indians were blankets, kettles, mirrors, rum, and one hundred and fifty dozen red-handled scalping knives. He subtracted twenty-five knives and three gallons of rum from the totals, wrote a voucher to the quartermaster for them, and sent the orderly out with the vouchers. Through the window he watched the fellow's trim red-clad figure saunter among groups of Indians and militiamen and vanish into a crowd of savages around the great storehouse on the other side of the parade ground. Then he took up his quill, and continued his letter to Governor Carleton at Quebec, which had been interrupted by the arrival of the Chippewas:

"*. . . since our last correspondence the Indians have been very busy, having brought in seventy-three prisoners, and one hundred and twenty-nine scalps, and have been paid handsomely for them, thanks to the continuing generosity of the Crown.*"

Reaching the bottom of the page, he sprinkled it with sand to dry the ink, funneled the sand back into its jar, drew forth another sheet of paper, dipped the quill and continued:

"As I have told you previously, sir, these Indians, certain tribes of them in particular, will stoop so far as to divide a scalp in half and try to pass it off as two, to collect a double bounty, but Major Hay has cultivated a keen eye for such deception and scolds them so soundly that it is doubtful the same brave tries that sort of merchandising more than once."

He paused, wiped the pen, thought, sighed, and then refreshed the pen and added:

"Be assured that I continually admonish the savages to spare the lives of such victims as are incapable of defending themselves, that I pay more generously for living prisoners than for scalps, and that I insist the Indians shew me every proof that they have not unnecessarily slaughtered the helpless. I have told that to Mr. Abbot repeatedly and implore you to believe it also."

Why should I keep making this apology, he thought angrily, rising from his chair and stalking about with his fists on his hips. If we did not hire the Indians, the bloody rebels would have overrun the Ohio Valley like ants by now! But those things need to be said, as long as Abbot goes on trying to shame our use of the tribes.

By God, if the Indians weren't raiding the settlements for our benefit, they'd be doing it for their own, to preserve their country from those land-greedy Yankees.

And who is to say the Americans themselves would not be using the Indians against us, if we couldn't afford to pay them better, he thought with grim satisfaction. The Indians know well the poverty of the bloody rebels! He returned to his desk. He had had this argument with himself countless times. And every time, he had been able to rationalize it to his satisfaction.

The simple truth is, he thought as he took up his quill again, I alone have had to bear the responsibility for keeping the rebellion under control here in these parts, and, by Jove, I am doing it.

Let him who could do better condemn my method!

10

BEFORE DAWN, GEORGE ROGERS CLARK WAS AWAKENED BY A VARIety of itchings, predominant among them being clusters of mosquito-bite swellings in the skin of his wrists and around his collarbones. Eyes still closed, he worried the bites with his fingernails, each deliciously, maddeningly tingling until it was scratched into submission. The Falls rushed in his ears; birds were beginning to twitter; men snored. He opened his eyes. It was still dark, but a gray-pearly softening of the night was beginning. In his nostrils was a commixture of wood-smoke from the smoldering fires, river mud, tang of fresh-cut hardwoods, flower perfume, and, when he moved in his blanket, the warm stale stink of his own body, which he had not had time to bathe for days. This condition, he presumed, was giving rise to some of his other itches, which ranged from his feet to his groin and scalp.

Tugging out the pouch he had used as a pillow, he groped in it for his lump of soap and a folded change of linen and stockings. He rose silently from his dew-damp blanket, made his way among the forms of the sleeping officers, went down to the riverbank, shushed a sentry who sat draped in a blanket with his long rifle across his knees, pissed on the ground, stripped, and went into the water. It was warmer than the morning air and its current tugged at him. He held his footing on the mossy slick bottom, stooped to submerge himself, shivering and exhilarated. He washed out his dirty linen and threw it ashore. He went into the deep water again to rinse off the soap, and lolled in the current as the morning light strengthened, and watched river-mist tumble in a breeze. For a few minutes he was enthralled by the simple wholeness of this moment, the animal contentment, the disregard of effort and consequence. He remembered a hot summer day before Dunmore's War when, passing time with a small party of Mingoes, he had sat smoking with the braves while squaws and children bathed naked nearby in a pebble-bottomed pool. Through that entire day his mind had been drugged by a primitive sense of suspended time, seduced from any thought of the surveying, clearing, or planting to be done, immersed in one boundless moment, driven by nothing. That idyll came into his mind as a picture now, then faded, leaving only poignancy and vague voluptuous yearnings. He heard a horse neighing softly down at the picket post on the Kentucky shore. Then he waded out and sluiced the water off his skin with the edges of his hands. He pulled back his hair and knotted it, let his hard body dry in the air, feeling like an inseparable element of the wild riverscape itself, then dressed and went back to the camp. When you're naked, he thought, it is only now. Clothes are the uniforms of time.

The officers were still sleeping. There was Helm, his hat over his face as a shield against the night damp; there was Joseph Bowman, curled on his side; there was his brother, John Bowman, hair lank with dew, breathing in long rumbles. There . . .

George paused, noticing that the bed of flattened leaves where Lieutenant Hutchings had been sleeping was empty; there was not even any bedding there. Would he have gone down to sleep near his men? George wondered about that, and then noticed that Captain Dillard's blanket had been thrown back and was empty. Hutchings and Dillard were members of the same contingent, and George felt a sudden, unexplainable rush of suspicion; he recalled dimly now a moment of uneasiness during the rum-enhanced excitement of the night before: Hutchings and some of the men in that contingent drawing aside into the shadows, looking darkly at him as he glanced at them. The moment had been too slight to dampen his exuberance but now the memory of it seemed full of portent.

Walking with soft tread but swiftly toward the west end of the encampment where that detachment was bedded, wading through a miasma of sleepers' breath, he was startled by the sudden appearance of Captain Dillard, who was rushing wild-eyed toward him. Dillard stopped before him, expressions of surprise, fear, then guilt fleeting in succession across his face. Before he could gather his wits to speak, a scrawny woodsman with no front teeth ran up behind him, then stopped and drew himself to an agitated stance of attention when he saw the commander. George felt a rush of anger and impatience.

"Well, damn you, speak, man!" he roared.

"Oh, God, Colonel, I'm mortified!" Dillard burst out, looking as if he might cry. "They's up and went! Hutchings took 'em, that weasel! He ..."

"Hutchings, you say!" Even with the rage and frustration pouring through him, George was appalled at himself for having made such a misjudgment of the young officer. "By God, I'll have his guts for garters, if I find him! How many went?"

"I don't ..."

"About twenty, sahr," interjected the skinny militiaman. "I jest took a muster. Some stayed."

"But damn them! We can't spare twenty! We can't spare a bloody one!" It was all he could do to speak through his rage. Twenty men deserted, out of this pitifully small excuse for an army! "How in blazes did they get away?" He had thought this island in fast waters deep in the wilderness would make desertion impossible; he had chosen it with that as well as its other attributes in mind.

"They found a wadin' place down yonder," the woodsman answered, pointing downstream. "Yestiddy when they was a-bathin' ..."

George was aware now of stirring and movement all about. Troops were awakening, propping themselves on elbows to hear this intriguing exchange. Some of them, doubtless, had entertained similar thoughts of leaving upon hearing last night of the formidable and dubious mission ahead of them in the remote western distances, this incredible mission into which, they might rightfully argue, they had been tricked. For a moment George simply did not know what he could do.

"Some of 'em ... eh, some of 'em," Dillard whined, as if trying to salvage what honor he could out of this betrayal, "... some of 'em wouldn't go ..."

"Is their trail cold?" George demanded. "When did they go?"

"Hanged if I know. I run down there when I woke an' saw Hutchings' bed gone. Before daylight sometime. No sentry saw or heard anything ..."

"Go wake Colonel Bowman and the others. Tell John we've got to borrow their horses. Never mind, I'll tell them." As he issued orders, he turned and strode toward the place where the officers were. Troops rising from their blankets were murmuring the rumor excitedly among themselves.

"By God," George snapped at Dillard, "any we catch that won't come back peaceably will be shot where they stand!"

As a party of twenty picked men thundered up the bluff into Kentucky on the borrowed horses, the rest of the force was summoned to an assembly around the same platform where they had so exuberantly received their orders the night before. Now they looked bewildered, scared, some sullen, as they stood puffy-eyed and rumpled under the blistering stare of their leader. They knew what the blaze of murder looked like in a man's eyes, and they recognized it now.

"I'll say this short and absolute for any here as might be doubtful," he began in a hard voice that cracked open the dawn. "A small and despicable company of cowards has sneaked off in the night, to avoid their duty. They are a crew of filthy squaws, not fit to be among men of purpose. Tell me what you think of that, now!"

"Aye," came their muttered reply. They seemed a half-hearted lot now.

"If there are any more such squaws here who think they're privileged to desert their country now or after and leave the fighting to the men, let them come one at a time and try to walk past me! Any who can and will is then free to go. If I stop him, he can swear his allegiance to this task and his folly will be forgot." He stared around. "Do I have any comers?" He felt at this moment so charged with the power of fury that he could dispatch five men at a time.

Several big men shifted their positions tentatively, but fell to examining their fingernails or the branches overhead when his eye struck them. Then a familiar voice came from behind him, a snarling brawl.

"Beg to ask, Cunnel, but don't y'admit we was summat tricked?"

George whirled on him. It was Sergeant Crump.

"You again! All right, Crump, do I take this to mean you'll try to leave?"

Crump hesitated; it was obvious that he had meant only to voice a thought that had been in many minds. Now he found himself directly challenged, though, and rather than back all the way down, he straightened up and said, "Wal, suh . . ."

George saw through his own anger suddenly and realized that he had put Crump on a spot he did not really deserve to be on; Crump surely was not the sort who would have deserted. But he was not the sort to back down from a challenge, either. George realized this now, and regretted that he would have to bait Crump, but he needed an object right now to make an important point to the whole troop, and Crump was the ideal object: he was brawny and formidable; he had spoken up before and he had spoken up now. If this expedition was to be held together and succeed in what lay before it, Crump would have to be made an example for the lesson of discipline.

George leaped down from the platform and advanced like a hungry cat on Crump.

The sergeant looked astonished for a moment, then his heavy black brows knotted in anger. George pressed on:

"Are you going to try to get through me, Crump? If y'are, then make your move!"

Crump turned his head slightly to one side to look at George warily through the sides of his eyes. He had no real idea what the full consequence of doing personal battle with a militia commander might be, and the situation was being unfolded on him faster than he could think about it. But he had been on the brink of his very life more than once, and was not one to shrink away from a provocation. He held up one palm toward the lithe red-haired officer before him. "I better warn you, Cunnel, when I git cornered, I'll chaw th' ears right off a bear!"

"Me too, Mister Crump. And you've defied me one time too many. Have at it, man!" George took a deep breath and prepared to move harder and faster than he ever had. There was a great risk involved here, he knew full well, not just for himself but for the entire expedition, perhaps for the preservation of the Kentucky frontier; Crump was indeed one of the fiercest creatures George had ever seen on two legs.

Crump suddenly handed his rifle to the man next to him, crouched, and hurled himself across the five feet of distance between them, hands reaching like grappling hooks.

George dodged to one side and brought both fists, one clenched inside the other, up in a mighty blow which thudded into the side of Crump's hurtling torso. It was like hitting a falling tree, but it did knock a loud grunt out of Crump. He landed on his hands and knees and was instantly back on his feet, but he was staggering and he had the round glassy eyes of a fish.

George stepped forward to finish him off with a gathered-up blow to the middle, but even as he threw it, Crump was coming at him through the air again and in the next instant George found himself straining to stand up under a huge, hard, sweat-stinking, tobacco-reeking, groping, bellowing, struggling wild man. One of the sergeant's merciless arms snaked around his neck and clamped down; George saw red and yellow blazes be-

hind his eyes, could not breathe, and thought his head was going to be torn off in that instant.

But something told him that he must stay on his feet as long
as he was alive, or everything he was trying to gain with these
men would be as good as gone.

So, refusing to buckle under Crump's weight and what
seemed like twenty of Crump's gouging hands, elbows and
knees, strangling in that great crooked arm, George kept
Crump's feet off the ground and ran with all his remaining
strength in the direction where he thought the platform stood.

They hit it with a force that collapsed the structure; Crump's
furious bellowing was punctuated by a yelp of pain, and the arm
loosened just enough for George to extract his searing head
from it and dump the big sergeant like a meal sack upon the
pile of clattering planks.

Crump was in an abandoned, pained rage now, and when he
clambered to his feet he brought up a plank with him, holding
it in both hands like some enormous broadsword, drawing it
back as if to deal the death blow.

But that moment of drawing back was just enough for
George to step in close and aim one blow at Crump's breastbone. It nearly stove in his wrist, but it sufficed. Crump dropped
like a poleaxed steer and lay face down among the yellow-white
boards, a pathetic rasping sound in his throat as he tried to draw
breath. George stood over him for only a moment, catching his
own breath and forcing his legs to remain steady. He was aware
that the men had not hooted and goaded as they usually did
while watching brawls; he presumed it was because he was not
just another backwoods scrapper but their commander. Some of
them, he thought, probably didn't know which of us they should
be cheering anyway.

Now he turned to them, hoping he did not look ridiculously
disheveled; from his sensations, he could not guess whether he
had any skin, hair, or even ears left on his head. Chest heaving,
standing straight, he looked around at their expressionless faces.
He hoped his voice would work.

"Now," he said calmly. "Is there anyone else disinclined to
follow me?"

No one moved. But slowly all the faces melted into grins.
Friendly grins.

He glowed inside. He turned and hauled Sergeant Crump to
his feet. The sergeant was just beginning to breathe. He was
rubbing his hip and shaking his head. He stooped to pick up his

fallen muskrat cap, beat the dust out of it on his thigh, and
jammed it on to cover the spot of skullbone in his scalp. Then
he shoved his face close to George's, gave him a raffish look
and a final shake of the head, and put his arm over his shoulder.
George's strained face managed a smile. Crump held him there
and turned a fierce vulpine grin on the onlookers.

"Now then, you motherless jackasses," he roared. "If they's
any of you who don't want t' go after that there prancin' British
hair buyer, y' jest come and try t' git past Cunnel Clark an'
me!"

GEORGE WORRIED ABOUT THE SUCCESS OF THE PURSUING PARTY
throughout the day, but continued with other business, supervis-
ing the erection of the fort and dividing the island into garden
land for the families.

Toward sundown a group of the pursuers returned leading
and dragging eight forlorn deserters whose skin and clothing
were awesomely scratched and torn. They had been overtaken
about twenty miles away, but, having seen their pursuers at a
distance, had scattered. Lieutenant Hutchings and about twelve
others had not been found. Riders from the chase party had
been sent ahead to advise the settlements to watch for the fugitives.

The captured deserters were held under guard, sitting in a circle, until late evening, watching sullen and shamefaced as the
industry proceeded all around them. From every passing man
and woman they received mean looks and verbal abuse.

By torchlight the men were hauled up after dark and forced
to watch as the soldiery prepared a special entertainment they
had dreamed up and George had approved: an effigy of Lieutenant Hutchings, made of clothing he had left behind and stuffed
with dry grass, was hanged and burned, to the tune of much
fierce cheering and jeering and the beat of Dickie Lovell's
drum. The fugitives now seemed totally terrified, unsure
whether they would themselves become the principals in a similar entertainment. Instead, George appeared before them and
gave them an opportunity to return to the ranks, upon taking an
oath that they would obey his subsequent orders to the letter
and would not try to desert again. "Do that," he told them, "and
you'll be welcomed back like brothers."

One of the fugitives dared to ask an obvious question. "What
alternative do we have, sir?"

"I'll let the men decide that," George answered with a grim smile.

Taking one look at the ring of menacing faces and the spilling sparks of the effigy, they all immediately gave their word. Their bonds were cut, their arms returned to them, and they were left to make themselves a part of the army again. George ordered that they should not be unduly harassed, but watched closely. "You'll have a certain amount of coolness to overcome," he told them. "But," he grinned, "welcome back among us." He looked at their wavering eyes and gulping throats, and dismissed them with a feeling that in trying to regain their honor they might well surpass the others in their conduct.

IN A FEW DAYS THE STRUCTURES WERE COMPLETED AND PLANTING was underway, and the troops were undergoing intensive drill which was aimed not so much at teaching maneuvers—"Leave ranks and files to the Redcoats," he told them—as at the instilling of morale and absolute discipline. George was forced to hurt one more unruly subordinate before this was complete; overhearing a gigantic Carolinian who was casting doubt on his sergeant's ancestry and refusing to stand at attention, George spun the astonished fellow about, grabbed his ample chin-whiskers and propelled him headfirst against a palisade pole. That man completed the day's drill in perfect obedience, his head swathed in a bloody turban of bandage.

The troops seemed to take heart from their young commander's obvious strength and decisiveness; they grew even tougher from the constant drill and labor, and more keen to fight, and whatever doubts they had shown in the first days on the island evaporated and they began talking about the upcoming westward raid as if it surely would be a lark. Every evening was given over to wrestling, running, and jumping matches or wild, earthshaking dances around the bonfire, to the tunes of a very facile fiddler from the Holston Valley contingent who had brought along a family heirloom violin his great-grandfather had made before emigrating from Scotland. As George watched these happy brutes cavort and whoop around the fire, he smiled to remember their consternation the night he had told them of Henry Hamilton's savage war-dancing.

Often George himself was prevailed upon to participate in the contests. He was outrun only once, by a nineteen-year-old Virginian built like a whippet, and in the jumping contests only Simon Butler cleared a higher bar than he did. The men watched him, marveled at his steel-spring physique, reveled in the colorful harangues and tongue-lashings he gave them on the drill field, and listened like children to the eloquent and cheerful predictions he made around the bonfire at night. Some who had been slouchers even began emulating his bearing. It gradually became apparent to every man that, even had George Rogers Clark not come to them armed with the authority of the governor's commission, he was the man among them who would have become their leader. George kept on a face of absolute confidence at all times, never giving an outward hint of his own trepidations. He wanted to give the impression of an iron fist in a doeskin glove, knowing that this would keep the men in assurance, keep them from fearing the unknowns that lay ahead. And even while constructing this image of himself for them, he felt his own need and his true affection for them growing. He saw the trust and camaraderie in their eyes when they looked at him and was aware that he, who in effect owned them for the short months of their enlistment, was actually their most cherished possession. "God in heaven, Joseph," he confided to Bowman one night as their departure down the river grew imminent, "these people are so in the palm of my hand that I should rather eat the aft end of a skunk than fail to keep them safe!"

Hunting parties went out. Venison, bear, and buffalo meats were salted or made into jerky in preparation for the expedition. Corn kernels left over from the planting were parched by the women to gray-black crunchiness in mud kilns; these would be carried in the troops' pouches as the trail substitute for bread.

There were days of heavy rain showers, which kept the river level high. George watched this with pleasure, as the long rapids could be run only when the water was high like this, and a portage of the heavy boats would have been a cumbersome task for this now highly keyed guerrilla force of his.

Two river messengers arrived in a pirogue from Fort Pitt one afternoon during such a downpour, bringing some mail and news, the best of which was that King Louis XVI of France had made an alliance with the Colonies. George thought an announcement of this information might further lift the spirit of his troops, then changed his mind. Their morale was good enough at present; they probably would see no immediate benefit from it here in the western frontier, but doubtless it might be used to some advantage upon his arrival among the French and Creoles at Kaskaskia. So he folded that information into his mind, revealing it not even to his officers.

On the twenty-third day of June, the new settlement being in good order, the seven men deemed not strong enough for the rigors of the march having been detailed to stay behind and garrison the island, George proclaimed a full day of amusement, broached a barrel of rum, enough to heighten the merriment but not so much as to debilitate the force next morning, and announced that they would leave the island by boat at daybreak to go against the British outposts on the Mississippi, some three hundred miles farther into the wilderness.

The sun went down, torches were lighted in a purple dusk, fresh meat was broiled over great fires, the fiddle squeaked and jiggled into the night, George danced with a gray-haired, gray-toothed grandmother in a gray dress while the troops cheered, and before midnight, all mellow, their granite faces all but melted by their complex emotions, the men sang a few melancholy songs around the dying fire, muttered a few embarrassed curses at their inner softness, then rolled into their blankets for their last night's sleep on Corn Island.

11

INTO THE ILLINOIS COUNTRY
June 1778

THE SUN WAS UP IN A BLAZING MORNING SKY OVER THE KENTUCKY bluffs when the men clambered into the boats and once again applied themselves to the oars they had pulled already for so many hundreds of miles.

George had announced only this morning, at muster, that they were going to be shooting the rapids, so that they would not have time to think about it. Many had blanched under their weathered skin at the news, but they had learned to keep their mouths shut and do as they were told. They had listened grimly as he told the helmsmen how to get through the channel. They were to follow his boat, which would be in the charge of Simon Butler during the three-mile descent. Butler had acted jolly and nonchalant, joking with the helmsmen and trying to make it seem like child's play.

Now, double-manning the oars, they rowed upstream against a fast current, heard the rush of the Falls with high-beating hearts, then turned the boats about a mile upstream, swung close to the northern shore and started down past Corn Island and into the intimidating maelstrom. They had a glimpse of two or three people watching them from the north shore of the island.

George was in the bow of the lead boat, the red-and-green Virginia flag rippling beside him, and Butler stood braced in the stern, directing Davey Pagan the steersman with cheerful orders. The crews of the following vessels, with orders to row faster than the current and stay on the tail of the command boat, whooped encouragement to themselves as the vessels plunged one by one into the glassy green and frothy white chute of water like corks on a flood.

At the awful moment when they seemed to be slipping over the very brink of the world, an eerie dim pall began to pervade the morning. And as the boats careened among the roaring spillways, dropping from one level to the next with water-cushioned jolts, rowers drenched with spray and lashed by the exhortations of the steersmen, the sun grew dark in the cloudless sky. Those who dared look up saw it diminish as if being gnawed away by some great black mouth, being reduced to a narrow shimmering crescent, then go black—a black hole in the hellish colored sky with a halo of misty rays. The helmsmen set their teeth on edge and aimed for the white water they could see, and there were as many prayers and curses and bewildered invocations as there were men in these boats.

"What in the name of God!" cried Joseph Bowman.

"It's an eclipse!" yelled George when at last he understood, as the boats leaped and rocked down through the hideous gloom. "A bloody omen to send us on our way!" He thought of his men. Surely they had never been as scared in all their adventurous lives as they were now, snatched down by the merciless swift power of the falling river and shadowed by this ominous malfunctions of their familiar and dependable sun. George's heart was in his throat and quavering; he felt as if he were riding pell-mell into the jaws of a cold and watery hell, and the Great Spirit of the wilderness was making one last desperate attempt to frighten him out of his purpose. From the stern, Simon Butler's now frantic orders bellowed, and Pagan grimaced and fought the rudder as if he were the mythical helmsman Charon of whom Mr. Mason had taught George in his boyhood. May God be with us in this moment, he thought. You mean something by this, I know!

And then, as Butler had predicted, the boats one after another glided out of the thundering turbulence into the gentle river below. The men were thoroughly shaken, giggling with relief; the superstitious among them were making of it what they would, and watched, squinting, with gaping jaws, as the sun emerged a bit at a time from behind the hard black disc of the moon, grew too bright to watch, and flooded once again the greenish waters and lush dark foliage of the river bluffs. It was hard to believe. Suddenly their world was normal again and they had come through the tumult of water.

"Hey, good work, Mister Forepoop Swabman!" someone yelled, and Davey Pagan took a bow.

But George gave them no time to ponder whether the eclipse had augured good or ill; ordering a quick cadence on the double-manned oars, he soon had the convoy speeding down the lower Ohio's mile-wide stream, the leagues measured by the bending and straining of bodies.

There was little talk. The men not rowing lay low in the boats with their long rifles loaded and primed, scanning the shore, or slept in shifts. These shores were hostile now; they were pulling steadily into regions under British control, leaving far behind the last outposts of American settlement. Here on the lower Ohio they could expect to meet no friends.

The blistering sun sank below the river bluffs; the air of dusk grew cool and damp; the rose tinge drained out of the western sky; the shores turned to purple and then receded into blackness; the stars came out; fresh hands took the oars, and those who had exhausted themselves lay down like rows of logs in the boats' damp bilges and plummeted into sleep. They were awakened in the slipping, gurgling, rushing darkness long before dawn and put back on the oars, and the night-rowers then slept as the eastern sky paled and became infused with pink. At midmorning the shifts were changed again, fed on cold meat, pone, and river water, sleeping and rowing and sleeping again; the sun set on the second day and rose again on the third. They passed the mouth of the great Wabash by morning light and the mouth of the Cumberland in the night, and when the fourth day dawned they learned that they were approaching the mouth of the Tennessee. They had come two hundred miles through heavily patrolled enemy country and, to their knowledge, had not yet been observed.

George led the boats toward a small uninhabited island called Baritaria in the mouth of the Tennessee, and the men murmured and groaned happily as the prows of the boats grated up onto the pebbly beach. Here the men were given a few hours to unbend and refresh themselves. A small, smokeless fire of white-oak bark was built and water was boiled for a kettle of powerful morning tea. Dozens of men squatted about, their lean white haunches exposed. "Ahhh!" crooned one. "Man jest ain't designed t'shit off the side of a boat!" Others simply stalked about stiffly, stretching their cramped limbs, grinning and holding their noses. When the troops had liberally fertilized the island and sipped the bracing tea, they moved back down to the shore near the boats to get their marching gear in order. George meanwhile conferred by the fire with his four company captains, Bowman, Helm, Harrod, and Montgomery.

"Three more leagues down the Ohio," he said, "is the old French Fort Massac. It's abandoned now, but we can't risk staying on the water past that point, because we're too nigh the Mississippi and all its unfriendly traffic." He showed them another map. "We'll row down here just above Massac, then debark on the Illinois side, conceal the boats there, and set out overland in a beeline to the northwest. That, in about a hundred and twenty miles, will fetch us up at the Kaskaskia River, which we'll cross by night and take the town and fort by surprise. That means, you understand, that we absolutely must not be seen until we're there . . ."

"Hi, sir!" rasped the sharp voice of a sentry at the shore. "A canoe!"

He pointed up the river.

"Get your men under cover," George ordered, watching the distant vessel approach the island. He and Bowman lay on their stomachs behind a shrub, a malodorous coil of stool on the ground between them. George watched the canoe, which seemed to have four or five hunters in it, coming parallel with the shore of the little island. Bowman glanced in disgust now and then at the great turd by his elbow.

"I'd say we could claim Baritaria now as true Virginia soil," he joked in a whisper.

"Aye," replied George. "By squatter's rights, eh?"

Bowman snorted laughter into the ground.

"They haven't seen our boats, yet," George said, "but they're bound to when they clear that point. I'm afraid we're going to have to bring 'em in. Get some men ready and man a boat, Joseph." Bowman scuttled off. Then George stood up and addressed a row of rifle muzzles which peeked out of the grass nearby. "Stand up and cover them," he said. Several riflemen rose out of the grass and brought their guns to bear on the canoe. "You there!" he shouted. The men in the canoe turned and saw him, and saw the long rifles aimed at them. They were clad in fringed yellow buckskins and wore bandannas around their heads. Their rifles were stacked amidships in the canoe, leaning on the carcass of a small deer. "Come ashore," George called, "or you're dead men." They stopped paddling for a moment, then saw Bowman's boatful of armed men slide out from beyond the point, coming to flank them. Bowman stood bareheaded in its bow, the sun blazing on his yellow hair, a pistol aimed at them.

The hunters shrugged, smiled nervously, dipped their paddles, and turned shoreward without a word.

They stepped ashore, rangy, sunburned, unshaven men, soiled and sweaty. Their eyes darted. They could not guess how many men lay in cover, but they saw the gleam of sunlight on gunmetal in many places as they strolled up to George, taking in his formidable bearing and cold eyes. "State who you are," he said.

"I'm John Duff," said the man in front, a freckled man with a broken nose. "This here's John Sanders, my guide. We're just hunters, sir."

"Americans?"

"Uh, formerly. Till we come here."

"What are you now, then?" He said it in a very menacing tone.

"Well, just hunters. Free agents, I reckon."

"Based where?"

"Kaskaskia."

"Now that's real interesting. Are you in the British pay?"

"Nope. Like I said, just free fer hire."

This John Duff is being shrewd, thought George. "How long out?" he asked.

"What, Mister Sanders? Eight days? Yup, I think eight days."

The troops were beginning to rise from cover and drift forward, curious. George turned and pointed at them. "Get back and work on your gear, all of you. There'll be plenty of time to meet our guests later. Now. Sit and have some tea, gents. If you're Americans, I must demand your oath of allegiance, or else you'll have to consider yourselves my prisoners. I have questions for you about the state of things at Kaskaskia."

The hunters took the oath amiably enough, though still bemused. George then introduced himself and began examining their knowledge of Kaskaskia. He tried to conceal his eagerness for their information. It had been a year since he had sent his spies Linn and Moore to Kaskaskia, and he knew the situation there might have changed drastically in the meantime. He had been running this expedition on very old intelligence. What rare luck to have these people show up from that very place, he thought.

His interrogation, which he kept on a polite and conversational tone, meanwhile weighing each fact against the others for consistency and any hints of untruthfulness, revealed that the fort was still under the command of Philippe de Rocheblave, functionary for the British, and that there were no British troops there at the moment. Rocheblave kept the French and Creole militia in a good state of readiness and well-trained, though perhaps as much for love of parade as for any expectation of attack. Duff said however that Rocheblave did maintain spies on the Mississippi and had ordered all hunters, Indians and other, to keep a sharp lookout for American rebels. There had been raids conducted recently against British settlements on the lower Mississippi by an American captain striking out of New Orleans with a gunboat. That raider, James Willing, had plundered and raised a great deal of havoc along the river, and news of his barbarities had reached as far north as the Illinois country, and the inhabitants, Duff said, were resolved to defend themselves.

Duff apparently was canny enough to see that George and his woodsmen were not here with a mere idle interest in the state of things as Kaskaskia; he offered the comment: "Them Frenchies is scared white o' the rebels. They been told by the British that the Americans—Virginians in pertickaler—is ten times worse'n any savage. They been told fer a long time now that Virginians 're the awfullest barbarians as ever got up off all fours. Heh! Anyhow, I reckon if they had any notice you was a-comin', they'd gather t' give you a hot reception, sure enough. But if you could surprise the place, I don't doubt you could have your way. Them Frenchies aren't exactly in love with th' British, either, y' understand." Duff estimated the population at Kaskaskia at something between five hundred and a thousand, depending on who was in town or out trapping and trading, and maybe five hundred at Cahokia up the river. And

the number of Indians about was always in flux. Duff didn't
know anything about Vincennes way over east on the Wabash,
he said, except that it was a big place.

George was satisfied with this information; it showed that not
much had changed since his previous intelligence, and when
Duff and his hunters asked leave to join the expedition, he welcomed them, first specifying that whatever knowledge of
Kaskaskia's defenses they might share in conversation with the
troops should be of a sort which would make them confident of
success.

As the force embarked and left the small island to row the
last three leagues down to their landing site on the Illinois
shore, George digested the information these hunters had
brought him. Of all he had heard, the most intriguing was that
the inhabitants considered Virginians to be such fiends. That
kind of a fear in itself multiplies our strength, he thought. It
makes up a little for those three hundred and fifty more troops
we ought to have had.

As the boats moved down the Ohio in the stifling heat,
George smiled and thought still more happily about this dreadful reputation of the Virginians. It was something he could improve upon if given any opportunity. The greater we can shock
them at first, he thought, the better they will respond when they
discover our humanity. The best way to get rid of an enemy is
by making him a friend.

Well, he thought, patting in his blouse the letter from Colonel
Campbell of Pittsburgh, the letter telling of the new alliance be-
tween France and America. Well then. We shall see about these
Frenchmen.

DUFF'S GUIDE JOHN SANDERS LED THE CONVOY, WHICH NOW IN-
cluded the hunters' canoe, into the mouth of a small creek
a mile above the ruins of Fort Massac. The stream here de-
bouched through a swampy place thick with saplings and scrub
and reeds which made it possible to hide the beached boats so
that one would have to step in them to find them. The men's
feet sucked in the black, rot-stinking muck, and clouds of mosquitoes bit and droned as the troops unloaded provisions for
four days of marching. George had never seen such an unhealthful sump of a place, and quickly formed the four companies of men into a single file and led them out.

It soon became apparent that a disproportionate part of their
four days would be spent in struggling through these first fifty

bottomland miles of the route to Kaskaskia, a hundred and twenty miles away. The region was a pathless maze of marshy bottoms, thickets of briar and thorns, great mats of vines, and acres of tall cane whose leaf edges sliced skin like razors. It was miserable going, but he chose not to get on the old trail from Massac to Kaskaskia for fear of being seen.

Throughout the steaming afternoon the single file of sweating, scratched, hard-breathing, wild-looking men in filthy buckskin and homespun slithered like a snake through the snarls of vegetation. There was no talk along the two-hundred-yard-long procession, there was just the swish of foliage over clothing, the thud of moccasins on soft earth, the crackling of twigs, creaking of leather, the occasional small wooden knock of a rifle stock against a knife handle or brandy flask, now and then a throat-clearing, a spitting, a breaking of wind, the drone of insects, a skin-smacking sound marking the death of some deerfly or mosquito.

It occurred to George once that Sanders might be leading them deliberately off course, or at least delaying them by taking them through the worst jungle he could find. But, referring often to his own pocket compass, he verified that this was the exact northwesterly heading that he had chosen himself. And it certainly was not the kind of country in which there was a likelihood of being discovered, there was no sign that any man, red or white, had ever been through here, and it would have been easy to understand why none had.

When the late sun quit flashing its red needles of light through the foliage in the west, darkness quickly filled the woods. With it came more mosquitoes, by the thousands, and the *glunk* and *peep* of innumerable frogs. Going without light, soaked by sweat and the crossings of creeks and swamps, the slogging men were beginning to stumble, to mutter curses containing the names of God, of Sanders, of Clark, of mosquitoes, of hidden roots, of lashing thorns. And so, when their progress brought them up on a slight rise of ground where the overhead foliage broke enough to show a few stars twinkling, George ordered the column to enter the glade, form in squares, halt, and settle for the night. No fires could be risked in the heart of hostile territory, so each man simply sat or hunkered in the darkness, munched stale johnnycake and parched corn or masticated leathery meat jerky out of his own pouch, curled up on the bare ground with his gun's flintlock between his thighs for protection against the damp, covered his face and hands as well as possible against mosquitoes, and dropped into the sleep of exhaustion. George had his captains post their sentries around the perimeter, with orders to keep an especially watchful eye on Duff's party, then he stretched out on the damp grass, felt the fatigue burning away in the muscle of his legs, and calculated gloomily that they surely had not managed to march more than fifteen miles through this tangle during the terrible afternoon. The next thing he knew was that it was morning.

All through the second day from dawn to darkness, stopping only to drink from streams and feed themselves from their pouches, they trekked through more of this stubborn country, occasionally emerging into pockets of ancient wood where gigantic black forest trees lay rotting and the only undergrowth was fern and mayapple. Here the progress was easier, and they surprised many deer, but despite their yearnings for fresh meat dared not fire a shot or build a fire which might give them away. Then they would plunge into still more areas of thicket and thorn, whose only recompense was that wild berries might be plucked in passing and popped into the mouth to relieve the monotony of corn and jerky. Again that night they dropped to the ground in alien darkness and slept like dead men, only to rise at dawn on the third day and continue.

At midday, having been through fifty miles of that wilderness, the army came out upon a level, nearly treeless plain, covered with waist-high grass rippling in the breeze as far as the eye could see. Grazing bison dotted the distance. The expanse of unbroken blue sky overhead made everyone look up and breathe deeply, as if they had crawled out of some dank tunnel into brave daylight, and they smiled to see the clear ground stretching away forever like a soft rug for their feet. After a few cheerful minutes for eating, resting, and stretching in the sunlight, they strode forward onto this great, clean prairie, the sun and wind drying the old humidity out of their clothes, so rejuvenated by the openness that their pace quickened to a lope which ate up the miles.

But George's pleasure at the freedom of such marching was marred by the realization that his line of riflemen could now be observed by anyone within miles. The grass was not high enough for concealment. There was nothing to do but keep the point men and flanking scouts out as far as possible, keep up the pace and hope for good luck.

The hundred and seventy men now sped rather like an arrow over the yellow-green plain toward the northwest; the point man and flankers fanned out in the shape of an arrowhead, the main column being the shaft and the rear flankers angling back like the fletch of the arrow. Each man stepped into the footprints of the man ahead so that anyone coming upon their trail could not have guessed how many they were.

They flopped along the line of march again at sundown, chewed their dwindling rations and washed them down with water or brandy from their canteens, relieved themselves, joked and laughed softly, and being dog-tired, stretched out in the dry, springy, fragrant grass, watched hawks circling in the high rosy sky, and prepared to go to sleep. But to their consternation, their young commander came back along the file, cheerfully urging them to their feet. "We can see where we're going out here," he told them as he moved along. "And we can travel at night with no danger of being seen. Up, now! Hey, Marr! You, Mayfield! Wake up, you beauties, and on your shanks! Get those sea legs in motion, Mister Pagan! I know this nice little walk can't be half as bad as beatin' around the Horn!"

They groaned, but rose, and soon the human arrow was again moving westward at a strenuous pace through the twilight, the stars winking on over their shoulders, fatigue blazing in the fibers of their legs. Still more hours of nothing but long breathing and light footsteps. They passed the point of pain now; they were numb and felt as if they could bear this dull discomfort forever if that danged Clark was so bent on making up for time they had lost in the thickets.

The sky was enormous. There seemed to be more stars, twinkling more cleanly from horizon to horizon, than they had ever seen. Passing nothing that gave them any sense of their progress, they had the strange sensation that the trail was simply slipping backward under them and they were stationary, the same stars standing in the same places overhead, the same silhouetted hats and shoulders bobbing up and down before them, the same aromas of old sweat and leather and gunpowder eddying backward like a wake, the same cushioned footfalls endlessly repeating after their own. Only at midnight did George bring the day's trek to a halt. The force was led aside a few yards from its trail, the companies formed into four squares, and sentries were named; the rest were dismissed, sank to the ground too tired even to eat, and were dreaming as soon as their heads touched the grass.

George stood in the starlight and looked at this little group of dark forms scattered about on the ocean of smooth pale plain.

Six hours of squirming through the forests this morning, he thought; six more racing along in the blazing sun, and now six more marching through the night. Eighteen hours on foot at this pace, and not one solitary straggler! He tipped up his flask and took a long pull of brandy, his eyes on the stars, the cool wind drying the sweat on his neck. He lowered the flask, continued to look up at the sky, thought of the eclipse that had so frightened the men a week ago on the Falls—a week it's been! he thought—and yet they had come on with him, overcoming the many fears they must be having, and still, even as he drove them on and on into this strange unfriendly country, they kept up, and kept up in good spirits. He listened to their sleep-breathing now, sighed, and looked at the high constellations and the stardust of the Milky Way. I thank Thee for bringing me men like these . . .

He was awakened to the sound of his flask dropping to the ground, and realized he had fallen asleep on his feet in the middle of a prayer. Shaking his head and smiling, he stretched out on the grass, put his hat over his face, and, with a sensation like lying on a raft in a whirlpool, spun slowly off to oblivion.

THEY HAD BEEN ON THE TRAIL FOR TWO HOURS THE NEXT MORNING when the sun rose behind them, lighting the high cumulus clouds piled above the horizon ahead. It was a glorious morning. Small birds flickered among the grasses and wildflowers, hunting, and as the sun climbed and burned off the dew that drenched the marchers' leggings, countless butterflies tumbled and drifted everywhere. Each step George took sent gray-green grasshoppers with black-banded legs scattering ahead through the grass, like the drops one splashes ahead when wading in shallow water.

The sun climbed higher and bore down on their heads and shoulders, the hot, dense ground-smell rose to their noses, and long brittle screeches of locusts drilled on the ear from everywhere. It soon became apparent, as they crossed miles without seeing any streams, that here was another price they must pay for this smooth passage: thirst. These woodsmen were accustomed to well-watered country, where clear brooklets babbled down every ravine, and springs trickled from mossy limestone. But now the hard march through the ovenlike air was drying them up and there seemed to be not so much as a mud wallow where they might find a little moisture.

"Sanders!"

"Sir?" The guide turned and waited for George to come abreast of him, then fell in step with him.

"D'you know of any water hereabouts?" he asked quietly.

"None for certain this time of year, sir."

"Oh? None for how far?"

"Well, Colonel, we'll be reachin' Missipp Valley tributaries sometime tomorrow, I reckon."

George marched with his eyes squinting against the shimmering prairie for a few paces, then glanced at Sanders, at the high, pockmarked cheekbones, the yellow complexion almost the color of his buckskins, the leached blue eyes. "Seems like if you knew how dry it is out here, you'd've told us before we left the river country, so we could fill up some. Didn't you think of that at all?"

"Nope," said the laconic guide. "First place, I never seen people guzzle water like these o' your'n. Second, I didn't know you'd be a-sweatin' 'em quite so."

"Hm." George sent him on ahead to the point. He looked back. Along they came, the long line of yellow and gray and brown, the black hats, glinting rifles, dogged expressions, sunken cheeks, chapped white lips drawn across their bristly faces. Bowman, just behind him, winked. George faced front again and strode on.

Well, he thought, they haven't asked about water yet. No sense telling them that bad news till they ask.

No one asked. Apparently it was quite plain to them that this was dry country, and that was just the way it was.

The thirst made parched corn and pone and jerky seem less appetizing, which in a way was just as well, as most were down to their last few crumbs. They had provisioned themselves for four days on the trail; but the overland journey by now had stretched to five days and they still were not in the Mississippi Valley country. They were tiring quicker without food or water, going at a slower pace, needing to rest longer. They watched the sky for signs of rain, but saw only an intense nacreous haze. Night brought cooler air but no rain.

On the sixth day they found a trapped pool in a dried-up westerly creek with barely enough murky water to half-fill their canteens. But it was enough to put them back in high spirits for a while. A few sips of water even gave them the temporary illusion that they had something in their shrunken bellies.

It was then that the guide's behavior began to arouse George's suspicion.

Sanders hesitated ahead, then made quite an obvious change in his course. He did this two more times within the hour; George grew annoyed and the men were beginning to mutter. George ran forward to the guide and grabbed him by the shoulder to spin him around. "Just what are you up to, Sanders?"

The guide's eyes were shifting and fearful. "Uhm, sorry, Colonel, I . . . I expected we'd meet up with the hunters' road to Kaskasky right about here, but I don't seem to recognize . . ."

"You *what?*"

Sanders stammered and glanced around at the horizons, sweat beading his lip. The troops had caught up and were drifting into a semicircle to listen. Their eyes were narrowed and they did not appear very happy. Sanders cleared his throat. "I think a way over there . . ." He raised his arm toward the north. When he saw the colonel's flashing eyes and grim mouth, he had to drop his gaze. George barked into his ear.

"What d'you mean, *think,* you scurvy fool? Don't you *know?* By God, man, if you've got us off the trail . . ."

The troops were muttering now, reacting as much to their commander's anger as to their own confusion. Among their murmurings could be heard the words "traitor" and "Tory."

"Hang th' scut," somebody suggested in a murderous flat tone.

"Yah," chuckled another. "If he can find us a tree."

George looked at the nervous guide, at his wavering, hunted-beast eyes, and felt the worst torrent of rage he had ever experienced in his life. He grasped the hilt of his sword with a shaking hand, ground his teeth, and nearly burst with fury. His head was roaring and every muscle was straining to draw steel and run Sanders through on the spot. *Control,* he warned himself. If this poxy scoundrel has led us into an entrapment it'll be up to me to extract us from it. Control. *Control!* He took several deep breaths and let them come quaking out, and the muscles of his arms and back relaxed a bit.

"Now, Sanders," he began, barely above a whisper. "Here I am wandering with my army, out in the open, in a country where any tribe of Indians could raise three or four times our number. These precious men have followed me more than a week by water and land, ready to do anything they're asked. But if they're asked to perish out here short o' their goal because you, a so-called *guide,* have got us lost, they may choose to cut you down, Sanders, an ounce at a time, and I personally shall start it by snipping off your manhood."

"Damn, I'm not *lost*, Mister Clark. I'm only *confused*! If you'd give me a little time . . ."

George glanced around at the terrain, which here had begun to undulate, with copses of oaks in the low places. "From the time I employed you, Sanders, you told me you knew the way well. This doesn't look like the kind of country a man would forget soon, if he really was acquainted with it. Frankly, Sanders, I don't find it in me to trust you any more."

"You can trust him, Colonel," offered John Duff, who had crowded forward.

"You! I trust you just as little, Duff."

"Please, sir," implored Sanders. "Just let me go out on yonder meadow there and look around. I'll get my bearings . . . There's a trail I can find . . ."

"Oh, aye?" growled Sergeant Crump from the edge of the menacing circle. "Let you go off alone? An' maybe bring back a few hunnerd Kaskasky soldiers, eh? You take Cunnel Clark fer a simpleton, do you?"

"No, Crump," George said. "We'll let him go find that trail. But Si Butler and yourself will go with him and watch 'im close. If he hasn't found the way in two hours, bring 'im back here and he'll be put to death with no further ado. Take your ease, boys," he told the troops. "Check your powder and enjoy a rest. One way or another we'll be on the move again in a couple of hours." He stalked about, cooling his temper, which had absolutely drained him, and watched Crump and Butler escort the miserable and disarmed Sanders down a long, grassy draw. Their forms shimmered in the heat as they went away.

George could not entertain the thought of turning back. He walked back and forth in the dry, ovenlike heat, slapping his hat against his thigh, imagining and discarding all sorts of consequences. The men lounged on the meadow, many of them stripped to moccasins and breechclouts against the heat, speculated on Sanders's loyalty, eyed Duff and the other hunters wordlessly, boasted of what they would do at Kaskaskia, carried on detailed reminiscences about splendiferous meals they had sometime enjoyed, rubbed their feet, wondered aloud about Frenchwomen, checked their rifles, or dozed, or examined the myriad cuts and bruises they had sustained coming through the swamp and thickets. Others simply watched their young commander in sympathy or wonderment as he waited.

Soon they saw him straighten up and, looking down the draw, beheld Si Butler summoning with sweeps of his arm.

Sanders had found the trail. He had indeed been not lost but only bewildered. George forgave him with comradely slaps on the back, and Sanders was almost in tears with relief and happiness. Soon the troop was running along a well-worn trail, cautious but in high spirits, and began descending into a wide and fertile valley.

By that evening, the fourth of July, they lay in the warm grass a few miles above the town of Kaskaskia, a cluster of handsome and well-built houses standing within the acute angle where the Kaskaskia River flowed southward into the Mississippi. They lay almost invisible in the meadow grass, mostly naked to catch any breeze of evening on their filthy, sweaty bodies, looking over the lazy valley and the broad, curving Mississippi, to the Indian villages north of the town, the gardens and fields and roads, the huge Old World windmill, the dim low bluffs on the distant shore of the Mississippi, and the blood-red sun setting over the Spanish territory beyond the gigantic stream; they waited here on the edge of a different world, light-headed with hunger and dreams of glory, bodies stinking and stomachs gnawing, for the darkness which would cover their attack on this strange, British-controlled little pocket of French civilization between two wildernesses.

"Them Frenchies down there is at heart a lazy, good-for-nothin' breed," John Duff observed. "It's a land o'plenty, and they work about half the time. Their niggers do most o' *that*. Git in their gardens with no effort a-tall, an' drink an' gossip the afternoons away. Never saw the like fer gossip. Guess they have a lot of fun, but I wouldn't give y' a shillin' fer the lot of 'em as men."

"I hear tell they git along famous with th' Indians," remarked a woodsman.

" 'Course they do," agreed Duff. "Just like 'em. Cunning. No ambition. They sell their furs and what little else they produce downriver in New Orleans and bring finery up by boat. But they act like the lilies of the field. Whatever the Lord sees fit t' give 'em that's all they 'spect. You won't often see a Frenchie out clearin' land fer corn. Grapes and herbs, maybe, but not corn." He spat.

"What kind of finery d'you mean, Mr. Duff?" one of the Virginians asked, laving his hands.

"Oh, high falutin' stuff. Like lace and silverware, candlesticks, delicate underwear, even jewelry. Imagine jewelry out here 'twixt nowhere an' nowhere else!"

"Them French ladies wear jewelry?" exclaimed a frontiers-man with four front teeth absent. "They pretty? Worth a-chasin' down?"

"Barefoot most o' the time," Duff chuckled. "But they put on their trimmin's fer special times, and you never seen nothin' so saucy."

He pointed out to them the big house within the fort where Philippe de Rocheblave lived, and the men stared down at it with malignant fascination. *Rocheblave.* They had memorized the French commandant's name from Colonel Clark's contemp-tuous pronunciation of it the night of their big powwow on Corn Island. And now, incredibly to their minds, here they were, two weeks and three hundred miles later, looking down from concealment onto the house of the notorious Rocheblave, just as his hireling Indians had so often lurked in the wilds around their own Kentucky and Virginia settlements waiting to attack and murder. Colonel Clark had made Rocheblave a proper villain for them to set their vengeful thoughts on, and it seemed to them neatly and wonderfully just that they should be stalking him now.

And it was their young colonel who had made this nice piece of justice possible. They glanced at him now and then, at that handsome and likable but sometimes soul-chilling young man who somehow, it seemed, could do the craziest things with the best of horse sense. They watched him study his Kaskaskia town map with his officers in the waning light. It was a map he had obtained a year ago from spies he had sent up here from Kaintuck, all on his own, a total secret.

"Daggonedest thing I ever did see," Sergeant Crump was saying to Duff. "He runs at things lookin' like a blind bull, then you find out he's done planned every step of 't." He rubbed his breastbone, which still ached whenever he recalled the fight Clark had coaxed him into on Corn Island. "B'lieve me, I *know*," he added.

"He always drive folks this hard?" Duff asked.

"Aye, oh, it ain't easy, Mr. Duff. It ain't easy. But all in all, I wouldn't a missed it fer anything."

In the meantime, George had been briefing his captains in a perplexing vein.

"Make every man understand that I'll tolerate not one act of plunder or savagery of any kind. There'll be no scalping, there'll be no looting, there'll be no raping, or even an ungentle gesture at any woman there. They'll use only what force they need to keep the civilians out of the way, and there'll be no intercourse of any kind with the inhabitants until I say so."

The captains looked at each other with raised eyebrows, then back to him. "No looting?" said Helm. "Th' boys won't like that; takes th' fun out of it. To th' victor goes th' spoils."

George gave him a hard, level look, indicating that such remarks deserved no comment. Then he went on:

"There is one other caution, most important. We'll take pains never to reveal how few we are. We must never be all together where we could be counted. If we can, we must seem a thousand. We'll simply have to be everywhere. You can negotiate only from a dominant posture, and that'll be no mean trick where we're outnumbered ten to one. But it has to be that way."

The officers looked confused, and a momentary apprehension flickered across their faces. They had not really let themselves think about numbers. "What d'you mean 'negotiate,' George?" asked Bowman.

"I mean first, their surrender. Then, this." He drew out Campbell's letter about the French-American alliance and showed it to them for the first time. They studied it with great curiosity, then looked back at him.

"It means," he said, "we invade them as enemy. Then with the help of God and what wisdom we have, we turn their loyalty around."

The officers scratched their scalps, squinted, grimaced. They had come all this way inspired by him into a simple raiding mood. And now he was giving them responsibilities far more complicated than that. He had had this treaty thing in his pocket for weeks and had waited until now to tell them about it. It was like the other trick of his, bringing them all the way down to Corn Island under a simpler pretext.

It was pretty perplexing, this matter of dealing with a man who always knew more than they did. But what choice was there, besides doing what he decided? And so the four captains shrugged, nodded, and agreed once again to do it his way.

He looked over the violet twilight in the valley, and pointed. "Y'see that big farmhouse just this side o' the river, below the old abandoned fort? Duff tells me there's a ferry of sorts there and we can acquire boats for the crossing. Now tell your companies what I said about their conduct, and tell 'em violations will be on pain of death. In ten minutes we'll move down the bluff to that farmhouse . . ." The severity of his tone suddenly softened, and in the dusk they could see him smiling. "Thank you, gents. Let's be about it now."

12

KASKASKIA, ILLINOIS COUNTRY
July 4, 1778

DON FERNANDO DE LEYBA, LOOKING MOST GUBERNATORIAL IN HIS long coat of black velvet, sat in the chair at Teresa's right, and his wife Maria, in a dress of black silk, sat on her left. It seemed to Teresa, who wore taffeta the color of old ivory, that their somber mien and sentry-like flanking positions must make any of the young Kaskaskians fearful of approaching her. The violins squeaked away busily at a minuet; many of the French militiamen and dandies gazed longingly her way as they danced past with their partners, but not one had dared to approach.

The de Leybas were being entertained as guests of honor by the wife of the merchant Gabriel Cerré. Monsieur Cerré was, as usual, away trading. The de Leybas had sailed down the river from St. Louis on a week-long excursion, and this ball was the culmination of their visit. They were to embark for their return to St. Louis the next morning.

Though Teresa was impressed by the elegance and voluptuousness of the French social life, she remained somewhat uncomfortable in the midst of it, never quite sure how far to unbend from that quiet reserve in which she had been conditioned since earliest memory. She had noticed that her brother's careful formality and studied hauteur were being eroded little by little as the weeks went by here in this remote little Franco-Spanish society strung along the banks of the Mississippi, but still, in comparison with the French, he was quite controlled, and a zealous warden especially of the properties surrounding a maiden sister.

No Frenchman had managed to penetrate the fine sieve of Don Fernando's discrimination, though there were four or five rather handsome and respectable ones who had, or whose fathers had, accrued substantial fortunes through trade in furs, hemp, tobacco, and grain. The few soldiers in the Spanish garrison at St. Louis were a rather coarse lot, some of them part Indian, and of course only an officer would have the right to play suitor to Teresa. Besides Don Fernando, who commanded the garrison, there were only two other Spanish officers, one of them, Cruzat, being middle-aged, married, and overfed. The other, Francisco de Cartabona, lieutenant of militia, was youthful, slender, and nearly as handsome as her brother. Teresa had met him but once before, at her brother's office in St. Louis.

At this moment, as if her thoughts had summoned him, Lieutenant de Cortabona appeared in the doorway at the far side of the ballroom. His intense gaze swept around the room and came to rest on her, and with a flush of self-awareness, Teresa lowered her eyes, and the lace-webbed fan in her hand began to fibrillate against her bosom. Maria, noticing these slight motions, sat up straighter, like a sentinel sensing danger; her sunken black eyes darted to the far side of the room just in time to see the lieutenant gather himself up and start making his way toward the de Leybas around the end of the ballroom, his cocked hat tucked under his left arm, his sword scabbard hanging from his belt. He stopped at attention before Don Fernando, bowing quickly and snapping his boot heels. "Good evening, Excellency," he said, not yet permitting himself to look at the ladies.

Don Fernando rose, returning the bow with a smile. "Good evening, Lieutenant. We see you so seldom. You've been seeing to the militia over at Ste. Genevieve, have you not? How do they stand?"

"Quite well, Excellency. For militia," he added with a mocking half smile. Then he turned to the ladies. "What a great pleasure to see you," he said, bowing again, now looking directly at Maria for just an instant, then at Teresa's eyes for a perceptible second longer. Teresa dropped her gaze with proper modesty.

Such fine skin and eyes, she thought. And so graceful. What a shame he is so little, no taller than I. She produced a guarded hint of a smile which, as she knew from a thousand past glimpses in her bedroom mirror, bowed her lips to the slightest degree and surely created a puzzle in the mind of any young man who saw it.

Lieutenant de Cartabona paused for a moment, as if interpreting that very enigma, then looked to Don Fernando. "It may be a little forward of me, Excellency, but would you allow your sister to dance with me in the next *cuadrilla*?"

"With her permission, gladly."

"Señorita?"

"Sí," she replied after a moment of conscious fan-fluttering which, she was sure, had its desired effect upon the anxious little lieutenant.

The next dance was indeed a quadrille. Being the sort of square dance that occasioned no more touching than that of hands on shoulders, it nevertheless permitted a succession of coquettish looks and other facial signals in passing, as well as the kind of innocent exuberance which allowed the partners to glimpse every few seconds each other's open-mouthed smiles and grace of movement. Lieutenant de Cartabona was indeed a lithe and exciting figure in movement, and would now and then introduce a manly Spanish stomp and fiery narrowing of the eyes, suggestive of flamenco. The lieutenant knew well how to project his fire.

By the time the quadrille was over, it was obvious to everyone that the sister of Lieutenant Governor de Leyba was involved in the process of courtship, to that limit of discretion imposed by the old Spanish code but modified by the casual circumstances in this remote outpost of Upper Louisiana. As the night wore on, Teresa admitted to herself that she was at least as happy as she had ever been in New Orleans.

13

KASKASKIA, ILLINOIS COUNTRY
July 4, 1778

THERE WAS A LAMP GLOWING IN ONE END OF THE FARMHOUSE WHEN Colonel Clark's little regiment filed silently in through the gate of the farmyard and squatted in the shadows along the foot of the stone wall. Beyond the dirt road outside the wall the Kaskaskia River sighed and gurgled among the pilings of the farm's landing dock. On the other shore of the river, just a few hundred feet away, lights of the town straggled up the bank. Now and then lanterns could be seen moving among those town buildings, and muffled voices or snatches of song and the yipping of village dogs would drift across the river. From somewhere in the town there came faint sounds of violin music, filtered through the constant din of frogs and crickets.

When his men were all concealed, George took Captain Bowman and two soldiers, with Sanders as interpreter, strode to the front door of the house, and knocked on it with his fist. There was a long moment of silence, then a query was called from within, just audible through the stout oak portal. Sanders answered:

"Ouvrez! Nous sommes les soldats de Rocheblave."

The sturdy French farmer who drew the iron bolt and swung the door open might have been surprised enough at a visit from Rocheblave's militiamen; he recoiled and almost fell backward over his family when a gigantic, gaunt, fierce-eyed, red-haired savage, pistol in hand, sweat and dirt burnishing the slabs and knots of muscle on his naked torso, pushed in, followed by others equally ferocious looking and bristling with weapons.

The family was herded into the parlor and seated, and huddled there wide-eyed, trembling in fear of their lives, as the leader of the intruders, without giving any explanation for his presence, began a rapid and demanding interrogation. The farmer was so awed by the man's glittering eyes that he dared not lie to him. George learned that a few days earlier Rocheblave, hearing rumors of a possible attack by the river raider Willing, had summoned all the militia and able-bodied townsmen to arms, but that the guard had been relaxed when no enemy appeared. Yes, the farmer assured him, the fort surely would be under minimal guard now. What would explain the music coming from the town? he was asked. He did not know, but presumed it might be the town's Negroes having one of their frequent entertainments. Would there be Indians about the town and the fort? Always, he replied, but one never knew how many; they constantly came and went in war parties and trading bands, dealing with Rocheblave and the traders.

"Consider yourselves prisoners," they were told by the intruder, "until our business in town is completed." A lieutenant entered the house and reported that five small boats had been procured, in addition to the two that lay at the farmer's landing.

It was about ten o'clock when the boats, with oars muffled

and without lights, began ferrying the men and their weapons across the Kaskaskia River. Few of the men could swim, but many hung to the gunwales and transom of the vessels, to facilitate the ferrying of so many troops in so few small boats. The men then lay low along the muddy riverbank in the darkness almost under the very doors and windows of the town, checking their powder and flintlocks in the damp stillness while the boats returned to bring over more men.

Shortly after midnight the crossing was completed. It had been done so stealthily that not even a dog had been aroused. Most of the lights of the village were out now, but from somewhere near the fort the music could still be heard.

George put Bowman in charge of two companies and sent them out to surround the town, and they vanished into the darkness. George, accompanied by John Sanders and Simon Butler, led the other company straight up through a darkened alley toward the gates of the fort, which stood silent and dark. He sent Butler ahead to reconnoiter the gate. Butler disappeared, silent as a ghost, then returned in ten minutes with the remarkable news that not only was one gate of the fort standing open, there was no sign of a single sentry. The music, he revealed, was coming from a fine private home near the fort, where about two dozen persons were having a dance to the music of fiddles and a flute. There was no sign of Indians within the fort, and the barracks building was dark, he said. George looked at the fort, a black, undefinable silhouette against the stars, looked back to the dark and silent file of frontiersmen who hovered in the alley behind him, then rose and went straight for the gate. There was no sound but the breathing of the nearest men. As the ghostly file passed a yard, a dog came forth to investigate; it gave a short growl, then was mysteriously silenced before it could emit a first bark. The music grew louder now as they approached the large stone house outside the fort.

Arriving at the open door of the lighted house, George halted the column, looked in for a moment at the swirling, laughing dancers, and thought of the countless happy occasions of this sort that he had attended as a young man in Virginia. Then, summoning a few men, he went to the door and stepped in.

A Negro servant leaning on the wall near the door, half asleep, looked up, saw him appear out of the darkness, and, taking a deep breath while his eyes grew large in the light of the chandeliers, gave a wavering, moaning cry which got the attention of the nearest dancers. In a moment the music trailed off in confused discord and a heavy silence filled the room, broken only by the gasps and murmurs of dancers whose eyes began to turn to this apparition in the doorway. Two women at once put their wrists to their foreheads and tried to swoon on the same fainting couch at the end of the room, resulting in a bit of clumsy confusion there.

George stood for a moment enjoying the incredulous expressions on the faces of the young officers, gentlemen, and ladies, then said to Sanders:

"Tell 'em they may continue their dancing, but to remember that they now dance under the flag of Virginia, not England." While Sanders announced this in his clumsy French, George sent a few of the half-clad, mud-smeared frontiersmen through the room to collect swords and pistols, then turned to go out. But a handsome, dark-eyed man, who had been standing in the company of two beautiful women, suddenly left them and came forward.

"Sir," he said in correct but strained English, "several of us here are Spanish citizens from St. Louis, and we are merely guests here of the French. Are we to be detained?"

George looked at the elegant little man, then said: "If you'll be patient, I'll attend to your situation. For the moment I must advise you and all the others not to stir from this house, for your safety. Is Chevalier de Rocheblave here, may I ask?"

"He went home not more than an hour ago," the Spaniard said.

George watched, over the man's shoulder, the younger of the two women who were with him, and felt a bittersweet pang in his breast. She was dark-eyed, oval-faced, transfixed by terror, but beautiful. He turned, ordered the musicians to continue, and left guards at the doors. He heard the fiddles resume hesitantly as he led his men on to the fort. The troops whispered their amusement as they came ahead in the darkness. Soon he saw the black bulk of the gates looming on either side of him, then knew from the starry space of open sky above him that he was within the compound of the fort.

He sent the men of his company around to infiltrate every corner within the walls, then followed Sanders directly to the house of Rocheblave. A dim light shone in an upstairs window. One hatchet blow opened the doorlatch, and a squad rushed silently into the house. George drew his pistol and mounted the staircase with three men at his heels. Lamplight showed through a door at the end of the upstairs hallway. He stepped into the room, a lighted bedchamber, in which a middle-aged man and woman, in nightcaps, sat against propped pillows, holding a bed sheet to shield themselves. A huge armoire stood open on each side of the room, one full of hanging uniforms and formal wear, the other of dresses and gowns. Cricket calls filled the room through open windows hung with mosquito cloth.

"Are you the Chevalier de Rocheblave?" George demanded.

The man only nodded, looking into the barrel of the pistol.

"It's my pleasure to inform you that you're now a prisoner of war and your town is under the control of the Virginia militia. I'm Colonel George Rogers Clark. This, I presume, is Madame Rocheblave?"

"Of course it is," croaked the man, whose look of astonishment was giving way to an ashen-faced expression of stark fear and dismay. George, nearly giddy with hunger now that the tension of the approach was past, felt a powerful urge to laugh at the absurd circumstances of the great and terrible Philippe de Rocheblave, but at the same time was moved by pity. What a mortification for a military commander, he thought, to be caught by complete surprise, cowering under a bed sheet. And looking like some gross dame in that silly nightcap! To keep himself from breaking out in hilarity, George went to the open window, leaned out into the night, discharged his pistol, and cried: *"Yaaaa, hooooey! Rocheblave is ours!"*

Immediately the night was filled with answering huzzahs and shouts from every corner of the town, and a babble of querying voices could be heard coming from everywhere. Soon the streets were full of the sounds of running men and the rattle and jingle of weaponry. Duff's French-speaking hunters, in response to George's signal, were racing through the streets ordering the awakening citizens to stay inside their houses on pain of death. Standing in the window, George grinned with thorough satisfaction and watched the town come alive with lights and cries as if some midnight festival had just begun. Finally he drew himself inside and turned to the speechless couple in the bed, who were contemplating the muzzles of the long rifles trained on them by the naked, hideously grinning woodsmen.

"Now, sir," he said, "you and Madame will kindly get up and dress. And you had best pack up the necessaries for a long journey."

"Journey?" Rocheblave asked, while his wife drew the bed sheet tighter around her and looked still more terrified.

"You'll be going under guard to Williamsburg," George an-

swered. "May I assure you, it is a long, long journey." He
thought back quickly over the thousand-mile odyssey which had
brought him here to this instant of bloodless victory, and the
recollection almost dizzied him. Noticing the panic in Madame
de Rocheblave's eyes now, he added: "You'll have privacy,
Madame. Contrary to whatever you may've heard, Virginians
are gentlemen. I shall take your weapons, Mister Rocheblave,"
he said, lifting the sword and brace of pistols from their peg on
the wall. His eye fell on a writing desk which stood in the adjoining room. "I must have your word that you'll not destroy
one scrap of paper. Do I have that?"

"Yes," muttered the Frenchman, who now pulled off his
nightcap, revealing a head of iron-gray hair, thus transforming
himself from a comic figure to a formidable, imperious, strong-
jawed man.

When George went downstairs and into the yard, he found
his men holding at gunpoint the officers of the French garrison,
most of them in drawers or shirt-sleeves, doing their poor best
to exhibit some semblance of dignity. "Put them in chains," he
said. "I'll deal with them later."

Going to the gate, he looked down the main street and saw
by the light of torches and lanterns that his troops were staging
their occupation of the town with all the sense of drama he
could have hoped for, and more. They ranged up and down the
streets half-clad, scratched, filthy, bewhiskered, rifles in one
hand, tomahawks in the other, glancing about with a kind of de-
praved, ferocious, wolfish authority which was thoroughly intimidating to any townspeople who dared come out to their
street gates or stay at their open doors and windows. As ordered, the troops were refusing to converse with those few inhabitants who had the courage to come to the street and try to
speak with them, and soon even those shrank from the wild,
glowering eyes of the raiders and withdrew from the streets.
Children could be heard crying, women simpering; soon all the
citizens had retreated into their homes, apparently to ponder
their fates; doors and shutters were being closed and latched everywhere. Good, George thought. We shall let their imaginations
work on them for a while. They'll be begging for their lives by
morning, I'll wager.

Captain Bowman arrived in a few minutes, and George sat at
the table in Rocheblave's parlor with him, reviewing a plan by
which Bowman would acquire horses, take about thirty
mounted men the next day and capture the smaller towns to the

north, Prairie du Rocher, St. Philippe, and Cahokia. He would use a tactic similar to this one which had succeeded so well at Kaskaskia. "You'll need to effect total surprise as we did here," George said, "so you'll have to leave in the morning. There'll be no time for rest before you go. I'm sorry. I don't know how the men have stayed on their feet this far."

Joseph Bowman shook his head and clucked instead of answering.

"To keep the alarm from getting ahead to those places," George continued, "take prisoner anybody you encounter along the road. White men or Indians either."

"I understand that," Bowman agreed.

"Now, if you'll excuse me, I think Mister Rocheblave has had enough time to get ready up there."

When he opened the door of the bedroom, he smelled smoke and found a guilty-looking Rocheblave and his wife huddled over a plate full of ashes. Drawing his sword in a rage, he forced the Frenchman to the wall and held him there with the swordpoint pressing his abdomen. With his left hand he fingered the ashes of what had been a quantity of papers. "By God," he hissed. "If the word of a French gent is so worthless, Heaven help us! I should run you through right now!" Rocheblave broke out in a sweat and looked as if he were expecting to die, while his wife began wailing. "Lieutenant," George called to one of his aides. "Put this 'honorable' polecat of a French lord in two suits of chains. So much as an unkindly glance from him should earn him a rifle ball straightway between his eyes. I'll decide at daylight whether to let him live or die." He whipped the sword away, slashing open Rocheblave's silken waistcoat, grabbed the gasping Frenchman's shirt-front and nearly jerked him off his feet, throwing him into the grasp of the lieutenant, then turned contemptuously from him. "You, Madame, who have the misfortune to be mated to such a scoundrel, you have my sympathy."

"He did not violate his word, m'sieur!" she cried with an imperious toss of her head. "*I* burned the papers!"

George glared at her in anger and admiration. "Go with him," he said finally. "I want you both out of my sight before I lose control of myself and hang him from the rafters by his own guts!"

IN THE GRAY LIGHT BEFORE DAWN, GEORGE WALKED DOWN THE main street, viewing the circumstances of his men and the cap-

tive town. He sensed the eyes of the townspeople peering out at
him through cracks in the closed shutters. His men, posted at intervals along the street, leaned on their guns, silent, emaciated,
some of them swaying with hunger and exhaustion, but each
grinned proudly at him as he passed. Others kept moving up
and down the streets in squads, as he had ordered, constantly
prowling, to give the impression that the force numbered in
hundreds. In his tour of five blocks, he encountered the same
squads two and three times, and each time they winked and
leered at him as cunningly as so many foxes. Starved though
they were, not one had entered any house to pillage a single
pantry. By the time he returned to his command post at
Rocheblave's house, his heart was in his throat and he was close
to laughter, or tears, or both.

Duff made arrangement with two American traders in the
town to supply meat, bread, and fruit to the fort; by the time the
sun was above the bluff on the other side of the Kaskaskia
River, makeshift tables in the yard of Rocheblave's house were
heaped with food, and the frontiersmen came through in orderly
details to be fed for the first time in nearly four strenuous days.
They ate standing in the yard, joking, exclaiming over the heav-
enly flavors, and accepting their colonel's praise in shuffling
embarrassment. By mid-morning he had thanked each man indi-
vidually.

And to substantiate the illusion of numbers he was trying to
create, his men ate enough for a thousand.

CAPTAIN HELM CAME IN BEAMING AS GEORGE SAT READING THE
documents that Rocheblave had not had time to destroy. "These
folks is in a perfect state of confusion," he said. "There's a delegation of their old men at the gate now to beg fer mercy.
They's a-cowerin' behind th' skirts of a little scarecrow priest.
They say they'll be our slaves if we'll jes' let 'em live. Hee,
hee! We got some reputation in these parts, George. If you was
t' walk down there an' say shit they'd all squat right in th'
street!"

George thought for a moment. "I think they ought to stew a
little longer. But bring them up. I want to get a look at this delegation. Judging by some of this correspondence, they ought not
be too hard to sway to our cause at all."

About six frightened old gentlemen and a remarkable-looking
priest were soon ushered in. The men seemed to shrink as
George rose behind the desk and stood staring at them. They

urged the priest forward. He was a gaunt, weathered man with
great, pious eyes and a beak of a nose, and when he removed
his round-crowned black hat and began turning it nervously before his middle, he displayed a pink tonsure with a fringe of
graying hair all around it. The priest visibly braced his spirit,
took two steps toward George, and searched his face. Obviously
the terrible appearance George and his officers made was
shocking them speechless. They all cringed in the middle of the
room and glanced about fearfully.

"What is it you want o' me?" George finally had to ask.

"Sir, I am Father Pierre Gibault. I have been asked by the
people of this town to make an appeal to your sense of humanity and beseech you not to harm their cherished families."
George did not answer, and at length the priest continued: "As
they expect to be separated and perhaps never allowed to meet
again, they beg that they might be permitted to spend some time
in the church to take leave of each other."

"I have no objection to that. Gather 'em there if you like, and
while they're assembled tell 'em that not a one is to try to venture out of town."

The priest bowed, his great bulging eyes going moist. "Thank
you, Colonel. I . . . I presume that our religion is obnoxious to
you, but to us it is all . . ."

"Mister Gibault, I have no concern with your church and
have nothing to say to it. Now, if you please, I am not at leisure."

The priest backed off quickly, still bowing, and led out the
gentlemen, who followed him like a flock of sheep.

Within a few minutes the streets were full of grim people
making their way down to the church. Mothers went carrying
babies in their arms and followed by little knots of subdued,
red-eyed children. They went with downcast eyes, led by their
menfolk; no one talked as they flowed through the streets past
the American sentries. George watched this procession from an
upstairs window. Soon the church was closed up with more people in it than one could have imagined it would hold, and all the
houses in the town stood open and vacant, the people apparently
having given up any hope for retaining their property. George
sent out an order that no American was to enter any house in
the people's absence.

The townspeople remained in the church for more than an
hour, and except for the endless dry whirring of locusts, the
town lay in utter silence as the sun rose higher and grew hot.

George could easily imagine the woeful consultations going on
inside that handsome little stone building. Now and then mourn-
ful snatches of song and chanting could be heard issuing from
the place.

WHILE THE POPULACE WAS IN THE CHURCH, GEORGE STROLLED OUT
to the place where Rocheblave sat ignominiously on the ground
chained to an elm tree, his wife kneeling beside him and com-
miserating. George looked down at him for two minutes, hard-
eyed, several times reaching for his sword and drawing it a few
inches out of its scabbard, as if trying to decide whether to let
him live. At length Rocheblave, white as flour, opened his
mouth to speak, but George snapped, "Not a word, man!

"From what I hear about you from your own people here,"
he continued after a moment, "y're a haughty and arrogant man,
more British than French in your heart, and if I was to take bal-
lots among the townsfolk, not many would vote to keep you
alive." He contemplated him for another minute, then shoved
the sword violently back into its scabbard. "I've been ordered
by Governor Henry to be as humane as I can in my treatment
of you, so I'll let you live long enough to be taken back to
Williamsburg. But let me advise you that any one of my boys
would enjoy taking a patch of your contemptible hide, in payment for what their people have suffered at the hands of your
Indians, and I can't guarantee what mightn't happen to you
when my back is turned."

He walked away then. That should be warning enough for
him, he thought. God, how can I spare the men to transport him
back east?

Captain Harrod met him at the door of the Rocheblave house.
"George, that Spanish gent and his party been askin' whether
they can go."

"Them! By heaven, I'd forgot about 'em altogether. I must be
getting faint in the head. Come in and sit with me while I have
some breakfast. Then maybe I can think straight."

"I gather they're pretty important folk over on the Spanish
side o' the Missipp," said Harrod, as George broke apart a small
roasted hen and began pulling the tender leg meat off the bones
with his teeth. Chew it up slow if you aim to keep it down, he
reminded himself. Your belly may not remember what food is.
A small portion of the bird and two bites of bread went wild in
his stomach; he forced down a wave of nausea, and soon felt all
right. He eyed longingly a decanter of liquor that stood on the

sideboard, but decided that one sip of it in his condition would probably floor him. I'm going to be needing whatever wits I have left before these next few days are over, he thought.

"All right, Bill," he said. "Bring on that Spaniard."

TERESA DE LEYBA HAD BEEN NEAR HYSTERIA SINCE MIDNIGHT; only by praying hour upon hour with her sister-in-law had she kept from giving in entirely to her terror. She and Maria had knelt and huddled together through the morning hours in a small downstairs room, saying Hail Marys over and over, now and then dozing with exhaustion but awakening from barbaric night-mares and hearing the frightful commotion out in the streets. Once, shortly before dawn, Teresa had at last drifted off to a deeper, calmer sleep, but had been jarred awake by Maria's ter-rible coughing. Crossing herself, she had risen and crept to the window, and through a narrow crack between its shutters could see only one person in the street a few feet outside the house, and the sight of him renewed her terror. He was one of the Americans, standing sentinel. His eyes were sunk deep in dark, pouchy sockets. Black hair hung in greasy strands to his shoul-ders, and from his cheekbones to his chin his face was hidden by patchy stubble. Around his head he wore a filthy band of homespun rag. He chewed slowly and absently, like a ruminat-ing cow, and occasionally spat vile-looking gouts into the street. His hands were folded over the muzzle of his long rifle and now and then he stopped chewing and rested his chin on his knuckles. He seemed to be wearing little besides dried mud and weapons; a powder horn, sheath knife, and bullet pouch hung from leather thongs over his shoulders, and the long slender handle of a tomahawk stuck through the waistband of his breechclout. The man was incredibly thin and rangy, muscled like a racing dog, his ribs standing out under taut, smudged, oily-looking skin. In her two months in this territory she had never seen an Indian of any tribe, even the scruffy, parched ones from the plains, who looked as evil and murderous as this American.

Teresa turned from the window, pressing her palm over her mouth to keep from crying. Maria was asleep on the divan. The graying light of early morning was beginning to seep into the shuttered room, and Teresa had a premonition that the whole population would be led into the open and slaughtered at the rising of the sun, perhaps even cannibalized. The man outside the window looked capable of that, and there were rumors that the Americans did eat the flesh of their victims, though her brother had chided her foolishness in believing such tales. "Governor Galvez is sympathetic to the Americans," he had scoffed. "Would he have dealings with cannibals?"

Teresa curled herself into a large soft chair and closed her eyes and held a handkerchief to her nose for comfort as was her habit. Beyond the door she could hear the men and officers talking, her brother's voice and Lieutenant de Carbatona's among them, but could not make out their words, just the murmuring of voices. They had been talking for hours, all night, sometimes excitedly, sometimes angrily, sometimes in low voices. Her brother's voice remained calm and reasonable at all times. He always reassures, she thought. He always expects the best to happen. He believes people are good because he is good. And he is so brave.

She huddled in the chair and thought of her brother's courage. She remembered how he had walked directly over to that gigantic, fierce American with red hair and spoken to him, while de Cartabona had hung back, sweating with fright.

Teresa shuddered at the memory of that moment, when she had feared that her brother would be struck and killed on the spot; and now the awesome image of that intruder stepped in through the door of her memory for the hundredth time, frightening and troubling her.

It was more than just fear of the man that was unsettling her. She kept remembering her own reaction to the sight of him. It was strange, something she had never experienced before. Though she had been stunned by his very murderous appearance, by the air of tension that had seemed to crackle about him, by his filthy, haggard look, she had nonetheless been shaken by a keen thrill and a flushing of blood all through her body. He was, in his terrible way, the most splendid man she had ever seen, one whose presence could, she feared, brush away as lightly as cobwebs all the reliable old defenses about her inner self, both those of her ingrained personal reserve and those of Spanish social custom, to strip her very soul and make it stand vulnerable. He was, somehow, like a keen-edged knife. And Teresa had always feared knives. She saw her father lying shirtless on a table, gushing crimson blood from a wound received in a duel . . .

"Maria! Maria! Teresa!" She awoke to the sound of her brother's voice and a rapping on the door, surprised that she had slept. She got up from the chair, nearly falling because one of her legs was asleep, hobbled to the door and unlocked it. Narrow stripes of sunlight, coming through the shutters, traced across the floor to Maria, who was beginning to stir.

Don Fernando de Leyba pulled his sister to him and put his lips to the part of her hair, and then knelt beside his wife and pressed his cheek to hers.

"The colonel of the Virginians has sent for me at last," he said. "I am going to the fort now to talk with him." He saw the panic in her eyes and smiled his ever-assuring smile. "He will give us safe passage, I am certain. We will be on the river to St. Louis by afternoon, and this unpleasantness can be forgotten."

"I'm afraid for you," Maria said with fervor. "I'm afraid for all of us!"

"Nonsense, Maria. As far as we can discern, these so-called 'barbarians' have not harmed one person, nor taken so much as a loaf of bread without asking for it. If you knew about war, you would realize how remarkable that is. Their commandant, this Colonel Clark, must be a superb fellow."

Clark, Teresa thought. No. Surely that is not the terrible one we saw last night. Such a person could not be a gentleman of rank.

"I know in my heart there is something unspeakable in store for us," Maria groaned.

"Only being frightened half out of our sense," Don Fernando insisted, rising to leave. Despite his vigil through the night, his eyes shone with excitement. Maria searched his face, uncomprehending, shaking her head.

"You seem to be actually *happy* about this awful thing!"

"As a soldier I can only be stirred by it," he exclaimed. "Think of it! The distance! The surprise! His Excellency will be delighted to hear of it. Maria, I am truly impatient to meet this Virginia colonel. You two go out in the salon now, and take some refreshment. All the townsfolk have gone to a meeting in the church. I'll be back for you shortly and we'll be going home." He kissed her.

When he went out, Maria sank to her knees and pulled Teresa down beside her. They began praying for his safety.

But even over the fervor of her praying Teresa kept seeing the image of the Virginian with the red hair. And so she had to beg forgiveness for the profanation of her prayer.

DON FERNANDO DE LEYBA WAS STARTLED TO SEE PHILLIPPE DE Rocheblave in chains in the shade of the elm tree, but was not led close enough to him to speak to him. In truth, he was glad. It would have been awkward.

Stepping smartly into the parlor of Rocheblave's mansion, de Leyba found about ten of the frightful-looking half-naked Americans standing or sitting about. It was immediately obvious that, despite their slovenly appearance, a very brisk and efficient command post was being operated here. Curt, spirited conversations were being conducted at a desk at the far end of the room. As one man left, another would go forward to the desk. Here, apparently, we meet this Colonel Clark at last, thought de Leyba, and he gathered his compliments on the tip of his tongue.

He was led straight through the mass of frontier soldiers, who were so malodorous in the close room that he had to breathe through his mouth. "George," Captain Harrod said loudly, parting the group and pulling de Leyba through by an arm, "here's the Spaniard who wants t' see you."

Don Fernando was astonished to see that the man who sat behind the desk with a quill pen in his hand was none other than the formidable youth who had interrupted the dance last midnight. Somehow he was surprised to see that the fellow could write. "Good morning," he said in his best English, glancing about for some sign of a uniformed officer. "I would be very happy to speak with Colonel Clark, if I may."

The young giant poked the quill point into its stand, then rose to his feet. "Then you should be a happy man, sir, because you're speaking to him. I am George Rogers Clark, and you are . . ."

The Spaniard covered his confusion quickly, clicking his heels and dipping his head. "Don Fernando de Leyba, lieutenant governor of Louisiana. What a pleasure to see you again, Colonel. Forgive me for not knowing you . . ."

The youth looked at him for a moment, eyes widening for an instant, waved the rest of the statement aside, and reached across to take de Leyba's hand, in a very firm and warm handshake. "We're honored to have you here, Governor. I hope we haven't distressed you any, but I really was a little too busy last night to hear you out." He broke into an engaging grin which shone through his unkempt aspect, and de Leyba, infected by it, smiled in return.

"It is a privilege, Colonel, to compliment you on a most enviable *coup*. I'm grateful that I happened to be here to see it."

Several of the listening frontiersmen looked from one to another blankly, and said, "Coo?"

"Boys, if you'd kindly back off into the hall for five minutes or so, I need to do some diplomatic business with the governor here, before his party leaves for St. Louis." As they moved off, elbowing each other and *coo*ing, George motioned de Leyba to a chair and sank back behind the ornate desk. "You've saved me the trouble of a trip up to St. Louis, Governor. I have greetings for you from Patrick Henry of Virginia."

"Thank you, colonel. I know Governor Galvez esteems his friendship highly. But I hope that this encounter need not preclude your visit to St. Louis at some time in the near future. We would be most pleased to show you our hospitality."

George studied this dark, elegant little man with ambivalent feelings. He was enjoying, after so many years on the frontier, that kind of gracious courtesy and polished speech which he had not experienced since his young years at Williamsburg and with George Mason's students at Gunston Hall. His own body itched and clamored for the feel of clean linen and fine cloth; his ear yearned for polite speech and genteel music, and for a momentary reprieve at least from the responsibilities of wartime leadership. At the same time he felt a little scorn for the Spaniard's apparent softness and delicacy, and for the political hypocrisy which he knew underlay Spain's friendly overtures to the American rebels. It's not for their love of us but their hatred of the British that they side with us, he was thinking. And by taking the Illinois from British control now I am just as much complicating Governor Galvez's eventual designs on it. Still, diplomatic friendship is reliable to a point, and there is precious little else to rely on in these times.

"There are two things I should like to mention before you embark, Governor," he said. "The first, which you may or may not know of yet, is that King Louis of France has of late signed an alliance with the Colonies, which I intend to announce here as soon as I have got this place under better order." The Spaniard's eyebrows went up and surprise flickered through his eyes; then he smiled as if at good news.

"You must be pleased," said de Leyba. George nodded, and went on.

"The other matter is that, although we've arrived here in considerable force . . ." he was careful not to smirk at his own lie, "we are nonetheless surrounded by a host of Indian nations whose minds have long been poisoned by the British. We hope that, in the unlikely event we should sometime be overwhelmed by their numbers, we might be assured asylum on your side of the Mississippi while we would regroup and await reinforcements from our army at the Falls of the Ohio." Again, at the thought of this imaginary force, he bit back his mirth.

"Be assured," said de Leyba. "I should be honored to serve you in any way I can." The Spaniard's expression and tone seemed sincere, and George felt a rush of real appreciation for him.

"Good, then. And I likewise am at your disposal, Governor, should you ever have need of me." In saying this, George suddenly had to gulp down an unexpected wave of emotion. I must be overly tired, he thought. I'm getting maudlin. He stood up quickly and went around the desk to grasp de Leyba's hand and go with him to the door. "When I have a proper government here," he said, "I will treat you to the ceremony that Virginians accord their worthiest associates. For now, forgive my informality. I'll have a detail escort your party to your boats, and I bid you Godspeed."

The Spaniard paused in the foyer, looking up at him with glittering wide obsidian eyes, as if searching under the grime and stubble for an outline of the true gentleman he felt must be inside. He clicked his heels again and bowed quickly.

"Until that day," he said. He was already anticipating the joy of his wife and sister.

CAPTAIN HELM, STANDING LIKE A SILHOUETTE IN THE WINDOW against the glare of the summer daylight outside, suddenly straightened up and turned to George. "Here comes that dang priest ag'in," he said, "a-leadin' his flock." He chuckled. "An' they look like he's leadin' 'em to th' slaughter!" George got up and watched them arrive in the yard. From the looks of them, only their spiritual dependence on the priest was giving them the courage to stay upright and place one foot before the other. "Bring 'em in," George said, returning to the desk and standing behind it. The delegation, now grown to about fifteen or twenty, followed the priest into the room, heads bared.

"What will it be now, gentlemen?" George asked the priest.

"Colonel," Father Gibault began, "we come to return thanks for the indulgence you have shown us, and beg your permission to address you further on a matter that is more dear to us than anything else."

"Speak," said George, clasping his hands behind his back and assuming a pose meant to express strained patience.

"We are resigned that our situation is the fate of war," the priest began his obviously rehearsed dissertation. "My friends here are reconciled to the loss of their property. But they pray that you might not part them from their families. They hope that the women and children might be allowed to keep some of their clothes, and perhaps enough tools and provisions by which they, ah, at your mercy, of course, might through industry support themselves wherever they are to be sent . . ." The priest's voice ended in a hanging tone, as if he hoped some sort of answer might be forthcoming. But when George only continued to stare at him, Father Gibault proceeded, a bit more desperately now, ". . . They wish to assure you that their conduct has always been influenced by their commandant, Monsieur Rocheblave, whom they always felt themselves bound to obey. They, ahem, they say that they have never had opportunity to inform themselves of the nature of the American war, but . . . but as much as they dared to, some of them have expressed themselves to be in favor of the Americans . . ." Here the priest paused to observe George carefully again, no doubt aware that this might sound very patently like a ploy to save their skins. Still George answered nothing, and his face betrayed no sign either of gullibility or skepticism. The priest did note from the corner of his eye, however, that some of the American officers were elbowing each other's bare ribs and smirking. He gulped, licked his mouth as if it were extremely dry, and then feebly finished his petition: "That is all they ask, Colonel. As for me, I . . . I ask only that some vestige of my church be permitted to remain. I mean, I . . ." His speech fell apart; he seemed to have run out of either hopes or words, and a painful silence filled the room.

This was the point to which George had hoped to bring them. He came around to the front of the desk, stood straight before the dismal-looking Frenchmen, and placed his fists on his hips.

"One moment, Father. D'you suppose you're speaking to savages? You must, judging by the tenor of your conversation. Don't insult me! Do you suppose Virginians mean to strip your women and children and take the bread out of their mouths? Do we look like the sort of people who would condescend to make war on the church?" He paused a moment; the suppliants stood with their mouths open, not yet comprehending the course of his words. "It wasn't the prospect of plunder that brought us here, but only to prevent the effusion of the innocent blood of *our own* women and children by the Indians, through the instigation of your vile commandant and his British friends. As for your church, our only concern with it is to punish anyone who does it insult. All religions are tolerated in America."

He paused again to let the priest translate this, and to watch the stir being created among the listeners by their gradual comprehension of his message.

"By thunder, people!" he went on now, loudly and rapidly, "we are *not* savages and plunderers. Listen, Father: it is so apparent to me that you've been influenced by lies and false information from your leaders, that I am willing to forget everything past. Now, as soon as I am able to turn the heads of certain nations of Indians hereabouts, I will be perfectly satisfied to conclude our business here and rejoin my main army on the Ohio . . ." His officers looked at each other and sucked on their tongues. The Frenchmen stood as if dumbstruck, absorbing all these unexpected words, and George continued:

"I expect an end to this war before long, as the King of France has joined the American cause." This information seemed to send still another wave of astonishment through them, and he waited until they had finished exclaiming among themselves about it. "Now," he resumed, "I am going to release your militia officers; but Mr. Rocheblave—who is so vicious and intemperate—he is going to be sent away. Now all of you might as well return to your families and tell them that they can conduct themselves as usual, with all freedom and without any apprehension of danger. My guards will be withdrawn from your town, with the exception of the home of a Mister Cerré, whose name has been put under question by some of your people. I shall post a proclamation shortly, and ask only that your people comply with it. You're free to ally yourselves with my purposes or stay neutral, and any who wish to remain belligerent will be given a chance to go and take up arms with the British, in which event we would rejoice in doing honorable battle with them. If you gentlemen understand me now, why, I am tired of talking and have nothing more I care to say."

The citizens simply stood there for a moment, staring at him or whispering to the priest, who appeared to be almost beside himself. "They . . . they beg your forgiveness that they seemed to take you for barbarians . . ." he stammered. "They only imagined that conquered property goes to the victors, and they want you to understand that they did *not* presume you're barbarians, ah . . ."

"No more on the subject. Now just go and relieve the anxiety of your people."

The priest stood swallowing, moist-eyed, his countenance glowing as if he had witnessed some sort of a miracle, and George fully expected him to drop straight-away to his knees. The citizens shuffled and hesitated, every sort of expression passing over their faces, and the American officers, moved by the transformation that had taken place in this room in the last few minutes, stood up straight and stared at their colonel, blinking with amazement.

At length the priest stretched out his trembling hands and took George's big, hard right hand, and clung warmly to it, saying, "Colonel Clark . . ." George himself, who had been engrossed mainly in making the most profound impression possible, now was growing relaxed and receptive, and felt suddenly almost overwhelmed by the love that was radiating out of this odd-looking priest like heat from an oven. It was a powerful and unexpected presence in the desperate war room, a remarkable spiritual power, and George began to suspect that this priest was not some mere cringing capon, but quite possibly the best man in the territory. Father Gibault finally seemed to have found his tongue again. ". . . Colonel, I can only say that I and whatever influence I have with my Lord are at your disposal."

He turned then and rushed the citizens out of the room. George's officers stood around with nothing to say; George sat down behind the desk, drained but somehow calm, and feeling his old familiar confidence returning to him.

And then in the buzzing midday silence a clamor of joyous voices began building up throughout the town; the bells of the church began to peal and people could be heard running through the streets, cheering and sobbing. George slumped behind the desk for a few minutes, swallowing hard, until he heard a commotion of women's and children's voices in the foyer; four or five young ladies and girls came sweeping into the room carrying vases of flowers, which they placed all over his desk, then curtsied and fled from the room like blowing petals. He got up and mounted the steps to the upstairs window again, and gazed out to see most of the populace thronging around the church, while others moved about in the streets decorating the fences with ribbons and flowers and putting up colorful pavilions. It was a spontaneous and extravagant scene, which strangely and unexpectedly wrenched his heart. Dear Heaven, he thought, I must find the leisure to write and describe this spectacle to my family and to George Mason. Why, these people are like children!

When he went downstairs again, Leonard Helm followed him to the desk, wreathed in smiles, drew up a chair and sat facing him, shaking his head. Finally he said, "George, it's the damnedest thing I ever seen. How in tarnation did y'ever dream up a vict'ry t' turn out this way?"

George leaned back in the chair and, with a great sigh, rubbed his palm across his clammy forehead.

"I didn't have much choice, did I? I told you, there's ten times as many people in this valley as we have, and God knows how many Indians attached to 'em. The only way to control 'em is to make 'em our bounden friends." He drew his hand down over his jaw now and sat forward, toying at the petals of a huge purple iris with his forefinger. "But we're a long way from finished. We'll lose our whole advantage if we don't do *everything* right for a long time to come. Now, listen . . ."

EARLY IN THE AFTERNOON, AS THE FESTIVITIES WENT ON, GEORGE ordered the people of Kaskaskia to provide some three dozen horses, with which Captain Bowman would take an expedition to the villages of Prairie du Rocher and Cahokia farther up the Mississippi. Some of the happy gentlemen, in bringing their horses, expressed their opinion that little more would be needed to win those villages than to have some of Kaskaskia's citizens go along with Bowman and convey the news of what had happened here. "There are many among us," said one of the released French militia officers, "who have been in sympathy with your rebellion, Monsieur. We do not care for Governor Hamilton nor for Monsieur Rocheblave, and you may be assured that you would be welcomed joyfully if only the truth about your cause and your benevolence could be explained." George pondered this, and wanted very much to believe it. But the attack on Kaskaskia and its attendant shock had been so dramatically effective in winning over the Kaskaskians that he felt a reenactment of it in those places would be more compelling.

"*Mon colonel,*" insisted the Frenchman, "your men are supremely fatigued. Surely they could use some help. Let some of my militiamen ride to the villages with your captain, at least. Then, when he has secured them, we can bring our influence to bear in convincing them."

The man seemed sincere, glowing with enthusiasm for the idea, and George thought it would be a good diplomatic gesture to demonstrate his faith in his newly won allies. But all this was happening so swiftly that he was not yet convinced that the Frenchmen could be trusted to take up arms and ride amid his troops. If they had been fickle enough to turn on their former leader this readily, he thought, *can I place such confidence in them?*

But there was not time to weigh the matter long; the villages were strung along the Mississippi for some sixty miles, and every passing hour increased the chances that warnings would reach them before Bowman could get there. Despite the attention George had given to security, it seemed probable that someone might have slipped away to carry a warning to those towns.

After considering the dilemma for no more than five minutes, George made his decision, and he made it on the basis of the only evidence he had at hand: the faces and demeanor of the French would-be volunteers. He looked at their eyes and listened to their cheerful tones of voice and decided that there was no treachery there. "Go with them, then," he said at last, and the French officer astonished him by grabbing his shoulders and kissing him exuberantly on one cheek and then the other, to the extreme amusement of the Virginians nearby.

"Do your best, then," George said, trying by stern aspect to cover his embarrassment. "Keep in mind this is the first time you've ever borne arms as free men, and thus a chance to do y'rselves proud." The Frenchman's eyes flashed at the thought.

Thus the little force, nearly half made up of French militiamen dressed up as if for parade, all mounted on some of the finest horseflesh George had ever seen, thundered out of the fort and up the river late in the afternoon, colored richly by a descending sun, cheered on by a good part of the Kaskaskia population, foremost among them the young ladies of the village. *That feminine urging,* George thought as the expedition was hidden in its own dust, *should do as much as anything could to make them behave honorably on our behalf. Much of the reward on their return,* he mused, *will be the company of these cheerful young women.* As he watched the colorfully dressed, animated ladies turn from the road and fall into little groups, laughing, chatting in their musical tongue, some of them casting coy sidelong glances at him, their shapely arms and calves bare and sun-kissed, he was washed over suddenly by a powerful wave of longing, of desire, of loneliness. A succession of faces, hands, arms, flickered through his memory: young women who had leaned in his arms in reels so long ago in Virginia, sunburned girls in homespun who had shared his few idle moments during the defense of the Kentucky settlements, the naked Mingo girls bathing in the shallows of clear creeks during his long-ago visits with Chief Logan's people before Dunmore's War, the adoring face of that chambermaid Nell in Williamsburg. And then, as he turned back to the fort to resume his administrative tasks, he saw the house where he had interrupted the ball the night before—it was the home of the prominent trader Cerré, he had learned, a man absent on commerce at present, a man apparently disliked and envied by many of the Kaskaskia townspeople, to judge by comments made by certain of the Frenchmen during the course of the morning, a man rumored to be strong in the British interest. Looking at the house now in the daylight, its doors closed and guarded by one of his own sentries, George remembered another face, one which had impressed itself on his mind even though he had had no time to think of it; he saw now the frightened, perfect oval face of the black-eyed Spanish girl who had been standing with Don Fernando de Leyba in the ballroom just before the young governor had come forward to speak. Seeing both of their faces in his mind's eye now, he was struck by their similarity, and, while he might have supposed that the girl was de Leyba's wife or lover, he now felt a notion that they seemed like brother and sister. Could that be? he wondered.

The question became lodged in his mind now as he passed through the gates into the fort.

And then, strangely, when he tried to envision the girl again beside de Leyba, he saw her instead seated beside himself on the porch of a great house overlooking the Ohio River Valley. That image came and then went in a moment.

"Huh," he muttered softly, and shook his head. Daydreams of an overweary fool, he thought. No time for that now.

14

The murders and assassinations of women and children and the depredations and ravages, which have been committed under those orders and policies of Governor Hamilton, cry for vengeance with a loud voice," George dictated.

"Les meutres et assassinations des femmes et enfants et les degats et ravages, qui ont été comise crie vengence a haute voix," the translator said slowly, and the scrivener's pen scratched furiously. George sat at the desk with his fingers steepled and searched the ceiling for the next phrases of his proclamation, which Father Gibault and Doctor Jean Baptiste Laffont had agreed to carry to Vincennes. Father Gibault, long fingers interlaced over his abdomen, eyes closed, sat in a large chair at the side of the room, nodded and listened. He had told George that the Vincennes inhabitants were so resentful against Rocheblave and the British that certainly they could be simply talked into joining the American side. George had come to have complete faith in the judgment of the priest in the four days of his occupation of Kaskaskia, and had decided to let the priest and the influential physician attempt their mission.

"Since the United States has now gained advantage over their British enemies . . ." he said.

"Les etats unis ayant appresent gagné la desus sur leurs ennemis brittanique . . ." recited the translator.

". . . and their plenipotentiaries have now made and concluded treaties of commerce and alliance with the kingdom of France . . ."

". . . et leurs plenipotentiaires ayant actuellement faite et conclus des traites de commerce et alliance avec le royaume de la France . . ."

". . . His Excellency the Governor of Virginia has ordered me

154

to reduce the different posts to the west of the Miami with a company of troops under my command, in order to prevent longer responsibility for innocent blood . . ."

"*Trop vite, m'sieur!*" groaned the sweating writer.

"What's he say?" George asked the interpreter.

"He says more slowly, *mon colonel*," said the translator.

Father Gibault laughed, a resonant, happy laughter that filled the room. He was looking at George now and shaking his head. "Ah, you Americans," he said. "Always such a hurry!"

"Well, Padre, I just haven't learned to think slow like you people."

"George, George, my son, you don't need to write all this out for me. I know what to tell them!"

"Ah, no, you don't," George laughed. "It has to be in my words. It has to be official. Shame on you, anyway, a priest dabbling in political matters." He had been delighted to discover the priest's jocose nature, and they had fallen into a habit of joshing each other.

"Oh, *mais non*!" protested the priest. "I have nothing to do with temporal affairs, I assure you, George. But," he added, putting his palms together in prayer and assuming an expression of piety, "I will give them such hints in the spiritual way that will be very conducive to the business!"

George laughed in delight. He had never suspected that a Roman Catholic priest could be droll and sly. George was, except for moments when he had to embroil himself in the infinite details of administering to this conquered territory, happier than he had ever been. A messenger had returned from Cahokia the day before with news that Captain Bowman was in control of all the upriver villages and had not lost a man in the effort. Bowman had ridden all night to cover the sixty miles to Cahokia, detaining every person met along the way, and thus had gotten inside the town before his presence was even discovered. The Cahokians had gone into a panic at the cry that the Big Knives had arrived, but soon had had their fears assuaged by the Kaskaskians in the expedition, who told them of all the happy events at Kaskaskia. Then Bowman had assembled all the Cahokians and had given them a speech which George wished he could have heard: He had told them that although resistance was out of the question, he would prefer their friendship; and that they were at liberty to become free Americans as their friends at Kaskaskia had, or else move out of the country, except those who had been engaged in inciting the Indians to war.

The Kaskaskians had dispersed among the Cahokians, and soon cheers of "Liberty!" and "Freedom!" had echoed throughout the town, and within a few hours Bowman and his men were snugly quartered in the old British fort. A large number of Indians encamped outside Cahokia had vanished into the countryside, but nothing had been heard of them subsequently.

Within three days, Bowman had taken all three of the villages in this manner, given the oath of allegiance to all their inhabitants, repaired the forts, and established a benevolent military government through that area. Only then had his troops, who had not slept for four strenuous days, gotten an opportunity to rest. George's heart was swollen with his appreciation of Bowman especially, and of all the other Virginia and Kentucky backwoodsmen of his little army who, transcending their rough, headstrong natures, were serving Virginia's cause in such exemplary fashion. He had expected them to have courage and endurance, but he had hardly dared hope they would behave in such a responsible and restrained manner in the delicate role of friendly conquerors. So far there had not been one complaint lodged against any one of his Americans by an inhabitant of the territory.

George thought of this while the scrivener caught himself up with the dictation. George picked up the glass of brandy which sat by his elbow, raised it to the priest, who in turn raised his own glass, and they sipped. Setting the glass down, George noticed a piece of fringe that had fallen off his buckskin jacket sleeve. He picked it up and contemplated it. "Tell me, Father, are the tailors hereabouts anything to speak of?"

"Wonderful," replied the priest, spreading the skirt of his shabby cassock and looking at it. "You have only to look at my splendid appearance to know the answer to that. And Frenchwomen are by birth and inclination seamstresses. Why do you ask?"

"Well, I've been thinking about the appearance of my people," he replied. "We came in here looking like so many savages and scared your people half out of their wits. Now that all my officers are busy conducting affairs of state, I wonder if we mightn't do better at it clad in some semblance of decorum. Listen, a few of my men have the remnants of Continental Army uniforms flapping about 'em . . . Perhaps the tailors here could copy those uniforms at least for those of us who are engaged in the public business . . ."

"Ah, I should have known! The pomp and the pride of mortals. And soldiers especially. Well, my son, as I've said, I have nothing to do with temporal matters, but ..."

"But perhaps you might show some tailor the spiritual way to dress us up a bit, eh? Ha, ha!"

The scrivener had begun clearing his throat and playing with his quill, so George finished dictating the proclamation for Vincennes:

"... I have taken possession of this fort and the munitions of this country ... and I have caused to be published a proclamation offering assistance and protection to all the inhabitants against all their enemies and promising to treat them as the citizens of the State of Virginia (in the limits of which they are) ... and to protect their persons and their property, if it is necessary, for the surety of which the faith of the government is pledged ... provided the people give certain proofs of their attachment to the states ... by taking the oath of fidelity in such cases required ... as prescribed by the law....

"I have been charmed to learn from a letter written by Governor Abbot to M. Rocheblave that you are in general attached to the cause of America....

"In consequence of which I invite you all to accept offers hereafter mentioned, and to enjoy all their privileges.... If you accede to this offer, you will proceed to the nomination of a commandant by choice or election ... who shall raise a company and take possession of the fort and of all the munitions of the king in the name of the United States of America for the Republic of Virginia ... and continue to defend the same until further orders....

"I have the honor of being with much consideration, sirs, your very humble and obedient servant, &c. &c.... There, now, M'sieur Priest," George said, banging his fist on the desk top, "how d'you reckon that will sit with 'em?"

"Superb," replied Father Gibault, raising his brandy glass again. "Eloquence worthy of the Church itself."

"Thank you, thank you. And now, to the health and the success," he said, "of my little black-robed diplomatic corps!"

A FEW DAYS LATER GEORGE MOUNTED A MAGNIFICENT DAPPLED warhorse which had been presented to him as a gift by the people of Kaskaskia, and rode out on the village road to see Father Gibault, Doctor Laffont, Simon Butler, and their little party off to Vincennes. George now wore a pair of fine buff trousers, boots, and a dark blue coat with buff lapels and gold-braid epaulets. He looked healthy and tanned; his firm jaw was clean-shaven, his thick coppery hair gleamed in the sunlight when he took off his hat to wish the priest goodbye. Father Gibault surveyed him up and down with admiration and affection, shook his head, and smiled. He was quite convinced now that the Lord had sent this splendid youth to inspire some strength of character into the villagers, whom he had been trying in vain to ennoble. When he had arrived in the Illinois country as vicar-general in 1769, he had found religion nearly extinct, free-thinking and irreverence rampant for lack of priests, and the people lazy, cunning, and litigious, with a passion for drunkenness surpassed only by that of the neighboring Indians. He had labored among the French souls for almost a decade, here and at Vincennes, achieving some small gains, but always sabotaged by the general cynicism and slyness occasioned by their situation under Rocheblave and the British. Now, with the excitement of their newfound allegiance, and their affection for the gallant and judicious American colonel, the villagers were beginning to act almost like a new people, bearing themselves more proudly and working harder. Or perhaps, he thought, it is simply their recent imagined escape from death that has so improved their attitude on life; that has been known to happen in human nature. At any rate, he thought, this lad will have his hands full governing these people, because though Our Father may visit us with miracles, I tend to doubt that He has changed their iniquitous souls all at once. He had warned George of all this, in a veiled way which did not altogether impugn the French character, of course, and now he leaned over from his own saddle and took George's hand in both of his own, while the horses fidgeted, and looked intently into his eyes. "Have faith in Heaven, my son," he said. "I feel in my heart that nothing will disappoint us on this mission. Expect me early in August. By then I should have this, um, *conversion* completed to your satisfaction. God be with you."

"And watch over you," George answered. He squeezed the priest's hand hard, struck Simon Butler on the shoulder, waved them away, then watched the party ride down to the wharf to be ferried across the Kaskaskia in the morning sunlight. He hated to see the priest go; it would be a little harder to administer to these people without his ready insights and sage counsel.

As he rode back toward the village and the fort, his thoughts grew heavy with other problems. The enlistments of his militiamen would expire soon, and there would be nothing in the world he could do about that but try to persuade as many as possible to reenlist, perhaps by offering them the glory of going to conquer Detroit. Some of them, he expected, would stay with him to achieve that, but many were already yearning for their families, who were as much as a thousand miles away, back in the Kentucky and Virginia settlements. And there was also the very baffling problem of continuing to pay his troops and provision his campaign here; the twelve hundred pounds of Virginia currency had been long since exhausted, and the problem of obtaining clothes, tools, munitions, and sundries for his men loomed huge and vague in the forefront of his mind. Already he had had to sign his own name to certain requisitions, with no notion of when or how the state of Virginia would reimburse him. He daily watched for dispatches from Williamsburg that might answer some of these questions for him; in the meantime he could only draw on his own resourcefulness and shape an answer to each dilemma as it arose. At this moment, the quickest relief seemed to lie in the hands of the wealthy American merchant Oliver Pollock in New Orleans, whom Patrick Henry had called a great patriot and a confidant of the Spanish Governor Galvez.

Arriving now at the gate of the fort, George halted his mount and gazed over the valley. All those uncertainties notwithstanding, it was a marvelous place to be, as rich, it seemed, as even the Ohio country. On the great floodplain north of the village, Indian corn grew nearly ten feet high without benefit of cultivation; there were vast fields of tobacco greening on the higher ground, and the plains beyond the Kaskaskia were dotted with hundreds of fat black cattle. Around the village there were orchards and vineyards of every sort. He smiled wryly at the dilemma he had posed for himself: All this provision and all the goods in town could have been his for the taking, had he come only as an ordinary victor, but by making the valley dwellers his allies he had placed himself in the position of having to buy from them everything he needed.

But if we had come as enemies, he reminded himself, we would never have held them even for this long, I'm sure.

Some of the troops were being drilled on the fort's small parade ground. Though they were fed now, and clean, all but a few were extremely ragged, many without shoes or shirts. That posed no particular problem in this hot weather, except the difficulty of maintaining a semblance of military dignity, but something would have to be done about it before winter.

It was growing less important to disguise the small size of his regiment now that the Americans were so affectionately regarded by the villagers, but George still insisted that only a squad or two at a time should be mustered in the public view. There were always *coureurs de bois* and river traders arriving and departing who might carry reports to Detroit, so he was determined to keep the size of his force a mystery. In every correspondence he made certain that the French scriveners and secretaries would hear him refer to his large army back at the Falls of the Ohio, and was confident that everybody hereabouts still believed in its existence.

As a private took George's horse and led it away toward the stables, Leonard Helm came out of the headquarters, looking comical and uncomfortable in his new Continental uniform, from which his huge hairy face and hands protruded incongruously; he looked like some great forest beast dressed up in costume. George laughed. "Leonard, I swear I might have to put you back in your deerskins. You look to me like a circus bear."

"Damned if I don't feel like one, too," he replied. "Looky here, George. The merchant Cerré has wrote you a letter from Ste. Genevieve."

George took the letter, which was written in French in a very fine hand. Going inside, he gave it to the translator, who read:

According to public rumor, my enemies there, jealous of the efforts I make to obtain a comfortable mediocrity, have profited by my absence, to blacken me and destroy me in the opinion of persons to whom I have not the honor of being known. I fear that in the first moment the false reports of my enemies may cause injury to my fortune, the only object of their hatred. . . . I venture to solicit you, sir, to have the goodness to grant me a passport to return home in order that I may be able to clear myself of the accusations that have been made to you against me, and attend to affairs that call me there. It is the favor that the most submissive subject hopes from you; and he has the honor of being with the most profound respect, sir, your very humble and very obedient servant,

CERRÉ

George remembered something Father Gibault had said about Cerré, not gossip, or any direct statement of Cerré's situation—as the priest never involved himself in "temporal affairs"—but just a few hints to the effect that the villagers who owed him money might like to have him banned from the villages as a British sympathizer. It was amazing to George how much understanding of Kaskaskia and the area he had absorbed just by being around the priest, even though he could remember hardly any specific secrets actually being stated to him.

"Well, we should give this Cerré a chance to face his accusers, I think, Leonard. We've let him hang around the other side of the Mississippi worrying about his reputation long enough."

A man of such wealth might be better as an ally to our impoverished company than as an enemy, he thought.

"I think," Helm remarked, "that any man brave enough to come flying home into the face of gossip desarves a chance t' do it."

Mr. Pollock, New Orleans

Kaskaskia, July 18, 1778

Dear Sir

I was ordered by the Executive Power of the Commonwealth of Virginia, to Attack the British Illinois and in case I succeeded to continue with a strong Garrison. I have succeeded agreeable to my wishes & am Necessitated to draw Bills on the State and have reason to believe they will be accepted by you the answering of which will be acknowledged, by his Excel^y the Governor of Virginia. I am happy to find the Inhabitants of this Country Unanimous in their Sentiments in favor of the American Cause. As for news Inquire of Monsr Crusat who promises to forward this Letter to you.

I am Dear Sir Your Humble Servant

G. R. CLARK

George folded the letter and put it in a packet of vouchers which would be carried down the Mississippi to Oliver Pollock in New Orleans by Francisco Crusat, an officer at St. Louis. A good correspondence with St. Louis, particularly with Lieutenant Governor de Leyba, had commenced soon after the capture of Kaskaskia, and the Spaniards there, with their constant traffic

up and down the Mississippi, promised to provide much of the
Virginians' contact with the American partisans in New Orleans. Having no money, George had begun issuing bills of credit
on Virginia in exchange for provisions; these so far had been
accepted gladly by the French and Spanish merchants and traders, who could anticipate that they would be paid at their face
value in silver by Pollock, the agent for Congress and for Virginia at New Orleans. Since the beginning of the Revolution,
Pollock had been doing a zealous business, securing assistance
from the Spanish authorities for the American cause. Much of
the military goods that had gone upriver throughout the war,
even as far as Fort Pitt on the Ohio, had been obtained through
his efforts, often at his own sacrifice.

Leonard Helm bustled happily into the room, in his shirt-
sleeves; he had given up trying to wear a uniform except on
formal occasions. He came in now with a bundle of papers
which he put down on George's desk. "Nothin' urgent," he said,
flinging himself back into a chair. "Just more of this danged
paperwork. Hey, George, I done learnt meself how t'talk
Frenchy already!"

"Already?" George asked with a slow smile, wiping his quill
clean on a rag. He needed some levity to take his mind off the
endless grim details of administration, and he knew that Helm
was bursting to provide some. "Tell me about it."

"Well, it's real easy, once y' git th' hang of it. All y' do is,
now, y'talk way up in your nose . . ." He began a sonorous,
twangy tone and continued: ". . . an' jes' 'bout ever' other word
y' hang an 'ay' or an 'oh' on it, an' y' turn yer voice up like
a question ever' half-a-dozen words, an' that's how y' do it,
George."

"Is that the truth now?" George laughed. "So let me hear you
speak some of this Frenchy of yours, then."

"Messy bo-koo, mohn coh-lo-*nel*! I am-*ay* at thees moh-
mohn speakin'-*ay* t' you-*oh* een Frenchy-*ay*! Coh-lo-*nel*
George-*ay* Rohjairs *Clark*, you air wohn boh-*day*-shus coh-lo-
nel of wohn boh-*day*-shus ar-*mee*! There. D'you understand that
all right?"

"I did, for a fact," George grinned. "But do the French?"

"Sure, I reckon they do; they look at me like they did. But
then, I can't understand their answers. I ain't learnt meself t'
hear Frenchy yet, jes' t' talk it."

"Ha, ha, ha! Agreed, Len, you're one bodacious linguist.
Vous parlez français assez bien, pour un Kentuckian."

"Say! Y' ain't doin too bad at it yerself, George! I dang nigh understood you thar fer a minute."

"Thank you. But now, listen, Leonard, I've been thinking about something that concerns you, and I hope you'll answer me yes. If the priest *has* managed to convert the people at Post St. Vincent, that place is going to need an American officer over its French commandant. For a while, anyhow. Can I assign you to that duty, Len? Will you sign over for another eight months or so?"

Helm contemplated his knees for a minute and frowned, chewing inside his lip. Then he looked up. "Y' need me, George?"

"I do."

"Then so be it."

"Thank you, Len. I really do thank you. You'll be a long ways off from the main body of us. You'll have all manner of problems solely on your shoulders, as I do here. Y'll have to keep the French happy, and the traders. And you'll probably have to treat with the Wabash Indian nations, and that as if from a position of strength, which we don't really have. I'm convinced that you have to be bold with 'em. I think if you give 'em presents and ask them to councils, they deem you weak. We don't have presents to give 'em anyhow." He laced his fingers and looked at notes on his desk, then frowned and sighed. "I've already heard overtures from the—let me see here—the Kaskaskias, the Peorias, the Michigamies, Potawatomies, and the Puans. They want to talk to us Big Knives."

Helm emitted a low whistle. "The word travels fast out here, don't it?"

"Aye. The French traders have been spreading the word about how strong we are. I'm letting the nations wait a bit. When they ask us direct to come and council, we'll go. Only then. You know, Len, I think we can do more real service out here even than I expected, if we approach it right. But my God, I think we've got more real work ahead of us than we've ever faced." He blew out a long breath. "I'd serve five years a slave to get some reinforcements. We're spread so thin now it's going to turn my hair white. And no idea whether Governor Henry is doing anything for us. I've written about our situation, but it'll be weeks before that gets to 'im. And more weeks before he can send succor if he hasn't already, which I doubt he has. Do what you can, Len, to influence your men to reenlist. I pray you, do that."

"Anything y' say."

"*Damnation!*" George slammed his palm on the desk. "With anything upwards of five hundred men like these, we could go straight up now and take Detroit, and all our worries'd be done with. Len, I want Detroit so bad I can *taste* it!"

"God dang you, I can't make out what kind of a crazy y'air," exclaimed Helm. "One minute you got us hangin' on t' th' bank o' th' Missipp by our fingernails, an' th' next minute you're set to go after Hamilton in his own lair! You . . ." He paused at the sound of excited voices outside the house. The lieutenant of the guard stepped into the doorway and saluted.

"Beggin' your pardon, sir," he said, "but Mister Cerré is here beggin' an audience with Colonel Clark, sir."

"Good!" George stood up. "Bring 'im in. I'm eager to see this man."

The merchant Gabriel Cerré entered the headquarters with an air of injured dignity. He was obviously a man accustomed to a place high in society, and did not easily wear the suppliant or defensive manner which his present circumstances now had forced him to assume. He was large, sleek, and pink-jowled, with a network of flaming capillaries running from his cheekbones into his nose. His coat of wine-colored velvet was rumpled and his white stockings were stained with the bilge water of the freight bateau in which he had been brought over from the Spanish side of the river. But he was freshly shaved, redolent of some sort of cologne, and his silvering, kinky dark hair was pulled back neatly and bound in a perfect queue. George confronted him with folded arms and expressionless visage, not taking his proffered hand. Cerré looked like one who would have heaped vituperation upon anyone else who had greeted him with such apparent indifference, but he was not in the least haughty before this Virginian who now seemed to be in charge of his fate.

"*Mon colonel*, please. The understanding I have is that certain people in this village accuse me of being very much in the British interest. But no. I trade at Detroit only because the British control the trade here. I am without politics, a world citizen, but with a deep love for France. No politics, sir. No politics at all."

"I've been told that some of your goods are used to pay the Indians for their depredations upon my people. That would be a bloody crime in my eyes, m'sieur."

"But it is not so! I abhor the practice of employing savages

in warfare! Sir, I truly suspect—I would wager—that the whole
body of my accusers are persons who are in my debt and would
love to see me ruined so that their obligations would be nulli-
fied!"

George ran his tongue over his eyetooth thoughtfully. All this
was as Gibault had hinted, and perhaps there was a way to verify it. "M'sieur Cerré, I don't want to hear any more of your
story at this time. Will you please retire to the antechamber over
there and close the door, and wait until I summon you. This little matter can be dealt with justly, I think, if you'll let me do
this my way."

Within fifteen minutes, all the citizens who had complained
against Cerré had been assembled in the parlor. They numbered
about a dozen, and sat or stood, fidgeting. George came in and
took a seat behind the desk. "We're here now," he began, "to
hear various charges made against the merchant Cerré . . ." A
babble of nasty voices went up in the room, and George silenced it by striking the desk top with the side of his fist. "Before you begin, messieurs—one at a time—I believe the accused
has the lawful right to face his accusers. Cerré!"

The antechamber door opened; Cerré stepped out and glanced
over the gathering. A look of contempt formed on his face and
the startled accusers began to squirm and look frightened. One
or two edged backward toward the door, and slipped out.

"This 'trial' is in session," George said. "Now who will be
the first to record his complaints against Monsieur Cerré formal-
ly?"

A dense silence followed, then the shuffling of feet and the
clearing of throats. Cerré stared from one to another. None
spoke. The merchant's countenance grew colder and colder. One
by one, eyes on the floor, the people got up and crept out. Soon
there was only one remaining, near the front of the room, a
lumpish fellow in peasant smock. He looked up and saw Cerré
staring at him; his eyes bulged and his Adam's apple worked.
When he glanced over both shoulders then and saw that all the
others had left, he turned pale, got up, and lumbered toward the
door, knocking aside two chairs in his haste.

Now Cerré stood looking across the empty room at the open
door, his lips drawn thin, hands clasped behind his back. He
turned slowly. "Well, *mon colonel*?" he said. George gripped
the edges of the desk top with both hands, stared back at him
for a minute, then leaned back and laughed.

"As I see it," he said, "the case is closed."

Cerré was delighted with the Virginian's system of justice. Within another half an hour he had taken the oath of allegiance to the United States, and ten minutes later was drinking brandy with George and discussing cheerfully the many ways in which his travels, goods, and influence might be used in support of the new Franco-American alliance.

GEORGE WAS SURPRISED IN THE NEXT FEW DAYS TO FIND THAT MOST of the citizens of Kaskaskia were as delighted with the handling of Cerré's trial as was Cerré himself, and the young commandant's reputation as Solomon soon augmented his renown as a benevolent conqueror. The citizens and traders continued spreading his praise far and wide among the Indians, and within a few days he had heard from chiefs of another half-dozen tribes, some as far away as the Great Lakes and four or five hundred miles west of the Mississippi. He began to plan a great council, to be held at Cahokia because of its importance as a center for Indian trade. There would also be an opportunity to see Joseph Bowman there, and perhaps to make a diplomatic call on Lieutenant Governor de Leyba at St. Louis across the river.

He delayed the departure, however, until the return of Father Gibault and Doctor Laffont from Vincennes. They arrived, as they had promised, on the first of August. Their joyful report was that the people of Vincennes, after reading George's proclamation and hearing about the state of harmony in the Illinois villages, had embraced the American offer almost unanimously, and had signed the oath of allegiance. The priest handed this document, covered with the signatures and marks of the Vincennes people, to George with a shy pride like that of a child presenting its parent with a handmade gift.

George sank back in his chair with a great sigh of relief. Now the whole Northwest territory, with the exception of Detroit and its environs, was, in a tenuous way at least, under American occupation. He smiled and silently gave thanks for the success of the expedition. But that was followed immediately by a strange sense of apprehension. Apparently it showed on his face; Father Gibault leaned toward him, asking, "What is troubling you, my son?"

"Nothing, nothing," George demurred. But what he wanted to say was, *It was too easy somehow.* Everything has been charmed and it doesn't seem real. Have we earned this success, he wondered, or has it been given to us?

Well, he thought then. Perhaps neither. We are still earning it,
I suspect.

GABRIEL CERRÉ HELD A BALL ON THE EVE OF GEORGE'S DEPARTURE
to Cahokia. For the first time in nearly three years, George had
the pleasure of holding women in his arms, feeling them sweep
and turn in the movements of the dance, feeling the suggestion
of their supple backs within the confines of hooks and stays.
Their bold and merry eyes stirred his blood; their laughter was
full of invitation. Several of them, who spoke a little English,
made inquiries about when he would return, and whether, when
he did, he might be disposed to attend any entertainments in
their homes. It was obvious that the leisure moments of his stay
here, if there should ever prove to be some leisure moments,
could become cozy and pleasurable. These Frenchwomen, it
seemed, could be quite forward, and he had become the main
object of their attention in these recent peaceful weeks. None of
them made any deep impression on his heart, but he did make
note of two or three of them who had left him in a state of lingering excitement. All in all these French and Creole ladies
seemed too fickle and spoiled and frivolous for his taste. The
women he had most admired in his youth were the young
pioneer women, with their attitudes of self-reliance and commitment and courage. Few of them were as attractive or provoca-
tive as these. But they were, he felt, of superior character.

He whirled about the floor now, in this same ballroom at
Cerré's house which he had invaded only a month before, and
that seemed like a vague dream now, an incident from the life
of someone else. Now he was well-fed, clean, comfortable in
fine fabrics, awash in polite words and lilting music, beguiled
by flashing eyes and by the intricate messages on young wom-
en's smiling mouths. Cerré fussed about in the far end of the
room with his stout wife, being the proud and perfect host, now
and then catching George's eye and saluting him with an expansive wave of the arm. George momentarily studied the delicate
neck, tawny shoulders, and scented bodice of the auburn-haired
maiden whose weight now swooped and swung cradled on his
right forearm; she was a daughter of some trader, whose name
escaped him at the moment because he had not yet mastered its
strange pronunciations; and the trader, resplendent in a coat of
forest green velvet and white summer breeches, watched from a
wall chair, smiling the smug but nervous smile of a father intent
on giving a daughter away to the right man. In this sense,

George mused, gazing down now at the voluptuous creature in
his arms, it's not unlike being back in Virginia.

"Vous êtes heureux, m'sieur?" she inquired, in a squeaky
voice that somehow did not seem to go with her ripe body and
adult face.

"Très heureux," he replied, understanding that simple question. "Yes, I am very happy, mademoiselle. *Et vous?"*

"O, mais oui," she squeaked.

I wonder, he thought, if the Spaniards try so avidly to pass
off their young women. Surely not. I understand they protect
them jealously.

We shall see soon enough, when we go to Cahokia, he
thought.

And that wan, vulnerable face, which he had seen only once,
in that month-old dreamlike moment, the face of de Leyba's
young woman, appeared once again in his mind's eye.

He was amazed that he remembered it so well.

"WELL, GEORGE," SAID LEONARD HELM, SITTING BY THE CAMP-
fire a few miles north of Kaskaskia, picking little chains of triangular green burrs off his trouser legs and flicking them into
the flames, "it's going to be a while, ain't it?"

"It is, and I surely do hate to divide us up." He sighed and
looked around the camp, where some forty Americans and
French volunteers sat by their cooking fires in the dusk at the
foot of the river bluff. Part of the force would split off here in
the morning and go eastward toward Vincennes, where Captain
Helm would assume the command of Fort Sackville and begin
making treaties with the Wabash Indians. The rest of the troop
would accompany George up the Mississippi Valley Road to
Cahokia, where he would stay at Joseph Bowman's garrison and
treat with the Illinois tribes. "I'm going to miss you, Len."

"Same here, George," Helm said, masking his sentiment and
his anxieties by turning back diligently to the removal of the
burrs, which he had picked up while dismounted at a drinking
spring earlier in the afternoon. George watched him, quietly,
thoughtfully.

Those little burrs carry seeds, George thought. They hook
onto clothes or animal fur going by, and they take a ride to
some new place where there aren't any burrs and fall there and
take root and become like they were in the old place. It's like
people coming to new places in boats across an ocean or down
a river, where they try to make a new world for themselves like

the old one, but with more space. The way we came to this continent from England and France, he mused, or the way we came down these rivers and made the Kaintuck settlements, or the way the French and Spaniards made these settlements here in the Mississippi and Wabash valleys.

People can think all that out before they go, and can design a boat, and bring familiar things along to make their new life somewhat like the old one, he thought. But how do burrs get smart?

He asked Helm what he thought about that, and the question made Helm stop and really examine a burr he was holding, as if he had never really seen one before.

"Bamboozles me," he said after a while, flicking the burr into the fire and looking long and seriously into the flames after it. Finally he grinned. "I've seen fruit seeds in bird shit. Them seeds been smart too, I reckon, but I think if I was a seed, I'd figure me out a nicer way to git around."

George chuckled and shook his head.

He really was going to miss Leonard Helm.

15

St. Louis, Upper Louisiana Territory
August 1778

Don Fernando de Leyba was in fine spirits. Word brought up the river from Kaskaskia day by day supported his good first impressions of Don Jorge Clark. And he had already had the pleasure of sending to Clark a bateau of American military stores which had come up the river from Oliver Pollock, the American agent in New Orleans. Colonel Clark and his shabby followers obviously were in great need of these goods, which had arrived at St. Louis before Clark had appeared at Kaskaskia.

De Leyba had a few days earlier written a long letter to Governor Galvez in New Orleans, describing Clark's astonishing arrival in the Illinois; now he was continuing his exuberant appraisal of the young American's progress. Putting quill to paper, he addressed the letter:

Señor Governor General,
My Dear and Most Respected Sir:

Colonel Clark deserves the greatest courtesy from all the inhabitants of this district since they are debtors to him for his pleasant manner, clemency, and upright administration of justice. Although his soldiers are bandits in appearance, he has them under the best of control. I am expecting this gentleman's visit from day to day. I shall show him all the courtesy I can and expect to have the best of dealings with him.

I remain with all respect at your Lordship's service. My dear Sir, the hand of your Lordship is kissed by your most devoted servant,

FERN^do DE LEYBA
Lieutenant Governor, Upper Louisiana

He folded the letter, melted wax over the fold, and was impressing his ring into the wax when the sound of walking horses and feminine voices came through the open front door of the mansion. Draining off the remains of a glass of Madeira, he rose, a little tipsy, from his desk and went toward the vestibule. He had been sipping the wine throughout his afternoon of correspondence, not heeding how often he had refilled his glass. Must regulate that a little better, he thought. His wife had been growing concerned over his tendency to be inebriated by the early evenings.

He stepped to the front door to greet the entourage. His wife, Maria, his sister, Teresa, and Lieutenant de Cartabona reined their horses in at the mounting block. His daughters, Maria Josefa, now nine, and Rita, six, in white cotton dresses and sun hats, were behind them in a tiny, two-wheeled cart pulled by a pony; the rear was brought up by four of the lieutenant's mounted militiamen. Black footmen went out, helped the ladies to dismount, unloaded from the cart a picnic basket from which hung the corner of a soiled groundcloth, and led the horses and pony out of sight toward the stables. The little girls ran squealing to their father, who stooped to embrace them and hear their excited account of their outing. Maria embraced him then, an expression of distaste fleeting over her face when she smelled the miasma of wine about him, then took the children into the house. Teresa stood near Lieutenant de Cartabona, who remained mounted. Fernando noted how often and how tenderly these two looked at each other. It was not entirely good, in his opinion. Cartabona was a charming fellow, and apparently alleviated Teresa's ennui here in these humid summer months, but he was a soldier of limited leadership qualities and had, before Teresa had begun to command his attention, built for himself some reputation as a gambler and rakehell. Only through the strict tradition of chaperonage could de Leyba permit them to spend so much time in each other's company.

"Much excitement in the countryside, Excellency," said de Cartabona. "I suspect a good half of our population has sailed over to Cahokia in the last few days to get a glimpse of the Bostonese, and they come back with the most fantastic giant stories!"

"Not so fantastic as you might think," de Leyba laughed. "They *are* giants, eh, Teresa?"

She frowned and came away to stand nearer her brother. He put his arm around her.

"Yes," he said. "She still has nightmares about it. And premonitions. What, little sister?"

She nodded, looking at the ground, troubled.

"Well, then, Tenente," said de Leyba. "Farewell, and thank you for escorting my dear ones."

"The pleasure was mine, Excellency. Adiós, Senorita, until I may have the honor again." And de Cartabona, always proud of his horsemanship, led his militiamen away down the cobbled street at a pretty canter, all obviously for her eyes.

16

CAHOKIA, THOUGH IT SAT IN A SPLENDID SITE, WAS A WRETCHED
place, reflecting the indolence of its inhabitants, who were more
committed to Indian trade than to farming or husbandry. It was
a straggling line of some thirty-five or forty dilapidated houses,
along a road which led from its mill to the juncture of the
Cahokia River and the Mississippi. Directly in the mouth of the
Cahokia stream nestled a picturesque wooded island; beyond
that, in the middle of the two-mile-wide Mississippi, lay a
smaller island, and on a bluff on the far side of the great stream
the distant buildings of St. Louis could be seen on a clear day.
To the east of the village of Cahokia was a long, curving lake
which apparently once had been part of the Mississippi's earlier
channel. Now all the lowland between the town and the lake
was full of the camps and horses of Indians who had come to
hold council with the Big Knives. The tribal camps sprawled
over the lush green grass in the humid summer morning mist of
the valley. Dominating the terrain was one ancient Indian
mound, huge as a hill.

George Rogers Clark, with Captain Bowman at his side,
stepped out of the large stone house which had been serving as
Bowman's command post and walked out through the gate of
the newly built palisade. Outside the gate, exactly between two
great fan-shaped elms, a long council table had been set up,
with benches at both ends and along the side nearer the fort. Sitting on the ground before the table in tribal groups were several
dozen Indian chiefs and chieftains, and behind them stood hundreds of warriors, a great, breathing semicircle of gleaming
brown faces, scalplocks, feathers, bead necklaces, greased skin,
knives in fringed sheaths, long breechclouts decorated with brilliant beads and quills, woven or metal armbands. Some of the

chiefs wore scarlet British uniform coats. They watched the American colonel with intense eyes but impassive faces as he strode to the table, bareheaded, the brass buttons on his buff-and-blue uniform glinting at them in the morning sunlight. A low murmur went among the Indians as they studied this lithe youth who had suddenly appeared in their country preceded by his own new legend. The Indians were not disappointed at the sight of him. Here was a man who looked like his legend. His hair seemed to burn like a flame in the sunlight and his eyes were like deep cold water.

George stepped behind the table, drew his sword and laid it across the tabletop, pointing toward the Indians. He took a deep breath and inhaled the smell of the huge body of Indians, that strangely pleasant, sweet, smoky, musky smell so evocative of his long-ago idylls among the Mingoes. His eyes flickered over the faces of the chiefs as he placed the sword, and as he reached for a bundle which Bowman handed to him.

Opening the bundle without looking down at it, George drew out two wide belts of bead wampum. One was white, and represented peace; the other was blood-red and represented war. The Indians knew the language of the belts and watched approvingly as the chief of the Big Knives laid them side by side across the table, arranging them so that several inches of the belt-ends hung over the forward edge, close before the eyes of the nearest chiefs. Now the chiefs rose, almost as one, to their feet, to face him and bring their eyes to a level with his.

An aged and dignified chief, his white hair in braids, his face brown and seamed as the leather of polished old boots, stepped forward, holding before him in both hands a long-stemmed peace pipe-tomahawk festooned with red and white feathers. Lighting it from a coal brought forward by a young brave, he then raised it out beyond his eyes, presenting it toward the Long Knife, then, turning, showed it to the four corners of the compass.

George came out from behind the table and stood directly before the old chief. Still no word had been spoken. The chief gave the stem of the pipe to George, who took it and puffed on it, drawing the rich, pungent tobacco smoke into his mouth. Damnation, he thought, whatever you do, don't choke on it. He returned the pipe to the old man, blowing the smoke into the air. The chief nodded, drew on it himself, then passed it around the first row of tribal leaders. When this was done, the Indians stood watching him.

"You are the solicitors of this council," George began, "so you will tell me what is in your hearts first. I have sent letters to you, desiring you to choose whether you shall lay down the tomahawk, or else behave like men and fight for the British as you have done. I told you that you'll see your so-called Great Father the British king given to the dogs to eat. I told you I care not whether you choose the white belt of peace or the red belt of war, because I am a warrior and I glory in war. But let me warn you that if you think of giving your hands to the Big Knives, give your hearts also. I believe when we are better acquainted you will find us to be of better principles than the bad birds of British rumor have made you believe."

George paused here to let them ponder what he had said, and looked them over as they thought. One chief, wearing a red military coat, a bloodstained belt about his neck and a small British flag like a bib upon his breast, watched George with an almost palpable intensity in his black eyes, a particularly hard and challenging look on his face. He seemed to be about thirty-five years old, very strong in the shoulders, where the English coat strained at the seams. His legs were sinewy; his cheeks sunken, his mouth very wide and thin-lipped and severe. George knew who this one was; he had been pointed out early in the morning, one of the first to arrive at the council table. It was Lajes, who was known as Big Gate because, as a mere boy, during the siege of Detroit by Chief Pontiac, he had shot and killed a soldier at a gate of the fort. He was a hero among his people, and he had a special sense of his own importance, having announced in a letter to the Americans that he would be attending the council. It was obvious that he expected to be recognized and singled out for attention very soon. Knowing this, George did not linger on Big Gate's face but quickly passed his gaze over the other chiefs. Then he continued: "You see that I do not cover my council table with rum or presents for your people, as the British do. That is because I have come here not as a weakling to bribe you, but to tell you the truth, and to hear you tell me the truth. Now . . ." he paused and folded his arms across his chest, "I wait to hear what you've come to say to me."

The chiefs murmured among themselves for a moment. George half expected Big Gate to come forward as their spokesman, but instead it was the old sage again.

"Chief of the Long Knife," this dignitary began, "we have come only to take your hand and hear your words. We come to say that we have warred against you because of the bad birds

of the English. We have come to hear what you have to say
about your war with them, so that we may understand who tells
the truth." The old chief was neither humble nor arrogant as he
made this request. "We hope," he went on, "that the Great
Spirit has brought us together here with you for good reason, as
he is good, and we ask you to blow the mist away from our
eyes." Concluding, he proffered his hand to George, who refused it. A murmur of consternation went among the Indians
now, and it was an ominous sound. George felt some apprehension, among these hundreds of savages, refusing that offered
hand, but he was determined not to show any signs of fear or
eagerness before this attentive public. Instead, he said:

"I have told you, there is time to give the hand when the
heart can be given also. You are many tribes; perhaps you're
not all of the same mind. Go and talk among yourselves. We
will meet at this same place tomorrow at the highest time of the
sun, and I will tell you why the Big Knives fight the British. I
do not believe that things of such importance as the making of
friendship can be done in haste, but only after men understand
each other. Tomorrow, then."

The interpreters gave the Indians this message then, and
George turned away. He picked up his sword from the table and
shoved it into its scabbard at his side with a quick, sure thrust.
He glanced at Big Gate, who still stood glaring at him, not falling into the general conversation among the other chiefs.
George turned then and walked off toward the little fort, followed by Bowman, who had gathered up the symbolic belts of
war and peace. They both breathed great sighs of relief when
they were inside.

TERESA DE LEYBA UNDRESSED BEHIND A FOLDING SCREEN IN HER
room upstairs in the governor's mansion at St. Louis, and
quickly drew a long white cotton gown over her nakedness.
Even in solitude she felt uncomfortable and insecure with her
body uncovered. The maid had brought up a kettle of hot water.
Teresa mixed it with cold water in a basin, soaked a cloth and
rubbed it with a small, fragrant piece of soap, then reached
under the nightgown to wash herself. These hot August days in
the river valley kept her in a constant state of humid discomfort,
and she had learned that, unless she repaired to her room to
wash two or three times a day, she tended to break out in a
prickly rash between her thighs and in the small tufts of black
flossy hair under her arms, and would even, at the most inaus-

picious times, become aware of unfresh smells from her own body.

Drying on a soft towel, she drew a light, lacy robe on over the nightgown, took the combs and pins from her hair, shook it out, sat at a mirrored vanity and began pulling a brush through it, looking at herself in the light of two sconces on the wall above. Through the open window casement came the faintest breath of a summer night breeze, barely enough to nudge the points of candlelight, and the night chorus of crickets and frogs.

Now and then, scarcely audible, almost as faint as a pulse-beat, the distant thumping of drums came from across the great dark river. This was the second night of the drums, and they had worried her sleep the first night, filling her head with thoughts of naked savages. Many Indians had passed through St. Louis in the last two days, members of the Missouri tribes, on their way to Cahokia for some mysterious council. They had gone through the streets, painted and gaudy with feathers, some carrying elaborately decorated ceremonial spears and shields as well as their British muskets.

Teresa paused in her brushing, listened to the faraway bump of the drums, and closed her eyes for a brief prayer for the safety of her brother, his family, and herself. Some Spanish subjects in recent months had been killed and scalped in their fields around St. Louis, and the atrocities were in general blamed, she had heard, on errant bands of warriors under the influence of British propaganda and British rum.

Now, plaiting her thick hair into two braids, she coiled them on top of her head, pinned them there, and pulled on a small white cap. As she did so, she heard hearty, happy voices on the veranda below her window, the voice of her brother and someone else, and the clink of crystal. She went to the window. Far across the river at Cahokia she could see many tiny, warm points of light, doubtless the Indians' fires. Below, at the edge of the veranda, a torch flickered on the end of a long pole stuck into the ground; moths tumbled through its light, occasionally singeing themselves and whirling to the ground. Just seating himself in a chair in the light of the torch was her brother, slim and fine-looking without a coat, wearing white breeches and hose and a lace-front white silk shirt with full sleeves. Facing him, seated in another chair with the back of his head to her window, was another man. The two touched the rims of their glasses. Drinking, Fernando saw her silhouette in the window.

"Ah, Teresa, my dear, you're still awake? You must come down, and say hello to our friend Vigo! He's been to Cahokia!"

The man had turned in his chair to look up at her, smiling with delight, rising to bow to her. "Hello, little beauty," he called up, in a voice that should have come from a giant, rather than this short, square, bustling little man with a pointed goatee.

"Uncle Francisco!" she cried in delight. He was not really an uncle, but had come to seem like one, and liked to be thus called. He was her brother's trading partner and closest friend here in St. Louis, hearty and generous and always cheerful. "But I'm not dressed," she protested.

"Come down, little beauty," insisted Vigo. "We'll pretend not to notice. Come and share the news."

Persuaded, she drew back into the room, tied a silken sash around the waist of her robe to give herself a feeling of being dressed, and went out of the room, past the sleeping-rooms of Maria and her daughters, and down the darkened staircase, feeling her way along the waxy hardwood banister. She felt a bit wicked, aware of her unlaced nakedness under the light gown, going down in the night to sit with the two men. She still had not grown accustomed to the suspension of propriety that seemed to prevail here so far from Spain. Emerging onto the veranda, feeling the cooler night air on her legs, she was met by the two men, who had stood to await her. Francisco Vigo took her hand and kissed it, while Fernando brought another chair out from the wall and wiped the dew from it with a handkerchief. Vigo wore his usual leather doublet and a belt at least four inches wide with a huge, square brass buckle. She had seen him several times, and whether he was in summer silks or in the furs and skins of the wilderness trader, there was always that doublet and that great buckled belt.

"My dear," he beamed, "what a pleasure to have you join us!" She sat in the chair between them, looking down and smiling in modesty, unsure how she should behave in this highly unusual circumstance, whether as a member of the conversation or simply as a listener. She watched Vigo sip his port. He was obviously in a high state of excitement. He was never able to contain his physical energy when he was enthusiastic about something; his eyes flashed, happy expressions played over his face, and he sat on the forward edge of his chair, looking as if he might jump up at any moment and begin running about. Sardinian by birth, he had been a muleteer, a common laborer, and then a Spanish soldier in the Old World before coming to Cuba, then New Orleans, and now to St. Louis where, even though he was only thirty-one, he had become very wealthy trading in furs with the trappers and Indians for the last five years. His trading centers were scattered from Kaskaskia to Cahokia and distant Vincennes, and he was seldom at his home base in St. Louis. He was free of any family ties and ranged continually about the territories, always welcomed by the important people on both sides of the Mississippi as a bearer of useful information. Being almost illiterate, he had the natural eloquence of a great raconteur and a bottomless memory for detail. He was a beloved favorite of the most influential man on the far side of the river, that gawky priest Father Gibault.

"Our friend," Fernando said now to Teresa, "has just seen an old acquaintance of ours!" Then he paused as if to let her guess.

"Who?" she asked. "Father Gibault? Señor Cerré?"

"Nay," Fernando replied, pleased that she had not been able to guess. "Colonel Clark, of the Americans."

"Colonel Clark?" Fortunately the torchlight was dim and uncertain; she felt herself flushing at the mention of that unsettling name.

"You remember," Fernando went on as Vigo nodded excitedly and grinned. "The one who burst in on us in the ballroom at Cerré's last month."

"That awful night! I shall always remember."

Fernando laughed and spoke to Vigo. "Teresa believes he is the most terrible man in the world."

"Name of God!" Vigo exclaimed. "On the contrary!" He fairly levitated off his chair for emphasis. "He has won the heart of every white man and woman in the Illinois! The women in particular, I daresay! And Father Gibault exults as if Our Savior has returned to walk on the earth. Ha, ha!"

Teresa gasped at this sacrilege, and Fernando exploded with a laugh, then checked himself and admonished, "Señor, if you please!"

"I'm only giving you my impressions. Gibault so loves this Clark that he went as his emissary to Vincennes and converted its people to Virginianism. Oh, you have never seen such a man ... but, yes, you have seen him, haven't you? Splendid, *splendid* ..."

Teresa twisted the ends of her sash in her hands, shaken with fright and confusion. Surely these men were wrong to have become so enthusiastic about that ... that ...

Yet she could not understand why her reaction to the thought of him was so unpleasant. Again the hard, naked, filthy image of the giant barbarian appeared behind her eyes, and she shuddered. "I . . . I'm sorry, but he frightened me worse than anything in my life, and I . . . I see him bringing only violence and grief upon us . . ."

"Nonsense, Teresa!" protested Vigo. "He is the fairest, most judicious man we've ever seen hereabouts. Surely as wise even as Gibault—though perhaps even less tolerant of nonsense and human frailty than that worthy. Ha, ha! And how vicious is a soldier who can subdue a whole territory without shedding a drop of blood, tell me that!"

Teresa fell silent. The men obviously were far beyond her fears.

". . . And the Indians, Fernando," Vigo rattled on. "They are buzzing with anxiety, let me tell you. There appeared to be nigh a thousand of them there this morning, yet he faced them down, and they're all but begging him—to the degree their dignity will allow, I mean—for the privilege of becoming his brother. Oh, Henry Hamilton would quail in his boots if he knew what is going on out here!"

"Not Hamilton," replied de Leyba quietly. "As I've heard of him, he is too arrogant to quail before anything."

"Aye, perhaps so. But I say he's met his better if he ever faces Clark. Ha, ha!" Vigo sat leaning forward with his elbows on his knees, rubbing his hands, smiling, alternately shaking and nodding his head. "But I tell you, Fernando, my friend, it is a good thing for all of us, I mean if this young man can prevail. Doing trade under the English flag was anything but ideal. Already, under the eyes of this Virginian, everything is proceeding in an easier and more natural way. I think that, if for no other reason than business itself, we should do whatever we can to help him. I, for one, feel absolutely right about it, clear down in my very bones."

Don Fernando de Leyba nodded. "Indeed," he said. "I've already extended an offer of Spanish hospitality to him, in person. Now that he's so close by, perhaps he can find a moment of leisure from his negotiations to come and visit us. Be so kind, dear friend, as to carry an invitation to him when you cross the river next, will you? I mean," he added with a grin at Teresa, "if my sister will permit me to bring such a *monster* into our house . . ."

"Permission?" she murmured. "But as you know, I am only a woman."

* * *

THE NOON SUNLIGHT STABBED DOWN THROUGH THE HIGH CANOPIES
of leaves in the twin elm trees, dappling the shaded ground and
tabletop with shimmering light. It was extremely pleasant and
cool in the shade, which spread wide enough to shelter Colonel
Clark and his aides, all the tribal chiefs, and a great number of
warriors as well. Sitting in view but off to one side near one of
the elm trunks was the priest Gibault, who was known and respected by all of the Indians except those who had come from
very distant places. He was known among all the Illinois and
Wabash tribes as a man who had never lied, and his presence,
George felt, could only lend credence to everything he planned
to say.

Now, as on the day before, he arrayed his sword and the belts
of war and peace on the table before the eyes of the Indians.
And as before, the northern chief Big Gate sat right in the foreground, his eyes flashing, haughty, the British flag on his breast
standing out like an insult. Again, George refused to pay any
special attention to him. Again, the old chief with the white
braids offered the tomahawk-pipe to the four winds, then
smoked it with George and the other chiefs. This time he offered it also to Bowman and several of the American lieutenants. "Get ready to sit a spell," George whispered to Bowman.
"I've got a long and ponderous speech to make." Bowman took
a bench at the end of the table, turned his strange pale eyes on
the Indians, crossed his legs, and folded his arms. George
picked up the red belt in his right hand, the white one in his
left, planted his feet wide, squarely in front of the table, stood
at his full height with the belts held before him in upturned
palms, and began in a loud voice, pausing for the interpreters:

"Men and warriors, pay attention. You informed me yesterday that the Great Spirit had brought us together, which you
hoped was good, as he is good . . ." A smile actually broke the
face of the old chief, upon hearing his own words thus cited.

"I also have the same hope," George went on, "and whatever
may be agreed upon by us at the present time, whether for
peace or war, I expect each party will strictly adhere to, and
henceforward prove ourselves worthy of the attention of the
Great Spirit."

They liked that. They sat straighter and their faces softened
for a moment. He continued:

"I am a man and a warrior, not a councilor. I carry War in
my right hand . . ." he raised the red belt over-head, then the

white belt, ". . . and in my left hand, Peace. I was sent by the Council Fire of the Big Knives and their friends to take control of all the towns the British possess in this country, and to remain here watching the conduct of the red men. I was sent to bloody the paths of those who continue the effort to stop the course of the rivers, but to clear the roads that lead from us to those who wish to be in friendship with us, in order that the women and children may walk in them without anything being in the way to strike their feet against; and to continue to call on the Great Fire for warriors enough to darken the land of those who are hostile to us, so that the inhabitants shall hear no sound in it but that of birds that live on blood." He paused here again for the interpreters, wishing meanwhile with all his might that it could be that easy to call more soldiers from the East.

"I know that a mist is yet before your eyes," he said, and again the old chief nodded approvingly at the echo of his own words. "I will dispel the clouds in order that you may see clearly the cause of the war between the Big Knives and the English, that you may judge for yourselves which is in the right. Then if you're men and warriors, as you profess to be, prove it by adhering strictly to what you may now declare, without deceiving either party and thus proving yourselves to be only old women." Here he let his eyes wander over the entire congregation, making a point of resting his eyes, for a change, on the face of Big Gate, whose lips grew tighter.

Then he leaned just slightly toward the Indians, and warmed the tone of his voice. "The Big Knives are very much like the red men. They do not know well how to make blankets, powder, and cloth; they buy these things from the English, from whom they formerly descended, and live chiefly by raising corn, hunting, and trading, as you and the French your neighbors do.

"But the Big Knives were daily becoming more numerous, like the trees in the woods, so that the land became poor and the hunting scarce, and having but little to trade with, the women began to cry to see their children naked, and tried to make clothes for themselves, and soon gave their husbands blankets of their own making. And the men learned to make guns and powder, so that they did not want so much from the English." The chiefs seemed to be hearing this quite sympathetically, as he had hoped. He knew how the Indians struggled for survival year after year, and he knew how they loved their women and children. Logan the Mingo had taught him that.

"Then," he said, "the English became very angry and stationed strong garrisons through all our country—as you see they have done among you on the Lakes and among the French—and would not let our women spin nor the men make powder, nor let us trade with anybody else. They said we must buy everything from them; and since we had become saucy, they would make us give them two bucks for a blanket that we used to get for one. They said we must do as *they* pleased, and they killed some of us to make the rest afraid.

"This is the truth and the cause of the war between us, which did not begin until they had treated us some time in this fashion. Our women and children were cold and hungry and continued to cry. Our young men were lost, and there were no counselors . . ." He stopped and gave the old chief a respectful look, "to set them in the right path. The whole land was dark, and the old men hung down their heads in shame, for they could not see the sun." The Indians, the whole great semicircle of them, sat in perfect stillness, listening to the words of the interpreters.

"Thus there was mourning for many years," he resumed. "At last the Great Spirit took pity upon us and kindled a great council fire that never goes out, at a place called Philadelphia. He struck down a post there and left a war tomahawk by it and went away. The sun at once broke out and the sky became blue. The old men held up their heads and assembled at the fire. They sharpened the hatchet and put it into the hands of the young men and told them to strike the English as long as they could find one on this side of the Great Water. The young men immediately struck the war post and blood ensued." He had been gradually raising his voice while describing this, and saw that the Indians were being stirred by the excitement in his tone. He dropped his voice now and went on, the Indians leaning forward to hear the rest:

"Thus the war began, and the English were driven from one place to another, until they became weak, and hired you red men to fight for them and help them.

"The Great Spirit became angry at this, and caused your *old* Father, the French King, and other great nations to join the Big Knives and fight with them against all their enemies, so that the English have become like a deer in the woods. From this you may see that it is the Great Spirit that caused your waters to be troubled, because you fought for the people he was angry with; and if your women and children should cry, you must blame yourselves for it, and not the Big Knives." He let that sink in, then he said:

"You can now judge who is in the right. I have already told you who I am. Here is a bloody belt and a white one. Take whichever you please. Behave like men and don't let your present situation, being surrounded by the Big Knives . . ." From the corner of his eye he saw Bowman suddenly uncross his legs and recross them, placing his hand over his mouth as if to keep from laughing. "Do not let that cause you to take up the one belt with your hands when your hearts drink up the other . . ." For a terrible moment, George was swept with mirth at the thought of Bowman's suppressed laughter, and at his own audacity, but he kept his face straight and silently thanked God for helping him do so.

"If you take the bloody path," he went on, "you shall go from this town in safety and join your friends the English; and we will try, like warriors, to see who can put the most stumbling blocks in the road and keep our clothes perfumed with blood the longest.

"If you should take the path of peace and now be received as brothers to the Big Knives and the French, but should hereafter listen to bad birds that will be flying through your land, you will no longer be counted as men but as persons with two tongues, who ought to be destroyed without listening to what you say, as nobody could understand you." He watched their faces as that was translated to them. It will put them on their honor, he thought with satisfaction, because they see each other here listening to it. And sometime soon, perhaps now, he knew, Tobacco's Son and other great chiefs of the Wabash tribes would be hearing essentially this same speech, getting this same challenge of their honor, from the lips of old Leonard Helm. He had rehearsed it over and over back in Kaskaskia with old Len, and could almost hear his own words now ringing over the Wabash in Len's ear-stabbing twang.

Now the interpreters were waiting and it was time to conclude. "Since I am convinced that you've never heard the truth before, I do not wish you to give me an answer before you've had time to council. We will part this evening, and when you're ready, if the Great Spirit will bring us together again, let us prove ourselves worthy by speaking and thinking with but one heart and one tongue."

With that, he turned on his heel, went around behind the table, and sat down, his sword and the belts before him. A cool breeze in the elm shade soothed his damp face. Birds twittered in the high foliage. A fly buzzed past his ear. Bowman shifted on his bench and rested his elbows on the end of the table and, his left profile to the Indians, winked his pale right eye at George. Beyond, Father Gibault sat beaming, his fingers laced across his midsection. And then the chiefs, following the example of their white-braided spokesman, stood up one by one and filed out of the shade into the sunlight, silent, straight, and dignified, their warriors falling in behind them. In two minutes they were all in their camps and the great pool of shade was deserted, ringing with the endless call of the summer locusts.

He awoke in the darkness, moaning low in his throat and taking deep breaths. Voluptuous thoughts, of arms and hips and long hair and bedding, roiled and grew vague as he became aware of the crickets outside and the dim gray square of the window, the stars glinting through the closed panes, the slick place under his hip in the sweat-soaked bedding. It had happened again, that curse of the lonely man, the seductive dream. It had been of a young woman he had bundled with one night in Caroline County. The constraint of the bundling-board had been ineffective, as it sometimes proved to be, and the occurrence of that night had repeated itself periodically in his dreams, as just now. Sleeping naked because of the summer heat in the closed room—security among the congregated tribes here at Cahokia forbade open windows—he lay now feeling the sensations ebb from his loins. He did not like it to happen. There was always the clammy discomfort afterward, and the sense of wasted energy. And what if the guard outside the door had heard him moaning, as he was sure he had been? And, too, it reminded him of his perennial loneliness.

He moved aside a bit in the narrow cot and considered that loneliness, which had become worse since his successes here in the Illinois. A private soldier could either bear his loneliness, which was part of being a soldier, or he could court or buy some temporary companionship when his energies ran too high in the night. The commander, though, especially one who had become such an object of public attention as he had, was forced to be totally discreet. Even though his successes in leadership seemed somehow to have made his yearnings even stronger, made every woman he saw seem more desirable, they had isolated him more than any private soldier ever could be. He could not take up with some common woman of the villages, or a squaw, or go to a brothel. Some commanders, less jealous of their example, might, but he could not. And gossip, which seemed to be the main preoccupation of the French villagers, made it almost impossible to imagine how he could have an affair of the heart—or even one of the loins—with any one of those respectable misses such as he had steered about the ballroom floor at Cerré's.

I am chaperoned by my role, he thought. I am as tightly chaperoned by my reputation as a Spanish noblewoman is by her *duenna*.

And now he had brought himself thus to thinking of that young woman again. *Teresa*, that was her name. *Teresa*. He had learned it from that trader yesterday, that Vigo. A fine fellow. Simply by mentioning de Leyba, George had brought down upon himself a torrent of praise and information about that lovely family. Vigo was enchanted by them all, by Teresa, especially, but apparently in an avuncular way. And she *was* de Leyba's sister; his guess about that had been right.

But how that Vigo had prattled on about her charms! As if advertising her. Could it be, George thought now, amused, that the little fellow is one of those congenital matchmakers who seem to exist everywhere, in every village? He smiled in the darkness and listened to the night sounds. Be that as it may, he thought, that fellow is a splendid character and promises to be an incomparable ally. One who ranges this whole territory, is trusted by everyone, knows the commercial ways, has goods and credit. And Gibault says you can trust him with your life if he's taken a liking to you.

George did not like to mix his thoughts of one's usefulness with his thoughts of one's friendship, but all American responsibilities out here being his own, he had to think in terms of everybody's usefulness. Someday, he thought, I'll have the luxury again of enjoying friends who are of no use to me. As for now, they have to be considered part and parcel of the plan to survive.

In his mind now he saw a connection, a sort of vein work, consisting of Gabriel Cerré in Kaskaskia, de Leyba in St. Louis, Vigo everywhere in the territory, and Oliver Pollock and Governor Galvez in New Orleans far down the river. Through them flowed the lifeblood of his triumphant but desperate little army. Lead and powder. Grain. Meat. Clothing. Tools and canvas and weapons and paper and rope, wax, cotton, quinine, tallow and salt and rum. And all of this flowed according to the power of

an ephemeral something called credit. His signature and the
name of the Virginia Assembly, written on hundreds of ledger
sheets and vouchers of paper. Paper. Scarcer even than gold. He
had made lists and vouchers on flysheets cut from books, on the
backs of letters, on anything made of that precious stuff. One of
his most worrisome burdens now, one that he felt must be
guarded at the cost of life almost, was his packet of records. He
had signed his name too many times, and in that network of
goods and credit imprinted on his brain there was not even a
shadow of a line leading directly to or from Virginia. Nothing
from there but silence. Someday there's going to be an accounting, he thought. He had faith in the word of Henry and Jefferson and their peers and in the state itself. But it was exceedingly
tenuous, that connection. He longed for messengers from Virginia as he longed for food. I've built a mountain of promises
out here in this valley, he thought, promises to the French, and
promises to my boys, and now promises even to the Indians, all
of which I have to trust Virginia will honor. Yet I can't seem to
get from that place even an inflated pound note or an able-
bodied rifleman. Nay, not even a *word*.

Five hundred men from that place—even four hundred,
perhaps—maybe even three hundred and fifty would be enough,
if they were like these—and I could go and reduce Detroit, and
the Northwest would be secure. *Detroit.* The image of the gate
of the great fort at Detroit burned in his mind now, as real and
detailed as if he had actually seen it.

Big Gate, he thought. That bloody English Indian there
among the chiefs: He has seen the gate at Detroit, and fought
there. His time will come. He'll need special handling. He
seems to have a sense of himself in the context of destiny.

Maybe that's my problem, too, George thought, with a sudden rush of clear understanding.

That, he thought, could be the worst kind of disease.

He thought then of another Indian who seemed to have a
sense of destiny: Saguina of the Chippewas, known as Mister
Black Bird. Mister Black Bird had not come to the councils, but
had, like Big Gate, sent a letter. And traders had brought word
that he was waiting to be invited. And so George had sent the
invitation back with them. Mister Black Bird was the chief of
a great band of warriors in the northern region of St. Joseph. He
had personally been among those treating with Hamilton in
1777, when Hamilton had danced at the fire with the savages.
Now he wanted to come and treat with the Big Knives. George

wanted very much to talk with Mister Black Bird, who was known as a wise man and probably could be brought to see the light. With him neutralized, the march against Detroit would be that much less perilous. Probably he is on his way here now, George thought. It would take him several days. But I would like to have him here while the others are still in council.

George reached for a corner of the sheet and wiped sweat from his face and chest and thought of the hundreds of Indians encamped at this moment not a half mile from where he slept. Or tried to sleep, he corrected himself.

These hundreds of savages I have surrounded, he thought, and puffed out voiceless laughter in the dark.

What a people, he thought, with his usual wonderment. How they yearn to trust! How they love ceremony, and the poesy in words and deeds! And, yet, damn! There's nothing like them for cruelty.

A ghastly memory arose in his mind, something from Dunmore's War: A white man, captive of the Mingoes or perhaps some allied tribe, had been stripped, his groin had been opened by a sharp knife, his small bowel severed at its lower end and tied to a sapling tree, and he had been forced to walk around and around the tree until the full length of his guts was wound around it. After he had fallen, or perhaps before, they had also lifted his scalp. The frontiersmen had found him kneeling there dead, still warm, bathed in the bloody slime of his own innards. What a people, he thought, remembering that, shuddering.

But our own people have done no less, he thought. A sergeant in Harrod's company, for instance, had as his most prized possession a bracelet made of a squaw's genitals.

Thank God my boys aren't all like that one, he thought, though many of 'em are: Insane when it comes to Indians. But give me men like Simon Butler. He's killed more Indians than any of 'em, but he's never killed one he didn't have to, and he won't take a scalp. George mused fondly on Butler, who was at this moment on his way to Kentucky to persuade them down there, if possible, to send men here for an assault on Detroit.

Outside the door the sentry moved. George heard the pop of his knee joints and a weary sigh. To have people lose sleep a-guarding you, he thought; what a sorry necessity that is. But it is a necessity. Sentinels awake, and guard squads sleeping clothed and ready, were stationed throughout the town. George knew he would be considered quite a prize, his new reputation

being what it was, for any band of braves who might have the
boldness to try to surprise him in the night and carry him off,
either dead or alive. Any warrior who could do that right now
would become a legend among the tribes and a prince among
the British. Another dubious benefit of my new-made fame, he
thought. Not only have I no privacy, but must be guarded like
a chest of gold.

He tried to give the Indians an impression that he was careless about his personal safety, that he had no anxiety whatsoever, and thus he kept his guard as unobtrusive as possible, and
lodged in a seemingly unguarded house outside the fort. But beyond that door sat the hidden sentry, and in an adjoining room
dozed a dozen more armed men. And directly across the street
in another house was a guard squad of French militia, volunteers from Kaskaskia.

But, my God, I might as well let them all rest and guard myself, wakeful as I am, he thought. He got up from the clammy
bed and stretched, licked his teeth and gums, leaned against the
windowsill, and looked out into the street.

What he saw sent a chill of alarm through him: Darting
across the pale starlit dirt of the street, crouched low, in a silent
file, moving directly toward his window, were Indians with
muskets. Perhaps a dozen of them, it appeared; two or three, he
saw now, were right outside the window already. His scalp
prickled.

Silently grabbing his breeches off a chair back, he pulled
them on and hastily knotted the string at his waist. Then he
picked up his pistol from the table, and went swiftly in bare feet
to the door of the adjacent room. Thrusting it inward, he groped
in the dark for the sergeant of the guard who slept on a cot just
inside. Getting a foot, he jerked the sergeant out of his sleep,
hearing him suspire loudly.

"Up!" George whispered sharply. "Get them up and out! Be
quiet about it. There's Indians outside the east window!" Instantly the room was full of rustling and excited whispering, the
rattle of weapons, the thump of moccasins on floorboards.
These woodsmen slept with the proverbial open eye, and could
be galvanized into action without so much as a yawn or a
groan. They were on their feet and bustling into his room when
suddenly a shout split the night outside.

"Guard! Hey, boys! Injuns out here!" It was the sentry outside the south entrance. He was cocking his flintlock at the moment George and the sergeant threw open the door and sprinted

out past him and around the corner of the house. George saw the intruders flitting across the street into the shadows, going toward the river. The French volunteers now were pouring out of their house, filling the air with sonorous cries and the sound of running feet. In a moment the whole town was aroused, and the night was shattered by a ragged rattling of gunfire down by the riverbank. That ceased, and there followed a few minutes of voices, talking voices, no more yells, from everywhere in the village. Then a large group could be seen walking up the street. The sergeant of the guard held up a lantern, and in its feeble glow the body of men was brought up before George.

It was a band of Puans, an evil-looking roving party called the Meadow Indians, who had been encamped on the island in the Cahokia while one or two of their chieftains hung around the edges of the council. Now guarding them was a squad of the French volunteers, whose captain bowed proudly to George. Other Frenchmen, soldiers and Cahokian civilians alike, were filling the street, bearing torches and lanterns, chattering with animation. George could also sense a great stirring and murmuring from the direction of the main Indian encampment. The Puans stood, bound, disarmed, their eyes darting in the lantern light. The French officer began interrogating them in a very abusive voice, and they responded plaintively or angrily by turns.

"We caught them running down by the creek, *mon colonel*," said the captain.

"They say they are innocent of any mischief, that they were fired upon by unfriendly tribes who crossed the creek. They say they were running from that, to get under the protection of our guard."

"I'm sure these is the ones," the sentry muttered to George. "Same headdress. Same paint on. I wasn't two yards from 'em, sir, an' I'd swear on it!"

"Voyez, voyez!" cried a villager who had been inspecting the captives. He held his lantern low, showing that the Indians' leggings and moccasins were wet and covered with mud. The French captain went into a tirade at them then, pointing at this evidence of their deceit and glaring into their furtive eyes. The Indians, some of whom appeared to be young chieftains, showed a variety of expressions ranging back and forth between indignation and shame.

"Now they have changed their story, *mon colonel*," said the officer. "They admit that they came across the stream, but say they did this only to test the loyalty of the French to the Long Knife. And they seem to have about a hundred various other explanations ready as well." Some of the American guards laughed aloud at this; the Indians stiffened as if the laughter had stabbed them.

Now George knew these were the ones who had tried to abduct him. He knew too that there was great risk in holding them captive. But in the back of his mind was the knowledge that most of the assembled chiefs considered this council a time of gravity and honor; they surely would not blame him for locking up a band of vagrants who had made a breach of the protocol like this. "Throw them in the guardhouse," he told the captain. "And put the chieftains among them in chains. We'll deal with them publicly at the council. Gentlemen, I thank you all for your alacrity." He gave the captain a warm squeeze of the hand and the Frenchman beamed with pride.

"Bon soir, mon colonel!"

It was three in the morning by the time the place was still again. Before retiring, Joseph Bowman tried to convince George that he ought to take lodgings inside the palisades.

"No," George said. "That would work against us in their minds. I'll increase the size of the guard in the house from now on, but they shan't know it. Don't you see, Joseph, they have to believe I'm protected by the Great Spirit?"

"I understand that, George. But what if you ain't?"

"Just pray to him that I am," he said, sending him off with a grin into the dark.

Dear Lord, he thought, returning to the lonely little bed. What a night.

IN THE INDIAN ENCAMPMENT, THE POWWOWS CONTINUED THROUGH the next day, perhaps, George suspected, complicated by the deadly prank the Puans had tried to conduct in the night. Probably the greater chiefs were embarrassed by that unthinkable impropriety and discussing how they might deal with it when they should meet him again. As for himself, he was sure his own legend could only have been enhanced by it. As further sign of his indifference to danger, he assembled a number of ladies and gentlemen of Cahokia and held a dance in the big house, a merry, loud affair that continued almost until morning.

The general council resumed the next morning, with even more ceremony than usual, as the chiefs seemed ready now to answer his offer.

But George began the meeting by having the chained Puan chieftains brought forth. They were herded into the space between the council table and the chiefs of the other tribes, their chains clinking and rattling. They would not look at the eyes of the chiefs, but stood there bedraggled, their legs encrusted with dried mud, looking very much, George noted with satisfaction, like a parcel of criminals. The assembled chiefs murmured and looked at them with disdain or pity.

He had their irons removed, and made them sit where they were, but would not permit them to speak. He stood in front of the table, and began a speech directed at them, which the whole assembly could hear.

"Your design was obvious to me," he said, his voice sharp with contempt. "A bird from your country has whispered in my ear; it said that all people believe you ought to die, which you yourselves must agree you deserve. I considered that, but on thinking of the meanness of your attempt to catch a bear sleeping, I decided that you're only old women, too mean to be killed by a Big Knife.

"Still, you ought to be punished for putting on breechclouts like men. Those shall be taken from you, and you'll be provisioned to go home, as women don't know how to hunt. As long as you remain here you'll be treated like squaws."

Abruptly he turned from the Puans, leaving them like that, and told the other chiefs that he was ready to resume the council. "You've talked among yourselves more than a day," he said. "You've considered the truths I have spoken, and I am ready to hear truths from your own mouths."

But before they could answer, the Puan chieftains, seeming very agitated, begged his attention. One came forward and began a speech, which George would not permit to be interpreted for himself. Then some other Meadow Indians came forward; a chieftain separated from them and laid a peace pipe on the table. He said through the interpreter that the Puans admittedly had intended to kidnap the Big Knife, but only because it had been put in their heads by bad men who had come among them from Michillimackinac. He said the Puans hoped the Big Knives would pity and spare their women and children and, as their own lives had been spared when they deserved to lose them, they were in hopes that peace would be granted them as it was to the other tribes here. George turned from him, went to the table, picked up his sword, smashed the peace pipe, and swept the pieces off onto the ground with the blade, then put the

sword back where it had been. As astonished murmur went up
from the crowd. "Tell him," George said to the interpreter, "that
I did not make war upon them, and that the Long Knife does
not treat with squaws. Tell them that when the Big Knives come
upon such people as them in the woods they might shoot them
as they would shoot wolves to keep them from eating the deer,
but would never boast about it."

Again he turned to the other chiefs, dismissing the Puans,
who began having a very earnest conversation among themselves. He was preparing to hear the old chief again when there
was movement among the Puans, and two young braves advanced grimly, sat on the ground nearly at his feet, and flung
blankets over their heads. Though George did not know what to
make of this, the crowd of Indians apparently knew what it
meant, and they began an excited whispering among themselves. Then two of the Puan chieftains came forward, holding
another peace pipe between them. One of them again told the
story about the bad influence of the Michillimackinac Indians.
Then he said, "We offer these two braves for your tomahawk,
as atonement for our guilt, and hope that we will be reconciled
with the Long Knife after this sacrifice." Again they offered the
peace pipe, which he refused again, but this time did not break.
He was almost speechless at this. In a tone just slightly warmer,
he told them to go and sit down. He stood looking down at the
two mounds of blanket at his feet. Dear God, he thought, they
must think the threat of the tomahawk hangs over their whole
nation and that nothing will save them but to get peace before
they leave here. The two braves remained kneeling under their
blankets, but after a time began raising the edges to peer out, as
if trying to see what was taking so long. Every person present
seemed to be in a suspended state, waiting to see what he would
do. The silence was broken only by the buzz of flies.

George turned to face the huddled forms now, and looked at
them for a long while, marveling that neither blanket was even
slightly trembling. He had been intending ultimately to make
peace with the Puans as well as with the others, but had not expected anything so extreme as this, and suddenly he felt so
moved by this display of courageous resignation that he reached
down, flung off the blankets, and told them to stand up. The
two rose slowly, trying to conceal the relief, the incredulity, the
joy that was flickering through their stolid faces. As if their
faces gave him the words to say, he turned to the chiefs, who

were stirring and breathing deeply; he began loudly now, his voice resonant with emotion:

"I have always chosen to believe that there are such men as these among all nations; I am happy to witness that there are at least two among these people." He turned to the two young men again, and said, "Only such men as you make true chiefs of a nation. I like to treat with such men, and so it is through you that the Long Knife grants peace and friendship to your people." He took one hand of each and raised them high, and said, "I take your hands as my brothers and as chiefs of your nations, and I expect everybody present will acknowledge you as such!" He led them to his own officers and had them shake hands, then to the French officers, where this was repeated, then to the few Spaniards, Vigo among them, who had come across the river again, and lastly to the Indians, who had all risen to greet them as chiefs as surely as if they had been so designated by their own elders. The air was full of cordiality now; and Father Gibault looked like a saint transported. Carried away by the happy outcome of this show, and it did seem like a fine show to him, George had his guard fire a rifle salute into the air in their honor. And as bits of elm leaf and twigs showered down on the assembly, he could not see an Indian whose smile did not match his own.

The whole event had come off splendidly, even though he had not planned it himself, and he decided that whoever had planted the crime in the minds of the Puans, the Great Spirit must have been working for him in the background.

THE NEXT DAY DAWNED COOL AND FRESH. THE INDIANS KINDLED A council fire a few yards beyond the elm trees, thus symbolically moving the proceedings onto their ground. There was more than the usual ceremony. George sat at the table, which had been moved out also, and awaited the business at hand.

The old chief advanced to the table and picked up the white belt of peace. He was flanked by two other chiefs, one bearing the pipe of peace and one carrying a stone bowl of coals with which to kindle it. This fire was presented first to Heaven, then to all the spirits, with an invocation for them to witness what was to be concluded.

The elder turned then to address the throng of Indians.

"We ought to be thankful," he said to them, in a voice incredibly deep and rich for one of his age, "that the Great Spirit has taken pity on us, and cleared the sky, and opened our ears and hearts so that we can hear and receive the truth." Then he turned to George and continued:

"Chief of the Big Knife, we have paid attention to what the Great Spirit put into your heart to say to us.

"We believe the whole of what you say to be the truth, as the Long Knife does not speak like the other white men we have heard. We see plainly that the British have deceived us with lies and have not told us the truth. Some of our old men have always told us this, and now we believe that the Big Knives are in the right, as the British have forts in our country.

"We understand now that if the British grow stronger in our country, they might treat us as badly as they have treated the Big Knives. Thus we the red people believe that we ought to help the Big Knives. With a sincere heart we have taken up the belt of peace, and spurned the other way. We are determined to hold fast the belt of peace, and we will have no doubt of your friendship, because of your way of speaking. There is no room for suspicion."

George felt a rich gratitude welling up in his breast, and nodded. The old chief continued:

"We will therefore call in all our warriors, and cast the tomahawk into the river, where it can never be found again, and we will suffer no more bad birds to pass through our land to disquiet our women and children. We will be cheerful to smooth the roads for our brothers the Big Knives whenever you come to see us.

"And also we will send to all our friends and let them know the good talk that we have heard here and what was done, and advise them to come and listen to the same. We invite you to send men among us with your eyes to see for yourself how we keep this word." The old man drew himself up even taller, and raised his voice, now quavering with emotion, to conclude:

"We are men, and we strictly adhere to all that has been said at this great fire that the Great Spirit has kindled here at Cahokia for the good of all people." Wave after wave of thrilling shivers swept through George, and he choked back an impending flood of tears.

The pipe then was rekindled and presented to all the spirits to be witnesses; the ceremony was concluded with handshakes all about; a great, harmonious murmur of conversation began, and in every Indian face now, with one exception, there glowed an expression of openness and affection.

That exception was Big Gate. Instead of moving among the

milling chiefs and white officers, he stood exactly where he had been throughout the councils, and stared expressionless at George.

"Excuse me, Joseph," George said to Bowman, who was all but hopping about with happiness now. "I think I'm going to have to give this fellow Big Gate some particular attention, or we're going to lose him." Striding through the hubbub, George advanced on Big Gate and stopped before him. His eyes passed quickly over the bloody belt and the British flag on Big Gate's breast.

"I know you," George said. "You're Lajes, the warrior famous as Big Gate."

The chief's short black eyebrows lifted almost imperceptibly as he found himself being addressed at last directly by the Long Knife. He nodded, his narrow lips still compressed.

"I have not spoken to Big Gate sooner," George said, "because among white people it is customary that when officers meet in this manner, even if they are enemies, they treat each other with greater respect than they do the ordinary people, and esteem each other the more in proportion to the exploits each has performed against other's nation."

Big Gate nodded again, his face still stolid even though his black eyes were virtually dancing in response to this tribute.

"And therefore," George added, "I invite you to dine with me in my house at a special council of the Big Knives."

Big Gate nodded gravely. And they parted without shaking hands.

BIG GATE ARRIVED AT THE HOUSE THAT EVENING AT SUNSET WITH A guard party of four warriors, whom he ordered to wait outside. George ushered him into a room where a dozen of his officers and subalterns were seated at two parallel tables. He introduced Big Gate to each of the officers, who rose in turn to face him, but there was no handshaking. George started to lead him to his place at the center of one of the tables, but Big Gate stopped in the middle of the floor. He was now definitely the center of attention. George moved away to let him claim the entire floor.

Big Gate struck his breast. "I am a warrior," he said. "You know I have been a warrior from the days of my youth."

He reached up, grasped the bloody belt at his neck and snatched it away, breaking it, and threw it to the floor. Then he ripped the British flag from his breast and threw that down beside the belt. George swallowed a smile. He was beginning to get the drift of the performance.

Big Gate now proceeded to rip open his red coat. Brass buttons sprayed about the room and rolled into corners. He stripped off the coat and threw it on the floor also, and now stood naked except for his breechclout and moccasins, his lithe physique gleaming.

"Big Gate delights in war," he pronounced loudly. "The English told me that the Big Knives were in the wrong. I have been to war against the Big Knives three times, and I was ready to go again. But I said instead, no, I will rest myself a while and come and see what sort of people the Big Knives are and how they talk.

"Now," he said, "I have been here for days and I have listened to everything that was said, and now I am convinced that the British are liars. They are wrong and the Big Knives are right! As a man and a warrior I will not fight in a wrong cause.

"Now I have flung away the bloody clothes the British gave me . . ." With that he began stamping on the discarded flag and apparel, and finally gave them a mighty kick which sent them across the room. The American officers kept their faces as straight as they could.

"From this day," the Indian said, "I am a Big Knife!" He stepped over to George then, and shook his hand, and all the officers erupted in cheering and applause. The chief went around both tables now, wreathed in a huge smile, shaking the hand of every officer. They laughed and praised him, and the room was full of a merry commotion.

"Captain McCarty," George cried, "our guest is quite naked. Would you fetch him something elegant from the village, please!"

The captain returned within minutes, having procured somewhere a suit gaudy with gold lace, which Big Gate put on, to the approbation of the whole company. He was easily now the finest spectacle at the table, and, exuberant in his new dignity, he ordered his warriors to come in and wait upon him. The food was good; rum flowed freely; the party was lively and continued far into the night, with this fancy new brother proving to be the merriest reveler in the house.

After the dinner, Big Gate made one more bid for special attention, saying that he wished to have a private conversation with Colonel Clark. He pointed to an adjoining room, which had a large window opening onto the street. George, though

somewhat drunk by now, became suspicious that his new
brother intended perhaps to stab him and flee through the window. But he saw no way to deny the interview, and so went in
with him and the interpreter, and closed the door. He waited,
poised, ready to fight if necessary. The officers grew quiet in
the dining room, and waited near the door, ready to burst in at
the first cry or sound of a scuffle.

"My brother," Lajes began. "I can tell you much about the
state of the defense of Detroit. I am free to go there and do
what I please. I can get any information from there that you
need. If you doubt that I can, I will prove it to you by going
there and getting for you a British scalp or a prisoner, and
bringing it back within forty days."

George relaxed. It was obvious that Big Gate simply wanted
an opportunity to prove himself further, this time for his new allies.

"I will be happy to have any information you can bring me
about Detroit," George said, "as I am somewhat interested in
that place. But we do not want the Indians to fight and kill for
us, but just to sit still and look on. I want you by no means to
kill anyone for us. But you may bring me news, or any prisoner
who might be full of information, if you can get one handily.
But do not hurt him; it's beneath us to treat prisoners ill."

The good cheer resumed when George and Big Gate returned
to the dining room. George gave Big Gate a medal and wrote
out for him a commission as a captain of the Big Knives, all of
which brought tears to the eyes of the stoic chief.

And when he departed into the night, being steered and kept
upright by his warriors, the Americans sent him off with three
cheers and gave him a final salute by firing their pistols out the
windows and doors into the night sky, waking the entire town
once again.

17

A PUFF OF WHITE SMOKE BLOSSOMED FROM THE PARAPET OF THE
little Spanish fort on the bluff and drifted away in the breeze. A
moment later the boom of the cannon rolled across the caramel-
colored river water to the Americans' boat.

George was sitting in the stern with Captain Bowman and
Lieutenant Jean Girault, a young import-house clerk from
Kaskaskia, whom George had made his official interpreter because of his command of the English, French, and Spanish
tongues.

"Well, now," said Bowman. "There's our salute."

Another cloud of smoke and another report rolled over the
river.

"Rather extravagant with their powder, aren't they?" observed George. "I would have preferred they give it to us in
kegs."

"They're terribly excited about your visit," said the slim, dark
Girault. "Monsieur Vigo told me so."

The cannon boomed again. The ten pairs of oars rose drib-
bling, dipped, rose, dribbled, and the boat crawled at an almost
imperceptible pace across the broad, sunflashing surface of the
great river. It was so broad, one had the impression of crossing
a bay instead of a river. As the cannon sounded a fourth time,
George gazed up the river and wondered about its sources. He
had a general notion of its origins around the huge lakes in the
north, whose routes were well known to the traders of several
nations, but he was most intrigued by reports of the huge
muddy tributary, called Missouri by the Indians, which poured
into it from the west a few leagues above St. Louis. He had
heard legends of endless plains, evergreen forest, deserts, and
sky-scraping mountains lying to the west, of areas more vast

198

even than all the half-explored lands east of the Mississippi.
These legends came from the Indians, as no known white man
had ever ventured far into those awesome distances. The Indians told of places where hot water shot out of the ground into
the sky, places where the ground was blood-red, places where
perpendicular towers of stone a mile high jutted from the plains,
places where not a blade of grass grew, and places where one
could ride for weeks and see nothing but grass. And somewhere
beyond it all, it was said, the continent ended at the Pacific
Ocean.

Here in this Mississippi valley, George fancied he could feel
the immense, tilted tables of the land, sloping gradually upward
to the far eastern mountains that he had crossed, and upward
also in the opposite direction toward the western mountains
which were said to be there. Down this river flows the drainage
of the entire continent, I suspect, George thought. God permit
me someday when these duties of war are over to follow those
western rivers and learn whence they come.

The reverie was broken by still another cannon shot, louder
now, and the faint, breeze-borne timbre of human voices from
the nearing western shore. He could see the Spaniards and the
west-bank French now, tiny and colorful, crowded on the wharf
at the foot of the village.

"Look perty hospitable to me," Bowman said with a smile.
"How long d'you reckon we can stay, George?"

"Not beyond two or three days, I think. There's a lot of Indian business left for us back in Cahokia. Weeks of it, I expect.
Mister Black Bird will show up any day, and I wouldn't care to
keep him waiting."

"Yeah. Sure hope he's as jolly a feller as ol' Big Gate. I ain't
had so much fun since Logan's gran'ma boiled a tit in th' cook
pot."

George chuckled and shook his head. Jean Girault looked at
Bowman for a moment with his mouth agape, then exclaimed,
"*Nom de ciel!* Did that really happen?"

"Might of," Bowman laughed.

"But how can one laugh?" Girault exclaimed. "It must have
been utter agony."

"*Udder* agony," said George, and Bowman nearly rolled into
the bilges.

LIEUTENANT GOVERNOR DE LEYBA HIMSELF, WITH A SQUAD OF IN-
fantrymen sweating at attention in their uniforms, met George

and his officers on the wharf. The entire population of the town seemed to have crowded down to the river's edge to see the Big Knives, and gazed in wonderment at them, at their extraordinary stature, their ruddy faces, their fierce but merry demeanor. Most of the officers were still in buckskins, though freshly scrubbed and clean-shaven; only George and four of the others had been fitted for uniforms in Kaskaskia. De Leyba appraised George's magnificent military appearance, greeted him with a proper Spanish salute, then a bow with smartly clicking heels, and finally gave in to his emotions and threw his arms around him in a French-style embrace. Flowers rained on the Americans as they filed off the wharf to the lively rattle of trap drums.

The Spaniard had brought down saddled horses to accommodate the American party, and George whistled in admiration at the sight of them. He mounted a glossy black warhorse of high spirit, and de Leyba made note of George's skill in establishing for the beast's edification who would be boss. Obviously this Virginian was as good a horseman as he was a trail runner, a fact which pleased de Leyba as much as anything else.

Another small but dashing uniformed Spanish officer rode forward. "Colonel Clark," said de Leyba. "Perhaps you remember Tenente Francisco de Cartabona, commandant of militia. He was with us at Cerré's ball."

"Very pleased, sir," said George, taking the soft but strong hand. "I have the greatest respect for militia, that being what my boys are themselves." The lieutenant bowed his head. The horses milled and pranced, impatient to go; the crowd maintained a cheerful uproar, laughing, shouting, and gawking.

"If we may, now," de Leyba said, "first a tour of the fort, and then an entertainment at my house." And the entourage clopped up the cobbled streets, between rows of neat stone houses. The sun was low in the west now and the streets seemed full of clean blue shadow. The procession wound upward until it was atop the bluff and in sunlight again. George turned in his saddle and looked back across the river to the far shore, to the distant white specks of Cahokia's houses, to the lake by the Indian camps, to the wide floodplain and the purple bluffs of the Illinois, that land which he and his little troop of rustics had so swiftly won and occupied. Bowman, riding beside him, watched his face, gazed back over the river himself, then looked back at George.

"I know what you're thinkin', George," he said softly. "And I'm just as confounded as y'rself. Believe me, I am."

* * *

TERESA DE LEYBA HAD CROSSED HERSELF AND JUMPED UP TO LOOK out the window five times already this afternoon, whenever she had heard hoofbeats on the road below. Now she heard them again, many horses this time. Almost faint with fright and anxiety, she knelt and crossed herself once more, and went to the dormer casement just in time to see the mounted party arrive at the mounting blocks below.

There was a rosy-gold sunset glow enhancing the colors of the various uniforms. The grooms were moving out from the portico to take the horses in hand; the last members of the column were drawing up and preparing to dismount; there was a swirling movement of dancing horses in the area below, and a hubbub of cheery voices. But Teresa's eyes, as if guided, immediately fell to the center foreground, upon one figure astride a nervous black warhorse; her heart suddenly frolicked in her breast and she clapped her hand over it as if to hold it in place. Blood rushed to her face.

He sat there, not ten feet below her window, between her brother and Tenente de Cartabona, controlling the great animal by the reins in his left hand without seeming even to pay attention to the task. The evening sunlight flamed in his sunbleached red hair and eyebrows, and modeled the hard, sharp bones in his brown face. He was looking up at the front of the house. And his eyes, those glittering dark falcon's eyes that had haunted her nightmares for more than a month, were full upon her. He had found her face in the window.

Her thighs began to quiver. Mother of God, she thought, Señor Vigo was right about him.

And now, but in a different way, she was more afraid of him even than she had been.

THERE, CENTERED IN THE OPEN WINDOW A FEW FEET ABOVE HIM AS if in a picture frame, was the face which even the whirlwind of recent events had not been able to sweep out of his memory. That delicate pale oval, those immense, frightened eyes. A shiver began in his scalp, cascaded down his back, through his loins, and to his knees. The noises close around him, the very presence of men and horses, seemed to slide away, leaving only himself and that face up in the window.

Tenente Francisco de Cartabona turned to speak to the colonel of the Virginians, to welcome him to the headquarters of the Spanish empire in Upper Louisiana. He saw the colonel looking up as if thunderstruck, and followed his gaze to the dormer window. He saw there Teresa, his own heart's only serious object, her eyes momentarily locked on those of the Virginian.

The little lieutenant felt his words stopped in his throat by a shock of despair.

JOSEPH BOWMAN, CHEWING A PIECE OF SPICED DUCK, SUDDENLY winced in pain. "Damnation!" he cried, drawing the attention of the thirty people who were seated along the sides of the great table.

"Watch your language," cautioned George, who sat several feet away at the head of the table.

"What is it, *capitán*?" queried Governor de Leyba, sitting at the other end.

With elaborate grimaces, Bowman worked his tongue around in his mouth, pushed something forward to his lips, and then spat it into the palm of his hand. George rolled his eyes toward the ceiling at the manners of his second-in-command. "This," said Bowman, glowering at the small metal pellet in his palm.

"Ah, I am so sorry!" explained de Leyba. The ladies were looking all around Bowman but not at him, hiding their smiles behind palpitating fans. "It's a piece of scattershot," the governor explained. "My hunters bagged these fowl in the marsh just yesterday. Expressly for you. One must bite gingerly, *capitán*. Forgive us."

"Scattershot?" exclaimed Bowman, laying the pellet on the linen beside his plate. "Why, that ain't hardly sportin'. Now, our boys'd bring 'em down with a rifleball, if it was us."

"On the wing?" said de Leyba, a mocking but good-natured smile tilting across his face.

"Heck, yeah," said Bowman, putting another piece of the bird in his mouth and masticating it very carefully. "On th' wing, sure. I always say, it ain't sportin' to kill a sittin' duck. 'Less he's bigger 'n you."

George grinned, shaking his head. "Joseph, I question the propriety of boasting when you're a guest."

"Sorry, George, but you know it's true. You've seen 'em shoot often enough." Bowman washed the duck down with another long draught of wine, which he had been pouring down like water.

"Well, then, if you say it, *capitán*, I take it to be so," said de Leyba. "But how remarkable! And so, here's to American marksmanship." He raised his glass and all drank. George, his own head swirling a little, remembered with a rush of nostalgia the turkey that his brother Edmund had decapitated with a rifle ball for the Clark family table the winter before, and opened his mouth to speak of it. Then he remembered his own admonition about boastfulness a moment ago, and held his tongue. It might be a bit gruesome for the ladies to hear anyway, he thought; and at the notion of protecting the ears of the exquisite Teresa from his own words, his heart skipped again. It had been behaving that way the entire evening. He was astounded by his feelings. One instant he felt like a hero, the next like a bumpkin.

He had been trying not to look too long or too often at her. He had the strange notion that he needed to protect her from the hunger of his own eyes. And each time his gaze would stray to her, she would be flushing, all along that sublime long neck and to her flaming ears, stirring the air with that dainty fan, which she seemed to hold more this evening than she did her fork and spoon. And each time he glanced at her, he had an instinctive certainty that she had just dropped her eyes from his own face. She seemed to be as agitated as he was.

There were musicians now moving into the next room. It meant that he soon would be, no doubt, swooping around the room with this fragile, timorous creature inside the curve of his arm.

His hand shook as he lifted his wineglass again.

Dear God, he thought. To touch her!

TENENTE DE CARTABONA, SEATED DIRECTLY ACROSS THE TABLE from Teresa, had not failed to notice the glances that passed between her and the Virginian. The lieutenant had not eaten anything either. He could not swallow. He was so heartsick he had not heard a half of the dinner conversation. He had prayed that the American colonel would make one of the awful gaffes that some of his oafish aides, like that Bowman, had made, so that Teresa with her perfect sensibilities would at last detect some flaw in him. But it seemed to be no use hoping that way. The damnable fellow seemed somehow, even in the primitive and churlish society of the American Colonies, to have acquired all the courtly graces.

De Cartabona's only immediate hope lay in the sight of the musicians' arrival. The fellow's as big as an ox, he thought. Surely he'll clump about and make a hopeless ass of himself.

The lieutenant's hopes lasted no longer than the first *cuadrilla*. The American moved with as much grace and ease as anybody de Cartabona had ever seen. The Spaniard's heart clenched each time Teresa's tiny white hand was lifted by the colonel's huge tan one, every time their wondering eyes met, every time that telling blush he had so long studied arose in her neck, every time she lowered her lashes before the colonel's adoring gaze, every time, especially, she swirled close to de Cartabona and was unable to meet his anguished eyes.

TERESA FELT AS IF SHE WERE A BUTTERFLY BEING BLOWN ABOUT IN the room by a warm zephyr. It was a thrilling sensation, but one not altogether good; it was frightening to have so little control over herself. The Virginian's hands and arms were as hard as steel, but warm and gentle enough, it seemed, that he might handle a butterfly without dusting its wings. Indeed, she felt a more palpable force from his eyes than from his hands. He seemed to be guiding her more with his intense, desperate will than with his physical body. He spoke no words, perhaps because he was, as was she, afraid any words would sound absurd.

Now and then, looking up from his broad chest to his chiseled face, she would recall the dread he had caused in her that first night, and she would be frightened again. Even the adoration in his eyes could not dispel that odd premonitory dread. In some strange way, it precipitated even worse fears, deep in the unfamiliar recesses of her inner self.

The night deepened. They drifted onward in the stream of music.

Governor de Leyba and his wife swept past the young couple and turned their heads to watch them go by.

"Maria," he hissed excitedly in her ear. "Look at them! Who could have foreseen this?"

She searched his face with her wise, cloudy, pain-darkened eyes, and he loved her keenly.

"Anyone," she said.

SEÑOR FRANCISCO VIGO SWUNG BY, GRINNING, EXUBERANTLY steering a dark lady who stood a head taller than he. The lady glanced enviously at Teresa.

Vigo winked at Teresa.

And Teresa flushed again at the sight of that sly, devilish wink, and felt perspiration trickle down the bare skin under her arm inside her gown.

He'll smell me! she thought, almost in a panic. I must go up and wash!

George stood near a table, waiting, drinking sherry. The musicians had stopped to rest. Teresa had curtseyed, ducked away from him with widened eyes, and disappeared up the stairs, followed soon by her sister-in-law. George was anxious, unable to imagine how he might have offended her.

Fernando de Leyba approached, filled a glass with the sherry, and touched it to George's glass. "Why, you seem upset, my dear colonel. What is it?"

"I—I don't know," George replied, glancing toward the stairs. "Is she all right, d'you suppose?"

"Who?" the governor asked, his lips pursed in a smile around his own joke.

It struck George then, and he coughed up an unexpected laugh, almost a hiccough. He raised his hand toward the staircase, then dropped it; his mouth opened and then closed and he said nothing.

"She'll be down in a moment," de Leyba laughed, giving George a reassuring squeeze on the elbow. "Womanly things, you understand." He shook his head. "Nay, on the other hand, don't try." He, too, seemed a little drunk. "Listen," he went on then, conspiratorially, "I told Maria to ask her to play the *guitarra* for us after the dancing. Just a little recitation. Would you like that? She's quite accomplished."

George was enchanted at the thought that one so beautiful to see might actually be capable of bringing beauty in other ways. "I'd love it," he breathed. He was unbelievably stirred inside.

"Of course she'll be reluctant," said de Leyba. "But she will do whatever I suggest." Suddenly his eyes brimmed. "My dear Don Jorge!" he exclaimed, his voice suddenly thick. "Somehow—somehow—I do believe this is one of the finest moments I've ever enjoyed. In a lifetime of fine moments!" He swallowed. "I'm so glad you—you and your Americans—are here! I'm so pleased that Teresa likes you . . ." He paused, as if he should not have said such a thing.

"She does, you think?"

De Leyba laughed. "She does, I think!"

"Then, Governor, I do believe this is one of the finest moments in *my* life!"

It was shortly before midnight. Teresa sat on a low chair, her head tilted in concentration over the instrument. She had played a gavotta, several minuets, a slow fandango, and now was performing a passacaglia. She had named each piece in a small voice before bending again over the *guitarra*. George understood none of the words, and vaguely wished he did. The violinist stood behind her, playing accompaniment on some of the pieces. Her nails plucked clear, sharp notes out of the higher strings, melodies of marvelous complexity, and her thumb stroked deep, soft-edged counterpoints from the lower strings. It seemed impossible that so much music could come from one small instrument and only two hands. The guests stood or sat in a semicircle about her, rapt. Candles on the walls bathed the room in a soft light, reflecting sometimes off the polished soundboard of the instrument. George had never in his life, even in the most enthralling moments of forest silence, felt so transported. The music, the light, the presence of these people, the vision of this girl playing—nay, caressing—the instrument, flooded over all his senses, and her agile, graceful fingers seemed to be lifting the melodies directly from his heart.

She finished the passacaglia; palms patterned approval; voices cooed and uttered constrained *bravas*.

"In a moment, a prelude of de Murcia," she murmured, looking once at George and then bending to tune the strings. George sensed someone beside him, then felt a hand on his shoulder. It was Bowman, who had just come forward and knelt beside him.

George reached up and patted the hand. Bowman squeezed his shoulder.

"By Heaven," Bowman said in a hushed voice. "I never thought I'd see it, but I do believe the Long Knife is reduced to helplessness."

George nodded, and blinked. The candlelight blurred and glinted through tears. His heart filled the room. He could say nothing.

Teresa again started to play.

TERESA QUIT PLAYING AFTER AN HOUR, THEN CURTSEYED, MURmured her thanks for the applause, and made another of her disappearances up the stairs, carrying the beautiful little *guitarra* by its neck. George was still entranced. He went to the table, decanted another bottle of sherry, looked toward the stairwell, and wished she would hurry back down. He had been trying to bring himself to the point of conversing with her, and now was at a loss for something to do with himself. He did not want to talk to anybody else; it was no time for words.

It was extremely hot in the room; he felt the humidity of his own body in his clothes, and so was drawn toward the wide doors which opened off the ballroom onto the terrace. Carrying his glass, he slipped swiftly toward that door and out into the cool, damp air, under the stars, in the cacophony of cricket song. For a moment he took deep breaths and let the fresh air carry off the fog of his muddled thoughts.

Suddenly, though he had not really heard a sound, he felt that he was not alone. He turned to his right. There, dimly visible in the light from the door, stood Tenente de Cartabona, wild-eyed, his face contorted in a pitiful mask of drunken rage. He said something harsh in Spanish, words which George did not understand but interpreted nonetheless as the invitation to a duel. He had been observing the lieutenant's behavior out of the corner of his eye during the evening.

But even before George could react, there was a breath of movement in the darkness, and de Cartabona found himself standing between two tall, smelly men in buckskins, his arms pinioned behind him, a knife-point pricking his throat.

George shook his head and grinned. He stepped closer to de Cartabona then, and spoke softly. "Can you understand me, Lieutenant?" The Spaniard nodded. His eyes were bulging in terror. "Now, hear me," George said, keeping his voice low so that the guests inside would not be attracted to this awkward scene. "I reckon I know what's vexin' you. But at this time we can't permit ourselves the indulgence of personal conflicts. There are things going on that are beyond our individual feelings. Quite plainly, man, we can't be spared. Neither of us. None of us. Are you hearing me?" The lieutenant nodded again. "If there comes a time," George continued, "when the two of us are expendable, then I shall be honored to give you satisfaction, and by any means you may choose. Until then, I most strongly recommend that you keep the interests of your governor and your most Catholic Majesty at heart. That means, sir, staying out of my way."

The lieutenant apparently was not stupid. He nodded again. George tilted his head and the guards released the Spaniard. They vanished, leaving only the sour smell of old sweat, and de Cartabona smoothed his clothes.

"Do I have it on your honor?" George asked, extending his hand. After a pause, the lieutenant took it. His chin was quivering, his eyes were wet with mortification and fury.

"Until we are no longer obligated, señor. As for Teresa . . ."

"Not a word on her, by God!" George withdrew his hand and raised it as a thick fist under the lieutenant's nose, and de Cartabona felt the proximity of the bodyguards again. He bowed abruptly, and ambled with bruised dignity back toward the door, wiping his face with a handkerchief and composing his features as he went. His shoulder bumped the doorpost; he staggered, then recovered his balance and steered himself into the candleglow. George watched him go in, then waved his woodsmen back into the darkness. He took a deep breath, jaw muscles working, then discovered the sherry glass he still held in his left hand. He drained if off and eased himself into a chair, not seeing, in the window above him, the silhouette of Teresa.

She stood, drawn close to the edge of the casement, steadying herself with one hand braced on it, the other in a fist over her mouth, and looked down at the top of the Virginian's head. Her brain was throbbing; her breast felt hollow; her mouth was dry. Prickling sensations raced all over the skin of her body.

She had been drawn to the window by the vicious rasp of Tenente de Cartabona's challenge. She had stood there watching the deadly minute, the knife of one of the Americans appearing at Francisco's throat. She had been certain that she would see his blood spilled. Then the instant of threat had simply ended, had dissipated into the night as if it had not really happened. Teresa felt her blood draining out of her head and shoulders now, and knelt by the windowsill to keep from swooning. She stayed there till the dizziness receded and was followed by a great weariness. She remembered the dancing, during which she had become so strongly and strangely aroused, aroused in the way she suspected a woman becomes aroused, not a girl; it was the first time she had felt anything quite like it. Not even during the summer's various dances and outings with the suave de Cartabona had it been quite this thing.

But even the excitement of dancing with the Virginian had not dispelled her fear that there was something lethal, something dreadfully hard and keen-edged about him, and so long as she had felt that fear, she had imagined herself still free of him— still able to resist his magnetic pull.

Only when she had looked up from her serenade and seen his face softened, transformed, only then had her heart melted into his; only then had she realized that she was fatefully and inexorably *for* him. She had rushed up the stairs after the recital, her heart going wild. She had put the *guitarra* away in its velvet-lined case, had soaked a cloth in cool water and pressed it to her burning neck, her cheeks, her brow, her shoulders. And then she had heard the voices below the window. And she had looked down on that scene which, once again, had seemed to confirm her fear of his killing edge.

Thus, now, she was doubly terrified. She was certain that there would be love, a binding, permanent love, between her and the American. And she knew, too, that she would always be in fear, somehow, of its consequences.

It's not that he would hurt me, she thought, trying to explain to herself this baffling ambivalence of her emotions. But he will be killed. Or lost from me somehow. With a man like that, fate is in charge.

I need to rest, she thought, putting both hands on the windowsill to rise. All this is fantasy because I'm tired.

She had worn herself out for days, dreading his arrival. She had lost sleep. She had been in his presence for all these tense hours this evening; she had been enervated by his vibrant attention to her, as if he had been drawing off her energies by the power of his senses. And then the terror of that minute's confrontation on the terrace below.

Francisco, she thought. Dear little Francisco. Such a fool you are.

"Ah, Colonel Clark! There you are! We've been looking for our honored guest. Eh, Vigo?" Teresa peered down over the windowsill. Her brother and Señor Vigo had strolled out onto the terrace, the American captain Bowman with them. They all carried full glasses. A servant followed them out, bearing a tray with clay pipes and a tobacco humidor, which he put on the table as they all drew chairs close to Colonel Clark.

"Getting some air," said the colonel's resonant voice. "This has been a night to remember. But thirty people do steam up a room."

"You were, ahem, were you conversing with Tenente de Cartabona?" inquired de Leyba. "I, ah, saw him come in. Then he excused himself and left. A bit too much drink and excitement, I suspect."

"We chatted. About little matters. Yes. A pleasant laddie."

How lightly he can speak of it, thought Teresa. Why, he isn't going to tell on Francisco!

"Well, my dear friend," de Leyba went on. He was being his most expansive, his most cheerful and charming self. Despite the warning of her conscience, Teresa remained stooped by the window, eavesdropping, rationalizing that she still felt too dizzy to get up.

"Señor Vigo tells me," de Leyba continued, "such marvelous reports of your dealings with the Indians. I nearly wept at the tale of the two young braves you spared."

"That!" the American laughed. "Aye! Oh, of course I had no intention of killing them. But they set the stage for a real dramatic show, didn't they? Ha! There's nothing like 'em for theatrics. And those two are strutting on the stage now, let me tell ye that! Pair o' nabobs they are. One of 'em came to me just yesterday, clothed in all the dignity of some old sagamore. He told me he had changed his name to Two Lives, to commemorate the occasion when I gave him a second life to live. Such a people!"

Vigo laughed. A whiff of tobacco smoke came in the window to the kneeling Teresa.

"They got a habit," came the slurring voice of Captain Bowman, "of naming themselves after occasions. Take that fellow Big Gate. Shot a soldier at the gate of Fort Detroit, and that's been his monicker ever since. Big Gate. Ha, ha! I ain't had so much fun since Logan's gran'ma . . ."

"Ahem! Right you are, Joseph. So much for that, eh?"

There was a thoughtful pause, filled with contented *hms*, sighs, and the screeching of night creatures. More tobacco smoke wafted into the humid night air. "Been a-puffin' a lot of this stuff lately, ain't we, George?" said Bowman's voice.

"Aye. And better get used to it, too. There's still a mighty passel of Indians we haven't parleyed with yet."

"As I've heard it, you've accomplished all this," said de Leyba, "without shedding a drop of blood!"

"Yes!" exclaimed Vigo's voice. "Isn't that the most remarkable thing!"

"It's real good fortune," said the American. "It makes me feel," he added with a pause, "that God's on our side."

There was more stillness, then de Leyba asked a question that Teresa knew was much on his mind; she had heard him discuss it often with military men. "Have you ever killed a man, Colonel?"

There was a long pause. Teresa prayed that he would say "No."

"I have. If I hadn't, I wouldn't be among you now."

There was more silence. Teresa shuddered. She had danced

with a man who had killed men! Then her brother pursued it
further:

"By bullet?"

"Aye."

"By, um, ever by sword?"

"That, too, Governor. Once." The Virginian's voice was
growing tight and unpleasant. De Leyba's voice persisted now,
in a rather breathy tone:

"That must be an experience. What is it like? I mean to
say, how did you f—"

"I felt bloody awful! Now . . . Excellency, with due respect,
sir," his voice dropped, " . . . could we direct ourselves at more
pleasant matters? I should hate to see the spell of the night
smirched by morbid . . ."

"Yes, yes. Forgive me, my dear colonel. It's just that as a
commanding officer, I have never actually . . . you know . . ."
He gave an embarrassed little laugh. "Even Father Gibault has
killed an Indian, I hear. But I . . ."

"In these times, I'm afraid you'll get your opportunity," said
the Virginian.

"I imagine so," de Leyba said, his voice coming up to the
window dispirited, as if he were now ashamed of his questions.
Teresa, as she had never once been before, was embarrassed for
her brother. There were several sighs in the darkness below, a
throat was cleared, the clink of glasses. Finally the cheerful
voice of Vigo broke the pause:

"Believe us, George, what we all admire most is the *humanity* of your conduct. Bloody victories may make better history,
but in men's hearts . . ."

"Eh, well! I'm only adhering to the language of my orders.
Governor Henry wrote that it should all be performed 'under
the direction of the humanity that has hitherly distinguished
Americans.' I quote the order. I take my orders to the heart,
gentlemen. I'm here to stop the flow of blood, not to shed
more."

"And that's just amazin', George," came Bowman's voice,
full of awe and drunkenness, "when you think that just 'bout
every man in yer whole wall-eyed army joined up t' git bloody
revenge . . ."

"Maybe so, but they'll get it in my way. I don't hear 'em
clamoring for blood any, now."

"No, I don't either. They're happy as pigs in sh—" Bowman

checked himself this time. "They feel pretty good," he mumbled.

"Of course," said de Leyba, "I'm sure most military orders advise humanity. It's what happens once the blood-letting begins, as I understand it. I hope you can control them then, sir."

"I do too, Excellency. Discipline will tell. I figure I'm not fit to lead 'em unless I can make them go, or make them stop, whichever the occasion demands."

"Wonderful!" exclaimed Vigo in his oversize voice. "Most honorable!"

"Most honorable," George reiterated, his own words now slurring some from the drink, "because I have this feeling about it, y'see, that th' kind of a nation we raise out of this war will depend largely on how we do it. Gentlemen, if I may change the topic," he said, abruptly rising, swaying. "D'you know what's the inmost desire of my bosom?"

"Only ask," said de Leyba, his voice cheerful again.

"To hear more of that music! God, I never heard anything like that music! Where could . . . she be?" His voice broke. And Teresa, huddled beside the window of her room above, heard it.

She crossed her closed fists over her breast, squeezed her eyelids shut, and shivered, and rejoiced at that small, piteous catch in that beloved voice. It meant that she had not been out of his thoughts even in all this talk about war and duty.

I will play for him again, she thought. I will, if he wants me to!

TERESA DID PLAY FOR ANOTHER HALF HOUR, FILLING THE ROOM with beauty and magic. She was playing only for the American colonel now, and the melodies were lilting ballads and gentle nocturnes. It soon was obvious even to the dullest guests in the room that George Rogers Clark was her whole audience.

It was after two in the morning when de Leyba, mellow and affectionate, moderately drunk, and very pleased with his entertainment, began making arrangements for lodging the guests. Most, being soldiers, were satisfied to pile up three or four to a bedroom or stretch out on rows of pallets in the ballroom. Several of George's men laid out their bedrolls in the corridor outside the upstairs guest room where he slept. Señora de Leyba agreed to give up the master bedroom to several of the lady guests, and stationed herself on a settee in the anteroom in Teresa's bed-chamber, while the governor took to the daybed in his office downstairs.

George, coat off, sweat-soaked shirt cooling against his skin, talked briefly to his officers, staying at large in the house as long as possible, in hopes of encountering Teresa somewhere. But she was put away for the night.

He took a half-empty bottle of brandy to bed with him, drank it in an effort to stupefy his rioting fancies, blew out the lamp, and lay there tossing, imagining that Teresa's bed must be exactly on the other side of the thick wall beside him. He held his palm against that wall; he listened; all he could hear was the cough of Señora de Leyba and the snores of sleeping men outside his door. At one point he contrived a daring plan for slipping into Teresa's room and kneeling beside her bed to take her hand and hold it, and for some time he imagined that over and over.

But then in his mind's eye he saw his own guards, sleeping lightly, virtually stacked like cordwood in the hallway outside his door, and he saw Señora de Leyba, kept wakeful surely by her own pitiful coughing, encamped in Teresa's antechamber. No. Impossible, he thought. Only the worst sort of a fool would try it.

He chuckled at a thought. I can't go to Detroit because I haven't enough people. And I can't go to Teresa because I have too many.

He went to sleep at last, his head full of her face and her music.

HE AWAKENED TO A STREAM OF BRIGHT SUNLIGHT BLAZING ON THE white bedding around him, and the sound of girls' voices outside his window. He propped himself on an elbow, appalled that he had slept so late. Then Teresa's plangent voice drifted in the window with the others, and, in a wave, the whole idea of Teresa—her face, her eyes, her hands, her music, the scent of her hair and her soap—invaded him.

He lay for a moment looking at the square of pearly blue morning sky, recalling the night of sheer enchantment, smiling at the foolish, drunken fantasy to which he had fallen asleep—it was all so vague, now; he could just remember lying with his hand pressed against the wall—and listened to the voices, which were like music, ranging from lilting to grave tones as the conversation went on. Often as a youth he had lain awake in the sleeping loft of the Clark home in Virginia, listening to his little sisters chattering downstairs. But this was different. The words being Spanish and unintelligible to him, he was listening not to conversation but to the tones and timbres of voices, the inflections, and it was more like music than speech, rather, he thought, like the birdsongs of the morning.

In the distant blue a tiny dark speck cut diagonally across the rectangular opening of the window, slanting downward and away. It was a hawk. It vanished, leaving again only the unbroken blue.

He rose, naked, feeling rested and strong, stretched and loosened his arm and shoulder muscles, washed his face quickly with cold water poured from a flowered pitcher into a porcelain bowl, dried on a small towel—which smelled like Teresa's soap, he fancied, that subtle and indefinable blend of spice and flowers—then went closer to the window to look down on the green river valley, the rooftops of the village of St. Louis, some thatched, some of splitwood shakes, even a couple of red curved pantiles, and then into the garden and terrace where the young ladies of the de Leyba household were having what appeared to be their lessons. The little girls sat on a carved bench rather like a church pew, with an open book lying between them; Señora de Leyba, in a white, long-sleeved high-necked dress of white cotton, only those hollow eyes and phthisic hands hinting at her frail health, sat on a chair opposite them, now and then intercalating their recitations with her words, and Teresa, dressed likewise, sat slightly apart, her back to the squared yew hedge, concentrating on a square of white cloth stretched in a wooden frame she held in her lap, doing something to it with a needle. The sunlight shone on the cloth and bathed her face in a soft reflective glow, limning her throat and her long, delicate neck. As George watched her, watched her quiet absorption, he wondered whether he was in her thoughts. He preferred to believe that he was. It had seemed to him last night that his presence was as important to her as hers was to him.

Birds twittered everywhere, shot among the hedges, hopped forward on the still damp grass in the shady places, looking for late worms. From the other side of the house he heard the voice of one of his own lieutenants drilling the guard. At that moment one of the children apparently said something funny in her recitation; Teresa and the Señora broke into trilling laughter and the girls began squirming and giggling. Teresa looked up as she laughed, and her glance caught him staring at her; their eyes met for an instant, then bounced away from each other like billiard balls. When he returned his gaze to her she was bent further over her needlework in elaborate concentration, and there seemed to be high color on her sun-washed neck.

George stood there for another full five minutes, wickedly trying to will her to look up again, determined that he would not look away next time.

She, perhaps by an equally strong exercise of will, did not look up once.

GOVERNOR DE LEYBA, AFTER SHARING A SUMPTUOUS BREAKFAST of fresh fruits, melons, and thin strips of peppery fried venison with the American officers, announced cheerfully that he had arranged a contest of marksmanship for midday, on a meadow north of the town, saying he had to see the frontiersmen's skill which Bowman had so lauded at dinner the night before. The officers met this with cheers and laughter. George and de Leyba then went down to an arbor in the corner of the grounds, sat in the shade of grape leaves amid the drunken drone of bees, and discussed matters of trade and supply. Encouraged by de Leyba's cheerfulness and his repeated offers to help the Americans, George told him of the poverty of his expedition, its lack of gold, currency, or goods, and the frustrating silence that prevailed in the direction of Williamsburg. He told him how Pollock and Vigo and even Cerré were extending their credit on his behalf, and then described his own method of signing his name personally on all bills for the provisioning of his army. But, he added, even in this short time the traders were becoming leery of accepting his personal notes. "Quite frankly," he said, "I brought my army to this place with nought but the shirts on our backs, and I'm not sure how long I can keep us alive if money doesn't come soon from Virginia."

"My dear Don Jorge!" exclaimed de Leyba, reaching across the table and putting a hand on George's wrist. "Trust me, I would not stand by and watch a great soldier and friend expend his faculties on such a mundane matter as credit! My name, sir, as of this moment, is pledged to underwrite yours. I have absolute faith in you and in Don Patrick Henry, and in the state of Virginia which has mothered such men."

George swallowed hard. "I cannot ask for such a kindness, Excellency."

"You are not asking for it, my friend. It is my pleasure to offer it. I know Governor Galvez would condone it; I know his sympathies. And believe me, it is small recompense for the hope and inspiration you have brought to us in this corner of exile."

"I'll use it sparingly," George said. "My people need no extravagances. But they do eat heartily, as you've seen, and they're about as naked now as an army ever was."

"Yes," de Leyba said. "Now tell me, is it true that they shoot as Captain Bowman says?"

George grinned. "You'll see that for yourself this afternoon. Excellency," he added as they rose to leave the arbor, "I must mention one other matter that is very much in my thoughts now."

"What is it?" de Leyba asked, pretending not to know.

"As my leisure permits, and with your blessing, sir, I should like to call now and then on your sister, who is surely the most ... the most ..."

"Nothing could please me more," said de Leyba, clasping his hands behind his back and taking a deep breath of the fragrant air. "Yes." He looked at the mansion as they strolled toward it. "You do have my blessing."

IT WAS A PERFECT DAY AND PLACE FOR SHOOTING. THE AIR WAS clear and cooler than it had been for days, with barely enough breeze to move the awnings of the blue and white pavilion that had been set up on the meadow to shade the ladies of the party, and not enough to complicate the aim of a long rifle. The meadow was flat, about two hundred yards across, and beyond it nothing but the river.

George had harangued his marksmen for a half hour before the ride out, telling them that their reputations in these parts, and the veracity of Captain Bowman, rested upon their skills and concentration. "And if that isn't enough for you," he had added with a hard-edged smile, "there's *my* pride to consider. And as you know, gents, I'm sorely jealous of my pride."

On the field, he provided a jug of taffia for the use of those who believed it whetted their eyesight or steadied their hands. The ladies spread a table with sweetmeats and other morsels, with a cloth over it to baffle the flies.

As the Americans loaded and primed their flintlocks, George looked for an opportunity to say something to Teresa. She busied herself at the center of the table while he stood at the end of it watching his marksmen. In a moment he heard the rustling of cloth close behind him. Seeming to be preoccupied with spreading the table cover, she had moved to the end of the table where he stood.

"Teresa," he said in a whisper, she looked up as if surprised to find him there. He searched her eyes, seeing in sunlight for the first time that they were not absolutely black, but burnished with a tinge of hazel. "For once," he said, "we don't have to look up or down through windows at each other, with a wall between us!"

She blushed at the reference and looked down at the table. "It's true," she murmured. "There is no wall between us, is there?"

"I hope never again," he whispered.

She went away then and joined the other girls and women under the pavilion's shade, patting her breast with a straw fan, and de Leyba came forward.

"My guard," he said, indicating the four Spanish soldiers who stood at ease nearby, "would be willing to shoot against yours, and make it thus a competition instead of an exhibition."

George looked at them and considered it; his people loved competition. But, he thought, from a diplomatic standpoint it might not be good for this kind but naive Spaniard to see his soldiers humiliated. "No doubt that would be an exciting match, Excellency," he ventured. "Your lads certainly look sharp enough. But if I may say so, it would be an unfair contest not of men but of weapons, I mean muskets against long rifles."

De Leyba professed to see the validity of that, and soon enough he was glad he had not insisted on the contest. The targets were peeled green willow switches stuck into the ground, each with a scrap of colored cloth tied to its upper end like a small banner. Standing at first for the short-range shots, then kneeling and finally lying prone as the switches were planted farther and farther away, the marksmen unerringly cut the yellow wands off with their bullets until the meadow grass for fifty yards out was littered with splinters and scraps of cloth.

The Spaniards watched, incredulous, as each frontiersman in his turn would step to the line in silence, level his slim, heavy weapon, take half a breath, and without pause send the ball cracking to its target. The only thing the sharpshooters seemed unable to control was their ungentlemanly whooping and howling of triumph, which drifted across the field as often as the puffs of blue-white gunsmoke. George had forgotten to warn them against their customary use of expletives.

Oh, well, he thought. Thank God these Spaniards have never heard those words before and couldn't know what they mean.

"I am duly impressed," de Leyba exclaimed. "God help any Indian who *won't* sign your peace treaties! But, ah, as for your own eyes, Don Jorge—I observe that you carry one of those remarkable long guns as well as your pistols . . . Do I presume that you shoot so well, too?"

"Tolerable, tolerable."

"Would you mind . . ."

"If you wish it. Key," he called, turning to his sergeant, "would you fetch me my piece?" The sergeant brought it to him. "And now if you'd plant me a target, out there at the farthest line . . . nay, maybe ten yards beyond." Key started off, and when the woodsmen saw that their colonel was going to shoot beyond their marks, they raised a good-humored jeering, first about his certain inability to do it, then about how unfair it would be if he did. George only grinned at them, shook his head at their remarks, loaded and tamped the charge, and primed the pan.

"What a fine-looking weapon," mused de Leyba, who stood close by. "May I try it, Don Jorge?"

George gave it to him. He didn't know whether his new Spanish friend was actually going to try a shot with it or not. He hoped he would not.

De Leyba held the rifle in both hands, turning it this way and that in the sunlight, admiring the lustrous golden-striped maple of the stock and the intricate scrollwork chased in the steel. "Very handsome," he murmured. Then he raised the barrel and sighted along it toward the willow switch, which from this distance looked narrow as a hair. George thought the governor really was going to try to shoot, until he noticed that the barrel was dipping. The Spaniard was having difficulty holding it up. His arm was trembling. Instead of shooting, then, he held it up before his eyes again and nodded. "Very handsome piece," he said again, handing it to George. "Surprisingly heavy, eh?"

"Makes for a steadier aim, Excellency."

George took his stance now, eyeing the target, de Leyba standing behind him, nodding, a little embarrassed. I believe he *was* going to try, George thought, but he couldn't hoist it. Hm.

He raised the rifle, and just as he brought the sights to bear on the tiny distant scrap of red, a flicker of movement off to the left caught his eye. A large rabbit had run onto the meadow toward the shooting party, had suddenly become aware of them, had stopped in confusion, then had leaped off at a sharp angle and was scampering toward the far edge of the meadow.

"The hare!" de Leyba cried excitedly. "Get him!"

George, responding to the lifelong instinct of one who hunts for food, was already bringing the muzzle around onto the fleeing animal; he led the scurrying brown shape by about half a foot and squeezed the trigger. The rifle roared and recoiled against his shoulder, and through the dissipating smoke he saw the animal tumble along the ground, flinging guts, then twitch and lie still.

At the same moment, a feminine voice emitted a shrill, short cry, followed by the huzzahs of the frontiersmen. Lowering the rifle, George glanced back at the pavilion to see Teresa turning toward her sister-in-law, her hands clapped over her eyes in horror. Instantly his satisfaction was overwhelmed by a pang of remorse, then anger at himself, for having so thoughtlessly exposed her to this needless instant of killing.

De Leyba himself was applauding and exclaiming in wonder at the shot, his voice raised along with those of the woodsmen, who were extremely and profanely proud of their colonel. But the deep, hopeful contentment George had been feeling since the previous evening was ruined. He had shocked Teresa, and couldn't imagine what he would be able to do to atone for it.

He was listening to de Leyba's joy and looking at Teresa's anguish when Lieutenant de Cartabona cantered onto the field, leading one of the American couriers.

The man brought word that Mister Black Bird of the Chippewas had arrived in Cahokia that morning and was awaiting his opportunity to meet with the Long Knife.

As George took the message and began making his excuses to Lieutenant Governor de Leyba, he saw askance that de Cartabona had wandered to the pavilion and was paying his compliments to the ladies there. Swallowing, frowning, feeling absolutely wretched, George watched the dashing little Spanish officer bow and kiss Teresa's hand.

And when George went to the pavilion to kiss the ladies' hands and take his leave for Cahokia, he felt Teresa try to withdraw her fingers from his just a telltale instant before he would have released them. She dropped her eyes when he tried to look into them, and just perceptibly turned her face aside.

"Until I have the honor of seeing you again," he said.

But he felt that there was a wall between them once more.

18

DETROIT WAS SWELTERING. GOVERNOR HENRY HAMILTON WAS working in his shirt-sleeves. All of the windows of his office were open, inviting any afternoon breeze which might come along.

Hoofbeats pounded to a halt outside, punctuated by the slobbery blowing of a winded horse. Hamilton leaned back in his chair, picked up a paper fan and tried to create a breeze of his own with it, wondering meanwhile what sort of fool would be riding so hard in this heat. Craning his neck, he could see through the window a bay horse caked with dust and lather, its sides heaving, and an equally dusty man dismounting. It looked like Maisonville, one of his agents for Indian affairs from the Wabash country. What the deuce is he doing here? Hamilton wondered.

Boot steps and heavy breathing sounded in the vestibule, and voices; the orderly stepped in and saluted.

"It is Mister François de Maisonville, wishing to see you at once, sir."

"Just a moment," said Hamilton, standing and drawing on his coat. Good, he thought. Maybe he can tell me what's going on with the savages down in those parts.

For some time virtually no Indians from the Wabash and Illinois tribes had come in to Detroit for munitions or gifts, or to bring scalps or prisoners. A strange silence had reigned in that quarter for weeks, and Hamilton had not been able to get any intelligence about it. "Show him in," he said, closing the last button of his coat.

Maisonville entered, reeking of sweat, horse, leather, and dried swamp mud, and grimly took Hamilton's hand. Before

Hamilton could speak, Maisonville braced himself and uttered the news.

"The rebels have invaded the Illinois and Vincennes, Excellency."

"What?"

"Rocheblave is in chains. All the tribes from Ouiatanon on down are over at Cahokia signing treaties with the Americans."

Hamilton was livid, speechless. His mouth was drawing down at the corners, showing his lower teeth; his heavy dark brows were drawn almost together over his nose in a frown; his hands were beginning to shake. All that territory! All under his jurisdiction and responsibility, that huge, rich chunk of British Canada, and now here stood this idiot of a Frenchman telling him it was infested with Americans. It was impossible! Any army large enough to take over all that country could never have passed unnoticed through the Ohio country, through his network of spies and roving war parties. They must have got a fleet up the Mississippi, somehow. That American river raider, Willing, he thought. That barbaric scoundrel must be behind this!

He found his voice at last. "When did this happen, Maisonville, for God's sake?"

"It started on the night of July fourth, Excellency, when they attacked Kaskaskia. They surprised all the Illinois posts and secured them within three . . ."

"July fourth?" screamed Hamilton, waving both fists over his head. "And I'm just now hearing of it? Good God, man, how can an army *surprise* a whole bloody territory, I'd like to know?" he began stamping about the room, gesturing with his arms, stopping now and then to throw questions at Maisonville's head faster than the flinching Frenchman could answer them.

"Where did they *come* from? Who led them? Where under the sun was that bedamned, mangy French militia all this time? God damn your eyes, Maisonville! You know this couldn't have happened if there'd been Englishmen there. But *Frenchmen!* God! The curse of my life is having to depend on *Frenchmen* . . ."

He checked himself, seeing Maisonville drawing himself up with flashing eyes, remembering that this partisan was French himself. Hamilton glowered at him, having no intention of apologizing; he was sick of dealing with Frenchmen and Indians and Canadians, all of whom he held in equal contempt. "What about casualties?" he said then.

"None, sir," the man muttered. "On either side."

"None? On . . . either . . . side?"

"None. As I said, Excellency, it was a surp . . ."

"Was there no resistance whatso*ever*?" Hamilton was turning red again.

"There was no opportunity . . ." Maisonville said lamely, rubbing his palms down over his stubbly jaw and blinking to keep tears of shame from coming.

"Do you mean to stand there and tell me that the entire French militia in all the Illinois are prisoners of the American army?" Hamilton said slowly, his voice rankling with sarcasm.

It was a while before Maisonville could answer that. "Actually, sir . . ."

"Well? Actually what?"

"They took allegiance to . . . to the American cause, Excel . . ."

"By the blood of Christ, I should have expected it from those traitorous cowards! Maisonville, don't you sometimes want to hide in shame at the thought of being French?" He didn't care now how much he offended the Frenchman. Dash the discomfiture of a mere Frenchman! Hamilton stalked about the room now almost sick with rage and disgust, stopped before a five-foot wall map of Canada, the Colonies, and the Northwest Territory, and stared at the wide fan-shaped network of Mississippi tributaries representing the lost territory, perhaps a half million square miles England had wrested away from French control some twenty years ago. His heart sank at the abysmal thought of it. For him it meant absolute disgrace unless . . .

. . . unless he could somehow regain it.

"As you know, Excellency," Maisonville was saying glumly, "France has after all made a treaty with the Americans . . ."

"Of course I know about it. But I didn't imagine the Illinois French would know about it already, or suspect that something so remote would make turncoats of them . . . They're British subjects, the scum!"

"The American commander gave them news of it when he got there. It had a profound effect on them, I hear . . ."

Hamilton turned a sidelong glance on Maisonville. "As for you?"

"Excellency, I protest! You know I am steadfast in your service!"

"Of course. Very well. Details, then. Details. Who is this American invader, and how big is his army? Is it Willing, that blackguard river pirate who calls himself an American officer?"

"No, sir. It is a Virginian, named Clark. A colonel of militia, I understand . . ."

"Militia!" Again Hamilton's scornful incredulity frosted the air. "You're telling me *militia* conquered the . . ."

"God knows what they are, sir. Rangers, criminals, murderers, who can say?"

"Some *murderers*, I'd say, with not one casualty! Jove, I believe a squad of *cutpurses* could have taken it from you!"

Maisonville compressed his lips and began wondering how this belligerent, pompous, evil-tongued Englishman could possibly be reputed as such a respected and effective leader. Through the wealth of the Crown, he thought. By using people like me and Jehu Hay and Rocheblave to buy the loyalty of savages. I guess that's how. But Maisonville enjoyed a good and privileged life from his activities, and he knew when to swallow his pride and remain respectful. So he held his retort.

"Clark, is it?" Hamilton was saying. "I never heard of a Clark." Blast, he thought; not even the honorable excuse of an illustrious opponent! "What size army has this Clark, then? Answer me that."

"Difficult to say, Excellency. They seem to be everywhere, but they never parade, so it has been impossible to make a count. They seem, though, to be an arm of sizable force stationed at the Falls of the Ohio. At times this Colonel Clark has proposed withdrawing to join his main army there and leave the French in control of their own towns. But, ahem, out of fear of your wrath, I suspect, sir, they implore him each time to stay on and protect them."

"Now, *that* I can believe," snarled Hamilton.

"You ought to know," said Maisonville, "that the Jesuit there, Gibault, has turned his whole considerable influence to the side of Clark. He's the worst of all Clark's champions, I'd say. You'll scarcely believe this, I expect, but . . ."

"I'll believe anything by now."

". . . it was the priest, one might say, who captured Vincennes." By now Maisonville was so inured to Hamilton's meanness that he was beginning to enjoy thus turning the knife in him. He smiled crookedly.

"What bloody nonsense is *that*?" Hamilton roared. "Explain yourself!"

Maisonville told Hamilton about the mission Father Gibault and Doctor Laffont had made to Vincennes with Clark's written proclamation, and the citizens' gleeful rush to sign the American oath of allegiance.

"That flea-bitten papist," Hamilton muttered blackly. "He'll suffer for that."

"There's much more to tell," Maisonville went on, now with grim satisfaction. "If you'd be so kind as to offer me a drop of something to wash the dust out of my gullet, I'll relate some helpful particulars . . ."

"There's brandy there. Go to it."

"As one might expect, the Spaniards across the river have extended open arms to the rebels . . ."

"God damn," muttered Hamilton. "Go on, man, I'm listening. Regale me with all the pretty details. I'd like to know everything there is to know about this ridiculous abomination before I take steps to rectify it."

HAMILTON'S RAGE HAD SETTLED TO COLD, PRACTICAL REASONING by the time Maisonville completed his report, and as the Frenchman went to guest quarters to clean himself up from his journey, Hamilton perused the map on the wall and began planning his counteroffensive. With his finger he traced the water route from Detroit across the west end of Lake Erie, up the Maumee River to its source, then a portage of a few miles to the headwaters of the Wabash and down its great southwesterly arc directly to Vincennes. Six hundred miles, almost all by boat, which would allow the transport of sufficient munitions, cannon, provisions, and enough gifts to recruit several hundred Indians along the way. And after Vincennes, which Maisonville had said was officered by just one of Clark's captains, it would be a quick march across Illinois, or perhaps a voyage on down the Wabash to the Ohio and thence up the Mississippi, to retake the Illinois outposts.

By God above, he thought, a fierce excitement beginning to build in him, it would be such a pleasant change of duty, to get away from this endless dreary administration, this constant, demeaning, compromising, spirit-sapping attention to the needs of spoiled Indians, venal Canadians, and drunken half-breeds, to embark on a mission worthy of an English officer for once!

Surely with a few British regulars, some well-drilled militia, and a few hundred handsomely paid savages, he could sweep this upstart Virginian and his backwoods bandits off the face of the earth, strike the fear of God into those treacherous gutless Frenchmen, and turn this entire farce to his own credit.

As he looked at the map the scope of his plan grew. Several of the objectives he had long been planning might grow swiftly and naturally out of the expedition. He could, after reducing the Wabash and Illinois posts, stop forever the rebel traffic on the Ohio and Mississippi; then march eastward to a general war council with all the tribes at the mouth of the Tennessee, and set out thence to open a total devastation of Kentucky and Pittsburgh and drive the Americans back over the Alleghenies. He had been planning this exact offensive for nearly a year; perhaps it had needed only this provocation by the upstart Clark and his mongrel gang of adventurers to set it in motion. Hamilton began writing in his mind a letter to Governor Carleton at Quebec, soliciting permission to begin the offensive. He was also looking at a mental calendar. Men and provisions and boats could be ready in two months or less, he thought. The journey might take a month or forty days.

We could be back in possession of the whole territory by November, he thought. We could winter there, in control of the rivers, await reinforcements, then overrun the entire Allegheny frontier early in the spring of '79.

He strolled around his office now in a growing state of excitement. After these years of moldering at Detroit, hiring Indians to do his fighting for him, and hating himself for it, here was the chance to effect his own rebirth as a soldier. There was no shortage of matériel or money for the campaign; there never had been. The want of good British soldiers here in Canada had always been a problem, but sufficient militia and Indians could make up for that. No, all that had kept him stagnating here had been a want of incentive. And now the incentive had presented itself, in the guise of a humiliating setback which urgently needed to be redressed. Now he *had* to move against the American frontiers, and that necessity lay before him like a great and unexpected serendipity.

Colonel Clark, whoever you are, Governor Henry Hamilton thought, you may be my salvation. I am delighted that you have appeared on my horizon! He pressed his palms together, twisted them, and strutted. You may end by being sorry for this provocation, Mister Clark, but I couldn't be happier.

19

CAHOKIA, ILLINOIS COUNTRY
August 1778

SAGUINA, THE CHIPPEWA CHIEF KNOWN AS MISTER BLACK BIRD, was so confident of his own power that he had made the long journey to Cahokia accompanied by a guard of only eight warriors. The fact made a deep impression on George Rogers Clark, and the impression was enhanced by his first sight of the chief.

Mister Black Bird, tall and broad, came wearing a fine lightweight red cloak which he held draped over one shoulder like the toga of a Roman senator. His headdress was a crest of eagle feathers bound into his scalplock and hanging down his spine. He had a slanting forehead, deep creases above the bridge of his nose which gave him an air of severity, and very prominent jaw muscles. His eyes were scarcely visible under their hooded lids.

He specified that he did not wish to spend time in ceremony. He had come to the Americans' headquarters alone like an important white man on a business mission. He looked at George forthrightly and shook hands with him, and the two of them took seats at opposite ends of a long table, with the interpreters sitting at both sides. Several American officers and French gentlemen sat on chairs around the walls of the room. George was reminded of the days when he had sat among the members of the Privy Council of the Virginia Assembly in Williamsburg, negotiating for aid in the defense of Kentucky.

Mister Black Bird opened the conversation. "I have much to say and many questions to ask," he announced through the interpreter.

"My time is yours, and I will be honored to satisfy your curiosity as well as I can," George replied.

"I have no confidence in what prisoners tell me," said the chief, sitting erect with his hands on his knees, "as they are generally afraid to speak. I have long wished to speak with a

real chief of the Big Knives, and you give me my first opportunity. I have engaged in the war on the side of the Englishmen,
but sometimes I have doubted the correctness of doing so. I
have heard only their side. There are some things which are
mysterious to me, and I wish to have them explained fully. Will
you please tell me how the war between the English and the
Big Knives came to be? Begin with the time when your people
came to this land as Englishmen."

George realized that this chief was not interested in hearing
the story told in the similes and figures of speech he had used
to convince the other chiefs; this man had that matter-of-
factness about him that Chief Logan of the Mingoes had exhibited.

And so George found himself having to recount the whole
history of the Colonies, from the first settlement on the Atlantic
seaboard. He told of the taxes and the restrictions the British
had tried to place on American trade and settlement, and recited
in detail the grievances which had caused the colonies to unite
despite their differences to declare their independence from
King George. Black Bird asked pointed and pertinent questions
which required comprehensive answers.

It was almost dark when Black Bird leaned back in his chair
and said that he now understood the story fully.

"I am convinced that the English have been deceiving us," he
said, "And that, as I long suspected, they wished to keep us in
the dark. Now I am certain that you are perfectly right."

"Thank you for hearing me with an open mind," said George.
"We have no doubt that we are right."

Black Bird nodded. "I am glad to find that my old friends the
French have joined the Americans, and I think the Indians
should do likewise. I would not blame you if you drove from
the face of this land all those who do not join you, for it is plain
to me that the British are afraid and know they are wrong. Otherwise they would not give us as many goods as they do to
fight for them.

"My sentiments are now fixed in favor of the Americans. I
will no longer pay any attention to the English, and will immediately cease taking any part in the war. You will please excuse
me that many of my young men are now out in their war paint.
As soon as they return, I will make them lay down their weapons, and not one of them shall again take up arms against you."

"Good. You now see the truth. Understand, Mister Black
Bird, that I do not blame you for receiving whatever presents

the British chose to give, but I think you know it's degrading for you to make war as hirelings. Such actions are beneath the dignity of real warriors, and I suspect that's why you've felt doubtful. I have respect for anyone who makes war against me on his own account; his scalp would be a great trophy. But the scalps of hired warriors would be given to the children to play with, or flung to the dogs."

Black Bird accepted this with the guiltlessness of one who has just learned the error of his ways. He stood up, and the two came together to shake hands again.

"As I return to my people," the Chippewa said, "I will tell the Indians of every tribe I meet what has passed between us, and tell them of the true cause of the war. I am sure that most of them will follow my example." The chief paused and thought, then continued. "It would have a good effect among them if you would let me take one of your young men back with me, under my protection, to help me carry your message among those nations. It would give great weight to what I will say to them."

"I will arrange that," George said. "If I have your word that he will be under your protection."

"You have my word, Long Knife. We shall view each other as friends from this day, and we shall keep a correspondence between us." The chief remained solemn, not giving way to something so undignified as a smile, but he stood close and breathed easily and there was warmth in his eyes.

"I am happy to see this business end so much to your satisfaction and mine," George said, warmly gripping Black Bird's hand, "and so much to the advantage and the tranquility of both our peoples. I will write immediately to the governor of Virginia and tell him what has passed here. It will give him and all Americans great pleasure to register you among our friends."

The conference with Mister Black Bird was thus concluded, with much dignified handshaking all around, and a modest quantity of rum decorously sipped. This man obviously was too stately to celebrate with the same sort of exuberance Big Gate had exhibited, a fact which Captain Bowman bemoaned, but the great Chippewa did seem reluctant to leave, and stayed on for several more days, visiting George at every opportunity, and holding long councils with the chieftains of other tribes as they arrived to meet the Long Knife. His influence invariably warmed them up for the treaty-making.

* * *

INDIANS CONTINUED TO TRAIL INTO CAHOKIA, FROM PLACES AS FAR as five hundred miles distant, and the treaty-making wore on through late August and well into the cooling days of September. In the shade of the yellowing leaves on the huge elms, or in the main room of his headquarters on bad days, George recounted again and again, several times each week, his figurative account of the British-American conflict, so often that he felt that he could have recited it in his sleep. In five weeks at Cahokia, he signed treaties of peace with the Chippewas, the Ottawas, Potawatomis, Missisaugas, Winnebagoes, Sauk, Fox, Osages, Iowas, and Miamis, as well as various wandering sects and bands of those tribes. Each conference was almost an exact reenactment of all that had gone before, and each was concluded in the same satisfactory manner. George lay exhausted from talking almost every night, thinking or dreaming of Teresa and hoping for a pause in the ceremonies which would allow him to go back across the river and try to restore himself in her favor. Evening after evening he would lie in his bed and remember that awful moment when he had shot the rabbit and turned to find her recoiling in horror. In his imagination he saw her dancing on the arm of Lieutenant de Cartabona or heard her talking to her sister-in-law about the barbarity of "that American colonel." Even if I had shot and killed an innocent man, he thought, I doubt I could more deeply regret squeezing a trigger.

But those fantasies were for the nights only. There was too much business to be conducted during the days. Hours not spent in council with the Indians slipped by in attention to the details of administration and supply and the enforcement of discipline. George realized that his only hope for hanging on in the Illinois, until such time as orders, money, or reinforcements might come from Virginia, lay in the strict subordination of his ragged little army. Thus he was, when not waxing eloquent for Indians, haranguing his soldiers on parade. With the greatest pleasure he would lecture to them on his resolutions, on the necessity of strict duty for their own preservation, on the importance of making a perpetually good appearance for the Indians, French, and Spaniards who kept them under such minute scrutiny.

The men, to his satisfaction, appeared to be sensible of the extreme delicacy of their situation, and seemed to derive from it a sense of special importance which inspirited them more every day. They answered him that they were zealous for their country and determined not to disgrace her through any sort of cowardice or misconduct, that they well understood their dangerous situation, that only good order would be conducive to their happiness and safety. The men improved daily, and George began to sense before long that probably no garrison anywhere could boast of better order or a more valuable contingent of men.

There would be moments, however, moments of insight which would come in the midst of that satisfaction, when he would feel that he was holding up a whole shaky empire with nothing but the sound of his voice, nothing but the breath of his speeches.

20

St. Louis, Upper Louisiana Territory
September 1778

AS YOUNG PEOPLE DO WHEN CONFUSED BY THEIR HEARTS, TERESA de Leyba was beginning to feel personally responsible for the long absence of her beloved.

The young Virginian was beyond doubt her beloved. She had come to understand that after a fortnight of thinking about him by day and dreaming about him by night. She would lapse into reveries while lace-making, while reading, while practicing on her *guitarra,* while entertaining her two nieces, while dining with her brother and his guests, even while dancing or riding with Lieutenant de Cartabona, and in those reveries she would see that red hair, that straight back, those broad shoulders, those keen, dark blue eyes. She deliberately, time after time, envisioned his face as it had looked that night when he was transported by her music, or that morning when he had stood in his window looking down at her in the garden; when the face came unbidden it would be shiny with sweat and smudged with dirt, as it had looked when he appeared in the ballroom at Kaskaskia, or it would be sunlit and full of astonishment as it had been the day of the shooting match when he had heard her scream and turned to look at her.

The shooting of the rabbit did not matter any more; it is man's nature, she realized, to kill game. What she now regretted was her reaction to it; she felt that her demonstration of horror and disapproval had driven him away and would make him stay away. She went over the scene every day in her thoughts, remembering his truly remarkable feat of marksmanship, recalling her foolish outburst, seeing the look of astonishment in his face, and the look of hurt in his eyes when she had pulled her hand back from his.

And now she felt that she would never see him again. Although Francisco Vigo and others came to the mansion almost every day with cheerful accounts of the Virginian's success with the Indians just across the river, they never brought news that he planned a visit. Obviously he was very busy with the Indians. But Cahokia was not more than five miles away and still he had not come back to St. Louis. If he loved her, as she had presumed he did, surely he would have found the time to come across the river and pay a visit. She had heard her brother express the same dismay two or three times. "I am surprised," he had said to Maria at the table, "that Don Jorge has not come back to see his good friends here! Ah, well," he had sighed. "The requisites of duty . . ."

The nights were growing cool in the valley. Leaves of certain trees around the mansion were sere, and there was a dry haze that made the eastern bank of the river look light blue on sunny days. At night the campfires and council fires of the Indians would glimmer like warm stars on the horizon. Teresa would blow out her lamp, sit on the edge of her bed, look across at those points of light, and concentrate on the name of George Rogers Clark, as if by doing so she could cause him to awaken in his bed and think kindly, even yearningly, of her. Once she even heard herself saying aloud: "It is not really important, my dear, about the rabbit."

"Our American friend," Vigo told de Leyba one day while stopping by on departure to his Vincennes trading post, "plans to go back down to Kaskaskia soon. Much of his business with the Indians seems complete, and he grows anxious about having been away from the main body of his men for so many weeks." Teresa, even though she had virtually given up hope of seeing him again, was stunned by this news. She dabbed at the corners of her mouth with a large napkin to hide her expression of alarm from the others at the table.

"What? Leaving?" de Leyba exclaimed. 'Then, Francisco,

there is nothing for it but to give him an *express* invitation to come see us before he departs. When you go across . . ."

"Oh, but never mind that," Vigo said, raising his hand and smiling. "He gave me this message for you." He drew a letter out of his blouse.

De Leyba broke the wax seal and read silently for a moment, a smile dawning on his face. "Good! He plans to come here the day after tomorrow, before sailing for Kaskaskia. Look, Teresa, he sends you his affectionate regards, and you, Maria, and the children . . ." He passed the letter around the table, winking at Vigo and indicating Teresa's sudden high color by a tilt of his head. She held the letter a moment as if touching its writer, and looked hungrily at the handsome, cursive script with its sure flourishes and that bold, flaring horizontal stokes at the end of each sentence. She noted with a self-conscious, foolish rush of pleasure the very large and ornate initial with which he had written her name.

"Oh, my," she laughed, reluctantly passing the letter along to Maria, "I had feared he was displeased with me."

"Child!" Vigo exclaimed. "How could he be? Why, on the contrary, whenever we speak of you, his eyes grow haunted and veer in this direction! Ha, ha! Fernando, what think you of the silly doubts of young lovers? Ha, ha! Teresa, my dear, he thinks it's *you* who are displeased!"

She put her hand on her bosom. "Has he said that?"

"Not in words," Vigo replied. "But with a face full of fretfulness."

Her laughter trilled, then ended abruptly. "But no. Now you're being fanciful. You're only teasing me. And how can you say . . . 'lovers'?" She was blushing mightily now.

"Pardon, my pretty," he said with a mocking bow. "A slip of my tongue perhaps. But now, my dearest friends, I must say *adiós*. I wish I could be here for your reunion with the Virginian, but I shan't return from Vincennes, I expect, until winter."

"Farewell," de Leyba said, rising, then added, with a laugh, " . . . Don Cupid."

A BLOOD-RED LEAF TUMBLED DOWN TO MEET ITS UPTUMBLING REflection on the pond's surface, and the reflection broke apart in tiny ripples. "Sweet gum," George said. "They always color before anything else. But to be falling so soon! I expect we're in for a hard and early winter."

"But a peaceful one, I hope," said de Leyba.

"I pray," said Teresa. She watched the leaf move slowly like a red sail toward the other side of the pond.

"As do I," George agreed. "And I've done everything in my power to assure that, God knows."

The trio turned away and strolled back to their horses. The sunlight was warm, the air cool. Long fine grass, bowed like waves of fading green, rustled under their feet. George walked slowly, looking down, watching with dumb wonderment as the toes of Teresa's tiny shoes poked forward alternately from under the hem of her riding skirt. He had never seen such small feet except attached to children, and a strange pang of tenderness made tears start to his eyes.

They took up the reins. The horses each ripped one last bit of grass from the ground as they raised their heads, and chewed. George's horse nuzzled the breast of his blue uniform coat and whickered softly. George stroked its powerful neck, smelled its sweet moist breath, and gazed at Teresa, who held her animal's rein in one small hand and drew a glove onto the other. At the sight of her hands, he felt the pang again. She looked at him and saw it in his eyes and felt the same. Don Fernando bent and cupped his hands to give her a step up into her saddle, but she was looking at George and didn't notice.

"My good friend," George said suddenly to him, "I'm sure you have pressing business, and you needn't spend your time wandering about with us. Why don't you go on, and we'll ride in shortly . . ."

"Why, I wouldn't hear of it!" the Spaniard exclaimed cheerfully. "How often do we see you? I have nothing more important to do, Jorge, I swear. Come, Teresa. Step up."

She put her foot in his hands and swung nimbly up onto the sidesaddle, where she sat smoothing her skirts and looking down with bemused resignation at George.

George sighed. He had been dropping hints and suggestions all afternoon, but de Leyba seemed oblivious to such cues, and blandly, innocently, continued to bless them with his cheerful presence.

It's their custom, George reminded himself for the tenth time, stepping into the stirrup and swinging up onto his saddle. He looked at Teresa, at the wry little smile that was beginning to pucker her lips and dimple the corners of her mouth. And she, he thought, of course understands it better than I.

They followed a path up the face of the bluff and emerged on the field where the shooting match had taken place. The splintered willow wands still stood about, and scraps of cloth, their colors now faded by August sun and September rains, could be seen in the grass. De Leyba reminisced excitedly about the shooting as they rode over the spot where the rabbit had fallen, and George looked from the corner of his eye at Teresa, to see if there would be any vestige of her displeasure. She only smiled at him and lowered her lashes, rocking gently back and forth with the horse's stride. Saddle leather creaked. De Leyba's horse dropped a trail of pungent dung. The sun was going down now and the sky beyond Teresa was a gauzy backdrop of enflamed cirrus clouds. A meadowlark reiterated its three silvery syllables. On the horizon, three other mounted figures rode in silhouette, rifles across their saddles. They were George's ubiquitous bodyguard, staying as usual just far enough away not to be obtrusive, but always watching and alert.

By Heaven, he thought, if I am ever to be alone with this dear person, it will have to be by stealth in the night.

THEY DINED ON FISH THAT EVENING AT TEN. THE LITTLE GIRLS stayed close about George for a half hour before bedtime, crowding close to hear him tell about his little sisters in Virginia, and about his smallest brother William. They made him promise to bring William to St. Louis someday. Now and then Rita, the six-year-old, would reach up and touch George's coppery hair, which was a source of constant wonderment to her. Maria Josefa, at nine already seeming to acquire the reserve of Spanish femininity, did not touch him but stood as close to his knee as she could without doing so. After they had been taken upstairs, he turned to Teresa, finding her regarding him in total absorption, apparently wrapped in a veritable cocoon of pleasure. She raised her eyebrows and sat up straighter when she realized he was looking at her.

"Teresa," he said, his voice almost quaking with emotion, "for weeks I've been hearing your music in my memory, but I'm beginning to forget how the melodies went. Would it be an imposition if I asked you to play them for me again? Would you play for me as your only audience?"

"You were my only audience then," she said, then flushed at her own audacity. De Leyba laughed.

"I knew that!" he exclaimed. "Yes, my dear. Please do."

AT THREE O'CLOCK IN THE MORNING, GEORGE ROSE FROM HIS BED. A rhombus of moonlight lay on the floor. He had lain awake for an hour after retiring, running the music of the *guitarra* through his heart, and finally had dozed. Now the house was absolutely still. De Leyba and his wife had closed themselves into their bedroom at the far end of the house, and this night all the men of the guard were bedded downstairs. The notion that nothing but empty darkness lay between his door and Teresa's now lodged itself in his mind like a seed in a furrow and inexorably began to grow to occupy him entirely. Naked, he prowled the room with the cool wooden floor under his bare feet, and warned himself that he could bring disaster upon himself and disgrace upon Teresa if he were to steal into her room and somehow be discovered. I would never be admitted to this house again, he told himself. This wonderful new ally of mine who guards his sister so diligently would no doubt become the most inveterate of my enemies.

Still, he found himself gazing at the dark rectangle of the oaken door and listening like a wild animal to the silence of the house.

Besides, he thought, her door might be locked.

You wouldn't know that unless you tried it.

What if I should enter, and she woke up alarmed—as she certainly would—and cried out? he wondered.

But maybe she's awake now, as I am, he argued. He felt that she was. Instinct told him that she was awake beyond that wall. He imagined he could hear her mind repeating his name. I could not be this desperately awake without my wakefulness awakening her, he thought. He was as certain of that now as he was certain his heart was beating.

It would ruin everything if we were discovered, his reason insisted.

But I'll never have a minute alone with her any other way, his heart argued.

He rubbed his palms down over his face and stared at the dark shape of the door. He shuddered. He turned away and padded to the window, to get away from that relentlessly beckoning door. A floorboard creaked as he stepped on it.

He stood by the window and stared over the darkened town while a whippoorwill uttered its throaty whistle a dozen times in the moonlight.

At last the idea became too strong to resist any longer, and the decision turned somewhere deep inside his head, turned silently but palpably like a well-oiled hinge of fate.

You just have to, he understood. There's no such thing as *not* going to her.

He crossed the room again, avoiding the loose plank in the floor, took his cotton breeches off the chair and pulled them on. He went to the door, took the cold brass knob in his hand, and turned it slowly, reminding himself that his guards could be awakened virtually by the fall of a snowflake.

The door swung open silently; the musty air of the hallway came in with it. He stepped into the black corridor and moved noiselessly the six steps to her door. His elbow bumped the wall softly as he groped for her door handle and he stood stock-still and waited. The silence prevailed. As he turned the handle, all the dire arguments of his reason whispered at him again to turn back. He continued to turn the handle, until the door moved. He pushed it open and the familiar scent of her soap eddied around his face. And the breath of camphor, the whiff of lavender.

He was inside now, and strained silently to ease the door shut. Cool air on the sweat-bedewed skin of his torso made him shiver again. The rectangle of her window stood gray opposite where he paused. He could hear her breathing now, and saw the dim shape of the white bedding, the high, square canopy, the open bed-curtains.

Now you're dead center in your own trap, he told himself. You're utterly daft to be doing this!

His body responded by going toward the bedside; fingers and toes felt for invisible obstacles, for things that might fall over; his heart walloped high in his breast and his nerves felt the night inches beyond the limits of his skin.

He knelt beside the bed; his knee cracked. Teresa moved in her bed, inches from him, bedclothes whispering, and her breath touched his face.

Now, he thought. You're this far, you fool. What now? Do you just look, just kneel here like a praying man, or try to wake her without waking the whole house?

Could just stay like this, he thought. You're alone with her now, and isn't that all you wanted?

No, that's not enough.

Wake her and she'll screech the whole house up, he thought.

Or else die of fright. What if she wakes up and thinks I'm an Indian? he thought.

Her name, he thought. Whisper her name.

Better, yet, just think it. Think it hard.

He thought it hard, and sweat bathed his forehead and she be-

gan to stir. A soft waking moan came from the dark shape of
her head on the pillow. *Now whisper,* he thought.

"*Teresa.*"

Again.

"*Teresa.*"

She moved her limbs and the sound of her breathing
changed.

She's awake now, he thought. Careful. *Oh, careful, man!*

"*Teresa.*"

She gasped. She sat bolt upright, the bed creaking loudly. Her
inhalation of breath warned him that she was about to scream.
Quickly as a striking snake he clapped his hand over her mouth;
her fingers clawed at his wrist and a high, strangled whimper
sounded in her throat. Her whole body was shuddering violently; he had terrified her fully as badly as he had feared to.

"*Teresa!*" he whispered into her ear. "*George! Hushhhh!*"

His pulse was hammering so loudly in his head that he could
hardly hear himself. He wanted to jump up and dash back to his
room. But he held her mouth with his left hand and began
stroking her hair with his right.

She began nodding then, stopped clawing at his wrist, and he
knew she recognized him. But she was quaking like a leaf and
might still cry out.

A new dread entered his mind. What if she takes this as a vi-
olation?

He had been thinking all along, in his desperate hopefulness,
that she would want him here beside her and would welcome
him once she was awake and calm. But what if her fear is followed by infuriation? It might well be. Even knowing it is I, she
might yet give the alarm.

She was not struggling now, though she still trembled in great
spasms. Slowly he relaxed the pressure of his hand on her face,
ready to clamp down again in an instant.

Now I'm in a predicament, he thought.

There was only one thing he could think of to make her understand and accept his awful intrusion.

"*Teresa,*" he whispered in her ear, the scent of her hair in his
nostrils, the warmth of her breath on his hand. "Teresa, *I worship you!*" A moment, then he took his hand from her face and
continued to stroke her hair.

For a long, long time, the vague shape of her face remained
turned on him; the air was full of their rapid breathing; her hair

moved under his hand; the silence was electric; she trembled violently; an outcry, a cataclysmic outcry, seemed imminent.

Then she whispered:

"Te adoro!"

SHE HAD AWAKENED IN MORTAL TERROR. SHE HAD THOUGHT HER heart would stop. Her oldest nightmare, that of a dark, live intruder in the privacy of her room, had come true. A steel-hard hand had stifled her outcry. She had struggled in vain; her body, every vulnerable inch of it, had flinched in anticipation of the knife. She had prayed *Holy Mary Mother of God pray for us sinners now and at the hour of our death amen Holy Mary Mother of God pray for us sinners now and at the hour of our death amen* in the wild rushing in her brain, certain that this was the very hour of her death. But then through the panic she had heard the intruder whisper the name of the man she had just gone to sleep thinking of, and had felt the hand gently caressing her hair, and then she had heard him whisper, "Teresa, I worship you," and she had known then that it was not her oldest nightmare but her newest dream that was coming true.

But even that was little less frightening; she was here almost naked without the armor of her hooks and stays and buttons and layers and layers of linen; here was this madman who had invaded the sanctity of her room; here he was inviting almost certain discovery by Maria or Fernando who were awake at any hour because of Maria's lungs; here was this man, kneeling by her bed and straining toward her, obviously undressed himself; but most frightening of all was the excitement, the desire, her delicious awareness of their proximity and dishabille. Nothing remotely like this had ever happened; no man had ever been this close to her, and she wavered between shame and this tingling desire for touch that was spreading over her.

That hand had continued to stroke her hair, sending chills of pleasure through her, stroking so gently. He had removed his hard hand from her mouth at last and now she breathed the man smell of him, and finally all the tenderness and longing that she had cultivated through the long, lonely weeks welled up in her until her breast was swollen with it, and she had whispered to him:

"Te adoro!"

* * *

HE TOOK A DEEP BREATH AND SIGHED. HIS LEGS BEGAN TREMBLING, twitching, from the awkward, tense kneeling. The house remained still. It was incredible that this enormous uproar of heartbeats and shrieking nerves had not roused the whole town; but it had been, of course, only a storm of rustlings and whispers, no more than a restless sleeper makes at any time in the night. The crisis of his intrusion was past. And she had whispered that she adored him!

His heart grew huge, and shivers raced around his temples. You, he told himself, have more blind good fortune than any man deserves!

He took her right hand now, and kissed the back of its fingers, turned it and kissed the fragrant pads of the palms. The fingertips touched his cheek.

Leaning then with his knees on the floor and his elbows on the bed, he cupped her face in his hands, tried to pierce the darkness to see what was in her eyes, memorized with his fingertips the tiny miraculous convolutions of those ears he had so often studied from a distance, those artfully sculptured ears which so often flamed with her embarrassments.

Though her panic surely by now was past, she continued to tremble in waves of intensity, causing such a tide of pity in him that tears burned his eyes and traced cool paths down both sides of his nose.

Teresa felt a teardrop fall on the skin of her bare arm—a teardrop, something she had so little expected ever from this hard man that at first she didn't know what it was; then she understood and was so moved by it that without thinking she reached out to embrace him like a child. The flesh under her hands, though, was not a child's flesh; it was smooth and rock-hard. Her thoughtless fingers wandered over the muscle-knots and the hollows of his back and shoulders; under the night-cooled skin his flesh was hot and hard as the powerful neck and shoulders of her riding horse. She felt gooseflesh rise on the skin of his upper arm and her fingers explored it with a curiosity of their own. Now her trembling had ceased and she was hot in the face and breast.

"My one," she whispered. "My one!"

George was growing weak from the sensation of her fingers moving on his back, weak and desperate for warmth; drawing his arms close to his chest he slumped until his cheek lay on her rising, falling bosom and her rapid heartbeat thudded against his right ear. The warm musk of her body bathed him now and the

fragrance, the faint floral and spice fragrance of her bedding and
thin nightgown, enveloped him. Her hand was stroking his temple now and exploring his hairline. Her breath sighed in and out
of her nostrils, her breast rose and fell and her heartbeat raced
in his ear. It seemed that this was home; this was the place to
which all his wanderings should have brought him to stay: here
upon this bosom where he could hear and feel the very life of
her beating and flowing and burning. Here seemed to be the
center of the universe toward which his restlessness had been
bringing him even though he had not known it. There was nothing more central to his soul than this; all about lay a cold room
hushing with the gray atoms of night, a sleeping village, an infinity of black and hostile wilderness, an icy blank moon and
shivering stars. But here was the hearth where he could warm
himself and rest and turn his back upon the doubts and dangers
that had preoccupied him for so many weeks. Now he doubted
that he could ever gather the strength to rise and go from here.

Yet even as he recognized this as the high, warm, sunny
home place of his life, he came gradually to realize that not all
yearnings ended here; the rest of himself was awakening to the
rest of her. If her bosom was his home, the rest of her body, extended beyond the embrace, moving now so slightly in the
warmth under her blanket, was like an unexplored territory,
beckoning him as unknown places always had done. He moved
his right hand, slipping it into the warmth of her back, feeling
the soft hollow of her waist, the nubby vertebrae, and the exquisite soft swelling of her nates, and his loins began to stir
with excitement.

But at the touch of his hand in that guarded region, Teresa
stiffened and he withdrew it.

Somewhere deep in the house, Maria's cough started disturb-
ing the stillness, and Teresa paused, tense, listening, lightly
pushing at George's shoulder. The coughing stopped, then began again in a few seconds. "Listen," Teresa whispered. "She'll
be getting up, looking in on the girls. She might find you here!
You have to go, before she comes out of her room!"

His awareness of the predicament returned full upon him
now, but the necessity of leaving the warmth of Teresa was
tragic. As he raised himself from the heat of her bosom the
night air coming between them was like a knife edge cutting
away a part of him. He knew he had to flee, but he had to make
some bond between them before he vanished. He stood, stooping over her, tense, willing himself toward the door, took her

hand and placed it to his lips. "My Teresa," he whispered. "I shall ask your brother for your hand! As soon . . ." They heard a door open in the corridor, and both started in alarm. ". . . as I see him!"

"Yes," she whispered. "Yes! But Maria . . ."

They could see a line of lamplight under the door. There was no exiting by that way now; the path between her room and his room had been cut by the vigilant Maria and her lamp.

He remembered then that Teresa's window overlooked the terrace, and, heart racing, darted toward the window. His bare foot struck something cold and hard, jarring it; the object fell with a metallic clang, a rolling, wobbling sound, and his heart jumped into his throat. He had kicked over her chamberpot in his haste, and Maria's voice came loudly through the door, calling Teresa's name, querying in Spanish, edged with alarm. The door handle clicked.

Teresa leaped from the bed and waved George toward the window, responding in Spanish: "It's nothing! I've only upset my necessary!"

And as the door opened and rays of lamplight angled into the room, George shinnied over the windowsill like a fleeing wildcat and dropped into the moonlit night.

JAMES JANUARY, A GRIZZLED KENTUCKY SCOUT ASSIGNED TO George Roger Clark's bodyguard detail, was just enjoying a great predawn yawn at his post on a garden bench half a dozen yards from a corner of the Spanish governor's mansion when he heard a clatter and voices issuing from an upstairs window. Jerking up his rifle and looking toward the window, he saw a sight that made his mouth drop open.

A man naked except for white knee-breeches suddenly emerged into the moonlight, hung from the windowsill for a moment by his fingertips, then dropped silently to the ground. In the instant it took the sentry to recognize his commandant, the figure ran around the corner of the house, looked up at the window of his own room, backed off twenty feet into the garden, ran at the house, sprang, caught the sill of his own second-story window, swarmed up the wall like a spider, and vanished inside.

A glow of lamplight had appeared in the other window, and the voices of two women came out, speaking in Spanish, one fussing, the other half-laughing, half-sobbing. Then there was silence again and the light faded from the window. James January found himself staring at a moon-washed stone house just as he had been doing since midnight. He blinked his eyes, shook his head, and lowered his rifle. He was not at all sure he had seen what he thought he had seen. It seemed more and more unlikely every second he thought about it. Perhaps he had dozed off and had a dream; that was a common affliction among sentries.

He decided, at any rate, that he was not going to report it to Colonel Clark.

George was kept awake until dawn by a smarting scraped knee, a bruised foot, a lover's ache in his groin, and a succession of worries and joyous recollections. After a short, fitful sleep, he rose to go down to breakfast and test the mood of the household. Teresa was not up yet, but de Leyba's cheerful countenance told him nothing was amiss.

"Teresa and I have agreed," George said, "to plight our troth, my dear friend. With your permission."

De Leyba rose to his feet at this astonishing announcement, tears of happiness gleaming in his eyes. Then he hesitated and looked puzzled. "But . . . when have you discussed this?" he asked.

"Ah, why, er . . ." George stammered, "let us just say it was a comprehension mutually arrived at."

That was sufficient for de Leyba, and the rest of the day was spent in sunshine and celebration.

21

Detroit
October 7, 1778

Though the gray sky looked pregnant with snow, General Henry Hamilton's regiment struck camp on the Detroit common and prepared to embark on the six-hundred-mile expedition against the American rebels at Vincennes and the Illinois. The soldiers stood shivering in ranks as the Articles of War were read to them, then took a renewed oath of allegiance to His Britannic Majesty. The venerable and imposing Father Pierre Pothier, Jesuit missionary for the vicinity, then conferred his blessing on the Catholics present. There was a large contingent of French-Canadian militiamen along with the King's Eighth Regiment, and a force of about sixty Indians, which General Hamilton had made arrangements to increase tenfold along the way. He was certain of having a striking force of seven to eight hundred soldiers and warriors upon his arrival at Vincennes. Waiting in the fleet of boats and large pirogues at the water's edge were ninety-seven thousand pounds of provisions and arms, gifts for the recruitment of Indians, and one large field cannon, the only one that could be spared from the fort. Hamilton then put the remaining garrison under the command of Captain Richard Lernoult, the troops embarked, and the convoy moved down the Detroit River toward Lake Erie.

An early snowstorm covered their first encampment, near the mouth of the river, and when it had subsided, the boats were reloaded for the thirty-six-mile passage across the end of the lake to the mouth of the Maumee. It was noon before the cold, flint-gray surf of the lake calmed enough to permit launching, and there was debate as to whether they should set out for the hazardous crossing. Hamilton squinted into the howling wind, considered that if he delayed any longer, the lake might freeze over, thus stopping him for good, and decided to make the push. Night fell while they were on the lake, rowing desperately and quartering against the bashing seas, an extremely dark night, and each boat raised a light to guide the ones behind. Shortly before midnight the wind shifted and increased, whipping the blinded convoy with icy rain and sleet, and the waves grew higher. Men prayed, bailed, and watched the pale, seething whitecaps march relentlessly toward them. General Hamilton knew that a rocky shore lay on their lee and for hours listened in mortal dread for the roar of the surf. Shaking with cold, a cloak drawn across his face, he consigned his soul to heaven but told the boatmen to keep rowing. It was almost morning when they rowed to land near the mouth of the Maumee, pulled the boats onto an oozy shore and waited for day. It was blowing too hard to permit them to pitch a tent or even make a fire, but they were warmed enough by the miracle of their escape.

They rowed up the Maumee to the foot of the Maumee rapids on the eleventh, and found there the British sloop *Archangel*, which had brought fourteen more tons of provisions for the journey.

Progress up the Maumee proved unexpectedly slow and fatiguing because of low water. The troops were continually having to drag the heavy boats through the cold shallows, often being forced to unload them entirely and carry the goods up the banks on their backs so that the vessels could be sledded over the mire and rocks, then reloaded. Hours were spent repairing stove boats, and the men at times felt like burdened slaves instead of soldiers.

After thirteen laborious days the expedition reached Post Miami far up the Maumee, where several previously summoned Indian tribes waited. Hamilton spent several days in war councils with these tribes, bestowing on them several tons of presents to induce them to join him. Several of the chiefs refused to go against the man they called the Long Knife, so Hamilton decided to make up for their numbers by sending messengers southeastward for the Shawnees, who he knew were still fully hostile toward the Americans. He also sent messengers ahead down the Wabash with presents inviting those tribes to join him, or at least to scout the activities of the Americans. In the meantime, the soldiers labored over the nine-mile portage to the upper reaches of the Wabash, working like ants to carry the heavy boats and goods to this second point of embarkation.

On reaching that place, expecting a leisurely float downstream to Vincennes with nothing more strenuous than a few recruiting councils along the way, General Hamilton was appalled to find the Wabash tributary even drier than the Maumee, and the excruciatingly slow business of loading, unloading, dragging and repairing resumed. When he had nearly decided to give up, the convoy came to a stretch of river where the water had been kept up by the great beaver dam. Reaching the dam, he offered jocular thanks and apologies to the beaver colony, ordered a work party with axes to cut through the dam, and the unloaded boats were taken through, then reloaded once more below.

The next obstacle was a vast swamp called les Volets, which had been reduced to little more than a tangled mud flat. Cursing the countryside, he finally sent a party of engineers and sappers down to build a dam below the swamp. After a long wait the water backed up into the swamp, eventually rising enough to float the vessels down to the new dam.

A similar dry stretch was met a few miles farther downstream at Rivière à l'Anglais, where another dam had to be built to raise the water.

By now, freezing had set in, further lowering the river. Floating ice cut the men as they worked in the water to haul the boats over shoals and rocks, and damaged the hulls of the bateaux, which had to be repeatedly unloaded, hauled, and caulked. Even the Indians, who were not by custom inclined to labor, were put to work at times to carry goods and lighten the boats. On some days, only a mile's progress would be made between dawn and dark. More days were spent in stopovers at the Indian villages, where there would be conferences and gift-giving to recruit more Indians. Often these conferences were in vain because the tribes had made treaties with Colonel Clark during the summer. The size of the expedition had, nonetheless, swollen to about seven hundred, the number varying from week to week as Indian bands joined and others wearied of the whole affair and turned back.

Thus the whole month of November went by in misery and toil, and Hamilton often fell asleep in his tent cursing Indians, cursing the drought, cursing the very terrain, and wondering whether after all this he would even reach Vincennes before a solid midwinter freeze of the Wabash. One thing is certain, he thought. If I make Vincennes in December, I shall winter us there. Never could an army cross the remaining two hundred and forty miles to Kaskaskia in midwinter. That would be impossible even for British regulars.

So that was settled. He would, if by miracle he reached Vincennes, wait there until the spring thaw to move against the rebels on the Mississippi.

At last, early in December, rains came and the Wabash began rising to a navigable depth. Hamilton stood on the bank, water trickling out of the three corners of his hat, and watched cheerfully the millions of raindrops making their circles on the rising brown water.

His satisfaction over the rising of the waters was short-lived; the flotilla was scarcely underway when bitter cold swept up the valley and the river froze from shore to shore in one night.

Well, by damn, the thought. We've not quite spent ourselves yet against this wretched climate, but we shall if we have to.

And so for the next few days, men stood in the prow of the leading boat, smashing at the ice with axes and pikes to make a channel, while General Hamilton stood grimly under an awning in the stern, watching the miles go by one foot at a time.

At last a few days' journey from Vincennes, the cold spell broke, the ice turned mushy and deteriorated, and for the first time in seventy days General Hamilton's fleet was borne toward its destination on smooth, deep, swift water.

Now, Colonel George Rogers Clark, or Long Knife, as your name may be, he thought, your ill-advised little adventure into the British domain is about to meet its inevitable outcome, which any intelligent man could have foretold.

FOUR FRENCH BUSHLOPERS, ONE A LIEUTENANT IN THE MILITIA, were making their way up the south shore of the Wabash just after dawn, trotting silently on the sodden brown turf, rifles at their sides. They wore winter suits of fur-lined skins, decorated with fur and beads, and fur caps, and carried bedrolls looped over their shoulders. They had been sent out by Captain Leonard Helm, the American commander at Vincennes, to investigate a rumor that a British force was in the valley. They were three days out of Vincennes and had not seen a soul, white man or Indian, in the wintry wilderness. Suddenly they sensed a great deal of movement around them, and stopped to find themselves surrounded by some twenty Indian braves in war paint, who had risen like ghosts from the brush along the path and stood with muskets trained on them. The men stood still, looking around and seeing that there was no gap through which to flee, then surrendered their weapons to a tall chieftain who came to where they stood. The Indians would answer no questions. They bound the Frenchmen's wrists tightly behind their backs with thongs, then fell into a file and continued in the direction the scouts had been following.

Emerging through a copse of leafless cottonwoods and sycamores, the prisoners were astonished to see a large fleet of bateaux and pirogues tied at the river's edge. A huge camp was being dismantled. White tents were being lowered; men were carrying equipment to the boats; food was being served from a steaming kettle over a huge bed of coals. The Frenchmen had never seen so many Indians in one place. There seemed to be hundreds of them.

And there were white men, in cloaks and red coats. Nearby troops of red-coated soldiers in tall, gold-trimmed hats were being formed into ranks. The glade was a buzz of activity.

The Indians led the Frenchmen to a slender, black-browed officer of apparent high rank, presented them to him, then stood back, apparently quite pleased with themselves.

The officer had the prisoners searched, and looked with avid interest at papers that were taken from the French lieutenant. He came to the lieutenant, appraising him with a mocking look.

"I find this rather remarkable," he said in a tone of heavy sarcasm. "You have here an officer's commission signed by my colleague Governor Abbot, and another officer's commission signed by the American, Clark. Pray tell, isn't it a bit confusing? Do you by chance know which side you are on?" The Frenchman's eyes fell before this mockery. The Englishman continued: "Governor Abbot having left Vincennes some time ago, I must presume that the other commission is current and you're in the pay of Congress?"

The Frenchman nodded.

"Then," the officer continued, "while you're in my care, I hope I can convince you of the error of your ways. Meantime, I give you a choice: You might sit with me and inform me of the state of things at Vincennes, or I could return you to your captors, and let them use you at their discretion. Which will it be, lieutenant?"

The Frenchman sighed unhappily. What a pity he could not take word of this army back to Vincennes. He had become so fond of the merry Captain Helm! But one must survive.

22

VINCENNES, WABASH VALLEY
December 17, 1778

LEONARD HELM STOOD ON THE PARADE GROUND IN FORT SACK-ville, using all his self-control to hold back tears of rage. The French militiamen of the garrison were dispersing out through the fort's main gate, carrying their personal effects, with all the shamefaced demeanor of whipped curs. They, who had been so cocky in parades and on guard duty, were deserting him en masse now that they had learned a British army was on its way.

Helm chewed tobacco furiously, his gray chin whiskers moving up and down with his ruminations, and watched the departing Frenchmen in disgust. He spat in their direction. He fingered the pistol in his belt and spoke to the American aide at his side.

"Last one out I got half a mind t' shoot in th' butt!"

"Aye."

"But that wouldn't do no good. Well, son, looks like that leaves you and me an' a score of Frenchies who ain't yet quite petrified, t' defend this trap again' General Hamilton's army and a half-thousand redskins. Hope you're feelin' perty spunky." The soldier nodded with a gray half smile. "Shut that gate once all th' mongrels has gone," Helm said, "an' turn that cannon on it. Maybe we c'd at least give Mister Hamilton a taste of grape-shot when 'e busts in. Now I got t' go write a letter to Cunnel Clark. Get one o' them lopers provisioned fer a quick run over t' Kaskasky, an' send 'im to me. One we can trust. If there is such a thing."

The soldier saluted and Helm set off across the dismal compound to his quarters. He hated having to write letters of any kind, but this was going to be the most distasteful one ever.

Good ol' George, he thought. This is gonna piss him somethin' turrible.

God damn this place to hell anyway, he thought. He looked around at the decaying palisades, where there were gaps big enough to stick a fist through. There wasn't a firing platform for marksmen. There wasn't even a serviceable well. The British had neglected the place before they left it in the hands of the French, and the French had neglected it as they neglected, it seemed to Helm, everything but their pleasures. Helm himself had not been able to get repairs started on the place because of his constant negotiations with Wabash tribes.

Just as well it's in this condition, he thought. Since we have no one to defend it, they's no sense giving Hamilton a good stockade.

Helm went into his cold, bare office, drew a small sheet of paper onto his desk, and trimmed a quill. Chewing his lower lip with the effort, he wrote.

December 17, 1778

Dear Sir—

    At this time there is an army within three miles of this place. I hear'd of their comin several days beforehand Sent spies to find the certainty the spies being taken prisoners I never got intelligence till they got within 3 miles of the town as I had calld the militia & had all assurance of their integrity I orderd at the fireing of a Cannon every man to appear, but I saw but few

Helm heard the rattle of drums in the distance and went to the door. Looking out over the palisade he could see a large body of men and flags coming over the brow of a rise beyond the town. He shook his head and started back inside. The courier he had sent for arrived at the door. Helm told him to wait and returned to his desk. The runner seemed very disconcerted by the sound of the drums. Helm dipped the quill again.

Ecuse hast as the army is in sight. my Determination is to defend the Garrison though I have but 21 men but what has lef me
The army is in three hundred yd of village   you must think how I feel   not four men that I can really depend on but am determined to act brave think of my condition   I know its out of my power to defend the town as not one of the militia will take arms thoug before sight of the army no braver men. their is a flag at a small distance   I must conclud

Yr humble servt
Leo^d Helm

Must stop.

Helm gave the letter to the courier. "Take it to Kaskaskia as quick as you can go, and go directly to Cunnel Clark. Answer him any questions as best ye can from what you've seen here. Godspeed, now!" The man nodded and vanished out the door.

Captain Helm took off his buckskin coat, hung it on a peg, and pulled on his blue uniform coat. He put on a black three-cornered hat, smoothed down with his hands the whiskers which tended to stick out in every direction from his jaws, and went out toward the gate. His few remaining French militiamen, pale and morose, looking as if they wished they had left with the others, hung about the walls, staring through the firing ports.

Climbing onto the platform, Helm looked out over the sharpened log-ends of the palisade and saw the entire village overrun with Indians, all hanging back and waiting near the cover of the

village houses and watching the fort. A regiment of enemy militia was drawn up in ranks along the far edge of the sloping
plain that lay between the fort and the town, and a company of
redcoated regulars stood in a square slightly in advance of them.
Four drummers and a flag-bearer stood in front and the drums
chattered. A chilly rain mixed with snow was now falling. *God,*
Helm thought. *Hopeless.*

A mounted British officer, seeing Helm, raised a red flag and
rode slowly across the field toward the gate. The drums
stopped. The officer reined in his horse within speaking distance.

"My I speak with your commandant, please?" he called.

"You are."

"I am Major Hay. I . . ."

"You mean Jehu Hay?" Helm snarled.

"The same."

"If it wasn't fer that truce flag, Major, I'd shoot you plumb
out of that saddle, you brigand," Helm twanged.

"Come, come, sir!"

"Come, come yerself," Helm retorted. "I won't talk to you.
If you have a *civilized* officer among you, send him to talk."

Hay hesitated, red with anger, then turned his horse and rode
back. Soon he returned with another officer, a slight man with
a long loose jaw and dark brows.

"I am General Henry Hamilton," this man said. "Whom am
I addressing?"

"Captain Leonard Helm. Militia of Virginia."

"Captain Helm, good day. In the name of his Britannic Majesty King George, I order you to surrender this post. I'm aware
of the straits you are in; it would be futile to resist."

Helm went down from the parapet, his heart racing, and ordered the private to throw open the gate. Hamilton found himself staring into the barrel of a cannon, beside which stood the
American captain and a private holding a lighted fuse match.
The captain said:

"Surrender on what terms, your Britannic lordship?"

Hamilton stared in amazement at the shaggy old man, then
smiled. Jove, what guts this one has, he thought. "With the full
honors of war, Captain."

Helm stood and looked at General Hamilton. What would
George do now? he wondered. It was impossible to imagine
him surrendering. But then I don't reckon he'd've ever let those
Frenchies cower out the way I done. Miserable, he turned and

looked around the compound. The only living creatures within were a score of trembling French militiamen, and thirty-two horses in a temporary corral. He turned again and looked at the hundreds of armed men in the distance.

One thing George don't like, he thought, is wastin' blood.

"If I let you and them savages of yourn come in this fort, can you keep 'em under control?"

"Certainly, Captain."

"That's a promise?"

"A promise."

"In that case, I accept your terms." He walked out the gate, tears running into his whiskers.

In fifteen minutes the British colors were again flying over Post Vincennes.

JUST BEFORE HIS ARRIVAL AT VINCENNES, GENERAL HAMILTON HAD dispatched Indian bands to lie along the trails leading from Vincennes to Kaskaskia and to the Falls of the Ohio, in order to intercept any communications the rebels might attempt along those routes.

Such a band was encamped, without a fire, in a thicket five miles west across the Wabash from Vincennes. Hearing a call in imitation of a barred owl, they rose swiftly and glided to the edge of the growth. One of their braves lay there, and he pointed toward an approaching figure in the gray distance: a white man trotting swiftly along the trail. As he drew near they recognized him as one of the Big Knives. Flintlocks clicked as five muskets were cocked and aimed. As the runner drew abreast of the ambush, several muskets fired in a ragged volley. He dropped to his knees, struck in several places in the body, and tried to raise his rifle, then dropped it. When the Indians surrounded him he was on hands and knees, coughing and spewing blood onto the path. One of the warriors, laughing, ran to him, grabbed the tail of his muskrat cap and snatched it off. Then he wound his fingers into the man's yellow hair, jerked his head up, and with two swift strokes of his red-handled knife, sliced a circular cut on the scalp. Then he yanked the hair, and the trophy came off with a soft *pop*.

The victim rallied enough to stagger to his feet. His eyes glazed with dying, he drew his long-bladed hunting knife out of its sheath and staggered toward the Indian as if to retrieve his scalp by force. The Indian backed away, still laughing and taunting, shaking the scalp just out of his reach. The white man sank to his knees again, and the Indian began slapping him back and forth across the face with his own scalp. In moments the man's face was smeared with blood and his eyes were full of it. As he began to fall forward, the other braves came close and each struck him a coup with tomahawk or warclub.

They searched his mutilated body and found a small, folded scrap of paper. They would take it with the scalp to the white father Hamilton. He would be very pleased and give them presents.

That was as far as Leonard Helm's letter to George Rogers Clark went that day.

GENERAL HAMILTON HAD DECIDED DEFINITELY THAT HE MUST WINter in Vincennes and wait until spring to start an expedition against the Illinois. The rivers were flooding, and covered with slabs of broken ice that would grind boats to pieces; the weather was raw and snowy. The ground was a chilly muck. Snow fell and melted, fell and melted again.

Hamilton scourged the Vincennes inhabitants with his tongue for their treachery and ingratitude in taking the oath to America, made them renounce that oath, and then read them a new one:

Vincennes, 19 December, 1778

We, the undersigned, declare and acknowledge to have taken the oath of allegiance to Congress, in doing which we have forgotten our duty to God and have failed in our duty to man. We ask pardon of God and we hope from the goodness of our legitimate sovereign, the King of England, that he will accept our submission and take us under his protection as good and faithful subjects, which we promise and swear to become before God and before man. In faith of which we sign with our hand or certify with our ordinary mark, the aforesaid day and month of the year 1778.

After hearing it read, the citizens of Vincennes kissed a crucifix at their altar and signed a copy of the oath. Hamilton perused the document in his new office with a sneer of disgust. This, he thought, is scarcely worth the paper it's on. But the formality of it is done. And maybe even Frenchmen aren't base enough to violate three oaths in a row.

Only a small group of citizens refused to sign the paper, among them two militia officers named Bosseron and LeGras, and a younger brother of Father Gibault. These men were placed under constant surveillance, and the young Gibault was brought to Hamilton several times to hear his brother denounced as a blackguard and a traitor in papal skirts.

Hamilton decided to spend the winter placing the wretched Fort Sackville in a perfect state of repair. Working his men six days a week, he began building a new guardhouse and barracks for four companies, sank a well, ordered the construction of two large blockhouses of oak, with embrasures for five pieces of cannon each, altered and lined the stockades, set up firing platforms, and laid the parade ground with gravel. In the meantime he sent war parties out to set up posts near the Falls of the Ohio and the mouth of the Wabash, and messengers to summon the tribes for the great spring war council.

He also authorized one enterprising Ottawa chieftain to go across to the Illinois country above Kaskaskia with a large body of warriors and some French guides, conceal himself there, and lie in ambush for an opportunity to capture Colonel Clark, who was known to travel with regularity on the road between Kaskaskia and Cahokia and to go often across the river to the Spanish settlement at St. Louis.

"If you bring him to me," Hamilton told the Ottawa, "you will have rewards beyond imagination. I will load you with gifts to make you rich, and all red men will speak your name forever. But you must bring him to me alive," he added. With such rewards as those in prospect, he knew, the chieftain might—indeed, probably would—try to bring in any scalp or carcass and claim it was Clark's. "Alive," he repeated.

ON DECEMBER TWENTY-FOURTH, FRANCISCO VIGO RODE EASTward on horseback along the Kaskaskia–Vincennes trail, sleet lashing the back of his coat. The sky was the color of iron. He had been on the muddy road for six days.

Five miles west of the Wabash, the band of Indians who had scalped Captain Helm's messenger crouched in the thicket and watched him come.

Vigo was very happy. His heart had been glowing ever since he had learned of the betrothal of his two favorite young people, Colonel Clark and Teresa de Leyba. They made the most beautiful pair of young lovers he had ever seen, and he could bring tears to his eyes just by imagining them together. He wondered sometimes how they would reconcile their two different religions, but Vigo personally believed that both their gods were the same and would show them a way.

And now he was on his way to see another favorite comrade, the rowdy and hilarious Captain Leonard Helm. He loved to visit with Helm whenever he was in Vincennes, and often would bring him gifts. This time he also had good news for Helm, a letter saying that Colonel Clark would soon be sending him a shipment of provisions and ammunition. Vigo sang softly to himself as he rode along, and did not see the Indians until his horse shied and several warriors in paint jumped into his path with their muskets aimed at him.

Surprised to find Indians acting this way in the region where the tribes had signed peace treaties with Colonel Clark, Vigo brought his horse under control. He did not reach for his pistols, but raised his hand in a greeting.

One of the young braves made a dash toward Vigo from the back. But he was stopped suddenly by a shout from the chieftain, who told him this man was not a Big Knife.

And by that fine a stroke of fortune, Francisco Vigo kept his scalp.

The Indians for some reason had not searched him—perhaps because he obviously was not an American—but they might at any time, and they were staying too close around him to allow him to dispose of George's letter.

They seemed to be taking him directly toward Vincennes, a fact which bewildered Vigo considerably. His captors, leading his horse by the reins, took him to the bank of the Wabash, where another band waited with canoes. Here there was a small armed camp with several wigwams; obviously it was a post set up primarily for ferrying people across the river, and he wondered why apparently hostile Indians had established such a network of permanent camps and stations hereabouts. It was not until the canoe was halfway across the river and Vigo saw through the slanting sleet that Fort Sackville flew a British flag that the answer became evident to him. Vincennes in control of the British! he thought. How could this be?

Obviously, then, he was being taken to the British headquarters there, which meant there was a distinct possibility that he could yet be hanged as a spy, if his captors should find Colonel Clark's letter on his person.

Vigo sat amidships in the canoe on his own saddlebags and searched his mind for a way to dispose of the letter without being seen. The paddler in front of him could not see him, of

course, but the one in the stern could. If he took the letter out
and dropped it over the side, he would give himself away.

He had a thought then. There was not much time. Reaching
under him into the saddlebag, he drew out a half a loaf of
bread. The Indian in the stern watched him warily. Vigo tore off
a chunk of the bread and, smiling, offered it to him. The Indian
nodded and reached for it, trailing his paddle with one hand. He
began tearing hungrily at the good bread with his teeth and
chewing it, nodding with pleasure. Vigo offered a piece forward
to the other paddler, but he shook his head. Then the trader tore
off bits and began eating them himself. Seemingly enjoying an
innocent repast, he bent forward over the loaf as if to shield it
from the sleet. Surreptitiously groping inside his coat, he drew
the letter out and slipped it under the loaf in his left hand. Then,
tearing a piece of the letter off with each morsel of bread, he
managed to devour it by the time the canoe touched the eastern
shore.

It had tasted awful and made tough chewing, but, in a manner of speaking, Vigo had never relished a meal more.

GENERAL HAMILTON SAT IN HIS OFFICE, ACROSS THE HEARTH FROM
his captive, the genial American Leonard Helm. Sleet hissed
against the window, but the fire radiated heat and cheer, and
Hamilton was enjoying one of the toddies Helm made so well.

Hamilton had admired Helm from the moment of their first
confrontation at the gate, and had since treated him well. They
had become companions, to the extent that inveterate enemies
could, and spent many hours in droll conversation. Helm's
coarse but wise humor somehow struck a strange chord in Hamilton's cynical mind, and the Englishman had come to prefer his
company over that of any of his own officers, whose talk was
always obeisant and predictable. One never knew what Helm
would say. He was a jolly adversary, and forever sniped at the
British character or told outrageous adventure tales emphasizing
the superior courage and integrity of the Americans. Hamilton
retorted always with observations on the recklessness, the oaf-
ishness, and the poverty of the Americans. "Why, just look at
yourself, Captain," he would laugh, "for a perfect example of
what I mean!" And Helm would accommodate him then with a
raucous belch, or break wind loudly, or feign to beg a shilling
for the purchase of a new American flag, which, he said, he
would be raising over Fort Sackville any day if the British made
the mistake of sleeping late.

Hamilton had a deep curiosity about the audacious Virginian, George Rogers Clark, who had materialized so suddenly in British territory to complicate his life, but chose to pretend indifference to the subject, for Helm's benefit. He would never actually ask Helm anything about Clark; on the other hand, Helm would never volunteer any information about him. But Helm enjoyed Hamilton's offhand efforts to fish him for observations about Clark. "Oh, he's a fairly good lad, as all Virginians air," was the most Helm would say about him, but his sly smirk as he said it was a constant taunt to Hamilton, who wondered what Helm was leaving unsaid.

All Hamilton knew was that Clark's name had the force of magic among most of the Indians. The Englishman had spent much of his stay here in Vincennes trying with all his considerable skill to buy back the allegiance of the tribes, and was infuriated every time some chief would refuse his presents with a condescending apology to the effect that he was now a brother of Long Knife. Tobacco's Son, chief of the nearby Piankeshaws, had spurned Hamilton with forthright rudeness, going so far as to declare himself a kinsman of Captain Helm and volunteering to be locked up in captivity with him to prove his devotion. Hamilton had not accommodated him. Some bands that had not even treated with the Long Knife would explain patiently to Hamilton that, although they were willing to go with him against Americans in the Kentucky or Pittsburgh or anywhere else, they would not strike where Clark was. That always awed Hamilton profoundly, because it was not the nature of warriors to profess fear of anyone. Hamilton made the error of telling Helm one day about such a refusal, but had since vowed he would never again; he didn't think he could again put up with that insufferable smirk on Helm's face.

The American, in turn, had discovered to his surprise and delight a certain prudishness in the British commandant. Hamilton would become extremely uneasy at any kind of bawdry. Like some other prigs Helm had met, Hamilton seemed repelled by lewdness because of a basic fascination with it, and Helm thus would use every opportunity to discomfit him with tidbits of erotic lore, particularly those he could attribute to Englishwomen. Helm had become acquainted with certain practices and devices enjoyed by the Creole women in Kaskaskia and Vincennes, in particular a stimulating artifact made from the soft-lashed eyelid of a goat, and would describe it and its use in detail to a horrified Hamilton, having transplanted the tale to the prewar colonies where, he claimed, the instrument was employed by most Tory wives. Helm once even inquired, with a conspiratorial man-to-man wink, whether Madame Hamilton had ever used one. That discussion had nearly terminated the relationship of the two officers. Hamilton had leaped to his feet, livid, and drawn his sword. "Enough, you filthy-tongued old freak!" he had shouted. "I've had all the leering obscenity I'll hear from you! What insolence, to talk that way to a superior officer and a gentleman! By God, Helm, I don't know whether to chain you to the guardhouse wall or run you through on the spot!"

"Possum shit, General!" Helm had roared back. "No man who buys the scalps of men has anything to say about obscenity!"

Reeling, then going into a paroxysm of rage, Hamilton had ordered Helm out of his sight, and they had not spoken for two days. Gradually, however, growing bored by the sycophancy of his junior officers, Hamilton had restored his welcome to Helm, and the topic of scalping had not yet been brought up again. Helm would from time to time, however, observe Hamilton's annoyance on some point or other by musing, "What's th' matter, Mister Hamilton, am I gittin' yer *goat*?"

They had called a truce for this day, however; it was Christmas Eve and both men were enjoying their toddies by the fire, and Hamilton had been waxing nostalgic about the Yule season in his homeland where, he insisted, the art of celebrating Noël had attained its highest form. "The food, the warmth, Captain, you can't imagine it, out here in this cruel wilderness!"

"Aye, it is cruel out here indeed, cold and heartless, General," mused Helm. "You know, Christmas is a special sad time for my friend George."

"You mean Clark?" Hamilton inquired. He couldn't believe that Helm was about to reveal voluntarily something about his commander. He sipped his toddy and gazed into the fire, feigning disinterest.

"Colonel Clark, aye," Helm continued. "It was on Christmas Day of '76 that a band o' Shawnees killed or captured his favorite cousin, Joseph Rogers. They were in your pay, quite likely . . ."

Hamilton drew his lips thin but said nothing. He was determined to hold his temper and not let this cozy moment be spoiled by Helm's insinuations.

"Did you ever hear of a prisoner by the name of Joseph Rogers, General?" Helm continued. "Nay? Well," he sighed, "it's a pity. George ain't no melancholy soul by any stretch, but at Christmas time, after a couple of my toddies, he don't fail to bring that up with considerable remorse." Helm chuckled. "Mebbe," he added, " 'cause he feels responsible, an' it's the only mistake he's ever been knowed to make."

"Come now," Hamilton growled. "We all make mistakes. I make mistakes even, myself . . ."

"Well, you're an Englishman."

"I'll disregard that. I flatter myself that I seem to make fewer than most men I know, but I have made a few. Trusting Frenchmen, for one . . ."

"Now that *is* perty dumb, all right," Helm nodded.

"But, you know, Captain, if I were to believe half of the myths I've heard about Mister Clark, why I should have to be jealous of him indeed!"

"Oh, but you really air," grinned Helm. "Why, a blind man c'd see that . . ."

"Pish! Why, I never even heard of the man until last summer!" Hamilton's voice was taking on an edge of annoyance.

"Well, give 'im time, Gen'ral. He's just a lad."

"What do you mean, 'just a lad'?"

"Why, he's, I believe, just twenty-five or so." Helm watched in pleasure as Hamilton's brow darkened at that humiliating news, then he added: "But he's a fairly good lad, as all Virginians air. Ha, ha!"

The orderly rapped on the door at this moment and came in. "Sir, the Indians have brought in a suspicious fellow they caught just across the river."

"Then pay them, and put him in the guardhouse. I'll see to him after the holiday."

"Begging your pardon, sir, but he appears to be a gentleman of substance."

"He does, eh? Very well, let's have a look at him."

Vigo and Helm were equally astonished to meet each other in this office of the British commandant; their eyes widened and they were about to burst into greetings, but both at once realized that a sign of recognition might show Vigo to be a partisan of the Americans and thus jeopardize him. So they checked themselves and merely nodded at each other politely, and Vigo went toward Hamilton with an outstretched hand and his best merchant's smile on his face.

"I am Francisco Vigo of St. Louis, Excellency, a Spanish subject and a poor fur trader in these parts."

"General Henry Hamilton, sir. I've never known of a *poor* fur trader, I must say. This is Captain Helm, my most privileged prisoner of war."

"A prisoner!" Vigo exclaimed, taking Helm's hand and squeezing it harder than he appeared to. "Why, sir, what an intriguing situation to find oneself in! I do hope you're being treated well."

"Tol'ably. He takes my chains off when I promise to mix 'im a toddy. Like one?"

"Indeed, thank you. It's bitter out there."

"Where from, Mr. Vigo?" Hamilton asked.

"By way of Kaskaskia, actually, sir. I have a branch there."

"Kaskaskia, eh?" Hamilton's eyelids lowered suspiciously. "And you say you're a trader, eh?"

"He is, Gen'l," interjected Helm from the sideboard. "I've heard of Mister Vigo. Trades here sometimes, too. Reputed to be a very honest merchant. You're here on business, I presume?"

"Indeed I am, Captain. Thank you. Gentlemen, to your health."

"God save the king," said Hamilton.

"Before it's too late," added Helm.

"Mr. Vigo," said Hamilton, swallowing. "I've heard some annoying reports that the Spanish inhabitants have been, shall we say, consorting rather blatantly with the American rebels. Would you know anything about that?"

"I know nothing about what you've heard, Excellency. I . . . as I said, I'm but a merchant, with no politics to speak of."

"So you say. Well, Mr. Vigo. I can't imagine why you're conducting trade in the depth of this season. Do you Catholics actually do business on the birthday of your Savior?"

"Careful of him," Helm said to Vigo. "He can be a real snot."

"Damn your eyes, Captain," Hamilton snapped. "Be still!"

"Actually," said Vigo, wide-eyed at such crossness between captor and captive, "I had expected to conclude all my duties here before the Holy Day, but the roads were abominable."

"Well, sir, I should like you to lay here a while at Vincennes. I have a great deal of work to do before the New Year, but I should certainly like to talk with you when I'm at leisure."

"Perhaps next time, Excellency," said Vigo. "I really cannot stay here long. A day or . . ."

"Mr. Vigo, I must insist!"

Helm looked at Hamilton through hooded eyes. Obviously, he thought, he wants to prevent word of his presence here from getting back to George.

Vigo was stroking his goatee now, looking less than happy. "Do you mean, sir, that you would detain me?"

"Until I'm satisfied, Mr. Vigo."

"Satisfied in what way, sir?"

"That you understand the consequences of consorting with enemies of His Majesty."

"When you drink toddies with me, Mister Hamilton," interrupted Helm, "you're consorting yourself with an enemy of His Majesty."

"There's as much truth as cheek in that, Captain. Maybe I ought to leave you in the guardhouse."

"Frankly, Gen'l, I'd be more comfy there than here listenin' t'you browbeating yer Spanish guest."

"To hell with you, you bloody bumpkin. All right, Mr. Vigo. You will stay, then."

"I should remind you, sir, that I am a Spanish subject."

"The orderly will prepare quarters for you, Mr. Vigo. Good day."

"Well, Mr. Vigo," said Helm with a hidden wink. "What an intriguing situation to find oneself in!"

GOVERNOR HAMILTON HAD DECIDED THAT HE COULD NOT LET THE rumored fraternization of the Mississippi Spanish and the rebels go unremarked, so he sat at his desk one day in January and wrote:

To His Excellency the Governor of Louisiana
Don Bernardo Galvez

Sir:

M^r Le Comte having desired permission to pass to New Orleans, I embrace the opportunity of kissing your Excellency's hands, and at the same time of acquainting you with the circumstance which procures me that honor.

The Rebel Americans having got footing in the Illinois country, and of course having opened a communication to the Colonies by taking post there and at this place, I thought it my duty to dispossess them as soon as convenient.

For this purpose I set out with a small force from the Detroit, so late as the seventh of last October, and arrived here on the 17th of December, having a few Chiefs and Warriors of thirteen different Nations of Indians along with me.

Having taken possession of the Fort, and received the submission of the inhabitants who laid down their arms and swore allegiance to His Britannic Majesty, I contented myself, for this winter, with sending out parties to different quarters.

Your Excellency cannot be unacquainted with what was common practice in the time of your predecessor in the Government of New Orleans, I mean the sending of supplies of gunpowder and other stores to the Rebels, then in arms against the Sovereign—Tho' this may have been transacted in an underhand manner by merchants, unknown to the Governor, I must suppose that under your Excellency's orders, such commerce will for the future be positively prohibited—

The several Nations of savages who accompanied me to this country may (if this traffic be continued) forget what instructions I have given them from time to time with relation to the subjects of His Catholic Majesty, but the native inhabitants of the banks of the Ohio River, must be particularly jealous of strangers coming up thro their country to supply the Rebels with whom they are at war. At the same time that I mention this to your Excellency, for the sake of individuals who might suffer from their ignorance of the English being in possession of this post, and of the communication by water to the Mississippi, I think it incumbent on me to represent further to your Excellency that the Rebels at Kaskasquias being in dayly apprehension of the arrival of a body of men from our upper posts accompanyed with the savages from that quarter, have declared that they will take refuge on the Spanish Territory as soon as they are apprized of their coming—

As it is my intention early in the Spring to take a progress towards the Illinois, I shall represent to the officers commanding at several small forts and posts for His Catholic Majesty, the impropriety of affording an asylum to Rebels, in arms against their lawful Sovereign—If after so candid a declaration the Rebels should find shelter in any fort or post on the Mississippi, it will become my duty to dislodge them, in which case their protectors must blame their own conduct, if they should suffer any inconvenience in consequence.

Perhaps I may be favor'd with a letter from your Excellency before the arrival of the reinforcements I expect the next Spring, at the same time that the officers acting under your Excellency's orders may receive notice how they are to act, whether as friends or enemies to the British Empire—

I have the honor to be, Sir

Your Excellency's most devoted and most obedient humble servant

HENRY HAMILTON
Lieutenant Governor of Detroit
St. Vincennes, 13 January 1779

23

KASKASKIA, ILLINOIS COUNTRY
January 15, 1779

THE FORTY INDIANS WHOM GENERAL HAMILTON HAD SENT TO KIDnap Colonel Clark had been lying in wait for several weeks, in a hidden camp alongside a creek three miles above Kaskaskia with that patience known only to single-minded warriors who see an opportunity to gain great glory. They had stayed there in constant jeopardy of being discovered, though the weather was so miserable that few people were abroad in the Mississippi valley.

Then, one bleak, snowy day in mid-January, it appeared that their opportunity had fallen into their laps. A small detachment of the braves, posted in hiding alongside the Kaskaskia-Cahokia road, heard voices and a jingling of harness coming toward them on the road. They shrank further into the brush and watched a small party of white men come up the muddy road from Kaskaskia. It contained seven armed horsemen who were obviously Big Knives, and two carriages full of French gentlemen. The carriages came on laboriously, their wheels clogged with mire or slithering in the deep snow. The horsemen rode slowly to allow the carriages to keep up.

Suddenly one of the carriages swamped, entering the ford of the creek, its right wheels sliding into an axle-deep rut, and nearly turned over. The weight of the passengers, which had shifted to the downward side, drove the wheels deeper until the body of the vehicle lay on the snowy mire. The group halted; the horsemen were ordered back to assist. Soon half the members of the entourage were up to their hips in the water and muck, cursing, flailing, laughing, hauling, and shouting advice, trying to help the floundering carriage-horse free the conveyance from the quagmire. One large young man sat on his horse nearby, waiting, talking with one of the riflemen. They were within one hundred yards of where the Indians lay in the snow. One of the French guides with the Indian band pointed out excitedly that the big man on the horse was the person they had come to capture. Are you sure? he was asked. Yes. That is the Long Knife, he swore.

Now the Indians were for the moment uncertain what to do. Their quarry sat in plain sight a few hundred feet from them, but his party looked too strong to attack without the rest of the band, which was encamped a half mile up the creek and unaware of his presence. The Indians could have stormed the group and killed them in the mud, perhaps, but the Long Knife had to be brought in alive, and he appeared too alert to be taken by surprise without a fight. And his life was said to be charmed. He was reputed to be as elusive as the water snake, and would have to be surrounded by many braves before he could be caught alive. Adding to the Indians' perplexity was the fact that the brush in which they lay was surrounded by a treeless field; they could not leave it to go and summon their brothers without being seen by the Long Knife. So they could only lie in hiding until the situation might change.

George Rogers Clark sat on his horse and watched the proceedings around the carriage with some amusement, now and then scanning the countryside. He thought of getting down and adding his strength to the effort, but had learned long since that an officer, especially an officer in command, upsets his people if he stoops to such things.

George was happy. He was en route to Cahokia and St. Louis after a long absence. Duties at Kaskaskia had kept him working almost around the clock throughout the winter, and he had been laid low for several weeks by some unnameable illness which had sapped all his strength and kept him in fevers for days at a time. He was recovered totally from it now, but it had set him many days behind in his work, and he had had to labor over pay and commissary records and judicial cases even during Christmas Day and New Year's Day. Now he was within two or three days of seeing his Teresa again, Teresa and her whole lovely family. He had missed her sorely. In retrospect it seemed that only his desire to see her again had pulled him through his sickness. It was this anticipation, it seemed, that offered any hope to him in his situation. The only thing he knew for a certainty these days was that he loved Teresa de Leyba.

He sat astride his stallion and considered, as he had to do every hour, his dubious circumstances. In nearly a year, since setting out down the Ohio from Pittsburgh, he had not had so much as a scratch of the pen from Patrick Henry. Despite the help de Leyba and Vigo were giving him with credit, he was finding it more and more difficult to acquire provisions in the valley. Farmers and provisioners, having little faith in the Americans' credit, had raised their prices steadily, until everything cost at least ten times as much as it had upon their arrival.

Worrisome from the standpoint of his army's safety was a flurry of unsubstantiated rumors about General Hamilton marching out of Detroit last autumn with a large force of troops and Indians. Where Hamilton was supposed to have been going was a mystery. The American General Lachlan McIntosh, who had succeeded General Hand at Pittsburgh, was rumored to have set out with an army to take Detroit in the fall, but there had been no word about the outcome of that expedition. In his private thoughts, George believed that Hamilton's sortie with the Indians had been an effort to head off and harass McIntosh. By now, George thought, either Detroit had fallen to McIntosh, or McIntosh has been turned back by Hamilton, or by winter, and Hamilton is probably back in his Detroit headquarters while the rumors remain at large.

Another possibility, a more dread one, was that Hamilton was on his way here to the Illinois country. If he is, George thought, we're in dire trouble. The Americans' manpower was even lower than it had been. Many of the volunteers had gone back to Kentucky and Virginia at the end of their enlistments, and with his remaining companies distributed among the Illinois towns, George doubted that he could provide eighty healthy

Americans in defense of his base at Kaskaskia. Simon Butler, whom he had sent to Kentucky last summer to request volunteers from there, seemed to have vanished off the face of the earth and as likely as not was dead in the forest somewhere.

If Hamilton is indeed on his way here with a large force, George thought, we may well have to fall back across the Mississippi and take asylum with the Spaniards until Virginia sends us some kind of help.

But surely, he thought, if he is in this territory, he is wintering somewhere. At Post Miami, perhaps. Or Ouiatanon on the upper Wabash. He cannot move a land force and all its matériel in this weather, and the rivers are too choked with ice for an expedition by water. And if he left Detroit for here in October, as rumor says, he would have fallen on us weeks ago. Nay, he's either sitting snug in Detroit where he belongs, or he's stranded somewhere on the Wabash. If it's the latter, Helm's scouts will find him, and we'll know soon enough. Relax yourself, he thought. You shouldn't expect news at this time of the year. No one's abroad. Except us, he thought, looking back at the carriage, which finally had been extricated. The gentlemen were clambering back in. George rode back onto the road and the party formed up again.

"Come on gents," he said. "It's nine miles to Prairie du Rocher, and the ladies are waiting!" A ball in the little village had been planned, to entertain them on the first night of their northward journey. The road rose onto slightly higher and drier ground here, and was comparatively clear; the horsemen and carriages clattered off now at high speed.

And the Indians, having lost their valuable prey through an inability to act, rose and waded back through the snow to their main party, to face the wrath of their fierce chieftain. The Ottawa berated his scouts for almost half an hour, promising that their names would be in disgrace in their nation from that day on. Then he stalked about in the snow for a while and tried to imagine some way to retrieve his lost opportunity. There must be a way, he thought, to lure the Long Knife back down this road . . .

THE VILLAGE OF PRAIRIE DU ROCHER HAD ONLY A FEW DOZEN INhabitants, but they were lively souls, and this evening were animated by the honor of playing host to Colonel Clark. The ball began at dark, after the travelers had had an opportunity to change from their wet and muddy clothes, and the music was good, the ladies coquettish, the gentlemen hearty. George danced cheerfully; his knowledge that he would be seeing Teresa within the next two or three days made the extravagant attentions of the ladies seem amusingly vain. George drank, laughed, danced, and talked, trying all the while to crowd the thoughts of his army's plight out of his mind and leave his reveries of Teresa in.

He was being toasted at midnight, as the fiddlers rested, when a mud-spattered messenger from Kaskaskia burst wild-eyed through the door, ran to him, saluted hastily, and blurted out before the startled assemblage:

"Colonel, sir, General Hamilton is outside Kaskaskia with an army of eight hundred!"

Panic and confusion put the room in a turmoil. "What is this?" George demanded, grabbing the courier by the front of his cloak.

"Aye, sir," the man stammered. "He's a-plannin' t' attack t'night, sir, and may already have done! I only got here by stayin' off th' road, sir!"

The guests had grown still now, and stood white-faced, crowding close to hear. "How come you by this?" George demanded. "Have they been seen?"

"Aye, sir. Rather, a party of their Indians was."

Every eye in the place was on George now, as if his next words were to determine their fate.

There seemed to be nothing to do but try to get back to the fort at Kaskaskia and direct its defense, if it were not too late for that already. Gasps and forlorn murmurings filled the room when he announced the intention and told his officers to get the horses saddled. "Get blankets for us all," he said. "In case the fort's already surrounded, we'll wrap in 'em and fall in with the Indians, and maybe get close to the fort that way. Then get let in at a signal." The officers rushed out to get the horses ready.

"You mustn't go back there, Colonel!" guests began imploring. "The town's no doubt taken already, the fort already under attack!"

"Let us row you over to the Spanish shore, Mister Clark," insisted the host. "Then you can study the situation in safety and decide tomorrow what to do."

"Listen, all of you," he said, raising his hand for quiet. "I appreciate your care, but I can't disgrace myself by fleeing with my life, when there's still a chance of doing service, as I reckon

I can. I hope you won't let this news spoil your diversion. Get those fiddlers back to work, and we'll take a few more turns till the horses are ready!"

The people gaped and hesitated for a moment, protesting and clamoring, until George went to a fiddler, took him by the arms and stood him up. "Play, damn you," he muttered. Within minutes the ball was back in progress, though considerably less joyous. Several young men of the village, obviously inspired by the determination of the Americans, volunteered to saddle up and go with him. "Thank you, but no. Stay, in case you have to defend your own. But I would like one fast rider to take a message to Cahokia."

"Here, *mon colonel!*"

George penned a brief note to Captain Bowman, ordering him to bring reinforcements to Kaskaskia as quickly as he could get them on the road and to send apologies across the river to the de Leyba house. The messenger vanished into the night.

Then, his own men and horses being ready, George said his goodbyes to the host and guests, cloaked himself, and led his horsemen off at a breakneck gallop through spitting snow and darkness back down the twelve-mile road toward Kaskaskia and whatever might await them there.

Teresa, he thought as the powerful mount lunged and panted between his legs. Will I ever see you again?

KNOWING THAT AN ARMY WOULD BE GUARDING ANY ROADS NEAR its objective, George led his horsemen off the road and southwestward toward the riverbank when they were within a few miles of Kaskaskia, thus unknowingly avoiding the Indian party which now lay in ambush for him at the fording place where they had seen him that afternoon. They rode across open, snow-covered country in the ghostly semi-darkness, forded a stream that was up to their horses' bellies, passed the old abandoned windmill, and plunged on through the snowdrifts. A mile above the town George brought the riders to a halt and listened for sounds that might tell whether the town was under fire yet. There was nothing.

He rode on, stopping every few yards to listen and watch for signs of enemy pickets, but met no interference. Soon his party was at the edge of the village. There was a hubbub of excited talking and shouting and sobbing to be heard in the streets, and when he rode in among the houses he was recognized and greeted by scores of tearful men and women who implored him to save their town.

Entering the fort he found his garrison already getting into a state of defense, and there were several of the young Frenchmen who had come in with arms to assist. Riflemen were on the parapets, outlined dimly against the snowy night sky, and ammunition was being hauled to all the firing stations.

George assembled his captains and lieutenants in his headquarters and asked for their observations. Most of them felt that the British force was waiting for the weather to clear up before attacking.

"From the looks of it, they might also be hangin' back to give us time t' abandon the place," said Captain Bailey. "I reckon it'd please 'em if we did."

"Likely enough," said George, "but if so, they aren't going to have that pleasure. If we have to lose this place, we'll sell it dear. Now what about the Frenchmen? Have they declared their intents?"

"Just them few as you saw in th' compound, George. The rest of 'em are havin' meetings all over the place. Reckon they'll let us know come morning."

"Aye. I think this is going to be the trial of their fidelity. I'm not sure I want 'em all anyway. If they take up arms to defend the town, we'll be obliged probably to go out with 'em and give the enemy battle on th' commons."

"We'd surely lose the whole that way, against an army of eight hundred," said Bailey.

"If I could have my choice," George said, "I'd prefer to have those without families in here to reinforce the garrison, and the rest lay neutral. Bowman ought to come in by the river by tonight, and then I don't doubt but with enough provision we could hold out a few weeks till Mr. Hamilton's Indians should tire of the entertainment, as they always do if they don't have immediate success. I won't pretend our situation isn't bad, but we've held forts in Kentucky against greater odds. What say you, boys?"

"Why, I say, bring 'em on," laughed Bailey. "My people come out here t' fight Englishmen and Indians, an' they ain't had th' chance t' shed a drop of blood yit."

"Aye!"

"My company's itchin' fer a little diversion!"

"Mine, too!"

"Good." George grinned, reassured by their spirit. "Come

daylight, then, we'll hear what the townfolk intend. We'll have to burn down the houses close around the fort if we're going to be under siege. Now, gents, see to your guards, and get a bit of sleep if you can before day comes. Jim, would you fetch me the priest, please? I need to talk with him."

Father Gibault came within ten minutes, his eyes bulging even more than usual, and embraced his friend. He had two pistols stuck in the sash of his cassock. He knocked a load of snow off the brim of his hat, accepted a glass of brandy and sat down.

"Well, Father, you've been among your flock. What d'you make of their resolve?"

Gibault looked down at his brandy. "If the enemy were not so numerous, George . . . if it were a more equal contest, I think they'd take your side, my son, but . . ."

George gritted his teeth. "They lack in character, Father."

"They won't be against you, you know, my boy. They'll have their ways of helping."

"A man stands fast or he doesn't," George said.

"You have to understand. This is not their war. They simply find themselves in the midst . . ."

"France is allied with America, Father."

Gibault sighed.

"Anyway," George went on, "what I brought you here to say, my friend, is that you stand in more personal danger yourself than any man of us here, including myself. I mean because of what you did for us at Vincennes. Hamilton will want your hide, Father, and so I should feel more easy if you were over on the Spanish side of the river. Would you be so kind as to take some papers and money across for me tomorrow?"

The priest's eyes filled. He blinked, drained off his brandy, and sighed. "It would be wise, wouldn't it?"

"It would."

"Very well. I'll go and have my servant pack. He and I can row; you won't have to spare any of your defenders for that." He rose. "I'll come for the papers at daybreak. God protect you, my son."

"And protect you too, my friend. When this adventure is over, Miss de Leyba and I will have need of a priest, I expect, and none other would be good enough."

AT DAYLIGHT THE TOWNSMEN WERE ASSEMBLED AT THE FORT AND George went before them. They were haggard and agitated, apparently having counciled all night about their plight.

"I want to know what you think of doing," George said. "Whether you want to defend the town or not. If you do, then I'll bring my troops down from the fort and lead you. If the enemy is waiting out the weather, we might even discover their camp and get some advantage of 'em. What will it be, gentlemen?"

A dignified elder of the town stood up and held his hat before him. "Colonel Clark," he began, "please understand that we are all in your interest. We have prospered and enjoyed the greatest happiness since your arrival here.

"But we have studied our situation maturely. Even with your whole force aiding us, we would make but a poor figure against so considerable an enemy. Have you thought, sir, of crossing the river and taking Spanish protection?"

"Not seriously, no."

"We fear, *mon colonel*, that surely you could not keep possession of the fort for more than a single day. The enemy would surely set the adjacent houses on fire and thus burn the fort as well.

"With sorrow in our hearts, then, *mon colonel*, and despite our extreme affection for you, we have voted to act neither on the one side nor the other . . ." The old man dropped his eyes. George swept his ferocious gaze over the assembly. They all looked at their hands and squirmed.

George felt his rage rising. He turned his back on the gathering and stalked into an anteroom where he might master his fury unobserved. There he stood for several minutes, fists balled and trembling before him, teeth clenched, eyes shut tight.

When the passion had subsided, he walked back out to face them.

"If ever there was a set of traitors," he said in a voice icy with contempt, "here they stand. I think then that you need no longer expect any favor from me. I am forced to conceive you as my secret enemies, and shall have to treat you as such! As for the enemy burning your houses, they shan't have the opportunity, as I've decided in my own interest to do that myself first. Now, damn you, out of my sight!"

The people began a whining and complaining among themselves, and two or three pressed forward. "Colonel, believe us, we are in your interest! Give us an order, and we will bring enough provision to the fort to hold you the entire winter! Don't think badly of us, sir!"

"By God, yes, I'll take your provisions if you choose to bring them! But if not, that's fine, too! Either way, I've had all of you my stomach can stand. If you don't bring it in, I'll have to burn it all to keep it out of the enemy's hands, so do as you will. But get away before you make me vomit!"

The people began leaving, some of the men even sobbing and wailing. Their distress moved him, despite his anger. Of course their sympathies are with us, he thought. Of course they're suffering. Their town about to be set afire by us whose favor they want; at the same time surrounded by savages they can expect nothing from but destruction.

But they have to understand how desperate and determined we are. And when it comes to defense, I can't have a mob of cowards in my way.

The citizens were not in such a state of lethargy that they had not taken his hint about burning provisions, and by evening they had brought into the fort enough stores of all kinds to last six months. They came up the hill bearing it in barrows and on their shoulders, many with tears streaming down their faces. The fort was soon in a good state of defense, and George sent several parties of men out with orders to find where the enemy was, hoping perhaps to attack their detachments swiftly and weaken them before they could take possession of the town. Other soldiers he sent out to burn down the houses that stood in the way of a good defense, and by late afternoon the immediate neighborhood was under a gray pall of dirty smoke. George stood on the parapet with Captain Bailey and they watched orange flames lick among the timbers, watched roofs and walls seep white smoke, then turn black and cascade roaring to the ground, watched cinders and ash billow into the sky to rain down on the snow everywhere. As he had expected, the heavy cover of snow on the roofs prevented the fire from spreading to any houses he had not intended to burn.

"Why is it, d'you think," he asked, "that a hearth fire smells so good but a burning house stinks so?"

"Don't know, George," Bailey replied with a sad shake of his head. "Guess it's just somethin' people put in wood by livin' in it."

The weather cleared that night. Embers smoked in the snow and mud. The Americans and a few bachelors of the town remained on guard around the palisades. Scouts returned to report that they had not yet turned up a sign of an enemy. The citizens stayed in their homes and prayed. There was no attack that night.

The next day Joseph Bowman arrived from Cahokia with thirty men of his own and a company of French volunteers from Cahokia, and a better spirit began to prevail everywhere in the fort. The Kaskaskians watched the Cahokia volunteers march proudly into the fort and looked more morose and ashamed than ever, even envious.

"Look at those people now," Bailey said. "Reckon they wish by now they'd behaved in a different manner?"

"I'm sure of it."

If the inhabitants had expected more severe treatment now that the Americans were reinforced, they were surprised. George altered his attitude toward them, treating them with kindness and a pleasant aspect whenever a man or group came into the fort with some request or another. Late in the afternoon a delegation of civilians came up, spent a half hour condemning themselves and saying he had indeed treated them as they deserved; they begged his forgiveness and swore that they would fight alongside him to the last man if the enemy did attack. Now the whole place was in a state of readiness and a fierce sense of happiness and strength prevailed.

The scouts soon were all back in, and reported that the only trace of an enemy they had found was a band of about forty Indians three miles up the Kaskaskia—Cahokia road, and that those warriors were in flight now northeastward along the road to Vincennes. George listened to this curious but heartening news and then decided to do something he had not been able to do thus far: trace the origin of the report which had caused all this alarm.

At length a French hunter and a small group of black men were brought to the fort and questioned. The hunter said he had discovered the Indians in their camp on the branch, and had quickly fled back to the fort. That, George reckoned, had been within an hour or two of the time when he and his party had passed the place and been delayed by the swamped carriage. The Indians, knowing they had been seen, apparently had revealed themselves to the Negroes, who had been going up the road on a wood-cutting party, and told them that they were part of a British army of eight hundred about to attack Kaskaskia. They had warned the Negroes not to take that information back to the town, knowing that of course they would. The result had been the alarm which had thrown the town into such a turmoil, and the express rider sent to Prairie du Rocher to summon the commandant home.

George listened to this account, chin in hand, shaking his head, piecing it all together, not sure whether to be joyous with relief or exasperated by the degree of panic that had resulted from so dubious a report. It certainly pointed out to him how edgy his force had become because of the winter's rumors and lack of news. When everybody had left but the American officers, George sat at his desk, one elbow resting on it, his fingers curved over his mouth, and looked from one to another of the officers, now and then emitting a puff of laughter through his nose and shaking his head ruefully.

"Well, boys," he said finally. "Let's us have a drink, and I'm going to make a vow never to leave this danged town again without taking everybody with me!" He burst into a paroxysm of laughter then, followed by all the others, and the brandy was passed around, and they had a long and uproarious party, most of it spent in laughing at themselves.

"But damn it all," he roared drunkenly late in the evening. "If it hadn't been for that fiasco, I'd be in the arms of my sweetheart right now!"

And beyond that point he didn't laugh any more.

TWO FACTS KEPT GEORGE FROM SETTING OUT FOR ANOTHER TRIP TO Cahokia right away.

The fleeing savages having gone in the direction of Vincennes had made him suspicious that Hamilton might be in that vicinity.

And there had not been one word of communication from Helm for more than a month. Even taking into account the weather and the distance, that long and total a silence was very suspicious. It had been his experience that only a blanket of Indian patrols could keep a place fully isolated. Even these vast and unpeopled wilderness regions were crisscrossed constantly by at least a few traders, military couriers, half-breeds, friendly Indians, bushlopers, or other solitary adventurers. He sent scouts toward Vincennes, but they were turned back by high waters.

These facts played on his imagination, and he suffered even more uneasiness than he had while expecting the attack, as he had more time to reflect on it. It seemed to him that unless reinforcements showed up from Virginia soon, the entire Illinois and Wabash country would be in possession of the British in a few months—except Kaskaskia, which he was determined never to surrender—and this whole campaign, which had been thus far attended by such incredible good fortune, would have been in vain.

In the height of his anxiety, on the evening of the twenty-ninth of January, the interpreter Girault came in while George was discussing the predicament with Joseph Bowman.

"Good news, Colonel, a long-lost friend of yours is here!"

"Who is it?" George asked, rising from his place before the fire.

"Señor Vigo!"

The trader bustled in, eyes sunken from weariness but a brilliant smile shining through his black whiskers. They had a noisy reunion, toasting each other with brandy, then Vigo grew somber and sat down in the firelight. "I have a great deal of news for you, Don Jorge. Hamilton has Vincennes."

"What! But I'm not surprised. And Helm?"

"He's, well, a prisoner, but with freedom within the fort. He spends his time aggravating General Hamilton, who through some perversity seems to enjoy it. But listen. I'll tell you how it came about, and I have accurate intelligence about the state of their defense, from my observation and from Captain Helm's. It seems, my friend, that Governor Hamilton descended on Vincennes on December seventeenth, frightening all the Frenchmen out of any resistance . . ."

He told the entire story, including details of Hamilton's skillful renovation of the fort. He drew a slip of paper out of his doublet. "Here is a manifest of all Mr. Hamilton's arms and stores, and a roster of his forces, British and French. He has two or three hundred Indians about the place now, but a larger number of them have gone home for the season or are out on raids against Kentucky. He expects a substantial body of reinforcements and shipment of goods down the Wabash at any time, and anticipates a return of several hundred more Indians when the weather breaks. That, my dear friend, is all the information I was able to obtain; anything I don't report herewith is probably insignificant."

George studied the papers, then handed them to Bowman, who whistled.

"Señor Vigo, this information is invaluable to me. I can't tell you how many doubts it resolves for me. I, personally, and the state of Virginia, and the American Congress, are in your debt. By Jove, I'm amazed that Hamilton let you leave that place!"

"I kept insisting I was a Spanish citizen. Finally, I suppose, he decided that was a valid point. He released me only after making me swear upon my honor that I would not come to you on my way home and tell you of his presence there."

"Oh?"

"Yes. A very perplexing dilemma, my honor in jeopardy, until the answer dawned on me: I went home *first*, touched the door, and then, my pledge thus fulfilled, came here as fast as I could!"

George stared open-mouthed for a moment. Then with a loud whoop, he grabbed the sturdy little Spaniard up in a bear hug and whirled him about the room.

24

KASKASKIA, ILLINOIS COUNTRY
February 3, 1779

KASKASKIA, ILLINOIS, 3 FEBRUARY 1779

To Governor Patrick Henry
   Commonwealth of Virginia

D^r S^r

As it is now near twelve months since I have had the least Intelligence from you I almost despair of any Relief sent to me, I have for many Months past had Reports of an Army Marching Against Detroit, but no Certainty. A Late Menuv^r of The Famous Hair Buyer General, Henry Hamilton Esqr. Lieut. Governor of Detroit, hath allarmed us much; on the 17th of December last he, with a Body of Six Hundred Men Composed of Regulars French Voluntier and Indians Took possession of St. Vincent on the Waubach what few men that Composed the Garrison not being able to make the least Defence He is Influencing all the Indians he possibly Can to Join him: I learn that those that have Treated with me have as yet Refused his offers. I have for some time Expected an

attact from him   he has Blocked up the Ohio R with a party
of French and Indians.

Yesterday I fortunately got every peace of Intelligence,
that I could wish for, by a Spanish Gent[1] that made his
Excape from M[r] Hamilton. No Attact to be Made on the
Garison at Kaskaskia until the Spring as passage is too difficult at present. Braves sent to war against different parts of
the countrey Especially Kentucky. Both presents and
Speaches sent to all the Nations South of the Ohio
Amediately to meet at a great Council at the Mouth of the
Tennessee R to lay the Best plans for Cuting off the Rebels
at Illinois and Kentucky & the Grand Kite and his Nation
living at Post St Vincent told Mr Hamilton that he and his
people was Big Knives and would not give their hands any
more to the English for he would shortly see his Father that
was at Kaskaskia Ninety Regulars in Garrison a few
Voluntiers and about Fifty Tawaway Indians that is Shortly
to go to war they are very Busy in Repairing the Fort
which will Shortly be very Strong, One Brass Six-pounder
two iron four pounders and two Swivels Mounted in the
Bastians plenty of Amunition and provisions and all kinds
of warlike Stores, Making preparation for the Reduction of
the Illinois & has no Suspition of a Visit from the
Americans this was Mr. Hamilton's Circumstance when Mr
Vigo left him.

Being sensible that without a Reinforcement which at
present I have hardly a right to Expect that I shall be obliged
to give up this Countrey to Mr Hamilton without a turn of
Fortune in my favour, I am Resolved to take the advantage
of his present Situation and Risque the whole on a Single
Battle I shall set out in a few Days with all the Force I can
Raise of my own Troops and a few Militia that I can Depend
on (whole to only one) Hundred (of which goes on) Board
a Small Galley turned out some time ago Mounting two four
pounders and four large Swivels one nine pounder on Board

this Boat is to make her way good if possible and take her
Station Ten Leagues Below St. Vincents until further
orders If I am defeated She is to Join Col. Rogers on the
Mississippi She has great stores of Ammunition on Board
Com[d] by Lieut. J[no] Rogers.

I Shall March across by Land my self with the Rest of My
Boys. the principal persons that follow me on this forlorn
hope is Cap[n] Joseph Bowman John Williams Ed[wd]

Worthington Rich^d MCarty & Fran^s Charlovielle Lieu^t Rich^d
Brashears Ab^m Kellar Ab^m Chaplin J^{no} Jerault And Jno
Bayley and several other Brave Subalterns. You must be
Sensible of the Feeling that I have for those Brave officers
and Soldiers that are Determined to Share my Fate let it be
what it will. I know the Case is Desperate but S^r we must
Either Quit   the Countrey or attack Mr Hamilton   No time
is to be lost   Was I sure of a Reinforcement I should not attempt to   Who knows what fortune will do for us.   Great
things have been affected by a few Men well Conducted
perhaps we may be fortunate

We have this Consolation that our Cause is Just and that
our Countrey will be grateful and not Condemn our Conduct
in Case we fall through   if so this western countrey as well
as Kentucky I believe is lost

The Expresses that you have sent I Expect has fallen into
the hands of Governor Hamilton

I have the Honour to be Sr Your Very Humble Servt

G. R. CLARK

After watching the messenger depart through the snowy
courtyard with the messages for Williamsburg, George paced
the room rapidly to dissipate some of the energy that always
seemed to build up unbearably in him whenever a course of action was at hand. He could scarcely contain his desire to act,
and, though the odds against the success of the expedition
seemed almost overwhelming, he could not keep down an inward assurance that, with the quality of men he had and the element of total surprise, he could succeed in defeating Hamilton
at Vincennes.

He smacked his fist into his left palm. "By Heaven, Joseph,"
he exclaimed with an intense breathiness in his voice, "at this
moment I would gladly bind myself seven years a slave in exchange for five hundred more troops! With that kind of a force
we could sweep through St. Vincents and on to Detroit, no
question about it! Come, I'm stifling in here. Let's walk down
to the river and see the *Willing* off."

In cloaks and boots they went aboard the sturdy,
broadbeamed row galley and strolled on the swept decks with
her commander. Young Lieutenant Rogers was a cousin of Colonel Clark's, and had been a veteran of two years in the Revolutionary army in lower Virginia before coming on the

Kaskaskia expedition as a lieutenant in Helm's company. George had absolute faith in him, and had reminded him a dozen times of the crucial importance of the galley's role in the upcoming attack on Vincennes. Vigo's report had shown the exact position of Fort Sackville's well-stocked powder magazine, and there was a distinct possibility that one accurately placed hot cannonball could blow half the fort away. It would be virtually impossible to attack a British fort without cannon, and because of the two hundred forty miles of snow and mud between Kaskaskia and Vincennes, there was no way other than by river to carry the cannon there. Even that would be a hazardous, barely feasible journey, because of the great crushing ice jams in the river this season and Henry Hamilton's numerous river blockades on the Ohio and Wabash. But the fort at Vincennes stood on the very bank of the Wabash, and a gunboat like this could do invaluable service, first by ferrying the foot troops across the Wabash, by delivering cannon and heavy stores to the ground force, then by bombarding the stockade from the river side, maybe putting that lucky hot shot into the magazine. It could also prevent Hamilton from fleeing down the Wabash if he were dislodged.

George stood with a hand on a stay-rope and gazed up at the mast, around which heavy snow was swirling. Then he watched work parties roll the last powder kegs and barrels of flour and salt pork up the gangway. A line of laborers passed along cannonballs, which disappeared into the hold. Cannon stood mute and black and solid along the gunwales.

"Jove," he said. "She's a moveable fortress. Imagine a fleet of these the length of the Ohio, John. What a line of protection for Kentucky!" It was an old dream of his, this of a river navy, and it had been intensified during the process of outfitting the *Willing*. He had named her the *Willing* after the American river guerrilla James Willing, but also because the name seemed to describe her stalwart and ready character. The French admired the vessel mightily, and there were now, as always, several villagers standing about on the wharf admiring her curving lines and sturdy oaken construction. There were rowlocks for thirty protected oarsmen. A berth was found for Davey Pagan as helmsman and maintenance man, but his comrades insisted on addressing him still as the Forepoop Swabman, and he was virtually in raptures to find himself once again upon a deck.

The Kaskaskians seemed to have become inspired by George's preparations for the offensive. He had told his officers to talk and conduct themselves as if they were confident without a doubt of defeating Hamilton; within a day or two the entire countryside had begun speaking of it as a *fait accompli*, and many of the male Kaskaskians, anxious to retrieve their honor after their recent show of cowardice, had turned out to join the expedition. The ladies of the village and countryside had become spirited about the expedition, and were sewing flags. Their interest had in its turn had its effect on still more young Frenchmen. Thus it was that by this fourth day of February, George could count on a force of a little over one hundred and eighty men, about a half of them French volunteers. About forty-five of them would accompany Cousin Rogers on the *Willing*; the rest, about one hundred thirty-five including a pack-horse master, would march with George himself across the Illinois country. Although the deep snow and wet ground made such a march appalling to consider, George was sure it would work in their favor, as General Hamilton would certainly be off guard.

At two o'clock, Father Gibault, back from the Spanish side of the river, came down to the riverbank to bless the vessel and give absolution to all her crew. The lines were cast off and, amid an uproar of cheering, the *Willing* was rowed out into the current, moved among the pans and chunks of ice, and grew dim in the snowy distance, finally vanishing upon the breast of the Mississippi's main channel.

George and Captain Bowman walked back up the hill to the fort with Father Gibault between them, all keeping cheerful countenances for the Kaskaskians who thronged the streets offering them greetings and good wishes. George noticed a shifting in the wind; it was coming from a more southerly direction now, with a milder temperature and a wet feel.

AFTER AN EVENING MUSTER, IN WHICH HE TOLD THE ASSEMBLED troops they would march the next day and gave a cheery dissertation on duty, he ordered rum broken out, toasted his own men and the French volunteers, then retired at dark to his quarters. Father Gibault walked with him to the door.

"Now, my son, if you need me to support you in praying for the success of this venture, say so. Or if you want to be alone, I'll leave now, and see you tomorrow."

"I'll pray alone, I think, Father. I need some time to myself. But I have a request. After we march tomorrow, I should like you at your convenience to go up to St. Louis and carry some letters for me to Governor de Leyba and his family. You might accompany Mister Vigo when he sets out for home, I was thinking."

"With pleasure. Good night. And don't hesitate to get on your knees tonight. You and I know God is already in your favor, but it might be prudent to let Him know that you know it."

"Right you are. Good night."

There was nothing more to attend to. Everything that needed to be done in preparation for the campaign had been done. But he could not yet sleep. He was too anxious. Having convinced every person in the region that the attack on Vincennes could not fail, he remained now the only one aware of the odds against succeeding. The Frenchmen, until he had convinced them to the contrary, had warned him that it would not be possible even to get an army to Vincennes in this season. Now they were persuaded it was possible, but he knew as he had known all along that they had been right; the hardship of it would be the supreme test of human endurance. This new warming wind from the south could make the entire route a quagmire of mud and slush, and surely the melting of so much snow would turn every stream into a flood. If there were no melt-off, on the other hand, the snow would pose an almost insuperable hindrance to their progress.

As for the attack itself, traditional military wisdom held that a well-stocked fort with artillery could hold out indefinitely against an attacking force five times the size of its garrison. *And we,* he thought, *even if by some miracle we all get there, won't outnumber them at all.*

To outfit the expedition, he had endorsed with his personal signature still more bills of credit drawn on Virginia, and the price of every item had been outrageously inflated. The thought of this awful financial over-extension made the innate perils of the expedition seem even more desperate; it gnawed at the back of his mind constantly.

Finally, he put a moratorium on worrying about such matters. *Worry accomplishes nothing,* he thought; *it only adds to the burden.*

And so now there was nothing more in his head to think about, and, as if into a vacuum, thoughts of Teresa came rushing in. This expedition could mean that he would not see her for still more months.

If ever, he thought suddenly.

Shaken by this first admission to himself that he might well be killed, he longed to send his thoughts to her. He drew a sheet of paper from the desk and opened the inkpot.

He grew extremely nervous about this. Writing orders and official dispatches was one thing; he had become adequate at that. Unburdening his heart was another. He had never written love letters. He was self-conscious about the writing of sentiments; and though he had confidence in his ability to sway people with oratory, he felt unsure with a pen in his hand. Never having quite grasped the rules of spelling as a youth, he had grown even more careless of it during a life in which action was his chief language. He preferred to dictate his letters through Monsieur Girault, his interpreter and secretary, whenever possible, rather than write them in his own hand. But Girault was not there now. And the things he wanted to say to Teresa were too personal to express through an amanuensis.

Come, now, he reprimanded himself. English isn't her language; your misspellings won't be evident to her.

Kaskaskia, February 4, 1779

Dear One—

Tomorrow I set out in a direction opposite to the pulling of my heart. Life's tenderest string, the bond of passion I have for you, shall have to be stretched farther still. Distance and time already has drawn it to the fineness of a spider's web. But my Charished One there are no Forces on earth that can break it

I am cognisant of no other substance more strong for its delicasy than what is spun out by a Spider, except it be the filament of Affection by which We Two are Betrothed.

George paused, looked at what he had written, and sipped brandy. What if, like most women, she is repelled by spiders, he thought. No, never mind that. He dipped the quill again.

I had allways thought the Fate that brot me to this Place was only Duty to my Countrey the Necessaty of preventing the Effusion of inocent blood upon our Frontiers.

But since those Few Remarkable Days we were in the Company of each other I have tho' that Fate perhaps carried me to this Remote place Equally for the Purpose of our

Meeting. Y^r Brother my Friend Fernando told me that you arrived in Post San Luis Less than a Month before I came to Kaskaskia and that my Belov^d seemes Suspitiously a manipulation of a Knowing Destiny

Y^r musick is allways in my thoughts I live for a time when I shall again have the Sublime enjoyment of Basking in those tunes and Observing the Beauty of y^r Tallent in such Concentration

There has not been a better Moment in my life than the

He stopped again. He had intended to write "the one moment when we were alone together in darkness and privacy," but, he thought, what if someone else in her family should by accident read this and demand an explanation? It would be an unforgivable injustice thus to place her under a suspicion of impropriety in her family. So, much as he wanted to refer to that moment when he had held her, that moment he had re-created so often in his reveries, he wrote instead:

than the moment when You my deare Maiden said Yes to my Suit for your Hand

I have wanted to tell You about a Dream I have Entertained sometimes which is that I sit on a Hill on the Terras of a fine house and look over a great River full of Peaceful commerce and beside me in another chair there sits a fine Lady growing old in my company   Until I first cast my gaze upon you the Lady in that Dream did not have a face that I could see   But since then she has worn y^r own faultless Visage

We Boath are young my Sweet Heart and I am of a Stock of People Prosperous Strong & Long-Lived & Sober & Industrious No better a People I expect this Conflict will be ended soon with our Side flourish^g in Independence and as of that Day I pray you will come and sit beside me to look with me across peaceful Valleys in the Sunshine until we grow old.

Dear Heaven Teresa how I yearn for such peace even as I go to the Opposite

Pray for us in our Endeavor as I am sure no prayer from so Pure a Heart c^d be Denied.

I am Teresa y$'^r$ humble & Most Devoted Forever

G. R. CLARK

P.S. My Sincear Compliments to Mad^m de Leyba and my two little Misses & not Least y^r Esteemed Broth^r

On the drizzly morning of February fifth, Master Dickie Lovell stood at attention on the slushy turf of the Commons at Kaskaskia wearing a black three-cornered hat and beating a spirited tattoo on his drum. A knapsack on his back counterbalanced the weight of the drum on his groin. Soldiers bearing the American, French, and Virginian flags stood behind him, and behind them in ranks were the French and American companies. Along both sides of the Commons all the people of Kaskaskia were gathered. Many of them were dabbing at their faccs with handkerchiefs, having just been moved to tears by Father Gibault's quavering voice.

Now the priest took Colonel Clark's hand, gazed earnestly into his face, and then embraced him, kissing him on both cheeks. The crowd cheered. Colonel Clark, in fringed buckskins and his black felt hat, swung with ease into the saddle and waved his arm. The officers of each company, likewise mounted, cried commands in English and French; the drumming changed to a marching cadence, and the squads began moving off in a file toward the river, rifles on their shoulders.

The snow of yesterday had turned to a drizzle of rain, and heaps and patches of melting snow and slush lay along the roadside down to the river. The civilians ran and tramped through this slush down to the river, cheering all the way. The troops were loaded aboard a motley collection of boats and ferried across to the eastern shore, and the people stayed on the Kaskaskia side, cheering them until they were out of earshot. Finally, becoming chilled by the rain on their shoulders and the wetness seeping through their shoes, they went up the hill to the old mission house where Father Gibault led them in prayer.

THE WIND BACKED INTO THE NORTHWEST AND RAIN TURNED TO sleet as the army slogged eastward above the valley. Two feet of snow that had been lying on the ground sinking and growing dense under the rainfall now acquired a half-inch crust of ice which boomed like thunder when feet and hooves crushed through it. The men stumbled more than they marched, flailing for balance. The edges of the ice cut at their knees and bruised their shins. The horses of the officers and the pack train were also hurt by the ice, and grew nervous from the pain and the constant crushing roar of the ice. The expedition had made a mere league by evening, and every man was gasping for breath and soaked to the thighs. Their leather leggings were freezing to their skin; their boots and moccasins were full of ice water. Freezing rain turned their hats to heavy helmets of ice. The sky was the color of lead.

At dark, George ordered the companies each to form a square camp with its baggage in the center. Large fires were built, rum was dispensed, meat was roasted, and soon the troops forgot their misery in singing and boasting.

George met with the captains and they voted to camp here and see if the ice would soften the next day. There were no tents; the men and officers rolled themselves into blankets or skins, made hollows in the snow to protect themselves from the wind, and fell asleep with their flintlocks protected between their thighs.

On the next morning they awoke to find the ice worse, and so George decided to devote the day to hunting, feasting, and war counciling, to keep the men's minds off their misery and immobility. The officers' horses were given to a hunting party to take some buffalo that had been found sheltering in a draw nearby. While the feast was being prepared, George kept up the spirits of the troops by telling them in as many various ways as he could that they soon would have their chance to get revenge on the Scalp-Buyer British general who had inflicted so much death and grief upon their families on the frontiers. As the festivities wore on, the sleet turned to rain again, and the wind grew warmer. "We'll be moving out tomorrow morning," he promised them, "and there'll be nothing to stop us till we reach General Hamilton and Major Hay!" The cry they sent up in response was fierce and joyous.

The morning of the seventh found most of the snow and ice gone, and the column set out early across the high plain under a cold drizzle. The ground, thawing on the surface but still frozen underneath, held the water of the rain and melted snow, turning it into a chilly brown soup as quickly as it was walked on. It squished and sucked at their feet and clung to their footgear in gobs heavy as anchors. In places, inches of standing water covered acres of ground along the route, and at once every man was wet to the knees again. The march was strenuous. By noon the column had struggled fifteen miles across the soggy plain and the men were famished from their exertions. Giving up their horses to a hunting party again, George and the other officers ran in the water and muck alongside the troops, telling jokes and yelling encouragement. They ate their midday meal on foot, munching parched corn and cold jerky, their feet kept moving by the promise of the hot roasted buffalo meat they would have at nightfall. They made nearly thirty miles that day in nine hours of marching and wading, again pitched camp in guarded squares, ate meat, dried their clothing around bonfires, drank rum, sang to the notes of jew's-harps and flutes, and held running, boxing, and knife-throwing contests to the amazement of the French volunteers, most of whom could barely stand up. Captain Bowman sat nearby and made an entry in his journal:

> *7th—began our March early, made a good days March for about 9 leagues—The roads very bad with Mud and Water. Pitched our camp in a square, Baggage in the Middle every Com'y to guard their own Square.*

The morning of the eighth began as had the day before, still drizzly and chilly, and the pace resumed as soon as there was enough light to see the way. The plain here lay flat as a tabletop and the water, with nowhere to run off, stood in sheets, looking like vast gray lakes, rippling in the cold wind, forlorn reeds and grasses sticking up above the surface. "Didn't need t' send the *Willing* around," remarked Lieutenant Brashears. "We coulda sailed 'er right along th' road with us."

During the afternoon the sky cleared a little, and the air grew colder, a weak sun going down behind the marchers, but before sunset it clouded over and began drizzling again. The men watched their feet endlessly plashing through the shallow water, drops spraying ahead with each step. They plodded on that day for nine hours, gasping from cold and weariness. Every hour or so each soldier might feel a hand on his arm and turn to see the cheerful face of Colonel Clark or one of the captains beside him, asking how he was getting along. "No complaints, sir," was always the answer, and the officer would trot ahead to pay attention to the next man.

"Jes' take a look at that rascal," said one private to the next, "don't he know he's doin' three miles to our one with all that there runnin' to an' fro?"

"Yup. Does yer heart good, don' it?"

They waded about nine leagues that day, and finally made camp on a small, wet rise which stood like an island no more than four or five inches above the surrounding inundation. Captain Bowman entered in his diary:

8th—Marched early thro' the Water which we now began to meet in those large and level plains where (from the Flatness of the Country) the Water rests a considerable time before it drains off, not withstanding our Men were in Great Spirits, tho much fatigued.

Knowing that the ceaseless misery and monotony of these clammy, exhausting days surely must wear down the men's will eventually, George took pains to see that every evening's encampment should be entertaining enough that they would look forward to it with eagerness. They mustn't fall to thinking in terms of two hundred miles or a hundred miles, he reasoned; they have to keep thinking in terms of this evening, this evening.

So the officers gave up their horses entirely to the hunting parties; and each day a different company would assume the duty of bringing in game. By turns, each company would kill and cook the food for the others, and invite the others to their feasts, and thus it became a friendly competition to determine which company could lay the greatest feast and stage the most uproarious entertainment for the others. Captain McCarty's company one night held a war dance in the Indian fashion, which the woodsmen seemed to enjoy for its fierce irony. As the men whooped and cavorted around the roaring bonfire, one soldier threw off all his sodden clothes, sprang into the firelight, his skin fish-belly white and wrinkled from the days of constant wetness, and frolicked about in the sleet with exaggerated movements and obscene gestures, whooping, "Hay-*oooop!* Looky me! I'm Lord Hennery Hamilton th' scalp-merchant! Yaaaaa-hooooey!"

9th—Made a moderate days March rain'd most of the day

The troops had forgotten what it felt like to be dry. Every day, besides the constant wading in standing water, they had to ford creeks which had overflowed their banks, often crossing in water to their chests, holding their precious powder horns and food pouches high over their heads. Thus thoroughly drenched by the icy water, they would wade on through mire and rain which gave their clothes no opportunity to dry. Only by their constant movement and the consumption of huge quantities of meat could they generate enough heat from within to keep from succumbing to the penetrating chill.

On the afternoon of the tenth of February, in a chilling downpour, they came to the fording place of La Petite Riviere, and finding the water so high it was over their heads, they took axes from the pack animals and felled trees. The horses were unloaded. The men strapped their freight onto the trees, then hung onto them themselves to be carried across to the far shore. The horses were led into the water and swam across. So much strength was spent on this crossing that an early camp was made near the river. The men spent that night under an open sky, whipped with rain and high winds.

> *10th—Crossed the River of the Petet Ford upon Trees that we felled for the purpose   the Water being so high there was no fording it; still raining and no Tents   encamped near the River   stormy and c.*

The next day a similar crossing had to be made at the flooded Saline River, further draining their energies. Truly restful sleep was impossible because of the incessant rain and cold; George, being stronger and more vigorous than most of his men, had only to heed the painful exhaustion in his own legs and the bone-shaking shivers to comprehend what they were suffering.

> *11th—Crossed the Saline River   nothing extraordinary this day*

They went on in this wretched condition all the next day, crossing a plain that was flooded knee-deep or more for a seeming infinity. George sent the hunters out on horseback with little hope that they would find anything in this flood. He turned aside from the head of the column and watched the men come on. He was growing light-headed from cold and exhaustion, and the drab light played tricks on his vision. It was like watching a nightmare: the pewter-gray ocean of water with black tree trunks sticking up from it, here and there gray-green moss and patches of lichen on the tree bark; the woodsmen's deerskins soaked black, their faces gray to white, lips and eye sockets bruise-blue, their whisker stubble wet with rain and snot, their red noses and knuckles providing the only color that indicated life in this dripping, hushing, flowing, gurgling universe.

And yet every one looked up at him and smiled or winked as

they slopped past gasping for breath. His heart clenched; he swallowed and blinked, then turned his face away from them and splashed forward to the head of the column again, shouting he knew not what phrases of encouragement, every muscle in his legs and torso protesting with a pain like a silent scream.

"Play," he said to the drummer. The lad began beating a cadence. The troops picked up the cadence and began singing soon, a long trail of voices faint over the splash and squish of their marching.

> There I sat on Buttermilk Hill,
> Who could blame me, cry my fill?
> An' every tear would turn a mill,
> Johnny has gone for a soldier.
>
> I'll sell my flax, I'll sell my wheel,
> Buy my love a sword of steel,
> So it in battle he may wield;
> Johnny has gone for a soldier . . .

George found himself gaining strength from it. He hoped the soldiers would too. But it doesn't fill a belly, he thought.

Night came on before they found a place high enough to camp on, the rain still pouring and the wind growing colder. He began to worry that some of the men might actually perish this night from exposure; there was no sign of the hunters with their life-giving red meat. Fires burned low and smoky because of the wetness of the fuel, and seemed to give too little heat to dry clothing or reach chilled muscle and aching bone. The weather showed no sign of improvement and the army was, he estimated, still some fifty miles from its destination, with two major rivers yet to cross.

And if we do get there, he thought, it's not to rest but to fight a battle.

Teresa, he thought suddenly. Are you still alive in this same world with me?

A shout sounded in the darkness. "Buffalo!" cried the voice. It was the hunting party. "Hey boys! Enough steaks here t' feed a thousand! Come on, boys!"

The wild-eyed horses emerged into the flickering fire light and smoke; their riders jumped down and began throwing off great red bloody haunches and briskets of meat they had strapped on behind the saddles. The camp had come back to life, roaring with laughter and war whoops, oaths in English and French. In moments the smoky wet glade was full of the maddening aroma of searing meat, the sizzle of dripping fat, and the almost delirious jabber of men on the very brink of anticipation.

They wolfed the meat half-raw, gorging themselves, their chins and hands shiny with grease. They clamored for the fat-riddled meat of the buffalo humps instinctively, knowing it was the best fuel for their clammy bodies. George ordered rum broken out.

The orgy of feasting subsided after a few minutes, and soon the entertainments began again, rowdy, boastful, punctuated by mighty belches, and George stood back, watched these great childlike celebrants, who had seemed near death an hour before, now cured by the miraculous medicine of full bellies. He grinned and watched them caper and shout, the warmth of life beginning to steal through his veins again, as the ruddy light of the fire illuminated the tree trunks and leafless branches overhead. He squinted into the high treetops, at the rain that came spitting into the fireglow, sniffed the wet and smoky smells, listened to the fine manly voices. There was a great knot in his throat.

Dear God, he thought. Thank thee for this thy bounty.

12th—Marched across bad plain saw and kilted number of Buffaloe the Roads very bad from the immense Quantity of Rain that had fallen, the Men much fatigued, encamped at the Edge of the Wood. this plain or Meadow being fifteen or more Miles across—it was late in the Night before the Troops and baggage got together—Now 21 leagues from St. Vincent.

A few hours' strenuous marching in sleet on the morning of the thirteenth of February brought the troops to the bank of the western branch of the Little Wabash. Here, according to maps and scouts, the two branches of this tributary ran parallel to each other some three miles apart. From the heights of one to the heights of the other was about five miles, and George saw, with a sinking heart, that the entire distance was under muddy, flowing water. The forests throughout the valley stood two to four feet deep in muddy flood. Bits of wood debris and rafts of spongy, half-melted ice moved slowly downstream among the trees.

Faith, he thought. We've got to cross this flood just to reach two greater rivers and then cross those. Is this possible?

He had the companies make camp on the height and set about entertaining themselves, so that they might not think about what lay ahead. His officers looked at him with eyes full of doubt, but he said nothing to them, and walked to the edge of the flood alone. He stood there for a few minutes, looking at the awful sheet of water.

"Come, man," he murmured finally. "You're doubting."

Afraid to hear a word from his officers for fear they would shake what little resolve he had left, he went back to the camp, ordered a party of men to get axes and adzes, and led them to a great poplar that stood on the shore. "Drop that tree," he said, "and hollow out a pirogue. We'll need it to scout up the easiest way across this puddle, boys."

Two men stood on opposite sides of the tree and, alternating their strokes, began cutting. The trunk was four feet thick. Two more men went to the tree to spell the workers. The axes chunked rhythmically for the greater part of an hour; then there were shouts and the rattling crash of branches, and a thump which made the soggy ground quake in the camp. The chopping then continued on the fallen trunk as a section twenty feet long was cut away. Soon the men had that section on blocks, and a team of four, wielding pikes and adzes and broadaxes, were removing the bark, hewing away the upper curve of the trunk and hollowing the log. A floor of fragrant yellow chips and shavings began to build up on the wet black ground.

George walked about in the camp, sat now and then to confer laconically with the officers, paced to the river's edge and looked across the expanse of water, then returned to the camp. A haggard woodsman, leaning against a tree near one of the campfires, looked at him and smiled. "Colonel, suh, be we lost?"

"Nay, Oreer. Not lost. Not a bit of it."

"Well, suh, if we do git lost, you can use me t' git th' bearin's. I got moss growin' on m' north side!"

The men around the fire laughed. George grinned. "So I see. We'll refer to you then, Oreer, if we do get confused."

Night was coming on. George ordered a fire built near the workmen so that their hewing could continue until late.

Captain McCarthy came and squatted near George to watch the workers. "Dunno, Colonel," he said. "One pirogue t' ferry a regiment. That be a slow process."

"We'll use her for scouting, mainly," said George. "We're going to have to wade most of that, and just ferry over the channels when we find 'em. Maybe send 'er downriver to find the *Willing*. We could sure use her right now."

"Aye. Them rivers scares me, George, runnin' fast like that. Don't reckon they's ten men in th' bunch as can swim. Even if they could, their gear'd drag 'em under."

"Come on now, Dick. We don't need dubious talk. This water's just a little diversion for these boys."

"Right y' are. Sorry, George." McCarty got up and walked away.

13th—Arrived early at the two Wabashes altho a league asunder they now make but one—We set to make a Canoe.

The chunking and ringing of the tools resumed early the next day. The troops stayed in camp, resting as well as they could in the rain and mud. Hunters were out all day but found little because of the flooding. Game had gone to higher country. Now and then George would find a man standing on the bank looking out over the flood, condensing breath drifting from his mouth like smoke in the dank air. He would joke with such men and turn them back toward the camp.. He didn't want them spending too much time considering it.

But he could imagine the thoughts going through their heads as they watched the water. Likely some of them were aware that once across these rivers, any hope of a retreat would be done away with. Once across this, he thought, they'll likely be happy to go forward and risk anything rather than suffer again what they've already experienced.

He looked up at the spitting gray skies. We've been lucky to have no freezing, he thought. A freeze would make the crossing impossible, unless the ice were strong enough to support us, and no chance of that.

14th—Finished the Canoe and put her in the Water about four o clock in the afternoon.

At daylight the next day George walked to the water's edge with the scouts who were to man the pirogue. "Now listen well, boys. I want you to pole the water for depth all the way. Find where the river channel lies. Find the opposite shore, and build a scaffold there to put baggage on so's we can swim the horses

over to pick it up. Got that? Blaze the route on tree trunks so
you can find your way back here. And mind this, now: Whatever it's like out there, you bring me back a *favorable* report. I
don't want this army going into that water with any doubts in
their heads. D' you follow me?"

The scouts looked at each other with raised eyebrows, then
back to him, and nodded. They clambered into the fresh yellow
trough of the vessel and he shoved them out into the stream.
"She floats like a swan, sir!" exclaimed the man in the bow,
who stood holding a long sounding-pole. The soldiers on the
bank sent up a cheer and hopeful laughter. The expanse of water
looked less formidable now that they understood it would not
be an absolute unknown. The canoe moved slowly away and
soon was out of sight among the trees.

Camp was struck and the men loafed on the ground waiting
for the return of the scouts. Finally, about midmorning, there
was a shout. "Here she comes!" The boat, now smeared with
brown mud, came slowly back, the scouts pausing at a tree every few yards to swing a tomahawk and chip away a spot of
bark.

The scouts were in good humor. "Found the channel, sir,"
they reported. "About thirty yards wide in all. Rest of the way
the water's two to four feet deep. We found t'other shore an'
put up a scaffold like you said, in about three feet of water."

"Fine work! All right, lads!" George shouted. "Let's get this
fine ship loaded with the baggage, and we're off!"

The loaded pirogue, burdened so heavily that her gunwales
were almost awash, moved out onto the flood again and George
waded into the brown water to follow her. "Come on in, boys!
Time t' get your feet wet again!" He braced his spirit against
the shock of the icy water that flowed into his moccasins and
crept further up his legs with every step.

"Yowee! Hoo ha!" the men shouted as they waded in after
him, one by one, gasping.

The file waded for an hour, the land disappearing behind
them, the bottom squishy and invisible under their feet. They
carried their rifles across their shoulders and their powder horns
around their necks. The water reached their knees, their thighs,
their hips, their waists, eventually their chests as they struggled
onward toward he river channel. Every breath was a gasp
through chattering teeth. Their skin grew too numb to feel; the
pain of the cold advanced inward to their bones and joints.

When the water was to his chest, George heard a chorus of

shivery laughter behind him. He turned to look. The men, their faces gray-blue, were watching Dickie Lovell, the little drummer boy, who had hauled himself up onto his drum and was lying on his stomach upon it, floating, hanging with one hand onto the fringe of Sergeant Crump's coat and thus being towed across. Responding to their laughter, the boy grew antic, splashing with his feet, grinning, finally letting loose of Crump's coat, and paddling himself along with his hands. George roared with happiness and turned to continue ahead, seeking the bottom carefully one step after another with his benumbed feet. His heart thudded rapidly in his breast and now and then a terrific shudder would shake him the whole length of his body. He turned again to look back and saw them coming on, their arms held high, each one close behind the other, rain dripping from their hats and noses, concentrating on their footing, not a one complaining or straggling. Some of the shorter men were immersed to their very necks, only their heads and forearms and hands above the surface. The current was becoming perceptible as the column crept closer to the channel of the river.

At last the scouts stopped the pirogue. "Here we are, sir, the channel!" George stopped the column. The men braced themselves against tree trunks or held on to the branches of scrub and waited while the pirogue was paddled across to the scaffold and unloaded. Then it came back; five or six men at a time were hauled into the dugout, an equal number threw in their guns and powder and then hung on to the gunwales with both hands to be towed across the depths.

In two hours of this, while those standing in wait gritted their teeth and fought with all their will to keep the last embers of life-warmth from ebbing out of their bodies, the ferrying of the troops was completed. The horses were swum wild-eyed over to the scaffold, found their footing, and standing belly-deep in the water, were loaded again.

And the march resumed up the gradually sloping bottom, the men growing more and more cheerful as the water level dropped below their waists. They began joking and cursing merrily as they went along. There was still no land in sight, but the awful fear of slipping under the murky waters and being drowned was past, and they grew intoxicated with that heady joy of having survived what had been for many the worst experience of their lives.

The column waded on for another three miles, a little warmed by their exertions again, but now feeling that awful gnawing emptiness in their bellies and knowing that there were no hunting parties out this day to bring them fresh meat for supper. Most had only a little corn and a few scraps of yesterday's meat in their pouches. "What're we eatin' tonight, sergeant?" somebody asked.

"Y'might search through yer clothes," came the reply. 'Y'may've picked up a catfish 'r two along th' way."

"Hey, Colonel Clark!" somebody called from back in the file. "Sir, where was all this water last July when we was a'goin't' other way crost Illynoy?"

"Hey, you remember that, do you?"

"Aye!"

"Well, think on it hard, then, and maybe that'll warm you a bit!"

"Ha ha!"

In that spirit they reached the channel of the second river, wading down again to their chests, then crossing in the pirogue or clinging to it, and it was a quicker crossing than the first, this river being not quite so wide nor deep and the men more familiar with the procedure. Dickie Lovell entertained them by floating on his drum once more, letting the boat tow him across.

By evening they were encamped on a half-acre knoll, the trackless water behind them. They were in high spirits, all laughing at each other in recollection of things that had happened in the course of what they were now casually referring to as "this ferrying business." George moved among their camps and encouraged their joking, here and there laying on a bit of praise. By nightfall they had begun to think themselves superior to other men, boasting that neither the rivers nor seasons could stop their progress. Their whole conversation now was about what they would do when they got to the enemy. They now began to view the Big Wabash ahead as a creek, and had no doubt that such men as themselves could find a way to cross it. They wound themselves up to such a pitch that they soon took Vincennes in their fancies and divided up the spoils, and before bedtime were far advanced on their way to Detroit.

George listened to all this with a catch in his throat, watched them feed themselves on imagination instead of hot food, watched them warm their gaunt, chilled bodies before the bonfires, and marvelled that they could laugh so, being now as it were stranded in enemy country with no way to retreat if the British or Indians should discover them, unless by some long chance they should fall in with the *Willing*. He was now convinced that they would find the whole low country of the Wabash drowned, and that today's accomplishment was but a prelude to what they would face in the next few days.

If the *Willing* has been unable to reach her station in this flood, he thought, we'll have to find and steal boats on this side of the Wabash to get across, even at the risk of an alarm.

Well, he thought. If that's what we'll have to do, that's what we shall do.

Captain Bowman sat by the fire that night and wrote:

15th—Ferried across the two little Wabashes—being then five miles in Water to the opposite Hills, where we encamped Still raining—Orders given to fire no Guns in future except in case of Necessity.

They set out early the next morning. It was still raining. They crossed another river and marched until nightfall, finding at last a rise of ground well-drained enough to sleep on, lay down wet and unfed, and lapsed into a state that was as much the swoon of exhaustion as sleep.

On the morning of the next day they set out again, plodding and squishing through the sopping gray-brown countryside, fording more flooded creeks, as if in an endless dream, bellies and heads empty. George sent four men down one of these creeks in the pirogue with orders to cross the Embarras River if possible and steal boats from a plantation that was known to stand on its eastern shore. The day was nearly gone when the troops reached the banks of the Embarras and were dismayed to see that all the land beyond it, as far as the eye could see, was under water. This river, sometimes known as the Troublesome River, flowed southward into the great Wabash a few miles below Vincennes, the two streams making a Y. George had hoped to cross the Embarras, then march five miles overland in the fork to meet the Wabash immediately opposite Vincennes, then make the final crossing of the Wabash and attack. But now it appeared that all the land between the two rivers was deeply inundated. There was nothing to do but detour down the west bank of the Embarras, find the Wabash below the juncture, and cross it there.

Turning the column southward now, he led the bedraggled woodsmen to lower and lower ground. Soon they were wading again, searching in the twilight for the Wabash.

After two more hours of struggling forward in that direction, they were rejoined by the scouting party in the pirogue, who had been unable to get across the Embarras because of driftwood, debris, and thickets. Now the immediate objective was not to find the Wabash but simply to find a spot of ground sufficiently above water to spend the night on. Rain started again, pelting down in the darkness, as the column floundered and splashed along in pitch blackness, keeping in touch with each other by voice. This was the worst circumstance yet, and George's mind was sinking toward abject despair, almost losing its orientation and slipping into panic, when his feet detected a barely perceptible rising of the slope. At eight o'clock they were at last on a rise of ground. Faint, aching, trembling so hard they were nearly incapacitated, they dragged up driftwood and built a dozen fires to dry themselves by.

> *17th—Marched early crossed several Rivers very deep sent Mr Kennedy our commisary with three men to cross the River Embara to endeavor to cross if possible and proceed to a plantation opposite Post Vincent in order to steal Boats or canoes to ferry us across the Wabash—About One hour before sunset We got Near the River Embara found the country all overflown, we strove to find the Wabash traveld till 8 o clock in mud and water but could find no place to encamp on still kept marching on but after some time Mr Kennedy and his party return'd found it impossible to cross the Embara River we found the Water fallen from a small spot of Ground staid there the remainder of the Night drisly and dark Weather*

The desolation Colonel Clark's army felt the next morning when they rose from their wet blankets and saw themselves surrounded by a sea of tan flowing water was dispelled by a single dull boom that rolled to them over the rushing of the flood:

It was the morning gun of Fort Sackville.

"Hear that, boys?" George yelled as soon as he realized what it was. "Hamilton's cannon! We're that close, lads!" The men cheered, shook their fists in its direction, pounded each other on the back, and went whooping and frolicking about the island. Having restored their circulation by that outburst, they loaded up and resumed the march southward through waist-deep water, nourishing themselves on a breakfast of marching songs and grim jokes.

At about two o'clock in the afternoon, their heads and bodies again benumbed by the painful progress, they came at last to a bluff which they knew would be the western bank of the Wabash. They had at last gotten below the mouth of the Embarras. They staggered up onto the high ground, spent, and made such camp as they could.

George reckoned that they were now about three leagues downstream from Vincennes. Now they had only to cross the Wabash to its eastern shore and march northward those nine miles and they would be at the destination they had suffered for so long to reach. Put in those terms, it sounded very simple. But looking across the great river, George saw that their greatest obstacle was indeed just ahead: There was no other side of the Wabash to be seen. The river swept by majestically below. But beyond its channel, as far eastward as he could see, there was nothing but floodwater, bristling with leafless trees, snarls of driftwood, and the tops of bushes. Beyond the place where he stood, he could not distinguish a foot of ground anywhere.

"You swim, Isaac?" he heard one man ask another behind him.

"Swim? Shoot, no," said the other scornfully. "Swimmin's fer a fish. A man walks on 'is two legs. But," he added after a thoughtful pause, "right now I'd give a lot to be a fish."

I need to ... I need to ... George blinked his eyes several times and shook his head to clear the rush of fatigue and confusion that was sweeping through it like a windstorm. The river and the drowned lands beyond were looking unreal, changing from brown to silver, coming close and then going away. Got to get to thinking straight, he thought, or I'm liable to make some foolish error! He took a deep breath and everything collected back into a semblance of normal vision.

Have to send scouts across there to seek a landing place, he thought. Find some dry ground.

He ordered a raft to be made by roping together dry logs, and putting four men on the raft, sent them across the Wabash channel to reconnoiter the far side. "If you find you can walk over yonder," he said, "go up to the town without discovering yourselves and get some canoes. Godspeed, now." He watched the raft angle off across the brown current.

"Captain," he said to McCarty, "there's ash and hickory hereabouts. Put some of your boys to making a small, fast canoe expressly for going up to the town for boats."

Should send the pirogue downriver to scout up the *Willing*, George thought. No, not yet, Can't spare 'er. She's the only thing we've got roomy enough to carry the goods or the sickly out of this place if it comes to that.

He looked over the bivouac area. The men were sitting or lying about now, listless, idle, drying themselves as best they could, eyes glassy, some beginning to moan about their hunger. Got to give them some direction while we wait on the scouts, he thought. Can't let them reflect on our plight. That would be most detrimental to their resolve.

So he instructed the company commanders to form work parties for the building of more canoes. The men hauled themselves painfully to their feet and went off to various sites along the bank and soon the sounds of axes and saws and mauls could be heard everywhere along this dismal shore. Thus the eighteenth of February, being the thirteenth day since their gala march out of Kaskaskia, passed into evening. Night came on and the raft with its scouts did not return. And the hunting parties he had sent out during the day came in empty-handed, swearing that every animal in the countryside must have gone somewhere else for the duration of the flood.

"They're all aboard Noah's Ark!" yelled someone.

"This food business is gettin' serious, George," Captain Bowman said quietly as they laid out their blankets for the night. "Frankly, I'm nigh to panic 'bout that."

"Shh, Joseph. A man can go longer without food than he thinks he can. They're still movin' and workin', aren't they?"

"Aye, but barely."

"Well, Joseph, keep this under your hat, but I'm not abandoning an expedition for want of provision while there's plenty of good horseflesh in our possession."

"Oh, yeh," Bowman whispered. "I hadn't thought o' that."

"Neither have the men," George replied. "But if you see any of these scoundrels lookin' at the corral and licking their chops, you come an' tell me about it."

Bowman chuckled in the dark.

George went to sleep thinking about the fine dappled warhorse the people of Kaskaskia had given him, seeing its lovely, deep brown eyes.

Dear God, don't let it come to that, he thought.

THE RACKET OF TOOLS RESUMED EARLY THE NEXT MORNING. The men worked steadily, looking like hollow-eyed scarecrows. They could still muster up a smile and a joke when George came around to watch their progress.

Some of the woodsmen had turned up edible roots of various kinds, which they distributed, but there was by no means enough to feed an army.

The French volunteers appeared to be running out of spirit. It had been George's observation that their instinct for self-preservation was far stronger than the desire for any greater achievement, and he knew he might soon have to deal with mutinous sentiments from them. They were looking sullen and tending to congregate off by themselves. He summoned Captain Charleville.

"M'sieur," he said calmly to him, "please look to the morale of your men. Assure them that we're not as crazy as we appear; I always know what I'm doing. Remind them, too," he added, "that they did volunteer for this adventure, eh? Thank you, sir."

There was a shout from the riverbank. The four scouts that had gone out on the raft the day before were paddling slowly back, lying on logs, looking like half-dead rats. They were assisted up the bank, stood, sagging in the knees, supported by their comrades, to report that they had failed to find any dry land on the other side except a low hill, known as the Lower Mammel, or Bubbie, totally surrounded by water. Their raft had been broken up by the current during their further exploration, and they had spent the entire night without rest, lying on old logs in the backwaters, half in and half out of the chilly water, waiting for daylight to show them the way back. Clenching his jaw muscles to fight off the shock of this forlorn report, George ordered a small, guarded fire built to make a hot gruel of roots fattened with tallow for them, then had them wrapped in blankets for a rest. Their extreme condition had the momentary effect of making the others feel comparatively well off, although their own was scarcely better.

The light canoe being finished, George quickly sent McCarty and three of his men up the river to make another attempt to steal boats. But within an hour, that party returned, reporting they had been stopped by the sight of four large campfires on the river shore about a league upstream, apparently some sort of a guard or scouting camp of British and Indians. "Damn the luck!" George muttered. Now it seemed that their only hope lay in the arrival of the *Willing*.

Captain Bowman concluded his journal entry for the nineteenth:

—Immediately Col. Clark sent two Men in the said Canoe down to meet the Batteau with orders to come on day and Night that being our last hope, starving Many of the Men much cast down particularly the Volunteers, No provisions of any Sort now two days hard fortune.

The camp was very quiet on the morning of the twentieth. Some of the men sat as if drugged, their eyes haunted and unseeing. Some sat leaning against trees, pounding their hands together either to keep the circulation going in them or as a gesture of despair. Captain Charleville told George that many of his Creole volunteers were talking about an attempt to return the way they had come.

"Come with me," George said. He led Charleville to the camp of the French company, feeling a fierce happiness now in having some sort of a challenge at hand. He was past all uneasiness.

"Do I understand that some of you want to go home?" he demanded, and was met by furtive eyes. He laughed. He decided not to dignify such a recourse by arguing them out of it. Instead he said, "Look at Lieutenant St. Croix there," indicating a sturdy old Cahokian with a snow white beard, who had throughout the march driven himself far beyond anything that could have been expected of one his age. "You don't see him sulkin', do you? You might pattern yourselves on him, I'd say." Old St. Croix drew up even straighter at this tribute. George went on: "Your trouble is, you want something to do. I should be very glad if you'd go out and kill some deer. How about that, now?" Confused by his reaction, they got to their feet and set out in different directions with their muskets to hunt.

He then went all about the camp talking up the certainty of success, talking about the imminent arrival of the galley, talking about the likelihood that so many hunters soon would be back with meat. If the galley doesn't heave into sight today, he thought, we'll have to effect the crossing tomorrow and march on the town without her. Two more days here and they'll have neither the strength nor the will. And damned if I want to feed 'em horses!

At noon the sentry on the riverbank decoyed ashore a passing boat carrying five Frenchmen who were on their way to meet a party of hunters down the river. They were astonished and delighted to see the Americans and some of their friends of the Kaskaskia and Cahokia volunteers. They told George that there was not the least suspicion of his presence in the vicinity, that the inhabitants were chafing once more under the arrogance of Hamilton and were well disposed toward the Americans. They said Hamilton's repairs on the fort were all but finished, and their count of the fort's garrison indicated that Francisco Vigo's report had been accurate and remained unchanged. They also reported that they had seen two small boats adrift up the river, and George sent Captain Worthington upstream in one of the new canoes to find them. The Frenchmen were detained as politely as possible; George had no intention of letting them go out and then double back to the fort and betray the presence of the Americans.

Worthington returned toward dusk, having found one of the drifting boats. Then a great cheerful shout from one end of the camp signaled that one of the American hunters had found and killed a small deer; he staggered into the camp with it over his shoulders, wearing a proud grin. Distributed among so many men, it provided no more than a couple of bites apiece, but was deemed most acceptable, and did as much as a feast for the morale of the camp. The deer, and the stray vessel Worthington had brought in, were small things in comparison with their needs, but George chose to consider them as the harbingers of a change in fortune.

Now, he thought, we've got the vigor of spirit again to undertake a hard task. We'll cross the Wabash first thing in the morning!

THE CANOES BEGAN FERRYING THE TROOPS OVER TO BUBBIE HILL early on the morning of the twenty-first. The crossing took much of the morning and it was necessary to leave the horses and most of the baggage on the western shore. The entire force now stood on this hill, finally across the river that had stood so long in the way of their progress, and were cheered by the prospect of covering the nine miles up to Vincennes by evening. The French hunters from Vincennes, however, were flabbergasted by the notion. They said it would be impossible to make the town that day, or at all. The nearest dry land in that direction, they said, was another breast-shaped hill called the Upper Mammel, a league to the north, and the next beyond that, a small rise still three miles beyond, where lay an abandoned sugar-making camp.

"It is absurd to imagine that you can go from here to the Mammel," they whined, "and surely never to the sugar camp."

But recollecting what the men had done thus far, George thought otherwise, and with a wave of his arm he went down the slope into the cold water, followed by a single file of his troops, each man gasping or cursing as he stepped in. He ordered the few small canoes to ply alongside near the men, ready to take on anyone who might succumb to cold or fatigue and start to sink. Once again the wretched procession through icy water, which seemed to have become their way of life, was underway, one cautious step at a time. The water was deep, and soon the men were soaked to their necks again. They grasped for support at the branches of bushes that protruded above the water, but learned that the same bush that gave them a handhold above the surface tripped them and snagged their legs beneath, and so began to steer clear of them. Once again the chill penetrated their muscles, even more quickly now that their bodies had no food to burn. Every step became what seemed like a last dying effort, with aching joints grinding in their sockets and breath rasping in their lungs. But then they would take the next final step, then the next, and the next.

They struggled throughout the rest of the day in that manner, not a man dropping out, and by evening, under a new rainfall, they had made the three miles to the Upper Mammel. They hauled themselves up the slope, laughing deliriously at this newest triumph, then flopped on the ground like wet flour-sacks and lay there whooping oaths and threats against General Hamilton. George turned a quizzical grin on the Frenchmen who had pronounced this passage impossible. The Frenchmen stammered, shrugged, raised their hands and let them fall to their sides. *"Mon colonel,"* one finally blurted, "this is superior to anything I have ever witnessed!"

He shook his head and rolled his eyes. George accepted that as the applause due his men, and as night fell another camp was made, and again the men fell into a stupor of sleep with nothing in their bellies but esprit de corps.

THE NEXT MORNING, GEORGE FED HIS MEN A BREAKFAST OF PRAISE and led them down the other side of the hill. As he started to plunge into the water, one of the Frenchmen began protesting in a wail that the water was deeper here and even such men as these could not cross it. George paused, impressed by the earnest tone, and sent two men out in a canoe with a sounding pole to test the depth. They vanished among the bushes, and soon returned, shaking their heads.

"They's no place to pass," said the man with the pole. "It's over their heads, sir."

"Give me that pole, man," George said. He scrambled into the canoe and they went out northward, probing for the bottom with the pole. It was shallow for a while. But a few hundred feet out it grew deep. Each time he brought the pole up, the waterline was as high as his neck or chin, which meant that it was indeed over the heads of most. This was a dismal discovery. It meant that the men would have to be ferried in the canoes much of the way to the sugar camp, which would use the entire day and probably also the whole night, as the vessels would have to pass so slowly through dense bushes. The loss of so much time to these starved men would be a matter of serious consequence. Damn, I'd give anything now for a day's provision, he thought. We should have slaughtered a horse or two while we had them, instead of leaving them over there where they do us no good. Damnation! He was very displeased with his judgment now; for the first time he was beginning to wish he had never left Kaskaskia. He had the paddler return very slowly to the island, giving himself time to think. The bushes parted, and as the canoe drew near the shore he saw numbers of the men trotting down close to the water's edge to hear what he would say. He stepped out of the canoe onto shore, looking as solemn as he felt, and as he started to tell Bowman what he had decided, he felt that every eye was on him. Forgetting to display his usual confidence, he whispered seriously to Bowman, and then realized what a mistake that was. Evidently taking it as the signal of their final despair, the whole troop became alarmed even without knowing what he had said, and began milling about, bewailing their fate.

George watched this desperate confusion growing for a short minute, and realized that he had to do something about it instantly. Whispering to the officers to follow his example, he scooped some water in his hand, poured gunpowder into it, blacked his face, gave a mighty war whoop, and marched into the water without a word of explanation. The officers followed him in. Their commotion got the attention of the troops, who stopped their lamentations, gazed at them for a moment, then fell in line one after another like a flock of sheep, following the officers into the water.

"Sing 'Katy Cruel,' " George told his officers. They began it, the troop's favorite marching song; it soon passed along the whole line as they marched cheerfully into the icy water.

When I first came to th' town,
They brought me bottles plenty.
Now they have changed their tune
*   and bring me bottles empty!*
Oh, diddle lully day
Oh, de little li-o-day!

Thro' the woods I'll go,
Thro' the boggy mire;
Straightway on the road
Till I come t' my heart's desire.
Oh, diddle lully day
Oh, de little li-o-day . . .

We'll just wade as far as we can and then start ferrying them when it gets too deep to go on, he determined. However long it takes. It's all we can do. We've just run plumb out of alternatives.

George was in water that had risen to his waist when one of the flankers called out that he thought he had discovered a path in the water. George went to him, and there did indeed seem to be a sort of footpath running northward, slightly higher than the surrounding bottom, and on the presumption that it would follow the highest ground, he led the line along it.

They progressed along it for hours, seldom getting in more than waist deep. It was a laborious process, as every step of the invisible path had to be felt out by moccasined feet numb with cold. Several of the men had to be hauled into the canoes, being by now too weak from hunger or twisted with muscle cramps to go on. But by evening they had reached the half-acre of soggy ground that had been the sugar camp, a sort of elevated grove of sugar maples bearing the old scars of the tapping spiles, and here they took up their lodgings, having surmounted one more major obstacle, and joyous to have survived one more day. They now believed themselves to be within three or four miles of the town. Captain Bowman was too exhausted to write in his journal that night, but made the entry next morning.

22—Col. Clark encourages his Men which gave them great Spirits Marched on in the Water, those that were weak and faintish from so much fatigue went in the Cannoes, we came one league farther to some sugar camps, where we staid all

*Night—heard the Evening and Morning guns from the
Fort—No provisions yet, Lord help us.*

General Hamilton inspected the rebuilt section of palisade
wall, grunting in satisfaction. He turned and looked about the
compound of Fort Sackville in the evening light. Now here is
what a British fort should look like, he thought. Not a rotten log
in her now.

"Now, then, Mister LaMothe," he said to the French officer
beside him, "a worthy labor well done, eh? I take a satisfaction
from the sight of all that bright new wood, don't you?"
LaMothe glanced about quickly and puffed a wordless syllable
of acknowledgment out of his sharp nose. LaMothe was seldom
good company; being laconic and hard-eyed, he made the
hearty British officers uneasy. But he was like a quick sword,
which Hamilton could use with swiftness and surety, and so the
British commandant favored him and endured his reptilian per-
sonality. "Come, Captain, I think our gentlemen deserve a spot
of refreshment for all this, eh?" They set off across the compound for the officer's quarters.

Soon an amiable celebration was underway, but it was interrupted shortly by the arrival of François de Maisonville, who
arrived from a scouting party on the Ohio with two Americans
he and his Indians had captured. During the business of con-
signing the prisoners to the guardhouse, Maisonville took General Hamilton aside. "On my way up the river last night, oh, I
would say, three or four leagues below the fort, I saw on the
eastern shore a number of campfires among the trees. I counted
fourteen all on one rise of ground. Something of a large party,
I thought, but whether of an enemy or of Indians, I couldn't
tell."

"Hm. I don't know of any of our savages down there now.
Wait. Captain LaMothe, would you hearken to this, please, and
see what you make of it . . ."

LaMothe's eyes flashed as he listened and he agreed that it
could bear looking into.

"Would you then take Lieutenant Schieffelin and a detachment down that way and find out who's there?"

"I'd be happy to lead you down, Captain, and show you
where I saw them," said Maisonville.

"That would be very much appreciated," said Hamilton,
"though I'm sure you must be exhausted already. . . ."

"My curiosity is piqued," Maisonville replied. "And one

can't be too watchful . . ." He had made much of his alertness ever since that humiliating day in August when he had had to bear to Detroit the news of Colonel Clark's invasion of the Illinois.

Twenty militiamen were armed and outfitted and, with LaMothe and Maisonville and the lieutenant riding at their head, set out from the strong new gate of the fort, went down through the village, and making a wide curve eastward to avoid the flooded lowlands, set out to find the mysterious party.

Within three hours, having wandered back and forth in the darkness trying to find a dry passage down the riverbank, they were lost. They settled down to make camp for the night, intending to continue their reconnaissance at daybreak.

"I regret having caused you this inconvenience," Maisonville said to LaMothe as they sat on a log by their campfire drinking taffia. "I have no idea whom we'll find, have you?"

"Madmen," LaMothe replied, managing to smile a mocking smile without in the least raising the corners of his mouth. "Only madmen would be out in this flood. And only madmen would be out here expecting to find someone!"

Maisonville laughed uneasily and gazed into the fire. "I take it you think I was imagining those fires?"

LaMothe merely shrugged, leaned forward with his elbows on the muddy knees of his leggings, and put a glowing brand to the bowl of his clay pipe.

THE SKY WAS CLEARING, AND FOR THE FIRST TIME IN THE TWO weeks of the expedition, stars were visible. But the cloudless sky also brought on a severe drop in temperature. The air which had hovered above the freezing point for so many rainy days now had an edge of stinging cold, which added to the extreme misery of Colonel Clark's wet and starving woodsmen. The Frenchmen who had become attached to the force two days before huddled together for a few minutes, glancing about uneasily, then came to speak to George and his officers.

"*Mon colonel,*" said their spokesman, "permit us to doubt that even these extraordinary people of yours can survive a cold night like this and another march tomorrow without some food. M'sieur, please let us take the canoes up to the town tonight and bring back provisions."

George hesitated, moved at first by the offer, then suddenly becoming suspicious. "Thank you for the offer," he said. "I should dearly love to see them break this long fast. But I'm going to have to decline, because we must effect a complete surprise. No one must suspect we're here."

"Mais non," protested the Frenchman. "We could bring food only from our own houses, without anyone knowing about it."

He wanted to trust them. He wanted desperately to see his men filling themselves on the nourishment they surely would need to go the last four miles to Vincennes. It seemed a proposition so easy to execute, and to so much advantage.

"George," hissed Bowman, "in the name of God, let 'em go do it!" His voice was quavering in the bitter cold darkness. George himself every few seconds would have an uncontrollable spasm of shivering and a feeling that his heart was going to stop. Bowman continued, pleading with him, "We could send a few of our men with 'em as a surety of their good intentions. What say you, George? These boys is like t' perish if they don't get het up from th' inside!"

But something beyond rationality told George not to risk it. Providence had after all helped them each time to go a little beyond the apparent limit and miraculously kept them from being discovered, and it seemed somehow to him that they had exploited the law of averages. Even if their intentions are right, he thought, they might simply by mischance give us away. "Joseph," he said finally, "don't press me on it. I feel as you feel, but something's telling me it should not be done, and so it shall not. No more on it, please, and messieurs, I thank you for your generous offer. Now let's snug down and rest as best we can. Good night all of you."

THOSE WHO HAD NOT SHIVERED THEMSELVES AWAKE IN THE BITING cold before sunrise were brought out of their stupor by the boom of the morning gun of Fort Sackville, which now was so close that it was loud and distinct. The men agonizingly brought themselves to their feet, literally white with the frost that had formed on them in the night. Some found their clothing frozen to the ground. Many of them were shivering visibly and constantly. Some tried to get their circulation going by pounding their arms across their chests and stamping their feet, only to find themselves exhausted by that little effort.

Had it not been for their intense suffering they might have been cheered by the sight of the morning. The whole world had a clean, sun-sparkling, crisp look, so greatly contrasted to the bleak, sodden black and gray and brown they had been seeing for so many terminable days. Now the sky was a pale blue whose quality was reflected on the frosty ground and on the skin of ice that had formed at the shores and in the still waters. It looked to George like a brave day, and he was certain it would be the day they would reach their destination.

He had them formed into ranks in the morning sunshine and braced himself to keep from shuddering. Facing them, breath condensing, he looked them over for a moment—the whole ghastly-looking parcel of them, their clothes soiled dirty gray, some having lost their shoes in the flood bottom, their faces chalk-white to blue, eye sockets purple as bruises, faces grimacing with cold, half of them trembling like aspen leaves, most sniffling and hacking, these men who had suffered so to come with him—and his affection for them was so overwhelming that for several minutes he could not speak. Each time he would open his mouth to form his words, the pronouncements would be strangled in a flood of pity and admiration. To gather himself and hide the sentimentality that must be, he felt, softening his authority, he turned his face away and looked northward in the direction of the town. Before him lay a flooded plain of some three miles in width, and visible at its far horizon was a narrow blue line of trees. The water looked blue under the bright morning sky, blue with its rim and sheets of new ice, less than an inch thick. There was not a tree or bush standing in the plain to give a handhold for a sinking man, and the bitter cold and starvation, he knew, would make this the most trying of all the difficulties they had faced. With a deep breath to steady his voice, George turned back to face the men, who were looking at the icy expanse with distrust or resignation.

"Gentlemen, listen now:

"You might be pleased with yourselves. I've long studied the history of wars, and I'll tell you that there never has been a march the equal of what you've done this month. In times when armies were routed and fleeing for their lives, they might have endured such hardships as these. But never did anyone go through this *on the way to a fight*!" Some of the troops began grinning and standing straighter; a few began to weep noiselessly.

"But then," George continued, his sight of them blurring with tears, "I reckon there never was a people of such a temper as we are." He turned and pointed across the flooded plain. "That," he said, "is the last obstacle between us and Fort Sackville. You see that line of woods yonder? There lies the end of your fatigues! Beyond those woods sits the object of your brave effort, boys: the Scalp-Buyer!"

Then without waiting for a response he turned and walked down into the water, followed by a loud *huzzah* and war whoops. The ice cracked and broke away in triangles and curving slabs, and he drew his sword to shove these pieces out of his way.

The ice water filled his shoes and leggings instantly and the cold shot up his spine like a bolt of pain. His heart fluttered and skipped and only with effort could he keep himself from whimpering aloud. But to display anything other than absolute stoicism now to these men could ruin everything. They were bearing all this because he seemed not to mind it. He knew that. They were trying to prove themselves to him; he knew that; he suspected it had become as important a drive as their patient motives of revenge.

But some of them might not be able to follow through this, George thought. The French volunteers. Some among them might not come along. George stopped and turned. About a third of the men were in the water with him now. A few of the French were hanging back.

"Captain Bowman!"

"Aye, sir!"

"Fall in at the rear with your company and have them shoot any man who refuses to march. We want no such people as that among us, do we, boys?"

"Right you are, Mister Clark!" yelled Sergeant Crump, and the rest gave a fierce cry of approbation. "Up, laddie!" Crump shouted, snatching up little Dickie Lovell and mounting him on his shoulders. "And beat that drum fer all y're worth!"

And in a few minutes the whole line was in the water, flanked by its canoes, heading northward toward that faraway line of trees that was its final horizon.

The benumbing cold sapped the men's vigor almost instantly, and they were only a few hundred yards out on the floodplain, thigh deep in water, before the marrow of their bones seemed to be frozen. The simple process of making their limbs work grew frighteningly difficult, not only because of exhaustion but because the nerves were not telling the mind where the feet were, or whether a knee or ankle was bent or straight, or what muscle might respond to what effort. Walking, difficult enough on mucky bottom, half-submerged, and weighted with arms and knapsacks, was reduced to a kind of gingerly, slow-motion stumbling, as if upon unfamiliar artifical limbs instead of responsive flesh and bone.

George was bewildered to find that he would have to force a leg forward, pause to determine whether the foot was planted on the bottom, then make a conscious decision to shift his weight to that dubious leg and start hauling the other one up. All this while his vision telescoped back and forth, went from blinding-bright to cloudy and back to blinding, and often he saw double. This was a new and awful thing, finding his powerful and athletic body unable to obey the commands of his will. George kept some fifteen or twenty of the biggest and strongest near him, those who most likely would have the strength to do his bidding in emergencies; and when the column was about half-way to its destination he began to feel himself sensibly failing, saw those strong men around him lurching along, gasping, moaning, and blowing, he was overcome with an almost panicky worry for the weaker men. There was nothing, not a tree or a bush, for them to cling to if their strength failed them, and he feared the weaker ones, if not the stronger too, might cramp up, collapse, and drown. Each time he looked back and saw them floundering along, their eyes wide with fright and strain, he grew more alarmed. He realized that he had always believed a man could force his body to go on as long as his will was determined, but for the first time began to suspect that it might not be so.

"Quick!" he called to the canoemen. "Go ahead and make land as fast as you can do it, unload the munitions and come back to pick up the men! Fast, now!" The canoes shot forward, soon diminishing in the distance. "Master Lovell, lay on that drum!" The boy, still perched on Sergeant Crump's shoulders, beat the drum forcefully right by the sergeant's ear. "Greathouse, and you, Freeman, come here." Two tall, rugged riflemen waded to his side. "I want you both to range on ahead, and holler back t' me now and then that the water's getting shallow."

"Aye, sir," said Freeman. "But what if'n it ain't?"

"Say so anyway. They need the encouragement. And when you get nigh th' woods, start hollering, 'Land!' Do that, now. Off you go."

As the morning wore on, that stratagem seemed to be having its desired effect. Heartened by the two men's hopeful shouts, the marchers exerted themselves far beyond any reasonable quitting point.

The unloaded canoes returned soon, took on as many of the half-conscious men as they could carry, and again sped ahead to the shore.

Freeman and Greathouse kept up their calls, but in actuality the water was growing even deeper as the column neared the woods. Now the smaller and weaker men were being held up by their stronger comrades, some being so weak they were supported with difficulty by one on each side.

The trees of the wood began to loom closer, growing with a maddening slowness. The fissures in the bark were visible; the fringe of white ice in the shadows by the shore grew wider. But the deepest part seemed to be here. George was appalled to find the water now risen up to his neck, and the shore only a few yards away. The canoes went back and forth in a great hurry now, picking up those who simply were not tall enough to keep their faces above the water. Shouts of relief and encouragement were coming from those who had already been put on the shore. The drummer boy beat with a thrilling agitation upon his drum, there was whooping and sobbing, and at last the column, in disarray, floundered into the flooded edge of the woods. Some with sufficient strength waded ashore and dropped to their knees or collapsed; others reached the first tree or bush they could find and clung there waiting for the canoes to come. Some reached shallow water and started wading out, only to find that without the water to buoy them they were too weak to stand. George came upon one woodsman, surrounded by broken ice, with an arm wrapped over a floating log, his stubbly cheek resting on the wet wood, whimpering something of which the only coherent word was "God." George got an arm under him and with his own last bit of strength dragged him onto the shore. Then he turned and watched.

Like gleaners, the canoes were going out and picking up the last dozen men whose heads and shoulders still dotted the sheet of water, and bringing them in. Bowman waded through the shallows, wet hair hanging over his shoulders in yellow strings, and came stumbling toward George with a rictus of a grin on his face; he looked like a skeleton in wet deerskins, shaking as with ague, but he was grinning.

"By God, George. By God in Heaven, it may be a miracle but we made it. D'you hear me, man? We *made* it! George, not a man went under!" He turned and gazed back over the bright expanse of ice and water to the tiny clump of distant trees where the sugar camp was, then at the edge of the woods, where some men were still lying half in and half out of the water trying to recover the strength to move. "Look at 'em, George! Dear *God*, I've never seen such people!" And suddenly his stretched grin crumbled; he buried his face in his hands and sobbed without constraint.

It was past noon. George ordered the able-bodied to build fires, regardless of the proximity of the town. It soon became apparent that the fires helped little; the men were frozen to the marrow. So two strong men would take a weaker by both arms and walk him staggering back and forth until he would recover enough to stand by himself. George was about to lean on a tree and pray for another miracle to send manna from Heaven when a shout came from the water's edge. The men in one of the canoes had discovered an Indian canoe full of women and children moving toward the town, and it was forced ashore. The squaws and children stood looking fearfully at the hideous crowd of wretches.

As if delivered by Providence—how often this has happened to us! he thought—the canoe carried half a buffalo quarter, some tallow, corn, and kettles. It was a small amount for a starving army but a grand prize nonetheless. George spoke to the oldest squaw, told her he believed that the Great Spirit must have sent them, and promised to pay her for the meat and corn as soon as possible. A hot broth was made and served out to the men. With careful rationing everyone got a little, but many of the stronger ones passed their portions on to the weakly, joking and making light of it. By Heaven, George thought, kings could learn something about nobility from these roughnecks of mine.

Warmed from outside by the strengthening February sunshine, from inside by their sips of broth and by the realization that the obstacles of their journey were all now behind them, the troops made an easy canoe passage of one more deep, narrow lake and marched a short distance to a copse of timber known as Warrior's Island. George led the men to the edge of that wood and then let them stay there at their ease for a few minutes to feast their eyes on the fort and the town they had suffered so hard and long to reach.

Less than two miles away, its outline hazy blue in the winter sunlight, stood Fort Sackville, its back to the Wabash: the long palisades, hip-roofed blockhouses at each corner, the huge, high gate of logs, the flag a mere speck above the headquarters building inside the compound. Sprawling alongside the road leading to the fort was the town of Vincennes. There they lay, in full view, and the men strained forward and stared like eagles, whispering, muttering, exclaiming in tight, snarling tones of voice, laughing a snickering, cruel, bitter laughter that had the edge of murder and revenge on it. Now and then they uttered the name *Hamilton* in voices choked with menace. Virtually every man, George suspected, was reviewing some act of murder, pillage, or destruction whose revenge he considered his personal responsibility. "There he sits, boys," George would insinuate to them as he passed. "The Scalp-Buyer, and all his agents. I ask you boys, was this worth the journey?"

"Aye!"

"What color'd you reckon *his* scalp is, Colonel?"

"Most likely a powdered wig, Mister Crockett."

"Good to be here, sir!"

"Glad to have you, Abe. Once or twice there I thought the going would get difficult."

"We're here by yer good policy, Mr. Clark."

"Thankee. Did you say that when you had ice in yer breeches?"

"Ha! It was nothing but what a man c'd bear."

"Or a soldier expect."

Such sentiments were like music to George. He knew they were all high-headed on hunger and eagerness, and had passed from one extreme to the other, from desperation to euphoria.

But now, he knew, that eagerness would have to be put to use while it existed, as the task ahead was as formidable as the one just completed. Here was his weakened band of one hundred thirty-five men, without the gunboat, provisions, reinforcements, or even cannon they had figured into their strategy, outside a massive, rebuilt fort that could be expected to stand off a thousand. Indians in the British pay ranged constantly in and out of the fort; British reinforcements were to be expected down the Wabash momentarily.

There was no way to retreat. It was as desperate a situation as any they had just survived.

George looked over the rolling plain that undulated between their present vantage point and the distant village, and pondered his strengths, his weaknesses, his abilities. We cannot wait for the *Willing*, not one day, even; we'd starve, freeze, or be discovered. The only strengths we do have are in surprise and spirit. We have to exploit those advantages. One thing I know, he thought. There's not an American here who'd quit short of dying.

The low places of the plain were covered with water, and several men from the town were out on horseback among those ponds, duck-shooting. Two or three of these hunters were within half a mile of the Americans' hiding place. George ordered some of the trustworthy French volunteers out onto the plain toward the duck hunters, with instructions to bring one in without alarming the others. When they brought him in, he looked with bulging eyes at the few Americans who stood, gaunt and severe, among the trees waiting for him. George had ordered the rest to conceal themselves. Questioned, the prisoner revealed that the repairs on the fort had been completed just the day before, and that there were a good many Indians in the town. Still there had not been any suspicion of the Americans' presence.

George wandered a few feet away and stood by himself, planning. Our fate will be determined in the next few hours, he thought. Nothing but the most audacious conduct can do this.

Must take into consideration the villagers. Many are secretly in our favor, and many lukewarm for either side. One thing we have to do is get them sorted out, then we can make our move.

Summoning Girault to come with pen and paper, George dictated, and Girault wrote in French:

> *To the inhabitants of the village of Post St. Vincent: Gentlemen, being now within two miles of your village and not being willing to surprise you, I take this step to request of such of you as are true citizens and willing to enjoy the liberty I bring you, to remain still in your houses. And that those, if any there be, that are friends to the King of England will instantly repair to the fort and join his troops and fight like men, and if such should hereafter be discovered that did not repair to the garrison, they may depend on severe punishment.*
>
> *On the contrary, those that are true friends of Liberty may expect to be well treated as such. I once more request that they may keep out of the streets, for every person found under arms on my arrival will be treated as an enemy.*

Signing it, George hoped it would encourage the friendly inhabitants, and that their confidence would make the others suppose he had enough troops to be sure of success.

The prisoner then was released and sent into town with the letter. George steadied himself against a tree and watched the messenger through a telescope until he entered the town. Then, in a few minutes, the glass revealed the villagers astir in every street. Soon large numbers of the villagers could be seen running or riding out onto the commons, as if to view the approach of the American army.

George kept scanning the fort and listening intently, but to his surprise there was no movement, or sound of drum or gun, to indicate that the alarm had been relayed to the garrison. That stillness worried him; he began to fear that the enemy knew of his presence and was already prepared. But he could only speculate about that, and deal with it however he must.

As the afternoon grew long, he had the companies formed up for the march into the village. In the first division he put Captain Williams's and Captain Worthington's companies, reinforced by the Kaskaskia volunteers; in the second he put Captain Bowman's company and the Cahokia volunteers. A detachment of fifteen sharpshooters under Captain Bailey was sent around the edge of town to pour harassing fire on the fort until the main force could take possession of the town.

Long poles were cut in the woods, and on the end of each was tied one of the many banners that had been made by the women of Kaskaskia. Soon almost every man carried a banner held high aloft. The men were ordered to march in absolute silence, and at unusually large intervals.

Shortly before sunset, he ordered the companies to start marching toward the town in a zigzagging course across the undulant plain, keeping mostly in the defilades. The officers, now mounted on horses taken from the duckhunters, rode repeatedly this way and that over the knolls. The purpose of this tactic was to give observers in the town a vastly exaggerated impression of the size of the invading force.

The sun set; the French villagers, having feasted their eyes on what obviously was a force of perhaps a thousand Americans—judging by the number of banners and officers—then followed the advice of Colonel Clark's proclamation and vanished into their homes, some apprehensively, some, familiar with the legends out of Kaskaskia, in a state of happy excitement. They opened their windows and watched the ominously silent army approach until dusk dimmed their view.

In a large stone house, half a dozen of the villagers who had refused to sign the oath of allegiance to the English king gathered, talking excitedly. Among them were the burghers Bosseron and LeGras and the young brother of Father Gibault. Moving aside a table and chair and peeling back a rug, they raised a section of flooring, climbed into a cellar, and began lifting up kegs of gunpowder and bars of lead they had kept hidden since December in anticipation of the Americans' return.

ONE OF THE GENTLEMEN OF VINCENNES WHO REMAINED PERPETUALLY under General Hamilton's suspicion, as spies or at least as secret American partisans, was the trader Moses Henry, who had been put under guard in the fort a few days earlier. His wife, under the pretense of bringing some of his personal effects, now visited him at sundown, and whispered to him the news of the American army's presence and the proclamation from Colonel Clark. Smiling with pleasure, Mr. Henry kissed his lady goodbye and then sauntered to the billet of the prisoner Captain Leonard Helm. Lighting a pipe from Helm's candle, he murmured:

"You would be pleased to know, Mister Helm, that the town has just now been occupied by your esteemed compatriot, Colonel Clark."

Helm sat up straight. His eyes sparkled. A broad, sly smile grew among his gray whiskers. "You don't say so! Thankee, Mister Henry, for that advice. And may I repay it by suggesting you keep your head down tonight, my friend."

25

VINCENNES, WABASH VALLEY
February 23, 1779

HENRY HAMILTON WAS UNEASY, AND COULD NOT QUITE EXPLAIN why. He stalked about in his headquarters, now and then sitting down at the hearth and sipping brandy. The evening had come down dry and cold, the kind of bracing weather that usually gave him a sense of well-being. But tonight his heart seemed to keep rising in anxiety. Perhaps it was the failure of LaMothe and Maisonville to return with some report on the mysterious fires downstream. Or that strange, unexplained bustling about that had taken place in the town that afternoon. Sentries had reported that for a few minutes everybody in the town had been in the streets, then had vanished back into their homes; yet not a word of explanation had come to the fort.

The orderly knocked and opened the door. "Sir, Captain Helm requests permission to see you."

"Ah, good!" said Hamilton. "Have him brought around." Maybe that genial old reprobate will dispel these spirits, he thought. And make me one of his great toddies for this cold night.

Helm entered, looking even more smug than usual.

"Good evening, Captain. What brings you here tonight?"

"Just payin' my respects, Mister Hamilton, and compliments on th' fine work you've done repairin' this fort."

"Thank you. Thank you very much indeed. Quite an improvement over the ramshackle thing it was when you commanded it, eh?"

"Aye, that it is, and we appreciate it. It'll save us a great deal of labor and expense."

"I'm afraid I don't follow you, Captain."

"Wal, surely, Mister Hamilton, sir, you don't think we're a-gonna let you keep it."

Hamilton laughed. "Oh, that again, is it? You amuse me, Mister Helm, with your absurd faith in that boy colonel of yours. Well, would you care to fix us one of your lovely toddies, mine fond enemy?"

"Honored! Honored!" Helm bustled to the sideboard, humming happily like some old servant, and clinked among the glasses and decanters. He shook cloves and cinnamon bark from two porcelain jars into mugs. Then he came to the fireplace and stuck two irons in the fire's embers. He sat by the fire, took the kettle off the iron swing-arm and poured hot water into the mugs. He stirred in the honey, stuck a red-hot iron hissing into each cup, gave Hamilton his cup, smiling and humming all the while, then held his own cup up for a toast. They clicked the vessels. "Success to Colonel Clark," Helm proposed.

"Blast your lights, you old sot. I'll drink to no such thing."

"As you will." Helm sipped, then sat looking about at no particular place in the room, leaning slightly forward in an attentive position. Hamilton finally laughed at him.

"You're a bloody imp this evening, Mr. Helm. What the devil are you listening to, the song of the leprechauns?"

Outside, a gunshot banged.

"That," Helm said, grinning and raising his cup again.

Four more shots were heard. General Hamilton cocked his head and looked askance at the window, still half smiling. "That?" he said. "Likely a party of the savages welcoming themselves home. They often do that, as you know. Or perhaps some frolic in the village." He sipped his toddy and shifted uneasily in his chair.

"Wal, General, I'll not argue with you. You're in command here. For th' moment, anyways."

There were shouts in the compound now, and as Hamilton rose to his feet scowling and reached for his cape and hat, there was a sharp *smack* as something hit the chimney, and mortar sifted down into the flames. As Hamilton opened the door, Leonard Helm went into gales of laughter. To the orderly, who stood bent half out of his chair, eyes wide in alarm, the general snapped, "Put that old fool back in his quarters." Then he stepped out into the cold, purple-gray twilight. British redcoats and French militiamen were scurrying over the parade ground in confusion, some mounting the parapets, carrying their muskets. Gunners were climbing to the blockhouses, on whose second floors stood the garrison's artillery.

What the devil is this? Hamilton wondered as he hurried toward one of the blockhouses. He could hear an uproar of whooping and laughter outside the walls. He couldn't believe the fort was under attack, and was growing indignant at the thought of this disturbance which, he was sure, stemmed from someone's drunken exuberance and would have to be punished severely, whether the culprit was Frenchman or Indian.

"Man the pieces!" he roared at the milling troops. "But hold fire until I know . . ."

He was interrupted by a scream of pain. A sergeant, lighting his fuse-match near the firing port of the cannon, caught a rifle ball in the chest, reeled out the blockhouse door and fell off the parapet, his body thumping to the gravel a few feet from General Hamilton. A shiver of awe spilled down the general's flanks as he stood looking at the twitching victim and heard the frightened shouts of the other soldiers who had witnessed this.

He rushed up the ramp to the parapet and peered out through a firing loophole into the early night. In the shadows among the dim houses and barns of the village, muzzle flashes winked and sparkled, the sporadic crackling and roar of rifles swept to and fro, and bloodthirsty howls and wailing laughter filled the air. The nearest houses were about two hundred yards from the fort, but the balls were hitting the palisade with intimidating precision, making their resounding *thwacks* or whistling mere inches overhead. When a ball thrummed through the loophole like a bumblebee and left its breath on his right ear, General Hamilton realized that he was silhouetted against the evening's red afterglow in the tiny porthole and quickly decided he had seen enough of the enemy's activity for the moment; he ducked away from the opening bathed in cold sweat and shouted:

"Return their fire! Gunners, rake those buildings!"

Soon the musket fire from the fort began banging, more resonant here within, against the distant crackling of the enemy's weapons. Then there was a flash of yellow-red from the nearest blockhouse and the roar of a four-pounder, followed immediately by another, and another, and the hearty shouts of the British gunners. The acrid sulphuric smell of gunpowder rankled like snuff in his nose, stimulating him as it always did, and momentarily his dread solidified into a happy, clearminded ferocity. He thought of Leonard Helm's mockery, and wondered how Helm had learned of this before the fact. It could be his friend Clark out there, Hamilton thought, though I don't see how he could have come here. But whoever it is, and whatever he has in mind, he'll find that he's dealing with Englishmen, not Creoles, this time.

At that moment, another of his English gunners yelled in pain and fell back from the palisade, his collarbone broken by a rifle ball that had whistled in through the embrasure.

Damn it! Hamilton thought. Where's LaMothe with his volunteers? We're going to need every man we have.

The British regimental surgeon trotted to Hamilton across the parade, huffing and blowing, eyes wild. "I just made it in through the gate," he exclaimed.

"I'm glad you're here, Doctor McBeath. I'm afraid we're going to need you."

"I was in the village when the shooting began," panted the surgeon. "The lady of the house told me Colonel Clark has arrived from the Illinois with an army of at least five hundred." Two cannon in the blockhouses boomed.

"Clark, eh? That's hardly credible. But never mind that, Doctor. Have the wounded moved into my quarters, out of this cold, and attend to them."

And another soldier yelped and spun to the ground.

IT WAS REMARKABLE THAT THEY WERE EVEN ON THEIR FEET. But they were, and they were doing with a fervid eagerness everything George needed done, and it seemed that he well might have more of a problem holding them back than driving them forward.

They're like wolves, he thought, made even more reckless and determined by their starvation.

He knew, from his own state, that they all were in an almost disembodied frame of mind from hunger and suffering, that clear-eyed and dauntless condition which he knew the Indians sometimes attained through deliberate fasting. They all seemed to be beyond fear or pain now, and he was certain that any one of them was worth ten British soldiers in this fight.

They had secured the town without firing a shot and now had surrounded the garrison completely. They had found natural cover behind houses, garden walls, ditches, and the riverbanks. Some of the woodsmen moved forward in the darkness and set up breastworks of logs and old timbers within twenty or thirty yards of the fort's walls, so close that the cannon muzzles could not be depressed enough to fire on them, and from this range they could put almost every shot right through a firing port or embrasure. The cannon belched smoke and fire over their heads as the night deepened, shattering a few walls and outbuildings, but so far not one of the Americans or their partisans had been wounded. The British soldiers on the walls poured out musketry as if powder and ball were inexhaustible, and their shots went whining and cracking everywhere but never found flesh. The Americans had found or made such good cover that they were almost as well protected as anyone within the fort. George knew he could not afford to lose men, and so had admonished his officers not to let them grow careless of themselves.

The hoarded supply of powder and lead turned over by Messieurs Bosseron, LeGras, and Gibault was, to George's mind, another of those small miracles that had come to his aid throughout this expedition. Marching on the town at sunset, with most of his ammunition still aboard the absent galley and the rest somewhat deteriorated by the conditions of the march, he had not expected to have firepower to spare. But when his allies had greeted him with the great cache, giving him the luxury of sustained fusillade, the effectiveness of his sharpshooters was vastly increased. A hail of rifle balls would riddle any spot where an Englishman showed his head, and it was not long before the British firing was nearly silenced.

At this time the woodsmen began to play with their enemy. "Hey, laddies," one would cry toward the fort in that maddeningly insolent tone that only an American hill man can produce, "stick yer arse up, an' I'll wager I can put a ball through it without makin' another hole!"

"Hey in there! How about Mister Hamilton's scalp, in trade fer th' one you took off my daughter?"

"Aye, you cowardly redcoat scuts! You dare come out from behind yer Indians an' meet a Kentuckian face to face?"

"Come out, you boneless buggers! Come on out! Come on, God blast you, an' have a taste o' long knife!"

"Hi bully boy! I'll snip off yer family jewels, if y' have any!"

"Here's the answer to your dumb ballyraggin'!" a voice would cry back from the fort; an embrasure would be thrown open and a cannon flash fire, but before its ball could even crash into the rubble, a dozen Kentucky rifles would be fired through the embrasure and a British gunner would spin away with an ear shot off or a ball through his shoulder.

And so this deadly riposte of word and gunshot continued into the night. Sometimes a volley of fire would come from one corner of the town, then stop instantly and a volley of nasal laughter would come from another quarter. A nasty snigger would draw fire, which would be returned instantly, tenfold. The British troops dared not go on relief, for fear that the walls might be stormed or sapped at any instant. Redcoats stood on the western parapet, tormented by the sounds of digging a mere thirty feet below, where Captain Bowman's men were undermining the wall near the powder magazine, but dared not raise their heads above the parapet to fire down because of the bullets and splinters that would meet them if they did.

George moved from one place to another watching this grim amusement, cheering the men on but warning them to protect their precious heads and save themselves for the morning. His men could not have performed more satisfactorily or with higher morale; he marveled that they could even lift their rifles after almost a week without food or warmth, yet here they were firing away in the darkness with the steady accuracy of starved hunters in the joyous pursuit of meat.

An ensign came to George shortly before midnight, where he had set up a command post in the old church, and told him that Tobacco's Son, the Grand Kite of the Wabash, had come to see him. The Piankeshaw chief, who had treated with Leonard Helm in the fall and proclaimed himself a Big Knife, strode into the candlelight, looked at George, smiled, nodded, then came forward with his eyes full of tears and gave him an earnest handshake. He was tall and proud, with deep parenthetical lines in his cheeks enclosing his thin mouth, with strands of gray in his greased and braided hair. He wore leggings and a hunting shirt of soft, nearly white deerskin, and had two pistols in his belt. His glittering eyes feasted on George for a moment as rifles crackled in the night outside. "You know," he said in a resonant voice, "that I am a Big Knife, your brother."

"I know that and I am content," George replied.

"I have told the Englishman Hamilton that I am a Big Knife, when he tried to buy my warriors to fight for him."

"Good. To fight for the British is a low thing."

"I have many warriors," said Tobacco's Son. "I have one hundred warriors with me near this place, and I wish to join my brother the Long Knife tonight and strike against the British fort." His straight white teeth glinted in the candlelight as he talked. A cannon boomed in the night outside and there was a shower of falling stone nearby but the Indian did not flinch.

George thought for a moment. Then he said, "I thank you for your friendly disposition." He did not want to risk the confusion that might result if a body of Indians mixed with the Americans in the dark, and was not altogether sure the chief could be trusted. "We are sufficiently strong ourselves," George said, "and would prefer that you keep your braves back. But I personally would like to have your counsel and your company, and invite you to stay at my side."

Tobacco's Son beamed with pride and pleasure. "This is a great honor. I have yearned to stand beside my brother the Long Knife, whom the Master of Life has sent among us to clear our eyes and make our paths straight. Now you are here and I am pleased with you."

"And I with you. Now let us take a walk and see how this business goes."

They found Captain Bowman outside in the street. He reported that his tunnel-diggers were being slowed by cave-ins as they tried to burrow under the fort's powder magazine. "By God, George," he breathed happily. "We've not had a man scratched yet, but I think we're playing havoc with 'em inside. Fine sport for the sons o' liberty, eh?"

"Fine sport indeed. Their hearts' desire. But this business has to be resolved quick, Joseph, before we get overrun by his Indians and reinforcements . . . What's that?"

There was a crackle of gunfire in a quarter of the town far

from the fort. "What could be happening over there?" Bowman asked.

An emaciated woodsman, one of the scouts who had been sent down the riverbank to watch for the *Willing*, soon came panting up with the answer. "They's a party of the enemy out south side o' th' town, colonel. 'Bout two dozen, it was. They tried to break through our line an' scamper into th' fort, it looked like. We turned 'em back and gave a chase but they just plumb disappeared."

"What, Indians? British?"

"One o' Charleville's boys said they was Canadians, an' said he heard th' voice of a Captain LaMothe."

"Aye, I know of that one," George said. "A dangerous rascal, I've heard."

"Captain LaMothe is like the fox," said Tobacco's Son. "He will be hard to find in the night."

"Tell Charleville to keep a detail looking for LaMothe," George said to the scout. "He could cause considerable mischief being at large thataway."

LaMothe, Maisonville, and the Canadians at this moment lay panting in a cold wet bed of straw and manure inside a barn south of the town. The fetid moisture soaked into their clothes. But the hazards of being outside were, for the moment, worse. LaMothe peered out between stones of the barn's wall. A tumbrel with a broken wheel leaned on its hub just outside, and now and then its outline would leap into clarity with the light from a cannon blast at the fort. LaMothe sent one of the Canadians out to seek a way into the fort. After a long wait, the man had not returned, and LaMothe sent out another.

He leaned against the stone wall and wrinkled his nose at the stench. His party had been returning from scouting the floodlands down the Wabash at sunset when the sound of cannon gave them their first knowledge that the fort was under attack. Returning to the village, they had made several rushes to get back into the cover of the fort, but had succeeded only in getting themselves pursued. And now here they were.

"Merde," cursed LaMothe with a bitter smile unseen in the dark. "Now I doubt they would let us into the fort even if we could get there."

Maisonville smiled. LaMothe was much more personable in danger. It seemed to bring him to life.

"Lieutenant," LaMothe said, "send another one out." Another Canadian crawled through the wall and vanished.

"Do you think they're getting caught? Killed?" Maisonville whispered.

"Non. Defecting, more likely," LaMothe whispered, then spat. *"Canaille!"* He spat again. *"Eh bien*, Maisonville, we'll have to get into that compound before daylight. They'll find us here otherwise."

"Listen. We might be of more service out here," Maisonville suggested. "We could go among the tribes and gather enough to trouble the rebels."

"What's this? Afraid to return to a besieged fort?"

"Mais non! Only that I could do better! Rather I should ask, are *you* afraid of being away from the fort among the *Bostonnais!"*

"Listen, m'sieur: LaMothe fears nothing!"

"Pardon."

"Lieutenant, send out another one. And warn this cur that if he doesn't report back, I'll find him someday and cut his throat."

Another Canadian went out, thus warned. The hours wore on, punctuated by constant gunfire, and he did not come back either.

THE SMELL OF GUNSMOKE WAS DENSE IN THE COLD AIR BEFORE dawn. George looked out into the fading darkness. The ring of muzzle flashes and verbal abuse around the fort continued as it had for the last twelve hours.

He was very pleased that despite all the lead the British had poured out into the surrounding darkness, not one of his men had been wounded. They were combining his cautionary orders with their own huntsmen's cunning to keep themselves virtually invisible, while at the same time doing more shooting than twice their number could have been expected to do. But George was growing anxious about Captain LaMothe. After midnight LaMothe had shown up in several places around the perimeter trying to make a break for the fort. Each time he had failed, but had escaped each time and was still thought to be hovering about the town waiting for his opportunity.

"Joseph, I've been thinking about this fox, LaMothe." He paused for a nearby fusillade of rifle fire to die down. "We've been trying to keep him from getting in the fort. But, you know,

I've been weighing it in the balance: If he got in, he'd reinforce the garrison by maybe twenty men, would you say?"

"Aye."

"But if he was to get discouraged and give up trying to enter, I suspect he'd soon think of going out to stir up the Indians against us. There's a lots of 'em in these parts, you know, that are inimical to our interest."

"I hadn't thought of that, but it's true."

"Well, weigh it: Where would we rather have an enemy like that, hemmed in or running loose?"

A cannon roared from the fort and simultaneously a shower of broken stone flew off the corner of a nearby house and rattled against walls and fences, leaving a rankling smell of stone dust.

"Why, put that way, George, I'd say inside, where he can be watched."

"Then I believe we should give him a chance to get in."

GENERAL HAMILTON OPENED THE DOOR OF HIS QUARTERS, WHERE four wounded soldiers lay or sat. He stepped out into the cold air, pulled his cloak about him, and listened. The gunfire had stopped, and the silence was as startling as the first gunshots had been twelve hours before.

The stars were fading. A smear of gray-pink light silhouetted the naked trees of the forest far to the east. The soldiers and militiamen along the parapets were cautiously peering over the palisades into the predawn gloom.

Hamilton crossed the parade and mounted a ladder to the parapet near the gate. He looked out over the window toward the town. There was total calm, not a sign of an enemy except the barricades and breastworks that had grown up in the meadow during the darkness since the moon set, and a fortified ditch that had been dug across the gate road.

Along the parapet the British soldiers were reloading their muskets, moving ammunition, blowing their noses, hawking and spitting, or simply stretching the stiffness and tension out of their shoulders.

"Surely they've not simply quit," said a lieutenant nearby.

"No such thing, I'll vow," said Hamilton. "Now, stand ready. They may be gathering for a rush. Load. Get the reserves up here!" He strained his hearing for the sound of troops moving in the distance, but heard nothing. He hated these stealthy methods of warfare. They seemed suitable only for Indians, and, to his mind, robbed warfare of its grandeur. Rationally, of course, he understood its superior effectiveness; as the perpetrator of Indian attacks against the rebel settlements, he was its chief advocate. But as a traditional British officer he deplored it, and often daydreamed of having a command in Europe where men still fought standing up on a field.

There was a sudden murmur of excitement along the parapet to his right. "Look you there, Gov'nor!" cried a soldier, pointing to the southeast quarter. Others were training their muskets there.

A group of men was halfway across the meadow, running at full tilt toward the fort, their forms dark against the pale, dead grass. As they drew near the palisade, feet thudding, arms rattling, one cried out:

"I'm LaMothe! Ladders! Ladders!"

Joy leaped in Hamilton's breast. "Drop over the ladders! Give them ladders!"

In seconds, Captain LaMothe, Lieutenant Schieffelin, and about fifteen of their men had swarmed over the eleven-foot palisade and leaped down into the arms of their comrades, panting and gasping. The soldiers cheered them and pounded their backs. "My God," LaMothe exclaimed shakily to Hamilton, "never was I so ready to feel a ball in my back, as when I topped that wall!" At that moment, a cackle of derisive laughter swept through the distance outside the walls, followed by a sudden hail of rifle balls which hummed past their ears and sent them all diving for cover. The Americans' harassing fire resumed full force.

"Congratulations on your safe return," Hamilton said with a trace of sarcasm as they crouched behind the palisade. "But I can't help feeling you were *let* in. Where's Maisonville?"

"He chose to stay outside," panted LaMothe, "to go among our Indians and rally them. We parted on that . . ."

"Damned good thinking!" Hamilton hissed. "You might have done better to stay with him."

Captain LaMothe's exuberance drained out of him.

Hamilton looked at him with a cold eye. It was altogether odd that a vigorous siege of the fort should have been totally suspended just long enough to let him get in safely.

Can I trust even LaMothe now? he wondered. Damn, damn, he thought. It's my perdition to serve among faithless Frenchmen. Well, then. I'll just have to watch him like the rest, he decided.

* * *

THE SUN ROSE, MAKING A MORNING OF GLITTERING FROST, YELLOW winter grass, long blue shadows, and bright, clear targets. The sun came up behind the town, at the Americans' backs, and shone blindingly into the eyes of the British defenders on the front wall of their fort.

Behind a jumble of stacked logs, carts, and barrels in the meadow, scarcely thirty yards from the looming fort, a company of American sharpshooters in filthy buckskins, fur caps or black hats, and mud-caked leggings, their toes showing through split-seamed moccasins, stood or crouched or lay prone, their cheeks sunken, eyes glittering, keeping up a tireless round of firing and loading. Blue-white smoke billowed constantly along this breastwork. Sunlight gleamed dull on the oily blue metal of hexagonal rifle barrels. Brass and hickory ramrods slid in and out of muzzles. Black powder trickled from powderhorns into flintlock pans; dirty thumbs cocked the hammers; callused forefingers fissured black squeezed the triggers; sinewy shoulders absorbed the recoil. If their shooting had been intimidating by moonlight, it was awe-inspiring now in the sunlight. The cannon fired a few rounds toward the village, but by now the merest crack in a gun port would admit well-aimed rifle balls; a rifleman watching a chink of light between two palisade logs would send a ball spinning through it the instant it was darkened by the movement of a body within. Soon the fort was buttoned up so tightly against this deadly hail that the cannon fell silent.

A young American private named Edward Bulger knelt behind the breastwork, diligently loading and firing. He trembled violently between shots, and sniffled constantly, but managed to pull his shivering body into a posture of statue stillness before each shot.

A shadow fell across the lad's gun as he reloaded, and a deep voice said:

"Wipe your nose, Mister Bulger, lest you wet your gunpowder."

Looking up, the private saw Colonel Clark standing before him, grinning. The lad beamed, ran the sleeve of his hunting shirt under his nose, poked the muzzle over a log, rested his cheek on the rifle stock, closed one eye, squeezed the trigger and shot the hat off an Englishman on the parapet.

Moving a few paces down the line, George and Bowman were amused at the sight of the lower half of a rifleman who lay firing from a prone position under an oxcart; the seat of his breeches was in shreds and his white buttocks shone through. Bowman laughed giddily. "Poor feller," he said, "Wonder whether them was blowed out or rotted out!"

"Now, Joseph," George said, "I have some nice news for you. The ladies o' Vincennes have kindly laid a great hot breakfast for us. If you'd relieve a half of your company at a time, so that they might go down and enjoy that welcome occasion . . ."

His words were drowned out by cheers.

"Lord help us, they've got Maisonville, sir!" exclaimed a British officer.

General Hamilton went up a ladder to the parapet and, eyelids trembling in anticipation of more of those precise American rifle balls, peered out through a gap in the palisade at a sight that made his blood run cold:

A mere thirty yards in front of the fort gate, François de Maisonville, arms bound behind him, was being led to an upright post in front of the American breastwork by two hideous, whooping woodsmen. The two tied the handsome French Indian agent to the post, exposing his chest to the fort, then stood behind him and, using his shoulders as rifle-rests, began with an air of confidence and immunity to snipe cheerfully at the fort, while Maisonville screamed his name frantically and begged the British not to return their fire.

Dear God, the wretch, Hamilton thought. He passed the word down the line not to risk hitting the captive. A shot fired by one of the snipers buzzed past General Hamilton's cheek, but he remained there, fascinated by the incredible sight, growing more furious and frightened with each passing second as this bizarre incident wore on.

The American Captain McCarty, drawn to this scene by the Frenchman's screams and the laughter of the riflemen, took one look at it, judged it as an unchivalrous way to use a prisoner, and ordered them to cease their amusement, untie the prisoner, and take him to the guard. The two men obeyed, but as they untied him, one of them, explaining to McCarty that this was the notorious Indian agitator Maisonville, drew his long knife, snatched a handful of hair and sliced off a patch of his scalp. Maisonville screeched in anguish and evacuated his bowels.

"Hey, you, Hair-Buyer!" the woodsman shouted back at the

fort as he led the stumbling Maisonville away, "You're next, yer
Lordship!"

On the parapet in the fort, Hamilton paled, turned away, and
went down the ladder, trying to shut out the abject wails of his
French ally.

He had paid for hundreds of scalps. But it was the first time
he had ever witnessed a scalping.

WHILE HIS SOLDERS ATE THE FIRST MEAL THEY HAD HAD IN SIX
days, George sat on a bench in the church in the village and wet
a quill in ink. He wrote:

Lt. Governor Henry Hamilton Esqʳ
Commanding Post St. Vincent
Sir

In order to save yourself from the Impending Storm that
now Threatens you I order you to Immediately surrender
yourself up with all your Garrison Stores &c. &c. for if I am
obliged to storm, you may depend upon such Treatment
justly due to a Murderer beware of destroying Stores of
any kind or any papers or letters that is in your possession
or hurting one house in the Town for by heavens if you do
there shall be no Mercy shewn you.

Febʸ 24th 1779

G. R. CLARK

At about nine o'clock the gunfire fell silent for the second
time, as the Americans waved a flag of truce. General Hamilton
crossed the parade, ordered one of the gates opened a few feet,
and stood inside waiting for the message. Captain Cardinal of
the Vincennes militia brought in the letter from Colonel Clark.
Hamilton broke the seal and stood reading the letter. His face
grew pale, then red. He looked up, scowling, at Cardinal.

"Wait," he said. Then he sent for all the officers of the garrison and had them come to his quarters, where he read them
the letter. They listened, some chewing the insides of their lips,
some pulling their noses; all were quite clearly frightened.
Some of them doubtless were recalling the spectacle involving
Monsieur Maisonville. Hamilton himself kept seeing that image.
It was unsettling to think of oneself on the other end of the

scalping knife, as it were, and that brutal act, always heretofore a remote abstraction in the business of governing, today seemed sickeningly real and proximate.

"My intention," Hamilton said, "is to undergo any extremity rather than give ourselves into the hands of such people. Has anyone an argument to that resolution? No? Good. Call assembly. I want to talk to the troops."

The occasion was brief. Hamilton read Colonel Clark's letter, told the troops what he and the officers had determined, and was assured by the British regulars that they would defend the king's colors to the last man. "Sir," barked one senior sergeant with a bulbous nose and ruddy jowls, "as the saying is, we'll stick to you like the shirt on your back, sir." The ranks gave three cheers. Hamilton clenched his molars, swallowed hard, and raised his chin.

"Thank you," he said huskily, and turned back toward his quarters. The French militia had not joined in the spirit of the demonstration; they hung their heads and shuffled their feet.

At his desk, Hamilton wrote:

> Govr Hamilton begs leave to acquaint Col. Clark that he and his garrison are not disposed to be awed into any action Unworthy of British subjects.

> *H. HAMILTON*

He gave the letter to Captain Cardinal, then sat slumped in his chair, gazing absently at a distant corner of the floor, and wondering what he might be bringing down on his brave people by this piece of defiance. He envisioned Captain Cardinal crossing the parade, going out through the gate, striding down the meadow to the American fortifications, handing the letter to Colonel Clark, the American reading it—

At that moment the crackle of rifle fire resumed, the booming of cannon, the rattle of splinters and spent balls on walls and roofs everywhere, the yelp of a defender nicked by a bullet. Hamilton sat at his desk listening to this mayhem. From the volume of the fire, he estimated that Clark must indeed have nearly a thousand attackers. My people can't stand in the face of that kind of fire long, he thought. Can't even use the bloody cannon! Damn, damn! He slammed his fist on the desk.

"Begging your pardon, Excellency," said the orderly, "Captain LaMothe sends word that a large body of the villagers have thrown in with the rebels, sir, and are firing on the fort."

"Blast!" the general barked, slamming his fist on the desk again. "Frenchmen!"

THE AMERICANS AND THEIR ALLIES, NOW FED, WARMED BY THE sun, certain that they had their long-hated enemies in their power, surfeited with ammunition, and presented with this huge fort which was a shooting gallery of such varied challenges, began competing with themselves for smarter and smarter shooting, with the result that the defenders by late morning had altogether stopped trying to return fire, either cannon or musket. It seemed incredible to George, but even without artillery, his marksmen had actually been able to silence a strong, well-defended British fort. He had never heard of such a thing; he felt that no man ever had been so happy, and was wondering just how to exploit this advantage when a truce flag appeared above the palisade, and he ordered a cease-fire.

The woodsmen reloaded and rested on their rifles as Governor Hamilton's messenger was brought through the lines. George opened the letter and read:

Lt Govr Hamilton proposes to Col. Clark a truce for three days during which time he promises there shall be no defensive works carried on in the Garrison, on condition Col. Clark shall observe on his part a like cessation of any offensive work   that he wishes to confer with Col. Clark as soon as can be and further proposes that whatever may pass between them two and any other Person mutually agreed upon to be present, shall remain a secret till Matters be finally concluded—As he wishes that whatever the Result of their conference may be to the honor and credit of each party—If Col. Clark makes a difficulty of coming into the fort Lt Govr Hamilton will speak to him before the Gate

24th Feb^y

H. HAMILTON

George pondered on the letter and passed it to his officers for their observations. He scratched his jaw, noting idly for the first time that a short but full-fledged beard had actually grown on him in the duration of this long and strenuous campaign. A fortnight since we left Kaskaskia, he thought. And not a moment's ease in all that time. And here we have Hamilton strapped really far tighter than we could have hoped; he's begging for a reprieve.

"I fear it's just a scheme t'get you inside that fort, George," said Captain Bailey.

"Aye," said Captain Worthington. "You'd be a prize hostage, all right."

"No," George replied. "A treachery of that nature would ruin his reputation. He wants those three days because—because—all I can see is, he has hopes of reinforcements by then."

"But so have we," Bowman said. "The galley must be nigh by now. She'll be on us in a day or two, if not this very afternoon."

"All's I know is this," said Captain McCarty. "Somethin's got t' change pretty soon. My boys is fed, fat, and sassy, an' been enjoyin' this shoot a whole lot, but some's sayin' they'd like t' get into that fort there, an' get to th' heart o' th' matter with the Hair-Buyer."

"Mine too," said Worthington. "I'm havin' a time making 'em keep down. They can git pretty rash, as y'know."

"Pen and paper, then," George said. He wrote:

Colonel Clarks Compliments to Mr Hamilton and begs leave to inform him that Col. Clark will not agree to any other terms than that of Mr Hamilton's surrendering himself and Garrison, Prisoners at Discretion—

If Mr. Hamilton is Desirous of a Conference with Col. Clark he will meet him at the Church with Captⁿ Helm—

Feb 24th 1779

G. R. CLARK

General Hamilton watched the messenger clamber through the barricade and return up the road and prayed that the American commander had made a reasonable response. The fort, meadow, and village lay almost silent in the wintry midday sunlight, save for the distant murmur of conversation and laughter behind the American breastworks and the screech of a hunting hawk that was crossing the bright sky. Then, from the commons beyond the town came faint yells and war whoops, followed by the rattle of gunfire. The buildings of the town blocked the general's view of that plain, and he had no idea what was happening there, but presumed that it might be one of his war parties returning from Kentucky, whooping in triumph and wasting ammunition. If it is, he thought, God help them now.

The messenger had entered the fort. Hamilton quickly looked over Colonel Clark's adamant letter, which was written with such sure, forceful slashes of the pen he thought he could sense its writer's mood.

Captain Helm was brought out of the guardhouse and escorted to General Hamilton's office, where the general sat looking very morose. The wounded had been removed and the general was alone. Helm greeted him with a flashing smile.

"Look at this," Hamilton said, thrusting Clark's letter at him. Helm read it, thrilling with pleasure at its forceful tone. He handed it back, smiling.

"Ol' George ain't changed a bit, I see. Is there sump'n about it you don't get? Surely it's plain enough."

"Obviously a rash and very stupid boy," Hamilton snarled. "Does he think I am without honor?"

"Guess he does."

"I . . . Damn you, Helm! Can't you remember the day of December seventeenth when you stood at the gate right out there, virtually all by yourself in the face of my army, and demanded honorable terms? And did I not grant them to you?"

"Yeah, you did, Guv'n'r," Helm said laconically, "and I 'preciated it. But y' see, th' big difference 'tween you and me is, I ain't never bought th' scalp of a woman or child."

Hamilton's mouth fell open and he went purple with rage. But he trembled and managed once again to contain his impulse to draw his sword and impale Helm. "I'll pretend I didn't hear that piece of insolence. You will please stand by, Mister Helm, while I confer with my officers. Then you will escort me and Major Hay down to the church to meet with this crass boy colonel of yours."

"You mean I'm to be seen in company of Hay and yerself? Bless me, I don't know if George'll ever speak t'me agin!"

CAPTAIN LAMOTHE'S VOLUNTEERS, HAMILTON LEARNED, WERE BEginning to mutter that it was difficult to be obliged to fight against their countrymen and relatives, who they now perceived had joined the Americans. LaMothe's men made up nearly half the garrison, and after such expressions of doubt obviously could not be trusted. There were less than a company of British regulars still unscathed and able-bodied, and apparently no immediate way existed to rally the various parties of Indians in the vicinity. Those red men within the fort had proved of little value as defenders; they were fickle mercenaries and it was not their nature to stand trapped in one place and fight to the death for someone else's honor. He fully expected them to go over the walls at nightfall and vanish.

"In short," he said to his officers now, "it appears that we have nothing much to expect from these rebels but the extremity of their revenge. Therefore I'm determined to go down and procure the most honorable terms I can, or else abide the worst.

"I must add, gentlemen, that if the defense of this fort depended on the spirit and courage of Englishmen only, the rebels would labor in vain. That is all, dear sirs. If you would inform your men of my intentions. And have them stand ready to cover me with musket and cannon in case something should go amiss at the church . . ."

The officers rose, swallowing hard, each harboring his personal sense of disaster.

Alone, heavy with dread, Hamilton sat at his desk and wrote out his proposed terms for surrender:

> *Lieutenant-Governor Hamilton engages to deliver up to Colonel Clark, Fort Sackville as it is at present with all the Stores, ammunition and provision, reserving only thirty-six rounds of powder & ball per man, and as many weeks' provision, as shall be sufficient to subsist those of the garrison who shall go by land or by Water to their destination which is to be agreed on hereafter.*
>
> *The garrison are to deliver themselves up prisoners of War, and to march out with their Arms, accoutrements & Knapsacks . . .*

He asked for guides and horses to give the garrison safe transport to its destination, for three days' time for baking bread and settling accounts with the Vincennes traders, and that prisoners with families should be permitted to swear neutrality and go to their homes, and concluded:

> *. . . Sick and wounded are recommended to the humanity and generosity of Colonel Clark—*

> Sign'd at Fort Sackville *Feby 24th 1779*
>
> *H. HAMILTON*

"So you are Colonel Clark."

"And you're General Hamilton."

They stood two yards apart facing each other, arms folded over their chests, in front of the battered church, each eagerly absorbing impressions of the other. George noted the Englishman's sensuous, somewhat pouty mouth and his drilling, dark gaze. Hamilton looked at the Virginian's imposing stature and his fierce, weathered, but surprisingly aristocratic countenance and felt a surprising kind of satisfaction. At least, he thought, no one can shame me for surrendering to a man like this!

But Hamilton was determined not to be stared down, even by this eagle. He believed that the man who can make the other drop his gaze establishes his own superiority. He had faced down dozens of subordinates, enemies, and Indian chiefs over the years, and not once in the course of his career as a general officer had he been forced to lower his eyes. Bracing himself for it now, he was astonished to see the young man's hard blue eyes suddenly crinkle, sparkle, glance aside at Leonard Helm, and wink. Clark stepped past Hamilton and embraced Helm, guffawing and pounding him on the back.

Hamilton, bewildered, suddenly felt one of his most cherished personal fancies shattered. The American, by dismissing his gaze as unimportant, had prevailed. Hoping no one had really noticed this, Hamilton glanced about to find the American Captain Bowman regarding him amusedly with his own ghostly pale-gray eyes. Then Bowman too stepped past him and joined in greeting Helm. Hamilton was mortified; he felt he had been dismissed as a less important personage than this yokelish Helm. Clenching his jaw, toeing the earth, and waiting for these arrogant louts to conclude their uproarious reunion, he found himself looking at the faces of some of the most piratical human beings he had ever seen; they were drifting close around, snaggle-toothed, evil of eye, lumpish in their rags and rotting buckskins, some barefoot, all unshaven and scrawny as jerky, stinking sourly even at this distance, but every one grinning with a happy mockery. A huge beast of a man stood smirking at him, testing the edge of a big hunting knife with his thumb, then suddenly reached up, snatched off his mangy coonskin cap, bent, and exhibited an ugly scar on the crown of his head, the white of skull-bone showing through. Then the man put his cap back on and winked at Hamilton, wrinkling his porous nose. Suddenly Governor Hamilton had the dispiriting notion that he would be unable to stare down any one of these fetid scoun-

drels; they were looking at him as if he were a swine ready for
the butcher block. Every last one of them felt superior to him!

Hamilton turned smartly away from them. He presented his
page of terms to Colonel Clark. "I trust you will find these reasonable and honorable," he said. He gazed at the Virginian's
hard brown hands and broad chest while the proposal was being
scrutinized.

Then George handed the document off to Captain Bowman
and came a step closer to Hamilton.

"Governor, hear me," he said. "It's as vain of you to try to
bargain with me as it is to think of defending yon fort. My
cannon'll be up in a few hours—though I doubt I need 'em—
and the bank side of your fort is already considerably undermined. You can't escape by water. Furthermore, I know, to a
man, which of your Frenchmen you can count on, and that's a
precious few. If you stand here trying my patience with hag-
gling, I shall have to make an assault. My boys 've begged my
permission to tear your fort down and get at you, and if they do
that, Gov'nor, I doubt that a single soul of you will be spared.
On the other hand, if you'll surrender at discretion and trust to
my generosity, you'll have better treatment than if you stand
here and haggle for terms." He stopped and waited, unblinking.

"Then, Colonel Clark, I'll have to abide the consequence, for
I'll never take so disgraceful a step as long as I have ammunition and provision. My numbers are small, but I can depend
upon my Englishmen."

The Virginian nodded, but replied, "You'll be answerable for
lives lost by your obstinacy. The result of an enraged body of
men like these . . ." he said, sweeping his arm in the direction
of those crowding around, "must be obvious to you."

"Mister Clark, I perceive you're trying to *force* me to a fight
in the last ditch!"

"Well you might suppose!" the American roared suddenly.
"Every fiber in me cries out to let these men avenge their massacred families and friends! If I let you live at all, it's more than
a man of your known barbarity deserves! Aye, it's true, I should
like nothing more than an excuse to put all your Indians and
partisans to death!"

"Colonel, for God's sake, I am not such a monster! Why,
your own captain Helm I am sure would verify that I am a
gentleman . . ."

"Captain Helm is a British prisoner, and thus it's doubtful
whether he can speak with propriety on the subject."

"Then he is from this moment liberated," snapped Hamilton, "and free to speak at his pleasure."

"I don't receive a prisoner's release on such terms. He'll return to the garrison and await his fate. If I get my friend back, I *take* him back!"

Hamilton looked at the obdurate American. "Then nothing will do but fighting?"

"I know of nothing else. Except surrendering, as I've said, at discretion. You're a murderer, you're caught, and you have no right to demand conditions. That's it, Mr. Hamilton!"

"George . . ." Leonard Helm began, stretching out his hand.

"Not now, Len," George said.

"Then, Colonel," said Hamilton, "will you stay your hand until I return to the garrison and consult with my officers?"

"Do that. You're at liberty to pass safely. Good day, Gov'nor."

PACING SOLEMNLY ON THE PARADE GROUND IN THE FORT, GENERAL Hamilton was aroused from a brown study by an awesome murmur coming from the men along the parapet. They seemed to be watching the village and the meadow. Hamilton climbed back up to the parapet, just in time to see a company of the Americans emerge from the village onto the gate road hauling forward six Indians covered with war paint. Each captive was being led by a rope around the neck. They were brought to the place where the street was crossed by the barricade, herded into a circle, and shoved to their knees. Hamilton recognized them; they were part of a war party he had sent to the Ohio weeks before, twenty Indians headed by a bloodthirsty Vincennes youth named St. Croix. Somehow on their return they had fallen into the Americans' hands. Numbers of the frontiersmen were leaving their places behind the barricade to crowd in a wider circle, jeering and howling, around these kneeling warriors, and Hamilton grew cold with the understanding that he was about to witness something most unpleasant.

Two or three Americans or Illinois volunteers now stood around each of the kneeling braves, threatening them with raised tomahawks, swords, and knives. A large group of the Tawaway Indians who had been sheltering in the fort came out onto the parapet to watch this proceeding. And then, from the church, Colonel Clark strode across the meadow toward the place where the captives were.

George moved into the circle where the painted Indians knelt.
"What have we here, Captain Williams?"

The captain's mouth was set in a bitter sneer, his eyes bulging with fury, the whites showing all the way around the irises.
"There was twenty of 'em comin' in with all these—" He
swung up from his side a heavy fistful of scalps, brown hair,
blond hair, white hair, black hair, red hair, each with its circle
of skin encrusted with brownish dried blood. A ferocious muttering swept among the American troops. George felt a shock of
fury; his hands clenched to fists, opened to talons, closed again
to fists, and he stared from one to another of the captives.
"They must of thought we was some of Hamilton's men coming out to greet'em," Williams went on. "They walked right up
t'us a-whoopin' an' hollerin' and a-poundin' 'emselves on th'
chest, jus' as jolly as you please. They didn't realize their mistake till they was right among us, and tried to turn tail an' light
out. We kilt fourteen of 'em an' caught these. Thought th' boys
might like t' have at 'em. What say you, George?"

George looked at the Indians and at the scalps, blood raging
in his veins. He remembered the Puans who had knelt with this
same fatal resignation before him at Cahokia six months ago,
awaiting the fate their warriors' minds accepted as fair, and he
remembered how well his purpose had been served by sparing
them.

Now the scene was similar, and once again he had the god-
like power to grant life or take it away, whichever would serve
him better.

He looked at his men, who were waiting his permission to
strike. He turned, then, to look at the Tawaways up in the fort,
who believed that the great English Father, Hamilton, could always protect them against their enemies. Then he looked at
General Hamilton and Major Hay on the parapet.

George knew that his marksmen had already struck terror into
the garrison, but Hamilton was hesitating and apparently needed
the final sign of his determination.

Looking for a while out of the corner of his eye at the watching Englishmen, his head tilted in an attitude of deliberation, he
then turned back to Captain Williams.

"John," he said in a loud, carrying voice, "let any man here
who has lost a blood relative to the Hair-Buyer's savages put
one of these murderers to the tomahawk."

There! He had said it!

A fierce shout of approval went up. Four of Williams's men

turned and looked around, then stepped back to let someone else take their places in the circle.

A wiry Kentuckian with crooked teeth stood over the chief of the Indian party. His tomahawk trembled in his right hand, its long narrow blade ruddy with rust. The chief straightened his spine, threw back his head, and began singing his weird, quavering death song. The other captives joined in with theirs. The Kentuckian's cap was made of a whole muskrat pelt, the little animal's head projecting out like a bill over the wearer's nose. Its dried up little eyeballs stared blindly at the Indian chief and he looked back at them as he sang.

Then the American said simply to the chief, "Here." And with a quick, whiplike movement of his arm, he swung the weapon at the painted forehead.

Chewk. It punctured the skull and stuck. The song stopped. The Kentuckian let loose of the handle and stood back, panting with excitement. The chief, quaking but still conscious, blood running down between his eyes and off the end of his nose, reached up and pulled the blade out, and handed the weapon back to his executioner. The woodsman took it, quietly muttered, "Sorry," then chopped a second and third time into the chief's skull. The other captives raised their eyes and continued singing their death songs. The chief slowly fell to the side, and two Americans, pulling on the rope around his neck, dragged him across the meadow, past the walls of the fort with its spectators perched aghast along the palisade, and down to the riverbank where they threw him in. The dying chief struggled a moment in the current, then slipped under, leaving a swirl of crimson on the turbid brown water.

Now the Indians on the fort wall all turned their heads toward where General Hamilton stood, glowered at him, began shaking their fists at him and berating him, demanding to know why he was not protecting the red man as he had always promised to do.

In slow succession, four more of the captives were struck down and dragged past the fort to be thrown in the river. The defenders in the fort watched these executions with an awful fascination, wincing, groaning, or inhaling sharply each time a tomahawk fell. Hamilton stood frozen in horror and indignation, his mouth hanging open. Such incredible barbarism! he thought over and over. But the delicious savor of his moral indignation was spoiled, repeatedly, by the whisper of his conscience reminding him that these murders were acts of revenge for his

own deeds. This realization twisted deeper and deeper in his
breast. It was the worst moment he had experienced in his life.
He felt the pillar of personal power crumbling inside him and
trickling away; or, rather, it was as if someone had grasped the
end of his spine and begun pulling it out of him bone by bone,
leaving him no way to stand.

GEORGE STOOD AND WATCHED THE EXECUTIONS, HIS FEELINGS IN AN
indescribable turmoil. Each time the steel split skullbone and
pierced brain, and a death song broke off, his body surged as if
he were driving the blow himself, his blood bubbling with the
powerful, joyous wrath of justice. But at the same instant his
bowels would grip with the shame of a murderer. By the time
the fifth warrior had been struck, George was dizzy with nausea
and seeing everything as if through a curtain of red mist.

One more. The last one of the condemned sang no death
song, but knelt, shaking uncontrollably; his doglike groan had
become louder each time one of his comrades fell. Standing behind this wretch to guard him was the white-whiskered Frenchman, lieutenant of Captain McCarthy's Cahokia volunteers,
named St. Croix. Despite his age, he had proved himself an ad-
mirable and durable campaigner throughout the grueling march
and the attack on the fort. He was an inveterate hater of the
British. Now he stood with his sword point between the shoulder blades of this doomed man as the executioner raised his
tomahawk.

Knowing this was the last moment, the kneeling man raised
his eyes to heaven and wailed, *"Mon Dieu! Au secours!"* And
despite his painted face, all realized at once that he was a *white*
man. The tomahawk hesitated, and at that moment, just as
George experienced a fresh rush of indignation at the thought of
a white scalp-taker, Lieutenant St. Croix yelped and clutched his
breast as if shot. He threw down his sword, jumped, shoved
away the man with the tomahawk, grabbed the kneeling man's
chin in one hand, and stared into his painted face, crying:

"Jacques! *Mon fils!*"

The painted face, its colors streaked by tears and slobber,
worked and grimaced, the eyes darting and uncomprehending
for a moment, then the youth cried: *"Papa! Papa! Aidez-moi!
Aidez-moi, Papa!"*

The old man sagged to his knees and embraced his son. Both
sobbed and blubbered for a moment as the Americans stood fro-

zen in their attitudes, just beginning to understand this appalling coincidence.

George, though astonished, could muster no feeling of mercy for such a monster as a white man who employed himself in taking white people's scalps, and, rather than subject himself to the old man's solicitations for his son's salvation, turned away and walked a few steps off. All his emotional stores were exhausted and he did not think he could endure this. He believed the youth should be executed swiftly for his murders, but he also knew that he could not bear to view the fine old man at the moment of his son's death. George stood, his back to the scene, looking over the horizon, his mouth open, breath quaking, waiting for it to be over. He heard footsteps and a sobbing voice approaching behind him, and the old man dropped to his knees beside him.

"My colonel," the old man begged, grasping George's hand, "I know he deserves to die. It would be just. He is a sinner. A paid murderer. I disown him. But, my colonel, in the name of God, and your great humanity, spare him. Or let *me* take his place! He is young, he is my *son*! Have I been a good soldier for you? Then do this for me!"

George pulled his hand free. But one word echoed in his mind. *Humanity*. He remembered something which, in this orgy of vengeance and victory, he had forgotten: those words he had committed to memory and made his creed, those words from his year-old orders from Patrick Henry: *that Humanity that has hitherly distinguished Americans, and which it is expected you will ever consider as the rule of your conduct and from which you are in no instance to depart . . .*

George stood there, breathing deeply, then he felt the presence of others around him, and turned to see several of his own officers, their faces drawn and beseeching. "George, please," whispered Bowman.

"For the old fellow's sake," said McCarty intensely.

The world composed itself around him: the blue sky, afternoon sun, the raucous cry of a distant crow, the slope of the frozen ground under his feet, the steam of his own breath in the cold air, and suddenly, the staggering weight and pain of his own exhaustion. And then a strange and incongruous image flashed upon his mind: Teresa de Leyba under a silken pavilion in a sunny, summer meadow, sobbing at the death of a rabbit. It was as if Teresa were watching him now. For an instant he saw her oval face, heard the delicate quavering notes of her *guitarra*, felt her bed-warm back on his hand.

"Yes," he said at last. "Yes, then. Let the man live."

THEY CAME BACK TO THE CHURCH IN THE MIDDLE OF THE AFTERnoon. Each looked as adamant to the other as before. But each in his own way had been changed by the spectacle of the executions.

Governor Hamilton spoke first. "Would you be so kind, Mister Clark, as to give me your real reason for refusing to accept my surrender as I offered it?"

"I have no objection to giving you my reasons once again," said George. "It is simply that I know the greatest part of the Indian partisans of Detroit are with you. I want an excuse to put them to death or otherwise treat them as I find proper." His eyes were red-rimmed and ferocious and unblinking as he spoke on, his voice rising, with a forefinger pointed at Hamilton's face:

"The cries of the widows and the fatherless on our frontiers now require their blood from my hands. I look on their commands as next to divine, and I do not choose to disobey them. General, I would rather lose fifty men and my own life than not to empower myself to execute this piece of business. It's that plain, sir, and if you choose to risk the massacre of your garrison for the sake of these few murderers, then that's at your own pleasure. I might perhaps take it into my head to send for some of those widows to see it executed. Can I make it any more clear? I think not."

"You dare call *us* murderers, after this slaughter just past?"

"You be murderers," George said. "I was an executioner."

Major Hay had stood listening to this with a raised eyebrow. "Pray, sir," he said, "who is it you call Indian partisans?"

George stepped quickly toward him, leaned close to him, stared into the small lashless eyes, and replied:

"Sir, I take Major Hay to be one of the principals."

Hay blanched and began to tremble; a sheen of sweat wet his brow and he looked as if he might faint. He clutched at his collar and looked scarcely able to stand. Never had George seen a man so struck with terror as Hay now seemed to be.

Glancing at Hamilton, George saw that the general was sneering and blushing, obviously much ashamed at Hay's cowardice. Looking then to Bowman, he saw Joseph's countenance seeming to alternate between expressions of disdain for Hay and sympathy for Hamilton's embarrassment. Somehow, without another word being spoken, George felt that Hamilton was, for all his arrogance and misdirection, a brave and proud man, that he was being crushed by circumstances out of his control, and that he was simply holding out for a vestige of his honor. *I can't execute more people simply to deny him that scrap,* he thought.

"Governor," he said, "let's return to our respective posts now. I'll reconsider the matter of terms, and let you know the result."

Hamilton turned to him, a flicker of hope in his eyes, a barely perceptible sigh escaping him.

"If I make further proposals, you'll know it by the flag," George said. "If not, be on your guard; our drum will mean we've chosen to storm you. Good day, Mister Hamilton, and please leave Captain Helm with me as a go-between."

Within a half hour, George had modified Hamilton's surrender proposal slightly, and sent Helm into the fort bearing these articles:

1st—Lt. Gov. Hamilton engages to deliver up to Col. Clark Fort Sackville as it is at present with all the stores, ammunition, provisions, &c.

2nd—The Garrison will deliver themselves up Pris^{rs} of War to march out with their arms accoutrements, Knapsacks &c.

3rd—The Garrison to be delivered up tomorrow morning at 10 o'clock.

4th—Three days to be allowed to the Garrison to settle their accounts with the traders of this place and inhabitants.

5th—The officers of the Garrison to be allowed their necessary baggage &c.

Post Vincents 24th Feby 1779

G. R. CLARK

George walked away from his officers and men. He wandered into the vestibule of the church to be alone. He stood inside, his back braced against the wall, head back, eyes closed, feeling the swells of weariness, the greatest weariness he had ever felt, surge down through him from his head to his feet. Pinpoints and clouds of light sparkled and billowed behind his eyelids. Somewhere between dream and thought, he saw a tomahawk split a skull, and a rabbit lying gut-shot, twitching. He heard a scream. *Teresa's voice,* he thought. He opened his eyes and the voice was that of Leonard Helm yelling his name. He

shook his head and went out the church door. Helm had returned with the articles of surrender. Under them on the same
sheet, Hamilton had written:

Agreed to for the following reasons, remoteness from suc-
cours, the state and quantity of Provisions &c the unanimity
of officers and men on its expediency, the Honble terms al-
low^d and lastly the confidence in a generous Enemy.

                              Lt. Gov & Superintend^t
                              H. HAMILTON

Thank God, George thought. Thank God. I don't think I
could've performed another minute!

THE MOON SLID DOWN THE SKY OVER A QUIET FORT AND TOWN. ITS
reflection danced on the moving water of the flooded Wabash,
and men on both sides of the conflict had the leisure to look at
it and think. The Americans and their allies were posted in
strong houses from which they could view the fort; guards were
set, and the rest plummeted off into the first comfortable sleep
they had had in weeks.

Henry Hamilton sat up by the hearth in his quarters most of
the night, sorting papers and preparing the countless details for
the next morning's disagreeable ceremony. He drank a little,
now and then growing so misty-eyed with misery and self-
reproach that he could not see what he was doing. Late at night,
he called in his orderly. "Tell the guard," he said, "not to raise
the colors in the morning, that we might be spared the mortification of hauling them down." The orderly gulped and blinked.

"Aye, sir."

GEORGE ROGERS CLARK AWOKE FROM A HEAVY SLUMBER NEAR
midnight. Moonlight shone in a rectangle on the wall of the
church near the head of his pallet, and when he rose on his elbow he could see the low moon through the transom above the
door. All was still after the eighteen hours of battle, whose af-
tershocks still seemed to pulsate in the back of his head. He
stood up, every muscle and joint aching, and threaded among
the sleeping officers and bodyguards on the floor. He looked
down at the dark shapes of them, heard their low, slow sleep-
breathing, recalled their long fatigue and bravery, and felt swollen with love and admiration for them, with gratitude for their

safety. Only one man under his command had been even slightly wounded, just enough to teach him not to saunter carelessly down a street during a gun battle. And now they were all sleeping, and the thought of their rest gave him the deepest sense of serenity.

He eased the church door open and whispered to the sentries, who nodded at him; then, with the icy air raising gooseflesh under his linen shirt, he strolled out to the place where he had negotiated with Hamilton for the surrender. He stood there for a moment watching the moon set over the river alongside the huge black silhouette of the fort. He could see sentries on the palisades where they had been afraid to show themselves before. Far off somewhere an owl's call repeated itself like the low note of a flute.

He had worried a little about letting the British remain in the fort overnight, but had decided that it would be impossible to guard them otherwise, as the victory was putting into his hands as many prisoners of war as he had men of his own—far too many prisoners to guard in any customary manner, and sure to become a problem.

George walked to a nearby tree, urinated steamily on its roots, then came back toward the door of the church. He looked into the northeastern quadrant of the sky, where the stars were cold and brilliant, and thought of Detroit lying under them, a mere six hundred miles away, that fort now weak and undermanned and its commander here a prisoner. This recapture of Vincennes and the imprisonment of Hamilton should by all rights open the door for the easy conquest of Detroit, he thought. If Congress or Virginia sends me even a mere two hundred men—never mind five hundred—I think I could go and reduce Detroit as quickly as we have this place.

But at least we have for the moment wrested this whole territory out of British hands. And though we'll still have to defend it, it's ours now. The most immediate value of this triumph, he realized, was that Hamilton's great spring offensive against the American frontier was ended before it could begin. Who, he thought, can even estimate the number of lives we've saved by this day's work?

The cold on his skin made him shiver, but it braced him and he felt strong as he had not felt strong since the start of their sufferings in the flooded valleys. It was still difficult to comprehend that this venture, which he had started as a forlorn and desperate hope, had ended in success of this degree. He couldn't yet rejoice because he couldn't yet believe.

He turned then for a last look at the setting moon. It was on the horizon now, its lower edge brushed by the bare tops of trees beyond the swollen Wabash. And the thought came to him then—it was as much a feeling as a thought—that somewhere in a direct line between him and that moon lay St. Louis. Somewhere, two hundred miles in that same straight line, in a spot marked for his eyes now by moonset, lay the village where Teresa would be sleeping. Under this very sky, he thought in wonderment; lighted by this same westering moon. Teresa, he thought. This deed is done. I can return to you soon.

Two tiny replicas of the moon glittered in his dark eyes for a few moments more, then were gone.

AT TEN O'CLOCK IN THE MORNING, COLONEL GEORGE ROGERS CLARK went through the barricade and strode up the road toward the fort. Behind him came the ragged Dickie Lovell, covered with gooseflesh, solemnly rapping t-tlt-t-t-t, t-tlt-t-t-t, t-tlt-t, t-tlt-t, t-tlt-t-t-t. Captain Bowman's company tramped across the meadow and turned off to halt and stand in ranks on one side of the gate road. Captain McCarty's company flanked left and took up its stand on the other side of the road. Then the companies of Captains Williams and Worthington marched up behind Colonel Clark, halted, and stood at parade rest. When the officers' commands trailed off, the drum stopped rattling. A soldier stood behind Colonel Clark with an American flag folded over his right arm and the red-and-green colors of Virginia over his left.

While the Americans stood waiting for gate to open, the inhabitants of Vincennes swarmed up the slope and gathered all around to watch: burghers in faded velvet coats, tradesmen in loose smocks, young women heavy with child, old women in bonnets or soiled wimples, *coureurs de bois* in their fur caps and Indian garb, small children with runny noses leading smaller children with runnier noses.

The ground was frozen hard; the tracked mud of the road had hardened to a yellow, ankle-twisting stucco. The shadows were blue, dusted with frost. The leafless trees were silvery and tan, but gilded with the weak sunlight. The great muddy Wabash, carrying limbs and forest debris and grinding slabs of ice, rushed and burbled beyond the corner of the fort.

Colonel Clark stood tall and straight before the gate of Fort

Sackville, looking up at the bare flagstaff above the fort.
Yellow-edged clouds crawled over and floated eastward.

Soldiers, civilians, and Indians kept stealing looks at the
American commander, at his broad back, his sharp profile, his
monumental stillness as he stood waiting for the gate to open.
Despite the condition of his buckskins, which were so torn,
soiled, and stained that they looked like something lifted from
the forest floor, he appeared grand and clean. He had shaved the
campaign stubble off his jaw, and wore a fresh white shirt and
stock. The brim of his black hat shaded his deep-set eyes. The
drab earthy color of his garb was set off by blue and red quill
designs. The mud-clotted, fringed leather gaiters around his
muscular calves were held up by blue garters fastened with silver knee buckles. His crisp linen, ruddy, clean skin, and the incongruous little silver buckles somehow imparted an edge of
genteel civility to his otherwise savage aspect as he stood there
waiting, and the bystanders were conscious of it even though
they could not have said why.

Drums rattled within the fort now; drill commands came filtering through the palisade; a wooden bolt rumbled and the
great twelve-foot gates groaned open to reveal the ranks of regulars at attention inside on the parade, in scarlet coats and white
breeches, their Brown Bess muskets at shoulder arms.

Now a British drummer began rapping his instrument slowly,
and Governor Hamilton appeared in the gateway, followed by
two other British officers, and marched down the grade toward
Colonel Clark.

Hamilton was resplendent. His coat was scarlet, breeches
white as snow, black knee-boots gleaming with polish. Gold
piping gleamed at his coat cuffs and lapels and his epaulets
were of golden board and braid. He wore a soft red velvet sash
around his waist, and from it depended his sword scabbard. But
Governor Hamilton's crowning glory this morning was a silvery
powdered wig, which glowed in the sunlight and framed his au-
tocratic features like a halo. He held his tricorn at his left thigh,
and strode, squinting against the sun, followed by his drummer
and officers, the few yards down the road to where Clark stood
waiting. The voices of sergeants rang out; the regulars marched
forward just far enough that their file leaders stood at the trodden timber threshold of the gate, then halted and stamped at
attention.

Hamilton stopped a yard in front of Colonel Clark. They saluted. Hamilton looked up at the young giant, then drew his

sword from its scabbard; with a flick of his wrist he tucked the blade under his right arm, so that the hilt projected within reach of the victor.

Colonel Clark, not taking his eyes off Hamilton's, reached for the sword and took it from him.

Hamilton now let his eyes stray to the ragged ranks of American woodsmen who flanked the gate. They stood, leaning on their rifles, clothes so filthy they were of indescribable color, many wearing red bandannas around their necks which furnished the only bright color to their general soiled gray, yellow, brown, and green drabness. Only their neckerchiefs and their predatory eyes were bright. They all had shaved. Many had nicked their chins and cheeks.

General Hamilton mentally summed up the little band, scarcely more than a squad, on his left, the one on his right, and the frazzled, weather-wasted knot of men backing up Clark. Then he swept his eyes over the meadow, and finally said:

"May I ask, Colonel Clark, where is your army?"

"This, sir," replied the Virginian with a sudden, dazzling smile, "is them."

After a minute of silence, Hamilton dropped his head forward, and gave a guarded, barely audible, strangled little whimper.

This man, George thought, waving his flag-bearer and Bowman's and McCarty's companies forward through the front gate, is going to spend the rest of his days making excuses to his Britannic Majesty for this, I expect.

George Rogers Clark turned from General Henry Hamilton, and held the fine English sword aloft. "Boys! Post Vincent . . . *is ours!*"

From their throats burst a deafening chorus of cheers and war whoops and shrill yokel yells; the company in the road broke ranks and stampeded for the gate, snatching Colonel Clark off the ground and bearing him laughing on their shoulders past the astonished redcoats into Fort Sackville.

Hamilton, stunned at first by this indecorous demonstration, watched the Americans disappear through the gate. Then his eyes fell on the morose faces of his regulars, whom he had failed. He turned his face from them and tears ran down his long shapely nose, as much from frustration and envy as from remorse.

Captain Helm was given the honor of raising the American and Virginian flags over Fort Sackville. The British and

LaMothe's French troops were marched out and disarmed, and Helm ran the victorious banners up the pole in the cool sunlight, as the woodsmen gave three cheers and threw their hats in the air.

Captain Bowman's company was then sent through the fort with permission to fire a salute with the cannon. Colonel Clark inspected the fort, looked over its general condition, its stores, its situation, and marveled that Hamilton had yielded such a stronghold. Bejesus, he thought, a company o' Kentuckians would've held this place for a year!

The cannon began discharging their salutes, and suddenly one battery erupted in a crackling roar of confusion. Smoke and orange flame billowed out of the northeast blockhouse, followed by screams and wailings.

George sprinted across the parade and up the ladder to that blockhouse. Sulphurous blue smoke boiled out its embrasures and doors. Inside on the floor lay Bowman and Worthington, and four of their men, writhing and coughing on the floor with their hands over their faces. Through the air in the blockhouse floated paper shreds of cannon cartridges. The men on the floor were blackened and burned, all these valuable people who had survived the campaign without a scratch; smoke rolled off their scorched clothing. George grasped his beloved aide under the arms and dragged him out into the fresh air, calling for help. Worthington and three others staggered out under their own power, and the fourth private was carried out. The skin of Bowman's face and hands was scorched and blistered, and embedded in it were black flecks, knurls, and gouts of hot powder.

Powder burns, George thought bitterly, as the men's wounds were being dressed with bear grease and rags. Always disfiguring, relentlessly painful, and so subject to fatal infection. The worst of accidents to befall these best of men. As well as an investigation of the shambles could determine, it had happened because the British gunners had left dozens of powder cartridges stacked in concealment near the guns, and those had been ignited by the firing of the victory salute.

There's always something to tarnish the perfectest joy, George thought. Always.

Bowman reached up and touched George's sleeve. "Hey, now, don't fret so," he mumbled through his bandages. "It's a small price t' pay for such a victory. We're all alive, ain't we?" He coughed. He had inhaled hot powder smoke. It hurt him to talk.

"Aye, Joseph," George replied. "Very much alive, thank you." He looked up at the colors flapping languidly around the flagstaff above the fort, and at the pale blue sky above, its downy clouds hinting at spring. Bowman held George's wrist, and said:

"Tell me what you're thinkin'."

George laid his hand lightly on Bowman's powder-scorched coat sleeve, searched the sky with tears in his eyes. "As I live, my dear friend, I think I'm just beginning to comprehend what we've done!"

"You happy, man?"

"Never so happy as this day."

"Likewise!"

26

VINCENNES, WABASH VALLEY
February 26, 1779

OVER THE INDIGNANT PROTESTS OF GOVERNOR HAMILTON, George ordered neck chains and fetters made for Major Hay and the other Indian agitators among the prisoners.

"I must remind you, Colonel Clark," Hamilton said, "that these persons are prisoners of war, included in the capitulation that you've so lately set your hand to. By the common courtesy, they ought not to be chained."

"And then I should apprise you in turn, Mister Hamilton, that I'm going to have my hands full keeping my boys from killing them. I can only hope that seeing them helpless in irons will partly assuage those passions."

"But those men were acting under my orders, and my orders were that they should never encourage barbarity among the savages."

George looked at him coldly. "That remark, sir, would be comical, if we could bear to laugh over the scalps of whole families of my people. Now, bother me with any more pleading on behalf of those polecats and I'll have a nice suit of chains tailored for yourself as well."

Hamilton threw back his head and scowled. "Sir, I would gladly wear them, rather than let this go unremarked."

"Then it is remarked. Let me say in candor, Mister Hamilton, that you have certain qualities and I regard you better than I thought to. For your safety's sake, I advise you to be humble and stick close to me until such time as I pack you off to Williamsburg."

LEARNING THAT HAMILTON HAD SENT A PARTY UP THE WABASH TO Post Miami to bring down ten boatloads of stores and provisions for the spring campaign, and that the convoy was expected to arrive at Vincennes at any moment, George on the twenty-seventh sent three armed boats, outfitted with swivel cannon, up to intercept and take it. He put Leonard Helm, with Moses Henry and two French militia officers, in charge of the expedition. "You're the only officer I've got who's had a chance to rest lately," George explained.

"Aye, by God, and spoiling for some action," Helm replied. "And," he said softly, with an exasperated glance at Tobacco's Son, "willing to put our good friend the chief thar int' yer care for a spell. He's been a-stickin' t'me like stink on a skunk ever since I come here, an' much as I like th' feller, I c'd stand to leave 'im dog somebody else's heels. Let 'im be *your* brother f'r a few days now, eh?"

George, with the grave and splendid chief now standing beside him on the parapet, watched Helm's three gunboats row up the swollen Wabash in a gray downpour. "He is my brother," the Piankeshaw said wistfully. "I told General Hamilton that I am a Big Knife. I told General Hamilton that while Helm is prisoner I too am prisoner. And you," he said, turning to meet his eyes with great emotion shaking his voice, "you are my brother. I request to come to your house at the end of the day and speak to you of a matter important to my people."

"I'll be happy to see you then."

The chief arrived that night accompanied by a young squaw, whom he directed to remain in the shadows near the door while he spoke.

Tobacco's Son stood tall and stolid as if in a ceremony, and George stood facing him in the candlelight, a little uneasy.

"It is true what they have said," the chief began. "Clark is the greatest of the Big Knives. The people of other tribes said Ham-

ilton was a god, but Tobacco's Son shut his ears. And now the
Long Knife has come to prove Tobacco's Son right. The Big
Knives are greater than the British, and Clark is the greatest of
the Big Knives." He paused, his eyes searching George's face
with pride and admiration. "The Piankeshaw people," he said,
"desire to have the powerful blood of the Long Knife Colonel
Clark running in the veins of their children." He raised his right
hand and summoned the squaw, who advanced silently into the
candlelight with small, graceful steps, the toes of her moccasins
turned slightly inward at each step. Her eyes were glinting obsidian, her eyelashes straight and long like those of a deer. The
skin over her high cheekbones was smooth, russet, and, under
the square, strong line of her jaw, her neck was tawny and
gleamed with unguent. She looked directly at George's face,
neither smiling nor not smiling, her eyelids half shut. Tobacco's
Son stepped behind her, put his hands on her shoulders and
pulled away the blanket.

The drunken laughter of the celebrating victors in nearby barracks came faintly into the hushed room. Rain rushed on the
roof.

The sudden sight of the maiden's nakedness had nearly made
George fall backward. Now he stood, speechless for the moment, trying to sort out the storm of thoughts and emotions that
rampaged through him. He was astonished by the instantaneous
flood of desire that rose up in him, galvanizing every animal
part of him, blood and humors; but that part of his soul which
was still Episcopal Virginian gentry was for the moment outraged by the chief's presumption. Yet there was, too, a powerful
satisfying notion that he was indeed a victor, a man of superior
blood, and that such a reward should be his.

But through the confusion of urges and instincts there came,
like a faint, haunting handful of delicate plucked chords, the
thought of Teresa. It cleared his head.

"Cover her," he told the chief, turning toward the hearth to
shut out the tormenting beauty of her nudity. Now for his sake,
George thought, I have to say the right thing. He is the best sort
of ally and must not be offended.

"My friend," he said, placing a hand on the chief's shoulder.
"The Piankeshaw are a great people and I am flattered that they
want my blood in their veins. The woman is of great beauty and
any man would want to lie with her. But I tell you this—and the
woman will understand it well—that I have pledged my troth
already to another woman, also of great beauty . . ." he thrilled

as he said these words that he had kept to himself for so long, "and among my people, the pledge of a man to a woman is as sacred as the pledge of one chief to another."

The chief's face, which had begun to look stricken with disappointment, softened, then broke into a smile. "Ah! This I did not know, that the Long Knife already has his woman." He turned to the squaw, now wrapped in her blanket and looking much cast down, and spoke to her briefly in their tongue. And suddenly a smile of happy comprehension broke through on her comely face, and she looked at George now with an expression compounded of admiration and girlish delight, and she stood there as if impatient to be dismissed. I suspect, he thought, that she's dying to tell this tale. He smiled back at her. What a stroke of luck, he thought. Now I'll doubtless be as much favored among the squaws as the warriors, which can do our cause no harm.

As Tobacco's Son was dismissing the young woman, another good idea emerged in George's mind.

"Wait," he said, after considering it for just a moment. "The Piankeshaw are said to be great healers."

"They are that," said Tobacco's Son.

"You know that the greatest of my chieftains," said George, "I mean Captain Bowman, was burned by fire from the British cannon powder. Being a Big Knife, he does not complain, but I know he suffers. This princess you've brought to me might nurse him and give him great comfort. Bowman," he added, "is one of a family of great chiefs among the Big Knives. There is no stronger blood than that in his veins."

Tobacco's Son spoke again to the woman, and she left.

Joseph, my lad, George thought, I only wish I could give you more.

IN MIDMORNING OF THE NEXT DAY, GEORGE WAS BROUGHT FROM his quarters by a sudden uproar of gunshots and cheerful yelling from the river side of the fort, and mounted the wall to see on the broad yellow-brown flood below the oaken prow of the long-lost *Willing*, making her tedious headway against the current, all oars lifting and falling. So laborious was her progress, foot by foot, that he at once understood why she had arrived these three or four days late. Taking the sentry's spyglass, George rested it on the top of a palisade and trained on the vessel. There in the prow stood his cousin, Lieutenant John Rogers, in turn scrutinizing the fort with his own telescope. He's seen our colors over the fort by now, George thought.

"Too late for the fight, m'lad, but by Heaven am I glad to see you all the same!" George greeted him as the vessel was moored at the landing below the palisade. The troops aboard the vessel were mortified that they had arrived too late to contribute to the victory, but quickly turned to rejoicing when they learned that not one of their comrades had fallen in the battle. "We need people," George said. "We've got almost as many prisoners as troops. I've decided there's nothing for it but to release the French Canadian militia on probation and let them go back to Detroit. From the change I've observed in their temper these last two days, I believe they'll actually do us more good there than harm. In truth, I've never seen so smug and merry a passel of captives. As for Hamilton and his partisans, I see no other way to get them back to Williamsburg but to take them in the *Willing* as far as the Falls, then march 'em the last eight hundred miles. But b'gad, cousin, d'you know these lads o' mine are all but screaming for a chance to go on to Detroit? What?"

Lieutenant Rogers had turned back to the galley. "Mister Myers!" he called, with a wave of his arm. George looked, and saw his old courier swinging off the gunwale onto the dock, a bag slung over his shoulder and his long Deckard rifle at his side.

"Bill Myers!" George yelled as the smiling, rangy runner approached.

"We picked 'im up off the riverbank," Rogers said. "He's got a packet for you from Patrick Henry. Thought you might be pleased t'see him."

The letters from Governor Henry seemed to have come from another world, and another age as well. They had been written in December, not long after the governor had learned the outcome of the summer 1778 campaign and the capture of Kaskaskia and the Illinois country. To remember that time, George had to make his mind span the more recent winter march, whose hardships loomed so enormous in recent memory that the summer campaign was like a dim and balmy dream.

W^{ms}burgh Decr 15, 1778

Sir:

Myers your Express has been kept here a long Time. I laid your Letters before the Assembly who are well pleased with your conduct & have thanked you. The Messenger waited for the passing the Act I send herewith.

I thank you also for your Services to the Commonwealth & hope you'll still have Success. Mr Todd is appointed to the County Lieutenancy. A Commandant as described in the Act is a civil Officer, & considering he is to hold his office during pleasure, it has been judged incompatible with any military office. You would have had it, had there been found any propriety in annexing it to military Command. Mr. Todd being a man of Merit, I have no Doubt he will be acceptable to you & all your Corps. Let me hear from you as often as possible.

I beg you will present my Compliments to Y^r Mr Gibault and Dr. Laffont & thank them for me for their good Services to the State.

I send you a Copy of the French Alliance & some other papers, by seeing which the people will be pleased, & attached to our Cause.

I refer you to the Instructions I send herewith, & wishing you Safety & Success am

Sir y^r mo. hbl Servant
P. HENRY

With the numerous letters in the packet were one from Governor Henry to Don Fernando de Leyba, whose seal George broke before noticing it was not addressed to himself; he put it aside. There was also, addressed to George, a letter from Benjamin Harrison, speaker of the Virginia House of Delegates:

W^msburgh Novr 24, 1778

Sir:

I have it on command from the House of Delegates to forward to you the enclosed Resolutions. I do assure you Sir it gives me the highest satisfaction to be the instrument of conveying this public testimony of the just sense your Country entertains of the very important Services you have render'd it.

You'll please take the proper method of communicating

the Resolutions to the intrepid officers and soldiers who have so nobly assisted you in the glorious enterprise.

I have the Honor to be your most obedient and very Humble Servant

BENJⁿ HARRISON
Speaker H. D.

George assembled his troops in the parade ground that evening at muster and read to them, in the last gray light of winter evening, the resolution which referred to last summer's successes and yet had by chance come so timely on the heels of this their most hazardous victory:

Whereas authentic information has been received that Lieutenant Colonel George Rogers Clark, with a body of Virginia Militia, has reduced the British posts in the western part of this Commonwealth on the River Mississippi, and its branches, whereby great advantage may accrue to the common cause of America, as well as to this Commonwealth in particular:
Resolved that the thanks of the House are justly due to the said Colonel Clark and the brave officers and men under his command, for their extraordinary resolution and perseverance, in so hazardous an enterprise and for the important services thereby rendered their country.

The troops sent up a hearty cheer for themselves, for each other, and for their colonel. It seemed to awe them somewhat that they were receiving recognition from the high and mighty in Williamsburg, a place some of them had only heard of and could not quite imagine, and it seemed to them that although this recognition was due them for their strenuous efforts, they had their young commandant to thank for it more than themselves.

"Boys," he said, after the cheering had died down, "what they say in this resolution, I myself say with a thousand times more feeling. I reckon you know my affections well enough. I'll ask you to recollect something. Remember that night in June last year on Corn Island, there by the bonfire, when I told you what our mission was to be?"

He watched the expressions in their faces as they turned their thoughts back to that other and lesser existence. He had re-

minded them, and now they looked back, and most of them realized that they were changed men, that they had indeed proved
themselves superior men. As if reading their thoughts, he said
now:

"You may know that General Hamilton had a plan to set out
from this place in the spring, retake the Illinois, and then destroy every American post this side of the mountains. Now,
boys, Mister Hamilton will indeed go east through our settlements this spring; but thanks to all of you, he goes there in
chains, not at the head of an army!" He let that sink in. The
men were quiet, but they were thoughtful, and were beginning
to understand what, in the larger picture, they had achieved in
the course of seeking their individual vengeance.

"Maybe you understand, now," he continued. "There's not an
army in the East, of any size, that's had a success as will compare with what four or five score Americans have done here in
this last month. Think o' that tonight before you go to sleep,
boys, and thank God we had the opportunity to serve so well."

They were already thinking of it. They stood on the parade
ground, gaunt, ragged, most still not half recovered from the
rigors of the march, but in their faces glowed a rare, calm, sure
light. Here, George thought, having to strangle back a huge up-
welling of emotion, here is a brotherhood that kings and priests
would envy.

But there was more news for them. Governor Henry had
promised five companies of reinforcements, which Captain John
Montgomery was to raise and lead to Kaskaskia. Montgomery
was also to bring ten thousand pounds in currency for the pay
of the troops. Both of these announcements were cheered
roundly. Myers also had picked up the news that Daniel Boone
had escaped from his Shawnee captors, fleeing one hundred
sixty miles in four days, and was back safe in Boonesboro. That
was a heartening report on one of their favorites.

George then added that he himself had been promoted to full
colonel by the governor's dispatches, which brought three
cheers, and announced that blank commissions had been sent,
which permitted him at his discretion to promote several of the
officers. "My first action on these," he said, "is the promotion
of our stalwart Captain Joseph Bowman to major's rank. I
gather you support me in that?" The three cheers were deafening, and were accompanied by the flight of half a hundred hats
into the air above the parade.

"And now, gents," he continued after the hubbub, "your officers and myself will go into a session right away to discuss the fate of Detroit, and you'll soon know about that. As for now, do as I said: think about what you've done, and be proud. As for me, I know as well as anybody that you're a company of heroes, to a man, and I salute you!"

ON MARCH FIFTH, LEONARD HELM RETURNED FROM HIS FORAY UP the Wabash, having surrounded the convoy party of forty British soldiers and partisans and taken them by complete surprise, without firing a shot; their booty included seven boats and forty thousand pounds' worth of stores, provisions, and Indian goods, as well as the person of Philip DeJean, Grand Judge of Detroit, who had in his possession a packet of letters from Detroit to Hamilton, revealing the present weakness and disrepair of Fort Detroit. The British loot was divided among Colonel Clark's soldiers, who had not been permitted to take a bit of plunder from the French of Kaskaskia, and now every soldier was, by his customary standards, almost rich.

Two days later one of the large captured riverboats was loaded with General Hamilton and his officers, Judge DeJean, LaMothe and Maisonville, and eighteen of the British soldiers, all under the guard of the newly promoted Captains Rogers and Williams, with twenty-five Americans, and the vessel was prepared for departure under raw, rainy skies. The Wabash was still high and swift. Provisions of pork and flour, and fourteen gallons of spirits, were loaded aboard for the trip to the Falls of the Ohio, and George and Captain Helm went down to see them off. Hamilton stood straight and dignified even in his leg irons, his red coat a bright contrast to the weathered oak of the boat, the soiled deerskins of his captors, and the gray and brown of the flooded, wintry countryside. Helm extended his hand. "Wal, Gov'nor, thankee for your hospitality. I have t' say, you're a gentleman for all your wrongheadedness, and I'm glad I met you. Now't you've et some humble pie and never can buy another scalp, I've hopes for your deliverance."

"And you, Mister Helm. I shan't forget you. Nor your splendid toddies, nor your gadfly wit. Mister Clark, what can I say to you? You've brought the world down around my head, and I could despise you. I can only wish you'd grown up a loyalist instead of a rebel. I have to pray for your failures, of course. But as I told myself when I first laid eyes on you, there's no shame in losing to a man like you."

"You lost to a few good men on a right cause, Mister Hamilton. Let me warn you now that the thousand miles ahead may be the most hazardous of your life, the settlers' sentiments being what they are. I've ordered your guard to care for you as best they can. I'd suggest you stay humble and be brave. Godspeed, Governor. I hope you'll think seriously on the meaning of all this. Shove off, cousin!" he bawled suddenly to Captain Rogers. "And God be with you!"

THE MESSENGER GAVE HIS MUD-SPATTERED HORSE TO THE GROOM, took off his muskrat cap and cloak, and was led to the pantry of the governor's mansion for refreshment and to await a reply or interview.

"Teresa," de Leyba called up the stairs. She was already on the landing, coming down. "Letters here from your sweetheart! One for you, one for me!" So! Then he is all right, she thought. Thank God! She smiled and took the sealed paper, her heart tripping. It would be hard to say who became more excited by word from the Virginian, she or her brother. Fernando had become very alarmed since February because Indian war parties, emboldened by the absence of the Americans, had made incursions onto the Spanish side of the river, killing a few innocent travelers and some slaves on work parties. De Leyba had only sixteen regular Spanish soldiers under his command, including a drummer, and knew that de Cartabona could raise scarcely forty militiamen in a crisis, as most able-bodied men were at large in the countryside trading and hunting, or boating goods down to New Orleans.

Now they opened their letters, too eager even to retire to their rooms.

Post St. Vincents, March 1, '79

Don Fernando de Leyba Esq.
Lieu't Governor, St. Louis
Per Mr. Murry

D[r] Sir:
  After a Fatiguing Journy of Nineteen days under going Every Difficulty that Could possibly have happened by High Waters and the want of Provisions, I arrived at this Town on the 23rd of Feb[y] at 7 o clock in the Evening and Attack the fort Amediately
  I never saw a Much pritier fire than Keep up on Both

Sides for Eighteen Hours. Governor Hamilton being ordered to Surrender he thought proper to Comply. I was Much Surprised after seeing his Men Stores Strength of Fort etc that he should think of Surrendering to a body of Men not Double his number. As I hope Shortly to have the pleasure of Giving you a Verbal Account of the Whole I shall Omit it in my Let'r.

Many Little Circumstances would divert you. the Express that I expected has arrived at this place all well   A Circumstance hapned that gave me Great uneasiness which was this in a packet of letters from the Governor General Henry there was one Directed to you among Many others of Mine and in breaking them Open one after another I unfortunately broke yours before I Knew whose it was and Read but two words before I discovered my Mistake

I hope Sir that you will pardon me for the Neglect as you may Rest assured that I will not Read it. I would Send it to you but I have orders to Deliver it with my own hands and at the same time I shall Acquaint you of Every piece of Inteligence   there is a Regiment of Troops now on their March to Illinois. I have ordered Mr. Murry to give you a Detail of Our expedition and attack on the Fort I hope it will meet with your aprobation.

I am Sir with the Greatest Respect your

G. R. CLARK

P. S. My Compliments to Madame Leyba and the young Ladies

"Ha, *ha!*" de Leyba whooped, throwing off any vestiges of his Spanish reserve. "The fellow is *invincible!* Marvelous! Ha, ha, *ha!* No more worry for us about the depravities of that Hamilton! Can you imagine that?" Without moving his feet he gave an impression of skipping all about the vestibule. He simmered down soon, and asked, "What does he say to you, little sister?"

"Fernando! Why, this is not a *public* letter!" She clutched it to her bosom.

"Oh, of course! Of course!" De Leyba turned to and fro in happy confusion for a moment. "Ah! Ah, yes, now where did that Murry go? Yes, the pantry. I must hear more about this wonderful expedition!" And he hurried deeper into the house, his excited voice echoing. Teresa seated herself slowly on a dark oak waiting bench, reading the letter again.

Teresa, my One love:

As I expect to be with you by April, I make this let'r brief, only to say that with the help of heav'nly Providence, the most strongheart'd of Friends, and the sustain'g thought of Returning to You I have succeeded in this Adventure beyond my fondest expectations. There are many things I must say to You that I can say to no one oth'r, as all Men hereabout are dependt on my Words and Action   I have played God by dealing the Choice of Life and Death, and thus am Isolated

Unbearably alone Save for You

The night of our Vict^{ry} I stood in moonlight and thought long on it that it Shone as well on You my Dear   Awaiting April I am ^{yr} devoted

GEORGE

This was the hardest decision George had ever had to make. His men, still strung taut as bowstrings with their desire to push on to Detroit, were ready to set out at once, disregarding their exhaustion. His officers were equally enthusiastic, as were the French volunteers, who promised to go along and assured him that their compatriots around Detroit would welcome him. George knew that Detroit was now at its weakest, and that the Indians were stunned and confused by Hamilton's surrender. All these circumstances told him to set out at once with his small force, despite the severity of the winter weather, and strike while the iron was hot.

On the other hand, reason told him he should wait for Captain Montgomery to come with the promised reinforcements. By June they should arrive, he thought, and then the travel will be less rigorous. My men, he reminded himself, are far more spent than they imagine themselves to be, and surely few of them could really effect another winter march. Besides, at least a half of them are needed here to guard all these prisoners.

But what if we never get all the reinforcements Montgomery is pledged to raise? he thought. What if we let pass this opportunity, in simple anticipation of more troops, and they never come? And in the meantime Detroit would be repaired and re-

inforced? I had to forsake that goal once before for simple want
of men; can I stand to do so again?

He and his officers counciled on it loud and long and, finally,
discretion prevailed. They decided to do what any ordinary military officer would have been expected to do: Wait for reinforcements, wait for spring.

Even as he uttered the announcement to the troops on the
parade, he felt a dreadful conviction that it had been the *wrong*
decision. It seemed that something went out of the troops, some
rigidity; and the fervor that had kept them up during and since
the long march was kicked out from under them like crutches
by the news of this delay, this loss of momentum. In the remaining two weeks before the army's return to Kaskaskia, many
of the men began to fall sick, and to be almost incapacitated by
the pains, the internal complaints, the chilblains resulting from
the severe exhaustion and exposure of the recent march. A solid
week of cold rain increased their miseries.

COL¹ HARRISON Speaker of the House D.
Williamsburg
Per Wᵐ Myers

Sᵗ VINCENT March 10, 1779

Dʳ Sir:

I receiv'd your letter with the thanks of the House inclosed. I must confess Sir that I think my country has done
me more honor than I merited but rest assured that my study
shall be to deserve that Honor that they have already con-
ferr'd on me.

By my public letters you will be fully acquainted with my
late successful expedition against Lᵗ Govʳ Hamilton who has
fallen into my hands with all the principal Partisans of Detroit. This stroke will nearly put an end to the Indian War,
had I but men enough to take the advantage of yᵉ confusion
of the Indian Nations. I could silence the whole in two
months. I learn that five hundred men is ordered out to reinforce me. If they arrive, with what I have in the country, I
am in hopes will enable me to do something Clever.

I am with respect Sir Yʳ very humble Servant

G. R. CLARK

A Warrant
To Wm MYERS

S^r as the letters you have at present contain matters of
great consequence and require a quick passage to
Williamsburg, This is to impower you to press for the service any thing you may stand in need of. If you cannot get
it by fair means, you are to use force of Arms. I request
of you to lose no time as you prize the interest of your
Country.

   I wish you success &c

                                        G. R. CLARK
                                      March 13, 1779

On the fourteenth of March, the courier Bill Myers set out by
land for a return trip to Williamsburg, bearing a packet of letters
and reports from Colonel Clark to Patrick Henry, among them
a day-by-day account of the battle of Vincennes.

The following day, parties of Miami and Peoria Indians came
to Vincennes to assure the Long Knife of their fidelity.

That evening, Tobacco's Son again sought audience with
George, this time bearing as his offering the deed to a huge
tract of land amounting to some one hundred fifty thousand
acres on the north side of the Ohio River, near the Great
Falls. "I wish that the Long Knife should build a great wig-
wam on that land and make it his home," said the
Piankeshaw. "The land shall hereafter and ever be the sole
property of our great father with all things thereto belonging,
either above or below the earth, shall be and is his, except a
road through this land to his door, which shall remain ours,
and for us to walk on and speak to our father. All nations
from the rising to the setting sun who are not in alliance with
us, are hereby warned to esteem the said gift and not to make
that land taste of blood, that all people either at peace or war
may repair in safety to get counsel of our father. Whoever
first darkens that land shall no longer have a name."

"I accept this generous gift of a great estate from my brother,
Tobacco's Son," George said. "I accept it in trust for Virginia,
which I serve. And the road will always be open for the red
man who wishes to come and talk to me." For a moment, his
mind slipped away to a familiar vision: the great house overlooking the peaceful valley where white-stone buildings grew;

the woman, now Teresa, sitting by his side in a chair on the porch. This, he thought, is still another of my dreams coming true.

But I won't have it, any of it, I'm afraid, until Detroit is mine and the war is over.

ON THE FIFTEENTH, WILLIAM MYERS RETURNED TO VINCENNES, having been unable to go by land to the Falls because the whole country seemed to be flooded. He stayed only long enough to trade his horse for a canoe and, with three other men, set off down the Wabash to take the water route to the falls. Within minutes the frail little vessel had ridden the seething rivercourse southward out of sight among the inundated woodlands.

The following day most of the French-Canadian prisoners took the oath of neutrality and set off on their return to Detroit, carrying with them a copy of the French-American alliance and a great deal of excitement for the new American cause.

It rained and snowed for the better part of the next two days as the *Willing* and five smaller armed boats were caulked and loaded for the return to Kaskaskia. On the night of the nineteenth, an entertainment marked by excesses of joy and melancholy was held in the fort, during which Tobacco's Son drank a great deal of Leonard Helm's toddy, and the more inebriated he became, the more dignified. He finally became so dignified that some of the revelers speculated that he had died and left his body leaning against the wall.

And the next day, after command assignments had been completed, George and Bowman stepped aboard the *Willing*, which was jammed to the gunwales with seventy soldiers. Reaching over the side to grasp the hands of Captain Helm and Lieutenant Brashear on the landing, George looked at their teary eyes.

"So we'll rally here in June, lads, to go for Detroit," he promised.

"Aye," said Helm, then he paused, interrupted by Bowman's sudden violent, phlegmatic cough. Bowman spat into the river and wiped his mouth on his coat sleeve. Helm looked at him, trying to hide the fear in his eyes.

"My regards," he said, leaning confidentially close to George, "to yer sweetheart and her brother." Then he stepped back and saluted; the lines were cast off, and the stout vessel, pressed by the current, swung ponderously away from the landing with

Davey Pagan standing proudly at the rudder post, trying to wink conspiratorially, with his one eye, at his commandant.

Bowman, shuddering under a tarpaulin, wrote in the papers of his journal.

March 20th—The Boats ready and loaded Capt. McCarty takes Charge with the Willing—Capt. Keller, Capt. Worthington, Ensigns Montgomery & Lawoin each of them to take charge one boat a Serg^t and Six Men to take charge of the Small Boat called the Running Fly—About 4 o clock the whole embarked leaving Lieut. Brashier, command^t of the fort with Lieut. Bayly Lt Chaplin 40 Men Serg^t & Corp. Includ'd to take care of the Garrison till reliev'd from Kaskaskias. Capt. Helm command of the Town in all Civil Matters and superintend^t of Indian affairs Mr Moses Henry Indian Agent Mr Patrick Kennedy Quarter Mast^r &c. The Boats after much rejoicing are now out of sight—God send us a good and safe passage.

Then he lay back and shut his smarting eyes and enfolded himself in memories of the bare, brown warm flesh and the tender ministrations of Mai-hah, his Piankeshaw princess, whom he was going to miss sorely.

When the fort had dropped out of sight astern, the rambunctious troops in the two boats grew quiet, and fell to gazing at the flooded landscape, each man turned inward upon his own private thoughts. At length, a woodsman sitting near the port side, his arm on the gunwale and his chin resting on his knuckles, swung his hand out and pointed at a low gray rise of land. "Yonder," he said quietly, "ain't that th' sugar camp, sir?"

"Right you are," George said, and several of the men, who had apparently been studying the route of their painful trek a month earlier, nodded in agreement.

"I can still feel where I woke up with m' arm froze to th' ground," somebody said.

George shuddered, remembering it. Wet snow sifted down, the little white flakes vanishing as they fell upon the brown water; the oars groaned in the rowlocks; the flood swashed and purled.

"Now," said somebody else, "I see down thar th' Bubbie."

"Bejeezus!" exclaimed another softly. "Hit's a looong hike. I can't quite believe it's true we done it."

"I can," said the first man, "I can feel in my bones that we done it."

Several laughed, understanding the jest well because they felt it too.

"Ay-*men*," George said. Then he lowered his head so that his hat brim hid his eyes.

And he tried to think of Teresa, to keep himself warm.

27

KASKASKIA, ILLINOIS COUNTRY
April 1779

THE WEATHER WAS MELLOWING FAST. A LIGHT GREEN PASTEL sheen of buds was beginning to lighten the gray woods when George Rogers Clark and his small convoy of returning victors reached Kaskaskia early in April, and were welcomed with shouting, dancing, gunfire, and parades by the exuberant citizens. The French Kaskaskian volunteers who had gone with him against Vincennes found themselves particularly lionized, even those who had been aboard the *Willing* and arrived too late to engage in the battle. George encouraged the attitude, feeling that it further solidified the new bond between America and the Illinois French. He wrote a proclamation giving great credit even to the French militia who had remained behind and guarded Kaskaskia.

Also on hand at Kaskaskia was the *Rattletrap*, the gunboat in which Captain James Willing had been terrorizing the British posts on the Mississippi since 1778. Willing had taken the sea route back to report to Congress on conditions in Louisiana, leaving the *Rattletrap* and her forty raiders in command of Captain Robert George, one of his subalterns and a distant relative of Colonel Clark's. Captain George had run the gamut of British Mississippi posts to get to Kaskaskia, and now placed himself and his vessel in Colonel Clark's service.

These circumstances, pleasant though they were, meant that

George had to pause several extra days at Kaskaskia even while he was champing at the bit to go on to Cahokia and St. Louis, to carry Governor Henry's letter to Fernando de Leyba and, above all, to return to Teresa.

She, her beauty, her gentleness, her vulnerability, had become his Siren, drawing him with a magnetic pull from his responsibilities, and like a *succubus* awakening him from night to night. Passionate French ladies of Kaskaskia danced him to exhaustion almost every evening as if determined, like the Piankeshaws of Tobacco's Son, to infuse his heroic blood into theirs.

No, by Heaven, he thought one April night as an auburn-haired lady of Kaskaskia (he was sure he had danced with her on some night long past) lay back against his arm and invited him with her eyes. No! You, no more than that naked squaw, cannot hope to divert me from my lady.

From Kaskaskia then he rode out with the returning Cahokia volunteers for their triumphal return to their town. It was a beautiful journey of sunny days and mild nights, the rich soil of the countryside bringing up brilliant green young grass, wildflowers in profusion, the stark silver-gray of the forests now softened by a lace-work of redbud and dogwood blossoms. The calls of cardinals and thrushes drifted through the young foliage like flakes of hope; the gentle spring sunlight warmed the riders' backs; gear jingled and leather groaned. Banners and guidons fluttered in the sun-charged motes of road dust. The Frenchmen, inspirited by pride, springtime, and their thoughts of home, broke into song every few minutes, and it was a happy trip indeed.

"I reckon you'll want to cross right away to St. Louis to see your sweetheart," Bowman said, riding close beside George.

"Aye. And to deliver Governor Henry's letter. You'll be crossing over with me, of course. They'll all want to see you."

"If it's all the same to you, George, I'd sooner stay in Cahokia. There'll be a lot for me t'do there . . ."

George didn't press him. He knew that Joseph simply did not want the ladies at St. Louis to see him in his wretched condition, with his face covered by this flaking pink and yellow burn scar and the freckles of embedded black powder, the constant draining of mucus from his nose, the sudden bursts of coughing. Mai-hah's nursing had been very good for Joseph's soul but had done little to heal his wounds. George had hoped that the arrival of warm weather would cure that awful coughing, but it seemed instead to grow worse, each day. George had begun to feel an awful sense of doom about Major Bowman; his lungs apparently had been burned and might not heal. Yet Bowman continued to conduct his duties with undiminished energy and obviously would not consider retiring for a convalescent leave while a Detroit campaign was but two months away.

I couldn't spare him anyway, George thought. Of all the great men I have, he's by far the best.

FERNANDO DE LEYBA GAZED OUT THE WINDOW OF HIS OFFICE, across the wide lawn, at the arbor where George and Teresa sat close together, both of her hands in both of his.

De Leyba sighed from the rich confusion of his feelings. It had been a glorious reunion for them all. George appeared to have aged ten years in the few months since they had seen him, growing leaner, harder, and more weatherbeaten, the fine squint lines beside his eyes more pronounced, the handsome dimples in his cheeks now deep lines that creased his face from cheekbone to jaw; the fine, fierce eyes now more sunken, and somehow more melancholy. The Virginia looked more like a man of forty now than a man of twenty-six. Yet he bore himself with even more authority than before, as well he might, and looked his part as a legend without playing it. De Leyba was thrilled and pleased at his presence, and felt as much his brother as if George had already married into the family.

On the other hand, there was this dreadful matter of the credit. De Leyba had continued throughout the winter to underwrite the bills drawn for the needs of the American posts at Kaskaskia and Cahokia, and lately these bills, even with his name, were beginning to be resisted by the Spanish traders. The state of Virginia would have to give George some major financial backing soon, or de Leyba might find himself on the verge of ruin. George had told him that ten thousand pounds was being brought by the coming reinforcements, but that would barely cover the back pay of the American troops and could not help at all in this financial plight.

Well, Virginia and the American Congress will not let us down, de Leyba thought. It's a matter of time. He turned back to his desk and, for reassurance, read the letter George had brought him from Governor Henry.

The Honorable
Spanish Commandant near the Illinois
Favored by Col. Clark

Williamsburg in Virginia
December 12, 1778

Sir:

Colonel Clark who commands the Forces of this Commonwealth at the Illinois will have the Honor to deliver this letter to you and at the same time to bear my high Regards to you. I beg leave to recommend that Gentleman to your friendly Notice and Regards which I also have to request towards all the Subjects of this State. At the same time, I tend to you sir and to all the Subjects of his Catholic Majesty, every Assistance, and friendly Interchange of good offices, which the mutual Happiness and prosperity of both People shall make necessary.

I shall be happy to embrace every opportunity of shewing my high regards to his Catholic Majesty's Interests, and that I am with great Truth Sir

Your most obedient Servant

P. HENRY

I trust you, your Excellency Señor Henry, de Leyba thought, as my governor Galvez and your Colonel Clark recommend you so. But pray attend to the needs of your commandant out here. He is having to conduct a very ambitious war from a very impoverished position. Indeed the only real currency he has to spend is his great soul.

De Leyba looked out the window again at the two lovers, who were talking and laughing as if there were no cares at all. Then he poured a small glass of Madeira, sat down at his desk, and began a reply to Governor Henry:

To his Excellency, Señor Don Patrick Henry

San Luis de Ylinueses, April 23, 1779

Your Excellency:

Colonel Jorge Clark has delivered to me your Excellen-

cy's esteem'd letter of the 12th of December just past. Its
contents gave me the greatest pleasure; first, because it is
very much in accord with the instructions which I have from
my General; and second, because your Excellency has
deigned to honor me with your letter.

From the time that my friend Colonel Clark arrived in
this place, fraternal harmony has reigned between the people
from the United States and the vassals of his Catholic Majesty.

The said Colonel Clark's wisdom and affability have
made him generally loved by all who know him, and I give
your Excellency a thousand thanks for having given me a
neighbor who by his friendly manners has made me his
debtor for the greatest courtesies, your Excellency's esteemed recommendation being under the circumstances not
the one of least consideration. I beg that your Excellency
will not regard me as negligent, if there is anything in which
I can be of service, since I offer your Excellency my most
sincere regards, and pray that God may keep you many
years.

He stopped writing and looked back over the letter. It seemed
terribly obsequious to him, but he had wanted to make the most
agreeable impression before bringing up the matter of Colonel
Clark's debts. It was going to be so difficult to write of that
business without seeming to complain about Virginia; it might
even seem that he had complaints against Don Jorge, an impression he did not want to give under any circumstances. He
drained off another glass of wine while musing upon this word-
ing. But now the wine was making his thoughts more fuzzy.

And what if a letter lamenting such private matters should
fall into the wrong hands, he thought. If the express should be
caught by a British party, revealing to them that I have committed myself that far to the rebel Americans, it could only embarrass Governor Galvez the more.

And what, he thought, if my dear friend Jorge should by
some chance read it and feel that I am expressing strain between him and myself? Not that he would open it . . . He is totally honorable, I know . . .

Yet, much as he hated to think of it, there was the matter of
that broken seal on Patrick Henry's letter.

I'm sure that was an accident, as he explained, de Leyba
thought.

Nonetheless, he decided to say nothing, in this initial letter to Governor Henry, anyway, about the finances. Surely Jorge's own correspondence to Governor Henry would convey well enough the desperate problems of the currency.

And so he simply concluded the letter:

Your Excellency's most obedient servant,

FERN^{DO} DE LEYBA

Teresa held her shawl tight; the day was cool though sunny. The color was high in her cheeks and she was looking directly into his face as she talked. "All my life I am told, it is too forward for the woman to tell her beloved of her feelings; it is his duty to profess his love, hers to listen. But, my beloved, while you were gone to the battle I was full of remorse every day . . . because I had not told you . . ."

"I knew of it. You've said to me that you'll be my wife. Those are enough words of love."

"No, listen. I dreamed that you were in danger. That you might be . . . that something would happen to you, and you would never have known!" She sighed; her eyes faltered and fell, then returned to his face. "Jorge, please hear this and try to understand: Jorge, I am afraid for you, but just as much I am afraid *of* you. No! Let me say this, for I have rehearsed these words the way I rehearse the playing of a song . . . Just let me say them, and help me have the courage to say them, because I have never been bold, never.

"My dear Jorge, from the beginning, I have seen signs that you will bring trouble upon us . . ."

"Teresa! I would no . . ."

"No, listen, please! I know you *would* not, as you are good. But you are a *force*, my Jorge, and where you go, consequences must follow. We all understand this, my brother, Maria, Vigo, Francisco de Cartabona . . . We all sense this, though we all love you more than any person . . ."

"Not Cartabona, I wager," he said, remembering the lieutenant's pathetic effort to challenge him the summer before.

". . . but I can say these things, things such as I've never dared say before to anyone, because, my cherished one, I have thought only of you for months. Jorge, you are like a . . . a *weapon*. And where a weapon is, danger is."

He searched her face, stunned by these revelations but understanding them somehow. Aye, he was a weapon; he understood that; he felt that he was a long weapon of Virginia. "But listen, Teresa," he said intently, "A weapon does not hurt the one who holds it. I am directed *away* from you, I am for your protection ..." He put a palm on each side of her face and made her look straight at him. How strange and unexpected this was. He had come to talk to her of love and peace, expecting her to be like music, like flowers, like rest; now he found himself having to talk to her, as to the Indians, in figures of speech, to assure her and convince her.

"I told you I have seen signs," she murmured. "The first were nightmares in which you appeared. Jorge, I am afraid of knives and swords. In my nightmares I see flesh cut and bleeding ..." She shuddered violently. "I ... In my dreams for so long you appeared with knives and swords. I was terrified of you ..."

"Forgive me for your nightmares," he said.

"But then you came and became our friend and I saw you were good, and those nightmares ceased. But then, dear Jorge, there was another thing; the night I saw your guard hold a knife to our friend Cartabona ..."

"You saw that, did you? Teresa, I would not have let them hurt him. He had thought to challenge me ..."

"I know, I know. But do you know what my nightmare is now, Jorge? Another sign. I see you shoot a frightened rabbit, just a rabbit that got unknowing into your way ..."

He remembered that, remembered her scream, remembered his confusion and remorse. His eyes fell.

"In my nightmare sometimes now," she went on, "I am that rabbit."

"Teresa!"

"Shhh! It's well enough! I know you would not have shot it, had you thought first of me!"

"No!"

"But, Jorge, you come here to do what you have to do, and you find us here in your way. Compared to you we are as weak as rabbits here ..."

"I do not think of the Spaniards as weak like rabbits," he contended.

"No. But Fernando. He is brave, but he is delicate and could be swept away so easily ..." Her eyes dropped again, and were wet as if with a sudden pity. "I am afraid for him," she said. "For Maria, for us all ..."

He stood up suddenly, breathing deeply, turning this way and that, peering out through the still leafless vines of the arbor toward the horizons. "This unsettles me. I had hoped to bring you happiness and confidence, not fear."

She grabbed his hand, and pressed her lips to it. "But you do! My dear, oh, my fine one! You bring happiness such as we have never had. Dear one, this family of mine has never been blessed with good fortune; we hardly know how to expect it. But you have brought a brave new kind of cheer into our hearts! Fernando, I believe, would be pleased to die for you. I would! But happiness, you see, has the seeds of sadness in it, because it cannot last."

He considered this and was surprised. Every young woman he had ever known had presumed that permanent happiness would be assured once she had gotten her way. Now here was this Teresa, a girl rather than a woman, always having been cloistered against the hardness of the world, who seemed to have a more realistic notion of the nature of happiness than any he had heard. It was not his own notion of happiness, or had not been, but in coming from her lips it came to seem most likely. She smiled at his perplexity, and continued: "There was a wise storyteller in my country who wrote this about happiness: 'It is seldom that there is a happiness so pure as not to be tempered by sorrow.' That is how my people see happiness, I think."

"Does that not make life harder to live?" he asked. Here, it seemed, was his only glimpse inside the Spanish character except for Fernando's preoccupation with the act of killing. It seemed to give him a clue to how Teresa might be made happy. Perhaps she could not.

"It might make life harder to live," she said. "Harder than what? How can I compare it with anything I have not known? But it makes the happiness of now—*ahora!*—brighter. This is why I am happy now, now that I am with you."

He dropped to one knee before now, his hand still held in both of hers. "I have never given thought to happiness," he said. "I've only felt it ... many times. I have felt it when crops I planted grew well. I feel it in the wilderness, and when I am with my family. I feel it greatly when I plan, and still more greatly when my plans succeed." He stopped and thought. "My greatest happiness ever is now, with you here. Before this, it was the moment when my men lifted me on their shoulders and carried me into the fort at Vincennes. I had not failed them, and they had not failed me. Teresa, I had a teacher in Virginia, a gentleman named George Mason, one of the best of the Virginians. He taught me from the *Meditations* of Marcus Aurelius that a man's happiness is in doing the things proper to a man. I am a happy man, Teresa, because I have always tried to do those things." He turned her palms upward and kissed the soft pads of her palms. He was in a dreamlike condition now; to be happy with her and talking of the nature of happiness was like a new world, a rapturous contrast to the hardships and hazards of the past year.

"I rejoice in your happiness," she said, smiling down on him with radiant tenderness.

"Beloved, listen: I think . . . I think it is impossible to be happy all by oneself. One can bear suffering alone, but not joy. I've felt more and more isolated with every success. I understand what has been happening to me. Listen, because discretion forbids me to say these things to anyone else:

"Because of my good fortune here, the destinies of everybody in this territory depend on what I do. I can say only certain things to people who look to me for their fates. I have held the power of life or death in my hands—I told you this in my letter . . ."

"And thus played God, you said."

"Aye. And am therefore alone. And I've also told you this, long ago: When peace comes and I settle down to prosper on the lands I've gained, I see you sitting beside me." He smiled. "Unlike you, my child, I don't foresee tragedy at the end of our joy." He shut his eyes and fell to kissing her hands, her wrists, her arms, now enveloped in a blissful blind world of birdsongs, drone of bees, sun's heat, tickling soft touchings, and the scents of moist earth, blossoms, her clothing, and the familiar but still exotic odor of her body.

"But I still do," her words came like a thunderclap. "I still see it."

He felt a chill at the certainty in her voice. "But how? What is it you imagine?"

"I don't know. It isn't clear, of course. But I have never seen us married in the eyes of my church. I have never seen us growing old together as you have. I see us split apart. By distance, by disappointment, by death—I have no words for it! I do not know what. I am heavy with it! But, Jorge: *ahora!* Now is all the more happiness, and all is well for us!"

He shook his head, frightened, but forced a chuckle and tried to reassure. "Then I shall simply have to change our fate.

Teresa, I always do what I attempt. You *will* sit beside me when I'm old. We shall see which prevails, your premonitions or my acts."

She smiled sadly, indulgently, down at his upturned face. "I pray for thee," she said. "But for now, in any event, we must have what we can have. In our eyes, just in our eyes, I swear that I am your wife and you are not alone."

The subtle trill of a redwing filled the pause. "You say, my wife?"

"I am, Jorge. In our eyes I am. I have prayed for guidance and the answer was made clear."

"And I agree. Teresa, you are my wife, and I am not alone."

SHE PLAYED SONGS ON THE *GUITARRA* FOR HIM AGAIN AFTER DINNER, the songs that he had carried in his head all the way to Vincennes and back, and some more vigorous and sensual *flamencos* that he had not heard before. There was a change in her demeanor in the recital now; instead of the furtive shy glances that she had raised to his eyes before, she now looked up from the instrument and met his gaze directly with eyes wide, black, and flashing. Her brother and Maria could not help noticing it, and knew that something important had transpired between the pair. Fernando was curious and wary. He was her guardian, and it was he who had so strongly advocated the Virginian to his family; now he was uneasy that his timid and cautious Teresa might have determined a course that would move her into harm's way.

It was after midnight when the family at last retired. George had stationed his guards downstairs, and lay in his bed waiting for the house to grow still, knowing that he could not sleep with Teresa's words still echoing in his soul: "I swear that I am your wife and you are not alone."

In her room, Teresa undressed and washed herself all over, and dried on a scented towel. She let down her hair and brushed it, and left it down. Naked save for her small crucifix, she studied her body in the mirror and was not now ashamed. She then drew on a crisp, white, loose nightdress on which she had embroidered a collar of silken flowers. And now in the candlelight she knelt at the icon beneath the crucifix on the wall, her knees on the hard bare wood of the floor, murmured the Lord's Prayer, crossed herself, and remained there for several minutes gazing at the crucifix. A great calm settled through her. She felt as she had always imagined a bride should feel. She had arranged this in prayer and was sure that this marriage was sanctified. She seemed purified and was not frightened. Now she rose from her knees and blew out the candles on the wall, leaving only the tiny candle flickering in a porcelain bowl under the crucifix. She climbed onto the bed and lay on her back on the covers, listened to the spring frogs and whippoorwills outside, and watched the small yellow smudge of light move on the white ceiling and on the wall, making the shadow above the crucifix bob and shift. The air in the room was cool and fresh on her brow and hands and bare feet. She lay and looked at the small gleaming bronze figure of the Christ on the crucifix, at its gaunt and graceful muscularity, the hard, stretched pectoral muscles and the long, ropelike muscles in the thighs; and once again in her mind's eye that lean muscularity merged with the image of George as she had first seen him. It had become a strange habit, this transposition; the first few times it had happened she had felt shame. But in the long lonely nights of his absence, she had grown more at ease with it. Once she had even stroked the bronze figure, running her fingertips down the hard flanks and thighs while in her imagination were the torso and limbs of her love. But only once had she done that. It had seemed that such a thing must be profane.

Now she did not know whether George would come to her room; she knew the hazards of it and would not have been surprised if he did not. But she had professed to be his bride and he seemed to have understood her and it was his right to come to her bed now if he chose to do it. If he did, she was ready to be his bride.

The seconds whispered by into minutes, and she did not seem to be drowsy, but when a draft of air from her closing bedroom door breathed over her body it woke her from a shallow sleep. The candle flame under the crucifix was leaping from that motion of air, and silhouetted against its leaping reflection on the wall he stood, looking down at her.

George stood for minutes looking at the white-clad form lying supine on the great bed, at the austere simplicity of her room, this room where she lived, where she lay alone when he was away, where she slept and dreamed and prayed; he was touched and pleased by its lack of clutter. The two dominant aspects of the room were the icon, with its candle and the crucifix above it, and the bed. Secondary in the room were the dark wardrobe, the *guitarra* case in a corner, a Bible, a sewing basket and a small shelf of books. It was as if the lonely gentility of this beautiful girl's life were depicted in symbols which made that life easy to understand. To have a home! he thought. And then a rush of warmth bathed his soul and he thought: More than anyplace else, this room is my home, because she is here.

He hesitated, his body poised like a great question mark, his world upon his shoulders, the cool night air on his sweat-bedewed skin. He had come to the room inflamed with the desire his imagination had built around her words, but now had paused to revere.

He was awed. Somewhere in this ascetic room this girl had found the audacity to abandon the constraints of her religion and culture and place her life in his care, whatever the risk, whatever the censure. I could turn about and return to my room, he thought, and not place her in the jeopardy of those consequences. I could not bear to cause pain and suffering to this vulnerable creature. He remembered what she had said about being the frightened rabbit, about fearing him. I must leave her inviolate, he thought. I must!

But as he stepped backward toward the door, looking at the dark shape of her head on the pillow, he saw a spark of candle-light in the shadowed hollow of her eye and realized that she was awake and looking at him.

He stood still. A timber joint in the great house popped apocryphally with the night cooling; a mouse rustled in the walls; Teresa breathed. Then the dim shape of her hand stole toward him across the pale counterpane upon which she lay, signaling for him where to sit; the doubt was gone then, and he moved to the side of the bed, sat, laid his broad hand on her damp cool brow, feeling the shape of her skull beneath the smooth skin, as if thinking through his hand: Here is where she is, this unique one; here within this case of skullbone is the essence; here is the astonishing will.

And from there, there was no such thing as retreating; only moist lips, straining, whispers, the gliding of hands over velvet skin, tears, moans caught in stopped throats, the carnal worship, bite of pain, tumescence, fibrillation, opening, the riot of membranes, breathing of vows, the creaking, the evanescent flowering, joyous sadness, gripping the throat, the long, cool, gray, slimy backsliding, and the gratitude: ah, the gratitude!

As silently as breathing they had effected it all, no outcries, no oaths, though their throats had been crowded with cries and oaths; then it was over, even while scarcely beginning. And for the two of them, the whole world had changed, within four stucco walls in the feeble light of an icon wick.

Now, he thought, we are married as she has told me. Now truly, he thought, as her hot breath tingled on his neck and his hand unclenched under the incredibly smooth, sweat-moist skin of her back: Now we are one. God help us . . .

AN EAR-SPLITTING CRACK AND A BRILLIANT WHITE FLASH JOLTED him awake. His heart was slamming. Rain lashed at the window and he saw the candle guttering under the icon. Another flash of lightning and thunderclap drove Teresa into his arms, quaking with terror. Blue-white light flashed and an incessant salvo of thunder crashed and rumbled, now sounding like cannon echoes, now sounding as if a heavy canvas sky were being ripped from horizon to horizon.

He should leave the room, he knew. This storm would awaken the household and he might be found here. He could not remember falling asleep; he could not believe he had so released his vigilance over himself as to let sleep overcome him in this precarious place. But now Teresa was clinging to him, her nakedness and warmth again enveloping his will. And seeing each other's eyes black and hungry in the flickering white light, their hearts racing, they blended again into one body, their souls flowing into each other like the confluence of two rivers. If the world ended now, it would be of little consequence.

They lay side by side then, hearing the storm bang and rumble eastward over the Mississippi.

"What, *querido mío?*" Teresa whispered, feeling him shaking with silent laughter.

"Listen to it. D'you know it sounds as loud as a rolling chamberpot?"

Her mouth fell open. Then she had to bury her face against his chest to smother her laughter and it was a long time before they could stop laughing.

MARIA DE LEYBA, AWAKENED BY THE CRASH OF THUNDER AND banging of shutters, then kept awake by a fit of morning coughing, pulled on a wrap and went to her daughters' room to look in on them. They were sleeping through the din. Little Rita lay neatly and calmly on her back, mouth open, arms outside the unmussed covers, as if she had just stretched out for a nap; Maria Josefa slept on her stomach, her bare foot sticking out from under her twisted blanket. Maria tugged the corner of the blanket down over the exposed foot, stood at the bedside for a moment gazing thoughtfully at the flashing rectangle of sky outside the window, sighed, then stepped back into the hallway and pulled the door closed. Turning from the door then she was startled by a movement at the other end of the hall. Going stock-still, she watched by lightning-flash as the tall, powerful figure of Colonel Clark, their honored guest, moved from Teresa's bedroom door to his own, opened it, slipped through, and eased it shut.

Maria stared at his door for a whole minute, slowly raising her fist to her mouth as she realized what she had just seen. Her jaw set, her eyes hardened, and she went to Teresa's door, turned the handle, and swung the door inward.

Teresa was naked, kneeling at her icon, her black hair hanging to the small of her back and spilling forward over her shoulder. Her face, just turning toward the door, was gilded on one side by the faint light of the candle; beside her on the floor lay her nightdress.

At the moment Maria's eyes were widening at this stunning sight, an eddy of air from within the room brought to her nostrils the moist, unmistakable musk of carnal sin.

The two women remained this way for many long seconds, only their eyes changing, as their complex, delicate kinship crumbled around them in the half light.

Teresa's haunch began to tremble as she knelt there. She sat back on her heels, reaching for the nightdress, lifting it from the floor, drawing it up to shield her nudity. Maria shut the door, took two steps into the room to stand over the kneeling Teresa, her face disintegrating into rage and hurt. "Mother of God!" she hissed. "To all I have to bear, you add this disgrace! Oh," her voice quavered, as she brought her hand up to her shoulder, "thou *whore!*" She lashed at Teresa and the back of her hand cracked on her temple, hurting them both, knocking Teresa off balance. She sprawled on her side on the cold floor.

Teresa gathered her legs under her and knelt under the crucifix again. She drew the nightdress on and lowered her head, eyes shut. She crossed herself, then stood up, looking to Maria not ashamed, but strangely beatific. Not like a *penitente*, Maria thought incredulously, but looking like a . . . a *bride*. Like a bride. And Teresa said, softly, "If you intend to tell Fernando, please, Maria, I ask you to think first of Fernando himself. I pray you."

Maria still stared, aghast, heartsick; slowly she began shaking her head and backing to the doorway. "No," she murmured. "No, I couldn't . . ." And then she was gone, with the creak of the closing door.

On the other side of the thick wall, George was washing the musk and dry sweat off his face and body. Water dribbled musically from the cloth into the washbowl; there was rainfall outside, and his head buzzed with happy exhaustion and the sacred imagery of the hours just past.

Thus transported still into the *penetralia* of Teresa's soul, thunder now grumbling away in the east and rain hissing down outside his window, he had not heard a sound from her room, and imagined her sleeping exhausted in her bed.

Our bed, he thought. God! As I live, I am surely the most favored man on the face of the earth. Teresa, he thought, savoring the words, I am your husband. You are my wife.

One day, he thought, everyone will know it.

HOPING TO HAVE A FEW MINUTES OF SLEEP BEFORE THE AWAKENING of the de Leyba household, George lay on his bed in a swirl of voluptuous new memories and swells of tender emotion, trying to sink into oblivion. But this attention was caught by the barking of dogs from the village below, then the drumming of approaching hooves through the rain. One horse. No doubt a messenger, he thought. He lay and listened.

Hallooing and a pounding on the door downstairs followed, then the voices of his guards. He raised himself up and drew on his clothing. His loins still tingled, and he was swept repeatedly by waves of an unaccustomed euphoria, followed by such poignancy that his eyes would tear. Then he opened his door and started toward the stairs. He glanced at Teresa's door, which was closed. De Leyba was just emerging from his room, buttoning his waistcoat; he smiled momentarily, then started down the stairs with George, brow knitted with curiosity.

The messenger, in drenched buckskins, saluted as George reached the bottom of the stairs. He looked quite downcast. "Colonel, sir, hit's about Bill Myers."

"What, man?"

"After he left Corn Island he got ambushed near the Bear Grass. Kilt an' sculped."

"Oh, God, no." George thought of the trusted courier, one of the swiftest and smartest frontier rangers he had ever known, and was stunned. Then he thought of the thick packet of laboriously written letters, reports, and confidential messages, and a chill went down his back. "And the messages to Williamsburg?" he said.

"A few tore up an' scattered where he laid, sir. Many thought carried off."

"And John Moore, who was with him?"

"Probably captured, sir. Here. Cap'n George sent up this letter from Jim Patten at the Falls. 'Twas 'e that found poor Bill."

George read the letter, whose inventory of the recovered papers indicated that a score of valuable and secret documents en route to Patrick Henry had been carried away by the savages. And probably are on their way to Detroit now, he thought.

"I am deeply sorry to hear this, friend Jorge," de Leyba muttered softly beside him.

"Aye. Well, it means I've got to cross back over and rewrite all those papers for Governor Henry." *Damn it all,* he thought. Days of laborious writing, just when he should be here taking leave with Teresa and her family. He looked toward the stairs as if hoping to see Teresa there, but instead there stood Maria, kerchief to mouth, staring hard-eyed. "Would you have my horse brought around and made ready, please?" he asked. "And I must see Teresa a moment before I go. Madam," he said to Maria, "will you tell Teresa I must have a moment with her, that I'm compelled to leave?" Maria stared at him for a moment with a strange expression which he first thought was hatred, then he decided that it must be his imagination. She turned then and disappeared upstairs.

AT HIS INSISTENCE, FERNANDO LEFT GEORGE AND TERESA ALONE for a few minutes, and let them sit together in his study to take their leave. Outside the rain had stopped, and water drops, catching the morning sun, fell like sparks from the trees beyond the windowglass.

She sat on a divan and he knelt beside her. He held both her hands raising them often to kiss the delicate fingertips. His heart was going wild. He was confused by the strange, angelic smile on her face and the sheen of tears glinting in her eyes. He released her hands and reached up to place both of his at the sides of her face. She grasped his wrists gently, her thumbs moving and caressing the wrist-bones beneath the skin. They looked at each other's eyes and remembered each other's bodies. For several minutes they languished in those reveries. She smiled.

"Had we been wrong," she said, "lightning would have struck us."

He smiled, then frowned. "I should be able to come back soon. I expect to go and attack Detroit in June, but I think I can come back here before then. This whole territory is at peace now. I ought not be too busy to come. I . . ." He found himself looking at her left hand, realizing that it had no ring upon it. No ring to symbolize their secret marriage. I'll have one made before I come back, he thought. She must have a ring on her hand. What . . .

"I have a keepsake for you, to hold until I can bring you back a ring." He reached into the deep pocket of his blue coat and drew out the two little athletic medals. He held them up, one between each thumb and forefinger, and she looked back and forth between them, bemused. "My teacher, George Mason, had these made for me," George said. "This one is for winning a footrace. This one is for winning a wrestling contest. They are a matched pair. Like you and me, Teresa. I shall give you one of 'em and keep the other. Then when we come back together, they shall come back together, eh?"

She smiled and nodded. Now tears were running down her cheeks.

"Which one for your keepsake, my love?" Her silent crying was infectious, and he found the two medallions to be swimming, vague, through his own tears.

She gazed at the one with the tiny running man in it. "I prefer to think of you running free as the wind rather than fighting," she murmured. "Should I take that one? No! No, wait. If you have the runner, maybe he will help speed you back to me. And I shall hold the wrestler medallion here, perhaps to keep you from conflict."

"So be it. I like that notion."

"I should like to attach it to the silver chain with my crucifix. And wear it always."

"Aye," he said softly. He could hear horses outside, and the voices of Fernando de Leyba and his own guards. He put the little medallion in the palm of her hand and pressed her fingers closed over it. She began sobbing.

"But I have no gift for thee," she said, sounding like a child rather than a woman.

He stroked her hair and tried to think what he could say. "Aye! You have, though!" he exclaimed. "The finest thing. You've given me what you can now give to no man else." She looked at him, puzzled, for an instant, then understanding dawned on her face and softened it. "And," he said, "I swear it binds us forever."

She swallowed and blinked, then began to rise. "They're waiting for you," she said. "Go now, while I can still bear it!" Teresa turned her face away and did not watch him leave the room.

MARIA STOOD AT A WINDOW UPSTAIRS AND WATCHED HER HUSBAND salute, then embrace the American colonel. Deep in her lungs there was the intolerable tickling pain, and her heart hurt as well, with agony and jealous rage. Be gone forever, *diablo*, she thought after him as he clapped his hat over his red hair and swung astride the stallion.

From the moment she had seen him appear naked and soiled in the doorway of that ballroom in Kaskaskia almost a year ago, she had thought of him in ways she should not have; she had been like a woman possessed. And this morning she had seen him leave the room of her sister-in-law, and she had smelled the scent of their intimacy. And at that moment her long, fantasized jealousy of the girl had broken completely, and was diverted to an utter hatred of this troublesome George Rogers Clark. Damn you, she thought. I wish thee all the failure and loneliness and disgrace a man can bear. Take my curse with thee! And God save me from ever seeing thee again!

George turned in the saddle and looked at the governor's house one more time before rounding a corner of the village street, where water flowed like a brooklet. His guard and the courier rode behind him, and watched him take that final look at the mansion. The house was yellow with the clean-washed early morning April sunlight.

I swear it binds us forever, he thought, remembering his last vow to his Teresa. He looked ahead down the street toward the brown Mississippi.

Vowing it to himself this way made it even more irrevocable than saying it to her. It works that way, he thought.

No other, he thought. Whatever our fates, no other for me.

28

KASKASKIA, ILLINOIS COUNTRY
May 1779

I WON'T GET BACK TO ST. LOUIS BEFORE JUNE, HE FINALLY ADMIT-
ted to himself.

Immediately upon his return to Kaskaskia, he became inundated in the myriad problems of administering a new frontier
county hundreds of miles from the seat of state authority, and of
preparing for a long-range summer offensive against Detroit.
Days and then weeks began to flow by in a blur of time, each
day distinguished from every other only by the good or bad
news it brought.

He was forced to declare war on the Delaware Indians after
a band of them killed a party of traders between Vincennes and
the Falls of the Ohio, and other Delawares came to Kaskaskia
where they became drunk and hostile and created a series of
disturbances, claiming that their great chief, White Eyes, had
been murdered in cold blood by white men. George sent Leonard Helm an authorization to make war on the Delawares near
Vincennes and destroy their camps as punishment for having
broken their treaty with the Big Knife. Helm's frontiersmen
struck swiftly and brutally; the Delawares sued for peace; and
ultimately Tobacco's Son and his Piankeshaw warriors took it
upon themselves to answer for the future conduct of the Delawares. The chief chastised them severely for breaking their
word and killing his friends, the Americans, told them they deserved the severe blow they had received, and swore by the Sacred Bow that he would decimate them if they did not return to
their hunting and remain peaceful. Thus ended the brief war between the new American regime and the Delawares, in such a
way that it strengthened further the legend of the invincibility of
the Big Knives.

Daily, George made preparations for the provisioning of the

Detroit campaign, and awaited the arrival of Captain Montgomery and his five companies of militia that Governor Henry had promised to send.

When Montgomery did at last arrive at Kaskaskia, long overdue, George felt with a sinking heart that history's misfortune was being replayed: Instead of the five companies, Montgomery had been able to bring only one hundred fifty half-starved and ill-clad men. They had been diverted to join an expedition against the Cherokees in the Western Carolina country.

This stunning disappointment was offset by his joy in the arrival of his young brother Richard, who at last had prevailed upon their father to let him join George in the Illinois country. Now nineteen, Dickie was lithe and determined, with an intensity that George easily recognized as a copy of his own demeanor at that age. After a short period of duty in Captain Robert Todd's company, Dickie was commissioned a lieutenant.

Because of the condition of Montgomery's little force, George now lamented that he had not marched on Detroit directly from Vincennes in April. He now fastened his dimming hopes for the Detroit campaign on the three hundred Kentucky volunteers Colonel John Bowman had promised to send to Vincennes by late June. With those added to Montgomery's one hundred fifty and his own veterans, George could hope to mount a force of some half thousand against Detroit, and he made himself believe that that number, if his fortunes held well, would be sufficient.

In June, he received a letter from Captain Helm which cheered those hopes. From a trader recently reaching Vincennes from Canada, Helm had learned that Detroit was as ripe for an easy conquest as any fort could be. Its commandant since Henry Hamilton's ill-starred departure, a Captain Lernoult, was apparently a man of little self-confidence and had only a handful of trustworthy royalists in the fort to help him defend it. The French-Canadian and Creole prisoners whom George had paroled and sent home to Detroit had spread his fame in the vicinity of Detroit, and many even declared openly that though they had sworn not to fight the Big Knives on their arrival, they felt themselves free to fight beside them. Helm's letter continued:

he says its not safe for a person to spake dispicably of the Americans that there is a Room for you and an other for me in every principle Gentlemans house in the Village furnished with Bowls and Glasses and Called Col° Clarks & Capt

Helms Rooms . . . that he seen Children in the Streets with
Cups of water drinking Success to Clack Success to Clack.

George smiled at those images and grew ever more impatient
to get his force underway to Detroit. His veterans talked of little
else, and soon they had infected Captain Montgomery's companies with Detroit fever as well.

Helm's letter also contained information that, in the wake of
the American victories in the territory, settlers were again pouring down the Ohio and through the Wilderness Road into Kentucky, and that the settlement he had founded at the Falls of the
Ohio was growing in population day by day. Helm had also
learned from a Delaware Indian informant that a large expedition of Kentuckians had departed from the Ohio to trounce the
Shawnees in their great town of Chillicothe. This, George presumed, was Colonel John Bowman's army, which was scheduled to rendezvous with him at Vincennes for the March against
Detroit. The news that John Bowman was making such a hazardous side excursion worried and irritated George. It was, it
seemed to him, a reckless attempt by Colonel Bowman to glo-
rify his own name on the frontier. George had heard often that
John Bowman was jealous of the fame of his brother Joseph
and, particularly, of George himself.

Damn you now, John Bowman, George thought. If you want
to make a brave name for yourself, just help me capture Detroit.
Don't waste all those lads you've got on a useless—nay, a
harmful—amusement against the Shawnees! God, man, there's
no need to rile those savages at this moment just to gain yourself a few laurels.

But, presuming that a brother of Joseph Bowman's could not
be utterly stupid, George told himself not to worry about it, and
continued with his efforts to provision his army. And that was
proving to be a difficult task. Prices for all sorts of stores had
been driven up as high as five hundred percent by traders
outbidding each other in his absence. This caused the French
and Spaniards to conceive of the Virginia currency as valueless,
and they were refusing to take it. The partnership of Vigo and
de Leyba, as well as Monsieur Cerré, had begun advancing considerable sums of their own property, which tormented George
despite his gratitude. They will be ruined, he thought, unless
some method can be used to raise the credit of the Virginia currency, or a fund sent to New Orleans. Oliver Pollock had by
now exhausted his own properties, and had not been reimbursed

by Governor Henry. With a heavy heart, George wrote to Pollock in June:

> ... I act by his Excellency's authority and I know that he
> will take every step he possibly can to make you a remit-
> tance which I expected would have been the case before this
> time. ... Virginia State will never let you suffer long for
> what you have done for her and if it has not been in her
> power to send you supplys she bears it with a greatful Re-
> membrance.

   Still with full faith in Virginia, not aware that she, like other
states, was heading toward insolvency, George authorized his
supply officer to obtain everything the army needed by drawing
bills on the state, which he endorsed himself. It did not seem a
prudent thing to do even as he did it, but he saw no other way
to carry out his mission.
   In this hectic and desperate manner the weeks were used up,
and the date for the June twentieth rendezvous in Vincennes
was imminent; there would be no opportunity whatsoever to go
up and see Teresa and her family before the campaign. Swallowing that disappointment, he sat alone in his office late one
night, sipping brandy and puffing on a clay pipe, and rubbing
the smooth silver of his lucky foot-racing medallion between
thumb and forefinger. It was unusual to have just one of the
lucky pieces. But he entertained himself by imagining that
Teresa in St. Louis might at the same time be touching its mate,
which he envisioned lying upon the moist smooth skin of her
breast, attached to the chain of her crucifix.
   For a good luck piece, it's luckier now than it ever was, he
thought. He smiled at his little joke, and slipped off into his reveries. It was a rare thing for him, this daydreaming. For over a
year he had seldom been able to detach his mind from his purposes long enough. Now he found himself succumbing to it in
the evenings when the demands of his position receded, and
would sit late in the quiet evenings drinking, thinking as much
now about Teresa as he did about Detroit.
   Two more glasses of brandy and he still could not pick up his
tired body from the chair and put himself to bed. He grew more
and more wakeful, his mind shuttling back and forth from Virginia to St. Louis to Vincennes to Corn Island; he mused on the
faces of people who had so unexpectedly forced themselves into
his affections during this remarkable odyssey: de Leyba's fam-

ily, Gibault, Vigo, Cerré, even the obsequious Tobacco's Son. What an array of unlikely friends and companions, he marveled, puffing breaths of wistful laughter out of his nostrils.

And Dickie here now, bringing all the poignant memories of home and family. . . .

He stirred. Must write to the family, he thought. There'll be no time for it on the way to Detroit.

He went to his desk. As he addressed the letter to his father, he was aware of pains in his wrist and elbow, and in his hips. These had been growing in him since the winter hardships in the Wabash. They were, he suspected, the stiffnesses and twinges of old age, and he had earned them early. It frightened him.

D^r S^r:

I Received your much Esteemed Letter by Dickie who arrived safe at this place. Happy to learn that all Friends are well. I have for a long time Injoyed a perfect State of Health under the greatest fatigues. My dispositions of War Hitherto have been Crown^d with great success but must Confess that Circumstances appear more serious at present than for some time past but I hope to Extricate myself as formerly no person Commanding on this Continent is in a more Critical Situation than I am Surrounded on all Sides by Numerous Nations of Indians with English officers among them Incouraging them to war but my Influance and Success of late hath been so great that I still keep the greatest number of them on our Side of the Question I dont doubt but you have before this time had a full account of my late Attack on post St Vincents after an Ingagement of Eighteen Hours the famous Governor Hamilton and his Murdering Band fell into my hands nothing extraordinary has happened Since my Last to you by Cap^{tn} Jack Rogers, I have Given Dickie a Lieutenants Commission if I Can get him to Imbrace the Air of an officer I dont doubt but he may make a good appearance in a short time I think he already improves. Expences in this Cuntrey is amasingly high it has not Cost me less than twelve or thirteen Hundred pounds since I have been in it. I Can give no account when Shall See you but as Soon as possible . . . You have for several years known the height of my ambition but I did not Expect to arrive at that so much determined Moment in so Short a time as I have done. Fortune in Every Respect as yet hath hovered Round me as if determined to direct me You may Judge Sir what Impressions it must have on a greateful Brest whose greatest Glory is to addore the Supreme director of all things.

George stopped writing, drank off the dregs of his brandy, and gazed into a far corner, suddenly so pressed by melancholy that he thought his heart would cave in. What would Father think if I told him of Teresa? he thought suddenly. No doubt his Episcopalian heart would miss a beat at hearing of my betrothal to a Catholic lady. He sighed and shook his head.

But this is a different world, he thought.

Sir it would give me the Greatest happiness to be assured that it was not a doubt in your Brest but that you had in me as dutifull a son as ever Father was possessed of. My dʳ Mother Brothers and Sisters is possessed of my sincear Regard

I am Sʳ with Esteem yours

G. R. CLARK

The second trek eastward across the Illinois to Vincennes was as pleasant as the first one had been miserable. In a party of mounted soldiers, George rode under hot blue skies across vast green and gold plains of waving grass dotted with the dark bulks of grazing buffalo; the earth underfoot, the same earth they had slogged through, wet to the knees, only four months ago, now was as firm and smooth as a highway, and the same two hundred forty miles that had taken them seventeen laborious days in February they now made in four. Montgomery, his men, and the supplies had started out early in June by boat to go around and up the Wabash and meet him in Vincennes, and Joseph Bowman was marching the main body of troops from the Mississippi posts overland, no doubt eager to return to the brown arms of his Mai-hah.

The sun beat down, melting the pain out of George's shoulders and hips, and he felt like his old self, capable of whipping any wrestling opponent unfortunate enough to draw a straw against him during the entertainments in the evening bivouacs. Esprit was high and heady. Now away from the tedium of administration, having left John Todd to deal with all that as the region's new civil governor, George was once again the exuberant warrior, confident of his plan and sure of his ability. He and his captains laughed, splashing now with such ease through clear, shallow, sun-dappled fording places in the Little Wabashes and the Embarras and the other streams across which they had waded or floated on trees during those desperate dank gray days of winter.

Now, in fact, these rivers were exceedingly low. It was a dry summer, the sky day after day being hot blue pearl. This worried George, who knew how much the traverse to Detroit would depend on the navigability of the upper Wabash and Maumee rivers. Although he thought three hundred men would be enough to storm and take Detroit, he knew it would require more than that to labor up and down sunken rivers with cannon and supplies, and also to make an impressive—and thus unmolested—passage through the lands of the Lakes tribes.

Their arrival at Vincennes was noisy and spirited, with Captain Helm throwing a huge celebration for the gathering army and being generous with the fort's plentiful stores of good food and drink. Helm did an imitation of Major Hay growing faint with fright, and then of Hamilton at the moment when he discovered that he had surrendered to one hundred thirty men instead of a thousand. Joseph Bowman vanished from the midst of the celebration early, and those who knew of his mission to enrich the blood of the Piankeshaw tribe smiled fondly at the thought of the tender circumstances he must be enjoying now with his comely nurse.

This merriment was increased by the appearance in their midst of Simon Butler, who for months had been presumed dead. Succinctly, Simon told them an incredible tale of capture, torture, and eventual escape. Caught by the Shawnees near Chillicothe, he had survived nine runnings of the gantlet and eventually had been taken half alive to Detroit, whence, after recovering his strength, he had escaped. He was prevailed upon to strip off his hunting shirt and show the scars of his ordeal—an array of half-healed cuts and burns that made even these seasoned men wince and curse. He parted his blond hair to show an inch-deep indentation in his crown where the blunt side of a tomahawk pipe, wielded by the famous Shawnee warriorchieftain, Blue Jacket, had broken his skull and pushed a disc of skullbone into his brain. The officers shuddered and mar veled at these tales, their imaginations filling in the details and descriptions that he omitted in his laconic account.

Much as he was taken with admiration by this awesome tale of survival, George was more interested in Butler's description

of the defenses at Detroit; he pressed him for details and was
pleased to hear that it was as feeble as other accounts had indicated. Butler in his turn listened with equal admiration to the
account of the winter march on Vincennes, and the two young
giants took leave of each other well after midnight, each inspired by what the other had done, and each more hopeful than
ever that men of their blood and spirit could end once and for
all the British influence in the western theater of the Revolution.

But this hope was dashed when the troops promised by Colonel John Bowman from Kentucky arrived. They came marching wearily into Vincennes, not three hundred as promised, but
thirty, led by a dispirited Captain Hugh McGary.

George and his officers sat that night with McGary, almost
weeping with frustration and rage, and listened to the account of
Bowman's attack on Chillicothe. It had been an even worse
blunder than George had dreamed it could be. Striking the town,
Bowman had failed to move decisively; most of the Indians had
escaped and the raid had quickly degenerated into an orgy of
burning and looting. Retreating then with goods and a hundred
of the Shawnees' horses, the Kentuckians had been harassed for
miles by a small sniping party of Shawnees. In the attack and
withdrawal, Bowman had lost thirty men killed and sixty
wounded. His attack had cost the Indians only two casualties:
the chieftain Red Pole had been slain, and the great and beloved
principal chief of the Shawnees, Black Fish, had been badly
wounded. "Colonel Bowman called it a great victory," McGary
said quietly, his chin trembling. "Most of us was so discouraged
by it all that much of the army disbanded when it returned to
Kaintuck. And this is all they is of us left to bring. Sorry, Mister
Clark."

Hugh McGary was known to be a reckless and murderous
Indian-hater, and if he was ashamed of a raid, it must have been
a fiasco indeed. George stalked about the room, lips drawn in a
white line, clenching and unclenching his fists, now and then
staring toward the ceiling and mouthing silent words, as if demanding God's explanation for this incalculable disappointment.
Finally he turned on the uneasy McGary.

"It's the most appalling thing I ever *heard* of!" he hissed. His
eyes were blazing. "Not only does he squander the force that
would have wiped out the British influence for good—but he
shoots *Black Fish! Black Fish!* God almighty damn, McGary!
D'you understand? We'd almost awed even the Shawnees into
peace by taking Hamilton and his partisans. And now John

Bowman gives the Shawnees an excuse to ally themselves more solid than ever with the British!" He turned and stalked the floor some more. Joseph Bowman, sick with shame for his brother's stupidity, rose from his bench and crept out of the room, swallowing bile, tears running down over his burn-scarred cheeks. George turned back to McGary. His voice was calm now, scarcely more than a whisper. "Thankee for comin', Captain. We welcome you." He sighed. "We'd better pray that Black Fish will live," he said. "If he dies, I predict Kentucky will run more blood than it did in '77."

THE DISASTROUS RESULTS OF JOHN BOWMAN'S RAID CRUSHED ANY hope of going against Detroit that season. George held a war council with his officers, and, though all but two still recommended the attack, the proposal finally was abandoned. Reasons were that the rivers were nearly dried up, that half the army was barefooted, that the summer was growing old, that three hundred fifty exhausted men might not be able to take Detroit, and, if they could take it, they might be too remote from supply to hold it long against a major British counterattack. To this rationale was added a newly arrived report that George Washington had sent an army of four thousand continental regulars, commanded by General John Sullivan, to attack British and Indian strongholds in the Finger Lakes region with the ultimate objective of Niagara. If successful, the campaign would choke the British supply line to Detroit and in effect put Detroit out of the Indian-inciting business. If Sullivan succeeded, it was felt, the Virginians' planned expedition would prove to be unnecessary and wasteful. But will he be? George wondered. McIntosh failed last fall, and Hand before him . . .

Late in the summer, word came that George's boyhood Virginia neighbor, Thomas Jefferson, had succeeded Patrick Henry as governor. That was good. Having been involved in the original authorization of the western campaign, he no doubt would continue to give George a long rein and receptive ear.

For now, with a Detroit campaign out of the question, George divided up his troops to garrison Vincennes and the Mississippi posts, and left them with orders to conduct feints and patrols throughout the territory, to confuse the British and Indians and "keep them in hot water and suspense," as he wrote in their orders. Then he bade his people farewell, left Joseph Bowman to take a recuperation leave in the care of his beloved Mai-hah and the Piankeshaw medicine men, and set out eastward with a small escort along the old Buffalo Trace to make his way to the Falls of the Ohio, to establish a permanent base there as the best place for overseeing the whole territory. Would I had someone to authorize me a long respite in the arms of my sweetheart, he thought as he rode ever farther from where she was. That, I think, might ease these disappointments a mite.

Teresa and Detroit, he mused. Both of 'em always hundreds of miles distant, it seems.

His reputation, his far-ranging sorties, and a variety of conflicting rumors circulated by his French friends through the enemy's country, did indeed keep the British officers on the verge of panic throughout the summer and fall of 1779. As far away as Mackinac, British leaders began setting themselves up for defense against parties of Big Knives who were reported to be building a fleet of boats at the place the Indians called Milwaukee; another report had still more Americans at the Chicago River on Lake Michigan. Months later the same British officers reported that Clark had gone down the Mississippi to Natchez, while other British reports circulated to the effect that fifteen to eighteen hundred Americans with cavalry and artillery were moving eastward across the Illinois country. To intercept one imaginary force of mounted Americans, three hundred British, Canadian, and Indian troops were sent out under a British lieutenant, but the fear of the Big Knives was now so great that the Indians deserted. Elsewhere, the British Indian leader Captain Henry Bird, trying to raise a force of Indians near Lake Erie to stop the anticipated American march on Detroit, could not find an Indian who would go to war against the American colonel called Long Knife. At Pittsburgh, Colonel William Crawford wrote to George Washington that even that far east, "Colonel Clark's affairs have changed the disposition of the Indians much. They have done very little mischief this summer."

Before leaving Vincennes for the Falls, George had instructed Montgomery to begin laying in provisions for another attempt on Detroit the following spring in the event that General Sullivan's mission might fail. He simply could not give up the notion.

"Never was a person more mortified than I was," he wrote in his promised report to George Mason that fall from the new town of Louisville he was building at the Falls, "to lose so fair an opportunity to push a victory: Detroit lost for want of a few men!"

While still reeling from the disappointment, George received

a messenger one day from Vincennes. The man came in, gaunt
and red-eyed, and took off his muskrat cap. He stood for several
seconds, unable to speak. His eyes filled with tears.

"Well, man, what is it? Are you dumbstruck?"

"Hit pains me to bear this, Colonel, sir," said the ranger,
handing George a letter. "They say his lungs jes' filled up from
th' powder burns or somethin' like 'at. But Major Bowman 'as
departed us, sir. So sorry, sir. Him such a young 'un. . . ."

George gave a brief memorial oration that afternoon, remembering, as he spoke, how Joseph had looked leaving the room
in shame over his brother's wildcat raid; and wondering what
would become of Mai-hah now. I hope, he thought, that Joseph
lives on now in her loins. I'm sure he tried his best. That was
just his way.

That evening, in the privacy of his new quarters redolent with
the tang of their fresh-hewn timbers, George wrote out Joe
Bowman's death certificate. Then he drank himself into oblivion.

In their own rooms, many of the other veterans of the Illinois
conquest did likewise.

29

St. Louis, Upper Louisiana Territory
September 5, 1779

LADY MARIA DE LA CONCEPTIÓN Y ZEZAR DE LEYBA WAS SIMPLY
letting herself die, and her husband could only sit beside her
bed helpless and desperate. Much of the time he sat there drunk
because it was too painful and maddening and bewildering to
try to understand it sober. The haze of drink softened the bony
outlines of her face before him, and muffled the tread of minutes and hours, and enriched his exquisite emotions of grief.

It was September fifth, and she had taken to her bed five
days before. She had been sinking ever since. For nearly two
days now she had said nothing to him.

Her decline was easy to explain to the family and to well-wishers in the society of St. Louis, as she had been consumptive and malarial even before her arrival. But Fernando de Leyba knew that she was dying not from consumption or malaria but from melancholy and shame.

Maria had endured this exile in the New World with Fernando only because she saw in her future a return to Old Spain with improved wealth and position. Now there was scarcely a hope of that left. By underwriting the credit of the Americans across the river, Fernando had finally lost his fortune, and fortunes of the Spanish traders he had influenced, and plunged into insurmountable debt.

Maria had seemed to understand their plight before he did. She was not an optimist, and did not have the same faith in people and institutions that he had. He still believed that the governor of Virginia would send real coin to his friend Jorge Clark, or, if not, Governor Galvez in New Orleans would intercede.

It seemed to Fernando de Leyba that everything would be all right if only Don Jorge would return to the Mississippi valley. Though matters had been difficult even when he was there, he had kept them under control. But since his departure to attack Detroit in June, his absence had been felt in serious ways.

Teresa had gone into depression. She was listless, pining, reticent, given to great sighs and unexpected outbursts of weeping. She seemed to be estranged from Maria. Now and then she would make an effort to cheer the household with her wit or music, but could not sustain her own vivacity long enough to inspire anyone else. She spent much of her time in her room praying, and was beginning to act like a nun.

Then there had been the Indian menace. After Don Jorge had led his army eastward out of the valley, bands of savages formerly allied with the British General Hamilton had become bold on both sides of the river. Two Kaskaskians had been killed and two others wounded by Indians. In the salt works at Ste. Genevieve two workers had been killed, and four men in a pirogue going from St. Louis to Ste. Genevieve had been ambushed from shore, murdered, and scalped. Many other alarms had occurred around the villages and in the fields. De Leyba was painfully aware of his limitations as defender of the Spanish honor in the region.

And since the small American detachment had returned to Kaskaskia from Vincennes without Don Jorge Clark, their relations with the French and the Spaniards had deteriorated. Don Juan Todd, the new civil governor of Illinois County, was a fine man, but seemed unable to deal diplomatically with the inhabitants. And Lieutenant Colonel Montgomery sometimes exhibited an abrasiveness, a certain arrogance, in his dealings with the Kaskaskians.

But all that was minor compared with the matter of currency and credit. Until lately, Spanish traders and boatmen through Señor Pollock of New Orleans had been able to redeem silver, dollar for dollar, for continental paper money they received for military stores sold to the Americans; thus the paper money had depreciated less quickly in the Mississippi valley than in the East. This had attracted American traders who came with large quantities of depreciated currency and unloaded it to buy pelts and skins. Gradually then the inhabitants had lost faith in the American paper currency, which made it ever more difficult for the American officers there to purchase supplies for their troops. The inhabitants did not want to yield up their goods even for receipts endorsed by the esteemed Colonel Clark, and so de Leyba, Vigo, and others who continued to honor the American credit became more and more overextended.

It was when Maria had questioned her husband about his gloom and immoderate drinking that he had revealed their plight; she had immediately thereupon taken to her bed with the weight of her mortification.

Fernando de Leyba leaned forward in his chair now to stroke Maria's ashen brow. Absently, he murmured, "Our friend Don Jorge will come from the Ohio to visit us one day soon. He will frighten the Indians away. He will make arrangements against the debts. He will make Teresa smile, and then thou, *querida mía*, can get up from this bed and be happy as before!" He leaned close and kissed her lips. For the first time in hours, she opened her heavy eyelids. She moved her lips to speak; they stuck dryly to her teeth. *"Borracho!"* she said, above a whisper. "You reek of wine."

"No matter. Maria, you hear me, don't you?" A smile was beginning to spread on his face; he imagined her past the crisis now. "Don Jorge will come to us and arrange everything, I said!"

She shut her eyes again; turned her face away. "Never say that name!" she hissed. *"Esta maldición . . ."*

He recoiled as if slapped. "Maria! I will not permit . . ."

"Estupido! He has ruined us. He has . . . despoiled the virtue

of thy sister, man! Go away, 'Nando. I am ready for the priest ... Is the priest ... Is the priest here? ... Holy Mary Mother of God pray for us now and in the hour ..."

She fell silent again and more limp still, sagging further into the great pillows, eyes shut, lids trembling, and Fernando lurched to his feet, stunned by what she had said and already casting out of his mind the veracity of it. God forgive her, he thought; she is crazy ...

He staggered down the corridor, bumping his shoulder on the wall and knocking down an iron sconce as he went to Teresa's door. He thrust it open. She was kneeling, muttering prayers as always, not even noticing his presence, transcendent, eyes radiant, virginal, and innocent, fixed on the crucifix. He backed out of the room and stumbled on the stairs, descending unsteadily to his office. Lies, he thought. Maria lies. Not dying. Shaming me ... for her disappointments. Doesn't need a priest ... not even sick ...

From a nearby room beyond a door came the reedy voices of the children, reciting with their tutor. De Leyba entered his study, glanced out at the early-coloring leaves, staggered to the sofa, and decanted brandy. To Don Jorge our friend and benefactor, he thought as he drained it. He will come and visit us from the Falls of the Ohio and repair all this nonsense. It is nothing, nothing. *Nada en absoluto.* Teresa is *virgen.*

He passed out eventually, without having another thought about summoning Father Gibault; and while he sprawled snoring and drooling on the sofa, Maria in their great bed upstairs quit living, without benefit of absolution.

By October the value of American currency was sliding downward so rapidly that John Todd wrote bills of exchange to a Spanish trader amounting to forty thousand pesos for twenty thousand pounds of hides and skins worth in reality about three thousand pesos, for the reason that he could always trade skins for provisions. The peltries were, in effect, a more stable currency than the American paper money, and became the "fund" by which the garrison could be kept in provisions for a while longer.

The trader, under persuasion from Fernando de Leyba, accepted the American notes for the skins though no one was by this time wanting to accept American paper. But because of the enormous discrepancy between the recent and earlier bills of exchange, de Leyba was afraid the matter might discredit the earlier bills, and so sat down on the eighteenth of October to write a letter which would advise Governor Galvez of the problem. It meant, of course, revealing his own involvement in trying to prop up the Americans' credit.

Looking sickly and ten years older than he had a few months before, feeling that he was at the very end of his rope, Fernando de Leyba sat drinking and writing, occasionally having to stop to wipe his tears and compose his thoughts.

My Dear sir and Protector—

The letters I sent your Lordship from the General of Virginia and Governor Clark will serve, I believe, as authentic documents to prove clearly to your Lordship my scrupulousness in the handling of this affair. I assure your Lordship with all respect that by courtesy alone I should not have been able to accomplish so much. It was my good works which forced them to live in harmony with the Spanish government of this side, but, my Governor, how dearly this little bit of idle splendor has cost me. My family weeps and I share with them in their just regret.

My undermined health does not promise me many years of life and, when this is ended, my poor daughters have no other resources to save them from beggary than the property that my hardships may have secured for them. By your Lordship's favor and protection I had well-founded hopes of freeing them from so bitter a potion, but the coming of the Americans to this district has ruined me utterly.

He had to stop; he was strangling on remorse. In his mind's eye he saw the face of his friend Don Jorge Clark, still his most beloved friend despite this catastrophe.

. . . Several inhabitants of this town, who put their property in the hands of these Americans to please me, find themselves in the same situation, and these losses are equally a matter of regret to me with my own since I consider myself the immediate cause of them. But what was there for me to do with your Lordship's orders except to come to their aid in view of the fact that even the principal leader, however many American documents he brought, had not a shirt to cover his nakedness. I accomplished this on my credit with all the inhabitants so that they might provide these Americans with whatever they needed.

This measure relieved them of their affliction and I was left as hostage, since I became bondsman for ten thousand pesos (as is clear from the receipts that I have in various places in this post, which must be paid). On their part I was paid by two bills of exchange which Francisco Vigo has taken to New Orleans, and they have not been paid. . . . I acted in this way, my Governor, thinking to do a service for your Lordship and please you. The result of this is that I am now overwhelmed with trouble not only for what I owe and cannot pay, but also by the chance that your Lordship may not approve my measures (this is what tortures me most) although all were intended to show you my blind obedience.

These inhabitants did not want to give up their goods even for Colonel Clark's receipts. They gave them immediately when I pledged mine. If I lose my credit by not being able to pay them, the service may be retarded as a consequence since it is certain that, if I need some unexpected aid for my troops, I shall not get it.

Finally, my Governor, my beloved wife, who came to this exile with so many hardships only to bring it about that at the end of it we should return to Spain, when she saw her hopes frustrated by the labyrinth of debts in which she found me involved, was overcome by such a great melancholy that after only five days of illness in bed, she passed from this to another life, without my repeated urgings that we could trust to your Lordship's favor being able to relieve her, that your Lordship, intervening, would not fail to look upon our cause with pity, but nothing was sufficient because the unexpected blow had been too much of a shock. Her loss makes me look upon that of my property as an affair of little importance. Therefore, in company with my weeping little daughters, I implore your Lordship's protection for the collection of these bills of exchange. I do not doubt that your chivalrous heart will grant it to me, at least out of pity for these innocent little girls, even though it be necessary to appeal to the court, inasmuch as whatever I have done has been purely an act of hospitality, fitting between any nations.

Your hand is kissed, your Lordship, by your most devoted and humble servant,

FERN^{do} DE LEYBA

Outside his window, a bitter wind was ripping leaves off the willows and maples and blowing them over the mansion grounds, bright flashes of yellow against a ragged, gusty, iron-gray sky. The leaves drifted up at the foot of the garden hedges and walls. Hard freezes had struck several times already, and a severe, comfortless winter seemed to hang like a grim and unmistakable threat in the offing. Fernando rose, heavy with regret and foreboding, and went toward the sitting room by the pantry, where the children's voices piped and whined through their lessons. The tutor had gone, and Teresa now sat on a straight chair before their divan, hearing their recitations. The children looked unwell, their eyes ravaged by sleeplessness and misery, their noses red from the chill in the house. Teresa was dressed in black simplicity, only a white collar showing, her thick hair drawn back as severely as Maria's had used to be. A child's face setting off the garb of a nun or matron, he thought; but with a strange, wise, serene sort of beauty about it now. After Maria's death she had emerged from her vacuity and her religious distraction back into reality, and was trying as well as she knew how to be a surrogate mother to her nieces.

The first day Fernando had seen her with them after Maria's death, he had swelled up with a wave of shame and anger, thinking for a moment that one who had thrown her virtue away was not fit to look after his daughters; he had thought for a moment of forbidding her to spend time privately with them.

But immediately his censure had been swept away by a warm rush of compassion.

Her only sin, he thought, was to give everything she had—even her honor—to the noblest and dearest man she had ever known.

And that, after all, he thought now as he looked at his sister, was in a way no more than he himself had done.

30

LOUISVILLE, KENTUCKY
September 1779

EARLY IN THE FALL OF 1779, COLONEL DAVID ROGERS, ONE OF George's cousins, brought a large boat up the Ohio to the Falls, carrying a valuable cargo of clothing, flour, and ammunition obtained from the Spanish at New Orleans and destined for the defenders at Fort Pitt. He had somehow managed to slip past the British posts at Manchac and Natchez on the Mississippi. George provided him with an escort of twenty-three veterans of the Illinois campaign to help ensure his passage the rest of the way up the Ohio. At the head of this detachment was Lieutenant Abraham Chapline. George went to the river one September morning and bade these old comrades goodbye, and watched the convoy go up the river.

In October one of the boats returned, its squad of men heavy with despair. On the fourth, they reported, Colonel Rogers and his party, numbering sixty men, had fallen into an ambush above the mouth of the Licking River. Over a hundred and thirty Indians led by the renegade Girty brothers had killed most of the party, taken the supplies, and captured Lieutenant Chapline and a few others. Colonel Rogers had died of wounds soon after the battle. Only this one boatload of men had escaped. For days thereafter, George was benumbed by grief for the loss of so many of his beloved heroes, and by the futility of Rogers' brilliant odyssey.

In November, nine months after capturing Henry Hamilton, George sent his conductor-general William Shannon to Williamsburg with a precious cargo of papers for the state auditor of Virginia: All his original vouchers, the twenty thousand papers of receipt and disbursement covering the entire Illinois campaign, that great and worrisome burden of meticulous records he had carried from one place to another. Here at last would be the settling of his public accounts and the clearance of all those innumerable liabilities to which he had signed his own name. The letter of passage told Shannon to wait on Governor Jefferson, then return to Louisville as quickly as possible with the auditor's receipt. George watched Shannon and his escort ride off through the snow, and felt as if a boulder had been lifted from his shoulders.

The winter of 1779–1780 was to be remembered for many years as "the hard winter." Snow did not melt for three months; streams froze to the bottom. Most of the settlers' cattle died, and innumerable buffalo, deer, wild turkeys, and other animals perished. Hunters were reduced to digging frozen animal carcasses out of the snow. People thawed the frozen meat of their dead horses. The price of corn quadrupled everywhere on the frontier. The typical meal for a Kentucky family was a fistful of hard johnnycake. John Sanders, released from military service, had gone into business with a group of hunters to serve as procurers of meat for the settlement and its garrison, but that winter they did precious little business. Many families starved to death trapped in their remote cabins, and many of the survivors suffered frostbite. The steel of axes and splitting wedges grew so brittle in the cold that they broke on striking. Trees split at night under the brilliant cold stars with cracks like rifle shots. The new settlement of Louisville at the Falls of the Ohio went on hard rations under George's orders, as nothing could be brought down the frozen Ohio, and messages between the winter-locked outposts almost stopped.

George yearned in vain for a thaw that might enable him to attempt a journey up to St. Louis, and had to content himself with reveries. He would sit late by the fire, maudlin with bad rum, roll the little silver runner's medallion between his thumb and forefinger, and try to imagine that Teresa with its mate was receiving his thoughts hundreds of miles away.

Little could be learned about the condition of the British posts and the Indians to the north, and he could only presume that something was being done to rebuild the power center he had shattered by his defeat of Hamilton. General Sullivan's expedition against the lakes country had petered out far short of its goals; that much George had learned before the winter had cut off the travels of his spies, and it had come as no surprise. It left Detroit as his objective.

What trade there was had reverted to barter, with skins or tobacco being used as a currency, as the value of an American dollar had dropped to less than a cent. In a way, therefore, severe and oppressive as the winter was, George dreaded the coming of spring, when he would have to begin the activities that would tax all his resourcefulness: holding the vast territory he had won. With the thaw, he was sure, would come a renewed wave of Indians led by British. He had confounded them for one year but knew that the effect could not last.

The winter broke suddenly and dramatically in February, and a spring as lush and invigorating as the winter had been severe surged into the territory. And virtually on the flood of the melting river came boats bearing American adventurers with their families. News in the East of Colonel Clark's taming of the Northwest Territory precipitated a flow of land-hungry settlers. Before May, three hundred boatloads of families had arrived at the Falls of Ohio. Half a dozen settlements sprang up on the Bear Grass, near where the courier William Myers had died a lonely death at the hands of Indians just a year earlier.

George watched this influx of immigrants with mixed feelings. Here was manpower aplenty for his offensive against Detroit, but he had not studied them long before he realized that they were not like the seven score men he had brought down the river two years earlier. These men were intent on gaining land, not defending it. Many seemed to have come to escape military service in the East, or to avoid taxation. Many were Pennsylvanians, prejudiced against Virginia and ready to dispute her Old Dominion claims and resist her government. It was not difficult to see the land-madness and its potential troubles growing. Soon the immigrants were disputing Virginia's jurisdiction over the Kentucky lands, and in this they were encouraged by the great land-scheme companies, whose agents quietly urged them to petition Congress to claim the territory and proclaim it a new state. As Virginia's commandant, George knew that he must resist this, and it was not long before powerful resentments began to build between the Virginians who had won the country and the newcomers who were compelled to help man and supply this desperate little force.

In the meantime, William Shannon returned, bringing George the auditor's receipt and authorization from Governor Thomas Jefferson to use his own discretion in the coming months; he could try to raise a force and go against Detroit, or build a fort at the mouth of the Ohio as suggested in Patrick Henry's original orders. The Revolution in the East was static, Shannon reported. Spain having entered the war against England, Governor

Galvez was capturing one British fort after another in the lower Mississippi. "It's good news now," George mused. "But once we're done with the British I fear we'll have Spain to put out."

As predictable as the natural quickenings of spring, the Shawnee raiding parties began sweeping southward and attacking the settlements. Their forays seemed exceptionally furious in this spring of 1780; the Indians were inflamed by the tide of white men pouring down the Ohio, were wanting revenge for the death of their great chief Black Fish, who had died of wounds suffered in John Bowman's attack the year before, and were once again being incited and equipped by Governor Hamilton's successors at Detroit. After several murderous raids had scattered settlements, the Kentuckians started beseeching George to lead a retaliatory expedition against them.

"No," he argued. "That would be like fanning the stink while letting the carcass lay. You gentlemen give me a thousand men and five months' provisions, and I'll take Detroit. And then you'll have *permanent* peace." Most of the county leaders, though, failed to see beyond the immediate threat and insisted that he go against the Shawnee towns. Now with the backing only of his veterans, he set workmen—on promise of eventual pay—to building a large number of boats for the Detroit offensive.

In the meantime, there was still a fort to be built at the confluence of the Ohio and the Mississippi, which would be the nucleus for the defense of the western rivers. It would control English river traffic. It would throw a net to capture the large numbers of Tories and deserters who had been escaping downriver, and would guard the channel of commerce and communication between Spain and the Colonies. But the most urgent reason was that the British were working hard to regain the support of Indians to recapture the Illinois country that he had held for two years; a strong fort there would be an invaluable defense against that threat. George knew he would get no help from impoverished Virginia in this matter. Governor Jefferson's letter had directed him to build the fort but added:

. . . The less you depend for supplies from this Quarter the less you will be disappointed by those impediments which distance and a precarious foreign Commerce throws in the way. . . . Take such care of the men under you as an economical house holder would of his own family doing everything within himself as far as he can and calling for as few supplies as possible.

In other words, George thought, I'll get about as much help from there as I've got in the last two years, that being virtually none, but now for a change I'm to be forearmed by the knowledge that hope and patience are useless. Well, in that sense I prefer Jefferson's way to Patrick Henry's; I can be realistic.

Late in April, with a convoy of troops and workmen, he arrived at the wide juncture of the mighty rivers and began surveying for a feasible site. Several great drawbacks immediately became apparent. To build the fort just below the confluence would be to put it directly in peril of being washed away by seasonal floodwaters; too, the lowlands here were humid; malarial, and unhealthful. Moving through brush and dense cane down the floodplain on the east bank of the Mississippi, his party at last came to a bluff which stood well above any flood danger. Though it was nearly five miles below the juncture of the two rivers, it commanded an immense view of the lowland and the broad, curving sheets of water. The bluffs were streaked with rusty red, which convinced him that it was the place the French river travelers had called the Mine au Fer, and the Americans the Iron Bluffs.

Drawing on everything he had learned about fortifications, George laid out plans for a good log fort with blockhouses covering each other and thick earthen redoubts, and his workmen and soldiers began a vigorous and well-organized construction project. Settlers began arriving soon by boat, attracted by the promise of four hundred acres of land to each family at a favorable price to be fixed by the General Assembly. In the mild spring weather, axes and mauls and hammers began chunking at daybreak each day and continued until the westering sun burnished the sluggish surface of the wide river. Oxen and horses dragged logs and stones and great wooden sledges of earth to and fro. At night the weary laborers rejuvenated themselves with fiddle and pipe music and tall tales, whooping and stomping dances, and athletic contests.

To gather an adequate force of men for this new stronghold, George sent orders to Fort Patrick Henry at Vincennes calling for the Americans there to leave that place garrisoned by a company of French militia and come to the new fort. He also sent orders to Colonel Montgomery to retire most of the American troops from the Illinois villages. Montgomery began making preparations for the pullout, and it was a move viewed with relief both by the Americans and the French; in the ten months since Colonel Clark's departure from Kaskaskia, the passionate friendship between his soldiers and the French inhabitants had been eroded steadily by disputes over the provisioning of the garrison. The impoverished Americans had virtually no buying power, and had been forced now and then to take food, provisions, and animals from the inhabitants against their will.

But before that evacuation from the Illinois villages could be effected, an alarming series of messages came to Colonel Clark from several quarters. Traders and spies came down from the north with reports of a stirring of British military activity. They said that Lieutenant Governor Patrick Sinclair at Michillimackinac was gathering loyalist traders and chiefs of northern and western Indian tribes for war councils. Along the upper Mississippi, tribesmen of several Indians, including the Ottawa, Winnegabo, Sauk, and Fox, were gathering in large numbers and being harangued about the presence of Americans in the Mississippi valley. The Indians were being incited to anger also against the Spaniards, who were now at war with Great Britain. Sinclair, the reports said, was promising exclusive control of the rich Mississippi fur trade to those traders who would help him regain control of the valley. A great Sioux chief named Wabasha was being assigned to attack the American rebels at Kaskaskia and then sweep on down the Mississippi as far as Natchez. A trader, Emanuel Hesse, was being authorized to seize and control St. Louis, and was collecting a mixed force of traders, servants, and Indians that was reported to number a thousand at least. A support party of Indians and Canadians, under the dreaded Indian partisan Captain Charles Henry Bird, was setting out from Detroit to go through the Shawnee country, gather warriors along the way, capture Clark's fort at the Falls of the Ohio, and then descend upon the central Kentucky settlements.

George was appalled at the task that was building for him. The numbers of enemy involved in those rumors could amount to two or three thousand, and their tactics would force him to be virtually in two places at once; his whole reliable force consisted of the one hundred fifty steadfast but unpaid and threadbare veterans under his direct command.

Any hope for his cherished offensive against Detroit had to be forgotten now. Nothing remained to him but to direct a desperate defense. He sent word for Montgomery to unpack and remain at Kaskaskia to organize a defense there. George rushed completion of Fort Jefferson at the mouth of the Ohio and pondered over the defensive alternatives he would have.

Early in May the first direct call of alarm came down from Cahokia, the northernmost and thus most imminently threatened of the French Illinois villages; the huge enemy force was in the vicinity. Almost immediately followed appeals from Montgomery at Kaskaskia and Don Fernando de Leyba at St. Louis. His course was now obvious: the defense of the Mississippi outposts first, then back to Kentucky. His old energy seemed to flood back into him now that the decision was made, and leaving a modest number of defenders at the new fort, he boarded his new boats with a small company of his best frontiersmen for a one hundred sixty mile dash up the Mississippi to Cahokia and St. Louis.

Never in the last two incredible years had he headed to battle with such a sense of urgency. Not only were his hard-won gains of 1778 and 1779 at stake; also in immediate danger were his Teresa, his generous and vulnerable friend, Don Fernando de Leyba, and his younger brother Dickie, who was serving with McCarty at Cahokia.

Now I am afraid, George thought as his fighters strained their oars against the yellow-brown current, that Fernando will soon satisfy his eternal curiosity about the sensations of killing. I can only pray that he shan't have been tested at it before I get there.

"Put some sinew in it, lads!" he cried. "You must admit it's a lark after swingin' axes and shovels!"

He was answered by a chorus of chuckles and groans.

LIEUTENANT COLONEL JOHN MONTGOMERY AND HIS JUNIOR OFFI-cers met George on the wharf when he stopped his little convoy there. Montgomery gave George a bear hug, to the cheers of a crowd of French Kaskaskians who had gathered on the shore to see the return of their old benefactor, and in a moment Father Gibault broke forth from the crowd and trotted out on the plank landing to embrace George and kiss him on both cheeks. The priest's gentle great eyes were brimming. "How long can you stay, my son?"

"Not at all. Only a look at the fort, and then on up to Cahokia and St. Louis."

"Listen to them people whoop an' holler," Montgomery sneered as they went up the bank toward the fort. Flowers rained on them as they went up the street, and hands reached out offering flagons of wine. "Couldn't hardly extrack a crust o' bread or pair o' shoes out of 'em all last winter. But now's th' British an' Injuns got their blood runnin' yaller again, they like us a lot."

"Never mind that, John. Bear in mind we promised 'em a lot of benefits that Virginia hasn't been able to deliver yet. A main one being protection, and it looks as if we have our chance to fulfill that one now anyway. How's their militia forming up?"

"They're good. With nowhere t' run to, I reckon they can be counted on."

George gave Montgomery a hard look. "I hope you'll improve that attitude, John. I can't ever forget that sixty o' these people marched with us to Vincennes last year. I can't ever forget that."

He met old campaigners he hadn't seen in a year, and was embraced by many weeping and laughing Kaskaskians. He inspected the defenses of the fort, went into the old Rocheblave house and trailed his fingers thoughtfully over the waxed desk where he had written so many orders and vouchers and proclamations as the new conqueror of the Illinois in the summer of '78. He went upstairs alone and gazed for a few minutes out of the bedroom window at the streets where the Kaskaskians had danced and sung and celebrated their deliverance on that long-ago July day. He looked down the street at Cerré's house where he had first seen Teresa de Leyba and her brother.

In less than an hour he was back at the wharf and ready to continue upstream, convinced that Kaskaskia was as ready as it could be if the invaders got this far.

"My affections to McCarty and to yer little brother, fine one that 'e is," said Montgomery.

"Aye, John. Now you keep alert; keep scouts far afield, an' make the most of this new morale. Seems it takes th' worst to bring out the best, eh, John? And now I give you one special charge: Protect this priest with your life if you must."

"On my word, George."

"May I have a word with you, Father?" The priest strolled to the end of the wharf with him. "If we get through this, Father, I need to know if there's a way under the sun for a Catholic lass to be married to the likes of me without losing her soul in the process."

The priest tilted his head and clapped his hands together under his nose, all his deep smile lines tilting upward around his wide, loose V of a smile. "My son, I shall say this: In my years

in this wilderness, I've married children of Manitou to backwoods barbarians whose Catholic souls were so far buried in in-
iquity and sloth that I could scarcely find them. If I could not
conceive some liberal way to bring two such pure and noble
souls as yours and Señorita de Leyba's together, I should think
I had lost my craft as a minion of our Savior. Yes, George, we'll
find a way, or if there is none, make one!"

CAHOKIA WAS BUTTONED UP FOR SIEGE WHEN GEORGE AND HIS LIT-
tle band of reinforcements arrived there on May twenty-fifth,
and the main enemy force was reported to be within a day's
river travel. His reunion with his old comrade McCarty and his
brother Dickie was joyous but hurried. Advance parties of the
enemy had already captured an armed boat from St. Louis with
thirteen men, and had taken seventeen prisoners at the lead
mines near Ste. Genevieve. The air was heavy with foreboding.
McCarty had learned that the Ottawa chief Matchikuis, who
was legendary for his daring capture of Mackinac in 1763 and
now wore the red coat, epaulets, and title of a British general,
was in charge of all the Indians under Emanuel Hesse. A
French bushranger had recognized him and brought back that
fearsome information. "So be it," grinned George. "But he has
never been up against the Big Knives, has 'e?" The officers
smiled and nodded.

The fort at Cahokia was a minimal defense, but not badly sit-
uated to offer clear fields of fire, as it was not obstructed by
town buildings as was Kaskaskia. George saw that McCarty had
already had the great elms cut down, the two under which he
had first negotiated peace with the Indians. Their obstruction of
the view of the approaching enemy would have been dangerous,
and now they lay on the ground, their sharpened limbs and
branches pointed outward from the fort as part of a well-made
abatis. George gazed over the palisade at them and recalled viv-
idly that portentous occasion: the sunlight dancing through the
canopy of leaves, the cool shade, the musk of the Indian crowd,
the tobacco smoke of the peace pipes. He remembered the long
table with the wampum belts lying across it, and Joseph Bowman sitting at the end of the table. Bowman, he thought, a sudden knot in his throat. Cahokia had been Bowman's command
and George wished with all his soul that that brave and capable
man had lived to be here for its defense now.

Soon having heard all the intelligence that they had on

Cahokia's defense and the approaching enemy, George licked his lips and announced:

"Gentlemen, in the remaining hours, I'm going over the river to St. Louis, to have a look at their defenses. Dickie, you'll come with me, and I'll take a squad of riflemen for our protection." Several of the officers started and stood up, their mouths dropping open, and McCarty protested:

"George, no! In Heaven's name, man, stay put! Forget the Spaniards! We got more'n we can handle right here!"

George buckled on his sword. "Mister McCarty, I won't have you arguing with me."

McCarty's eyes blazed. "George, hear me, there's too much at stake f'r you t'be dashin' off t' dally in th' arms o' yer sweetie!"

There followed a shocked stillness in the room and a few murmurs of agreement, and George barely constrained his fist as a curtain of red fury rippled through his brain. "I'm going to forget you made that remark," he said in a low voice. "Do I have to remind you that without Governor de Leyba you'd have been starved out of this place long months ago? Now he's sent for me and, by my honor, I go. You know how to fight Indians, all of you. De Leyba doesn't. I'll simply advise him, and be back here before anything falls on you. Take my word for it." He winked then, and squeezed McCarty's right shoulder with his right hand, and McCarty nodded in resignation.

"Get on with you then. I know we're much beholden to 'im. Damn you, don't get reckless. This whole territory'd cave in in a day if you was lost."

"Then I shan't be lost! Come, brother o' mine, there's some very kindly folk across the river I want you to meet."

"So I have heard, George," said Richard Clark, adjusting his sword and moving with a sureness that looked like a copy of his brother's. "So I have heard, and I'd be delighted."

31

THE SIGHT OF THE DE LEYBA ESTATE WRENCHED GEORGE'S HEART, not because it looked so familiar, but because it looked so different: It had been turned into a fortress. The high stone walls in whose shadow he had courted Teresa a year ago bristled with the muskets of militiamen. Outside the walls were entrenchments, their raw red earth marring the emerald grasses, and these diggings also were occupied by a mixture of Spanish soldiers and armed villagers. George surveyed the arrangements as he and Dickie galloped up, and he was pleasantly surprised. The primary weakness he saw was that no part of the barracks wall could be covered by fire from any other part, and, once through the trenches and reaching the wall, an enemy could begin breaking through it with impunity.

Inside the house of his tenderest memories George found an even more poignant scene. The place was swarming with Spanish and half-breed soldiers, short in stature, swarthy, their skin shiny with sweat and oil, their gaudy uniforms dingy and faded. They chattered in their incomprehensible tongue and made an effort to prevent him from entering the house until he and Dickie grasped their muskets and shoved them aside to enter the great oaken front door. There in the foyer George was confronted with a familiar face, a handsome goateed face whose expression flickered for a moment between gladness and disdain.

"Ah! Richard, may I present Lieutenant Francisco de Cartabona," said George. "Señor, my brother, Lieutenant Richard Clark of the Virginia militia." The two nodded, de Cartabona taking his intense eyes off George's face only long enough to make a momentary appraisal of the young man. He's still hostile, George noted.

411

From the interior of the house, which had glowed gracious and enchanted in his memory for the last year, came dense, unfresh smells and a cacophony of distressful sounds: the squalling of infants, lamentations of women, groans, and an undercurrent of sobbing and praying. All the fine pictures and sconces and tapestries were gone from the walls and mud was tracked all over the board floors. Stepping into the ballroom, where he had so long ago danced amid the glitter of chandeliers and silver and listened to Teresa's exquisite recitals, George was stunned to see it had been transformed into a refugee camp of women, children, old people, shabby baggage, and even goats and chickens. The people lay about on filthy litters, sat with their backs against the walls, strolled about, nursed the infants, prayed, or held each other and gazed about disconsolately. He glanced over this abject scene, sensed the terror of these people, remembering the awful, fetid crowding of people and animals in the little Kentucky forts during the incessant Indian raids of 1776 and 1777, and his old fury against the British policy of waging war with Indian mercenaries was greater than it had been since his defeat of Hamilton. "It is my honor," de Cartabona said, "to protect these helpless ones if the enemy penetrates the walls."

"A task to break your heart, I know," said George, and de Cartabona's haughty face softened for an instant at these words of compassion from the man he so hated and feared.

George was searching the room and the hallways. "You are looking for his Excellency," de Cartabona ventured, with a bitter half smile and no mention of Teresa.

"I am. And the señorita . . ."

"This way."

In the study they found Fernando de Leyba sitting behind his desk, alone, his face in his hands. Their entrance startled him. When he looked up, bewildered and disoriented, not at first recognizing him, George was appalled at his wretched appearance. It was incredible that one year, even such a grievous one as de Leyba had endured, could have wrought such change in a man. His eyes were red-rimmed and sunken, their sockets deep and gray-brown like bruises; his face was blotchy and pasty, his cheeks sunken and unshaven; he looked as cadaverous as some of George's men had looked after their arrival at Vincennes. His lower lip hung slack like an idiot's as his mind reached to recognize these intruders.

Suddenly he lurched to his feet, his eyes filling with tears, and stood swaying. "Don Jorge, dear friend!" he cried, and George saw with a shock that this once-elegant wretch was not only very sick but quite drunk. De Cartabona had quietly backed out of the room and closed the door as if to avoid looking at him. Don Fernando staggered out from behind his desk and threw himself into George's arms, sniveling and moaning.

"Nombre de Dios!" he strangled. "Forgive, amigo, that you should see me brought so low! I think I am at the end of my string . . ."

"Nonsense!" George snapped, grabbing de Leyba's shoulders and shoving him back to arm's length, hoping to shock him out of this miserable condition. "No man is low until he's disgraced himself, and you've not done that!" De Leyba blinked, and as the statement penetrated his despair he began to draw his bony frame up taller, a vestige of his old pride beginning to flicker in his eyes. "You have my deepest sympathies for your losses," George went on, "but it was Heaven took your lady and my government that ruined your fortune . . . there's no disgrace on you, man! Stand up and collect yourself, and tell me what you've done to defend this place. And I must see Teresa. Quick, man, get yourself together. I have an hour at the most to stay here."

"You . . . you haven't come to help us . . .?"

"Aye, friend, to help and advise, but my command is the other side of the river. The only business I have here is love and friendship. Excellency, this fine lad with me is my brother, Lieutenant Richard Clark, Virginia militia . . ."

De Leyba drew his sleeve across his eyes and smiled, standing straighter now, and with a bow said: "I am most honored and surprised! Ah, Lieutenant, how proud you must be of this . . . of this . . ." And he burst into blubbering again, turning and stumbling back to his desk. There he wiped his face with a kerchief. "I am so ashamed! I am weak, Don Jorge; it exhausts me to stand . . . Yes, Teresa, you must see Teresa . . . Comrade, just let me gather my wits. . . . I'm afraid that drink and sleeplessness . . ."

The door swung open and Teresa, in black but with a soiled peasant smock over her dress, stood in the entry, her black eyes wide and wild, almost a bit mad-looking, one hand on her throat, staring at George.

"They said you were here. I did not dare hope. . . ." And then she was across the room, and into his embrace, sobbing and snuffling at his bosom, one arm around his waist and the other stroking his neck, while he held her there and smoothed the thick black hair and felt under his palm the bone-shape of her beloved head within, an enormous wave of emotion swelling in his chest and the ghastly realization in the back of his mind that this timid, delicate person, so full of piety and music, but strangely also of passion and resolve, was in mortal danger. In his memory there rose unbidden the vision of a pioneer woman in Kentucky, found dead in the bloody mud of a wilderness road, clothes ripped away and buttocks striped with knife slashes, a patch of bloody skullbone peeking through her glossy black hair, glossy like this, where the crown of her scalp had been . . .

God, he thought, dismissing the awful image, anything but that such a horror should befall her . . .

He introduced her to Richard, then turned to de Leyba. "Don Fernando, it is your sacred duty to keep the British and their savages out of this fortification. By Heaven, I swear that your honor lies in that. If any harm comes to your sister through your cowardice or ineptitude, I shall call thee a disgrace!"

The threat electrified de Leyba. His eyes bugged and he grew three inches in stature. "I have sworn to Governor Galvez," he shot back, "that the honor of Spanish arms shall never be tarnished on my account! Now I swear the same to you!"

"Good, then. Now let us hear what you've done."

Now looking like a soldier, de Leyba led George to the desk and showed him a plan of the village with defenses drawn in. "You saw the entrenchments. They will be manned by twenty-nine regulars and two hundred eighty-one villagers under the command of Lieutenant de Cartabona. I have scouts abroad, and a troop of cavalry stationed here and here as pickets. The rest of the regulars, under my command, as well as twenty militiamen borrowed from Ste. Genevieve, will man the walls here—and the men from the entrenchments will fall back and join us if necessary. The cannon will be trained on the gate at the end of this street. And, as you see, the women and children are here in my house, which is our last redoubt. If," he sighed, "things go so badly for us, de Cartabona and his survivors will fall back and make their stand here. A lamentable duty which they have vowed to fulfill to their last breath." He straightened up, not ashamed of his plan.

"Fair. Nay, better than fair. But you have five cannon, and you plan to use 'em only if the enemy reach the gate? That's a waste."

"Unfortunately the terrain within the walls does not permit us to fire down over them."

"Then you must build a platform along the inside of the wall and set them up higher so they can rake the slope here. Like this." Quickly he sketched the works. "Your artillerymen can survey to tell you how high to mount them."

De Leyba looked at the sketch with admiration, while Teresa stood clinging to her lover's arm. "I had felt so helpless about that," de Leyba said. "But, yes! This would do it!"

"The Indians fear cannon. A four-pounder well placed is worth a company of muskets. But as you know, hired savages won't expend themselves against a strong defense. They'll range the countryside rather and pick off the helpless. So get as much of your population inside as you can. And quickly. I believe they'll fall upon us by tomorrow if not tonight." He felt Teresa shudder at his side.

De Leyba looked up, imploring with his reddened eyes. "My friend . . . I . . . I wish you could be induced to take command of our defense as well as across the river. I . . . have no experience, little confidence . . ."

George looked at him, a little ashamed for him, then at Teresa, and weighed the offer. But no. He knew very well that his first duty lay on Virginia's territory on the eastern banks.

"I have no choice. And I'm sure beyond a doubt that they'll land on that side first. If they do, we'll take a great deal of hide off 'em and then they may not feel up to attacking this height o' yours. Listen, my friend: I may not see you again for a long while. If we're successful at Cahokia, I have to leave at once for Kentucky. The British have Shawnees headed there, and Shawnees are a more formidable lot than the mongrel mob coming here. Faith in yourself, man." He turned to look down into Teresa's eyes again. She was trembling in waves, and looking at her brother in pity. George again stroked her hair, and traced her ear with a fingertip. "Listen," he added, "if they strike here I cannot come to your aid, though my heart will cry for it. I've only a handful of men, and not enough boats to bring but a part o' those. And against their numbers, that would be in vain. Just remember this: once that motley band finds you're not weak, they surely won't storm you. I don't expect 'em to get even to your walls. But . . ." He paused, squinting, musing, "if they by chance should overrun your trenches, signal us with a slow cannon salvo . . . and maybe we can come and do something. God knows what . . ." His voice fell off after this hope-

less amendment, which he knew he'd had no official right to
make, even if he did have a moral one. Into the pause came the
bleating of goats and some shouts and a hubbub of talking from
the ballroom beyond. A timorous smile broke on de Leyba's
face.

"Theresa," he said, looking her up and down, "I should take
thee for a nun." Turning to George, he said, "She cares for the
sick and feeble in there. Whatever she has done . . . she is pure
in her soul, I swear I know it. Ah, don't look so baffled; I know.
Maria told me, on her deathbed . . ." His eyes filled up again,
but he blinked back the tears and strained at a smile. "There is
no dishonor, my friend. Not for a moment—no, perhaps for half
of a moment—my grandee pride told me to demand satisfaction
from you. Ha. But you were a hundred leagues away. And like
Teresa, I ached instead for your companionship. So you see,
amigo, we two love you, and we are as always in your hands."

Bewildered by this abject declaration, George looked from
one to the other for a moment, into their eyes, then reached for
Fernando's shoulder and pulled the pair close to his bosom. He
stood there speechless for a minute, his head bent, eyes closed,
his mouth pressed to the white line of scalp revealed by the part
in Teresa's ebony hair. She began shaking with sobs.

George stepped back, releasing them. He took the athletic
medal from his pouch and held it before her eyes. He took in
his fingers her thin gold neck chain and lifted it until the crucifix and the other medal appeared from the edge of her collar.
Then he touched the medals to each other. "Look," he said.
"And soon we'll match them together once again. I promise."
She nodded, still sobbing, looking down at the two pieces of silver. The floor creaked; the door whispered open and shut, and
they found themselves alone. Fernando and Richard had left the
room.

George put away his medallion and stood stroking the sides
of Teresa's face gently. She turned her face and kissed the heel
of each hand, then sagged against him. He grew dizzy with an
overwhelming, bittersweet agony, torn between a protective tenderness and a turgid desire to feel her long-remembered nakedness. Lifting her from the floor then with an easy sweep, he
carried her to the divan and stooped, lowering her upon it. He
began stroking her forehead, and she lay with eyes closed for a
moment, tears squeezing out between her lashes, breathing
through parted lips. But then the noise of people and animals
beyond the door intruded and she began rolling her head to and

fro, and opened her eyes for an apprehensive glance at the door.
"*Querido mío,* I'm afraid," she whispered. "To find us now
would break his heart."

"Aye." He knew she was right, and so resigned his desire and
let her sit up. And when Fernando reentered the room five minutes later with de Cartabona, George was kneeling at Teresa's
side with his lips pressed to her hand while with her other she
stroked his sun-bleached hair.

De Cartabona looked away and followed de Leyba to the
desk, where he was shown a sketch for the gun platforms.
George rose, held Teresa close for an instant, then bowed to the
two Spanish officers. "My affectionate regards to the two little
misses," he said. "I should like to see them, but it's growing
late. As it is, it may require stealth as well as haste for me to
get back to my boys."

The three men shook hands. "Remember," George said, "the
signal if they seem to be overrunning you . . ."

"A slow cannon salvo," said de Leyba, forcing a wistful
smile. His face was again chalky with fear, making his sunken
and inflamed eyes look even more terrible, but at least he was
standing now like a man with a backbone.

"You may be obliged to kill at last," George said softly, below Teresa's hearing, then grinned and added: "but I pray you'll
be careful of yourself."

Teresa went with him to the door, clinging to his arm as they
walked through the narrow aisles among the refugees encamped
in the ballroom. They stood facing each other at the door, their
hands knotted tightly between them. Richard stood outside the
door with the horses, "You'll play music for me next time we're
together," George said. She nodded. She did not tell him that
her *guitarra* had been crushed under the foot of a burly muleteer unloading provisions in the parlor. George gathered her
close in his arms and kissed her with a bruising pressure on the
mouth. Then she stood in the doorway with Fernando at her
side as the broad backs of the Clark brothers vanished in the
dust of their horses' hooves, down through the wall gate,
through the late-slanting sunbeams, while Spanish soldiers and
militiamen lounged at ease about their stacked muskets in the
yard and curiously watched them go.

IN THE STILL DARKNESS BEFORE DAWN OF THE NEXT DAY, A LINE OF
silent riflemen waiting on the parapet of the fort at Cahokia began hearing the soft rustling and knocking sounds of large num-

bers of Indians infiltrating the unseen fields beyond. George
was summoned from his quarters, mounted the parapet, and
stood listening. Down by the river, the hollow bumping of boats
and groan of oarlocks could be heard. By this evidence he deduced that the savages were concealing themselves in the weeds
and grasses and behind fences and hedgerows as close to the
fort as they could steal, probably for a rush about daybreak.

"This little amusement ought not last long," he whispered
confidently to his officers. "They won't be expecting the kind
of fire we've got awaiting."

The woodsmen stood silent as hunters in a blind, their deadly
long rifles already lying across the top of the palisades. They
were so still that the enemy might well have supposed the fort
deserted. The eastern sky began to thin from black to gray; the
stars faded; the brittle buzz insects hung in the cool air; then
birds began to awaken, and trees, fields, fences, houses, and
roads began to separate themselves from the fading gloom and
take shape. Even before the leading rim of the sun had winked
over the horizon, most of the frontiersmen had with their practiced eyes already picked out shapes and shadows in the fields
below as their particular targets.

Behind every man on the parapet slouched another rifleman,
ready to step forward and shoot while his alternate stood back
to reload. A morning breeze stirred, and along the walls eddied
a scent of lived-in buckskins, tobacco-tainted breath, and gunpowder.

"I wager they'll move just as th' sun peeks up," George
whispered.

"Aye," whispered McCarty.

Down by the river now there came a trundling sound, which
presumably was cannon being rolled off boats or up shore
gravel. "Soon as you can get a location on their cannon, spot
'em for the artillery," George whispered to his brother. "Maybe
we can knock one or two out even before they get a fix on us."
Richard nodded and disappeared, silent as a ghost.

A spark of sun winked on the eastern horizon; a meadowlark's clear notes rippled through the air. And as George
watched over the wall, the fields outside seemed to come alive
with movement; Indians were rising as if to a man at that meadowlark's song, rising into their low, crouching run, some carrying ladders, obviously believing they were going to reach the
walls undetected. George shuddered in the morning air, thinking, God, what if we hadn't known they were coming! Some of

the Indians in front paused as they heard scores of flintlocks being cocked above them, a tiny rattle of clicks; and then George yelled in a voice that shattered the morning:

"Now, boys!"

Fifty long rifles cracked and flashed almost simultaneously around the perimeter of the fort; a rankling cloud of blue smoke billowed and rose, and fifteen or twenty Indians in the foreground pitched, reeled, groaned, or screamed, some killed, some wounded, some merely stunned. The rest stopped, looked to each other or dropped to the ground for cover, or surged forward with their pulsating, ululating war screams, only to be spattered with another hailstorm of hot lead.

Now it was the defenders' turn to shrill the murderous high-pitched cry, and as the Indians milled about in the field, crawling, firing wildly at the fort, grabbing up their wounded brothers, or sprinting for safety of distance, they were pelted by a third withering volley as the first rank of riflemen returned to the palisade and discharged their reloaded weapons.

"Pick your targets and fire at will!" George yelled, joyously urging the defenders to do what they already were doing with relish, and at the same time he waved at the drummer boy, who began beating an excited tattoo. In that moment, two of the fort's cannon belched flame, and out of the corner of his eye George caught the sight of a boat flying apart at the river's edge and tiny men falling. Miscalculating their landing in the dark, the attackers had beached several vessels in full sight of the fort. A cannon flashed and fumed from the edge of a copse of sycamores near the water's edge, and a ball whiffed over the rampart, ten feet too high; immediately another of the fort's cannon billowed smoke and noise in reply and the enemy cannon leaped up and fell in the light of its own exploding powder cartridges. Good boy, Dickie! George thought with a rush of pride. It was as if he himself had done something just right, this pride in the alacrity of another Clark. The cannon of the fort erupted several more times in the next few minutes; the riflemen on the ramparts practiced their deadly skill on the figures retreating to the boats, and the enemy seemed to be in full rout.

For a few minutes then as the sun rose red and shimmering in the east, there was no more shooting, and the men craned and watched, congratulating themselves in low voices and with whickering laughter, and George passed praise along the line. Ten minutes later, sporadic firing rattled at a far corner of the fort, and George hurried there just in time to see another salient

of enemy braves and troops, who had tried to shove in from a
point farther down the river, disintegrate and turn tail under the
deadly fire.

That, George thought, ought to do it.

By eight o'clock buzzards were circling the fort in the morning sunlight, and the only sign that an attack had been made
was the scattering of bodies in the fields around the fort, many
of them in and near the great fallen council elms on the east
side of the fort. George and several of his men went out into the
field to inspect the dead. They wore the peculiar dress of western tribes, quilled headbands and moccasins, and among them
were two half-breeds or Canadians in green-dyed buckskins and
tricorn hats. An American private was bending to slice away a
scalp when George grabbed him by the nape of the neck and
propelled him back toward the fort.

At ten o'clock a stiff wind arose from the southwest, bringing
a sharp-edged shelf of blue-black clouds pregnant with rain.
Spoor detected along the bank of the Mississippi indicated that
the enemy had retreated upstream on foot and in their boats.
Without doubt we've disheartened them entirely, George
thought. Traders and Canadians and western Indians, he thought
with scorn. Bejesus, what a ragtag and immoral excuse for an
army, born obviously in desperation by that fool Sinclair up in
Michillimackinac.

MIDDAY OF MAY TWENTY-SIXTH CAME AND WENT, AND FERNANDO
de Leyba paced the yard of his mansion under the ragged, dismal sky and began to believe that there would be no attack
against St. Louis.

But at one o'clock in the afternoon, a rattle of musketry began down in the entrenchments, and he realized that the time of
his ultimate test had come.

De Leyba kissed his sister and daughters, ordered them to
stay within the safety of the house, and strode down across the
grounds toward the new artillery platforms, which had been
constructed on thick log pilings during the night according to
George's plans. The platforms gleamed white in the sunlight
and smelled of raw new wood, and the cannon sat upon them,
muzzles projecting between high, spoked wheels, aimed down
over the stone wall and over the heads of the defenders in the
entrenchments outside. De Leyba went up a ramp onto the platforms, was saluted by the gunners who stood sweating at attention around the weapons, and, his flesh almost twitching in

anticipation of harm, looked down over the panorama: the lush
meadow sweeping away to the north, fresh emerald green, white
clouds of powder smoke drifting away over the trenches but
constantly renewing itself as the muskets of the defenders rattled and roared. Ever the elegant horseman, Lieutenant de
Cartabona was riding back and forth behind the trenches, shouting orders and encouragement, waving his saber, controlling
with apparent ease his great white warhorse, which pranced and
reared nervously amid the din of shouting and gunfire. At the
bottom of the meadow another curtain of gunsmoke billowed in
the strong breeze, and from its midst came a shrill keening of
Indian war cries, barely audible because of the distance and the
breeze. Much of the enemy fire was coming from a row of
stone houses and garden walls at the foot of the meadow, where
the attackers seemed to have fortified themselves. It appeared to
de Leyba that most of the shooting was very ineffectual; he
could see hardly any of the enemy, only a small dark figure
now and then flitting from one sheltered place to another, and
those were amorphous and indistinct in the drifting smoke.

De Leyba turned to the nearest gunnery officer, who stood
looking nervously at him, apparently awaiting orders, and realized that he was, indeed, in charge of this defense and should
not be standing here musing as a spectator. "Find the range and
fire at will!" It truly is a magnificent vantage point, he congrat-
ulated himself, here on this platform commanding the meadow
and the town. And to the east beyond the village lay the enormous yellow curve of the river, so open to surveillance from
this point that any attempt by the enemy to flank St. Louis from
the river side would be perceived long before it could begin. A
stretch of fields and gardens to the south was being watched by
the mounted patrols, who could alert the defenders at once if the
enemy decided to shift their attack to that flank. Really, thought
de Leyba, his pride beginning to swell as the cannon emitted
their earthshaking booms beside him, I believe we have an ad-
mirable defense and a very good prospect of holding. The cannon thudded with regularity, jolting the gun platform; the
gunners and loaders cheered and shouted, and geysers of earth
and stone burst from the gardens and houses where the enemy
lay, apparently discouraging them from any attempt to storm the
hill. The Indians' cries still came faintly from below with the
distant crackle of their musketry; now and then a ball would
whack into the platform or whish overhead, nearly spent by the
distance. Twice the wind brought from the house the sound of

smashing window glass and the pitiful wailing of the helpless
refugees inside, and de Leyba prayed that Teresa and the girls
were obeying his orders and staying low, away from those windows.

Now the firing was subsiding, and there were cheers from the
entrenchments. De Leyba looked down over the meadow and
saw that the puffs of musket smoke from the enemy positions
were diminishing. Down at the entrenchments, de Cartabona
was still galloping to and fro, now waving his hat instead of his
sword, and pointing with it down a street of the village through
which numbers of the attackers could be seen withdrawing.

For the first time in months, some of the weight of hopeless-
ness began to lift off Fernando de Leyba's soul. If he actually
had repulsed this enemy, if he had been successful in his first
trial by war, surely Governor Galvez and his homeland would
not let him suffer the disgrace of financial ruin; surely his conduct here at St. Louis on this day would vindicate him and
Galvez would underwrite his credit as he had underwritten that
of his friend Don Jorge Clark. Thinking how proud his friend
would be of his conduct, just beginning to breathe deeply with
the joy of this returning hope, and the joy of realizing that his
daughters and sister might yet be saved from the atrocities of
the Indians, Fernando stood tall and stepped to the forward edge
of the platform, when he was staggered by a sharp bolt of pain
under his right jawbone and a red flash in his vision. His legs
caved in under him, and as the gunfire dropped off to a few
sporadic rounds, he lay looking up at the dirty gray clouds,
against which loomed the silhouettes of his artillery officers
who bent over him. He felt his own hot blood leaking into the
collar of his tunic, and the awareness of it made him nauseous.
He strained to keep from gagging and felt a chilly sweat spread
like dew over his face and body.

ACROSS THE RIVER AT CAHOKIA, GEORGE STOOD ON THE PARAPET
of the fort and strained to listen to the distant sounds of combat
at St. Louis. But the wind, blowing out of the southwest, carried
the noise away from his ears. Now and then, faint as the sound
of fingertips tapping on a tabletop, would come a patter of musketry, and at random intervals the thud of cannon. He paced
with his anxiety about Teresa and her brother. But he was certain that the signal guns had not been fired. And by midafternoon even those indefinite sounds of battle had subsided to
stillness. Now George lingered in an excruciating state of sus-

pense, not knowing how to interpret that quick cessation of fire. "They've either repulsed the attack mighty quick, or given up with hardly a struggle. Damnation! I wish I knew!"

"I don't know," mused Dickie, shaking his head. "That Spaniard surely didn't impress me as a lionheart."

"I know," George admitted with a look of pain and sadness. "And that does worry me."

As the afternoon wore on, the damp wind brought an occasional crackle of musket fire across the river but no cannon, and now it sounded as if it came from an area south of St. Louis. "What d'you take that to mean, George, to make a guess?"

"Guess is all I can do. Knowing the Indians, I'd have to reckon they broke off from St. Louis when they found a strong defense, and are taking out their spite by raiding the countryside. That's how they always did in Kentucky."

Soon George's scouts began bringing in deserters from the enemy force, mostly French-Canadians, and these were interrogated in the middle of the little parade ground. They confirmed the earlier report that Captain Bird was on his way from Detroit to Kentucky with nearly a thousand English and Indian troops and a train of artillery. The news agitated George visibly. "I've got to go there as quick as I can," he told his officers. "If they overrun our people at the Falls and the inner frontier, the Illinois and Fort Jefferson as well are cut off, as good as doomed." He paced the room, grim with frustrated energy, waiting for information upon which to act.

Shortly before dark it came. A Spanish courier from St. Louis had braved the infested valley to cross the river in a canoe and bring word from Governor de Leyba. George clasped his hands behind his back to keep them from shaking as the messenger's report was translated for him.

"The enemy turned back from St. Louis after about two hours," he said. "We had only three or four wounded. The enemy was more like a mob than an army. Governor de Leyba is certain they will not attack the town again. Most of them have been seen retreating up the river. But there are hundreds ravaging the plantations along the riverside. That God may have pity on those who did not take refuge in St. Louis." He crossed himself.

"Then the governor and his family are safe?"

The courier's eyes shifted when he heard the question. "Excellency," he said, "the governor asked me not to tell you, but he was struck in the neck by a splinter of wood. It is not serious; it cut no artery. He was sitting up when I saw him, propped on pillows at his headquarters."

George blinked at the sting of tears. A wave of pride for his poor tragic friend swept through him. So, he thought, thank God he was no coward after all. "And his family?"

"Quite safe. His daughters and his sister. They hover over him like nuns. No man could be better comforted."

WHEN DARKNESS FELL, FERNANDO DE LEYBA ASKED TO BE MOVED out of the hot and noisome house onto the terrace so that he might breathe fresh air. His chair was carried out by two burly soldiers, and Teresa took a seat by his side. A torch was lighted a few feet away and the soldiers retreated into the shadows. From the house came the murmur of the refugees' many voices, less panicky now but still full of woe and commiseration. The wind had diminished to a light breeze from the west, whence it brought whiffs of smoke from the burning plantations and cabins outside St. Louis. In the distant countryside here and there burned a dirty red glow, and faint on the wind would come distressing sounds of gunfire and human screams. Though St. Louis had successfully repelled its attackers, it was still only an island of security in a sea of enemies, and all its defenders remained at their posts in the entrenchments and on the parapets. Lieutenant de Cartabona had been placed in direct command of all the defenders, but was still responsible to his wounded commandant.

He came through the house now and paused at the doorway to the patio, looking at de Leyba and Teresa, whose backs were to him. De Leyba's neck was encased in a thick white bandage which reached up to his chin and earlobes. Teresa, still in her soiled smock, sat at his left side and held his hand. Beyond them, moths circled the smoky flame of the torch. De Cartabona sighed, then came forward into their view, saluting de Leyba and then bowing to Teresa, his eyes dark with that eternal hopeless devotion.

"Ah, Francisco," gurgled de Leyba. Talking and swallowing were painful to him. "Tell me what goes."

"It's quiet, Excellency," said de Cartabona. He paraded himself a bit self-consciously before Teresa, showing rather proudly the powder smudges on the legs of his tight white breeches and on his jaw, which was shiny with oil and sweat. He did look heroic, he thought, and fittingly so, having proved his courage and ability during the defense at the trenches. De Leyba smiled fondly at the young officer's posturings.

"You are a fine soldier indeed, Francisco. We owe you more than I can say. To you and Colonel Clark, I would say, goes the credit for our survival." Then he saw the twinge of anger in the young man's face and realized he should not have mentioned the American at that moment. "Take a glass of the Madeira there, sit," he coughed, "and tell me what you think."

"The men are in a growing rage," said de Cartabona. "They hear the sounds of murder out there," he swung the decanter out to indicate the countryside, "and are helpless to put a stop to it."

"*Sí*. But it would be suicidal to go out there. The Ingleses and their savages are five times our number. But Francisco, we defeated them today!" Again the saliva gurgled in his throat, and he fell silent.

"Will they attack again?" Teresa asked. She was not certain that she could endure another day of the noise and bloodiness. Her brother did not know it, but she had been forced to crawl under a table and bite down on the cloth of her sleeve today to keep from coming unhinged when the wounded were brought in. Her jaws still ached from that long, desperate clenching.

"I think not," the lieutenant said. "They failed today at Cahokia and here. Their army is disintegrating, retreating up the river. Their Canadians desert, ashamed, and surrender to us for amnesty. They were no army, but a crowd of opportunists, with neither bravery nor honor." De Cartabona contemptuously spat a mouthful of the Madeira into the bushes. "No, they'll be gone by morning, I'll wager, with the scalps of those poor innocents out there!" Teresa shuddered at the mention of scalping. "Half of our people at a time are posted on guard," the lieutenant continued. "Now, by your leave, Excellency, Señorita, I bid you good night." He saluted, bowed, and left them.

The dear fool, Teresa mused. He could still call me by my name, but never has, since George came . . .

George, she thought, with an exquisite pain in her heart, as if a velvet noose were being squeezed around her heart.

"What, Teresa?" her brother said.

"What?"

"You sigh. One who loves you must always inquire into your sighs." He squeezed her hand.

"I didn't know I had."

"It is about Jorge, I suppose."

"Yes, brother."

"And what about him? Will you share your thoughts?"

"Will this hideous warfare never stop, Nando? While it goes on I see him but a day or two in a year! He is forever leaving, to tie up some leaking corner of his ungrateful commonwealth!"

Dios! he thought. How well said!

"But," she continued, "he is my husband."

"Teresa. I must forbid you to say that until it is so in the eyes of the Church!"

"Please don't get excited. It is so in the eyes of Our Savior. How does your wound feel?"

He gripped her hand again, tiredly. "It's a small matter. Pray only that there shall be no infection."

"Do not even speak of it. You were foolish to stand up in the open. But I am proud that you were brave." She sighed. "Bravery and foolishness! Of these, men are made."

I should not let her speak with such disrespect, he thought. But she is so right! "Listen," he said after a while in a pained whisper, "do you know why I did expose myself?"

"Why?"

"I imagined him watching the battle. Don Jorge. And I wanted to be worthy of his respect. Ha! Does that amaze you? No doubt you must think me a fool among men!"

"No. I understand you. Remember, I too exposed my life for him."

De Leyba sat, thoughtful. "Yes. And finally I understand that."

They watched the moths tumbling through the torchlight. They were wrapped now in the richness of their feelings.

"Now," de Leyba whispered after a while, "I am most grateful to him for this. For this understanding. Do you know how difficult it is for a Spanish man and a Spanish woman to comprehend each other?"

"If not impossible."

"For example I have never said to you how I love you, my sister."

"Nor have I told you how I love you."

They held hands and their eyes grew dim. The crickets filled the night with their piercing sound. There was no more gunfire to be heard.

"You know, do you not," he said in a strangled voice, "that when Maria decided to die, she also decided to blame him for it."

"Yes, I think I knew that."

"It was the financial ruin. She thought it was a matter of shame."

"And she thought my love for him was a matter of shame equally."

He smiled sadly. "Anyone who did not know us, Teresa, might say he had wounded us both very badly."

"*Sí*. Or anyone who did not know *him*."

"Look at the moths," he said after a while. "They throw themselves into the flame until they singe their wings. And then they do it again. Can you guess whom they remind me of?"

"Yes, Fernando. Of you and me."

He nodded and was quiet for a while, watching them. Then he said, "Do you know, dear sister, this may prove to have been the best day I have ever lived?"

32

CAHOKIA, ILLINOIS COUNTRY
May 29, 1780

JOHN MONTGOMERY FELT THAT HE HAD RENDERED ENOUGH SERVICE, for the time being, to Virginia. He had come with Colonel Clark against Kaskaskia almost two years before; he had conducted the prisoner Rocheblave back to Virginia for him; he had exhausted himself trying to recruit a force for Clark's expedition against Detroit in 1779; he had struggled to command the Kaskaskia garrison amid the faithless and corrupt Creoles and had now in the spring of 1780 participated in the defense of the Illinois country against the British and Indians. Lieutenant Colonel Montgomery was a prominent citizen of western Virginia, and was more than ready to return to his family there. He had thus respectfully and regretfully submitted a request to be relieved of duty. One evening a few days after the battles of Cahokia and St. Louis, George summoned Montgomery up to Cahokia. They sat down on opposite sides of a table covered with maps. The young commandant looked haggard and thin;

Montgomery knew he had been kept sleepless with the chills and fever of malaria, as had half the people in the valley, and by his anxiety to get down to the Ohio and intercept Captain Bird's offensive there.

"John, you've served hard and well, and you deserve a leave. But I need you, man, for one more little task, and I've no one else can do it." George watched Montgomery's face grow wary. "Will you say yes now, John, or will you require me to persuade you over a cup o' rum?"

Montgomery drew a hard dry hand down his stubbled sharp chin with a rasping sound, squinted, prodded among his molars with his tongue tip, stood up, flung his felt hat across the room, turned in a circle with both fists clenched at his sides; then his shoulders dropped, he sat back down at the table, laid both palms on the maps, and stared at George.

"I'll take the rum," he said. "But o' course, I canno' refuse you—I mean, if it's anything less'n six more months."

"I should estimate three months at the outside, if you're swift, as you must be."

"All right, George. Provided it don't involve Frenchies an' Creoles."

"It does precisely that, John. Sorry."

"Damn yer eyes! You could a said so 'fore I agreed!"

George smiled and tilted his head, and set the cup of liquor on the table before Montgomery.

"As you well know, John, ever since I first treated with the savages at this very place in '78, I've been warning 'em to keep the peace with us or suffer the consequences."

"Aye."

"I'm obliged to stand by that. The scoundrels hired out to the British once again and fell on this place. When we stopped 'em here, they crossed to St. Louis and there they were stopped again. Whereupon they infested the countryside, slaughtered a score of innocent Spaniards, and carried off maybe seventy others. Now they've retreated up the Illinois River, leaving their trail littered with the murdered and scalped bodies o' them as couldn't make the march. You see our duty is plain, John. If we let this go unpunished, the boasts of the Big Knives will be meaningless to 'em, and we're doomed from this day on." He paused, frowning down at a sketch of Illinois river courses, then looked up and exclaimed:

"John, by my life, I'm jealous of our reputation! I've strutted and bluffed and cracked heads, and waded to my neck in ice water to maintain it!"

Montgomery's scalp tingled at the crackling tone of voice and the hard blue eyes. He took his cup from his lips and sat up straighter.

George continued: "Since I cannot be on two frontiers at the same time, I must ask you to chase these murderers up the Illinois and punish 'em, while I try to head off Bird in Kentucky. So, I must direct you to pursue 'em, plumb up to Lake Michigan and the Rock River if you must, strike their towns, and distress 'em however you may. They'll be weak, probably having just disbanded by the time you get there. Do it, John. They must learn we'll retaliate whenever they join the British emissaries!"

Montgomery looked up from the map, where he had been following George's finger up the great, bent Illinois River, almost to the Indian place called Milwaukee on the shore of the big lake. "You keep saying *I'm* to go all the way up yonder an' give 'em a drubbin'. Now, I'm no mean fightin' man, but I hope you don't mean to send me up there alone t'do all that."

George grinned. "I wish I could give a regiment o' Virginians t' help you. But as you know, I don't even have one o' my own. You take this company of ours, and for th' rest, French and Spaniards."

Montgomery groaned and hid behind his forearm in mock horror. George laughed.

"Nay, listen, John. They're rabid to avenge the massacre around St. Louis. Governor de Leyba offers near two hundred Spaniards, fighting mad. Cahokia can give you enough to bring your roll up to three-fifty or four hundred. I'll need only eight or ten for my escort back down to Fort Jefferson; the rest are yours."

Montgomery digested that. "Then Frenchies and Spaniards it is." He leaned forward over the map, then cocked his head and squinted at George. "And pray tell, who's a-goin' to go with you against Bird's army?"

"I'll pick up what Fort Jefferson can spare, on my way. The rest I'll raise in the settlements, if they haven't gathered already. Maybe four, maybe six hundred. I don't know what sort o' men they'll be—certainly not like our old regiment, from what I've seen o' the newcomers. But they'll be after savin' their own scalps, and that is a spur."

On the fourth of June, George set out in a swift boat for the mouth of the Ohio with a small escort of scouts and riflemen.

Once out on the stream of the Mississippi, he could gaze astern and see diminishing slowly the hazy blue bluffs and tiny distant buildings of St. Louis, once again feeling that intangible web of his attachment to Teresa stretching, slowly stretching, to the measure of oars and the murmur of the great river.

And when the town had dwindled too far to see, he kept gazing at the low, blue line of the bluff. When it receded from sight behind a bend, he released a bittersweet sigh and turned to face forward.

"Lay on, boys. Let's see if we can make Fort Jefferson by tomorrow evening."

They looked at each other, blinked in disbelief, and did lay on.

TWO DAYS LATER, FERNANDO DE LEYBA WAS HELPED ASTRIDE HIS horse and rode down past the fortifications and through the shell-battered town of St. Louis to the wharf, and there watched his armed Spanish volunteers load themselves and their munitions on board the fleet of boats for their mission of revenge up the Illinois River. They looked grim, determined. He was proud of them and wished he could go with them. But it was all he could do to sit his horse and keep his head up. The pain in his throat felt enormous and corrupt, and he was dizzy with fever. An armed boat with French, Spanish, and Virginian flags in the bow bumped the wharf nearby, and Colonel Montgomery of the Americans debarked, came before de Leyba, and saluted.

"Compliments to your Excellency and your family from Colonel Clark, and from myself."

"Don Jorge is well?"

"At Fort Jefferson by now, no doubt." He turned and perused the embarkation, then back to de Leyba. "I wish you could go with us, Gov'nor. George tells me y'r quite an officer."

De Leyba's eyes misted. He smiled and braced himself with both hands on the pommel of his saddle. "From him, that is something! I too am sorry, Colonel Montgomery. But this . . ." He indicated the yellowing bandage around his neck which, though Teresa had changed it for this occasion, already enveloped him in a smell of putrefaction.

"I sh'll have your people back here in eight or ten weeks, God willing," said Montgomery, looking at the grimacing gray face with its swollen red eyelids and sheen of sweat. Montgomery tried to hide his pity.

Short of a miracle, he thought, this poor dandy is seeing 'em
for the last time.

CAPTAIN HENRY BIRD, ENCAMPED NEAR THE SHAWNEE TOWN OF
Chillicothe on June third, sat in his bell tent and wrote to his
commandant, Major Arent de Peyster, who was Henry Hamilton's successor at Detroit:

> Colonel Clark is said to be at Fort Jefferson & will not be
> able to join the Rebels assembling at the Falls before the
> 15th of this month. He has certainly 200 soldiers with him.
> I could wish to proceed immediately to the Falls.
>
> It is possible, before Colonel Clark's arrival, they may
> raise 800 men, probable they may raise 600, certain they can
> raise 400. It is possible we may beat 800, probable we can
> beat 600, certain we can beat 400. Colonel Clark's arrival
> will add considerably to their numbers, and to their confi-
> dence; therefore the Rebels should be attacked before his ar-
> rival. Now it is possible he may return by the 14th, probable
> by the 22nd, certain by the first of July. Tho' possible for us
> to get to the Falls by the 10th of this month, certain by the
> 14th.
>
> The Indians have their full spirits, the ammunition, and
> everything plenty, and in the state we could wish it. After
> taking the Falls, the country on our return will be submissive
> and in a manner subdued; but if we attacked the nearer forts,
> in Fayette county, first as we advanced, we would have a
> continual desertion of Indians, our ammunition expended,
> and our difficulties would increase as we advanced, and Col-
> onel Clark would be at the Falls, with his people collected to
> fight us.
>
> I have another reason for attacking the Falls: Should we
> succeed, we can ambuscade Mr. Clark as he returns.
>
> If this plan is not followed, it will be owing to the Indians,
> who may adopt others.
>
> I am Dear Sir Yr most humble and Obt Servant,

> H. BIRD

For the truth is, thought the handsome, graceful-looking captain, putting down his quill and gazing out the tent door into the
crowded, dusty, sunlit glade, though we purport to be in command, seven hundred Shawnees really can hardly be controlled.

* * *

AT FORT JEFFERSON ON THE MORNING OF JUNE TENTH, SOLDIERS
and workmen loading munitions and rolling cannon in the parade ground paused in their work and watched in astonishment
as three tall, muscular, bare-chested Indians in leggings, feathers, breechclouts, and war paint, emerged from the doorway of
Colonel Clark's quarters with Captain John Slaughter and strode
across the sunny enclosure toward the fort's gate.

Their surprise turned to incredulity as the three savages
passed near them with their long rifles cradled in their arms; the
Indian at the head of the trio had a strange, ruddy coloration,
and on his chest, where a small, round, circular silver medallion
hung by a thong, golden chest hair caught the sunlight.

"By the eternal!" exclaimed one of the soldiers, a veteran of
the original Illinois regiment, pointing, "That'n's Cunnel Clark
or I don't know my own name!"

"Damn me if it ain't," breathed another, "an' them two's Major Harlan an' Captain Consola!"

The three "braves" went out through the gate with the American captain and stood for a moment with him, looking eastward
over the stump-dotted clearing and fields of waist-high, green
young corn, toward an infinity of dark-green treetops.

"Let's pray," smiled the red-haired one, "that we won't be so
easily recognized by the Indians 'twixt here and the Falls."

"Then better pray, George, you don't get that close to any of
'em," said Captain Slaughter. "You're the only Indian I ever
seen with redder hair than skin. You sure this ain't a folly? I'd
feel a heap safer if you'd an armed company around you."

"I know that, but there's not time, and we'd be too easily discovered. Besides, I rather relish traveling light for a change.
Now, see that you have that convoy on the way up the Ohio by
tomorrow. God and our shanks willing, we'll have a defense organized and waiting by the time you sail up." He gave the captain a handshake and a hard squeeze on the shoulder, then
turned to the two other disguised officers who, with their
straight black hair and craggy, weathered features, might have
had little trouble passing for Indians. "Now, my chieftains,
d'you feel fit for a three-hundred-mile run through yon pristine
forest?"

"We'd best start now afore I have time to think on't," grinned
Major Harlan.

George turned back to the fort and saluted the men who had
stopped working and stood along the parapets and the road

down to the boats at the water's edge looking at him. "See y'at the Falls, boys!" he yelled, then turned and led his companions at a long-legged lope down through the clearing and into the shadowy green wilderness, the huzzahs and farewells of the garrison soon being blotted up by the dank green curtain of foliage that closed behind them.

They sped single file among the gigantic hardwoods, heavy rifles now at their right sides, now at their left. They ran with the Indian stride, moccasin toes pointed slightly inward, both to avoid entanglement in roots and to leave no obvious whitemen's spoor. Within an hour they were breathing like horses, deep, slumping breaths in rhythm with their softly thudding feet, ignoring the pain, their sweat-stung eyes darting constantly among the columnar tree trunks ahead, with that woodsman's determination always to see an Indian first.

The forest floor was moist and springy, free of almost all undergrowth except shade-dwelling fern, mayapple, and the minute wildflowers of the deep woods. The sun was evident in this green gloom only as an occasional spark of light on the eye when the runners would pass through some thin sunbeam that penetrated the lofty canopy of leaves. Musty black carcasses of giant oaks and maples lay decaying among the ferns, flecked with shelf fungi and lime-green mosses. Orioles, tanagers, cardinals, buntings darted away from their approach, shooting through the woods like flakes of red and indigo. So swiftly and quietly the runners came on that they surprised several deer where they stood; George once had to leap to clear the back of a fawn which had spraddled in terror in his path, too petrified to flee.

Squirrels swarmed up trees; opossums peered up myopically, then blundered away among the ferns; once a black bear and its cub, surprised, scampered behind a hollow-beech honey tree and peered curiously out at the passing runners. George smiled with joy at these sights, and his mind slipped back to those carefree days, seven and eight years before, when he had roamed the inner frontiers where no white man had ever trodden before, then as now surprising animals who didn't know what to make of him.

Miles, leagues unwound backward under their padding feet. The little footrace medallion jounced upon his chest with every step, and he thought now of Teresa, with the other medallion on a chain around her neck, lying in the musky valley between those apple-firm little breasts. He had learned long ago that the burning agony of long-distance running could be blanked out if the runner allowed his mind to go elsewhere. In the runner's wakeful trance, then, he led Harlan and Consola relentlessly eastward until, on the slope of a gully, Harlan fell to the ground and lay face down in the humus, sucking breath with a rasping sound, his legs twitching. A probing vertical finger of sunlight told the time as noon, and the three rested near a trickling mossy spring to eat strips of jerky and starchy crumbs of parched corn, which they chased down with a nutritious brew made by mixing a powder of corn flour and maple sugar with the crystal spring water. Now that they had stopped, they were beset by the nettlesome bites of huge black-and-tan deerflies, the nasal drone and toxic nips of mosquitoes. They anointed their sweating shoulders and backs with more bear grease to fend off these annoyances, looked each other over for wood ticks, then rose on twitching limbs to resume their progress. Shunning the bank of the Ohio, which they were sure would be heavily patrolled by Indians, they were heading eastward over untracked ground toward the Tennessee River—which they would have to contrive a means to cross—then some twenty miles farther on, they would have to cross the great Cumberland River. The mouths of both of these rivers would be watched, George was sure, and he intended to cross them far upstream from their junctures with the Ohio.

They sped onward through that first afternoon, through that deep green humid gloomy silence, hearts slamming, lungs burning. Their perceptions grew unreal with their increasing exhaustion, and at times it seemed to George that they were progressing across the bottom of some fantastic green sea. They paced on until the last flickering peeps of sunlight turned red-gold and winked out. Then it was less than an hour before the foliage grew black and the terrain too dim to travel.

Reconnoitering for a few minutes in the darkening woods, they found no sight or sound of Indians, discovered a trickling spring in a steep-sided ravine, and decided to risk a small fire, as the place was so sheltered.

Having refreshed their burning skin with the chilly spring water, they heated strips of jerky over the fire to create the illusion of having a hot meal. They chewed strenuously on the smoky fibers, munched parched corn, chased it down with water, then sat, embracing their knees, gazing into the licking yellow flames and orange coals and feeling their stomachs transform the food into new vigor for their spent limbs. George began to smile as he studied the scene: the mossy stone from which issued the spring; the ferns and the great twisted root-knees and fissured trunks of the venerable trees all softly illuminated by the firelight; the encircling blackness with its choruses of night-creature sounds probably unchanged for eons; his companions with their berry-stained skin and sweat-streaked war paint, bear-claw necklaces, fringed breechclouts, and beadwork moccasins, gazing mesmerized into the campfire. Major Harlan yawned, the firelight shining into his great cave of a mouth with its bad teeth like stalactites and stalagmites, then caught George gazing at him with that half smile on his lips.

"You seem amused, sir."

"Aye, Major. Reckon I am, thinking about things in general." He shook his head and gazed at the flames another moment, still smiling. "As a boy I had the scriptures drummed into my head at home. Then a hard Scot tutor filled me with history, and geography, mathematics, and the ancient tongues. Mr. Mason then imbued me with moral precepts and philosophy, and I learned to minuet at the hands of pink misses of the Tidewater aristocracy ..." Harlan and Lieutenant Consola were listening blank-faced to this unexpected recitation. "... and now," he concluded, indicating with a sweep of his hands their primitive little enclave, "look how far all that civilizing has brought me!"

THEY WERE OFF THE NEXT MORNING AS SOON AS THE WOODS WERE light enough to see their way in. Their feet and muscles protested with stiffness and pain for the first few miles, until it was all worked out by the relentless moving. They ate their noon meal on the run, following the easterly tributaries toward the Tennessee River.

They reached the Tennessee shortly before sundown. They estimated that they had made sixty or seventy miles in their first two days. They scouted the wooded banks of the deep stream, finding evidence of recent Indian landings but seeing no Indians. As evening fell, they pitted their reluctant muscles against the task of binding two logs together with grapevines to make a raft. They slept beside it on mossy ground, too exhausted to try an evening crossing.

They awoke before dawn, to a sensual chaos of itchy mosquito bumps, bleeding fly bites, dewy gooseflesh, and aching joints, the watery murmuring and gulping of the Tennessee a few feet away immediately reminding them of their hazardous first duty, the crossing. In the semi-darkness they dragged the heavy makeshift raft down to the river's slippery edge and launched it, wading it up to their waists in flowing water which was, fortunately, warmer than the morning air. The ooze of the river bottom dragged at their moccasins as they strapped their precious rifles, food, bullet pouches, and powder horns atop the raft with leather thrums cut from the fringe of their leggings. They then covered the cargo with brush from the shore. As gray light began dissolving the darkness, they saw that a mist hovered over the river surface, obscuring everything more than ten feet away. Major Harlan and Lieutenant Consola worked grimly, trying to hide the dread in their faces. Neither of them could swim, and the narrow raft was too small for both men and baggage to ride upon.

"Very well now, gents," George whispered, bracing his legs against the pressing current. "I don't have to tell you to hang on tight. Keep your heads low. Kick, but kick deep and don't splash the surface, if you please."

"We know how, sir," Harlan whispered back, almost testy in his uneasiness. "God knows we've snuck acrost many a river since we met you."

George grinned. "Then get hold, and shove off!"

The mucky bottom released its grip on their feet; they felt themselves borne away into the liquid flow; the shore dissolved from sight behind them. George commenced making powerful frog kicks under the water, and felt that he must be doing all the work while the other two hung on for their lives. "Give me some power, boys, or we'll be in th' Ohio 'fore we make the other shore!" Soon their surging breathing told him they were at work.

It was a delicate balancing act in the disorienting mist. Consola tended to pull down hard on his side with each kick and George had to strain to keep the narrow conveyance from rolling over several times. Being rudder as well as propeller, George had no reference for navigation but the faint sense of current on his right side. He was aware of the invisible and unknowable depth below him, and he was sure that the others were doubly conscious of it. A fragment of cut bough slipped off the raft and drifted downstream; he hoped no Indian patrol down near the mouth would find it and paddle up to investigate.

A low black shape materialized out of the mist at that moment, heading straight at the raft. "Consola! Look right!" George hissed, just as the object, a splintery-ended drift log, bumped the front of the raft and began to swing around, as if to crunch Consola's head between itself and the raft. George thrust the aft end of the raft downstream with a powerful kick of his legs, and the log swung off and dissolved in the mist downstream. Consola, eyes wide in his red-stained face, edged forward hand over hand to check the condition of the forward end of the raft.

"Busted a vine," he whispered back. "Pray it'll hold t' shore."

They prayed, and it did. After half an hour in the current, they saw through the thinning fog the dark foliage of the east bank looming a few yards ahead, then their feet found the squishy bottom.

They unloaded the raft, slung on their gear, and put dry powder in their rifles' flash pans. While Major Harlan was checking his flintlock, George waded back into the river, drawing his long skinning knife to cut the grapevines and dissassemble their telltale raft.

As he slashed at the tough vines, something slithered suddenly under his hands. He recoiled and grasped, the spade-shaped head of a huge water moccasin suddenly jabbing the air where his hand had been. The glistening serpent cocked its head for a second strike, and George stared in horror at the wide, white maw of its mouth, his hunting knife at the ready, wondering if he could be quick enough to decapitate it without being pierced by the venomous fangs.

But suddenly the reptile's head disintegrated with a cracking roar, bits of it spattering on the river. The mottled body convulsed and fell off the raft. George, with a metallic taste in his mouth and his heart slamming at his ribs, looked up at the cloud of gunsmoke billowing away from Harlan's rifle. The report's echo was repeating itself between the riverbanks.

George's eyes explained everything to Harlan. Gratitude and reproach.

"Sorry," said the major, reloading. "Wa'n't no time t' think."

George finished cutting the vines and floundered ashore. He picked up his rifle, gripped Harlan on the shoulder, meanwhile listening like a wild animal, his long nose pointing as he turned this way and that. "Listen," he breathed. From downstream very nearby came guttural voices, then faint splashing sounds, either of wading or paddles. George pointed violently up the riverbank into the forest and, brushing over their trail in the slippery bank as well as he could, disappeared after Harlan and Consola into the woods.

He overtook them and led them at a swift, silent run through the forest, their water-filled moccasins squishing and slapping. Coming to the bank of a small tributary creek, he leaped into it. The others followed him, knee-deep, as he went downstream a hundred feet, tracked the other bank there, then waded backward into the stream again and returned eastward against the current.

They flitted up the stream a mile, emerged in a grove of hickories and plunged on at full tilt for another mile before drawing up to a halt, chests heaving, to listen for sounds of pursuit. There was nothing. Birdcalls, which had fallen still at their frantic approach, resumed all about.

Their wind recovered, they took up their less strenuous woodman's lope. Throughout the morning they made their way eastward in a gradual climb out of the valley of the Tennessee, then trotted through forests and lush, flowery meadows through a gentle decline into the Cumberland Valley. They reached the Cumberland with two hours of daylight to spare, scouted quickly along the banks for Indian camps, found none, made another bound-log raft, and on the fourth morning of their trek crossed that river under cover of a steady rainstorm. Now the two major river crossings were behind them, and the greater part of their distance lay before them: two hundred more miles through the rolling, untracked Kentucky countryside on a northeasterly course. The next major river to cross would be the Green, about a hundred miles ahead. Drawing as much nourishment as they could from every scrap of jerky and crumb of corn, supplementing these now and then with berries and edible weeds and roots, they steeled themselves against the burning agony of fatigue and pushed on.

33

June 14, 1780

CAPTAIN BIRD ARGUED WITH HIS INDIAN CHIEFTAINS, THEN pleaded with them, then gave up in disgust. He sat back in his tent on the bank of the Ohio, a hundred miles above the Falls which were to have been his army's first target, and resolved to let the Indians make their plans without him.

The Indians had received a report two days earlier that George Rogers Clark was already at the Falls of the Ohio, and flatly refused to go there. Henry Bird was certain that the report was erroneous, that Clark could not possibly have gotten there by the twelfth, the day of the report. Now it was the fourteenth. The Indians had vented the hot air of their blustery oratory for two days in council on this riverbank, wasting time, weakening their resolve, and in general depressing their purported commander a great deal. It was becoming apparent that they would prefer to make a foray instead against two populous but ill-defended settlements on the Licking River, Ruddle's and Martin's Stations, which were inhabited primarily by placid and industrious Pennsylvania Germans. Toward the close of the second day of their squabbling, the chiefs announced to Bird that they had agreed to go against the Licking River settlements instead of the Falls, and were ready for Captain Bird's soldiers and artillery to lead them there.

"So you choose not to strike at the Falls, even though it would be a more important strategic move?" Bird said, just as sarcastically as he dared.

"What is the strategy of the Englishmen?" retorted the Indians' spokesman. "On Licking River many Americans grow crops and drive game out of the sacred hunting grounds of Cantuc-kee. To stop this is our strategy."

Bird turned his eyes to the three white men who had joined

his force with the Shawnees: Simon, James, and George Girty.
Simon, short, black-haired, and black-eyed, seemed to be the
most influential of them, and was, for that matter, perhaps the
best interpreter and the most influential white man among
the Shawnees. The Girty brothers had been adopted captives of
the Indians since boyhood but, unlike many such adoptees, they
would not remain submerged in the tribes and were constantly
appearing on the margins of conflict, goading and scheming. All
along the course of this expedition, Bird knew, they had kept
exhorting the Indians to avenge the death of Chief Black Fish.

"Mr. Girty," said Bird, "tell these people of yours that we are
attacking the settlements as soldiers, not as a vengeful mob. We
will force surrender, take prisoners back to Detroit, and not
harm women and children. I must have them understand that
this is a British military operation, and I will not lend my men
and artillery to it except under those terms."

Simon Girty's eyes looked straight into Bird's, but it was as
if reptilian eyelids had suddenly veiled them.

"I'll tell 'em," he replied, then went away without telling
them.

WHEN GEORGE ROGERS CLARK AND HIS TWO COMPANIONS AR-
rived at the Falls, identified themselves as white men and were
admitted, they were astonished to see that the settlement was
manned by scarcely more than its basic garrison. "Where in
blazes are the people who are supposed to be gathering here to
meet Bird's army?" he raged.

The explanation was that much of the regional population
was at Harrodsburg by the Kentucky River, milling about the
newly opened land office where entries were being made on a
million and a half acres of choice new Kentucky land. "They're
in a fever about it, sir," said an officer of the garrison. "A call
to arms is the last thing in their minds."

Learning also that Captain Bird's army had veered away from
the Falls into the interior, George quickly outfitted himself in
his old uniform, formed an escort, and set off on horseback for
Harrodsburg, rankling with indignation over the greed and irre-
sponsibility of these new immigrants.

Galloping into Harrodsburg at midmorning with his troop of
old Illinois veterans, George was astonished at the appearance
of boom-town disorder. A motley horde of men, in shabby velvet, homespun, Continental uniform remnants, and even some
scarcely clad at all, milled around in the compound, lounged at

the gates, whooping, buzzing, trading pieces of paper. Many of them were roaring drunk, even though the sun was still over the eastern hills, blazing off the surface of the Kentucky River. The main part of this scruffy mob was concentrated around the land office. They scattered and stumbled out of the way as he rode among them to James Harrod's house. Some in the crowd recognized him and shouted his name as he rode through, and for a moment his arrival diverted the attention of the land-office crowd. Then they turned back to their business.

Colonel Harrod, grown stockier in his prosperity and beginning to turn gray at his side-whiskers, met George with a mixture of joy and embarrassment.

"You do know that Henry Bird's somewhere within a hundred miles o' this place, Jim."

"That I do."

"Then why isn't that crowd out there under arms, man? You're the county lieutenant!"

"They won't serve," Harrod said, his eyes falling.

"*Won't* serve?" George exploded.

"They say they won't defend a country where they have no land yet. They . . . they tell me your soldiers are paid to defend the state; let *you* do it . . ."

George's fist pounded a cloud of dust out of Harrod's desk. "Aye, by God, they are right about that! *I'm* the one that'll do it! But my men are strung out everywhere from here to the Missipp', hanging on by their toenails to this empire they've won! So now, Jim Harrod, I need more men to keep this Kentucky o' yours together, and that rabble out there . . ." he flung his arm in the direction of the land office, "th . . . they are going to be a good part of it, if I have to shut down that land office to get their attention!"

"You really don't have the authority to do . . ."

"Damn having the authority! I've had to make my own authority for two bloody mean years now and I'm an old hand at it. Come on. We're going to walk over their right now."

Harrod hesitantly got up and followed, not meeting the eyes of his own men or George's officers as they filed out of the house.

George barged into the land office, followed by a cheer from some of the old-timers, shouldering aside several dickering newcomers who were between him and the land register. This official, a large, rangy, cold-eyed man with gray hair and bored-looking eyes, looked up from his table of deeds and papers to identify the cause of the commotion. He saw the red-haired colonel standing there glowering down on him.

"Yes?" he said.

"I'm Clark. I've come to request in the public's safety that you suspend the business in this place!"

"Ah, so you are Colonel Clark. Honored, sir. But I can scarcely close. There are claims in progress . . ."

George's eyes narrowed. "I advise you to reconsider, mister, real quick."

The hubbub in the room fell still as judges, claimants, and brokers became aware that something was happening at this table.

The register bowed his head slightly, smiled with his lips only, looking at George with annoyance, and shrugged. "I'm sorry, Colonel."

"You're saying no, I take it? Very well, then if you can't suspend this business, *I can*!" Drawing his sword, he used it swiftly to sweep the documents off the table onto the floor. The register cringed before the blade, which George then immediately sheathed, turning to the men who crowded about.

"This court is closed," he bellowed. "There'll not be one deed signed while Kentucky is endangered. Out, all of you, out! Get into that yard there and hear me!"

He herded them all out of the building and soon stood on the stoop of the building, as if on a dais, glowering over his unsettled audience. They had come to the land office this morning preoccupied with claims, rights, profits, and grudges, all their myriad self-concerns, but now everybody in Harrodsburg, those who had known him for years and those seeing him for the first time, were attentive to the same thing: the urgent and severe force of his presence.

"Now hear me!" he shouted, sweeping a pointed finger over the crowd. "This land office for this moment is nothing. You may have deeds in your pockets and no scalps on your skulls this very week, unless you put aside your private greed and behave like principled men! Open your eyes, damn you! Or you'll have nought but a title to your own burial plot. But the Shawnees won't even respect that! Rather they'll leave you lie to stink and feed the buzzards!

"Now, listen. I give you no choice: you will stand and fight for this place. And I do mean *no choice*! I've put pickets on the Wilderness Road to turn back any craven who tries to flee out of Kentucky. Look about you! I have men here who marched with me and *won* this land you're dickerin' over. They're right among you now—d'you know the man at your shoulder, eh?—and they have my order to stop any able-bodied man from leaving! I tell you, there's honor in fighting alongside those boys, and a lot to learn. If you refuse to serve, then, by your leave—or *without* it—we'll at least put your horses in the service and take your guns and ammunition to put in the hands of braver boys—ten-year-olds, maybe, who haven't yet learned to put avarice over honor!"

He paused and studied the crowd. Many looked sullen, some scared; here and there in the mob stood lean men with familiar faces, with hunters' eyes and vulpine grins, old campaigners leaning on their rifles, delighted with what was happening here.

"I reckon I've made my intentions plain," George continued. "Anyone too dense to understand what I say would be of little use to this country. As of now, this land office is a recruiting office . . ."

Suddenly the crowd's attention was distracted by hair-raising sounds coming from the fort gate behind them: women wailing, and the throaty, tearing, sobbing cries of some tormented creature.

The women led him in through the gate: a straw-haired boy of fifteen or sixteen, the front of his homespun clothing spattered with blood and smudged with mud and soot. His scraped, bruised face was distorted beyond recognition by agony, his nose drained into his lips, his lips onto his chin. The crowd parted as the women led him to Colonel Clark, supporting him by his arms as his legs wobbled and threatened to buckle.

The boy slid to the ground before George, and sat there snuffling and gagging, trying to talk but totally incoherent. But the women, all trying to talk at once, told what the boy had said to them, and it sent a shock through the crowd:

"He run all the way here! Ruddell's Station was massacred! Shawnees and Redcoats by the hundreds! O, Gawd, Gawd! He's the only one got away, the rest is took! His whole family! Almighty help us!"

The boy, who had fallen apart upon reaching the safety of Harrodsburg, was soon calmed enough to sit on a bench in the land office and relate what had happened.

"Thursday," he whimpered. "A guard called down from the wall . . . We looked out . . . They was hundreds, hundreds out there . . . They shot a cannon at us . . . It busted open a blockhouse. Mr. Ruddell he waved a white flag . . . Went out to talk

to three redcoats on horses . . . They said surrender to King
George and the womenfolk and chillun could come here safe
. . . Mr. Ruddell he says yes . . .

"But when the gates was open, the Indians run in yellin' . . .
They kilt ladies an' babies . . . with their tommyhawks . . .
sculped 'em. Miz Ruddell had her boy baby . . . Indian grabbed
'im an' thrown 'im in a fire . . . She jumped for to save 'im, an'
they kilt 'er and thrown 'er on th' fire too . . . They sculped Mr.
Ruddell when he run to help. . . .

"They kilt maybe twenty 'fore the British officer could stop
'em . . . He called 'em cowards. Made 'em promise they
wouldn't murder at Martin's Station . . . Lines us all up to
march . . . But them too sick or old or little to walk was . . . was
just kilt standin' there an' sculped an' left to rot . . ."

The men in the office listened and looked at each other and
their faces were white and their mouths bitten narrow. "What
else?" George coaxed. "What about Martin's Station?"

"The . . . the British officer told the Indians to promise no
murderin' at Martin's or he wouldn't use his cannon for 'em.
He made 'em promise to give him the prisoners to take to
'Troit, he said. So they said yes . . . We was all loaded with all
we could carry, an' went over to Martin's. They gave up with
no fight. Indians killed all the cattle an 'swup th' horses . . . We
walk an' walk. Anyone stumbles gets their head split. They was
goin' back t'ward th' big river. I see a holler sycamore and see
no one's lookin' an' slip in till they all gone past. Then I lit out
fer here . . ." His face went aghast again and now that the duty
of reporting was done, he began blubbering. George stroked the
boy's hair and reviewed the images the boy's words had created. His eyes smoldered. He thought of Captain Bird, his newest enemy, who was perhaps a principled man who had bent his
principles a long way and realized too late the inhumanity of
employing savages. It reminded him of Henry Hamilton. He
shall have to live with it—if he lives, George thought.

A CLOUD OF GLIDING BUZZARDS SHOWED THEM WHERE RUDDLE'S
Station was before they rounded a hill and saw the splintered
blockhouse standing above the trees.

They rode into the compound and were assailed by the stench
of rotting flesh. Bodies, scalped and crusted with brown dried
blood, lay about in all attitudes, swollen in the sunlight, some
having burst, many already partly flayed and picked by the
hunchbacked scavenger birds, which raised their messy beaks,

shook their wattles, and lumbered into flight as the horsemen
rode among them swinging at them with swords and rifles.
Black flies by the thousands droned and swarmed through the
enclosure. Every foot of ground was covered with trash: bits of
paper, broken crockery, feathers, smashed furniture, scraps of
cloth, tools, corn husks, skeins of wool and flax, smashed drinking gourds, pewter implements, split trunks, a homemade doll
covered with dried blood lying beside a scalped child; it was as
if the lives of the four hundred inhabitants had been shaken up
in a huge box and dumped within the palisade.

More buzzards and more mutilated bodies—an old woman
with her dugs sliced off, a man with a bandage on his leg and
his teeth smashed in, a small boy with his genitals sliced off and
the wound alive with black flies—marked the road to Martin's
Station five miles away. There were fewer bodies at Martin's,
where the burned shell of the fort still smoldered.

After the viewing of those ruins, there was no more difficulty
raising an army.

34

OHIO VALLEY
July 25, 1780

THEY ASSEMBLED LATE IN JULY AT THE MOUTH OF THE LICKING
River: a thousand mounted and armed men, in response to Colonel Clark's call to arms. It was three times as large an army as
he had ever been able to gather when he had needed numbers
to march against Detroit. This time they could see the immediate result of their fighting: revenge. They left their settlements
defended only by their sons and wives and old men, left their
crops standing in the fields, hoping to massacre the Shawnees at
Chillicothe and Piqua and get back in time to harvest.

Some of the best leaders and Indian fighters in the territory
arrived at the great camp. Daniel Boone came, quiet-talking,
catlike, with eyes that seemed to see for miles. Levi Todd and

William McAfee came. Simon Butler was there; he was appointed a captain and put in charge of all scouts and spies. Five companies were formed, a colonel in charge of each company: Benjamin Logan, John Floyd, James Harrod, George Slaughter, and Benjamin Linn. This time the settlers of the Kentucky frontier had a brass cannon to use against the Indians. A brass cannon captured two years earlier at Kaskaskia had been brought up the Ohio by the convoy from Fort Jefferson.

The training period was brief but rigorous. Among the transients drafted at the land office were many accomplished scoundrels and malingerers who had to be thrashed to learn that Colonel Clark had no tolerance for insubordination or wheeling and dealing. Some saw the light while sitting chained to a post in the middle of the camp. The veterans who had served with him in previous campaigns found Clark just as energetic, efficient, and severe as ever, but there was something missing now: he seldom joked and seldom laughed. This expedition, they sensed, was somehow different to him from the others.

On the evening of August first, with the army ready and the crossing of the Ohio scheduled for the next morning, George left his tent and strolled in the late sunlight to the perimeter of the camp, hands behind his back, barely nodding in response to the greetings his troops uttered as he passed among their cookfires. He walked out of the camp and went up a sloping meadow to a place where a dozen freshly cut wood crosses stuck up above the brown earth of fresh graves. Henry Bird and his Indians and their four hundred captives from the raids on Martin's and Ruddle's Station had crossed the river here a few weeks earlier on their return to Detroit, and for various unknown reasons a number of the captives had been killed instead of ferried across. The first Americans arriving here for the rendezvous had found their corpses lying about in the grass and reeds, scalped, putrefying, half devoured by animals and insects, and had buried them on this pleasant meadow overlooking the site of their final horror. George walked among the nameless graves, then stopped to gaze down over the big encampment at the river mouth. Hearing a cough, he turned suddenly and saw a familiar figure sitting with his back to a tree at the top of the meadow, looking at him. He walked over to the giant woodsman, and knelt beside him, and they looked at the long shadows.

"You ready for tomorrow, Simon?"

"I am."

"You'll remember to keep your advance scouts moving ten or twenty miles ahead of the army."

"Aye."

They sat quietly for a few more minutes. This was one of the characteristics George always had admired about Simon Butler. He never seemed to feel obliged to talk just to be talking. But now Simon drawled:

"It may be none o' my concern, but I'd say as how they's something gnawin' you away down in your vitals."

"Yes, you'd be right to say that, Si."

"I care what it is."

Though accustomed to keeping his own counsel, George yearned to say what was on his mind; maybe it would lift off some of his melancholy.

"Well, y'see, Simon, I think there are better things we could be doing with this size an army than raiding Shawnee towns for revenge."

"You mean Detroit."

"Detroit. Two years now I've been drawn up at the end of my tether, just a few companies shy of going there. Meantime, all this going back and forth for vengeance, Shawnees against Kentucky, Kentuckians against Shawnees, is never going to end as long as the British sit up there selling their guns and gew-gaws for scalps. In a week there'll be more blood spilt, ours and theirs, but it'll have to be done all over again in another season, then another. But after Ruddle's and Martin's, why, these people have to get even, and so I guess I'm their man as usual." He cleared his throat and sighed. There! he'd said it, and Simon, who knew Detroit's condition, was nodding in agreement. But now George was wishing he'd kept as circumspect as usual about his feelings. He knew the reason for his discontent was that fate had taken the initiative out of his hands, but it could do no good for a commandant to express his doubts this way to a subordinate. "Anyhow," he said briskly, shifting his weight and rubbing his hands briskly, "we'll give 'em a good enough drubbing to last a season, eh?" Then he glanced aside at Simon's massive, leonine head, his imperturbable eyes, and changed the subject. "Tell me, if you care to, this yarn I've heard about you changing your name to Kenton."

The big youth sat wrapped in thought, smiling. Then he said, softly: "Simple. Simple. Kenton's my true name. Back in '71, just sixteen, I was, I whup a man. Over a girl. Lost my head an' pounded 'im long after he was out. When I calmed down I lis-

tened for his heart; thought 'e was dead. Lit out, never went
home. Changed my name to Butler, after a man who took me
in. Kept to m'self, as you know. Thought a lot. Coulda gone
back and turned myself in, but instead come to th' frontier an'
stayed Simon Butler. Hope you won't think less of me for
runnin' away, but I didn't want t' hang; I'd whup 'im in fair
fight, an' didn't think myself no murderer, but I knowed they
would."

"All those years an alias! And famous by it, too. But why are
you Kenton again?"

"Well, here's th' funny part on't," Kenton went on wistfully.
"I run onto some tenderfeet up t' Three Islands a few months
back, an' they was from Prince William County. We got t'
talkin', and I find out that man *didn't* die. In fact, he stood trial
for murderin' *me*, as I couldn't be found. But he was acquitted
on 'count of no evidence." He chuckled. "So that is my story,
sir. Don't it make you think?"

George mused on it, and marveled. There were so many
untalkative men here on the frontier, loners who never spoke of
their origins; his beloved old Illinois regiment had had a score
of such. How many odd stories there must be, he thought.
"Well, then, my congratulations to you on recovering your iden-
tity. Now you'll have to build a reputation as Simon Kenton to
equal that of Simon Butler, eh?"

"Well, but it ain't reputation I care about. It's just keepin'
m'self alive. And any as I can help. Now, sir, why I come up
here was not to tell you my story, but to give you this letter. It
was left off just now by a trader on the way to Fort Pitt from
th' Missipp.'"

It had the Church seal, George noted as he broke the wax,
and he knew it could only be from Father Gibault.

St. Louis, June 28, 1780

Dear Friend:

The poste being so dubious in these hazardous times I
have made it my sad duty to send you news which you may
have or may have not received from other sources, being
that our beloved ally Fernando de Leyba succumbed to the
complications from his wound, and has been buried this day
beside his wife Maria at the church of St. Louis.

I was with him in his final days and know that two concerns most occupied his soul: first, that he had through neg-

ligence let Maria slip from his life without benefit of the last rites; second, that support of his daughters Maria and Rita should be given to the care of their maternal uncle Fernando de Zezar, New Orleans, and Teresa also if any harm should befall you in your present campaigns. Our friend spoke of his love and admiration for you several times in his last hour, and I believe was despite his misery almost happy because he had conducted himself in a fashion you would have deemed manly.

Mlle. Teresa, so fragile of spirit when I first knew her, bears herself in the face of all this with a granite fortitude, but is I fear quite brittle and holding herself together with the divine mastic of Faith, in Our Savior and in yourself, whom I think sometimes she confuses, the one for the other. But she is for the moment well. At her request I enclose herewith a billet to you in her own hand.

All matters at this place are in the care of Lieutenant de Cartabona until such time as Fernando's successor shall arrive from N. Orleans.

The people of his vicinity are in perpetual contention with the representatives of Virginia whose aid and protection they were promised. Most disputes involve quartering of troops and provisioning due to the worthlessness of currency. Your guiding hand is sorely needed here. The sole cheerful news I have to give is that our droll friend Leonard Helm and I did meet in our travels once and I confess that I veered from the path of temperance to toast with him all our dear remembered comrades one by one, yourself several times. It was a night to remember, most of which I can't recall.

Any correspondence you may have time to send me should be addressed to Ste. Genevieve where I return within a few days and shall be indefinitely.

May God be with you in all your righteous endeavors, and bring you back to us sound and victorious. In the name of Our Lord I remain

Your most affectionate and devoted servant

P. GIBAULT

Kenton saw the emotions working in George's face and turned away, not to intrude. George opened the little letter inside with shaking hands.

St. Louis, June 29, 1780

Querido Mío,

Fernando is dead, God ease his torment. After a long bad fever he passed away with your praise on his lips.

Coming to this place has cost us everything. One would not believe such complete disaster could come so fast, this in a land that looks so like the Paradise—until one looks closer and sees the distress and death among the flowers. But Fernando and I did not in the end curse this place. Here we learned how much we could bear, and that, I believe now, though I never supposed it before, is perhaps the essential truth one should know.

Your precious trophy is as always privately upon my breast above my heart.

I am sustained now by your dream, that of sitting beside you on a plaza watching the sun go down on a peaceful country. To live without that hope is unthinkable. Defend yourself, and may God protect you.

I await you and pray for you every hour and if anything should happen to me I would watch over you from Heaven.

I remain with Fidelity and Adoration,

Yours
TERESA

"Go away, Simon," George said in a strangling voice. But Kenton had already gone.

35

MIAMI RIVER VALLEY
August 2, 1780

THE MARCH TO CHILLICOTHE UP THE EAST BANK OF THE LITTLE MI-ami River was swift but strenuous. Because of the cannon, roads had to be cut through seventy miles of the way, through thickets and windfalls and snarls of bottomland driftwood. A great part of the march was under heavy rainfall. Then a sultry sun came out and steamed the valley. Gasping, some collapsing from the close August heat, stung by sweatbees and tormented almost to madness by the clouds of mosquitoes and giant flies that feasted on their blood, the woodsmen with the sharp axes engineered roadways and log fording-bridges along the wild valley.

The new soldiers learned that being driven by George Rogers Clark was even more grueling than legend had it. In the five days required for the winding two-hundred-mile approach to Chillicothe, virtually every man of the thousand found his endurance stretched miles beyond its supposed limit. Some of the men, their feet and ankles chafed constantly by the wet leather of their moccasins, developed the excruciating condition known as scald feet, which made every step an agony. Young men who had entered manhood inspired by tales about Boone and Kenton and Clark were almost in a state of joy as they plodded along through the sun-dappled greenery looking at the very backs of their heroes. In hundreds of fatigue-numbed minds there were stories forming, destined to be heard by thousands of children and grandchildren, nephews and nieces, cronies and constituents as yet unborn.

The approach of such a force could not go unnoticed, particularly by the vigilant Shawnees. And so when the mounted troops thundered down from the woodlands and through the cornfields to the great Indian town of Chillicothe, seat of the Chalahgawtha sept of the Shawnees, they found the town already deserted and partially burned. The tribe had departed so abruptly that corn and green beans were still warm in English iron kettles over the cooking fires. It was a ghost town of hemispherical wigwams of bark and hide, some reduced by fire to their charred skeletons of bowed saplings; of long, well-built council houses, one of which caved in with a roar of flame and lay crackling even as the vanguard of Kentucky officers rode by it; and a small fort of sharp-tipped palisade stakes. Just west of the village the river made a double bend under a spectacular wooded bluff, and to the north was an extensive marsh with a single gigantic oak standing on a knoll in its center.

Kenton's scouts had already crossed the river, and returned in late afternoon to report that the Chalahgawthas were withdrawing to Piqua town on the Mad River fork of the Great Miami,

thirteen miles to the northwest, where they probably would join
with Delawares, Mingoes, Wyandots, and Piqua's Shawnees to
make a stand. George ordered a strong defense set up in the
ruins of Chillicothe against counterattack, and bivouacked his
army in the town, where they had a supper of fresh corn and
beans to enhance monotonous trail rations. Legend had it that
the Chalahgawtha Shawnees in this town owned a ton of silver,
which they had been mining for generations from river gorges
nearby, and a number of the Kentuckians who knew of this
made feverish, secretive searches through every corner of the
town until they were satisfied that either it was untrue or that
the treasure had been carried away by the fleeing tribe. At last
the army gave in to bone-weariness and settled to rest for the
next day's march.

George ordered the Shawnees' crops cut down and burned or
thrown in the river before dawn, leaving only a few acres standing to provide ears of sweet corn for their return trip, and then,
the heavy smoke still in their nostrils, the Kentuckians set off at
a canter in the delicate light of sunrise, heading for Piqua,
rested, lusting for vengeance, and confident that with Clark
leading them they should surely have it.

JOSEPH ROGERS LAY ON HIS PALLET IN THE HUT OF HIS ADOPTED
Shawnee family at Piqua, too excited to sleep; so excited was
he that he went into fits of trembling every few minutes.

Outside, all night long, he had heard the footsteps and low
voices of the Shawnee warriors who were preparing for the defense of Piqua town. From snatches of conversation he had
heard that Shemanese, or Big Knives, were at Chillicothe, that
they numbered many hundred, maybe a thousand, that they had
at least one cannon, that they probably would attack Piqua at
midday or early afternoon unless they stayed longer at
Chillicothe. He had heard that among the Kentuckians were
such great fighters as He-Whose-Gun-Is-Always-Loaded, whose
American name was Simon Butler; and Sheltowee, or Big Tur-
tle, who was Daniel Boone.

But the most electrifying rumor he had heard was that the
Shemanese were led by Long Knife, their *nenothtu oukima*, or
great warrior chief, the man named Clark who had a charmed
life.

Clark! With hair the color of *outhowoququah*, which was
copper. Joseph Rogers had been hearing about Long Knife since
the summer of 1778, and by now was certain that it could be no

one but his first cousin, George Rogers Clark, with whom he had been bringing gunpowder to Kentucky when he was captured by the Shawnees near Limestone on Christmas Day of 1776. It was three and a half years that he had been living among the Shawnees, and had not talked to a white man, except the Girty brothers, since; but now, by this wonderful turn of fate, his own cousin, one of the last Virginians he had seen, was coming to defeat the Shawnees and, if the day went well, would free him and return him to his own people.

Joseph lay awake now in the wee hours, trying to remember their faces: His cousin George he could remember quite well, as his intensity and fine appearance were quite unforgettable; his own father George Rogers, the Long Knife's namesake, he could never forget; and his father's sister, Ann Rogers Clark, he could remember too, with her wheat-colored hair and freckles, commanding blue Rogers eyes, and her fine, strong features; and as Joseph Rogers lay awake now in the ominous night, his adopted Shawnee parents sleeping a few feet away, his life as a Shawnee son fell away little by little until, by the time the gray of morning outlined the door of the hut and the moccasined feet of the defenders of Piqua passed the door and weapons rattled and war drums began to thump, Joseph Rogers was a Virginian again, fully a Virginian, a Rogers. He began to contemplate how he might in the confusion of battle effect his escape.

The warriors had taken his hunting rifle from him yesterday, not trusting him to use it against his fellow white men even though he had been a model Shawnee son and had never in his years at Piqua tried to escape. So he would have to face the holocaust of the coming day unarmed except for his skinning knife, and probably would be kept in or near the stockade and watched from the corners of the warriors' eyes during the battle.

But there would be much confusion in the battle, he imagined, and surely there would be a time when he might slip from his captors' sight and hide until the white men were near enough to hear his cries and sweep him into their protection. "*I am a Virginian!*" he would cry. "*I am a Virginian!*" In his imagination he rehearsed it and saw them recognizing him and embracing him with joy, and tears came to his eyes as he trembled and daydreamed to the solemn drums.

At midmorning on August eighth, a column of five hundred armed Kentuckians crossed the Mad River about a mile below Piqua town, at a fording place where scouts had found the water only knee-deep. The horses splashed through the clear water; flags fluttered, harness jingled, and the iron-rimmed wheels of the six-pounder ground over the stony shore. Directly behind George Rogers Clark rode two men bearing the banners of Virginia and the United States, then more cavalry, then files of woodsmen afoot. The sky was clear and blue.

George stood in his stirrups and turned to watch Colonel Ben Logan's regiment marching up the other side of the river. Logan was to go up around the horseshoe bend and ford the river on the far edge of the town, attack from that side, and prevent the Indians from escaping in that direction.

George stopped and deployed Colonel Harrod's regiment in ranks off to the left after the crossing, in preparation for the advance over the intervening ground, and to give Logan time. He surveyed the rolling plain ahead, noting a few wooded hillocks and a zigzagging pole fence off to the left. To the right lay a large cornfield, along whose margin ran another pole fence, generally parallel with the river. Beyond it was a wooded elevation marking the outskirts of the town. George could see the motions of large numbers of Indians along that fence and all about the town itself. Partly visible through the trees at one end of the town was a new, triangular log fort, which he knew would be the Shawnees' final stronghold in the event that Logan could bottle them in on the far side.

The morning grew still; horses blew, birds twittered and darted over the sunny meadow. After a seemly wait, with the ranks formed for an advance across the plain, George drew his sword and pointed to the drummers. One of them was Dickie Lovell, the lad who had gone with him to Vincennes, and that boy held the same drum upon which he had floated through the icy Wabash floodwaters.

George dug his heels into the flanks of his horse and swung his blade around toward Piqua. Two long ranks of men, in gray linen or buckskin hunting shirts and breechclouts, began moving forward in a crouch, their long rifles cocked and sweeping the field ahead of them. Drums rattled; leggings whispered in the grass. Within a minute after the start of the advance, far to George's left, and scarcely fifty yards in front of Colonel Harrod's regiment, the zigzag fence and nearby wood suddenly emitted a cloud of white smoke and crackling of musket fire. it was immediately answered by a chorus of cheers and a withering volley from the front rank. As that rank knelt to reload, the following line poured another volley through the fence, and

George saw a sudden flurry of Indians, perhaps a hundred tiny figures, break from the shelter, scatter through the grass at a fast run for about two hundred yards, then rally on a timbered hillock. Almost at that moment, a greater hail of fire roared out of the cornfield and from the pole fence on the right flank of the advancing Kentuckians.

Instead of stopping in the face of the fire, the companies screamed wildly, and broke into a swift run toward the enemy, gaining many yards before the Indians could reload. Routed by his headlong rush, several hundred braves scattered from behind the fence and swarmed like bees into the high corn, and the Kentuckians, carrying down the fence with their onrush, vanished into the cornfield after them. Keep going, George thought as he galloped toward that point, if you stop and let 'em reload and rally, it could be deadly in there! But the swaying corn tassels and moving heads, visible from his mounted height, showed that the Indians were not stopping, but curving left toward the elevated wood where the smaller party had fled.

Galloping into the cornfield behind his troops, he urged them on toward the woods. It was an unnecessary encouragement, as they were whisking forward through the stalks like a swift wind, screaming a bloodthirsty war cry as they went. In minutes the cornfield was behind them and they were into the edge of the woods, where they were met by a shower of ineffective musketry from the shade. George and the mounted officers rode back and forth behind them, re-forming the double ranks, which had become disarranged in the blind charge through the corn. "Press on 'em!" he roared at the top of his voice. "Don't let 'em shoot twice from behind the same tree!" Riding past a captain named Haskins, George saw the captain's dusty tricorn hat leap from his head with a puff of dust and spin to the ground; Haskins reached up with a perplexed look, touched a bullet furrow that had taken off some hair and a layer of skin, then rushed with a happy shriek deeper into the woods.

Darting from tree to tree and firing at puffs of musket smoke, the frontiersmen within an hour had the Indians driven to the far side of the woods. So far George had not seen a single white man fall. He kept listening for sounds of battle above the town, where Logan should have been attacking by now, but heard none. Logan was either meeting no resistance or had not attacked yet.

Now some of the Indians, in parties of twenty or thirty, detached themselves from the main defense line and sped toward

the ends of the American line, trying to get around and attack
the flanks or rear. But the woodsmen, who had learned their lessons well under the intensive drilling at the camp on the Licking, simply wheeled, delivered two or three volleys, and
dispersed those sorties.

The battle for the woods consumed nearly two hours. Smoke
filled the green shade; bullets whacked through the foliage,
making a continuous shower of twigs and leaves. Balls
thrummed past George's ears every few seconds, as the
mounted officers like himself offered the best targets, but he felt
invulnerable, as if the Indians' own Great Spirit had thrown a
protective aura around him.

As the enemy retreated through the woods, they picked up
and carried off their wounded, but the frontiersmen were now
passing among Indian dead, stopping to bend and lift scalps as
they went. George now began to ride among brown-skinned
war-painted corpses lying amid blood-speckled ferns and undergrowth in contorted positions, the hair and skin gone from the
crowns of their heads. One body appeared to have been slashed
to ribbons by some frenzied knife-wielder; dozens of deep cuts
had been made across the flesh of the chest and arms and the
abdominal cavity had been ripped open violently. Another lay
sprawled supine over a log, his breechclout cut away, a jagged
red wound where his genitals had been. As George was bracing
himself against the grimness of that sight, a runner came and
told him that Bill McAfee, one of the best of the Indian fighters,
had been shot through the body and was down but still conscious and talking.

At last driven from this wood, the Indians darted across open
ground to the next, where another battle of the same nature
raged for another two hours. The casualties on both sides
seemed to be light despite the constant uproar of gunfire, both
the Indians and the attackers being masters at concealment.

It was late afternoon when the Indians were at last driven to
the edges of their town, and they retreated gradually through the
gardens and the huts and cabins, at last darting a few at a time
into their fort, and the gunfire diminished.

Their triangular stockade seemed to cover half an acre, sitting
near the end of the horseshoe bend of the river that looped
around the town. A rear guard of the retreating warriors kept up
a prolific fire and then withdrew into the enclosure through its
one gate, which was on the side facing the town.

Now George recalled his tiring troops and formed them in a

hollow square on an elevation some two hundred yards from the stockade. The brass six-pounder cannon was brought forward, pulled by a four-horse team and followed by packhorses laden with powder and cannonballs. The piece was unlimbered in the middle of the hollow square, and wheeled to bear on the stockade. The Kentuckians watched with undisguised glee as the wheels were chocked, the powder and ball rammed home, and the smoking match brought up. George sat his horse a few feet from the cannon, looked in vain for any sign of Logan's regiment, decided not to wait for it, and then raised his hat to the gunner.

"Fire!" he bellowed, slapping the hat down against his knee. The cannon spat orange flame and blue-gray smoke, kicked, and settled, its roar echoing from the bluffs opposite, and the Kentuckians cheered as chunks and white splinters of the palisade flew into the air.

"Fire when ready, boys," he cried. "Work on that gate!"

The cannon roared fourteen more times, as fast as it could be swabbed and reloaded, accompanied each time by the cheers of the Kentuckians, and segment after segment of the palisade was shivered. One of the big log double doors of the gate burst, sagged, then fell to the ground in a cloud of dust. The Indians fired for a while toward the cannon with their muskets, but at this distance the fire was ineffectual and they soon gave it up.

Unobserved from the cannon position, however, several hundred warriors had shimmied over the wall of the fort on the river side, crouched in the cornfield which grew almost to the wall, and crept through the stalks, gaining the woods behind the regiment.

Then, between rounds from the cannon, the Indians within the fort performed a singular maneuver. They marched out of the broken gate and began forming a single long rank on the flatland before the front of the fort.

"By Jove," George muttered to Colonel Harrod. "I do believe they're coming out to treat for peace. Hold your fire!" he told the cannoneers. He rode out of the square of troops and guided his horse a few yards down the slope toward the fort, trying to pick out someone among the Indians who would be coming forward as spokesman. The whole area was quiet in the hot afternoon sunlight, long calls of the locusts drawing out.

No Indian came forward with the white wampum belt or flag of truce. Instead, the whole long line suddenly drew their muskets up at the ready, gave vent to a chilling war cry, and began charging up the slope at a dead run, firing as they came. At the same moment a storm of gunfire began pouring into the regiment from the woods behind the squared regiment, and George, wheeling his steed and galloping back in among his troops, understood the Indians' tactic. It infuriated him to have been so fooled, but he was not alarmed. The troops on the rear side of the square flattened themselves against the ground and began a brisk return fire which soon had the Indians in the rear all but immobilized behind the trees. In the meantime the line of Indians from the fort came running up the slope in a desperate frontal charge, their shrieks pulsating back and forth along the line. George felt his scalp prickle at such desperate bravery on the part of the Indians. "Damn, damn," exclaimed Harrod, apparently thinking likewise, "I never seen them charge exposed like that!"

"Aye," said George as they came closer. "Because you never saw 'em fighting for their own place. Hey, boys!" he roared, "hold fire till they're too close to miss!"

"Heyo, laddies!" cried an officer nearby, "don't shoot till you can singe their eyebrows!"

The horde came on, their feet patting the earth, cries piercing, painted faces looking demoniacal. They came now like an onrushing wall of pent-up murder. George's heart was in his throat; the savages were almost upon the square now.

"First rank," he yelled, *"Fire!"*

"Fire!" the command was relayed up and down the line, and nearly a hundred rifles barked at once. Indians pitched forward, spun and pirouetted to the ground.

"Reload! Reload!" yelled the officers to the first rank. "Fire!" they commanded the second rank, which had stepped forward. The rifles sputtered again. The few Indians still coming flung up their arms and reeled; others, who had stopped in confusion or were trying to reload, now turned tail and sprinted or limped, crawled, and squirmed back down the hill, many of them leaving trails of blood.

The company on the rear side of the square, meanwhile, had repulsed that charge entirely and was cheering itself roundly, and at that moment George faintly heard drums and fifes in the distance at the upper ford of the river. He stared toward a line of cottonwood and willow, and saw the flags and ranks of Logan's regiment at last coming up the riverbank. But George didn't want him now; the Indians were already in retreat, through another cornfield, invisible to Logan's regiment, and obviously were making their escape straight toward the ravine and ford that Logan had just vacated. "Go back, damn you, Ben!" George bellowed, but the distance was far too great, and Logan's half thousand marched blithely on toward the fort which was by now nothing but a shattered empty shell.

The Kentuckians around the cannon, who obviously felt they had obeyed long and well enough, were breaking their rank now, disregarding the commands of their officers, and running down the slope to collect scalps from the dead and wounded Indians they had just mowed down. They swooped down like vultures on the scattered casualties in the waving grass, wielding their long hunting knives, slashing viciously and lifting hair. George watched this breach of discipline with disgust, watched Logan's regiment marching gallantly toward an empty fort while several hundred Shawnee, Wyandot, Mingo, and Delaware braves stole unseen around him and swarmed through a ravine which led out of the valley and into the safety of the surrounding high forest land.

The sun was setting now, illuminating the whole disorderly scene with a rich, tawny glow. Shadows of the leaping and hooting soldiers were long and distorted; the distant drums and fifes sounded like some ironic, meaningless air to another war somewhere, as remote and detached from his own battle, George felt, as the eternal movements of Washington and Greene and Steuben and Sullivan in the east. Everything was out of kilter somehow; somehow Logan had been so tardy that he had robbed the force of a decisive victory; somehow these riflemen had just demonstrated a sloppy disobedience which marred their generally commendable performance throughout the day, and it came as a great insult to George in a way he would have been unable to define. He had defeated the Shawnees, of course, and by burning their crops and villages now would forestall any more raids on Kentucky for the year. But the victory was ignoble somehow, a mockery compared to the miraculous victory over Hamilton in '79 . . .

Ah, he thought, as the shadows purpled and Logan's men marched on in the distance, the distant fife-notes somehow off-key, that's it, I reckon; maybe you just can't be satisfied that well but once. It spoils you for anything that follows . . .

These thoughts, unlike anything he had ever considered before, had flickered through his head in a moment, making him feel old and bitter in the midst of what others seemed to be enjoying as a triumph, and as he was bringing his attention back from that reverie he thought he heard someone calling him by his first name in the distance, beyond the cackling and cheering of the troops: "George! George!" came a young voice into the margins of his attention. He turned in the direction of the sound, as did several of the frontiersmen nearby, and saw an inexplicable sight: one lone Shawnee, in breechclout and moccasins and war paint, running toward him up the slope in a plunging, lunging stride, like some crazed fiend on a sacred suicidal mission. Some of the troops and officers gathered nearby also deduced immediately that an assassin was almost upon their commander; and with the instant reflexes of Indian fighters leveled their rifles at him and fired.

Six rifle balls struck Joseph Rogers in the chest, hurling him backward and blinding him with a silver-blue blot of pain and knocking all the breath out of him.

Joseph lay on his back in the long grass, feeling numb and smashed inside, hearing blood gurgling in his lungs with every attempt to breathe, seeing the evening azure sky overhead go silvery, then black, then silvery, then black. In a part of his mind he reprimanded himself for having forgotten to shout what he had rehearsed: *I am a Virginian! I am a Virginian!*

Silhouetted faces under felt hats and coonskin hats and cocked hats loomed between him and the fluctuating sky, and voices came from the silhouettes, talking about somebody being a white man, not an Indian. Then an arm was slipped under his shoulders and he was raised up a little, and there was a face close over him now, and damned if it wasn't Cousin George, big Cousin George holding his head cradled and looking at him with such an agonized expression in his face that Joseph felt pity for him. Joseph choked back and swallowed the salty blood that seemed to keep filling his mouth up like brine, and took a bubbling breath into his hot wet numb chest and said, "George . . ." He couldn't say the rest yet because the brine was filling him up again and he swallowed and swallowed, determined to get it said.

George was looking down on him and said, "In the name o' God eternal, Joe, why didn't you slip out last night and come to us? Why'd you wait till *now*?"

Joseph kept swallowing and swallowing the brine, looking up into those dark blue eyes, those Rogers eyes, until he felt able to say what he had meant to say. "George," he gurgled as the sky went from silvery to black one last time, "I am a Virginian."

36

St. Louis, Upper Louisiana Territory
September 20, 1780

"But you must come with us! There is nothing left for you here but loneliness and sickness and danger!"

Lieutenant de Cartabona paced back and forth in the parlor of the de Leyba house, emphasizing each word by flinging his hands downward, palms upturned. He had been pleading thus with Teresa for two days. He had used every means of persuasion he could think of, from tender cajolery and logical arguments to dire warnings and, a time or two, outbursts of anger. But Teresa responded the same way to all the different manners of entreaty: She sat looking at her small white hands clenched on the lap of her black mourning dress and shook her head or simply gave no sign of hearing at all.

Now de Cartabona knelt before her, as he had many times, looked into her face, and wrung his hands. "Listen, Teresa. Your dear brother and his wife are dead, God take them. There is no one here to take care of you. There will be no money coming here for your keep. The nieces who are all the family you have left in this world are packed to go to New Orleans on the boat tomorrow. They themselves plead with me to make you consent. They cannot bear to have you stay behind, as you are just as much their whole family as they are yours! For their sakes, Teresa, if no other form of good sense will move thee!"

Only a twinge of pain passing over her brow indicated that she was even hearing him. She seemed to have put a wall of adamant about herself; she seemed to be bearing all this begging as one bears a siege: determined not to surrender to it, waiting with stolid patience for the assailant to go away.

"Think of these things, then," he pleaded. "It is September. Soon it will be cold. Do you not remember the suffering last winter in this country? We with Spanish blood are not meant to

461

huddle at fireplaces, shivering and choking on smoke! In New
Orleans it is not like that in the winter.

"And then if one survives the winter without dying of consumption, or starving, Teresa, all one can expect in the spring is
more war from the British and Indians. They will come down
the rivers as fast as the melting snow. And this time we can expect no help from the Americans. Your Clark is far to the east
in an Indian war. He will never come here again, and it is foolish to believe . . ."

"He will!" Her voice was small but emphatic. She laved her
hands and shook her head back and forth, eyes squeezed tightly
shut, and de Cartabona gritted his teeth with pain and annoyance, not only because she would respond to nothing but her
lover's name but because she had such unshakable faith in him
as the savior of any circumstance.

"He will not!" he exploded in exasperation. Even his mute
devotion to Teresa was tried beyond patience by her stubborn,
blind faith in that Virginian. The lieutenant had sworn to himself that he would protect her with his life, and felt that he had
indeed done so in May. It was your brother and I, not Clark,
who defended St. Louis, he wanted to shout at her.

"He will be here, Francisco," she said with finality, getting
up suddenly and leaving him for a moment kneeling awkwardly
by the divan. She left the room as he was rising, and pulled the
door shut after her.

It may become necessary, he thought, to drug her and place
her aboard the boat. Could he do that? It was a hateful thought,
a shameful thought, but it seemed better somehow than having
to force her aboard, screaming and crying, as she probably
would be. Obviously she was not going to be persuaded in these
remaining hours to go willingly.

Either way, he thought, she is going to hate me for doing this
in her interest. That was the worst of it. He had always nurtured
a hope that her indifference to him might someday revert to affection if the accursed American finally dropped out of her life.
But if he had to do something like this which would make her
hate him . . .

De Cartabona sat at the lieutenant governor's desk, tracing
his front tooth with a thumbnail and looking at the small vial of
laudanum left over from de Leyba's sufferings, when he heard
hoofbeats outside the house. In a moment, a servant ushered in
one of the American couriers from Cahokia. The man had two
letters from Colonel Clark, one for de Cartabona and one ad-

dressed to Teresa. "I shall see that the Señorita gets this," he said. "Please have a cup of brandy while I see whether I need reply." He put Teresa's letter on the desk and broke the seal of his own, as the rough-looking messenger helped himself to a draught of liquor that should have knocked an ordinary man off his feet.

Louisville, 23 August 1780

Dear Sir:

I must presume that the command of St. Louis has fallen to You upon the Tragick death of our Great Friend Governor de Leyba words can not Express my Feelings of Remorse at the Loss of that Brave Man I am certain that you are similarly Distraut having lost not only his Friendship but his wise Leadership as well.

The News came to me on the Eve of a Successfull expedition from which I have Lately Return^d in which with the Force of a thousand Kentuckie settlers the Principal Shawnese towns were invaded & Destroy^d crops burned & some 70 Indian scalps lifted by the Kentuckians who went burning for the Revenge of Atrosities done Hereabouts in June. these Ohio tribes I Suspect will be too busy Hunting and Foraging to make any Mischief before next Year of our People 17 were Kill^d & some 40 wounded, the battle at Pickaway haveing continued hotly through the whole of a day with very Clever and Confident resistance on the part of Chief Blackhoof who escaped with most of his Warriors due to a Piece of Mismanagement in one of our Divisions. tho' I had entertained a thought of proceeding with that large Body of Men to reduce Detroit I was forced to abandon that perennial Hope once again the men for the most part haveing left their Settlements and Homes unguarded and not being of the same Temper as those that marched with me 2 Years Ago. Also the extream heat Uncertainty of Provision shortness of the Season &c

I hope you will inform my good Friends Vigo Gibault Cerré & all on the Spanish side that tho every part of the Western Department under my responsibility is in desperate Straits undermanned impoverish^d &c &c I will try to come to that place before Depth of winter. I send by this same Express a letter to Miss Terese offering my Condolences which I know will be Insuffic^t on the death of her Brother.

A great deal of business awaiting me on my Return to the Head Quarters here I can not Continue at more Length in This let'r but anticipate a personal audience with you in the near Future.

I am Sir you most hb¹ & obdᵗ Serv

G. R. CLARK

De Cartabona, pensive, put aside that letter and fingered the one addressed to Teresa. In all of his life he had never opened a letter addressed to someone else. But never before in his life had he suffered a strong enough temptation to do so. Everything he was trying to do toward carrying Teresa out of this place could be undone by one mere hint that Clark might come to St. Louis. And surely this letter to her would contain such a hint.

He slipped her letter under his own, and picked up both. "Rest," he said to the messenger, who had dispatched his gill of brandy and was huffing and blowing and rocking on the balls of his feet. "Have another potion, and I shall be with you presently."

"Thankee, suh," the ruffian exclaimed, reaching for the decanter.

Stepping into the adjacent anteroom, de Cartabona crossed himself and made a small prayer pertaining to the matter of using foul means to a fair end, and broke the seal of the second letter.

Louisville, 23 August 1780

My Dear Teresa

I was embarked on a Major Expedition at the time of receipt of the unhappy news of Fernando's death. I could not even attempt to express to you then my Consternation & Sadness, nay, I can not even now But I am return'd safe from that adventure, in whose duration I had some Moments to reflect upon what course might be most Agreeable to Human Nature regarding our present Circumstance & have decided that the Time is upon us when I must take you under my personal Protection as my Wife

This place is probably somewhat more Secure than St. Louis tho its Accomodations are rough and wanting Niceties After a brief Respite here from the River Journey I would then take you to my Family in Virginia where you would enjoy the most Compleat comforts & Safety & their incomparable Devotion until my Responsibilities in this department of the War shall have been done.

I expect to Journey to Virginia in the coming Winter to petition for all the Necessaries for one more Attempt on Detroit and that trip would enable me to take you to Virginia in my own company and with an Armed escort for your Safety

I implore you therefore my Beloved to wait for me in St. Louis for the few weeks it will take me to come for you. This War can not go on much longer & it will be my Pleasure then to lay down my Arms haveing served my Countrey as Energetically & Faithfully as I was able & abide in Peace for ever & ever with you at my side according to those dreams we have shared

With the tenderest concern for Your Happiness & Well being I am Y^r devoted

GEO.

De Cartabona, sweating, inflamed by jealousy and guilt, folded the paper into his own letter and stood for a moment in the little room, pulling his nose and squinting. Then he returned to the waiting messenger. "A brief reply," he said, and sat down to write.

San Luis, September 20, 1780

Sir:

Thank you for yours of 23 August and Compliments on still another Conquest, the particulars of which were most impressive. As for passing your sympathies to the Señorita . . .

He paused here and prayed silently for the audacity to do this. If anyone were to find this out! he thought. But I shall be in New Orleans. And this is after all a private matter, not public business. His hand trembled as he wrote:

being left without Family or Guardians in this harsh & remote corner of the Domain and wrapped in the most inconsolable dolour, she begged to be returned to the comfort of her Mother Country and is by now well on her way, probably being at or near New Orleans by this time. I fear that she left no message for you, only expressing her horror at the

bloodiness of this wilderness and its denizens both white &
native.

Your most humble Svt.

de C.

He scrawled the last with such a flourish as to make it illeg-
ible, then folded and sealed the paper and addressed it to
Colonel Clark at Louisville, Falls of the Ohio.

The lieutenant stood at the window and watched the messenger fling himself into the saddle with all the agility of a sober
man, and watched him gallop down the road and out through
the gate, past the artillery platforms which had been left standing since the battle in May.

Then, in a state of awful, guilty excitement, trembling like a
criminal, he tore both of Colonel Clark's letters into quarters,
knelt, and dropped them on the small fire that burned in the
hearth. He stood up, feeling a little dizzy, leaned on the mantel
until he felt steady, went to the decanter and sloshed a strong
measure of brandy into a glass, threw it to the back of his
throat, swallowed, poured another, and gulped it. Eyes watering,
he drew a kerchief out of his sleeve and daubed at his eyes and
nose. He picked up the vial of laudanum and slipped it into a
pocket. He squared his shoulders, repeated to himself his conviction that he was doing all this for the welfare of Teresa, flung
open the double doors, and strode through the great foyer, now
scuffed and scarred from the occupancy of the refugees, and
mounted the steps leading to her room. He paused outside the
door, took a deep breath, and rapped softly. There was no answer. He turned the latch and pushed inward, and found her
kneeling before her little altar with the black lace veil over her
head and face.

He shut the door and moved to her side. Her lips were moving. At last she crossed herself and looked up at him.

"Teresa . . ." He reached for her hands and held them as she
arose. Behind the veil her eyes were large and unblinking, as if
she were in a fervid trance. "Sit," he said. "I have something to
say." She obeyed, sitting on the edge of her bed. He stood before her, still holding her wrists, which she seemed not to notice. "Now hear me," he said, "and may God help you. An
American messenger was here. He brought forlorn news. Your
Colonel Clark fought in a battle with the Indians of Ohio . . ."

Her eyes were beginning to return from their otherworldly stare now, were seeing him, and were beginning to dart over his face, the eyelids trembling as if she anticipated a slap. "And he was shot to death," de Cartabona blurted out. God forgive me, he prayed, as he watched the serene mask of her faith crumble, watched her hands go into claws, felt the stiffening in her arms and body and waited, ready to stifle her screams, ready to fight her into submission if necessary, ready to dose her with the sedative.

But no scream erupted from her slack lips; no whimpering sounded; she did not struggle. It was worse. In total silence, as he stared at her face, something seemed to snap behind her eyes, that elemental strand of spirit which connects the inner and outer worlds of a sentient being. With his words he had severed that as surely as if he had cut it with a knife.

It would have been better if she had shrieked and protested and fought it with disbelief. But this, this abject, helpless, silent break . . . it had been like smothering a baby under its pillow.

The lieutenant shivered and began to sob. Then he stumbled to his feet, groping toward her washstand. She sat on the side of her bed with an idiot's incomprehension in her face and her hands lying palms up on the lap of her black skirt while the lieutenant retched dryly over her porcelain washbowl.

The next morning before daylight Teresa was taken on a litter down to the river galley and put in the small covered cabin in the stern, with a nurse to watch over her. Maria and Rita were brought down after sunrise with their baggage, looking pale and forlorn and red-eyed. But they brightened when they saw that Teresa's trunk was on board also.

"Yes," said the nurse. "Señorita Teresa is going, too. But she is sick now. Perhaps later you may talk with her."

The lieutenant got aboard last, ashen-faced, spoke to the citizens and soldiers on the wharf, and then saluted.

The line was cast off and the boat that had carried the de Leyba family from New Orleans to the outpost of St. Louis two years earlier swung into the wide brown current of the Mississippi to bear its survivors back down to civilization.

PART THREE

1812–1818

37

Locust Grove, Kentucky
1812

Major Wm Croghan
Locust Grove K^y

Dear Sir:

The enclosed certified copy of a law which passed both branches of the Virginia legislature yesterday, I hasten to forward, thro you, to General Clark. I can truly declare that no event in my life has given me more pleasure than I derived from being the instrument of Justice and Honor, in preparing, presenting, and urging the passage of the inclosed act. Whether I may be permitted to congratulate you and General Clark upon the success which attended my efforts, I know not; but, of this, I am persuaded, that had you been present, you would have approved of the course which I pursued, which sustained the honor and dignity of General Clark, while it interested the tenderness, the generosity, and the magnanimity of the General Assembly of Virginia. Our house was dissolved in tears: my voice was almost drowned in my own emotion. I told them the Story of the Sword, and urged as a reason why they should present to the gallant veteran another, that he had, with a haughty sense of wounded pride and feeling, broken and cast away that which this state formerly gave him.

I hope the whole transaction of yesterday will afford to your illustrious friend the pleasure which it gave, not to me alone, but to more than two thirds of the Virginia legislature.

I write in great haste, that my letter may not be delaid and

with it the enclosed bill. Be pleased to present my most respectful compliments to General Clark and to Mrs. Croghan,
and your gallant son if he is with you, and permit me to sub-
scribe myself with my best wishes for your happiness.

Your friend and very Hum^ble^ Servt,

CH^s^ FENTON MERCER

"Do you suppose he might do something hotheaded again
this time?" Diana Gwathmey asked. She gazed out the window
of the kitchen house at the old man in his wheelchair in the sun
on the veranda. There was a yellow-fringed black shawl around
his shoulders and his black hat lay on a table beside him. He
had put aside his book and newspapers and letterbox and was
gazing northward toward the Ohio valley as he seemed to do
most of the time these days.

"I think not," said Lucy Croghan, now pouring strong tea
into two cups on a tray.

"I'm not sure it's tea he's a wanting," said Diana, giggling,
nodding toward her uncle. Lucy looked out the window in time
to see the old man lift a small jug and tilt it to his lips. Then
he put the jug back on the table and replaced the hat over it.
The maneuver was awkward because he had little control of his
right hand.

"Ah, the old fox," Lucy breathed. "Now, what varmint smug-
gled that'n to 'im, I'd like t' know!"

"Not I," said Diana. "But sometimes I fancy the orchard's
full of his old scouts—Mister Kenton, perhaps—and they creep
out like Indians when we aren't a-watchin' and bring it to 'im."
She stirred honey into both cups of tea. "Maybe he had been
sipping on the sly like this when he broke the first sword.
D'you think maybe so, Auntie?"

Lucy frowned at the memory. "No, dear, I'm sure he was just
as sober as you or me. He was insulted, I know that. And
rightly so. Oh, he did embarrass those well-meaning dignitaries
something awful! Embarrassed me, too, but I could understand
how he felt. A fancy secondhand sword the state of Virginia
bought for him, from some dandy gent who'd 'hardly ever used
it,' as his reward for all he'd done! Well, I was embarrassed but,
by Heaven, I was proud of him! That Colonel Hancock put that
silly little token in his hands, and stood back, beamin' like
they'd just done him a great favor. But George he just looked
down at it as if it was a toad, and he turned that hard eye 'o his

on that man and said, I remember it exactly, he said, 'Young man, when Virginia needed a sword, I gave her one. Now she sends me a toy, when I need bread!' And he took the sword, an' he stuck it between two bricks in that veranda there, shoved it way into the ground, put his foot on it, and snapped it clean off, right at the hilt. Don't know where he found the strength. Well, it was an awful minute, but like I said, I was proud. And he *was* sober, I'll swear to that! Now you take 'im this tea, an' have a nice visit. He just dotes on you, an' you do 'im a world o' good, dear."

Diana sighed, looking out at him as she balanced the tray. "He's such an adorable old bear. But you're sure all my chitchat don't bother him?"

"Honey, go on with you. He tells us y're his sweetheart. And it keeps his mind alert, recollectin' all those tales."

"Hello, Uncle George," Diana chirped as she set the tea tray on the table. "You look very handsome today, sir!" She curtseyed and extended her hand, and held it there while he gathered his attention from wherever it had been. He turned his head slowly and brought his dark eyes to bear on her face. His eyebrows had turned to white bristle since his stroke three years ago. The crown of his head was bald, mottled with great freckles and age spots, and his long white hair, with just a few strands of faded red in it, hung down to his shawl. His mouth, so finely shaped only a few years ago, was turned down bitterly at the corners and crumpled inward, and the cheeks were sunken under the cheekbones, all his teeth being gone now, and the flesh on the right side of his face—eyelid and mouth corners—drooped. Sometimes Diana imagined that all the flaccid, weathered, thin skin of his face might slide off were it not held up so tightly stretched over the narrow bridge of his patrician nose.

"Annhh, hn," he gurgled phlegmatically and reached to her with his huge, gnarled, brown-flecked left hand. His cheek dimpled as he smiled and the sadness went out of his eyes. "Ah, it's about time, Missy. You left me fer a long spell . . ."

"Nonsense, now, Uncle, you know I . . ."

"Eh?"

"I say you know very well I come every fortnight to see my sweetheart! I was here two weeks ago and here I am again . . ."

"Aye, aye, you do, eh? Heh!" His hand, trembling, held hers and drew it insistently toward his breast, and she stepped closer and with her other hand stroked his bald dome, as he liked.

"Well, sir, what've you been thinking of today, sitting here on this fine afternoon?" That was, she knew, the way to get him started. She was always amazed at what she found when she would dip into his stream of reveries that way.

"Oh, I was puzzling on a strange thing," he began, going far into the distance. "You know, when William and Mr. Lewis were way out there in the West, where there had never been a white man before 'em, they found a squaw there, and d'you know, there was a tattoo on that woman's arm. It said 'J. Bowman.'" He clucked his tongue. "'J. Bowman,'" he repeated. "Now, I've thought on that many and many a time, Missy, and if there's an explanation for it, why, it must be wonderful indeed . . ." He fell back into his musings and was still for several minutes. Then he looked up at her as if she had just appeared there. "Ha, Diana! Well, sit down there, and tell me anything you know." His voice was growing louder and more animated now, and she knew she was once again successfully pulling him out of that great, turbid river of long memories.

"Well, I know that some fine gentlemen of Virginia will be here today and they have a magnificent new sword to present to you, and you shall be a gracious, fine Virginian yourself as you accept it . . ."

"Ah, ha, Missy. I know what you're trying to say, that I should be a good boy, rather than a spiteful one, and not break their toy, eh?"

"Well, I should hope! They've come a long way."

"That they have. Well, we shall see, Missy. But you know," he added with a mischievous twinkle in his eye, "I don't always have the control of my temper; no, I never have had."

"But you will today, or I shall be very, very put out. I came today to have a nice day with you, and no tantrums. And they're going to give you a nice pension, too, Auntie Lucy tells me."

"About time, by God," he rumbled. "D'you know, I never got a penny of my officer's pay for all those battles, all those years? And d'you know, they ended up givin' all my boys one hundred and eight acres of land for their valor, not the three hundred they were promised. And wouldn't't've give 'em *any* of it, if I hadn't badgered 'em the way I did so many years . . ."

"Drink this nice hot tea, now, and don't fret so."

"Ah, thankee. Tea, eh? Hm." He reached to his hat, put it on, and tipped the little jug over the teacup.

"Now what on earth!" Diana exclaimed, feigning surprise.

"Just a special sweetening, that's all, that I prefer over honey . . ."

"Aha. Well, just don't get yourself *too* sweetened up before those gentlemen come . . ."

"La, la, la; one'd think you was a wife, Missy!"

"And pray what d'you know about wives, Uncle!"

"All my friends've got 'em, that's what . . . ah . . ." A frown gathered on his brow suddenly, and his vision seemed to recede inward again.

"What is it, Uncle?" Diana asked, leaning close. She always strove to keep him jolly during her visits, and felt personally responsible whenever he would have a slump in spirits or lapse into his reveries.

He picked up the cup and took a long drink from it, and wiped the back of his hand across his mouth. Then he gave a deep sigh, and gazed off over her shoulder, his eyes watery. "Ah Missy! If the fates had treated me fair, you'd've had an elegant aunt you'd've loved very much, so fine and gentle was she, like you be fine and gentle." He blinked rapidly, then raised a handkerchief up, dabbed his mouth with it, and returned it to the sleeve of his half-dead right arm. Diana patted the back of his hand. He took her hand and began stroking it, still seeming to look at a point miles beyond, and said, "Aye, fine and gentle."

After a while, Diana said, "The Spanish lady, Uncle?"

"The very one. The Spanish lady."

Diana did not ask any of the many questions she would have liked to ask. She had asked before, asked questions about the lady's name and age and all sorts of inquiries, fishing for details of a story which she imagined must be unbearably romantic. Diana lately had become a reader of novels, and in her mind's eye she had often seen her uncle as a dashing young cavalier, intermingling gusty sighs with a dark-eyed beauty in a voluminous satin gown of exotic design. But the old soldier could never be prevailed upon to confirm such details. He would only mention the Spanish lady on occasions when he was somewhat in his cups, and would give only mere fragments of allusion, as if his mind were fluttering around the margins of a memory too painful to look at directly. Once when Diana had pressed him for more details to make her heart race, he had admonished: "You ought to read history, girl. Novels will make you silly."

But Diana was remembering something now. "Uncle George,

you said something a few months back when you dictated that letter to Mister Vigo. D'you remember . . ."

"Vigo!" Again the old man's face contorted with emotion.

"You said that about 'life's tenderest string.' D'you remember that? I suspect it was about your lady. . . ."

"Vigo," the old man repeated. "Missy, pray would you read me his letter again? It's there in the letterbox. . . ."

She found it near the top of his cherished correspondence. She unfolded it. She had had to read it to him every visit since it had come.

Vincennes, July 15, 1811

Sir:

Permit an old man who has witnessed your exertions in behalf of your country in its revolutionary struggles to address you at the present moment. When viewing the events which have succeeded those important times, I often thought that I had reasons to lament that the meritorious services of the best patriots of those days were too easily forgotten and almost taxed my adopted Country with ingratitude. But when I saw that on a late occasion, on the fourth of July last, the Citizens of Jefferson County from a spontaneous impulse of gratitude and esteem had paid an unfeigned tribute to the Veteran to whose skill and valor America and Kentucky owe so much, I then repelled the unwelcome idea of national ingratitude and my sentiments chimed in unison with those of the worthy Citizens of Kentucky towards the Savior of this once distressed Country. Deprived of the pleasure of personal attendance on that day, I took this method of manifesting to you, sir, that I participated in the general sentiments.

Please, sir, to accept this plain but genuine offering from a man whom you honored once with your friendship, and who will never cease to put up prayers to Heaven that the evening of your days may be serene and happy.

I have the honor to be, Sir, Your most obed. Serv.

VIGO

"Vigo," the old man said again, shutting his eyes and shaking his head. Then he stared hard, seeming to be in another search through memory. "D'you know, that man cashed drafts upon

Virginia for me for—what was it—twelve thousand dollars or thereabouts, that Virginia has never paid 'im?"

But Diana was more interested in romance than finance. She said, "And then you wrote to him that you'd not have that 'serene and happy evening' because Providence had 'cut asunder life's tenderest string.' Uncle, I know you meant by that the Spanish Lady!" Diana exclaimed with a knot in her throat and a mist in her eyes, as it was the favorite one of all her reveries, and she yearned to have it confirmed from his own lips. "He knew the Spanish Lady, didn't he?" If I ever meet Mister Vigo, she thought, I must ask him all about her.

"Vigo," the General murmured. "De Leyba. And Cerré, and Gratiot, and Pollock. All of 'em ruined like me, due to some great meanness in the Capital." He seemed to be gnawing mentally at the familiar old lament, which she had heard him speak of a dozen times. "Virginia wouldn't honor my expenses of the Western campaign. They said I didn't send 'em an accounting. Well, God knows what a task it was to keep records in the heat of that war . . . but I was meticulous in public matters, and by Heaven . . ." he banged his fist on the arm of his wheelchair, "I sent every account book and every voucher—*twenty thousand bloody vouchers*, so help me, writ on any shred o' paper as we could scrounge! I sent Bill Shannon to the state auditor at Williamsburg in November of '79 with all those packets, and he took receipt for 'em." Diana marveled at his recall of such details thirty years later, though he might forget what he had done yesterday or last week. "Every blasted transaction! No matter how little. A bottle o' rum or a washerwoman's hire, I made a voucher. How many a candle did I burn up, sitting up at night over them pestilential accounts, when my mind ought to've been on strategy! Bill Shannon couldn't even carry all that paper by himself. Seventy packets, it was. I remember exactly. Paper, and paper, and paper! How could anybody lose that much paper? I mean, unless they *wanted* to?"

He was thumping on the chair arm with his fist as he labored once again through his lament. "And then the auditor said those records didn't exist! We showed the receipt for 'em, and then 'e says, 'Well, they must was destroyed when Benedict Arnold burned the Capital at Richmond.' Well, maybe they was, an' then again maybe they wasn't. But they was never found and many a good patriot went broke to 'is grave since!" He kept thumping on the chair for a while, his eyes blazing into the distance, then he stopped and vented a huge sigh and seemed to shrink with weariness. Diana never knew what to say when he was on this pet tirade. It seemed too absurd a story to her, and much as she liked to believe her uncle, she wondered sometimes if he had fabricated this explanation out of his disappointments and come to believe it was true.

It seemed more likely to her that he would not have been able to keep such precise records during those campaigns, or that Shannon had not delivered them to the Capital, or some other explanation stemming from the vicissitudes of those troubled times. At any rate, it was all too complex and remote and businesslike for her turn of mind, and she had to make herself patient as he repeated the woeful old litany, which she had heard so many times before. But today it was upsetting her. Here he sat, drinking more than a little and worrying the scabs of those old wounds of state injustice while at this moment, probably—she looked up at the shadows on the walls of the great four-chimneyed brick Croghan house—emissaries of that state were on their way here to present him with another token sword. Young and romantic-headed though she was, Diana Gwathmey could sense another mortifying storm of temper a-brewing.

If only he'd go to sleep for a while, she thought, so I could steal away that awful little jug. Though doubtless another would appear from somewhere if I did . . .

But the old general was not nodding. He was still brooding. "It all got worse when Virginia turned over its war debts to Congress," he grumbled. "Congress was worse than the Virginia Assembly. One would think they'd never heard of the war in the West. We spent most of our time applying for reimbursement, did Jonathan and me. Years and years . . . Jonathan . . ."

His voice broke on the name. Jonathan, closest in age of the Clark brothers and George's boyhood playmate, had died suddenly the previous year and it had been a crushing blow. "Old Jonathan," he mused now. "It was hard, Missy, that he who wanted to live should die, while I, wanting to die, should live."

"Now, Uncle, I won't hear again such nonsense! 'Wanting to die,' indeed!"

"And Dickie," he murmured. "And John." This morbid brooding about his long-dead brothers was no better. Dickie had vanished in the wilderness between the Falls of the Ohio and Vincennes in 1784, never to be heard of again, and John had died that same year of consumption and other ailments contracted during six years as a British prisoner of war. Their parents, John and Ann Rogers Clark, had died within three months of each other in 1799. The old general's thoughts were often on death, which, he claimed sometimes, "is ever calling in the neighborhood, but afraid to come to see me."

"Let me fresh up your tea, Uncle," she said, getting up and carrying off the tainted cup before he could give it a thought. She emptied it in a mint bed outside the kitchen door as she went in, hoping it wouldn't kill the mint.

"Mercy!" she exclaimed to Lucy Croghan as the tea was poured. "Those gentlemen are going to believe all they've heard about his intemperance. But I'm afraid to just take his jug right away from 'im."

"Oh, never you mind," said Lucy. "I'll just tell William to give 'em a deep whiskey when they arrive, an' they'll never even notice how 'e is."

THE HONORABLE CHARLES FENTON MERCER, BRINGER OF THE sword, was a lean, straight-backed man with thin, sandy hair, grand flaming ears, light blue eyes with brows so light and sunbleached they were imperceptible, a profusion of freckles, long, delicate upper lip and hard chin which his military bearing caused him to keep pulled in close to his Adam's apple. He was also quite obviously awed to be in the presence of George Rogers Clark, and extremely pleased with having been the Virginia legislator whose bill had created the memorial sword and pension for the conqueror of the Northwest Territory.

"General Clark, sir," asked Colonel Mercer, to make conversation as the visitors and family were gathering on the terrace for the ceremony, "what are your thoughts on this new war with England?"

"I know little of it but what confused reports I get here to read. But I suspect we should have had little to suffer from it in these parts, had I been enabled to throw Detroit and the Lakes into our hands when I so desired it."

"Ah, yes," mused Mercer, his hands clasped behind his back. "I understand what you mean."

"I did everything in my power for the state of Virginia," the old man said, looking up at Mercer through his now redrimmed eyes, "being stopped only by lack of support from the state."

"Yes, I know," said Mercer, a bit abashed.

"The state of Virginia turned my laurels into thorns," the old soldier said.

Oh dear, thought Diana Gwathmey. I'm afraid he's going to take them to task again.

The officials and family members were placing themselves about now, before and behind the wheelchair, self-consciously sidestepping to make room for other sidesteppers, most with timorous smiles and murmured politenesses, their hands mostly clasped before them. Diana came close to the side of the General's chair and stood there with one hand protectively on its back, and once reached over to smooth down a strand of his hair in back. The general himself sat nodding and rocking to and fro just perceptibly, as if halfway between dozing and preparing to fight.

Colonel Mercer stood directly in front of the wheelchair now, his shadow cast by the weak fall sunlight lying across the general's laprobe. His two aides flanked him, and one of them held a sheathed sword. Mercer turned, took the hilt of the sword and pulled it out, the fine steel chiming faintly as it came free.

"Now, sir," said Mercer, placing the naked blade in the hands of the old general, who laid it across his lap and held it and gazed down at it. "General George Rogers Clark, as a Virginian, I have long been inspired by your foresight and daring, and by the unspeakable hardships you and your soldiers endured to protect the West. To think on your deeds has always moved me to great humility. Last February it was my honor to introduce a bill in the legislature which would provide you with a pension for the rest of your life, and to order the manufacture of a fine weapon especially made for you as a symbol of our regard. I am happy to say that the bill passed through both houses of the legislature in one day. You may not be able to understand the enormous satisfaction this measure provided to my humble soul, but . . ." Mercer's voice broke, and General Clark looked up from his contemplation of the blade to see Mercer's chin trembling. "I take great pleasure to read to you the following letter from His Excellency James Barbour, governor of the state of Virginia:

" 'Sir—The representatives of the good people of Virginia, convened in general assembly, duly appreciating the gallant achievements during the Revolutionary War of yourself and the brave regiment under your command, by which a vast extention of her empire was effected, have assigned to me the pleasant duty of announcing to you the sentiments of exalted respect they cherish for you, and the gratitude they feel at the recollection of your unsullied integrity, valor, enterprise, and skill. Having learned with sincere regret that you have been doomed to drink the cup of misfortune, they have requested me to tender you their friendly condolence. Permit me, sir, to mingle with the discharge of my official duty an expression of my own feelings.' " Mercer cleared his throat and read on.

" 'The history of the Revolution has always engaged my deepest attention. I have dwelt with rapture upon the distinguished part you acted in that great drama, being always convinced that it only wanted the adventitious aid of numbers to make it amongst the most splendid examples of skill and courage which any age or country has produced. I feel a conspicuous pride at the recollection that the name of Clark is compatriot with my own. I, too, most sincerely sympathize with you in your adverse fate, and deeply deplore that the evening of your life, whose morning was so brilliant, should be clouded with misfortune. The general assembly of Virginia have placed among their archives a monument of their gratitude for your services, and, as a small tribute of respect, have directed that a sword should be made in our manufactory, with devices emblematic of your actions, and have also directed that four hundred dollars should be immediately paid, as also an annual sum to the same amount. I lament exceedingly that any delay should have occurred in this communication. You will readily believe me when I assure you it arose from the tardiness of the mechanic employed in completing the sword. It is now finished and is sent herewith. I shall take pleasure in obeying your commands as to the transmission of the money to which you are entitled. You will have the goodness to acknowledge the receipt of this as soon as your convenience will permit. I am, sir, with sentiments of high respect, your obedient servant, James Barbour.' "

Mercer stood, swallowing hard, rustling the paper as he folded it. Major Croghan, standing directly behind his brother-in-law's wheelchair, stroked his jutting chin, then smudged a tear from the corner of his eye with his thumb. Lucy Croghan and young Diana Gwathmy glanced at each other, their eyes brimming and anxious. A cold breeze rattled the bare branches of trees in the yard.

George sat with the new cold steel held in both hands, its blade lying across his right thigh and the stump of his left. The end of the hilt was fashioned in the style of an eagle's head. A gold-braid tassel was knotted to a lanyard hanging from the guard. On a small oval plaque of silver in the handle was engraved a picture representing General Hamilton surrendering his sword to Colonel Clark at the gate of the fort at Vincennes, an angel flying over them blowing a trumpet. On the blade just below the hilt there were engraved words of tribute too small for him to read with his failing eyes.

In the stillness he was seeing his little detachment of ragged, emaciated, frostbitten, mud-stained volunteers dressed in motley rags and rain-soaked hats, and their faces: Bowman, McCarty, Williams, Worthington, Helm ... And behind him the little drummer boy Dickie Lovell rattling away solemnly with his sticks. He seemed to hear the drum, seemed to hear a distant fife, seemed to hear the gurgling flow of the flooded Wabash, the imagined sound making him feel cold. And then, that sound he would never forget, the *huzzahs* of his beloved victors.

Oh. They were waiting for him to reply.

He looked up at Colonel Mercer's shadowed face, his bared head. Then he took a deep breath. His voice came out quaking and feeble.

"You've made a very handsome address. This sword is very handsome, too. When ... when Virginia needed a sword, I gave her one." He ran his fingers along the gleaming blade. "I am too old and infirm, as you can see, to ever use a sword again, but ..." now everything before him blurred through a curtain of tears, "but I am glad that my old mother state hasn't entirely forgot me ... I reckon I was imprudent to get so indebted in her public affairs ... But a country was at stake, and I suppose I'd do the same again, if I had similar field to pass through ... So, now, I thank Virginia for the honor, and I thank you, sir, for your kindness and friendly words."

He sat there in the silence, his thoughts drowned in bittersweet emotion.

Then Diana's hand stole down over the shawl on his shoulder and she kissed him on his bald scalp. "I'm proud of you," she whispered.

He smiled. "Aha. Aye. I was a good boy for you, was I not?"

38

IT WAS UNSEASONABLY MILD. DIANA GWATHMEY HOPED IT MIGHT
be a sign of an early spring. For nearly two months the winter
weather had kept her Uncle George confined inside his downstairs room of the Croghans' big Georgian house, but now they
sat together on the terrace as they had during her visits for so
many years. She was nearly twenty now, and engaged to be
married soon to a respectable young gentleman named Tom
Bullitt, but as she had done for half of her lifetime, she still
came every other week to visit her uncle and sit by his side, do
needlework and keep him company.

It was different now. For the last five years there had been no
more of their tender and intriguing conversations. A massive
stroke in 1813 had destroyed his speech and scrambled his wits
and he had lived on these last five years as a huge, silent ruin.
The stroke had ended his long career as Commissioner of the Illinois Regiment Grant, had robbed him of his last great pleasure, reading, and left him inert and helpless as a newborn baby.
His great old wreck of a body simply would not cease to func-
tion and his heart beat on day after day, month after month, year
after year. So now Diana would sit with him in silence.

But she knew her visits were not wasted. When she arrived
at Locust Grove and came around in front of his chair and
stooped to show him her face, his toothless mouth would open
slightly as if he were smiling, and a little life would show in his
eyes. She would sit on a low stool close by his wheelchair, on
his left, and he would stroke the hair on her head by the hour,
and sometimes he would make strenuous, futile efforts to speak.

Her friends sometimes asked her if it was not tedious or bor-
ing to spend those hours sitting by the side of a speechless old
hulk. "No," she would say, and that would be her whole reply,

because she could not have explained why it was a good thing for her, and why she always anticipated the visits, and why these hours filled her with such warmth and serenity instead of the depression one might have expected.

"Why didn't he have a wife, if he was so great and so handsome?" her friends would say. "It should be a wife sitting by him all these years, not a niece."

"He didn't get married because something happened to the only lady he loved," Diana would try to explain from her limited knowledge. "And then, too, I suppose, he could think of courting no one else afterward because of his poverty."

The sun was going down now. It was growing melon-colored and descending toward the bare treetops. Diana did not know how well Uncle George could see, but she knew that he would tend to face the sun as it went down.

With the lengthening of the afternoon came a chill in the air, and the terrace bricks gave up the little warmth they had absorbed from the February sun.

He won't want to go in till he's seen the sunset, Diana thought. But he'll need a blanket or a heavier shawl. And so will I.

"Excuse me, Uncle," she said in the stillness, and rose from the stool, squeezing his hand and laying it on the chair arm, then crossed the bricks toward the door and went in.

The old man's heart hurt because the girl had gone away.

The sun, now a cooling, indistinct orange disc, eased down through a violet haze.

As he watched it sink, the crown of a distant cloud began creeping up to obscure the bottom of the disc. Little by little, the sun was eclipsed.

In his mind there was an eclipse of the sun and a great rushing sound, like a waterfall. Faint shouts. Distant roars and rattlings. Singing, or was it a fife? It was too faint under the rushing. And then a sweet chord, like a handful of plucked strings.

Soon there was only a thin arc of red in the haze in the western sky; it grew thinner, smaller, became a glowing dot.

He felt cold. Cold as when brown icy water had flowed about his body, brown water as far as the eye could see.

Diana came out of the house toward his wheelchair, bringing a black wool blanket. He heard her speak to him through the rushing, but it was too late to try to reply. He looked down from where he was and watched her bending to spread the blanket

around the shoulders of a big old man in a black hat in a wheelchair and he wished he could go back just for a moment to
thank her for caring so much. Now the girl and the old man and
the brick house grew smaller and smaller and the fields and
trees and the curving Ohio River with its island and its falls
and the old log house on the point on the other side of the river
grew smaller, and he followed that red ember of the sun. Somewhere under that same sun Teresa must be . . .

THEY CAME ON HORSEBACK DOWN THE NEW ROADS FROM THE UP-
river settlements, or by canoe down the deep wintry-gray rivers,
or on moccasined or booted feet through the silent, frozen
woods, white men and red, bent on reaching Louisville before
Wednesday. Members of the Bar at Louisville voted to go to the
funeral en masse, and to wear black crepe on their sleeves for
thirty days, and they elected their most eloquent orator, Judge
Rowan, to deliver an elegy at the graveside. Those living too far
away to reach Louisville before Wednesday sat at their tables at
home and wrote letters.

William Clark, now the governor of the Missouri Territory,
arrived, having been on the Buffalo Trace Road en route to
Louisville on business when his brother died.

The body of the old general lay in a waxed walnut coffin in
a cold room at the Croghan house for five days and men and
women came through the room to stand and look in at him. The
newspapers printed solemn and laudatory recapitulations of his
victories and public services, and militiamen in a detachment
came and camped at Locust Grove and drilled for the precise
maneuvers of a military funeral. Old Davey Pagan, in charge of
Major Croghan's ferry boat, brought many an old comrade
across the river from the Indiana Territory where their land
grant lay, and his one eye teared when some of them recognized
him and remembered to call him the Forepoop Swabman.

On Wednesday the eighteenth of February, the people came
to Locust Grove through a bitter wind and blowing snow and
gathered in and around the house. A brief ceremony was conducted inside the house and then the coffin was carried out
through the snow and along a path through the garden to the
family burial ground a few hundred feet from the house. At intervals of one minute, the militiamen fired their long rifles into
the air. Dick Lovell, now fifty years old, paced behind the pall-
bearers through the dry snow, rapping slowly on the muffled
drum, remembering how he had tapped this same old drum be-

hind this same broad and tall man in '79 through the bone-chilling waters of the flooded Wabash and before the gate of Fort Sackville while General Hamilton handed over his sword, and at the Shawnee towns in '80, and he remembered as well tapping his drum outside the log house on Clark's Point across the river nine years ago while surgeons cut away the general's leg. Dick Lovell could scarcely see where he was going now through his tears, but it was just a matter, as it had always been, of following the progress of Mister Clark.

At the graveside there was a remarkable gathering of people, considering the weather. Several hundred were there, much of the town of Louisville being on hand. Diana Gwathmey stood wrapped in a cloak, eyes smarting from tears and cold, and looked from the long, deep, final hole in the ground to the dark wood of the closed coffin to the faces of people she recognized and people she had never seen before. She wished the Indian, Two Lives, could be among them. But his tribe lived too far away. That heavy, stooped man with straw hair and the profusion of capillaries in his cheeks, that was John Sanders, an old guide and hunter turned merchant. That enormous hulk in deerskins and cloak, his nose almost touching his chin, was Kenton; William Clark, whose deep-set blue eyes had beheld an ocean called the Pacific, stood gulping. Major Croghan stood near the coffin with his incredibly handsome son George Croghan, the hero of Fort Sandusky in the War of 1812; while Lucy Clark Croghan, the general's sister, stood between and slightly in front of them, stolid but red-nosed and red-eyed as the dry snow whipped through the leafless branches of the orchard.

There were so many old men in the crowd, on canes or crutches, bent, hardly able to stand, but standing there on this bitter day nonetheless, with a look in their rheumy eyes which hinted that they were someplace else as well as here.

The coffin was lowered into the gaping ground, and Judge Rowan droned on sonorously, while Diana daydreamed: What if, she thought, what if I could look up just now from this sad hole in the ground and see standing here among them a Spanish lady in a woolen cowl and a great comb in her black—no, gray now—hair? But Uncle George would scold me, if he could see my thoughts now (as he surely can!) for reading so many novels and making myself silly!

". . . The mighty oak of the forest has fallen," Judge Rowan concluded. "And now the scrub oaks may sprout all around."

William Clark lingered at the graveside as the crowd thinned.

He watched the workmen throw the cold Kentucky earth onto the dark coffin below. The shovels rang; the clods thumped on the walnut wood.

"Tuck 'im in snug, boys," said Governor William Clark. "He always had trouble stayin' warm."

Epilogue I

SUNLIGHT WAS BRILLIANT ON THE STONE WALLS OF CONVENTO DE la Incarnación, but inside in the hallways and cells it was eternally dank and cool.

Holding the letter in both hands against her bosom, Sister Dolores moved down a long corridor lined with closed doors. Her heels clicked on the polished stone floors and echoed the length of the corridor.

Poor crazy Sister Terese, she was thinking. I'm sure she doesn't understand what these letters say. She sits and nods and seems to listen but her eyes never change and she says nothing.

Sister Terese was a nun of the order, but in truth was as much a patient as a nun, simple, vague, ethereal, and all but helpless. She had been in the convent longer than any of the present sisters—since the 1780s, according to the records, and was treated as a special case, being supported by a grant from His Catholic Majesty. She had been the victim, it was rumored, of some unexplained tragedy in the wilds of New Spain. Her mind had been broken by it somehow. A portrait miniature of her had been among her possessions, and was now in the convent library, and it showed that in her youth she had been exquisitely beautiful in an aristocratic way. Sister Terese, now gray and frail and sixty-six years old, with a few long gray hairs growing out of her puckered upper lip, was a subject of wonder and speculation among the new postulants and novices every year, but with familiarity the mystery would evaporate and she would be simply "poor Sister Terese," a saintly and useless little inmate who neither read nor sang nor did any of the hard or complicated duties of the convent. Rather, she only prayed fervently in her room or went about in a beatific daze, making little or no sense when she spoke unless she was talking about her room, the food, the flowers in the garden, or butterflies on the flowers. One or two letters would come to her each year from her niece, Señora Maria Josefa de Leyba Sarti in Madrid, and in recent years it had been Sister Dolores who undertook the task of reading the gossipy, innocuous letters to her.

"Now," Sister Dolores said, seating herself on a stepstool beside the cot upon which the frail gray nun sat with folded hands, "here is what your niece Maria Josefa says to you:

" 'Dear Aunt, I write to you again so soon because something very interesting and puzzling has been brought to my attention. At a ball with Ramon I was approached by an officer who some time ago had served at St. Louis, and asking me if I were not a daughter of Governor de Leyba he said then, surely you knew the great American General Clark who died recently. Determining that he meant our dear Don Jorge Clark—as I understand he had one or two brothers who were of high rank—I said I knew of his death but would hardly call 1780 recent, upon which the officer corrected me, saying no, Señora, I have read that he died only two or three years ago, quite old and ill. I am surely at a loss to explain it, dear Terese, but the gentleman was so sure of his information that I . . .' "

Sister Dolores looked up in astonishment. The old nun had risen from her cot and stood tottering, at this moment beginning to fold at the knees and waist, her mouth wide open, emitting a strange, strangling wheeze, her eyes seeming to bulge nearly out of their sockets. As Sister Dolores rose in alarm to help her, Sister Terese drew herself down into a crouch and fell sideways on the stones of the floor, where now an animallike whimper, broken by rasping inhalations, issued from her. Sister Dolores, skin crawling with fright, struggled to raise her from the cold floor and called for aid. In a moment the door was flung open by another astonished sister and the clattering footsteps of others were approaching in the corridor.

They took turns constraining Sister Terese on her cot for the next two hours, by twos, with a big-boned, wide-eyed postulant, who had been a peasant girl, leaping forward to hold her down when her fit renewed itself most violently. They could not imagine where in her bony little body she was finding this strength. They caressed her brow as they held her down, and the Superior came in and prayed grimly for a while at the foot of the cot.

By evening the little old woman had exhausted herself, her incoherent sounds had trailed off, and suddenly she fell into a deep slumber. Sister Dolores remained to sit a vigil by her bedside, praying with the light of one candle shining on her broad and placid face. At midnight she left the room, relieved by a sturdy novice who stationed herself on a temporary cot in the corridor, ready to summon help if poor Sister Terese should awaken unruly again. There was no sound heard from her room for the rest of the night.

Before daylight, Sister Dolores arose in her cell, went to the chapel and prayed, then came down the corridor. She awoke the sleeping novice and they eased the door open and went in, preceding themselves with a candlestick. They recoiled, gasping, at the sight that lay within.

Sister Terese lay naked on the cot, her hands clenched on her breast, her white body a pathetic bundle of ribs and swollen joints and loose skin hanging on bone, her flat, withered dugs sagging on her rib cage. Her cropped white hair stuck out in sprigs. Her sunken eyes were shut and her mouth was open, a dark hole. On the floor where she had cast them off, a dark puddle of cloth, lay her habit and wimple. Her old bronze crucifix that she had carried to New Spain and then brought back hung on the end wall of her cell overlooking the dismal and shocking scene, the tilted face of the Christ seeming to study the emaciated old body with unutterable pity.

Sister Dolores grabbed the clenched hands to awaken her, tongue ready to scold her for this revolting and profane behavior which no grief or mental aberration could excuse in such a house of holiness. But the arms were cold and rigid under the loose wrinkled-silk skin and could not be pried away.

Sister Dolores fell to her knees and crossed herself. "Holy Mary Mother of God," she breathed. "She is dead!"

When they were preparing Sister Terese's body for interment they had to break the bones of the hands to open them and free their grip on her necklace.

In the left hand they found her crucifix pendant. In the right was a strange small silver medallion bearing the figure of an athlete.

Epilogue II

ONE HUNDRED AND THIRTY-TWO YEARS AFTER GEORGE ROGERS Clark sent to the Virginia auditor his vouchers and account books detailing the expenses of the Western campaigns, an assistant state librarian named E. G. Swem obtained permission to examine seventy large unopened bundles of papers that had been found lying in the dusty chaos of an unused room of the Auditor's Building at Richmond.

Setting up a long table under a good light and donning a green eyeshade, Mr. Swem carefully opened a few of the packages, whose papers had turned brown and flaky. He looked in wonderment at some vouchers selected at random. Most were written in the same bold copperplate hand with flourishes and sure strokes at the end of each line.

To Oliver Pollock Esqr
New Orleans

Kaskaskias Novr 23rd 1778

$800
Sir

At Thirty Days sight of this my first of Exchange, Second of same Tenor and Date not being Paid Please Pay to Mr Charles Gratiot or to his Order the sum of Eight Hundred Dollars for Sundries furnish'd the State of Virginia and charge same as per former advice from—

Sir your very Obdt
most Hum Servt

G. R. CLARK

G. R. Clark? Swem thought, an old inkling of half-remembered history nudging in the back of his mind. Oliver Pollock?

He sneezed in the dust, then took up a stained, blotted itemization written in that same hand on a limp yellow square of linen paper:

The United States of America to Dan Murray.
To 20 Bottles Rum furnished Colo. George Rogers Clark's Detachment for a Refreshment after their taking possession of the Illinois Country ....100. . . .
To 4 Bottles ordered by Colo. Clark to Refresh Captn. Bowmans party on their arrival from Cahokia ......20. . . .
To Colo. Clarks ord in favr. of Michael 1 pint ....2. . 10.
To 5 quarts Rum furnished by Party that came from Caho by water .... 25.

147.10

Augs 14th.—78

Mr. Swem sneezed again, and blew his nose into a handkerchief, almost too engrossed to heed what he was doing. Vaguely recalled details of that old story came back to him as he sorted through the papers. Long ago Mr. Swem had read the memoir of the Western campaign that General Clark had written at President Madison's request, and he could remember particulars of that incredible march to Vincennes. . . .

Here now was a voucher in a different hand, on a stained, crumbling strip of paper scarcely three inches wide, evidently torn from the top of a full sheet of paper:

To the Isuing Commasary
Sir
    Isue to that Squa that Firnesh[d] our men with Provisions on our way to Attact Governor Hamelton one Bush[l] of corn and five Pound of Pork.

March 12th 1779
JOS BOWMAN

Author's Note

THE TALE YOU HAVE JUST READ IS AS MUCH HISTORY AS NOVEL. IT is true to the documented facts of the events it describes, to that degree revealed in the letters and memoirs of its principal characters. All the characters were real; their lives were intertwined as told.

I am not one of that recent breed of novelists who believe that great license may be taken with history; I have not written in any encounters that could not have happened. The military actions, treaties, and friendships of George Rogers Clark I have reconstructed from the journals and papers of Clark himself, of Joseph Bowman, Leonard Helm, General Henry Hamilton, Francisco Vigo, Lieutenant Governor de Leyba, Thomas Jefferson, Patrick Henry, the hero's illustrious brother William Clark, and of other participants in these events.

As is anyone who would tell this story, I am indebted to Dr. Lyman C. Draper, who spent thirty years of his life in the nineteenth century ranging through the country, tracing and collecting documents relating to the career of General Clark. Those documents, now resting in fragile condition at the Wisconsin State Historical Society in Madison, have been used by perhaps a dozen writers who have sought to retell the conquest of old Northwest Territory in the nonfictional mode; many of them have done it well, and I attach a bibliography hereafter for any reader who would wish to follow it. Dr. Draper interviewed many persons who had known General Clark in their lifetimes, and was so moved by his historical quest that he wrote to a correspondent:

"I do not wonder that you sh^d have your heart's memories and affections deeply stirred within you when such a man's worth and services were brought to your notice. The life services of Gen'l Clark have so long been a subject of profound study with me, that I have long learned to reverence him as I never have any other public character."

I echo those sentiments. Living in an age in which literature focuses so much on self-indulgence, cynicism, brutality, and weakness of character, I find myself braced and inspired by Clark's story, despite its tragic outcome.

My imagination has been at work on George Rogers Clark since boyhood, when I was nearly overwhelmed by a painting by F. C. Yohn of the surrender of Vincennes, used as an illustration for *The Youth's Companion*. At that time I began to people the event in my imagination. Being something of a ridge-runner at that age (and still), I was able to conjure all the sounds, the sights, the sensations of that audacious wilderness venture simply by seeing the illustration. In 1976, the Bicentennial year, interest was awakened when a friend, Ruth F. Banta, wrote to me on behalf of Indiana historians and asked if I would be able to do a dramatization of Clark's life. Now, a man past the age of forty, I have spent the last two years applying the same imagination to that same story. If this novel fails to recreate the feelings or actions of its characters as they really were in those days exactly two hundred years ago, my imagination is to blame.

Lest I be suspected of trying to pass off some fiction as fact, I must specify that there is one dimension of this story in which my imagination has had to invent particulars where documentation is scarce: the outcome of young Clark's romance with Teresa de Leyba. That the two were betrothed is generally accepted as true by most scholars of the man's career; that the betrothal was dissolved and Teresa de Lebya died a nun in a Spanish convent in 1821 is recorded as a historical fact. But to tell no more of this one great affair of his heart than exists in known records would leave too large a hole in the fabric for the novel reader to forgive. Therefore I have written between those sparse recorded lines, to tell their love story as it could have happened in view of their characters and customs and the vicissitudes of communication during such a conflict in that vast and hazardous wilderness. As no known letters between the lovers survive, I have invented them, three by Clark and one by Teresa, as well as one from Father Pierre Gibault and one from de Cartabona relating to the pair. A letter from Clark to de Cartabona, and one to Teresa from her niece, complete these. All other letters in the book are genuine.

The hardest test of my imagination was to get inside the mind of this vigorous, principled, and audacious character, to portray the inner being of a true hero as he went from vision to triumph to despair. Fortunately, I was given hints in his own words. Many of his thoughts and conversations in this novel are borrowed directly from Clark's own language, as found in his report to George Mason, in various letters, and in the memoir which he prepared in 1789 and 1790 at the request of James Madison.

I followed this same procedure in trying to dramatize the scenes involving Henry Hamilton, Fernando de Leyba, and others whose writings were available.

The reader may well wonder at my leap across the years 1781 through 1809 in General Clark's career. I have given only glimpses of those long, discouraging years, and have chosen to do so because I believe it is the storyteller's duty to distill the most powerful and significant moments out of life, to make the most essential statements and color the distinct contrasts. In the case of George Rogers Clark, the contrast between his triumph and his tragedy makes the essential statement.

Biographical details of those middle years are complex and impressive: While in Virginia in 1781, trying once again to raise an army for his coveted campaign against Detroit, he was engaged in a defensive battle against the troops of Benedict Arnold, conducting the only successful American ambuscade against Arnold's forces. Once again in that year, the Detroit campaign fell through because of circumstances beyond his control, even though he had the blessing of Commander-in-Chief George Washington, who wrote to Governor Thomas Jefferson:

I have ever been of opinion that the reduction of the post of Detroit would be the only certain means of giving peace and security to the whole western frontier. . . . I do not think the enterprise could have been committed to better hands than Colonel Clark's. I have not the pleasure of knowing the gentleman; but, independently of the proofs he has given of his activity and address, the unbounded confidence, which I am told the western people repose in him, is a matter of most importance.

As the British-Indian alliance continued to harass the settlements of Kentucky to and beyond the end of the Revolution,

Clark was prevailed upon to lead retaliatory expeditions in 1781, 1782, and 1786. Troop desertions marred the 1786 campaign, and an elaborate defamation plot engineered in the East by the infamous powergrabber James Wilkinson capitalized on that failure and succeeded in removing Clark from leadership. An appalling story could be written on that complicated treachery, which involved a series of fraudulent, forged, and anonymous letters. False rumors that drunkenness had destroyed Clark's leadership abilities were also circulated in the East by ambitious men jealous of Clark's influence in Western lands.

Clark resigned as the government's western Indian agent and principal surveyor for the Virginia state line late in the 1780s and retired to the home of his parents at Mulberry Hill near Louisville to prepare a memoir.

In the 1790s, when Spain kept the lower Mississippi closed to Kentucky trade and the new United States government refused to intercede, Clark as usual took matters into his own hands. He pledged his allegiance to France and assumed command of French Republic forces in the West. This venture, highly unorthodox but not illegal, gave his enemies more ammunition to fire at his reputation.

Meanwhile, Henry Hamilton, whose defeat was Clark's greatest triumph, fared better in his twilight years. After being released in a prisoner exchange, he returned to the Lakes region, served as lieutenant governor of Quebec, and later concluded his career as governor of the Bermudas.

During the next few years, Clark was the companion and mentor of his younger brother William, and secured for him his appointment as co-leader of the Lewis and Clark Expedition to the Pacific. It was, ironically, an expedition George Rogers Clark had turned down in 1783 in order to remain and protect Kentucky settlements. It must have been one of the few satisfactions of his later years that that magnificent adventure was led by a Clark.

Still another story could be told of George Rogers Clark the naturalist and archaeologist. He was the first to advance the now accepted theory of the origins of the Mound Builders civilization. And John James Audubon sought him out as the authority on bird species in the West.

All this time, Clark was so plagued by financial difficulties brought on by his commitment to the Revolution that he found it impossible to own property or even receive an inheritance from his father's estate. The efforts of George, Jonathan, and

William Clark to obtain justice in that matter would make a story so relentlessly dismal that surely few readers could endure it. We may presume that the last forty years of his life tried his faith and fortitude harder even than the rigorous feats of his youth.

In discussing my interest in George Rogers Clark over the last few years, I find that almost everyone presumes that by Clark I mean William Clark. Somehow William's legend has got what is known these days as the better publicity.

I suppose there are two factors contributing to the obscurity of the Clark whose exploits won for America the rich Midwest:

First, the printing presses which ground out what became the history of the Revolution were east of the Alleghenies. Clark's brilliant deeds on the other side of the mountains were so distant from the instruments of publicity that they might have been conducted on the moon.

The other reason for his obscurity is, ironically, one which should reflect all the greater glory on him: his victories were almost bloodless. He was an officer who, using surprise and bluff and mercy as his weapons, made great conquests without killing hundreds or thousands of human beings in the process. He secured the Northwest Territory in 1778 and 1779 without losing a single man in combat. With that kind of cleverness he assured his place as the hero history forgot.

It was exactly two hundred years after George Rogers Clark's bloodless capture of Kaskaskia when I drove down to the Ohio to see the places where he spent his last years. I had just completed the first draft of this novel; I was spent; my imagination was charged with the events of his career. I live, as I have almost all my life, in the heart of what used to be the old Northwest Territory, so it was a short and beautiful trip down through the Southern Indiana hills to the Louisville area.

I wanted to go first to Clarksville, on the Indiana side of the Ohio River, to find the place known as Clark's Point where the first chapter of this novel was set. I knew there was a stone monument there marking the site where his log house was thought to have been.

My map having no notation on it of a Clark Memorial, I stopped at a Shell service station and made inquiry of its proprietor, whose petroleum-smudged face gleamed oily in the July sunlight.

"A what? Memorial?"

"Yes. A marker that's supposed to show where he lived in his old age."

"Where *who* lived?"

"George Rogers Clark. The founder of this town, and of Louisville."

"A monument, eh?" He seemed to be anxious to get back to draining crankcases.

"Yes. A stone marker."

"Only monument I know of is over to Jeffersonville. Take this road, veer right till you hit Tenth Street, then go left. Somebody there could prob'ly tell ya. Might be the same guy."

A succession of such encounters followed as I drove among shopping centers, roller rinks, mobile home parks, chain restaurants, filling stations, discount stores, and ice cream shops where men and women with listless eyes and overstuffed shorts waited in line to be served. I had talked with a dozen persons before I found a youth in an auto parts store who had gone to George Rogers Clark School and knew where the monument stood. He gave me directions to the place on the flood wall along Harrison Street where the marker stood. The sun was low when I reached the site.

The marker stood across the street from a row of modest residences. The evening was full of the snarling racket from a chain saw somewhere nearby. The words on the monument's bronze plaque were dwarfed by the spray-painted declaration, "I hate Debbi." Cars rolled by on the street; the river flowed below. Two tanned blonde girls rode by on bicycles, looking back to smile and giggle at the sight of this man standing on a flood wall gazing at a monument. The air was dirty. Upriver and downriver, great steel bridges spanned the Ohio. Smokestacks jutted into the horizon. Louisville's tall, square downtown buildings crenellated the skyline to the south. High-tension lines spanned the river, like a string of Eiffel Towers. There was no Falls of the Ohio anymore, nor any Corn Island; locks and dams and erosion, I knew, had smoothed them out many decades ago. The wide river was slate-gray, fast and eddying. Trotline fishing floats were strung along the near shore. The roadside was strewn with empty beer six-packs. Traffic droned and whispered by; spillways of the hydroelectric plant across the river hissed and hushed. Rock music was coming from somewhere.

My imagination strained against all this to see the Ohio from Clark's Point as the old soldier had seen it in my first chapter. I was about to give up. But the sun was descending just as I have described it; the broad river curved away south and west; the wooded ridges diminished into the hazy distance. And then, I'll swear, a flock of martins swooped down past me toward the river. Yes, it was the same evening I had described from my imagination. The detritus of the twentieth century had faded momentarily to let me see through my real eyes what my imagination had seen through the failing eyes of that embittered old hero.

A panting black and tan beagle came by and explored me. A man and a woman in a pickup truck drove into a lovers' lane among the horseweeds and parked and watched impatiently for me to leave.

The sun had set. The gray haze in the west held a fading rose stain. My pilgrimage had been a success after all. It was time for me to fold up my imagination and go.

Bibliography

Temple Bodley. *George Rogers Clark—His Life and Public Services*. Boston: Houghton Mifflin Co., 1926.

Allan W. Eckert. *The Frontiersmen*. Boston: Little, Brown, 1970.

William Hayden English. *Conquest of the Country Northwest of the River Ohio*. Indianapolis: The Bowen-Merrill Co., 1896.

The French, the Indians, and George Rogers Clark in the Illinois Country. Proceedings of Indiana American Revolution Bicentennial Symposium. The Indiana Historical Society, 1977.

James Alton James, ed. *The George Rogers Clark Papers*. Illinois Historical Collections, 1912.

————. *The Life of George Rogers Clark*. Chicago: University of Chicago Press, 1928.

Ross F. Lockridge. *George Rogers Clark: Pioneer Hero of the Old Northwest*. World Book Co., 1927.

Fredrick Palmer. *Clark of the Ohio*. New York: Dodd, Mead & Co., 1930.

Milo M. Quaife, ed. *The Capture of Old Vincennes*. New York: Bobbs-Merrill Co., 1928.

Dr. George Waller. *The American Revolution in the West*. Chicago: Nelson-Hall, Inc., 1976.

They came to North America 300 years before Columbus, mingling their blood, their legends, and their dreams with the New World's Native peoples.

THE CHILDREN OF FIRST MAN

by
James Alexander Thom

Sweeping from the blood-soaked castles of medieval Wales to the landmark expedition of Lewis and Clark, from virgin wilderness to native villages, based on the legendary story of the Madoc people.

Published by Ballantine Books.
Now in bookstores everywhere.

New in paperback!

Frances Slocum, kidnapped from her frontier home when she was five by the Lenape,
was raised by them to become an honored
leader and healer of her adopted people.

When she has a chance, as an adult, to
return to her white family, there is no doubt
in her mind that her heart is a red one.

THE RED HEART

by

James Alexander Thom

This powerful story about a real woman out
of history adds another strong chapter to the
large contribution James Alexander Thom is
making to American literature.